THE MODERN TRADITION

THE MODERN TRADITION

An Anthology of Short Stories

Second Edition

Edited by

DANIEL F. HOWARD

Rutgers University

LITTLE, BROWN AND COMPANY   BOSTON

LIBRARY OF CONGRESS CATALOG CARD NO. 74-186062

NINTH PRINTING

Printed simultaneously in Canada by
Little, Brown & Company (Canada) Limited

PRINTED IN THE UNITED STATES OF AMERICA

ACKNOWLEDGMENTS

JOHN BARTH. "Lost in the Funhouse," copyright © 1967 by the Atlantic Monthly Co. "Life-Story," copyright © 1968 by John Barth. Both reprinted from *Lost in the Funhouse* by John Barth, by permission of Doubleday and Company, Inc. Photograph used courtesy of Lurton Blassingame.

DONALD BARTHELME. "See the Moon?" from *Unspeakable Practices, Unnatural Acts* by Donald Barthelme. Copyright © 1966, 1968 by Donald Barthelme. Reprinted by permission of Farrar, Straus & Giroux, Inc. "Margins" from *Come Back, Dr. Caligari* by Donald Barthelme. Copyright © 1961 by Donald Barthelme. Reprinted by permission of Little, Brown and Co. Photograph used courtesy of Farrar, Straus & Giroux, Inc.

SAUL BELLOW. "A Father-to-Be" from *Seize the Day* by Saul Bellow. Copyright © 1955 by Saul Bellow. (Originally appeared in *The New Yorker.*) "Leaving the Yellow House" from *Mosby's Memoirs and Other Stories* by Saul Bellow. Copyright © 1957 by Saul Bellow. Both reprinted by permission of The Viking Press, Inc. Photograph by Jeff Lowenthal used courtesy of The Viking Press, Inc.

JORGE LUIS BORGES. "The Secret Miracle" from *Labyrinths* by Jorge Luis Borges, translated by Harriet de Onís. Copyright © 1962 by New Directions Publishing Corporation. Reprinted by permission of New Directions Publishing Corporation. "Funes, the Memorious" from *A Personal Anthology* by Jorge Luis Borges, translated by Anthony Kerrigan. Copyright © 1967 by Grove Press, Inc. Reprinted by permission of Grove Press, Inc. Photograph by Jill Krementz used by permission.

ANTON CHEKHOV. "Misery" from *The School Mistress and Other Stories* by Anton Chekhov, translated from the Russian by Constance Garnett. Copyright 1921 by The Macmillan Company, renewed 1949 by David Garnett. Reprinted by permission of The Macmillan Company, Chatto and Windus Ltd., and David Garnett. Photograph used by permission of Novosti Press Agency.

JOSEPH CONRAD. "Youth" and "The Secret Sharer" are reprinted by permission of J. M. Dent & Sons Ltd. and the Trustees of the Joseph Conrad Estate. Photograph used courtesy of J. M. Dent & Sons Ltd.

WILLIAM FAULKNER. "Dry September" from *Collected Stories of William Faulkner.* Copyright 1930 and renewed 1958 by William Faulkner. "Pantaloon in Black" from *Go Down Moses* by William Faulkner. Copyright 1940 and renewed 1968 by Estelle Faulkner and Jill Faulkner Summers, copyright 1942 by William Faulkner. Both reprinted by permission of Random House, Inc. Photograph by Ralph Thompson used courtesy of Random House, Inc.

Acknowledgments

Nathaniel Hawthorne. Photograph used by permission of Brown Brothers, New York.

Ernest Hemingway. "Big Two-Hearted River" from *In Our Time* by Ernest Hemingway. Copyright 1925 Charles Scribner's Sons; renewal copyright 1953 Ernest Hemingway. Reprinted by permission of Charles Scribner's Sons. Photograph used courtesy of Charles Scribner's Sons.

Henry James. Photograph used by permission of Brown Brothers, New York.

James Joyce. "Araby" and "The Dead" from *Dubliners* by James Joyce. Originally published by B. W. Huebsch, Inc., in 1916. Copyright © 1967 by The Estate of James Joyce. Reprinted by permission of The Viking Press, Inc. Photograph by Ruth Asch used courtesy of The Viking Press, Inc.

D. H. Lawrence. "The Prussian Officer" from *The Complete Short Stories of D. H. Lawrence,* Volume I. "Odour of Crysanthemums" from *The Complete Short Stories of D. H. Lawrence,* Volume II. Both reprinted by permission of The Viking Press, Inc. Photograph used courtesy of The Viking Press, Inc.

Norman Mailer. "The Man Who Studied Yoga" and "The Language of Men" from *Advertisements for Myself* by Norman Mailer. Copyright © 1959 by Norman Mailer. Reprinted by permission of G. P. Putnam's Sons. Photograph by Jerry Bauer used courtesy of Little, Brown and Company, Inc.

Bernard Malamud. "Angel Levine" from *The Magic Barrel* by Bernard Malamud. Copyright © 1955, 1958 by Bernard Malamud. "Black Is My Favorite Color" from *Idiot's First* by Bernard Malamud. Copyright © 1963 by Bernard Malamud. Both reprinted by permission of Farrar, Straus & Giroux, Inc. Photograph used courtesy of the photographer, Janna Malamud.

Carson McCullers. "The Sojourner" and "The Jockey" from *The Ballad of the Sad Cafe* by Carson McCullers. Copyright 1955 by Carson McCullers. Reprinted by permission of the publisher, Houghton Mifflin Company. Photograph by John Vincent Adams used courtesy of Houghton Mifflin Company.

James Alan McPherson. "On Trains" and "Of Cabbages and Kings" from *Hue and Cry* by James Alan McPherson. Copyright © 1968, 1969 by James Alan McPherson. Reprinted by permission of Atlantic-Little, Brown and Co. Photograph by Phil Troyer used by permission.

Vladimir Nabokov. "First Love," copyright 1948 by Vladimir Nabokov. (Originally appeared in *The New Yorker.*) "That in Aleppo Once . . . ," copyright 1943 by the Atlantic Monthly Co. Both reprinted from *Nabokov's Dozen* by Vladimir Nabokov, by permission of Doubleday and Company, Inc. Photograph by Marc Riboud used by permission of Magnum Photos, Inc.

Joyce Carol Oates. "Where Are You Going, Where Have You Been?" from *Epoch* (Fall 1966). Copyright © 1966 by Joyce Carol Oates. "How I Contemplated the World from the Detroit House of Correction and Began My Life Over Again" from *Tri-Quarterly* (Fall 1967). Copyright © 1967 by Joyce Carol Oates. Both reprinted by permission of the author and Blanche C. Gregory, Inc. Photograph by Jack Robinson used courtesy of Blanche C. Gregory, Inc.

Flannery O'Connor. "Good Country People" from *A Good Man Is Hard to Find and Other Stories* by Flannery O'Connor. Copyright, 1953, by Flannery O'Connor. Reprinted by permission of Harcourt Brace Jovanovich, Inc. "Everything That Rises Must Converge" from *Everything That Rises Must Converge* by Flannery O'Connor. Copyright © 1961, 1965 by The Estate of Mary Flannery O'Connor. Reprinted by permission of Farrar, Straus & Giroux, Inc. Photograph used courtesy of Farrar, Straus & Giroux, Inc.

Acknowledgments

JOHN UPDIKE. "A & P," copyright © 1962 by John Updike. "The Doctor's Wife," copyright © 1961 by John Updike. Both first appeared in *The New Yorker* and are reprinted from *Pigeon Feathers and Other Stories* by John Updike, by permission of Alfred A. Knopf, Inc. Photograph by Peter Simon used courtesy of Alfred A. Knopf, Inc.

KURT VONNEGUT, JR. "Next Door," copyright © 1955 by Kurt Vonnegut, Jr., and "EPICAC" copyright © 1950 by Kurt Vonnegut, Jr., from *Welcome to the Monkey House* by Kurt Vonnegut, Jr. A Seymour Lawrence Book/Delacorte Press. Both reprinted by permission of the publisher. Photograph by Jill Krementz used by permission.

RICHARD WRIGHT. "Big Boy Leaves Home" from *Uncle Tom's Children* by Richard Wright. Copyright 1936 by Richard Wright; renewed 1966 by Ellen Wright. Reprinted by permission of Harper & Row Publishers. "The Man Who Lived Underground," copyright 1944 by L. B. Fisher Publishing Corporation, reprinted by permission of Paul R. Reynolds, Inc. Photograph used courtesy of Harper & Row, Publishers.

PREFACE

Two distinct principles motivate this book. The first is that a reader of fiction should have as much opportunity as possible to build up a sensitivity to one writer's range of appeals before moving on to another's. There are of course practical considerations: perhaps ideally one should read all of Joyce's *Dubliners,* at least five or six stories by D. H. Lawrence, etc.; but such concentration is rarely desirable in introductory courses designed to stimulate interests in *various* authors – some of whose works may inspire the student to study them in depth in more specialized courses. Thus there are here not The Forty-four Best Stories of Modern Times but two excellent, representative stories by each of twenty-two major writers who constitute the modern tradition in short fiction. Of course these twenty-two haven't fashioned the tradition alone; there are others who could be included to round out the picture, but there can be no doubt about the originality and influence of those represented here. With two stories by each the reader has the chance to put to use, as he reads a second story, the perceptions gained from having read and discussed the first. There is no attempt to furnish mere variety, for it is the editor's view that concepts of "variety" and "difference" among works of literature have little meaning unless one understands exactly what the story read today is supposed to be different *from* – and unless he is moved to pay special attention to today's story because he knows that it will enrich his reading of tomorrow's.

Stories are grouped by individual authors (rather than by such abstractions as "theme," "technique," "the urban experience," "growing up," etc.) in order to emphasize integral connections between them – connections involving imaginative organization: the writer's selection of detail, his projection of voices, his development of theme, his relating of environment to character, etc. Because the stories of any one writer are the products of a single distinctive imagination, this arrangement encourages the reader to make meaningful comparisons and contrasts within each writer's stories, and, having developed a set of reactions to one writer, to measure more intelligently the different achievement of the next. It is then finally on the basis of his own experience of particular short stories that the reader can develop a sense of what the "modern tradition" is.

The second principle of this book is that a reader benefits most not from an editor's supposedly definitive analysis of a given writer but from a number of suggestions about "what to look for" as he reads. A serious reader wants to learn how to generate his own reactions, to be able to say something about what he has read. To help him do so at that crucial time when he is ready to reflect upon the story before him is the intention of the introductions to each writer. They are directed toward the disclosure of ranges of possible reaction to an author, not toward making a statement that encapsulates everything that should be said. The editor's comments are in this sense unlike professional critiques, for they deliberately put on display exactly what a professional critic hides: the steps taken to find and develop an idea. In short, the critical aid is designed to invite students to think along with an observer who is not committed to a particular interpretation but who is engaged in discovering what can be said – the essential question behind the commentary being not "What do this writer's stories mean?" but "What interesting questions can be asked about them?"

The format consists of a general introduction to ways of thinking about short fiction, and one essay on each of the authors.

CONTENTS

INTRODUCTION

As one reads the stories in this book it is well to keep in mind the one principle of organization that underlies them all: each story's characters, events, scenes, props, are pulled together by being parts of a *short* story – "short" not in terms of an absolute maximum length (which can in exceptional cases extend to a hundred pages or so) but in terms of the writer's assumption that his reader is continuously available to him during an uninterrupted period of time. This concentration of attention is the source of the short story's unity. In the novel, the assumption is different: that the reader will pick up the novel, read what he can, put it down, come back to it, and so in stages get through it. The novel is available in episodes, as for example the Bible has always been, even for leisurely reading aloud evening after evening, or serialized for monthly consumption in a magazine (which often took almost two years to publish all of it). Certainly there may be people who read a Dickens novel straight through from page 1 to page 800 in a single sitting, and clearly there are people who of necessity interrupt their reading of a short story – but what counts is the assumption of either a continuous or a discontinuous experience by the reader. Dickens wrote his novels for an audience which picked up the parts month by month, gradually acclimatizing themselves to his fictional terrain. Short stories have to work much faster: there is no time to stroll through the countryside getting to know one family after another; a more intense central focus is required, and this changes the quality of detail.

The short-story form became popular during the same period, the mid-and-late nineteenth century, in which the taste for serialized novels was at its height, and the large reading public fond of novels-in-parts influenced the short-story writer. It was a post-Romantic public that more and more preferred prose to poetry, but, having lived under the influence of two generations of romantic poets, it also valued the emotional intensity and metaphorical expansiveness of poetry. Thus its preference for fiction was combined with a taste for poetic intensity. The short-story writer confronted an audience which, though it appreciated the lifelikeness, the expansive structure, and the multiple plots of huge Victorian novels, also yearned for a literary form more gripping – one that carried them off into a less extensively fabricated, more immediately emotional world. The short story's compactness made it potentially more thrilling than the novel because, relying upon the reader's unceasing attention during a short period of time, it could elevate the reader into intense states of fear, or terror, or joy under the pressure of time. The tacit agreement between writer and reader that the story's spell was not to be broken by an intrusion of everyday reality made all the difference.

What, then, are some of the implications of this special time relationship between the short story and its reader? One certainly is that because the short story has room for but a small fraction of the data of life, the writer must not only select carefully but must choose facts that suggest more than themselves – those that have a kind of radiance capable of extending the limited area of the story to give it the illusion not only of life but of a kind of superintense life. Of course all art selects: even a massive novel does not report everything; and though a novelist may offer elaborate information about hats, shoes, dresses, jewelry, and may thereby encourage the reader to imagine that he could go out and buy the characters' wardrobes, were he to try to do so, he would discover the *illusion* of inclusiveness that has been produced. Even the most elaborately specific novels exclude, necessarily, more details of experience than they include, despite the fact that the novelist, as opposed to the short-story writer, can afford to indulge many kinds of interest, and so may represent his characters' shoes as indicative of this, their hats and gloves of something else, and so on – weaving all of these indications into the fabric of the novel. The range of concern of the short story, on the other hand, is so sharply narrowed that a character must be summed up by details that naturally, within the context of the story, must simultaneously both give a sense of real life and expand metaphorically to connect the character to everything else in his fictional world.

Take as an example the apparently casual gesture of Gabriel in Joyce's "The Dead" when he arrives at the Misses Morkan's party. There is snow on his shoes, and he (as perhaps most of us would) flicks it off. There is nothing especially odd in this: it is typical of Gabriel to be ill-at-ease and to be looking for some gesture to relieve his self-consciousness – and perhaps it is also typical of him to show his fastidiousness by trying to keep his shoes dry. But in the context of the story this casual flicking of snow suggests much more than a merely natural-seeming action: it takes its place in a pattern of meaning involving Gabriel's dissociation from nature, from Dublin society, and finally from his personal relationship with his wife. Thus the gesture joins other facts that define Gabriel's distaste for and yet participation in a kind of death, the external locus of which is the cold and snow that descend on Ireland. A pattern like this, generated by perfectly chosen details, raises Gabriel's apparently casual flicking away of a bit of snow to a superlifelike act. To put it another way, we can imagine that if Gabriel were a real person rather than a character in a short story, he might have as he came in also straightened his tie, hiked up his pants, and rubbed his itchy nose (certainly we can be sure that Gabriel would not have stood there like a stone); but Joyce, the short-story writer, invents a gesture both suggestive of something that a real person might do *and* that connects Gabriel with an evolving synthesis of the people and the things around him.

Of course, the snow on Gabriel's shoes is a "symbol," but it is not a static or simple one, and in reading "The Dead," or any of these stories, we will do well not to hunt for symbols that unequivocally "mean" other things (snow equals death, for instance). The world of a short story is an organic unity in which words are under pressure, and under pressure they suggest more than they do in the loose context of everyday life; but instead of labeling them symbols "meaning" something else, we do better to become aware of the way in which a story's details form a whole, and of how the whole is often made credible by the development of a strong mood, a dominant emotion, such as Gabriel's fevered desire for his wife – which at the end of "The Dead" sustains the Hell-like details of the setting through which he moves – and later his ensuing depression – which justifies the cosmic significance of the snow falling over all of Ireland.

Now moods and emotions belong to people, and it is not surprising to find that short-story writers, in utilizing the possibilities of their form, often put the reader in the presence of characters who are obsessed and whose obsessions are contagious. The character may be the narrator, who wants to tell us his story because it seems to have a special significance that he may think he understands; or the narrator may be mysteriously disturbed and may be trying in the very act of telling his story to work out its significance. An obsessed character offers the author a focus for whatever emotion or mood dominates the story and connects its details. Not that the author is "with" his narrator's state of mind all the way. Maybe in a pure thriller the reader is asked to identify completely with a character who is obsessed by, say, a series of terrors leading to some final horror that presumably both character and reader will share together. In such a thriller (if it exists) there is no divergence between the reader and the character who acts as the story's emotional center: the identification of one with the other is complete, as it occasionally is in real life, as when we identify completely with one of our friends reporting what happened to him. In good fiction such a complete identification is impossible, for a pure thriller denies the reader the active role that makes fiction interesting: in it the reader is asked merely to *accept* a character's response.

In good short stories there are elaborate variations of the distance between the reader and the characters. Often, for example, a narrator does not see the meaning of his own story, and by not perceiving it acts as a foil to the reader, who has the fun of finding significance *in spite of* the participant's lack of understanding. The reader in effect is encouraged to play fiction-maker, entering the artificial world of the story as an all-seeing detective-like observer. His excitement, unlike the narrator's, builds up from his growing apprehension of a reality more complicated than the one understood by the characters who live it.

We have said that certain possibilities follow from the short story's being short, encompassable within one sitting. It follows that all details and actions must fit, and fit in a special resonant way so that they suggest the complexity of a world – perhaps a superworld in the sense that it is so perfectly connected in all its parts. This means that the language of short stories tends toward metaphor, because metaphor is one way of connecting separate facts to suggest a unified, complicated experience. And one way of making metaphor seem natural, appropriate to realistic-seeming fiction, is through the personality of an emotionally charged character, often the narrator. But sometimes the dominant mood comes not from a character at all but from what we might call a "focus of sensibility," an unlocatable voice, an arrangement of details that invests the events being narrated with emotion. Since there are no pure thrillers in this book, the reader is never expected either to identify completely with the characters or to accept uncritically the focus of sensibility: we shall have to be actively engaged in establishing the terms of our relationship to the characters and to the special feeling of the story. We shall find tricky narrators, those out to mesmerize us and force us to agree that their world is exactly what they imagine it to be; others who would limit our seeing so that they can convince us that the events of the story are to be understood as merely logical – or emotional, or social – phenomena; and there are apparently dumb narrators who cannot find their story in the facts that comprise it, and so seem to leave the matter to us.

If we begin to question the appeal made by a story's focus of sensibility, we find ourselves involved in helping the author to make his fiction; we accept our position as mature readers, different from that, say, of school children accepting the story of Little Red Riding Hood as a report of a real happening rather than a deliberately created story. As mature readers we create our own story out of materials presented. The author is guiding us, of course – by his arrangement of details, by balancing one character against another, by language that reveals unrecognized levels of feeling – but for his guidance to work we must actively seek our position with respect to the characters and/or the focus of sensibility in the story.

The reader will also find it rewarding to be aware of the relation established in these stories between people and concrete things. Again, because the form is so intense, the things that surround characters have to serve as indices to their mental and emotional states. In Nabokov's "First Love," the subject of the narrator's recollections is the narrator himself as a youngster. The young boy is revealed not only by the strong nostalgia with which the narrator describes his boyhood trip from St. Petersburg to Paris, but also by the details of the Pullman car in which the journey is accomplished. Seen by the narrator in memory as a model in a travel-agency window, the Pullman car evokes the feel of a pre–World War I life that the narrator recognizes as gone forever; but the intense reaction to this lost moment in history comes from the fact that at that time the Pullman car and the boy were conjoined in a yearly ritual of travel. In a sense the car was an extension of the boy's personality; and it is this identity, now lost and existing only in memory, that contrasts with the narrator's present dissociation from things. The story's effect centers on the narrator's fondness for the innocence that made the elegant Pullman car an extension of one's self — a state of almost mystical identification of one's personality with the objects surrounding it, a state of mind which was, on one level, his "first love."

Many of the narrators in these stories attempt to impose *imaginary* connections between themselves and objects, connections outside the reality otherwise represented in the story. The boy in Joyce's "Araby," for example, is so saturated with the romantic literature of the Arabian Nights (as well as with the ceremonies of the Roman Catholic Church) that as he walks with his aunt through downtown Dublin he transforms the details of the scene before him — the groceries, the smells, the sounds — into an imagined romantic-religious quest. Joyce temporarily lets us participate in the vision the boy is creating for himself. We find his naive world as lovely as it is unreal, though we see that, regrettably, it does not correspond to the solid Dublin that Joyce reveals behind the boy. Our understanding of "Araby" grows as we become aware of the difference between the construction that the boy puts upon the materials of Dublin and what the rest of the story establishes is really there. When at last the boy also perceives that the supposedly fabulous land of Araby is made up of exactly the same things as everyday, unromanticized Dublin, we are very close to him, for he has caught up to what we have been aware of. Still, there is a distance between us, created by our *sympathy* for his burning disappointment (rather than our direct participation in it), and by our closer association with the gentle older narrator who is no longer the boy he once was. It is the distance between us and the boy that makes the story.

The short story, then, is intense. Characters are more identified with things and actions than in the novel, in which they at least tend to maintain a greater independence. To say this is another way of pointing to the special "singleness" of short stories — a singleness of action, character, and effect. However many separate problems and issues the short story may seem to raise, it drives relentlessly toward a unification of all into a single (albeit complicated) synthesis. This synthesis is accomplished under the kind of heat and pressure not common in daily life, and it is justified in realistic terms by the presence of some extraordinary mood in which human beings make and accept connections that are neither strictly logical nor limited in significance by ordinary standards of relevance. For this mood to work, the short-story writer has to solicit his reader's participation in making the fiction, in "being there," in feeling for the characters' circumstances at the same level of intensity — even though always rather differently. Thus, more than many other kinds of art, short stories are for participants rather than for spectators.

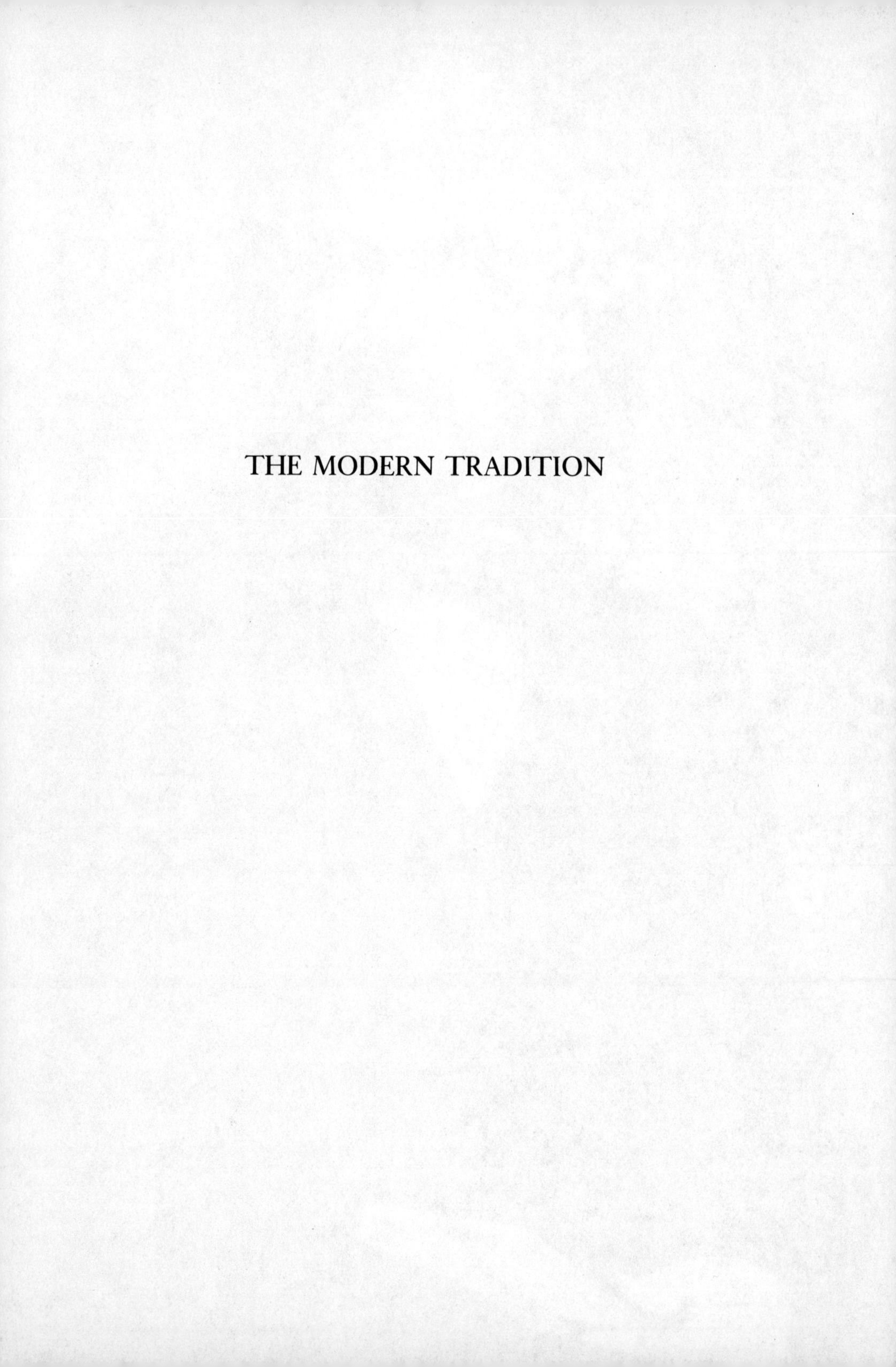

THE MODERN TRADITION

NATHANIEL HAWTHORNE 1804–1864

Hawthorne was born on the Fourth of July, 1804, in Salem, Massachusetts, a town preoccupied with its witch-hunting past and left in the wake of a more vigorous, secular America. His life reveals a pattern of brooding isolation and retreat interspersed with periods of conventional, non-literary employment. As a youth he read widely in romantic works and cultivated a taste for wilderness and natural scenery. Following his graduation from Bowdoin in 1825, he retired to his family home for twelve years, preparing for a literary career that began with his first published collection of stories, *Twice-Told Tales* (1837), followed by a series of works that culminated in novels like *The Scarlet Letter* (1850) and *The House of the Seven Gables* (1851). Hawthorne's marriage to Sophia Peabody in 1842 rescued him from gloomier moments of introspection and made him aware of nuances of feminine psychology. He was the friend of the great literary figures of his time: Emerson, Thoreau, and Melville. And fortunately for his financial well-being, he was also a classmate and friend of Franklin Pierce, the fourteenth president of the United States, whose influence secured him positions at the Boston Custom House and as United States consul in Liverpool.

When Henry James looked back at Hawthorne, his distinguished American predecessor, he saw a writer who to his mind had wasted a remarkable talent on too narrow a society – one lacking in variety, in opportunities for the interplay of personality and society that James so loved. Hawthorne seemed to him burdened by a "sombre lineage" of Puritanism in which a writer had to see right and wrong as always unambiguously evident, people as either good *or* bad, honest *or* dishonest, truthful *or* lying. James, as we can see from his stories here, considered such absolutes abhorrent; nothing was farther from his mind than labeling complicated human beings according to any rigid system. He could not, for example, have dealt with the first view that we have of Hester Prynne in Hawthorne's *The Scarlet Letter*: her identity apparently contained in the letter *A* that she is forced to wear on her breast. True, she is indeed what the *A* declares that she is, an adulteress; and though that fact is not irrelevant the announcement of it is too crude for James. He preferred to deal with characters who generate their identities as they engage the world – constantly changing as nuances of light and shadow play upon them, not measured against some Puritan caricature of themselves.

So James pitied Hawthorne, confined in his "simpler" America by such coarse conceptions. But his pity was misplaced, for Hawthorne deliberately set out to make use of that simpler America, which did not, after all, exist in his time any more than it did in James's. Hawthorne saw that he could use a colonial world fully two generations behind him, and therefore imaginatively reconstructed it. He recognized in Puritan moral absolutism a background against which he could establish his special kind of complicated experience; for him Puritanism defined the extreme ends of a scale of conceptions of people, all of which he perceived could be valid simultaneously. Always at issue in Hawthorne's stories is the way in which characters can or cannot transcend the limitations of labels, of which Hester's *A* stands as an extreme example; always there is a more or less successful effort to break out of whatever conception society uses to encapsulate the individual. Not that society's conception is ever all wrong: it does point to one area of the individual's personality; but it is never valid alone.

In "My Kinsman, Major Molineux," for instance, the boy whose consciousness dominates the story is young enough to have only partially absorbed the Puritan habit of labeling people. He walks through the town trying to find people as free from preconceptions as he is; but everywhere he finds his kinsman labeled a despot, conceptualized as a false god to be cast down. He watches in amazement as this concept of his kinsman rises out of the secret hearts of individuals until, collectively possessed by it, they yield their independent imaginations to a dehumanized mob impulse to destroy Major Molineux. By the time the Major passes by, tarred and feathered, the people whom the boy has encountered as individuals have been transformed into a host of demons, utterly wanting in human sympathy and devoid of any recognition of their "kinship" with the suffering Major. Despot he may be, but a suffering human being he also is, though their hysteria makes it impossible for the mob to recognize this crucial kinship.

James's appreciative amazement that Hawthorne could have had even partial success with such materials ("[he] transmuted this heavy moral burden into the very substance of the imagination," James says in wonder) points us to the difference between the way a James story generates, out of an interaction of all its materials, the standards by which its action is to be measured, and the way in which a Hawthorne story characteristically sets up polarities that are *not* resolved in some middle ground but are simultaneously valid throughout. If we "listen" to a Hawthorne story we hear an authoritative voice, the voice of history almost, that assures us that the issues in the story are perfectly clear-cut, the facts certain, the attitude to be adopted obvious to all reasonable people. What this voice assures us of is not wrong, but we soon become conscious that other interpretations (even seemingly contradictory ones) are simultaneously right — that, for instance, the boy's "kinsman" may in one sense be akin to him and in another be terrifyingly remote. By contrast, when James in his fiction brushes with Puritan certitudes (as in his novel *The Europeans*), the reader knows at once that they are to be regarded as grotesque extremes, and that to have any value at all they will have to be qualified by a broader, more sophisticated Europeanism. Consequently, in James a dialogue ensues between "simpler America" and Europe, out of which a flexible view emerges. The extreme positions, which constituted one side of the dialogue but were never believed in, are then discarded. In Hawthorne there is no blending: Major Molineux *is* a graven image to be cast down, *and* he is a suffering human being to be pitied — both at once, just as the townspeople are both ordinary folk and devils too.

To watch Hawthorne construct a world in which even opposing views can be valid, we should strain to hear voices other than that of the authoritative speaker, and to catch, even within his voice, human dimensions which the confident speaker's rationality may unconsciously be excluding. What Hawthorne is constantly doing is adding dimension to rigid conceptions of life, whether about moral matters or about what constitutes reality. As he says,

> We who are born into the world's artificial system can never adequately know how little in our present state and circumstances is natural, and how much is merely the interpolation of the perverted mind and heart of man. . . . It is only through the medium of the imagination that we can loosen those iron fetters, which we call truth and reality, and make ourselves even partially sensible what prisoners we are.
>
> —"The New Adam and Eve"

The psychological state which best expresses the desired freedom from the "world's artificial system" and an awareness of the truth that lies in opposing views is a half-waking, half-sleeping state, often as in "My Kinsman, Major Molineux" intensifying into nightmare. The characters are then perceived halfway between the literalness of the waking day and the uncontrolled creativity of the imagination; and the reader becomes aware of the continuousness of the spectrum from pure naturalism to pure imagination. Thus he is not moved to ask the question that the "world's artificial system" prompts: "Is it a dream or is it real?" For it is both: the naturalistic world working upon the imagination, and the imagination upon the world, to weave the mysterious and wonderful fabric that is Hawthorne's reality.

THE MAYPOLE OF MERRY MOUNT

There is an admirable foundation for a philosophic romance in the curious history of the early settlement of Mount Wollaston, or Merry Mount. In the slight sketch here attempted, the facts, recorded on the grave pages of our New England annalists, have wrought themselves, almost spontaneously, into a sort of allegory. The masques, mummeries, and festive customs, described in the text, are in accordance with the manners of the age. Authority on these points may be found in Strutt's Book of English Sports and Pastimes.

Bright were the days at Merry Mount, when the Maypole was the banner staff of that gay colony! They who reared it, should their banner be triumphant, were to pour sunshine over New England's rugged hills, and scatter flower seeds throughout the soil. Jollity and gloom were contending for an empire. Midsummer eve had come, bringing deep verdure to the forest, and roses in her lap, of a more vivid hue than the tender buds of Spring. But May, or her mirthful spirit, dwelt all the year round at Merry Mount, sporting with the Summer months, and revelling with Autumn, and basking in the flow of Winter's fireside. Through a world of toil and care she flitted with a dreamlike smile, and came hither to find a home among the lightsome hearts of Merry Mount.

Never had the Maypole been so gayly decked as at sunset on midsummer eve. This venerated emblem was a pine-tree, which had preserved the slender grace of youth, while it equalled the loftiest height of the old wood monarchs. From its top streamed a silken banner, colored like the rainbow. Down nearly to the ground the pole was dressed with birchen boughs, and others of the liveliest green, and some with silvery leaves, fastened by ribbons that fluttered in fantastic knots of twenty different colors, but no sad ones. Garden flowers, and blossoms of the wilderness, laughed gladly forth amid the verdure, so fresh and dewy that they must have grown by magic on that happy pine-tree. Where this green and flowery splendor terminated, the shaft of the Maypole was stained with the seven brilliant hues of the banner at its top. On the lowest green bough hung an abundant wreath of roses, some that had been gathered in the sunniest spots of the forest, and others, of still richer blush, which the colonists had reared from English seed. O, people of the Golden Age, the chief of your husbandry was to raise flowers!

But what was the wild throng that stood hand in hand about the Maypole?

It could not be that the fauns and nymphs, when driven from their classic groves and homes of ancient fable, had sought refuge, as all the persecuted did, in the fresh woods of the West. These were Gothic monsters, though perhaps of Grecian ancestry. On the shoulders of a comely youth uprose the head and branching antlers of a stag; a second, human in all other points, had the grim visage of a wolf; a third, still with the trunk and limbs of a mortal man, showed the beard and horns of a venerable he-goat. There was the likeness of a bear erect, brute in all but his hind legs, which were adorned with pink silk stockings. And here again, almost as wondrous, stood a real bear of the dark forest, lending each of his fore paws to the grasp of a human hand, and as ready for the dance as any in that circle. His inferior nature rose half way, to meet his companions as they stooped. Other faces wore the similitude of man or woman, but distorted or extravagant, with red noses pendulous before their mouths, which seemed of awful depth, and stretched from ear to ear in an eternal fit of laughter. Here might be seen the Salvage Man, well known in heraldry, hairy as a baboon, and girdled with green leaves. By his side, a noble figure, but still a counterfeit, appeared an Indian hunter, with feathery crest and wampum belt. Many of this strange company wore foolscaps, and had little bells appended to their garments, tinkling with a silvery sound, responsive to the inaudible music of their gleesome spirits. Some youths and maidens were of soberer garb, yet well maintained their places in the irregular throng by the expression of wild revelry upon their features. Such were the colonists of Merry Mount, as they stood in the broad smile of sunset round their venerated Maypole.

Had a wanderer, bewildered in the melancholy forest, heard their mirth, and stolen a half-affrighted glance, he might have fancied them the crew of Comus, some already transformed to brutes, some midway between man and beast, and the others rioting in the flow of tipsy jollity that foreran the change. But a band of Puritans, who watched the scene, invisible themselves, compared the masques to those devils and ruined souls with whom their superstition peopled the black wilderness.

Within the ring of monsters appeared the two airiest forms that had ever trodden on any more solid footing than a purple and golden cloud. One was a youth in glistening apparel, with a scarf of the rainbow pattern crosswise on his breast. His right hand held a gilded staff, the ensign of high dignity among the revellers, and his left grasped the slender fingers of a fair maiden, not less gayly decorated than himself. Bright roses glowed in contrast with the dark and glossy curls of each, and were scattered round their feet, or had sprung up spontaneously there. Behind this lightsome couple, so close to the Maypole that its boughs shaded his jovial face, stood the figure of an English priest, canonically dressed, yet decked with flowers, in heathen fashion, and wearing a chaplet of the native vine leaves. By the riot of his rolling eye, and the pagan decorations of his holy garb, he seemed the wildest monster there, and the very Comus of the crew.

"Votaries of the Maypole," cried the flower-decked priest, "merrily, all day long, have the woods echoed to your mirth. But be this your merriest hour, my hearts! Lo, here stand the Lord and Lady of the May, whom I, a clerk of Oxford, and high priest of Merry Mount, am presently to join in holy matrimony. Up with your nimble spirits, ye morris-dancers, green men, and glee maidens, bears and wolves, and horned gentlemen! Come; a chorus now, rich with the old mirth of Merry England, and the wilder glee of this fresh forest; and then a dance, to show the youthful pair what life is made of, and how airily they should go through it! All ye that love the Maypole, lend your voices to the nuptial song of the Lord and Lady of the May!"

This wedlock was more serious than most affairs of Merry Mount, where jest and delusion, trick and fantasy, kept up a continual carnival. The Lord and Lady of the May, though their titles must be laid down at sunset, were really and truly to be partners for the dance of life, beginning the measure that same bright eve. The wreath of roses, that hung from the lowest green bough of the Maypole, had been twined for them, and would be thrown over both their heads, in symbol of their flowery union. When the priest had spoken, therefore, a riotous uproar burst from the rout of monstrous figures.

"Begin you the stave, reverend Sir," cried they all; "and never did the woods ring to such a merry peal as we of the Maypole shall send up!"

Immediately a prelude of pipe, cithern, and viol, touched with practised minstrelsy, began to play from a neighboring thicket, in such a mirthful cadence that the boughs of the Maypole quivered to the sound. But the May Lord, he of the gilded staff, chancing to look into his Lady's eyes, was wonder struck at the almost pensive glance that met his own.

"Edith, sweet Lady of the May," whispered he reproachfully, "is yon wreath of roses a garland to hang above our graves, that you look so sad? O, Edith, this is our golden time! Tarnish it not by any pensive shadow of the mind; for it may be that nothing of futurity will be brighter than the mere remembrance of what is now passing."

"That was the very thought that saddened me! How came it in your mind too?" said Edith, in a still lower tone than he, for it was high treason to be sad at Merry Mount. "Therefore do I sigh amid this festive music. And besides, dear Edgar, I struggle as with a dream, and fancy that these shapes of our jovial friends are visionary, and their mirth unreal, and that we are no true Lord and Lady of the May. What is the mystery in my heart?"

Just then, as if a spell had loosened them, down came a little shower of withering rose leaves from the Maypole. Alas, for the young lovers! No sooner had their hearts glowed with real passion than they were sensible of something vague and unsubstantial in their former pleasures, and felt a dreary presentiment of inevitable change. From the moment that they truly loved, they had subjected themselves to earth's doom of care and sorrow, and troubled joy, and had no more a home at Merry Mount. That was Edith's mystery. Now leave we the priest to marry them, and the masquers to sport round the Maypole, till the last sunbeam be withdrawn from its summit, and the shadows of the forest mingle gloomily in the dance. Meanwhile, we may discover who these gay people were.

Two hundred years ago, and more, the old world and its inhabitants became mutually weary of each other. Men voyaged by thousands to the West: some to barter glass beads, and such like jewels, for the furs of the Indian hunter; some to conquer virgin empires; and one stern band to pray. But none of these motives had much weight with the colonists of Merry Mount. Their leaders were men who had sported so long with life, that when Thought and Wisdom came, even these unwelcome guests were led astray by the crowd of vanities which they should have put to flight. Erring Thought and perverted Wisdom were made to put on masques, and play the fool. The men of whom we speak, after losing the heart's fresh gayety, imagined a wild philosophy of pleasure, and came hither to act out their latest day-dream. They gathered followers from all that giddy tribe whose whole life is like the festal days of soberer men. In their train were minstrels, not unknown in London streets: wandering players, whose theatres had been the halls of noblemen; mummers, rope-dancers, and mounte-banks, who would long be missed at wakes, church ales, and fairs; in a word, mirth makers of every sort, such as abounded in that age, but now began to be discountenanced by the rapid growth of Puritanism. Light had their footsteps been on land, and as lightly they came across the sea. Many had been maddened by their previous troubles into a gay despair; others were as madly gay in the flush of youth, like the May Lord and his Lady; but whatever might be the quality of their mirth, old and young were gay at Merry Mount. The young deemed themselves happy. The elder spirits, if they knew that mirth was but the counterfeit of happiness, yet followed the false shadow wilfully, because at least her garments glittered brighest. Sworn triflers of a lifetime, they would not venture among the sober truths of life not even to be truly blest.

All the hereditary pastimes of Old England were transplanted hither. The King of Christmas was duly crowned, and the Lord of Misrule bore potent sway. On the Eve of St. John, they felled whole acres of the forest to make bonfires, and danced by the blaze all night, crowned with garlands, and throwing flowers into the flame. At harvest time, though their crop was of the smallest, they made an image with the sheaves of Indian corn, and wreathed it with autumnal garlands, and bore it home triumphantly. But what chiefly characterized the colonists of Merry Mount was their veneration for the Maypole. It has made their true history a poet's tale. Spring decked the hallowed emblem with young blossoms and fresh green boughs; Summer brought roses of the deepest blush, and the perfected foliage of the forest; Autumn enriched it with that red and yellow gorgeousness which converts each wildwood leaf into a painted flower; and Winter silvered it with sleet, and hung it round with icicles, till it flashed in the cold sunshine, itself a frozen sunbeam. Thus each alternate season did homage to the Maypole, and paid it a tribute of its own richest splendor. Its votaries danced round it, once, at least, in every month; sometimes they called it their religion, or their altar; but always, it was the banner staff of Merry Mount.

Unfortunately, there were men in the new world of a sterner faith than these Maypole worshippers. Not far from Merry Mount was a settlement of Puritans, most dismal wretches, who said their prayers before daylight, and then wrought in the forest or the cornfield till evening made it prayer time again. Their weapons were always at hand to shoot down the straggling savage. When they met in conclave, it was never to keep up the old English mirth, but to hear sermons three hours long, or to proclaim bounties on the heads of wolves and the scalps of Indians. Their festivals were fast days, and their cheif pastime the singing of psalms. Woe to the youth or maiden who did but dream of a dance! The selectman nodded to the constable; and there sat the light-heeled reprobate in the stocks; or if he danced, it was round the whipping-post, which might be termed the Puritan Maypole.

A party of these grim Puritans, toiling through the difficult woods, each with a horseload of iron armor to burden his footsteps, would sometimes draw near the sunny precincts of Merry Mount. There were the silken colonists, sporting round their Maypole; perhaps teaching a bear to dance, or striving to communicate their mirth to the grave Indian; or masquerading in the skins of deer and wolves, which they had hunted for that especial purpose. Often, the whole colony were playing at blindman's bluff, magistrates and all, with their eyes bandaged, except a single scapegoat, whom the blinded sinners pursued by the tinkling of the bells at his garments. Once, it is said, they were seen following a flower-decked corpse, with merriment and festive music, to his grave. But did the dead man laugh? In the quietest times, they sang ballads and told tales, for the edification of their pious visitors; or perplexed them with juggling tricks; or grinned at them through horse collars; and when sport itself grew wearisome, they made game of their own stupidity, and began a yawning match. At the very least of these enormities, the men of iron shook their heads and frowned so darkly that the revellers looked up, imagining that a momentary cloud had over-cast the sunshine, which was to be perpetual there. On the other hand, the Puritans affirmed that, when a psalm was pealing from their place of worship, the echo which the forest sent them back seemed often like the chorus of a jolly catch, closing with a roar of laughter. Who but the fiend, and his bond slaves, the crew of Merry Mount, had thus disturbed them? In due time, a feud arose, stern and bitter on one side, and as serious on the other as anything could be among such light spirits as had sworn allegiance to the Maypole. The future complexion of New England was involved in this important quarrel. Should the grizzly saints establish their jurisdiction over the gay sinners, then would their spirits darken all the clime, and make it a land of clouded viasges, of hard toil, of sermon and psalm forever. But should the banner staff of Merry Mount be fortunate, sunshine would break upon the hills, and flowers would beautify the forest, and late posterity do homage to the Maypole

After these authentic passages from history, we return to the nuptials of the Lord and Lady of the May. Alas! we have delayed too long, and must darken our tale too suddenly. As we glance again at the Maypole, a solitary sunbeam is fading from the summit, and leaves only a faint, golden tinge blended with the hues of the rainbow banner. Even that dim light is now withdrawn, relinquishing the whole domain of Merry Mount to the evening gloom, which has rushed so instantaneously from the black surrounding woods. But some of the black shadows have rushed forth in human shape.

Yes, with the setting sun, the last day of mirth had passed from Merry Mount. The ring of gay masquers was disordered and broken; the stag lowered his antlers in dismay; the wolf grew weaker than a lamb; the bells of the morris-dancers tinkled with tremulous affright. The Puritans had played a characteristic part in the Maypole mummeries. Their darksome figures were intermixed with the wild shapes of their foes, and made the scene a picture of the moment, when waking thoughts start up amid the scattered fantasies of a dream. The leader of the hostile party stood in the centre of the circle, while the route of monsters cowered around him, like evil spirits in the presence of a dread magician. No fantastic foolery could look him in the face. So stern was the energy of his aspect, that the whole man, visage, frame, and soul, seemed wrought of iron, gifted with life and thought, yet all of one substance with his headpiece and breastplate. It was the Puritan of Puritans; it was Endicott himself!

"Stand off, priest of Baal!" said he, with a grim frown, and laying no reverent hand upon the surplice. "I know thee, Blackstone![1] Thou art the man who couldst not abide the rule even of thine own corrupted church, and hast come hither to preach iniquity, and to give example of it in thy life. But now shall it be seen that the Lord hath sanctified this wilderness for his peculiar people. Woe unto them that would defile it! And first, for this flower-decked abomination, the altar of thy worship!"

And with his keen sword Endicott assaulted the hallowed Maypole. Nor long did it resist his arm. It groaned with a dismal sound; it showered leaves and rosebuds upon the remorseless enthusiast; and finally, with all its green boughs and ribbons and flowers, symbolic of departed pleasures, down fell the banner staff of Merry Mount. As it sank, tradition says, the evening sky grew darker, and the woods threw forth a more sombre shadow.

"There," cried Endicott, looking triumphantly on his work, "there lies the only Maypole in New England! The thought is strong within me that, by its fall, is

[1] Did Governor Endicott speak less positively, we should suspect a mistake here. The Rev. Mr. Blackstone, though an eccentric, is not known to have been an immoral man. We rather doubt his identity with the priest of Merry Mount.

shadowed forth the fate of light and idle mirth makers, amongst us and our posterity. Amen, saith John Endicott."

"Amen!" echoed his followers.

But the votaries of the Maypole gave one groan for their idol. At the sound, the Puritan leader glanced at the crew of Comus, each a figure of broad mirth, yet, at this moment, strangely expressive of sorrow and dismay.

"Valiant captain," quoth Peter Palfrey, the Ancient of the band, "what order shall be taken with the prisoners?"

"I thought not to repent me of cutting down a Maypole," replied Endicott, "yet now I could find in my heart to plant it again, and give each of these bestial pagans one other dance round their idol. It would have served rarely for a whippingpost!"

"But there are pine-trees enow," suggested the lieutenant.

"True, good Ancient," said the leader. "Wherefore, bind the heathen crew, and bestow on them a small matter of stripes apiece, as earnest of our future justice. Set some of the rogues in the stocks to rest themselves, so soon as Providence shall bring us to one of our own well-ordered settlements, where such accommodations may be found. Further penalties, such as branding and cropping of ears, shall be thought of hereafter."

"How many stripes for the priest?" inquired Ancient Palfrey.

"None as yet," answered Endicott, bending his iron frown upon the culprit. "It must be for the Great and General Court to determine, whether stripes and long imprisonment, and other grievous penalty, may atone for his transgressions. Let him look to himself! For such as violate our civil order, it may be permitted us to show mercy. But woe to the wretch that troubleth our religion!"

"And this dancing bear," resumed the officer. "Must he share the stripes of his fellows?"

"Shoot him through the head!" said the energetic Puritan. "I suspect witchcraft in the beast."

"Here be a couple of shining ones," continued Peter Palfrey, pointing his weapon at the Lord and Lady of the May. "They seem to be of high station among these misdoers. Methinks their dignity will not be fitted with less than a double share of stripes."

Endicott rested on his sword, and closely surveyed the dress and aspect of the hapless pair. There they stood, pale, downcast, and apprehensive. Yet there was an air of mutual support, and of pure affection, seeking aid and giving it, that showed them to be man and wife, with the sanction of a priest upon their love. The youth, in the peril of the moment, had dropped his gilded staff, and thrown his arm about the Lady of the May, who leaned against his breast, too lightly to burden him, but with weight enough to express that their destinies were linked together, for good or evil. They looked first at each other, and then into the grim captain's face. There they stood, in the first hour of wedlock, while the idle pleasures, of which their companions were the emblems, had given place to the sternest cares of life, personified by the dark Puritans. But never had their youthful beauty seemed so pure and high as when its glow was chastened by adversity.

"Youth," said Endicott, "ye stand in an evil case thou and thy maiden wife. Make ready presently, for I am minded that ye shall both have a token to remember your wedding day!"

"Stern man," cried the May Lord, "how can I move thee? Were the means at hand, I would resist to the death. Being powerless, I entreat! Do with me as thou wilt, but let Edith go untouched!"

"Not so," replied the immitigable zealot. "We are not wont to show an idle courtesy to that sex, which requireth the stricter discipline. What sayest thou, maid? Shall thy silken bridegroom suffer thy share of the penalty, besides his own?"

"Be it death," said Edith, "and lay it all on me!"

Truly, as Endicott had said, the poor lovers stood in a woeful case. Their foes were triumphant, their friends captive and abased, their home desolate, the benighted wilderness around them, and a rigorous destiny, in the shape of the Puritan leader, their only guide. Yet the deepening twilight could not altogether conceal that the iron man was softened; he smiled at the fair spectacle of early love; he almost sighed for the inevitable blight of early hopes.

"The troubles of life have come hastily on this young couple," observed Endicott. "We will see how they comport themselves under their present trials ere we burden them with greater. If, among the spoil, there be any garments of a more decent fashion, let them be put upon this May Lord and his Lady, instead of their glistening vanities. Look to it, some of you."

"And shall not the youth's hair be cut?" asked Peter Palfrey, looking with abhorrence at the lovelock and long glossy curls of the young man.

"Crop it forthwith, and that in the true pumpkin-shell fashion," answered the captain. "Then bring them along with us, but more gently than their fellows. There be qualities in the youth, which may make him valiant to fight, and sober to toil, and pious to pray; and in the maiden, that may fit her to become a mother in our Israel, bringing up babes in better nurture than her own hath been. Nor think ye, young ones, that they are the happiest, even in our lifetime of a moment, who misspend it in dancing around a Maypole!"

And Endicott, the severest Puritan of all who laid the rock foundation of New England, lifted the wreath of roses from the ruin of the Maypole, and threw it, with his own gauntleted hand, over the heads of the Lord and Lady of the May. It was a deed of prophecy. As the moral gloom of the world overpowers all systematic gayety, even so was their home of wild mirth made desolate amid the sad forest. They returned to it no more. But as their flowery garland was wreathed of the brightest roses that had grown there, so, in the tie that united them, were intertwined all the purest and best of their early joys. They went heavenward, supporting each other along the difficult path which it was their lot to tread, and never wasted one regretful thought on the vanities of Merry Mount.

MY KINSMAN, MAJOR MOLINEUX

After the kings of Great Britain had assumed the right of appointing the colonial governors, the measures of the latter seldom met with the ready and generous approbation which had been paid to those of their predecessors, under the original charters. The people looked with most jealous scrutiny to the exercise of power which did not emanate from themselves, and they usually rewarded their rulers with slender gratitude for the compliances by which, in softening their instructions from beyond the sea, they had incurred the reprehension of those who gave them. The annals of Massachusetts Bay will inform us, that of six governors in the space of about forty years from the surrender of the old charter, under James II., two were imprisoned by a popular insurrection; a third, as Hutchinson inclines to believe, was driven from the province by the whizzing of a musket-ball; a fourth, in the opinion of the same historian, was hastened to his grave by continual bickerings with the House of Representatives; and the remaining two, as well as their successors, till the Revolution, were favored with few and brief intervals of peaceful sway. The inferior members of the court party, in times of high political excitement, led scarcely a more desirable life. These remarks may serve as a preface to the following adventures, which chanced upon a summer night, not far from a hundred years ago. The reader, in order to avoid a long and dry detail of colonial affairs, is requested to dispense with an account of the train of circumstances that had caused much temporary inflammation of the popular mind.

It was near nine o'clock of a moonlight evening, when a boat crossed the ferry with a single passenger, who had obtained his conveyance at that unusual hour by the promise of an extra fare. While he stood on the landing-place, searching in either pocket for the means of fulfilling his agreement, the ferryman lifted a lantern, by the aid of which, and the newly risen moon, he took a very accurate survey of the stranger's figure. He was a youth of barely eighteen years, evidently country-bred, and now, as it should seem, upon his first visit to town. He was clad in a coarse gray coat, well worn, but in excellent repair; his under garments were durably constructed of leather, and fitted tight to a pair of serviceable and well-shaped limbs; his stockings of blue yarn were the incontrovertible work of a mother or a sister; and on his head was a three-cornered hat, which in its better days had perhaps sheltered the graver brow of the lad's father. Under his left arm was a heavy cudgel formed of an oak sapling, and retaining a part of the hardened root; and his equipment was completed by a wallet, not so abundantly stocked as to incommode the vigorous shoulders on which it hung. Brown, curly hair, well-shaped features, and bright, cheerful eyes were nature's gifts, and worth all that art could have done for his adornment.

The youth, one of whose names was Robin, finally drew from his pocket the half of a little province bill of five shillings, which, in the depreciation in that sort of currency, did but satisfy the ferryman's demand, with the surplus of a sexangular piece of parchment, valued at three pence. He then walked forward into the town, with as light a step as if his day's journey had not already exceeded thirty miles, and with as eager an eye as if he were entering London city, instead of the little metropolis of a New England colony. Before Robin had proceeded far, however, it occurred to him that he knew not whither to direct his steps; so he paused, and looked up and down the narrow street, scrutinizing the small and mean wooden buildings that were scattered on either side.

"This low hovel cannot be my kinsman's dwelling," thought he, "nor yonder old house, where the moonlight enters at the broken casement; and truly I see none hereabouts that might be worthy of him. It would have been wise to inquire my way of the ferryman, and doubtless he would have gone with me, and earned a shilling from the Major for his pains. But the next man I meet will do as well."

He resumed his walk, and was glad to perceive that the street now became wider, and the houses more respectable in their appearance. He soon discerned a figure moving on moderately in advance, and hastened his steps to overtake it. As Robin drew nigh, he saw that the passenger was a man in years, with a full periwig of gray hair, a wide-skirted coat of dark cloth, and silk stockings rolled above his knees. He carried a long and polished cane, which he struck down perpendicularly before him at every step; and at regular intervals he uttered two successive hems, of a peculiarly solemn and sepulchral intonation. Having made these observations, Robin laid hold of the skirt of the old man's coat, just when the light from the open door and windows of a barber's shop fell upon both their figures.

"Good evening to you, honored sir," said he, making a low bow, and still retaining his hold of the skirt. "I pray you tell me whereabouts is the dwelling of my kinsman, Major Molineux."

The youth's question was uttered very loudly; and one of the barbers, whose razor was descending on a well-soaped chin, and another who was dressing a Ramillies wig, left their occupations, and came to the door. The citizen, in the mean time, turned a long-favored countenance upon Robin, and answered him in a tone of excessive anger and annoyance. His two sepulchral hems, however, broke into the very centre of his rebuke, with most singular effect, like a thought of the cold grave obtruding among wrathful passions.

"Let go my garment, fellow! I tell you, I know not the man you speak of. What! I have authority, I have – hem, hem – authority; and if this be the respect you show for your betters, your feet shall be brought acquainted with the stocks by daylight, tomorrow morning!"

Robin released the old man's skirt, and hastened away, pursued by an ill-mannered roar of laughter from the barber's shop. He was at first considerably surprised by the result of his question, but, being a shrewd youth, soon thought himself able to account for the mystery.

"This is some country representative," was his conclusion, "who has never seen the inside of my kinsman's door, and lacks the breeding to answer a stranger civilly. The man is old, or verily – I might be tempted to turn back and smite him on the nose. Ah, Robin, Robin! even the barber's boys laugh at you for choosing such a guide! You will be wiser in time, friend Robin."

He now became entangled in a succession of crooked and narrow streets, which crossed each other, and meandered at no great distance from the water-side. The smell of tar was obvious to his nostrils, the masts of vessels pierced the moonlight above the tops of the buildings, and the numerous signs, which Robin paused to read, informed him that he was near the centre of business. But the streets were empty, the shops were closed, and lights were visible only in the second stories of a few dwelling-houses. At length, on the corner of a narrow lane, through which he was passing, he beheld the broad countenance of a British hero swinging before the door of an inn, whence proceeded the voices of many guests. The casement of one of the lower windows was thrown back, and a very thin curtain permitted Robin to distinguish a party at supper, round a well-furnished table. The fragrance of the good cheer steamed forth into the outer air, and the youth could not fail to recollect that the last remnant of his travelling stock of provision had yielded to his morning appetite, and that noon had found and left him dinnerless.

"Oh, that a parchment three-penny might give me a right to sit down at yonder table!" said Robin, with a sigh. "But the Major will make me welcome to the best of his victuals; so I will even step boldly in, and inquire my way to his dwelling."

He entered the tavern, and was guided by the murmur of voices and the fumes of tobacco to the public-room. It was a long and low apartment, with oaken walls, grown dark in the continual smoke, and a floor which was thickly sanded, but of no immaculate purity. A number of persons – the larger part of whom appeared to be mariners, or in some way connected with the sea – occupied the wooden benches, or leather-bottomed chairs, conversing on various matters, and occasionally lending their attention to some topic of general interest. Three or four little groups were draining as many bowls of punch, which the West India trade had long since made a familiar drink in the colony. Others, who had the appearance of men who lived by regular and laborious handicraft, preferred the insulated bliss of an unshared potation, and became more taciturn under its influence. Nearly all, in short, evinced a predilection for the Good Creature in some of its various shapes, for this is a vice to which, as Fast Day sermons of a hundred years ago will testify, we have a long hereditary claim. The only guests to whom Robin's sympathies inclined him were two or three sheepish countrymen, who were using the inn somewhat after the fashion of a Turkish caravansary; they had gotten themselves into the darkest corner of the room, and heedless of the Nicotian atmosphere, were supping on the bread of their own ovens, and the bacon cured in their own chimney-smoke. But though Robin felt a sort of brotherhood with these strangers, his eyes were attracted from them to a person who stood near the door, holding whispered conversation with a group of ill-dressed associates. His features were separately striking almost to grotesqueness, and the whole face left a deep impression on the memory. The forehead bulged out into a double prominence, with a vale between; the nose came boldly forth in an irregular curve, and its bridge was of more than a finger's breadth; the eyebrows were deep and shaggy, and the eyes glowed beneath them like fire in a cave.

While Robin deliberated of whom to inquire respecting his kinsman's dwelling, he was accosted by the innkeeper, a little man in a stained white apron, who had come to pay his professional welcome to the stranger. Being in the second generation from a French Protestant, he seemed to have inherited the courtesy of his parent nation; but no variety of circumstances was ever known to change his voice from the one shrill note in which he now addressed Robin.

"From the country, I presume, sir?" said he, with a profound bow. "Beg leave to congratulate you on your arrival, and trust you intend a long stay with us. Fine town here, sir, beautiful buildings, and much that may interest a stranger. May I hope for the honor of your commands in respect to supper?"

"The man sees a family likeness! the rogue has guessed that I am related to the Major!" thought Robin, who had hitherto experienced little superfluous civility.

All eyes were now turned on the country lad, standing at the door, in his worn three-cornered hat, gray coat, leather breeches, and blue yarn stockings, leaning on an oaken cudgel, and bearing a wallet on his back.

Robin replied to the courteous innkeeper, with such an assumption of confidence as befitted the Major's relative. "My honest friend," he said, "I shall make it a point to patronize your house on some occasion, when" – here he could not help lowering his voice – "when I may have more than a parchment three-pence in my pocket. My present business," continued he, speaking with lofty confidence, "is merely to inquire my way to the dwelling of my kinsman, Major Molineux."

There was a sudden and general movement in the room, which Robin interpreted as expressing the eagerness of each individual to become his guide. But the innkeeper turned his eyes to a written paper on the wall, which he read, or seemed to read, with occasional recurrences to the young man's figure.

"What have we here?" said he, breaking his speech into little dry fragments.

" 'Left the house of the subscriber, bounden servant, Hezekiah Mudge, – had on, when he went away, gray coat, leather breeches, master's third-best hat. One pound currency reward to whosoever shall lodge him in any jail of the providence.' Better trudge, boy; better trudge!"

Robin had begun to draw his hand towards the lighter end of the oak cudgel, but a strange hostility in every countenance induced him to relinquish his purpose of breaking the courteous innkeeper's head. As he turned to leave the room, he encountered a sneering glance from the bold-featured personage whom he had before noticed; and no sooner was he beyond the door, than he heard a general laugh, in which the innkeeper's voice might be distinguished, like the dropping of small stones into a kettle.

"Now, is it not strange," thought Robin, with his usual shrewdness, – "is it not strange that the confession of an empty pocket should outweigh the name of my kinsman, Major Molineux? Oh, if I had one of those grinning rascals in the woods, where I and my oak sapling grew up together, I would teach him that my arm is heavy though my purse be light!"

On turning the corner of the narrow lane, Robin found himself in a spacious street, with an unbroken line of lofty houses on each side, and a steepled building at the upper end, whence the ringing of a bell announced the hour of nine. The light of the moon, and the lamps from the numerous shop-windows, discovered people promenading on the pavement, and amongst them Robin had hoped to recognize his hitherto inscrutable relative. The result of his former inquiries made him unwilling to hazard another, in a scene of such publicity, and he determined to walk slowly and silently up the street, thrusting his face close to that of every elderly gentleman, in search of the Major's lineaments. In his progress, Robin encountered many gay and gallant figures. Embroidered garments of showy colors, enormous periwigs, gold-laced hats, and silver-hilted swords glided past him and dazzled his optics. Travelled youths, imitators of the European fine gentlemen of the period, trod jauntily along, half dancing to the fashionable tunes which they hummed, and making poor Robin ashamed of his quiet and natural gait. At length, after many pauses to examine the gorgeous display of goods in the shop-windows, and after suffering some rebukes for the impertinence of his scrutiny into people's faces, the Major's kinsman found himself near the steepled building, still unsuccessful in his search. As yet, however, he had seen only one side of the thronged street; so Robin crossed, and continued the same sort of inquisition down the opposite pavement, with stronger hopes than the philosopher seeking an honest man, but with no better fortune. He had arrived about midway towards the lower end, from which his course began, when he overheard the approach of some one who struck down a cane on the flag-stones at every step, uttering at regular intervals, two sepulchral hems.

"Mercy on us!" quoth Robin, recognizing the sound.

Turning a corner, which chanced to be close at his right hand, he hastened to pursue his researches in some other part of the town. His patience now was wearing low, and he seemed to feel more fatigue from his rambles since he crossed the ferry, than from his journey of several days on the other side. Hunger also pleaded loudly within him, and Robin began to balance the propriety of demanding, violently, and with lifted cudgel, the necessary guidance from the first solitary passenger whom he should meet. While a resolution to this effect was gaining strength, he entered a street of mean appearance, on either side of which a row of ill-built houses was straggling towards the harbor. The moonlight fell upon no passenger along the whole extent, but in the third domicile which Robin passed there was a half-opened door, and his keen glance detected a woman's garment within.

"My luck may be better here," said he to himself.

Accordingly, he approached the door, and beheld it shut closer as he did so; yet an open space remained, sufficing for the fair occupant to observe the stranger, without a corresponding display on her part. All that Robin could discern was a strip of scarlet petticoat, and the occasional sparkle of an eye, as if the moonbeams were trembling on some bright thing.

"Pretty mistress," for I may call her so with a good conscience, thought the shrewd youth, since I know nothing to the contrary, – "my sweet pretty mistress, will you be kind enough to tell me whereabouts I must seek the dwelling of my kinsman, Major Molineux?"

Robin's voice was plaintive and winning, and the female, seeing nothing to be shunned in the handsome country youth, thrust open the door, and came forth into the moonlight. She was a dainty little figure, with a white neck, round arms, and a slender waist, at the extremity of which her scarlet petticoat jutted out over a hoop, as if she were standing in a balloon. Moreover, her face was oval and pretty, her hair dark beneath the little cap, and her bright eyes possessed a sly freedom, which triumphed over those of Robin.

"Major Molineux dwells here," said this fair woman.

Now, her voice was the sweetest Robin had heard that night, yet he could not help doubting whether that sweet voice spoke Gospel truth. He looked up and down the mean street, and then surveyed the house before which they stood. It was a small, dark edifice of two stories, the second of which projected over the lower floor, and the front apartment had the aspect of a shop for petty commodities.

"Now, truly, I am in luck," replied Robin, cunningly, "and so indeed is my kinsman, the Major, in having so pretty a housekeeper. But I prithee trouble him to step to the door; I will deliver him a message from his friends in the country, and then go back to my lodgings at the inn."

"Nay, the Major has been abed this hour or more," said the lady of the scarlet petticoat; "and it would be to little purpose to disturb him to-night, seeing his evening draught was of the strongest. But he is a kind-hearted man, and it would be as much as my life's worth to let a kinsman of his turn away from the door. You are the good old gentleman's very picture, and I could swear that was his rainy-weather hat. Also he has garments very much resembling those leather small-clothes. But come in, I pray, for I bid you hearty welcome in his name."

So saying, the fair and hospitable dame took our hero by the hand; and the touch was light, and the force was gentleness, and though Robin read in her eyes what he did not hear in her words, yet the slender-waisted woman in the scarlet petticoat proved stronger than the athletic country youth. She had drawn his half-willing footsteps nearly to the threshold, when the opening of a door in the neighborhood startled the Major's housekeeper, and, leaving the Major's kinsman, she vanished speedily into her own domicile. A heavy yawn preceded the appearance of a man, who, like the Moonshine of Pyramus and Thisbe, carried a lantern, needlessly aiding his sister luminary in the heavens. As he walked sleepily up the street, he turned his broad, dull face on Robin, and displayed a long staff, spiked at the end.

"Home, vagabond, home!" said the watchman, in accents that seemed to fall asleep as soon as they were uttered. "Home, or we'll set you in the stocks by peep of day!"

"This is the second hint of the kind," thought Robin. "I wish they would end my difficulties, by setting me there to-night."

Nevertheless, the youth felt an instinctive antipathy towards the guardian of midnight order, which at first prevented him from asking his usual question. But just when the man was about to vanish behind the corner, Robin resolved not to lose the opportunity, and shouted lustily after him, —

"I say, friend! will you guide me to the house of my kinsman, Major Molineux?"

The watchman made no reply, but turned the corner and was gone; yet Robin seemed to hear the sound of drowsy laughter stealing along the solitary street. At that moment, also, a pleasant titter saluted him from the open window above his head; he looked up, and caught the sparkle of a saucy eye; a round arm beckoned to him, and next he heard light footsteps descending the staircase within. But Robin, being of the household of a New England clergyman, was a good youth, as well as a shrewd one; so he resisted temptation, and fled away.

He now roamed desperately, and at random, through the town, almost ready to believe that a spell was on him, like that by which a wizard of his country had once kept three pursuers wandering, a whole winter night, within twenty paces of the cottage which they sought. The streets lay before him, strange and desolate, and the lights were extinguished in almost every house. Twice, however, little parties of men, among whom Robin distinguished individuals in outlandish attire, came hurrying along; but, though on both occasions, they paused to address him, such intercourse did not at all enlighten his perplexity. They did but utter a few words in some language of which Robin knew nothing, and perceiving his inability to answer, bestowed a curse upon him in plain English and hastened away.

Finally, the lad determined to knock at the door of every mansion that might appear worthy to be occupied by his kinsman, trusting that perseverance would overcome the fatality that had hitherto thwarted him. Firm in his resolve, he was passing beneath the walls of a church, which formed the corner of two streets, when, as he turned into the shade of its steeple, he encountered a bulky stranger, muffled in a cloak. The man was proceeding with the speed of earnest business, but Robin planted himself full before him, holding the oak cudgel with both hands across his body as a bar to further passage.

"Halt, honest man, and answer me a question," said he, very resolutely. "Tell me, this instant, whereabouts is the dwelling of my kinsman, Major Molineux!"

"Keep your tongue between your teeth, fool, and let me pass!" said a deep, gruff voice, which Robin partly remembered. "Let me pass, or I'll strike you to the earth!"

"No, no, neighbor!" cried Robin, flourishing his cudgel, and then thrusting its larger end close to the man's muffled face. "No, no, I'm not the fool you take me for, nor do you pass till I have an answer to my question. Whereabouts is the dwelling of my kinsman, Major Molineux?"

The stranger, instead of attempting to force his passage, stepped back into the moonlight, unmuffled his face, and stared full into that of Robin.

"Watch here an hour, and Major Molineux will pass by," said he.

Robin gazed with dismay and astonishment on the unprecedented physiognomy of the speaker. The forehead with its double prominence, the broad hooked nose, the shaggy eyebrows, and fiery eyes were those which he had noticed at the inn, but the man's complexion had undergone a singular, or, more properly, a twofold change. One side of the face blazed an intense red, while the other was black as midnight, the division line being in the broad bridge of the nose; and a mouth which seemed to extend from ear to ear was black or red, in contrast to the color of the cheek. The effect was as if two individual devils, a fiend of fire and a fiend of darkness, had united themselves to form this infernal visage. The stranger grinned in Robin's face, muffled his party-colored features, and was out of sight in a moment.

"Strange things we travellers see!" ejaculated Robin.

He seated himself, however, upon the steps of the church-door, resolving to wait the appointed time for his kinsman. A few moments were consumed in philosophical speculations upon the species of man who had just left him; but having settled this point shrewdly, rationally, and satisfactorily, he was compelled to look elsewhere for his amusement. At first he threw his eyes along the street. It was of more respectable appearance than most of those into which he had wandered; and the moon, creating, like the imaginative power, a beautiful strangeness in familiar objects, gave something of romance to a scene that might not have possessed it in the light of day. The irregular and often quaint architecture of the houses, some of whose roofs were broken into numerous little peaks, while others ascended, steep and narrow, into a single point, and others again were square; the pure snow-white of some of their complexions, the aged darkness of others, and the thousand sparklings, reflected from bright substances in the walls of many; these matters engaged Robin's attention for a while, and then began to grow wearisome. Next he endeavored to define the forms of distant objects, starting away, with almost ghostly indistinctness, just as his eye appeared to grasp them; and finally he took a minute survey of an edifice which stood on the opposite side of the street, directly in front of the church-door, where he was stationed. It was a large, square mansion, distinguished from its neighbors by a balcony, which rested on tall pillars, and by an elaborate Gothic window, communicating therewith.

"Perhaps this is the very house I have been seeking," thought Robin.

Then he strove to speed away the time, by listening to a murmur which swept continually along the street, yet scarcely audible, except to an unaccustomed ear like his; it was a low, dull, dreamy sound, compounded of many noises, each of which was at too great a distance to be separately heard. Robin marvelled at this snore of a sleeping town, and marvelled more whenever its continuity was broken by now and then a distant shout, apparently loud where it originated. But altogether it was a sleep-inspiring sound, and, to shake off its drowsy influence, Robin arose, and climbed a window-frame, that he might view the interior of the church. There the moonbeams came trembling in, and fell down upon the deserted pews, and extended along the quiet aisles. A fainter yet more awful radiance was hovering around the pulpit, and one solitary ray had dared to rest upon the open page of the great Bible. Had nature, in that deep hour, become a worshipper in the house which man had builded? Or was that heavenly light the visible sanctity of the place, — visible because no earthly and impure feet were within the walls? The scene made Robin's heart shiver with a sensation of loneliness stronger than he had ever felt in the remotest depths of his native woods; so he turned away and sat down again before the door. There were graves around the church, and now an uneasy thought obtruded into Robin's breast. What if the object of his search, which had been so often and so strangely thwarted, were all the time mouldering in his shroud? What if his kinsman should glide through yonder gate, and nod and smile to him in dimly passing by?

"Oh that any breathing thing were here with me!" said Robin.

Recalling his thoughts from this uncomfortable track, he sent them over forest, hill, and stream, and attempted to imagine how that evening of ambiguity and weariness had been spent by his father's household. He pictured them assembled at the door, beneath the tree, the great old tree, which had been spared for its huge twisted trunk and venerable shade, when a thousand leafy brethren fell. There, at the going down of the summer sun, it was his father's custom to perform domestic worship, that the neighbors might come and join with him like brothers of the family, and that the wayfaring man might pause to drink at that fountain, and keep his heart pure by freshening the memory of home. Robin distinguished the seat of every individual of the little audience; he saw the good man in the midst, holding the Scriptures in the golden light that fell from the western clouds; he beheld him close the book and all rise up to pray. He heard the old thanksgivings for daily mercies, the old supplications for their continuance, to which he had so often listened in weariness, but which were now among his dear remembrances. He perceived the slight inequality of his father's voice when he came to speak of the absent one; he noted how his mother turned her face to the broad and knotted trunk; how his elder brother scorned, because the beard was rough upon his upper lip, to permit his features to be moved; how the younger sister drew down a low hanging branch before her eyes; and how the little one of all, whose sports had hitherto broken the decorum of the scene, understood the prayer for her playmate, and burst into clamorous grief. Then he saw them go in at the door; and when Robin would have entered also, the latch tinkled into its place, and he was excluded from his home.

"Am I here, or there?" cried Robin, starting; for all at once, when his thoughts had become visible and audible in a dream, the long, wide, solitary street shone out before him.

He aroused himself, and endeavored to fix his attention steadily upon the large edifice which he had surveyed before. But still his mind kept vibrating between fancy and reality; by turns, the pillars of the balcony lengthened into the tall, bare stems of pines, dwindled down to human figures, settled again into their true shape and size, and then commenced a new succession of changes. For a single moment, when he deemed himself awake, he could have sworn that a visage — one which he seemed to remember, yet could not absolutely name as his kinsman's — was looking towards him from the Gothic windows. A deeper sleep wrestled with and nearly overcame him, but fled at the sound of footsteps along the opposite pavement. Robin rubbed his eyes, discerned a man passing at the foot of the balcony, and addressed him in a loud, peevish and lamentable cry.

"Hallo, friend! must I wait here all night for my kinsman, Major Molineux?"

The sleeping echoes awoke, and answered the voice; and the passenger, barely able to discern a figure sitting in the oblique shade of the steeple, traversed the street to obtain a nearer view. He was himself a gentleman in his prime, of open, intelligent, cheerful, and altogether prepossessing countenance. Perceiving a country youth, apparently homeless and without friends, he accosted him in a tone of real kindness, which had become strange to Robin's ears.

"Well, my good lad, why are you sitting here?" inquired he. "Can I be of service to you in any way?"

"I am afraid not, sir," replied Robin, despondingly; "yet I shall take it kindly, if you'll answer me a single question. I've been searching, half the night, for one Major Molineux; now, sir, is there really such a person in these parts, or am I dreaming?"

"Major Molineux! The name is not altogether strange to me," said the gentleman, smiling. "Have you any objection to telling me the nature of your business with him?"

Then Robin briefly related that his father was a clergyman, settled on a small salary, at a long distance back in the country, and that he and Major Molineux were brothers' children. The Major, having inherited riches, and acquired civil and military rank, had visited his cousin, in great pomp, a year or two before; had manifested much interest in Robin and an elder brother, and, being childless himself, had thrown out hints respecting the future establishment of one of them in life. The elder brother was destined to succeed to the farm which his father cultivated in the interval of sacred duties; it was therefore determined that Robin should profit by his kinsman's generous intentions, especially as he seemed to be rather the favorite, and was thought to possess other necessary endowments.

"For I have the name of being a shrewd youth," observed Robin, in this part of his story.

"I doubt not you deserve it," replied his new friend, goodnaturedly; "but pray proceed."

"Well, sir, being nearly eighteen years old, and well grown, as you see," continued Robin, drawing himself up to his full height, "I thought it high time to begin in the world. So my mother and sister put me in handsome trim, and my father gave me half the remnant of his last year's salary, and five days ago I started for this place, to pay the Major a visit. But, would you believe it, sir! I crossed the ferry a little after dark, and have yet found nobody that would show me the way to his dwelling; only, an hour or two since, I was told to wait here, and Major Molineux would pass by."

"Can you describe the man who told you this?" inquired the gentleman.

"Oh, he was a very ill-favored fellow, sir," replied Robin, "with two great bumps on his forehead, a hook nose, fiery eyes; and, what struck me as the strangest, his face was of two different colors. Do you happen to know such a man, sir?"

"Not intimately," answered the stranger, "but I chanced to meet him a little time previous to your stopping me. I believe you may trust his word, and that the Major will very shortly pass through this street. In the mean time, as I have a singular curiosity to witness your meeting, I will sit down here upon the steps and bear you company."

He seated himself accordingly, and soon engaged his companion in animated discourse. It was but of brief continuance, however, for a noise of shouting, which had long been remotely audible, drew so much nearer that Robin inquired its cause.

"What may be the meaning of this uproar?" asked he. "Truly, if your town be always as noisy, I shall find little sleep while I am an inhabitant."

"Why, indeed, friend Robin, there do appear to be three or four riotous fellows abroad to-night," replied the gentleman. "You must not expect all the stillness of your native woods here in our streets. But the watch will shortly be at the heels of these lads and" —

"Ay, and set them in the stocks by peep of day," interrupted Robin, recollecting his own encounter with the drowsy lantern-bearer. "But, dear sir, if I may trust my ears, an army of watchmen would never make head against such a multitude of rioters. There were at least a thousand voices went up to make that one shout."

"May not a man have several voices, Robin, as well as two complexions?" said his friend.

"Perhaps a man may; but Heaven forbid that a woman should!" responded the shrewd youth, thinking of the seductive tones of the Major's housekeeper.

The sounds of a trumpet in some neighboring street now became so evident and continual, that Robin's curiosity was strongly excited. In addition to the shouts, he heard frequent bursts from many instruments of discord, and a wild and confused laughter filled up the intervals. Robin rose from the steps, and looked wistfully towards a point wither people seemed to be hastening.

"Surely some prodigious merry-making is going on," exclaimed he. "I have laughed very little since I left home, sir, and should be sorry to lose an opportunity. Shall we step round the corner by that darkish house, and take our share of the fun?"

"Sit down again, sit down, good Robin," replied the gentleman, laying his hand on the skirt of the gray coat. "You forget that we must wait here for your kinsman; and there is reason to believe that he will pass by, in the course of a very few moments."

The near approach of the uproar had now disturbed the neighborhood; windows flew open on all sides; and many heads, in the attire of the pillow, and confused by sleep suddenly broken, were protruded to the gaze of whoever had leisure to observe them. Eager voices hailed each other from house to house, all demanding the explanation, which not a soul could give. Half-dressed men hurried towards the unknown commotion, stumbling as they went over the stone steps that thrust themselves into the narrow footwalk. The shouts, the laughter, and the tuneless bray, the antipodes of music, came onwards with increasing din, till scattered individuals, and then denser bodies, began to appear round a corner at the distance of a hundred yards.

"Will you recognize your kinsman, if he passes in this crowd?" inquired the gentleman.

"Indeed, I can't warrant it, sir; but I'll take my stand here, and keep a bright lookout," answered Robin, descending to the outer edge of the pavement.

A mighty stream of people now emptied into the street, and came rolling slowly towards the church. A single horseman wheeled the corner in the midst of them, and close behind him came a band of fearful wind-instruments, sending forth a fresher discord now that no intervening buildings kept it from the ear. Then a redder light disturbed the moonbeams, and a dense multitude of torches shone along the street, concealing, by their glare, whatever object they illuminated. The single horseman, clad in a military dress, and bearing a drawn sword, rode onward as the leader, and, by his fierce and variegated countenance, appeared like war personified; the red of one cheek was an emblem of fire and sword; the blackness of the other betokened the mourning that attends them. In his train were wild figures in the Indian dress, and many fantastic shapes without a model, giving the whole march a visionary air, as if a dream had broken forth from some feverish brain, and were sweeping visibly through the midnight streets. A mass of people, inactive, except as applauding spectators, hemmed the procession in; and several women ran along the sidewalk, piercing the confusion of heavier sounds with their shrill voices of mirth or terror.

"The double-faced fellow has his eye upon me," muttered Robin, with an indefinite but an uncomfortable idea that he was himself to bear a part in the pageantry.

The leader turned himself in the saddle, and fixed his glance full upon the country youth, as the steed went slowly by. When Robin had freed his eyes from those fiery ones, the musicians were passing before him, and the torches were close at hand; but the unsteady brightness of the latter formed a veil which he could not penetrate. The rattling of wheels over the stones sometimes found its way to his ear, and confused traces of a human form appeared at intervals, and then melted into the vivid light. A moment more, and the leader thundered a command to halt: the trumpets vomited a horrid breath, and then held their peace; the shouts and laughter of the people died away, and there remained only a universal hum, allied to silence. Right before Robin's eyes was an uncovered cart. There the torches blazed the brightest, there the moon shone out like day, and there, in tar-and-feathery dignity, sat his kinsman, Major Molineux!

He was an elderly man, of large and majestic person, and strong, square features, betokening a steady soul; but steady as it was, his enemies had found means to shake it. His face was pale as death, and far more ghastly; the broad forehead was contracted in his agony, so that his eyebrows formed one grizzled line; his eyes were red and wild, and the foam hung white upon his quivering lip. His whole frame was agitated by a quick and continual tremor, which his pride strove to quell, even in those circumstances of overwhelming humiliation. But perhaps the bitterest pang of all was when his eyes met those of Robin; for he evidently knew him on the instant, as the youth stood witnessing the foul disgrace of a head grown gray in honor. They stared at each other in silence, and Robin's knees shook, and his hair bristled, with a mixture of pity and terror. Soon, however, a bewildering excitement began to seize upon his mind; the preceding adventures of the night, the unexpected appearance of the crowd, the torches, the confused din and the hush that followed, the spectre of his kinsman reviled by that great multitude, — all this, and, more than all, a perception of tremendous ridicule in the whole scene, affected him with a sort of mental inebriety. At that moment a voice of sluggish merriment saluted Robin's ears; he turned instinctively, and just behind the corner of the church stood the lantern-bearer, rubbing his eyes, and drowsily enjoying the lad's amazement. Then he heard a peal of laughter like the ringing of silvery bells; a woman twitched his arm, a saucy eye met his, and he saw the lady of the scarlet petticoat. A sharp, dry cachinnation appealed to his memory, and standing on tiptoe in the crowd, with his white apron over his head, he beheld the courteous little innkeeper. And lastly, there sailed over the heads of the multitude a great, broad laugh, broken in the midst by two sepulchral hems; thus, "Haw, haw, haw, — hem, hem, — haw, haw, haw, haw!"

The sound proceeded from the balcony of the opposite edifice, and thither Robin turned his eyes. In front of the Gothic window stood the old citizen, wrapped in a wide gown, his gray periwig exchanged for a nightcap, which was thrust back from his forehead, and his silk stockings hanging about his legs. He supported himself on his polished cane in a fit of convulsive merriment, which manifested itself on his solemn old features like a funny inscription on a tombstone. Then Robin seemed to hear the voices of the barbers, of the guests of the inn, and of all who had made sport of him that night. The contagion was spreading among the multitude, when all at once, it seized upon Robin, and he sent forth a shout of laughter that echoed through the street, — every man shook his sides, every man emptied his lungs, but Robin's shout was the loudest there. The cloud-spirits peeped from their silvery islands, as the congregated mirth went roaring up the sky! The Man in the Moon heard the far bellow. "Oho," quoth he, "the old earth is frolicsome to-night!"

When there was a momentary calm in that tempestuous sea of sound, the leader gave the sign, the procession resumed its march. On they went, like fiends that throng in mockery around some dead potentate, mighty no more, but majestic still in his agony. On they went, in counterfeited pomp, in senseless uproar, in frenzied merriment, trampling all on an old man's heart. On swept the tumult, and left a silent street behind.

. . .

"Well, Robin, are you dreaming?" inquired the gentleman, laying his hand on the youth's shoulder.

Robin started, and withdrew his arm from the stone post to which he had instinctively clung, as the living stream rolled by him. His cheek was somewhat pale, and his eye not quite as lively as in the earlier part of the evening.

"Will you be kind enough to show me the way to the ferry?" said he, after a moment's pause.

"You have, then, adopted a new subject of inquiry?" observed his companion, with a smile.

"Why, yes, sir," replied Robin, rather dryly. "Thanks to you, and to my other friends, I have at last met my kinsman, and he will scarce desire to see my face again. I begin to grow weary of a town life, sir. Will you show me the way to the ferry?"

"No, my good friend Robin, — not to-night, at least," said the gentleman. "Some few days hence, if you wish it, I will speed you on your journey. Or, if you prefer to remain with us, perhaps, as you are a shrewd youth, you may rise in the world without the help of your kinsman, Major Molineux."

HENRY JAMES 1843–1916

The circumstances of James's death reveal his character so well that they seem like materials for a last and very personal tale. As he collapsed from the stroke that within weeks killed him, James reported that he heard a voice say, "So here it is at last, the distinguished thing!" A few months before he had become a British subject, after having lived in England for most of his adult life; yet a few months later, in accord with his wishes, his ashes were carried across the Atlantic and buried in the Cambridge, Massachusetts cemetery where his parents, brothers, and sister lay – the Mount Auburn cemetery that in life had often moved him to melancholy reflection on his divided allegiances to an America in which he could not live yet which commanded his deepest loyalties.

James's divided selves are implicit in the events of these months surrounding his death. One part of him speaks in that poised voice with its precise understatement: "at last, the distinguished thing." The voice is not identical with the mortally stricken human being, but it is not separate either; it has something of the same relationship to James as does the voice in Spencer Brydon to Spencer Brydon, a voice that tries so sensitively to state his case objectively but that will not acknowledge the psychological terror Brydon is going through. For Brydon is on the point of realizing that for thirty years he may have denied his real self.

James was fascinated by the way in which the attempt to understand experience tends to remove one from the possibility of feeling it. He often created narrators who understand more than they feel, and so constructed his stories that the distance between a strictly objective, esthetic kind of perception and a fuller, more subjective kind – including emotion – is revealed. An example of the remote, somewhat too cool narrator is the man in " 'Europe' " who is just a bit too eager to discern a "perfect story" in the agony of the old lady and her three daughters. The effect of his enlightened, but not very feeling, interest is to make the reader all the more aware, by contrast, of dimensions beyond the esthetic – the "perfect story" – in the troubles of the mother and her three daughters. The narrator's presence is necessary if we are to measure the distance that lies beyond merely intellectual perception — just as James, dying, needed that precise voice to register the moment and yet reveal by indirection so much that it does not say.

Equally apparent in the circumstances surrounding James's death is the conflict within him regarding Europe and America. As in both of the stories here, there exists the crude concept of "Europe" as the highest form of civilization, the place where intellect, sensibility, and a feeling for one's place in history flourish, and the correspondingly crude concept of America as a place marked by raw energy and unbounded expansionism. Of course, as James knew very well, that wasn't the way it was at all. Europe was often marked by a certain renunciation of the vigorous and genuine; often was morally corrupt, and sometimes (as in the story here) was associated with death; whereas America even in its exaggeration commanded respect and loyalty: its purity and force could not be denied. When James at the end of his life took on British citizenship he was doing the honest thing, acknowledging the major role that the old civilization had played in his life; but at the same time he directed that his ashes be returned to that jolly corner in Massachusetts which, like Spencer Brydon's in New York, represented a terrifying acceptance of another self.

James remained a bachelor all his life. He feared the role of the merely disinterested observer, the role that the lack of intimate ties can impose upon one; and fearing it in his life he confronted it in his fiction. The son of a rich father who devoted himself to philosophical writings, James was born in New York and spent his boyhood in a cosmopolitan atmosphere. The family travelled extensively and were well acquainted with the social and intellectual leaders of the age. His elder brother William became a famous psychologist, a professor at Harvard, but Henry James's talent was clearly marked for literature. From the time he abandoned the study of law at Harvard in 1863 he began writing reviews and short stories — and, later, novels and plays — at a prodigious rate. The finest of his early work is the novel *The Portrait of a Lady* (1881), and his later career is marked brilliantly by three major novels, *The Wings of the Dove* (1902), *The Ambassadors* (1903), and *The Golden Bowl* (1904).

Whatever his ostensible subject, James always wrote about education — not the kind that is carried on in schools and colleges but that which people of an inquisitive turn of mind achieve (or sometimes, tragically, do not achieve) by examining their own experiences. In the stories that follow the nature of the education is different but the issue involved the same: what can one learn from living?

The learning in these stories is varied, and perhaps to understand it better we should begin by asking what the characters regard as an ordinary event and what as an extraordinary one. In this way we shall find a clue to the level of reality on which they assume that they live; for James's characters tend to satisfy themselves by, on the one hand, elevating apparently humdrum facts into something mystically significant or, on the other, comforting themselves by reducing to merely naturalistic phenomena events that *should* fill the mind with wonder.

The key to dealing with the narrator in relation to his assertion (or his denial) of the magic quality of the world is to become aware of the disparity between *his* presentation of the world and the reality more objectively defined in the story. We can perceive this by listening to the character's (or the narrator's) language in relation to other languages in the story. For example, the urgency felt in Boston for the European experience is expressed in a language that is to be heard against the narrator's urbane, low-keyed description of the household. In "The Jolly Corner," too, there are contrasts leading similarly to an awareness of the distance between a character's sense of his own uniqueness or magical destiny (something that he may be trying to talk himself into) and the established norm of the story. The character need not be hyperexcited for the contrast to work, for, as in " 'Europe,' " we can equally well perceive the distance between an emotionally deficient narrator and a melodramatic reality.

For James, to learn from one's experience is to learn not only something about how one's imagination deals with external reality, but also to achieve morality, to achieve, that is, a proper balance between self-assertiveness (the tendency to demand that others yield themselves to you) and those qualities of sympathy and honor and loyalty which require a yielding of oneself. In James this kind of moral integrity must be derived first from an intelligent understanding of one's experience – and the stories reveal to the reader the difficulty within his fictional world of discerning exactly what demands are being made by other people and what demands one makes on them. But even then, having discerned this, enormous difficulties attend the characters as they try to act morally.

The trouble is that there is never one moral prescription that can be applied to all circumstances, for James, like the other late nineteenth- and twentieth-century writers represented here, insists that morality emerges only from particular contexts. James's fiction presents life as constantly evolving, so that when and if one does learn, he does not learn a set of maxims that he can use to control his next personal and social involvement; rather, he learns that every set of human circumstances is unique. And thus the virtues that allow one to live life at its most elevated, noble, heroic even, are those of awareness – both of oneself and of oneself in relation to the world – and responsibility to other human beings. That is why the continuous shaping and reshaping of context in a James story is such a delicate process, for the context is in fact the definition of the moral problem, the only terms in which education – intellectual and moral – can be carried on.

THE JOLLY CORNER

I

"Every one asks me what I 'think' of everything," said Spencer Brydon; "and I make answer as I can – begging or dodging the question, putting them off with any nonsense. It wouldn't matter to any of them really," he went on, "for, even were it possible to meet in that stand-and-deliver way so silly a demand on so big a subject, my 'thoughts' would still be almost altogether about something that concerns only myself." He was talking to Miss Staverton, with whom for a couple of months now he had availed himself of every possible occasion to talk; this disposition and this resource, this comfort and support, as the situation in fact presented itself, having promptly enough taken the first place in the considerable array of rather unattenuated surprises attending his so strangely belated return to America. Everything was somehow a surprise; and that might be natural when one had so long and so consistently neglected everything, taken pains to give surprises so much margin for play. He had given them more than thirty years – thirty-three, to be exact; and they now seemed to him to have organised their performance quite on the scale of that licence. He had been twenty-three on leaving New York – he was fifty-six today: unless indeed he were to reckon as he had sometimes, since his repatriation, found himself feeling; in which case he would have lived longer than is often allotted to man. It would have taken a century, he repeatedly said to himself, and said also to Alice Staverton, it would have taken a longer absence and a more averted mind than those even of which he had been guilty, to pile up the differences, the newnesses, the queernesses, above all the bignesses, for the better or the worse, that at present assaulted his vision wherever he looked.

The great fact all the while however had been the incalculability; since he *had* supposed himself, from decade to decade, to be allowing, and in the most liberal and intelligent manner, for brilliancy of change. He actually saw that he had allowed for nothing; he missed what he would have been sure of finding, he found what he would never have imagined. Proportions and values were upside-down; the ugly things he had expected, the ugly things of his far-away youth, when he had too promptly waked up to a sense of the ugly – these uncanny phenomena placed him rather, as it happened, under the charm; whereas the "swagger" things, the modern, the monstrous, the famous things, those he had more particularly, like thousands of ingenuous enquirers every year, come over to see, were exactly his sources of dismay. They were as so many set traps for displeasure, above all for reaction, of which his restless tread was constantly pressing the spring. It was interesting, doubtless, the whole show, but it would have been too disconcerting hadn't a certain finer truth saved the situation. He had distinctly not, in this steadier light, come over *all* for the monstrosities; he had come, not only in the last analysis but quite on the face of the act, under an impulse with which they had nothing to do. He had come – putting the thing pompously – to look at his "property," which he had thus for a third of a century not been within four thousand miles of; or, expressing it less sordidly, he had yielded to the humour of seeing again his house on the jolly corner, as he usually, and quite fondly, described it – the one in which he had first seen the light, in which various members of his family had lived and had died, in which the holidays of his overschooled boyhood had been passed and the few social flowers of his chilled adolescence gathered, and which, alienated then for so long a period, had, through the successive deaths of his two brothers and the termination of old arrangements, come wholly into his hands. He was the owner of another, not quite so "good" – the jolly corner having been, from far back, superlatively extended and consecrated; and the value of the pair represented his main capital, with an income consisting, in these later years, of their respective rents which (thanks precisely to their original excellent type) had never been depressingly low. He could live in "Europe," as he had been in the habit of living, on the product of these flourishing New York leases, and all the better since, that of the second structure, the mere number in its long row, having within a twelvemonth fallen in, renovation at a high advance had proved beautifully possible.

These were items of property indeed, but he had found himself since his arrival distinguishing more than ever between them. The house within the street, two bristling blocks westward, was already in course of reconstruction as a tall mass of flats; he had acceded, some time before, to overtures for this conversion – in which, now that it was going forward, it had been not the least of his astonishments to find himself able, on the spot, and though without a previous ounce of such experience, to participate with a certain intelligence, almost with a certain authority. He had lived his life with his back so turned to such concerns and his face addressed to those of so different an order that he scarce knew what to make of this lively stir, in a compartment of his mind never yet penetrated, of a capacity for business and a sense for construction. These virtues, so common all round him now, had been dormant in his own organism – where it might be said of them perhaps that they had slept the sleep of the just. At present, in the splendid autumn weather – the autumn at least was a pure boon in the terrible place – he loafed about his "work" undeterred, secretly agitated; not in the least "minding" that the whole proposition, as they said, was vulgar and sordid, and ready to climb ladders, to walk the plank, to handle materials and look wise about them, to ask questions, in fine, and challenge explanations and really "go into" figures.

It amused, it verily quite charmed him; and, by the same stroke, it amused, and even more, Alice Staverton, though perhaps charming her perceptibly less. She wasn't however going to be better off for it, as *he* was – and so astonishingly much: nothing was now likely, he knew, ever to make her better off than she found herself, in the afternoon of life, as the delicately frugal possessor and tenant of the small house in Irving Place to which she had subtly managed to cling through her almost unbroken New York career. If he knew the way to it now better than to any other address among the dreadful multiplied numberings which seemed to him to reduce the whole place to some vast ledger-page, overgrown, fantastic, of ruled and criss-crossed lines and figures – if he had formed, for his consolation, that habit, it was really not a little because of the charm of his having encountered and recognized, in the vast wilderness of the wholesale, breaking through the mere gross generalisation of wealth and force and success, a small still scene where items and shades, all delicate things, kept the sharpness of the notes of a high voice perfectly trained, and where economy hung about like the scent of a garden. His old friend lived with one maid and herself, dusted her relics and trimmed her lamps and polished her silver; she stood off, in the awful modern crush, when she could, but she sallied forth and did battle when the challenge was really to "spirit," the spirit she after all confessed to, proudly and a little shyly, as to that of the better time, that of *their* common, their quite far-away and antediluvian social period and order. She made use of the street-cars when need be, the terrible things that people scrambled for as the panic-stricken at sea scramble for the boats; she affronted, inscrutably, under stress, all the public concussions and ordeals; and yet, with that slim mystifying grace of her appearance, which defied you to say if she were a fair young woman who looked older through trouble, or a fine smooth older one who looked young through successful indifference; with her precious reference, above all, to memories and histories into which he could enter, she was as exquisite for him as some pale pressed flower (a rarity to begin with), and, failing other sweetnesses, she was a sufficient reward of his effort. They had communities of knowledge, "their" knowledge (this discriminating possessive was always on her lips) of presences of the other age, presences all overlaid, in his case, by the experience of a man and the freedom of a wanderer, overlaid by pleasure, by infidelity, by passages of life that were strange and dim to her, just by "Europe" in short, but still unobscured, still exposed and cherished, under that pious visitation of the spirit from which she had never been diverted.

She had come with him one day to see how his "apartment-house" was rising; he had helped her over gaps and explained to her plans, and while they were there had happened to have, before her, a brief but lively discussion with the man in charge, the representative of the building-firm that had undertaken his work. He had found himself quite "standing-up" to this personage over a failure on the latter's part to observe some detail of one of their noted conditions, and had so lucidly argued his case that, besides ever so prettily flushing, at the time, for sympathy in his triumph, she had afterwards said to him (though to a slightly greater effect of irony) that he had clearly for too many years neglected a real gift. If he had but stayed at home he would have anticipated the inventor of the sky-scraper. If he had but stayed at home he would have discovered his genius in time really to start some new variety of awful architectural hare and run it till it burrowed in a gold-mine. He was to remember these words, while the weeks elapsed, for the small silver ring they had sounded over the queerest and deepest of his own lately most disguised and most muffled vibrations.

It had begun to be present to him after the first fortnight, it had broken out with the oddest abruptness, this particular wanton wonderment: it met him there – and this was the image under which he himself judged the matter, or at least, not a little, thrilled and flushed with it – very much as he might have been met by some strange figure, some unexpected occupant, at a turn of one of the dim passages of an empty house. The quaint analogy quite hauntingly remained with him, when he didn't indeed rather improve it by a still intenser form: that of his opening a door behind which he would have made sure of finding nothing, a door into a room shuttered and void, and yet so coming, with a great suppressed start, on some quite erect confronting presence, something planted in the middle of the place and facing him through the dusk. After that visit to the house in construction he walked with his companion to see the other and always so much the better one, which in the eastward direction formed one of the corners, the "jolly" one precisely, of the street now so generally dishonoured and disfigured in its westward reaches, and of the comparatively conservative Avenue. The Avenue still had pretensions, as Miss Staverton said, to decency; the old people had mostly gone, the old names were unknown, and here and there an old association seemed to stray, all vaguely, like some very aged person, out too late, whom you might meet and feel the impulse to watch or follow, in kindness, for safe restoration to shelter.

They went in together, our friends; he admitted himself with his key, as he kept no one there, he explained, preferring, for his reasons, to leave the place empty, under a simple arrangement with a good woman living in the neighbourhood and who came for a daily hour to open windows and dust and sweep. Spencer Brydon had his reasons and was growingly aware of them; they seemed to him better each time he was there, though he didn't name them all to his companion, any more than he told her as yet how often, how quite absurdly often, he himself came. He only let her see for the present, while they walked through the great blank rooms, that absolute vacancy reigned and that, from top to bottom, there was nothing but Mrs. Muldoon's broomstick, in a corner, to tempt the burglar.

Mrs. Muldoon was then on the premises, and she loquaciously attended the visitors, preceding them from room to room and pushing back shutters, and throwing up sashes – all to show them, as she remarked, how little there was to see. There was little indeed to see in the great gaunt shell where the main dispositions and the general apportionment of space, the style of an age of ampler allowances, had nevertheless for its master their honest pleading message, affecting him as some good old servant's, some lifelong retainer's appeal for a character, or even for a retiring-pension; yet it was also a remark of Mrs. Muldoon's that, glad as she was to oblige him by her noonday round, there was a request she greatly hoped he would never make of her. If he should wish her for any reason to come in after dark she would just tell him, if he "plased," that he must ask it of somebody else.

The fact that there was nothing to see didn't militate for the worthy woman against what one *might* see, and she put it frankly to Miss Staverton that no lady could be expected to like, could she? "scraping up to thim top storeys in the ayvil hours." The gas and the electric light were off the house, and she fairly evoked a gruesome vision of her march through the great grey rooms – so many of them as there were too! – with her glimmering taper. Miss Staverton met her honest glare with a smile and the profession that she herself certainly would recoil from such an adventure. Spencer Brydon meanwhile held his peace – for the moment; the question of the "evil" hours in his old home had already become too grave for him. He had begun some time since to "crape," and he knew just why a packet of candles addressed to that pursuit had been stowed by his own hand, three weeks before, at the back of a drawer of the fine old sideboard that occupied, as a "fixture," the deep recess in the dining-room. Just now he laughed at his companions – quickly however changing the subject; for the reason that, in the first place, his laugh struck him even at that moment as starting the odd echo, the conscious human resonance (he scarce knew how to qualify it) that sounds made while he was there alone sent back to his ear or his fancy; and that, in the second, he imagined Alice Staverton for the instant on the point of asking him, with a divination, if he ever so prowled. There were divinations he was unprepared for, and he had at all events averted enquiry by the time Mrs. Muldoon had left them, passing on to other parts.

There was happily enough to say, on so consecrated a spot, that could be said freely and fairly; so that a whole train of declarations was precipitated by his friend's having herself broken out, after a yearning look around: "But I hope you don't mean they want you to pull *this* to pieces!" His answer came, promptly, with his re-awakened wrath: it was of course exactly what they wanted, and what they were "at" him for, daily, with the iteration of people who couldn't for their life understand a man's liability to decent feelings. He had found the place, just as it stood and beyond what he could express, an interest and a joy. There were values other than the beastly rent-values, and in short, in short – ! But it was thus Miss Staverton took him up. "In short you're to make so good a thing of your sky-scraper that, living in luxury on *those* ill-gotten gains, you can afford for a while to be sentimental here!" Her smile had for him, with the words, the particular mild irony with which he found half her talk suffused; an irony without bitterness and that came, exactly, from her having so much imagination – not, like the cheap sarcasms with which one heard most people, about the world of "society," bid for the reputation of cleverness, from nobody's really having any. It was agreeable to him at this very moment to be sure that when he had answered, after a brief demur, "Well yes: so, precisely, you may put it!" her imagination would still do him justice. He explained that even if never a dollar were to come to him from the other house he would nevertheless cherish this one; and he dwelt, further, while they lingered and wandered, on the fact of the stupefaction he was already exciting, the positive mystification he felt himself create.

He spoke of the value of all he read into it, into the mere sight of the walls, mere shapes of the rooms, mere sound of the floors, mere feel, in his hand, of the old silver-plated knobs of the several mahogany doors, which suggested the pressure of the palms of the dead; the seventy years of the past in fine that these things represented, the annals of nearly three generations, counting his grandfather's, the one that had ended there, and the impalpable ashes of his long-extinct youth, afloat in the very air like microscopic motes. She listened to everything; she was a woman who answered intimately but who utterly didn't chatter. She scattered abroad therefore no cloud of words; she could assent, she could agree, above all she could encourage, without doing that. Only at the last she went a little further than he had done himself. "And then how do you know? You may still, after all, want to live here." It rather indeed pulled him up, for it wasn't what he had been thinking, at least in her sense of the words. "You mean I may decide to stay on for the sake of it?"

"Well, *with* such a home – !" But, quite beautifully, she had too much tact to dot so monstrous an *i,* and it was precisely an illustration of the way she didn't rattle. How could any one – of any wit – insist on any one else's "wanting" to live in New York?

"Oh," he said, "I *might* have lived here (since I had my opportunity early in life); I might have put in here all these years. Then everything would have been different enough – and, I dare say, 'funny' enough. But that's another matter. And then the beauty of it – I mean of my perversity, of my refusal to agree to a 'deal' – is just in the total absence of a reason. Don't you see that if I had a reason about the matter at all it would *have* to be the other way, and would then be inevitably a reason of dollars? There are no reasons here *but* of dollars. Let us therefore have none whatever – not the ghost of one."

They were back in the hall then for departure, but from where they stood the vista was large, through an open door, into the great square main saloon, with its almost antique felicity of brave spaces between windows. Her eyes came back from that reach and met his own a moment. "Are you very sure the 'ghost' of one doesn't, much rather, serve — ?"

He had a positive sense of turning pale. But it was as near as they were then to come. For he made answer, he believed, between a glare and a grin: "Oh ghosts — of course the place must swarm with them! I should be ashamed of it if it didn't. Poor Mrs. Muldoon's right, and it's why I haven't asked her to do more than look in."

Miss Staverton's gaze again lost itself, and things she didn't utter, it was clear, came and went in her mind. She might even for the minute, off there in the fine room, have imagined some element dimly gathering. Simplified like the death-mask of a handsome face, it perhaps produced for her just then an effect akin to the stir of an expression in the "set" commemorative plaster. Yet whatever her impression may have been she produced instead a vague platitude. "Well, if it were only furnished and lived in — !"

She appeared to imply that in case of its being still furnished he might have been a little less opposed to the idea of a return. But she passed straight into the vestibule, as if to leave her words behind her, and the next moment he had opened the house-door and was standing with her on the steps. He closed the door and, while he re-pocketed his key, looking up and down, they took in the comparatively harsh actuality of the Avenue, which reminded him of the assault of the outer light of the Desert on the traveller emerging from an Egyptian tomb. But he risked before they stepped into the street his gathered answer to her speech. "For me it *is* lived in. For me it *is* furnished." At which it was easy for her to sigh "Ah yes — !" all vaguely and discreetly; since his parents and his favourite sister, to say nothing of other kin, in numbers, had run their course and met their end there. That represented, within the walls, ineffaceable life.

It was a few days after this that, during an hour passed with her again, he had expressed his impatience of the too flattering curiosity — among the people he met — about his appreciation of New York. He had arrived at none at all that was socially producible, and as for that matter of his "thinking" (thinking the better or the worse of anything there) he was wholly taken up with one subject of thought. It was mere vain egoism, and it was moreover, if she liked, a morbid obsession. He found all things come back to the question of what he personally might have been, how he might have led his life and "turned out," if he had not so, at the outset, given it up. And confessing for the first time to the intensity within him of this absurd speculation — which but proved also, no doubt, the habit of too selfishly thinking — he affirmed the impotence there of any other source of interest, any other native appeal. "What would it have made of me, what would it have made of me? I keep for ever wondering, all idiotically; as if I could possibly know! I see what it has made of dozens of others, those I meet, and it positively aches within me, to the point of exasperation, that it would have made something of me as well. Only I can't make out *what*, and the worry of it, the small rage of curiosity never to be satisfied, brings back what I remember to have felt, once or twice, after judging best, for reasons, to burn some important letter unopened. I've been sorry, I've hated it – I've never known what was in the letter. You may of course say it's a trifle – !"

"I don't say it's a trifle," Miss Staverton gravely interrupted.

She was seated by her fire, and before her, on his feet and restless, he turned to and fro between this intensity of his idea and a fitful and unseeing inspection, through his single eyeglass, of the dear little old objects on her chimney-piece. Her interruption made him for an instant look at her harder. "I shouldn't care if you did!" he laughed, however; "and it's only a figure, at any rate, for the way I now feel. *Not* to have followed my perverse young course – and almost in the teeth of my father's curse, as I may say; not to have kept it up, so, 'over there,' from that day to this, without a doubt or a pang; not, above all, to have liked it, to have loved it, so much, loved it, no doubt, with such an abysmal conceit of my own preference: some variation from *that,* I say, must have produced some different effect for my life and for my 'form.' I should have stuck here – if it had been possible; and I was too young, at twenty-three, to judge, *pour deux sous,* whether it *were* possible. If I had waited I might have seen it was, and then I might have been, by staying here, something nearer to one of these types who have been hammered so hard and made so keen by their conditions. It isn't that I admire them so much – the question of any charm in them, or of any charm, beyond that of the rank money-passion, exerted by their conditions *for* them, has nothing to do with the matter: it's only a question of what fantastic, yet perfectly possible, development of my own nature I mayn't have missed. It comes over me that I had then a strange *alter ego* deep down somewhere within me, as the full-blown flower is in the small tight bud, and that I just took the course, I just transferred him to the climate, that blighted him for once and for ever."

"And you wonder about the flower," Miss Staverton said. "So do I, if you want to know; and so I've been wondering these several weeks. I believe in the flower," she continued, "I feel it would have been quite splendid, quite huge and monstrous."

"Monstrous above all!" her visitor echoed; "and I imagine, by the same stroke, quite hideous and offensive."

"You don't believe that," she returned; "if you did you wouldn't wonder. You'd know, and that would be enough for you. What you feel – and what I feel *for* you – is that you'd have had power."

"You'd have liked me that way?" he asked.

She barely hung fire. "How should I not have liked you?"

"I see. You'd have liked me, have preferred me, a billionaire!"

"How should I not have liked you?" she simply again asked.

He stood before her still – her question kept him motionless. He took it in, so much there was of it; and indeed his not otherwise meeting it testified to that.

"I know at least what I am," he simply went on; "the other side of the medal's clear enough. I've not been edifying – I believe I'm thought in a hundred quarters to have been barely decent. I've followed strange paths and worshipped strange gods; it must have come to you again and again – in fact you've admitted to me as much – that I was leading, at any time these thirty years, a selfish frivolous scandalous life. And you see what it has made of me."

She just waited, smiling at him. "You see what it has made of *me*."

"Oh you're a person whom nothing can have altered. You were born to be what you are, anywhere, anyway: you've the perfection nothing else could have blighted. And don't you see how, without my exile, I shouldn't have been waiting till now – ?" But he pulled up for the strange pang.

"The great thing to see," she presently said, "seems to me to be that it has spoiled nothing. It hasn't spoiled your being here at last. It hasn't spoiled this. It hasn't spoiled your speaking – " She also however faltered.

He wondered at everything her controlled emotion might mean. "Do you believe then – too dreadfully! – that I *am* as good as I might ever have been?"

"Oh no! Far from it!" With which she got up from her chair and was nearer to him. "But I don't care," she smiled.

"You mean I'm good enough?"

She considered a little. "Will you believe it if I say so? I mean will you let that settle your question for you?" And then as if making out in his face that he drew back from this, that he had some idea which, however absurd, he couldn't yet bargain away: "Oh you don't care either – but very differently: you don't care for anything but yourself."

Spencer Brydon recognised it – it was in fact what he had absolutely professed. Yet he importantly qualified. "*He* isn't myself. He's the just so totally other person. But I do want to see him," he added. "And I can. And I shall."

Their eyes met for a minute while he guessed from something in hers that she divined his strange sense. But neither of them otherwise expressed it, and her apparent understanding, with no protesting shock, no easy derision, touched him more deeply than anything yet, constituting for his stifled perversity, on the spot, an element that was like breathable air. What she said however was unexpected. "Well, *I've* seen him."

"You – ?"

"I've seen him in a dream."

"Oh a 'dream' – !" It let him down.

"But twice over," she continued. "I saw him as I see you now."

"You've dreamed the same dream – ?"

"Twice over," she repeated. "The very same."

This did somehow a little speak to him, as it also gratified him. "You dream about me at that rate?"

"Ah about *him!*" she smiled.

His eyes again sounded her. "Then you know all about him." And as she said nothing more: "What's the wretch like?"

She hesitated, and it was as if he were pressing her so hard that, resisting for reasons of her own, she had to turn away. "I'll tell you some other time!"

II

It was after this that there was most of a virtue for him, most of a cultivated charm, most of a preposterous secret thrill, in the particular form of surrender to his obsession and of address to what he more and more believed to be his privilege. It was what in these weeks he was living for – since he really felt life to begin but after Mrs. Muldoon had retired from the scene and, visiting the ample house from attic to cellar, making sure he was alone, he knew himself in safe possession and, as he tacitly expressed it, let himself go. He sometimes came twice in the twenty-four hours; the moments he liked best were those of gathering dusk, of the short autumn twilight; this was the time of which, again and again, he found himself hoping most. Then he could, as seemed to him, most intimately wander and wait, linger and listen, feel his fine attention, never in his life before so fine, on the pulse of the great vague place: he preferred the lampless hour and only wished he might have prolonged each day the deep crepuscular spell. Later – rarely much before midnight, but then for a considerable vigil – he watched with his glimmering light; moving slowly, holding it high, playing it far, rejoicing above all, as much as he might, in open vistas, reaches of communication between rooms and by passages; the long straight chance or show, as he would have called it, for the revelation he pretended to invite. It was a practice he found he could perfectly "work" without exciting remark; no one was in the least the wiser for it; even Alice Staverton, who was moreover a well of discretion, didn't quite fully imagine.

He let himself in and let himself out with the assurance of calm proprietorship; and accident so far favoured him that, if a fat Avenue "officer" had happened on occasion to see him entering at eleven-thirty, he had never yet, to the best of his belief, been noticed as emerging at two. He walked there on the crisp November nights, arrived regularly at the evening's end; it was as easy to do this after dining out as to take his way to a club or to his hotel. When he left his club, if he hadn't been dining out, it was ostensibly to go to his hotel; and when he left his hotel, if he had spent a part of the evening there, it was ostensibly to go to his club. Everything was easy in fine; everything conspired and promoted: there was truly even in the strain of his experience something that glossed over, something that salved and simplified, all the rest of consciousness. He circulated, talked, renewed, loosely and pleasantly, old relations – met indeed, so far as he could, new expectations and seemed to make out on the whole that in spite of the career, of such different contacts, which he had spoken of to Miss Staverton as ministering so little, for those who might have watched it, to edification, he was positively rather liked than not. He was a dim secondary social success – and all with people who had truly not an idea of him. It was all mere surface sound, this murmur of their welcome, this popping of their corks – just as his gestures of response were the extravagant shadows, emphatic in proportion as they meant little, of some game of *ombres chinoises.* He projected himself all day, in thought, straight over the bristling line of hard unconscious heads and into the other, the real, the waiting life; the life that, as soon as he had heard behind him the click of his great housedoor, began for him, on the jolly corner, as beguilingly as the slow opening bars of some rich music follows the tap of the conductor's wand.

He always caught the first effect of the steel point of his stick on the old marble of the hall pavement, large black-and-white squares that he remembered as the admiration of his childhood and that had then made in him, as he now saw, for the growth of an early conception of style. This effect was the dim reverberating tinkle as of some far-off bell hung who should say where? – in the depths of the house, of the past, of that mystical other world that might have flourished for him had he not, for weal or woe, abandoned it. On this impression he did ever the same thing; he put his stick noiselessly away in a corner – feeling the place once more in the likeness of some great glass bowl, all precious concave crystal, set delicately humming by the play of a moist finger round its edge. The concave crystal held, as it were, this mystical other world, and the indescribably fine murmur of its rim was the sigh there, the scarce audible pathetic wail to his strained ear, of all the old baffled forsworn possibilities. What he did therefore by this appeal of his hushed presence was to wake them into such measure of ghostly life as they might still enjoy. They were shy, all but unappeasably shy, but they weren't really sinister; at least they weren't as he had hitherto felt them – before they had taken the Form he so yearned to make them take, the Form he at moments saw himself in the light of fairly hunting on tiptoe, the points of his evening-shoes, from room to room and from storey to storey.

That was the essence of his vision – which was all rank folly, if one would, while he was out of the house and otherwise occupied, but which took on the last verisimilitude as soon as he was placed and posted. He knew what he meant and what he wanted; it was as clear as the figure on a cheque presented in demand for cash. His *alter ego* "walked" – that was the note of his image of him, while his image of his motive for his own odd pastime was the desire to waylay him and meet him. He roamed, slowly, warily, but all restlessly, he himself did – Mrs. Muldoon had been right, absolutely, with her figure of their "craping"; and the presence he watched for would roam restlessly too. But it would be as cautious and as shifty; the conviction of its probable, in fact its already quite sensible, quite audible evasion of pursuit grew for him from night to night, laying on him finally a rigour to which nothing in his life had been comparable. It had been the theory of many superficially-judging persons, he knew, that he was wasting that life in a surrender to sensations, but he had tasted of no pleasure so fine as his actual tension, had been introduced to no sport that demanded at once the patience and the nerve of this stalking of a creature more subtle, yet at bay perhaps more formidable, than any beast of the forest. The terms, the comparisons, the very practices of the chase positively came again into play; there were even moments when passages of his occasional experience as a sportsman, stirred memories, from his younger time, of moor and mountain and desert, revived for him – and to the increase of his keenness – by the tremendous force of analogy. He found himself at moments – once he had placed his single light on some mantel-shelf or in some recess – stepping back into shelter or shade, effacing himself behind a door or in an embrasure, as he had sought of old the vantage of rock and tree; he found himself holding his breath and living in the joy of the instant, the supreme suspense created by big game alone.

He wasn't afraid (though putting himself the question as he believed gentlemen on Bengal tiger-shoots or in close quarters with the great bear of the Rockies had been known to confess to having put it); and this indeed – since here at least he might be frank! – because of the impression, so intimate and so strange, that he himself produced as yet a dread, produced certainly a strain, beyond the liveliest he was likely to feel. They fell for him into categories, they fairly became familiar, the signs, for his own perception, of the alarm his presence and his vigilance created; though leaving him always to remark, portentously, on his probably having formed a relation, his probably enjoying a consciousness, unique in the experience of man. People enough, first and last, had been in terror of apparitions, but who had ever before so turned the tables and become himself, in the apparitional world, an incalculable terror? He might have found this sublime had he quite dared to think of it; but he didn't too much insist, truly, on that side of his privilege. With habit and repetition he gained to an extraordinary degree the power to penetrate the dusk of distances and the darkness of corners, to resolve back into their innocence the treacheries of uncertain light, the evil-looking forms taken in the gloom by mere shadows, by accidents of the air, by shifting effects of perspective; putting down his dim luminary he could still wander on without it, pass into other rooms and, only knowing it was there behind him in case of need, see his way about, visually project for his purpose a comparative clearness. It made him feel, this acquired faculty, like some monstrous stealthy cat; he wondered if he would have glared at these moments with large shining yellow eyes, and what it mightn't verily be, for the poor hard-pressed *alter ego,* to be confronted with such a type.

He liked however the open shutters; he opened everywhere those Mrs. Muldoon had closed, closing them as carefully afterwards, so that she shouldn't notice: he liked – oh this he did like, and above all in the upper rooms! – the sense of the hard silver of the autumn stars through the window-panes, and scarcely less the flare of the street-lamps below, the white electric lustre which it would have taken curtains to keep out. This was human actual social; this was of the world he had lived in, and he was more at his ease certainly for the countenance, coldly general and impersonal, that all the while and in spite of his detachment it seemed to give him. He had support of course mostly in the rooms at the wide front and the prolonged side; it failed him considerably in the central shades and the parts at the back. But if he sometimes, on his rounds, was glad of his optical reach, so none the less often the rear of the house affected him as the very jungle of his prey. The place was there more subdivided; a large "extension" in particular, where small rooms for servants had been multiplied, abounded in nooks and corners, in closets and passages, in the ramifications especially of an ample back staircase over which he leaned, many a time, to look far down – not deterred from his gravity even while aware that he might, for a spectator, have figured some solemn simpleton playing at hide-and-seek. Outside in fact he might himself make that ironic *rapprochement;* but within the walls, and in spite of the clear windows, his consistency was proof against the cynical light of New York.

It had belonged to that idea of the exasperated consciousness of his victim to become a real test for him; since he had quite put it to himself from the first that, oh distinctly! he could "cultivate" his whole perception. He had felt it as above all open to cultivation – which indeed was but another name for his manner of spending his time. He was bringing it on, bringing it to perfection, by practice; in consequence of which it had grown so fine that he was now aware of impressions, attestations of his general postulate, that couldn't have broken upon him at once. This was the case more specifically with a phenomenon at last quite frequent for him in the upper rooms, the recognition – absolutely unmistakable, and by a turn dating from a particular hour, his resumption of his campaign after a diplomatic drop, a calculated absence of three nights – of his being definitely followed, tracked at a distance carefully taken and to the express end that he should the less confidently, less arrogantly, appear to himself merely to pursue. It worried, it finally quite broke him up, for it proved, of all the conceivable impressions, the one least suited to his book. He was kept in sight while remaining himself – as regards the essence of his position – sightless, and his only recourse then was in abrupt turns, rapid recoveries of ground. He wheeled about, retracing his steps, as if he might so catch in his face at least the stirred air of some other quick revolution. It was indeed true that his fully dislocalised thought of these manoeuvres recalled to him Pantaloon, at the Christmas farce, buffeted and tricked from behind by ubiquitous Harlequin; but it left intact the influence of the conditions themselves each time he was re-exposed to them, so that in fact this association, had he suffered it to become constant, would on a certain side have but ministered to his intenser gravity. He had made, as I have said, to create on the premises the baseless sense of a reprieve, his three absences; and the result of the third was to confirm the after-effect of the second.

On his return, that night – the night succeeding his last intermission – he stood in the hall and looked up the staircase with a certainty more intimate than any he had yet known. "He's *there,* at the top, and waiting – not, as in general, falling back for disappearance. He's holding his ground, and it's the first time – which is a proof, isn't it? that something has happened for him." So Brydon argued with his hand on the banister and his foot on the lowest stair; in which position he felt as never before the air chilled by his logic. He himself turned cold in it, for he seemed of a sudden to know what now was involved. "Harder pressed? – yes, he takes it in, with its thus making clear to him that I've come, as they say, 'to stay.' He finally doesn't like and can't bear it, in the sense, I mean, that his wrath, his menaced interest, now balances with his dread. I've hunted him till he has 'turned': that, up there, is what has happened – he's the fanged or the antlered animal brought at last to bay." There came to him, as I say – but determined by an influence beyond my notation! – the acuteness of this certainty; under which however the next moment he had broken into a sweat that he would as little have consented to attribute to fear as he would have dared immediately to act upon it for enterprise. It marked none the less a prodigious thrill, a thrill that represented sudden dismay, no doubt, but also represented, and with the selfsame throb, the strangest, the most joyous, possibly the next minute almost the proudest, duplication of consciousness.

"He has been dodging, retreating, hiding, but now, worked up to anger, he'll fight!" – this intense impression made a single mouthful, as it were, of terror and applause. But what was wondrous was that the applause, for the felt fact, was so eager, since, if it was his other self he was running to earth, this ineffable identity was thus in the last resort not unworthy of him. It bristled there – somewhere near at hand, however unseen still – as the hunted thing, even as the trodden worm of the adage *must* at last bristle; and Brydon at this instant tasted probably of a sensation more complex than had ever before found itself consistent with sanity. It was as if it would have shamed him that a character so associated with his own should triumphantly succeed in just skulking, should to the end not risk the open, so that the drop of this danger was, on the spot, a great lift of the whole situation. Yet with another rare shift of the same subtlety he was already trying to measure by how much more he himself might now be in peril of fear; so rejoicing that he could, in another form, actively inspire that fear, and simultaneously quaking for the form in which he might passively know it.

The apprehension of knowing it must after a little have grown in him, and the strangest moment of his adventure perhaps, the most memorable or really most interesting, afterwards, of his crisis, was the lapse of certain instants of concentrated conscious *combat,* the sense of a need to hold on to something, even after the manner of a man slipping and slipping on some awful incline; the vivid impulse, above all, to move, to act, to charge, somehow and upon something – to show himself, in a word, that he wasn't afraid. The state of "holding-on" was thus the state to which he was momentarily reduced; if there had been anything, in the great vacancy, to seize, he would presently have been aware of having clutched it as he might under a shock at home have clutched the nearest chair-back. He had been surprised at any rate – of this he *was* aware – into something unprecedented since his original appropriation of the place; he had closed his eyes, held them tight, for a long minute, as with that instinct of dismay and that terror of vision. When he opened them the room, the other contiguous rooms, extraordinarily, seemed lighter – so light, almost, that at first he took the change for day. He stood firm, however that might be, just where he had paused; his resistance had helped him – it was as if there were something he had tided over. He knew after a little what this was – it had been in the imminent danger of flight. He had stiffened his will against going; without this he would have made for the stairs, and it seemed to him that, still with his eyes closed, he would have descended them, would have known how, straight and swiftly, to the bottom.

Well, as he had held out, here he was – still at the top, among the more intricate upper rooms and with the gauntlet of the others, of all the rest of the house, still to run when it should be his time to go. He would go at his time – only at his time: didn't he go every night very much at the same hour? He took out his watch – there was light for that: it was scarcely a quarter past one, and he had never withdrawn so soon. He reached his lodgings for the most part at two – with his walk of a quarter of an hour. He would wait for the last quarter – he wouldn't stir till then; and he kept his watch there with his eye on it, reflecting while he held it that this deliberate wait, a wait with an effort, which he recognised, would serve perfectly for the attestation he desired to make. It would prove his courage – unless indeed the latter might most be proved by his budging at last from his place. What he mainly felt now was that, since he hadn't originally scuttled, he had his dignities – which had never in his life seemed so many – all to preserve and to carry aloft. This was before him in truth as a physical image, an image almost worthy of an age of greater romance. That remark indeed glimmered for him only to glow the next instant with a finer light; since what age of romance, after all, could have matched either the state of his mind or, "objectively," as they said, the wonder of his situation? The only difference would have been that, brandishing his dignities over his head as in a parchment scroll, he might then – that is in the heroic time – have proceeded downstairs with a drawn sword in his other grasp.

At present, really, the light he had set down on the mantel of the next room would have to figure his sword; which utensil, in the course of a minute, he had taken the requisite number of steps to possess himself of. The door between the rooms was open, and from the second another door opened to a third. These rooms, as he remembered, gave all three upon a common corridor as well, but there was a fourth, beyond them, without issue save through the preceding. To have moved, to have heard his step again, was appreciably a help; though even in recognising this he lingered once more a little by the chimney-piece on which his light had rested. When he next moved, just hesitating where to turn, he found himself considering a circumstance that, after his first and comparatively vague apprehension of it, produced in him the start that often attends some pang of recollection, the violent shock of having ceased happily to forget. He had come into sight of the door in which the brief chain of communication ended and which he now surveyed from the nearer threshold, the one not directly facing it. Placed at some distance to the left of this point, it would have admitted him to the last room of the four, the room without other approach or egress, had it not, to his intimate conviction, been closed *since* his former visitation, the matter probably of a quarter of an hour before. He stared with all his eyes at the wonder of the fact, arrested again where he stood and again holding his breath while he sounded its sense. Surely it had been *subsequently* closed – that is it had been on his previous passage indubitably open!

He took it full in the face that something had happened between – that he couldn't not have noticed before (by which he meant on his original tour of all the rooms that evening) that such a barrier had exceptionally presented itself. He had indeed since that moment undergone an agitation so extraordinary that it might have muddled for him any earlier view; and he tried to convince himself that he might perhaps then have gone into the room and, inadvertently, automatically, on coming out, have drawn the door after him. The difficulty was that this exactly was what he never did; it was against his whole policy, as he might have said, the essence of which was to keep vistas clear. He had them from the first, as he was well aware, quite on the brain: the strange apparition, at the far end of one of them, of his baffled "prey" (which had become by so sharp an irony so little the term now to apply!) was the form of success his imagination had most cherished, projecting into it always a refinement of beauty. He had known fifty times the start of perception that had afterwards dropped; had fifty times gasped to himself "There!" under some fond brief hallucination. The house, as the case stood, admirably lent itself; he might wonder at the taste, the native architecture of the particular time, which could rejoice so in the multiplication of doors – the opposite extreme to the modern, the actual almost complete proscription of them; but it had fairly contributed to provoke this obsession of the presence encountered telescopically, as he might say, focussed and studied in diminishing perspective and as by a rest for the elbow.

It was with these considerations that his present attention was charged – they perfectly availed to make what he saw portentous, He *couldn't*, by any lapse, have blocked that aperture; and if he hadn't, if it was unthinkable, why what else was clear but that there had been another agent? Another agent? – he had been catching, as he felt, a moment back, the very breath of him; but when had he been so close as in this simple, this logical, this completely personal act? It was so logical, that is, that one might have *taken* it for personal; yet for what did Brydon take it, he asked himself, while, softly panting, he felt his eyes almost leave their sockets. Ah this time at last they *were,* the two, the opposed projections of him, in presence; and this time, as much as one would, the question of danger loomed. With it rose, as not before, the question of courage – for what he knew the blank face of the door to say to him was "Show us how much you have!" It stared, it glared back at him with that challenge; it put to him the two alternatives: should he just push it open or not? Oh to have this consciousness was to *think* – and to think, Brydon knew, as he stood there, was, with the lapsing moments, not to have acted! Not to have acted – that was the misery and the pang – was even still not to act; was in fact *all* to feel the thing in another, in a new and terrible way. How long did he pause and how long did he debate? There was presently nothing to measure it; for his vibration had already changed – as just by the effect of its intensity. Shut up there, at bay, defiant, and with the prodigy of the thing palpably proveably *done,* thus giving notice like some stark signboard – under that accession of accent the situation itself had turned; and Brydon at last remarkably made up his mind on what it had turned to.

It had turned altogether to a different admonition; to a supreme hint, for him, of the value of Discretion! This slowly dawned, no doubt – for it could take its time; so perfectly, on his threshold, had he been stayed, so little as yet had he either advanced or retreated. It was the strangest of all things that now when, by his taking ten steps and applying his hand to a latch, or even his shoulder and his knee, if necessary, to a panel, all the hunger of his prime need might have been met, his high curiosity crowned, his unrest assuaged – it was amazing, but it was also exquisite and rare, that insistence should have, at a touch, quite dropped from him. Discretion – he jumped at that; and yet not, verily, at such a pitch, because it saved his nerves or his skin, but because, much more valuably, it saved the situation. When I say he "jumped" at it I feel the consonance of this term with the fact that – at the end indeed of I know not how long – he did move again, he crossed straight to the door. He wouldn't touch it – it seemed now that he might *if* he would: he would only just wait there a little, to show, to prove, that he wouldn't. He had thus another station, close to the thin partition by which revelation was denied him; but with his eyes bent and his hands held off in a mere intensity of stillness. He listened as if there had been something to hear, but this attitude, while it lasted, was his own communication. "If you won't then – good: I spare you and I give up. You affect me as by the appeal positively for pity: you convince me that for reasons rigid and sublime – what do I know? – we both of us should have suffered. I respect them then, and, though moved and privileged as, I believe, it has never been given to man, I retire, I renounce – never, on my honour, to try again. So rest for ever – and let *me!*"

That, for Brydon was the deep sense of this last demonstration – solemn, measured, directed, as he felt it to be. He brought it to a close, he turned away; and now verily he knew how deeply he had been stirred. He retraced his steps, taking up his candle, burnt, he observed, well-nigh to the socket, and marking again, lighten it as he would, the distinctness of his footfall; after which, in a moment, he knew himself at the other side of the house. He did here what he had not yet done at these hours — he opened half a casement, one of those in the front, and let in the air of the night; a thing he would have taken at any time previous for a sharp rupture of his spell. His spell was broken now, and it didn't matter — broken by his concession and his surrender, which made it idle henceforth that he should ever come back. The empty street — its other life so marked even by the great lamplit vacancy — was within call, within touch; he stayed there as to be in it again, high above it though he was still perched; he watched as for some comforting common fact, some vulgar human note, the passage of a scavenger or a thief, some night-bird however base. He would have blessed that sign of life; he would have welcomed positively the slow approach of his friend the policeman, whom he had hitherto only sought to avoid, and was not sure that if the patrol had come into sight he mightn't have felt the impulse to get into relation with it, to hail it, on some pretext, from his fourth floor.

The pretext that wouldn't have been too silly or too compromising, the explanation that would have saved his dignity and kept his name, in such a case, out of the papers, was not definite to him: he was so occupied with the thought of recording his Discretion — as an effect of the vow he had just uttered to his intimate adversary — that the importance of this loomed large and something had overtaken all ironically his sense of proportion. If there had been a ladder applied to the front of the house, even one of the vertiginous perpendiculars employed by painters and roofers and sometimes left standing overnight, he would have managed somehow, astride of the window-sill, to compass by outstretched leg and arm that mode of descent. If there had been some such uncanny thing as he had found in his room at hotels, a workable fire-escape in the form of notched cable or a canvas shoot, he would have availed himself of it as a proof — well, of his present delicacy. He nursed that sentiment, as the question stood, a little in vain, and even — at the end of he scarce knew, once more, how long — found it, as by the action on his mind of the failure of response of the outer world, sinking back to vague anguish. It seemed to him he had waited an age for some stir of the great grim hush; the life of the town was itself under a spell — so unnaturally, up and down the whole prospect of known and rather ugly objects, the blankness and the silence lasted. Had they ever, he asked himself, the hardfaced houses, which had begun to look livid in the dim dawn, had they ever spoken so little to any need of his spirit? Great builded voids, great crowded stillnesses put on, often, in the heart of cities, for the small hours, a sort of sinister mask, and it was of this large collective negation that Brydon presently became conscious — all the more that the break of day was, almost incredibly, now at hand, proving to him what a night he had made of it.

He looked again at his watch, saw what had become of his time-values (he had taken hours for minutes — not, as in other tense situations, minutes for hours) and the strange air of the streets was but the weak, the sullen flush of a dawn in which everything was still locked up. His choked appeal from his own open window had been the sole note of life, and he could but break off at last as for a worse despair. Yet while so deeply demoralised he was capable again of an impulse denoting – at least by his present measure – extraordinary resolution; of retracing his steps to the spot where he had turned cold with the extinction of his last pulse of doubt as to there being in the place another presence than his own. This required an effort strong enough to sicken him; but he had his reason, which over-mastered for the moment everything else. There was the whole of the rest of the house to traverse, and how should he screw himself to that if the door he had seen closed were at present open? He could hold to the idea that the closing had practically been for him an act of mercy, a chance offered him to descend, depart, get off the ground and never again profane it. This conception held together, it worked; but what it meant for him depended now clearly on the amount of forbearance his recent action, or rather his recent inaction, had engendered. The image of the "presence," whatever it was, waiting there for him to go – this image had not yet been so concrete for his nerves as when he stopped short of the point at which certainty would have come to him. For, with all his resolution, or more exactly with all his dread, he did stop short – he hung back from really seeing. The risk was too great and his fear too definite: it took at this moment an awful specific form.

He knew – yes, as he had never known anything – that, *should* he see the door open, it would all too abjectly be the end of him. It would mean that the agent of his shame – for his shame was the deep abjection – was once more at large and in general possession; and what glared him thus in the face was the act that this would determine for him. It would send him straight about to the window he had left open, and by that window, be long ladder and dangling rope as absent as they would, he saw himself uncontrollably insanely fatally take his way to the street. The hideous chance of this he at least could avert; but he could only avert it by recoiling in time from assurance. He had the whole house to deal with, this fact was still there; only he now knew that uncertainty alone could start him. He stole back from where he had checked himself – merely to do so was suddenly like safety – and, making blindly for the greater staircase, left gaping rooms and sounding passages behind. Here was the top of the stairs, with a fine large dim descent and three spacious landings to mark off. His instinct was all for mildness, but his feet were harsh on the floors, and, strangely, when he had in a couple of minutes become aware of this, it counted somehow for help. He couldn't have spoken, the tone of his voice would have scared him, and the common conceit or resource of "whistling in the dark" (whether literally or figuratively) have appeared basely vulgar; yet he liked none the less to hear himself go, and when he had reached his first landing – taking it all with no rush, but quite steadily – that stage of success drew from him a gasp of relief.

The house, withal, seemed immense, the scale of space again inordinate; the open rooms, to no one of which his eyes deflected, gloomed in their shuttered state like mouths of caverns; only the high skylight that formed the crown of the deep well created for him a medium in which he could advance, but which might have been, for queerness of colour, some watery under-world. He tried to think of something noble, as that his property was really grand, a splendid possession; but this nobleness took the form too of the clear delight with which he was finally to sacrifice it. They might come in now, the builders, the destroyers – they might come as soon as they would. At the end of two flights he had dropped to another zone, and from the middle of the third, with only one more left, he recognised the influence of the lower windows, of half-drawn blinds, of the occasional gleam of streetlamps, of the glazed spaces of the vestibule. This was the bottom of the sea, which showed an illumination of its own and which he even saw paved – when at a given moment he drew up to sink a long look over the banisters – with the marble squares of his childhood. By that time indubitably he felt, as he might have said in a commoner cause, better; it had allowed him to stop and draw breath, and the ease increased with the sight of the old black-and-white slabs. But what he most felt was that now surely, with the element of impunity pulling him as by hard firm hands, the case was settled for what he might have seen above had he dared that last look. The closed door, blessedly remote now, was still closed – and he had only in short to reach that of the house.

He came down further, he crossed the passage forming the access to the last flight; and if here again he stopped an instant it was almost for the sharpness of the thrill of assured escape. It made him shut his eyes – which opened again to the straight slope of the remainder of the stairs. Here was impunity still, but impunity almost excessive; inasmuch as the side-lights and the high fan-tracery of the entrance were glimmering straight into the hall; an appearance produced, he the next instant saw, by the fact that the vestibule gaped wide, that the hinged halves of the inner door had been thrown far back. Out of that again the *question* sprang at him, making his eyes, as he felt, half-start from his head, as they had done, at the top of the house, before the sign of the other door. If he had left that one open, hadn't he left this one closed, and wasn't he now in *most* immediate presence of some inconceivable occult activity? It was as sharp, the question, as a knife in his side, but the answer hung fire still and seemed to lose itself in the vague darkness to which the thin admitted dawn, glimmering archwise over the whole outer door, made a semicircular margin, a cold silvery nimbus that seemed to play a little as he looked – to shift and expand and contract.

It was as if there had been something within it, protected by indistinctness and corresponding in extent with the opaque surface behind, the painted panels of the last barrier to his escape, of which the key was in his pocket. The indistinctness mocked him even while he stared, affected him as somehow shrouding or challenging certitude, so that after faltering an instant on his step he let himself go with the sense that here *was* at last something to meet, to touch, to take, to know — something all unnatural and dreadful, but to advance upon which was the condition for him either of liberation or of supreme defeat. The penumbra, dense and dark, was the virtual screen of a figure which stood in it as still as some image erect in a niche or as some black-vizored sentinel guarding a treasure. Brydon was to know afterwards, was to recall and make out, the particular thing he had believed during the rest of his descent. He saw, in its great grey glimmering margin, the central vagueness diminish, and he felt it to be taking the very form toward which, for so many days, the passion of his curiosity had yearned. It gloomed, it loomed, it was something, it was somebody, the prodigy of a personal presence.

Rigid and conscious, spectral yet human, a man of his own substance and stature waited there to measure himself with his power to dismay. This only could it be — this only till he recognised, with his advance, that what made the face dim was the pair of raised hands that covered it and in which, so far from being offered in defiance, it was buried as for dark deprecation. So Brydon, before him, took him in; with every fact of him now, in the higher light, hard and acute — his planted stillness, his vivid truth, his grizzled bent head and white masking hands, his queer actuality of evening-dress, of dangling double eye-glass, of gleaming silk lappet and white linen, of pearl button and gold watch-guard and polished shoe. No portrait by a great modern master could have presented him with more intensity, thrust him out of his frame with more art, as if there had been "treatment," of the consummate sort, in his every shade and salience. The revulsion, for our friend, had become, before he knew it, immense — this drop, in the act of apprehension, to the sense of his adversary's inscrutable manoeuvre. That meaning at least, while he gaped, it offered him; for he could but gape at his other self in this other anguish, gape as a proof that *he,* standing there for the achieved, the enjoyed, the triumphant life, couldn't be faced in his triumph. Wasn't the proof in the splendid covering hands, strong and completely spread? — so spread and so intentional that, in spite of a special verity that surpassed every other, the fact that one of these hands had lost two fingers, which were reduced to stumps, as if accidentally shot away, the face was effectually guarded and saved.

"Saved," though, *would* it be? — Brydon breathed his wonder till the very impunity of his attitude and the very insistence of his eyes produced, as he felt, a sudden stir which showed the next instant as a deeper portent, while the head raised itself, the betrayal of a braver purpose. The hands, as he looked, began to move, to open; then, as if deciding in a flash, dropped from the face and left it uncovered and presented. Horror, with the sight, had leaped into Brydon's throat, gasping there in a sound he couldn't utter; for the bared identity was too hideous as *his,* and his glare was the passion of his protest. The face, *that* face, Spencer Brydon's? — he searched it still, but looking away from it in dismay and denial, falling straight from his height of sublimity. It was unknown, inconceivable, awful, disconnected from any possibility – ! He had been "sold," he inwardly moaned, stalking such game as this: the presence before him was a presence, the horror within him a horror, but the waste of his nights had been only grotesque and the success of his adventure an irony. Such an identity fitted his at *no* point, made its alternative monstrous. A thousand times yes, as it came upon him nearer now – the face was the face of a stranger. It came upon him nearer now, quite as one of those expanding fantastic images projected by the magic lantern of childhood; for the stranger, whoever he might be, evil, odious, blatant, vulgar, had advanced as for aggression, and he knew himself give ground. Then harder pressed still, sick with the force of his shock, and falling back as under the hot breath and the roused passion of a life larger than his own, a rage of personality before which his own collapsed, he felt the whole vision turn to darkness and his very feet give way. His head went round; he was going; he had gone.

III

What had next brought him back, clearly – though after how long? – was Mrs. Muldoon's voice, coming to him from quite near, from so near that he seemed presently to see her as kneeling on the ground before him while he lay looking up at her; himself not wholly on the ground, but half-raised and upheld – conscious, yes, of tenderness of support and, more particularly, of a head pillowed in extraordinary softness and faintly refreshing fragrance. He considered, he wondered, his wit but half at his service; then another face intervened, bending more directly over him, and he finally knew that Alice Staverton had made her lap an ample and perfect cushion to him, and that she had to this end seated herself on the lowest degree of the staircase, the rest of his long person remaining stretched on his old black-and-white slabs. They were cold, these marble squares of his youth; but *he* somehow was not, in this rich return of consciousness – the most wonderful hour, little by little, that he had ever known, leaving him, as it did, so gratefully, so abysmally passive, and yet as with a treasure of intelligence waiting all round him for quiet appropriation; dissolved, he might call it, in the air of the place and producing the golden glow of a late autumn afternoon. He had come back, yes – come back from further away than any man but himself had ever travelled; but it was strange how with this sense what he had come back *to* seemed really the great thing, and as if his prodigious journey had been all for the sake of it. Slowly but surely his consciousness grew, his vision of his state thus completing itself: he had been miraculously *carried* back – lifted and carefully borne as from where he had been picked up, the uttermost end of an interminable grey passage. Even with this he was suffered to rest, and what had now brought him to knowledge was the break in the long mild motion.

It had brought him to knowledge, to knowledge – yes, this was the beauty of his state; which came to resemble more and more that of a man who has gone to sleep on some news of a great inheritance, and then, after dreaming it away, after profaning it with matters strange to it, has waked up again to serenity of certitude and has only to lie and watch it grow. This was the drift of his patience – that he had only to let it shine on him. He must moreover, with intermissions, still have been lifted and borne; since why and how else should he have known himself, later on, with the afternoon glow intenser, no longer at the foot of his stairs – situated as these now seemed at that dark other end of his tunnel – but on a deep window-bench of his high saloon, over which had been spread, couch-fashion, a mantle of soft stuff lined with grey fur that was familiar to his eyes and that one of his hands kept fondly feeling as for its pledge of truth. Mrs. Muldoon's face had gone, but the other, the second he had recognised, hung over him in a way that showed how he was still propped and pillowed. He took it all in, and the more he took it the more it seemed to suffice: he was as much at peace as if he had had food and drink. It was the two women who had found him, on Mrs. Muldoon's having plied, at her usual hour, her latch-key – and on her having above all arrived while Miss Staverton still lingered near the house. She had been turning away, all anxiety, from worrying the vain bell-handle – her calculation having been of the hour of the good woman's visit; but the latter, blessedly, had come up while she was still there, and they had entered together. He had then lain, beyond the vestibule, very much as he was lying now – quite, that is, as he appeared to have fallen, but all so wondrously without bruise or gash; only in a depth of stupor. What he most took in, however, at present, with the steadier clearance, was that Alice Staverton had for a long unspeakable moment not doubted he was dead.

"It must have been that I *was.*" He made it out as she held him. "Yes – I can only have died. You brought me literally to life. Only," he wondered, his eyes rising to her, "only, in the name of all the benedictions, how?"

It took her but an instant to bend her face and kiss him, and something in the manner of it, and in the way her hands clasped and locked his head while he felt the cool charity and virtue of her lips, something in all this beatitude somehow answered everything. "And now I keep you," she said.

"Oh keep me, keep me!" he pleaded while her face still hung over him: in response to which it dropped again and stayed close, clingingly close. It was the seal of their situation – of which he tasted the impress for a long blissful moment in silence. But he came back. "Yet how did you know – ?"

"I was uneasy. You were to have come, you remember – and you had sent no word."

"Yes, I remember – I was to have gone to you at one today." It caught on to their "old" life and relation – which were so near and so far. "I was still out there in my strange darkness – where was it, what was it? I must have stayed there so long." He could but wonder at the depth and the duration of his swoon.

"Since last night?" she asked with a shade of fear for her possible indiscretion.

"Since this morning – it must have been: the cold dim dawn of today. Where have I been," he vaguely wailed, "where have I been?" He felt her hold him close, and it was as if this helped him now to make in all security his mild moan. "What a long dark day!"

All in her tenderness she had waited a moment. "In the cold dim dawn?" she quavered.

But he had already gone on piecing together the parts of the whole prodigy. "As I didn't turn up you came straight – ?"

She barely cast about. "I went first to your hotel – where they told me of your absence. You had dined out last evening and hadn't been back since. But they appeared to know you had been at your club."

"So you had the idea of *this* – ?"

"Of what?" she asked in a moment.

"Well – of what has happened."

"I believed at least you'd have been here. I've known, all along," she said, "that you've been coming."

" 'Known' it – ?"

"Well, I've believed it. I said nothing to you after that talk we had a month ago – but I felt sure. I knew you *would,*" she declared.

"That I'd persist, you mean?"

"That you'd see him."

"Ah but I didn't!" cried Brydon with his long wail. "There's somebody – an awful beast; whom I brought, too horribly, to bay. But it's not me."

At this she bent over him again, and her eyes were in his eyes. "No – it's not you." And it was as if, while her face hovered, he might have made out in it, hadn't it been so near, some particular meaning blurred by a smile. "No, thank heaven," she repeated – "it's not you! Of course it wasn't to have been."

"Ah but it *was,*" he gently insisted. And he stared before him now as he had been staring for so many weeks. "I was to have known myself."

"You couldn't!" she returned consolingly. And then reverting, and as if to account further for what she had herself done, "But it wasn't only *that,* that you hadn't been at home," she went on. "I waited till the hour at which we had found Mrs. Muldoon that day of my going with you; and she arrived, as I've told you, while, failing to bring any one to the door, I lingered in my despair on the steps. After a little, if she hadn't come, by such a mercy, I should have found means to hunt her up. But it wasn't," said Alice Staverton, as if once more with her fine intention – "it wasn't only that."

His eyes, as he lay turned back to her. "What more then?"

She met it, the wonder she had stirred. "In the cold dim dawn, you say? Well, in the cold dim dawn of this morning I too saw you."

"Saw *me* – ?"

"Saw *him,*" said Alice Staverton. "It must have been at the same moment."

He lay an instant taking it in – as if he wished to be quite reasonable. "At the same moment?"

"Yes – in my dream again, the same one I've named to you. He came back to me. Then I knew it for a sign. He had come to you."

At this Brydon raised himself; he had to see her better. She helped him when she understood his movement, and he sat up, steadying himself beside her there on the window-bench and with his right hand grasping her left. "*He* didn't come to me."

"You came to yourself," she beautifully smiled.

"Ah I've come to myself now – thanks to you, dearest. But this brute, with his awful face – this brute's a black stranger. He's none of *me,* even as I *might* have been," Brydon sturdily declared.

But she kept the clearness that was like the breath of infallibility. "Isn't the whole point that you'd have been different?"

He almost scowled for it. "As different as *that* – ?"

Her look again was more beautiful to him than the things of this world. "Haven't you exactly wanted to know *how* different? So this morning," she said, "you appeared to me."

"Like *him*?"

"A black stranger!"

"Then how did you know it was I?"

"Because, as I told you weeks ago, my mind, my imagination, had worked so over what you might, what you mightn't have been – to show you, you see, how I've thought of you. In the midst of that you came to me – that my wonder might be answered. So I knew," she went on; "and believed that, since the question held you too so fast, as you told me that day, you too would see for yourself. And when this morning I again saw I knew it would be because you had – and also then, from the first moment, because you somehow wanted me. *He* seemed to tell me of that. So why," she strangely smiled, "shouldn't I like him?"

It brought Spencer Brydon to his feet. "You 'like' that horror – ?"

"I *could* have liked him. And to me," she said, "he was no horror. I had accepted him."

" 'Accepted' – ?" Brydon oddly sounded.

"Before, for the interest of his difference – yes. And as *I* didn't disown him, as *I* knew him – which you at last, confronted with him in his difference, so cruelly didn't, my dear – well, he must have been, you see, less dreadful to me. And it may have pleased him that I pitied him."

She was beside him on her feet, but still holding his hand – still with her arm supporting him. But though it all brought for him thus a dim light, "You 'pitied' him?" he grudgingly, resentfully asked.

"He has been unhappy; he has been ravaged," she said.

"And haven't I been unhappy? Am not I – you've only to look at me! – ravaged?"

"Ah I don't say I like him *better,*" she granted after a thought. "But he's grim, he's worn – and things have happened to him. He doesn't make shift, for sight, with your charming monocle."

"No" – it struck Brydon: "I couldn't have sported mine 'downtown.' They'd have guyed me there."

"His great convex pince-nez – I saw it, I recognised the kind – is for his poor ruined sight. And his poor right hand – !"

"Ah!" Brydon winced – whether for his proved identity or for his lost fingers. Then, "He has a million a year," he lucidly added. "But he hadn't you."

"And he isn't – no, he isn't – *you!*" she murmured as he drew her to his breast.

"EUROPE"

I

"Our feeling is, you know, that Becky *should* go." That earnest little remark comes back to me, even after long years, as the first note of something that began, for my observation, the day I went with my sister-in-law to take leave of her good friends. It is a memory of the American time, which revives so at present — under some touch that doesn't signify — that it rounds itself off as an anecdote. That walk to say goodbye was the beginning; and the end, so far as I was concerned with it, was not till long after; yet even the end also appears to me now as of the old days. I went, in those days, on occasion, to see my sister-in-law, in whose affairs, on my brother's death, I had had to take a helpful hand. I continued to go, indeed, after these little matters were straightened out, for the pleasure, periodically, of the impression — the change to the almost pastoral sweetness of the good Boston suburb from the loud, longitudinal New York. It was another world, with other manners, a different tone, a different taste; a savour nowhere so mild, yet so distinct as in the square white house — with the pair of elms, like gigantic wheat-sheaves in front, the rustic orchard not far behind, the old-fashioned door-lights, the big blue and white jars in the porch, the straight, bricked walk from the high gate — that enshrined the extraordinary merit of Mrs Rimmle and her three daughters.

These ladies were so much of the place and the place so much of themselves that, from the first of their being revealed to me, I felt that nothing else at Brookbridge much mattered. They were what, for me, at any rate, Brookbridge had most to give: I mean in the way of what it was naturally strongest in, the thing that we called in New York the New England expression, the air of Puritanism reclaimed and refined. The Rimmles had brought this down to a wonderful delicacy. They struck me even then — all four almost equally — as very ancient and very earnest, and I think theirs must have been the house, in all the world, in which "culture" first came to the aid of morning calls. The head of the family was the widow of a great public character — as public characters were understood at

Brookbridge – whose speeches on anniversaries formed a part of the body of national eloquence spouted in the New England schools by little boys covetous of the most marked, though perhaps the easiest, distinction. He was reported to have been celebrated, and in such fine declamatory connections that he seemed to gesticulate even from the tomb. He was understood to have made, in his wife's company, the tour of Europe at a date not immensely removed from that of the battle of Waterloo. What was the age, then, of the bland, firm, antique Mrs Rimmle at the period of her being first revealed to me? That is a point I am not in a position to determine – I remember mainly that I was young enough to regard her as having reached the limit. And yet the limit for Mrs Rimmle must have been prodigiously extended; the scale of its extension is, in fact, the very moral of this reminiscence. She was old, and her daughters were old, but I was destined to know them all as older. It was only by comparison and habit that – however much I recede – Rebecca, Maria, and Jane were the "young ladies."

I think it was felt that, though their mother's life, after thirty years of widowhood, had had a grand backward stretch, her blandness and firmness – and this in spite of her extreme physical frailty – would be proof against any surrender not overwhelmingly justified by time. It had appeared, years before, at a crisis of which the waves had not even yet quite subsided, a surrender not justified by anything that she should go, with her daughters, to Europe for her health. Her health was supposed to require constant support; but when it had at that period tried conclusions with the idea of Europe, it was not the idea of Europe that had been insidious enough to prevail. She had not gone, and Becky, Maria, and Jane had not gone, and this was long ago. They still merely floated in the air of the visit achieved, with such introductions and such acclamations, in the early part of the century; they still, with fond glances at the sunny parlour-walls, only referred, in conversation, to divers pictorial and other reminders of it. The Miss Rimmles had quite been brought up on it, but Becky, as the most literary, had most mastered the subject. There were framed letters – tributes to their eminent father – suspended among the mementoes, and of two or three of these, the most foreign and complimentary, Becky had executed translations that figured beside the text. She knew already, through this and other illumination, so much about Europe that it was hard to believe, for her, in that limit of adventure which consisted only of her having been twice to Philadelphia. The others had not been to Philadelphia, but there was a legend that Jane had been to Saratoga. Becky was a short, stout, fair person with round, serious eyes, a high forehead, the sweetest, neatest enunciation, and a miniature of her father – "done in Rome" – worn as a breastpin. She had written the life, she had edited the speeches, of the original of this ornament, and now at last, beyond the seas, she was really to tread in his footsteps.

Fine old Mrs Rimmle, in the sunny parlour and with a certain austerity of cap and chair – though with a gay new "front" that looked like rusty brown plush – had had so unusually good a winter that the question of her sparing two members of her family for an absence had been threshed as fine, I could feel, as even under that Puritan roof any case of conscience had ever been threshed. They were to make their dash while the coast, as it were, was clear, and each of the daughters had tried – heroically, angelically, and for the sake of each of her sisters – not to be one of the two. What I encountered that first time was an opportunity to concur with enthusiasm in the general idea that Becky's wonderful preparation would be wasted if she were the one to stay with their mother. They talked of Becky's preparation – they had a sly, old-maidish humour that was as mild as milk – as if it were some mixture, for application somewhere, that she kept in a precious bottle. It had been settled, at all events, that, armed with this concoction and borne aloft by their introductions, she and Jane were to start. They were wonderful on their introductions, which proceeded naturally from their mother and were addressed to the charming families that, in vague generations, had so admired vague Mr Rimmle. Jane, I found at Brookbridge, had to be described, for want of other description, as the pretty one, but it would not have served to identify her unless you had seen the others. *Her* preparation was only this figment of her prettiness – only, that is, unless one took into account something that, on the spot, I silently divined: the lifelong, secret, passionate ache of her little rebellious desire. They were all growing old in the yearning to go, but Jane's yearning was the sharpest. She struggled with it as people at Brookbridge mostly struggled with what they liked, but fate, by threatening to prevent what she *dis*liked, and what was therefore duty – which was to stay at home instead of Maria – had bewildered her, I judged, not a little. It was she who, in the words I have quoted, mentioned to me Becky's case and Becky's affinity as the clearest of all. Her mother, however, on the general subject, had still more to say.

"I positively desire, I really quite insist that they shall go," the old lady explained to us from her stiff chair. "We've talked about it so often, and they've had from me so clear an account – I've amused them again and again with it – of what is to be seen and enjoyed. If they've had hitherto too many duties to leave, the time seems to have come to recognise that there are also many duties to *seek*. Wherever we go we find them – I always remind the girls of that. There's a duty that calls them to those wonderful countries, just as it called, at the right time, their father and myself – if it be only that of laying up for the years to come the same store of remarkable impressions, the same wealth of knowledge and food for conversation as, since my return, I have found myself so happy to possess." Mrs Rimmle spoke of her return as of something of the year before last, but the future of her daughters was, somehow, by a different law, to be on the scale of great vistas, of endless aftertastes. I think that, without my being quite ready to say it, even this first impression of her was somewhat upsetting; there was a large, placid perversity, a grim secrecy of intention, in her estimate of the ages.

"Well, I'm so glad you don't delay it longer," I said to Miss Becky before we withdrew. "And whoever should go," I continued in the spirit of the sympathy with which the good sisters had already inspired me, "I quite feel, with your family, you know, that *you* should. But of course I hold that every one should." I suppose I wished to attenuate my solemnity; there was something in it, however, that I couldn't help. It must have been a faint foreknowledge.

"Have you been a great deal yourself?" Miss Jane, I remember, inquired.

"Not so much but that I hope to go a good deal more. So perhaps we shall meet," I encouragingly suggested.

I recall something – something in the nature of susceptibility to encouragement – that this brought into the more expressive brown eyes to which Miss Jane mainly owed it that she was the pretty one. "Where, do you think?"

I tried to think. "Well, on the Italian lakes – Como, Bellagio, Lugano." I liked to say the names to them.

" 'Sublime, but neither bleak nor bare – nor misty are the mountains there!' " Miss Jane softly breathed, while her sister looked at her as if her familiarity with the poetry of the subject made her the most interesting feature of the scene she evoked.

But Miss Becky presently turned to me. "Do you know everything – ?"

"Everything?"

"In Europe."

"Oh, yes," I laughed, "and one or two things even in America."

The sisters seemed to me furtively to look at each other.

"Well, you'll have to be quick – to meet *us,*" Miss Jane resumed.

"But surely when you're once there you'll stay on."

"Stay on?" – they murmured it simultaneously and with the oddest vibration of dread as well as of desire. It was as if they had been in the presence of a danger and yet wished me, who "knew everything," to torment them with still more of it.

Well, I did my best. "I mean it will never do to cut it short."

"No, that's just what I keep saying," said brilliant Jane. "It would be better, in that case, not to go."

"Oh, don't talk about not going – at this time!" It was none of my business, but I felt shocked and impatient.

"No, not at *this* time!" broke in Miss Maria, who, very red in the face, had joined us. Poor Miss Maria was known as the flushed one; but she was not flushed – she only had an unfortunate surface. The third day after this was to see them embark.

Miss Becky, however, desired as little as any one to be in any way extravagant. "It's only the thought of our mother," she explained.

I looked a moment at the old lady, with whom my sister-in-law was engaged. "Well – your mother's magnificent."

"Isn't she magnificent?" – they eagerly took it up.

She *was* – I could reiterate it with sincerity, though I perhaps mentally drew the line when Miss Maria again risked, as a fresh ejaculation: "I think she's better than Europe!"

"Maria!" they both, at this, exclaimed with a strange emphasis; it was as if they feared she had suddenly turned cynical over the deep domestic drama of their casting of lots. The innocent laugh with which she answered them gave the measure of her cynisicm.

We separated at last, and my eyes met Mrs Rimmle's as I held for an instant her aged hand. It was doubtless only my fancy that her calm, cold look quietly accused me of something. Of what *could* it accuse me? Only, I thought, of thinking.

II

I left Brookbridge the next day, and for some time after that had no occasion to hear from my kinswoman; but when she finally wrote there was a passage in her letter that affected me more than all the rest. "Do you know the poor Rimmles never, after all, 'went'? The old lady, at the eleventh hour, broke down; everything broke down, and all of *them* on top of it, so that the dear things are with us still. Mrs Rimmle, the night after our call, had, in the most unexpected manner, a turn for the worse – something in the nature (though they're rather mysterious about it) of a seizure; Becky and Jane felt it – dear, devoted, stupid angels that they are – heartless to leave her at such a moment, and Europe's indefinitely postponed. However, they think they're still going – or *think* they think it – when she's better. They also think – or think they think – that she *will* be better. I certainly pray she may." So did I – quite fervently. I was conscious of a real pang – I didn't know how much they had made me care.

Late that winter my sister-in-law spent a week in New York; when almost my first inquiry on meeting her was about the health of Mrs Rimmle.

"Oh, she's rather bad – she really is, you know. It's not surprising that at her age she should be infirm."

"Then what the deuce *is* her age?"

"I can't tell you to a year – but she's immensely old."

"That of course I saw," I replied – "unless you literally mean so old that the records have been lost."

My sister-in-law thought. "Well, I believe she wasn't positively young when she married. She lost three or four children before these women were born."

We surveyed together a little, on this, the "dark backward." "And they were born, I gather, *after* the famous tour? Well, then, as the famous tour was in a manner to celebrate – wasn't it? – the restoration of the Bourbons —" I considered, I gasped. "My dear child, what on earth do you make her out?"

My relative, with her Brookbridge habit, transferred her share of the question to the moral plane – turned it forth to wander, by implication at least, in the sandy desert of responsibility. "Well, you know, we all immensely admire her."

"You can't admire her more than I do. She's awful."

My interlocutress looked at me with a certain fear. "She's *really* ill."

"Too ill to get better?"

"Oh, no – we hope not. Because then they'll be able to go."

"And *will* they go, if she should?"

"Oh, the moment they should be quite satisfied. I mean *really*," she added.

I'm afraid I laughed at her – the Brookbridge "really" was a thing so by itself. "But if she shouldn't get better?" I went on.

"Oh, don't speak of it! They want so to go."

"It's a pity they're so infernally good," I mused.

"No – don't say that. It's what keeps them up."

Yes, but isn't it what keeps *her* up too?"

My visitor looked grave. "Would you like them to kill her?"

I don't know that I was then prepared to say I should – though I believe I came very near to it. But later on I burst all bounds, for the subject grew and grew. I went again before the good sisters ever did – I mean I went to Europe. I think I went twice, with a brief interval, before my fate again brought round for me a couple of days at Brookbridge. I had been there repeatedly, in the previous time, without making the acquaintance of the Rimmles; but now that I had had the revelation I couldn't have it too much, and the first request I proffered was to be taken again to see them. I remember well indeed the scruple I felt – the real delicacy – about betraying that *I* had, in the pride of my power, since our other meeting, stood, as their phrase went, among romantic scenes; but they were themselves the first to speak of it, and what, moreover, came home to me was that the coming and going of their friends in general – Brookbridge itself having even at that period one foot in Europe – was such as to place constantly before them the pleasure that was only postponed. They were thrown back, after all, on what the situation, under a final analysis, had most to give – the sense that, as every one kindly said to them and they kindly said to every one, Europe would keep. Every one felt for them so deeply that their own kindness in alleviating every one's feeling was really what came out most. Mrs Rimmle was still in her stiff chair and in the sunny parlour, but if *she* made no scruple of introducing the Italian lakes my heart sank to observe that she dealt with them, as a topic, not in the least in the leave-taking manner in which Falstaff babbled of green fields.

I am not sure that, after this, my pretexts for a day or two with my sister-in-law were not apt to be a mere cover for another glimpse of these particulars: I at any rate never went to Brookbridge without an irrepressible eagerness for our customary call. A long time seems to me thus to have passed, with glimpses and lapses, considerable impatience and still more pity. Our visits indeed grew shorter, for, as my companion said, they were more and more of a strain. It finally struck me that the good sisters even shrank from me a little, as from one who penetrated their consciousness in spite of himself. It was as if they knew where I thought they ought to be, and were moved to deprecate at last, by a systematic silence on the subject of that hemisphere, the criminality I fain would fix on them. They were full instead – as with the instinct of throwing dust in my eyes – of little pathetic hypocrisies about Brookbridge interests and delights. I dare say that as time went on my deeper sense of their situation came practically to rest on my companion's report of it. I think I recollect, at all events, every word we ever exchanged about them, even if I have lost the thread of the special occasions. The impression they made on me after each interval always broke out with extravagance as I walked away with her.

"*She* may be as old as she likes – I don't care. It's the fearful age the 'girls' are reaching that constitutes the scandal. One shouldn't pry into such matters, I know; but the years and the chances are really going. They're all growing old together – it will presently be too late; and their mother meanwhile perches over them like a vulture – what shall I call it? – calculating. Is she waiting for them successively to drop off? She'll survive them each and all. There's something too remorseless in it."

"Yes; but what do you want her to do? If the poor thing *can't* die, she can't. Do you want her to take poison or to open a blood-vessel? I dare say she would prefer to go."

"I beg your pardon," I must have replied; "you daren't say anything of the sort. If she would prefer to go she *would* go. She would feel the propriety, the decency, the necessity of going. She just prefers *not* to go. She prefers to stay and keep up the tension, and her calling them 'girls' and talking of the good time they'll still have is the mere conscious mischief of a subtle old witch. They won't have *any* time – there isn't any time to have! I mean there's, on her own part, no real loss of measure or of perspective in it. She *knows* she's a hundred and ten, and she takes a cruel pride in it."

My sister-in-law differed with me about this; she held that the old woman's attitude was an honest one and that her magnificent vitality, so great in spite of her infirmities, made it inevitable she should attribute youth to persons who had come into the world so much later. "Then suppose she should die?" – so my fellow-student of the case always put it to me.

"Do you mean while her daughters are away? There's not the least fear of that – not even if at the very moment of their departure she should be *in extremis*. They would find her all right on their return."

"But think how they would feel not to have been with her!"

"That's only, I repeat, on the unsound assumption. If they would only go to-morrow – literally make a good rush for it – they'll be with her when they come back. That will give them plenty of time." I'm afraid I even heartlessly added that if she *should* against every probability, pass away in their absence, they wouldn't have come back at all – which would be just the compensation proper to their long privation. And then Maria would come out to join the two others, and they would be – though but for the too scanty remnant of their career – as merry as the day is long.

I remained ready, somehow, pending the fulfillment of that vision, to sacrifice Maria; it was only over the urgency of the case for the others respectively that I found myself balancing. Sometimes it was for Becky I thought the tragedy deepest – sometimes, and in quite a different manner, I thought it most dire for Jane. It was Jane, after all, who had most sense of life. I seemed in fact dimly to descry in Jane a sense – as yet undescried by herself or by any one – of all sorts of queer things. Why didn't *she* go? I used desperately to ask; why didn't she make a bold personal dash for it, strike up a partnership with some one or other of the travelling spinsters in whom Brookbridge more and more abounded? Well, there came a flash for me at a particular point of the grey middle desert: my correspondent was able to let me know that poor Jane at last *had* sailed. She had gone of a sudden – I liked my sister-in-law's view of suddenness – with the kind Hathaways, who had made an irresistible grab at her and lifted her off her feet. They were going for the summer and for Mr Hathaway's health, so that the opportunity was perfect and it was impossible not to be glad that something very like physical force had finally prevailed. This was the general feeling at Brookbridge, and I might imagine what Brookbridge had been brought to from the fact that, at the very moment she was hustled off, the doctor, called to her mother at the peep of dawn, had considered that *he* at least must stay. There had been real alarm – greater than ever before; it actually did seem as if this time the end had come. But it was Becky, strange to say, who, though fully recognising the nature of the crisis, had kept the situation in hand and insisted upon action. This, I remember, brought back to me a discomfort with which I had been familiar from the first. One of the two had sailed, and I was sorry it was not the other. But if it had been the other I should have been equally sorry.

I saw with my eyes, that very autumn, what a fool Jane would have been if she had again backed out. Her mother had of course survived the peril of which I had heard, profiting by it indeed as she had profited by every other; she was sufficiently better again to have come down stairs. It was there that, as usual, I found her, but with a difference of effect produced somehow by the absence of one of the girls. It was as if, for the others, though they had not gone to Europe, Europe had come to them: Jane's letters had been so frequent and so beyond even what could have been hoped. It was the first time, however, that I perceived on the old woman's part a certain failure of lucidity. Jane's flight was, clearly, the great fact with her, but she spoke of it as if the fruit had now been plucked and the parenthesis closed. I don't know what sinking sense of still further physical duration I gathered, as a menace, from this first hint of her confusion of mind.

"My daughter has been; my daughter has been – " She kept saying it, but didn't say where; that seemed unnecessary, and she only repeated the words to her visitors with a face that was all puckers and yet now, save in so far as it expressed an ineffaceable complacency, all blankness. I think she wanted us a little to know that she had not stood in the way. It added to something – I scarce knew what – that I found myself desiring to extract privately from Becky. As our visit was to be of the shortest my opportunity – for one of the young ladies always came to the door with us – was at hand. Mrs Rimmle, as we took leave, again sounded her phrase, but she added this time: "I'm so glad she's going to have always – "

I knew so well what she meant that, as she again dropped, looking at me queerly and becoming momentarily dim, I could help her out. "Going to have what *you* have?"

"Yes, yes – my privilege. Wonderful experience," she mumbled. She bowed to me a little as if I would understand. "She has things to tell."

I turned, slightly at a loss, to Becky. "She has then already arrived?"

Becky was at that moment looking a little strangely at her mother, who answered my question. "She reached New York this morning – she comes on to-day."

"Oh, then – !" But let the matter pass as I met Becky's eye – I saw there was a hitch somewhere. It was not she but Maria who came out with us; on which I cleared up the question of their sister's reappearance.

"Oh, no, not to-night," Maria smiled; "that's only the way mother puts it. We shall see her about the end of November – the Hathaways are so indulgent. They kindly extend their tour."

"For *her* sake? How sweet of them!" my sister-in-law exclaimed.

I can see our friend's plain, mild old face take on a deeper mildness, even though a higher colour, in the light of the open door. "Yes, it's for Jane they prolong it. And do you know what they write?" She gave us time, but it was too great a responsibility to guess. "Why, that it has brought her out."

"Oh, I knew it *would!*" my companion sympathetically sighed.

Maria put it more strongly still. "They say we wouldn't know her."

This sounded a little awful, but it was, after all, what I had expected.

III

My correspondent in Brookbridge came to me that Christmas, with my niece, to spend a week; and the arrangement had of course been prefaced by an exchange of letters, the first of which from my sister-in-law scarce took space for acceptance of my invitation before going on to say: "The Hathaways are back – but without Miss Jane!" She presented in a few words the situation thus created at Brookbridge, but was not yet, I gathered, fully in possession of the other one – the situation created in "Europe" by the presence there of that lady. The two together, at any rate, demanded, I quickly felt, all my attention, and perhaps my impatience to receive my relative was a little sharpened by my desire for the whole story. I had it at last, by the Christmas fire, and I may say without reserve that it gave me all I could have hoped for. I listened eagerly, after which I produced the comment: "Then she simply refused – "

"To budge from Florence? Simply. She had it out there with the poor Hathaways, who felt responsible for her safety, pledged to restore her to her mother's, to her sisters' hands, and showed herself in a light, they mention under their breath, that made their dear old hair stand on end. Do you know what, when they first got back, they said of her – at least it was *his* phrase – to two or three people?"

I thought a moment. "That she had 'tasted blood'?"

My visitor fairly admired me. "How clever of you to guess! It's exactly what he did say. She appeared – she continues to appear, it seems – in a new character."

I wondered a little. "But that's exactly – don't you remember? – what Miss Maria reported to us from them; that we 'wouldn't know her.' "

My sister-in-law perfectly remembered. "Oh, yes – she broke out from the first. But when they left her she was worse."

"Worse?"

"Well, different – different from anything she ever *had* been, or – for that matter – had had a chance to be." My interlocutress hung fire a moment, but presently faced me. "Rather strange and free and obstreperous."

"Obstreperous?" I wondered again.

"Peculiarly so, I inferred, on the question of not coming away. She wouldn't hear of it, and, when they spoke of her mother, said she had given her mother up. She had thought she should like Europe, but didn't know she should like it so much. They had been fools to bring her if they expected to take her away. She was going to see what she could – she hadn't yet seen half. The end of it was, at any rate, that they had to leave her alone."

I seemed to see it all – to see even the scared Hathaways. "So she *is* alone?"

"She told them, poor thing, it appears, and in a tone they'll never forget, that she was, at all events, quite old enough to be. She cried – she quite went on – over not having come sooner. That's why the only way for her," my companion mused, "*is*, I suppose, to stay. They wanted to put her with some people or other – to find some American family. But she says she's on her own feet."

"And she's still in Florence?"

"No – I believe she was to travel. She's bent on the East."

I burst out laughing. "Magnificent Jane! It's most interesting. Only I feel that I distinctly *should* 'know' her. To my sense, always, I must tell you, she had it in her."

My relative was silent a little. "So it now appears Becky always felt."

"And yet pushed her off? Magnificent Becky!"

My companion met my eyes a moment. "You don't know the queerest part. I mean the way it has *most* brought her out."

I turned it over; I felt I should like to know – to that degree indeed that, oddly enough, I jocosely disguised my eagerness. "You don't mean she has taken to drink?"

My visitor hesitated. "She has taken to flirting."

I expressed disappointment. "Oh, she took to *that* long ago. Yes," I declared at my kinswoman's stare, "she positively flirted – with *me!*"

The stare perhaps sharpened. "Then you flirted with *her?*"

"How else could I have been as sure as I wanted to be? But has she means?"

"Means to flirt?" – my friend looked an instant as if she spoke literally. "I don't understand about the means – though of course they have something. But I have my impression," she went on. "I think that Becky —" It seemed almost too grave to say.

But *I* had no doubts. "That Becky's backing her?"

She brought it out. "Financing her."

"Stupendous Becky! So that morally then —"

"Becky's quite in sympathy. But isn't it too odd?" my sister-in-law asked.

"Not in the least. Didn't we know, as regards Jane, that Europe was to bring her out? Well, it has also brought out Rebecca."

"It has indeed!" my companion indulgently sighed. "So what would it do if she were there?"

"I should like immensely to see. And we *shall* see."

"Why, do you believe she'll still go?"

"Certainly. She *must.*"

But my friend shook it off. "She won't."

"She shall!" I retorted with a laugh. But the next moment I said: "And what does the old woman say?"

"To Jane's behaviour? Not a word – never speaks of it. She talks now much less than she used – only seems to wait. But it's my belief she thinks."

"And – do you mean – knows?"

"Yes, knows that she's abandoned. In her silence there she takes it in."

"It's her way of making Jane pay?" At this, somehow, I felt more serious. "Oh, dear, dear – she'll disinherit her!"

When, in the following June, I went on to return my sister-in-law's visit the first object that met my eyes in her little white parlour was a figure that, to my stupefaction, presented itself for the moment as that of Mrs Rimmle. I had gone to my room after arriving, and, on dressing, had come down: the apparition I speak of had arisen in the interval. Its ambiguous character lasted, however, but a second or two – I had taken Becky for her mother because I knew no one but her mother of that extreme age. Becky's age was quite startling; it had made a great stride, though, strangely enough, irrecoverably seated as she now was in it, she had wizened brightness that I had scarcely yet seen in her. I remember indulging on this occasion in two silent observations: one to the effect that I had not hitherto been conscious of her full resemblance to the old lady, and the other to the effect that, as I had said to my sister-in-law at Christmas, "Europe," even as reaching her only through Jane's sensibilities, had really at last brought her out. She was in fact "out" in a manner of which this encounter offered to my eyes a unique example: it was the single hour, often as I had been at Brookbridge, of my meeting her elsewhere than in her mother's drawing-room. I surmise that, besides being adjusted to her more marked time of life, the garments she wore abroad, and in particular her little plain bonnet, presented points of resemblance to the close sable sheath and the quaint old headgear that, in the white house behind the elms, I had from far back associated with the eternal image in the stiff chair. Of course I immediately spoke of Jane, showing an interest and asking for news; on which she answered me with a smile, but not at all as I had expected.

"Those are not really the things you want to know – where she is, whom she's with, how she manages and where she's going next – oh, no!" And the admirable woman gave a laugh that was somehow both light and sad – sad, in particular, with a strange, long weariness. "What you do want to know is when she's coming back."

I shook my head very kindly, but out of a wealth of experience that, I flattered myself, was equal to Miss Becky's. "I do know it. Never."

Miss Becky, at this, exchanged with me a long, deep look. "Never."

We had, in silence, a little luminous talk about it, in the course of which she seemed to tell me the most interesting things. "And how's your mother?" I then inquired.

She hesitated, but finally spoke with the same serenity. "My mother's all right. You see, she's not alive."

"Oh, Becky!" my sister-in-law pleadingly interjected.

But Becky only addressed herself to me. "Come and see if she is. *I* think she isn't – but Maria perhaps isn't so clear. Come, at all events, and judge and tell me."

It was a new note, and I was a little bewildered. "Ah, but I'm not a doctor!"

"No, thank God – you're not. That's why I ask you." And now she said good-bye.

I kept her hand a moment. *"You're* more alive than ever!"

"I'm very tired." She took it with the same smile, but for Becky it was much to say.

IV

"Not alive," the next day, was certainly what Mrs Rimmle looked when, coming in according to my promise, I found her, with Miss Maria, in her usual place. Though shrunken and diminished she still occupied her high-backed chair with a visible theory of erectness, and her intensely aged face – combined with something dauntless that belonged to her very presence and that was effective even in this extremity – might have been that of some centenarian sovereign, of indistinguishable sex, brought forth to be shown to the people as a disproof of the rumor of extinction. Mummified and open-eyed she looked at me, but I had no impression that she made me out. I had come this time without my sister-in-law, who had frankly pleaded to me – which also, for a daughter of Brookbridge, was saying much – that the house had grown too painful. Poor Miss Maria excused Miss Becky on the score of her not being well – and that, it struck me, was saying most of all. The absence of the others gave the occasion a different note; but I talked with Miss Maria for five minutes and perceived that – save for her saying, of her own movement, anything about Jane – she now spoke as if her mother had lost hearing or sense, or both, alluding freely and distinctly, though indeed favourably, to her condition. "She has expected your visit and she much enjoys it," my interlocutress said, while the old woman, soundless and motionless, simply fixed me without expression. Of course there was little to keep me; but I became aware, as I rose to go, that there was more than I had supposed. On my approaching her to take leave Mrs Rimmle gave signs of consciousness.

"Have you heard about Jane?"

I hesitated, feeling a responsibility, and appealed for direction to Maria's face. But Maria's face was troubled, was turned altogether to her mother's. "About her life in Europe?" I then rather helplessly asked.

The old woman fronted me, on this, in a manner that made me feel silly. "Her life?" – and her voice, with this second effort, came out stronger. "Her death, if you please."

"Her death?" I echoed, before I could stop myself, with the accent of deprecation.

Miss Maria uttered a vague sound of pain, and I felt her turn away, but the marvel of her mother's little unquenched spark still held me. "Jane's dead. We've heard," said Mrs Rimmle. "We've heard from – where is it we've heard from?" She had quite revived – she appealed to her daughter.

The poor old girl, crimson, rallied to her duty. "From Europe."

Mrs Rimmle made at us both a little grim inclination of the head. "From Europe." I responded, in silence, with a deflection from every rigour, and, still holding me, she went on: "And now Rebecca's going."

She had gathered by this time such emphasis to say it that again, before I could help myself, I vibrated in reply. "To Europe – now?" It was as if for an instant she had made me believe it.

She only stared at me, however, from her wizened mask; then her eyes followed my companion. "Has she gone?"

"Not yet, mother." Maria tried to treat it as a joke, but her smile was embarrassed and dim.

"Then where is she?"

"She's lying down."

The old woman kept up her hard queer gaze, but directing it, after a minute, to me. "She's going."

"Oh, some day!" I foolishly laughed; and on this I got to the door, where I separated from my younger hostess, who came no further. Only, as I held the door open, she said to me under cover of it and very quietly:

"It's poor mother's idea."

I saw – it was her idea. Mine was – for some time after this, even after I had returned to New York and to my usual occupations – that I should never again see Becky. I had seen her for the last time, I believed, under my sister-in-law's roof, and in the autumn it was given to me to hear from that fellow-admirer that she had succumbed at last to the situation. The day of the call I have just described had been a date in the process of her slow shrinkage – it was literally the first time she had, as they said at Brookbridge, given up. She had been ill for years, but the other state of health in the contemplation of which she had spent so much of her life had left her, till too late, no margin for meeting it. The encounter, at last, came simply in the form of the discovery that it *was* too late; on which, naturally, she had given up more and more. I had heard indeed, all summer, by letter, how Brookbridge had watched her do so; whereby the end found me in a manner prepared. Yet in spite of my preparation there remained with me a soreness, and when I was next – it was some six months later – on the scene of her martyrdom I replied, I fear, with an almost rabid negative to the question put to me in due course by my kinswoman. "Call on them? Never again!"

I went, none the less, the very next day. Everything was the same in the sunny parlour – everything that most mattered, I mean: the immemorial mummy in the high chair and the tributes, in the little frames on the walls, to the celebrity of its late husband. Only Maria Rimmle was different: if Becky, on my last seeing her, had looked as old as her mother, Maria – save that she moved about – looked older. I remember that she moved about, but I scarce remember what she said; and indeed what was there to say? When I risked a question, however, she had a reply.

"But *now* at least—?" I tried to put it to her suggestively.

At first she was vague. " 'Now?' "

"Won't Miss Jane come back?"

Oh, the headshake she gave me! "Never." It positively pictured to me, for the instant, a well-preserved woman, a sort of rich, ripe *seconde jeunesse* by the Arno.

"Then that's only to make more sure of your finally joining her."

Maria Rimmle repeated her headshake. "Never."

We stood so, a moment, bleakly face to face; I could think of no attenuation that would be particularly happy. But while I tried I heard a hoarse gasp that, fortunately, relieved me – a signal strange and at first formless from the occupant of the high-backed chair. "Mother wants to speak to you," Maria then said.

So it appeared from the drop of the old woman's jaw, the expression of her mouth opened as if for the emission of sound. It was difficult to me, somehow, to seem to sympathize without hypocrisy, but, so far as a step nearer could do so, I invited communication. "Have you heard where Becky's gone?" the wonderful witch's white lips then extraordinarily asked.

It drew from Maria, as on my previous visit, an uncontrollable groan, and this, in turn, made me take time to consider. As I considered, however, I had an inspiration. "To Europe?"

I must had adorned it with a strange grimace, but my inspiration had been right. "To Europe," said Mrs Rimmle.

JOSEPH CONRAD 1857–1924

Conrad's parents were educated and well-to-do Polish patriots whose land became Russian territory when Poland was partitioned between Russia and Germany. When Conrad was four, his father was arrested for advocating the cause of Polish freedom, and the family followed him into a humiliating exile north of Moscow. His mother died soon thereafter, and seven years later his father succumbed too. Conrad's memories of family life were warm but understandably marked by a deep sense of transitoriness and loss; he came to feel himself a permanent exile and wanderer. The life of a sailor was perhaps an inevitable acting out of his childhood feeling; at any rate, after a few years of desultory schooling and without ever having even seen the sea, he went to Marseilles and signed onto a French ship. Like most educated Poles his second language was French, and he got on well in the French merchant marine. He either sought out or at least was extremely available to the most romantic sorts of voyages, for in the four years he sailed out of Marseilles he was involved in South American revolutions, smuggling guns to Carlist plotters in Spain, an affair with a Basque beauty, and a duel with an American sea captain (which left him with a bullet wound just over his heart).

In reaction to or in flight from these adventures, Conrad at twenty-two embarked on a career in British ships, which he determined would lead to a captaincy. Since he knew almost no English, to change to the British flag was a brave move, but in eight years he had his master's papers, and in ten his first command. By the time he was thirty-six Conrad was ready for a new career. He put the sea behind him and began to write in his adopted language. A hard and very careful worker with an almost inexhaustible store of adventure to draw upon, Conrad soon began to be noticed by connoisseurs – though his real fame did not begin till after the publication of *Chance* in 1913. Perhaps because in a sense he was always learning English, he was particularly receptive to various ways in which he could use the language to express the significance of his adventures. Unlike some authors who repeat one or two successful story-telling formulas, Conrad was always experimenting, and fortunately he was encouraged to do so by his brilliantly inventive friends: writers like James, Ford Madox Ford, and Stephen Crane.

"Youth" is one of the many tales inspired by Conrad's own adventures on the sea. In reality the old ship called the *Judea* in the story was the *Palestine,* which burned and sank on the coast of Java. The second mate was Joseph Conrad on his first voyage to the East, and in the story the immediate excitement of the events comes through very clearly. But as a writer Conrad is interested in many other, subtle questions. To keep in the foreground the meaning of trying to tell the story, Conrad insists upon Marlow as a character talking to friends twenty years after the experience. It is not only Marlow's reactions on the ship twenty years earlier that are called into question but also his later interpretations of them. He points out differences between his instinctive responses then, which he ascribes to "youth" and the seeming irrationality of those responses when they are remembered later. His narration questions whether "youth" is an abandonment of self, a pleasurable cooperation with events that seem fated, or a collection of clichés that nostalgic older people use. He also questions whether the East as youth sees it is a romantic place with a Secret Soul or just a dirty harbor at the end of a foolish voyage. There is of course no definitive answer to these questions because the story asserts the ambiguity of human perception and understanding – in this case the special truths *and* distortions that "youth" (itself a shifting concept) produces.

"The Secret Sharer" is much more markedly psychological than "Youth." The first paragraph announces a dream landscape of neither land, sea, nor air but of some inward geography; and the story turns on the captain's giving up the security of his seaman's expertise to enter such a dark underworld of unconsciousness where his other self, Leggatt, exists. It is a perilous but necessary journey – rather like the one that takes place (in radically different surroundings) in James's "The Jolly Corner." The story is a particularly fine example of Conrad's extension of his own real-life adventures into areas of psychological and mythic significance without compromising the reality of either kind of experience.

YOUTH

This could have occurred nowhere but in England, where men and sea interpenetrate, so to speak – the sea entering into the life of most men, and the men knowing something or everything about the sea, in the way of amusement, of travel, or of bread-winning.

We were sitting round a mahogany table that reflected the bottle, the claret-glasses, and our faces as we leaned on our elbows. There was a director of companies, an accountant, a lawyer, Marlow, and myself. The director had been a *Conway* boy, the accountant had served four years at sea, the lawyer – a fine crusted Tory, High Churchman, the best of old fellows, the soul of honour – had been chief officer in the P. & O. service in the good old days when mail-boats were square-rigged at least on two masts, and used to come down the China Sea before a fair monsoon with stun'sails set alow and aloft. We all began life in the merchant service. Between the five of us there was the strong bond of the sea, and also the fellowship of the craft, which no amount of enthusiasm for yachting, cruising, and so on can give, since one is only the amusement of life and the other is life itself.

Marlow (at least I think that is how he spelt his name) told the story, or rather the chronicle, of a voyage: –

"Yes, I have seen a little of the Eastern seas; but what I remember best is my first voyage there. You fellows know there are those voyages that seem ordered for the illustration of life, that might stand for a symbol of existence. You fight, work, sweat, nearly kill yourself, sometimes do kill yourself, trying to accomplish something – and you can't. Not from any fault of yours. You simply can do nothing, neither great nor little – not a thing in the world – not even marry an old maid, or get a wretched 600-ton cargo of coal to its port of destination.

"It was altogether a memorable affair. It was my first voyage to the East, and my first voyage as second mate; it was also my skipper's first command. You'll admit it was time. He was sixty if a day; a little man, with a broad, not very straight back, with bowed shoulders and one leg more bandy than the other, he had that queer twisted-about appearance you see so often in men who work in the fields. He had a nut-cracker face – chin and nose trying to come together over a sunken mouth — and it was framed in iron-gray fluffy hair, that looked like a chin-strap of cotton-wool sprinkled with coal-dust. And he had blue eyes in that old face of his, which were amazingly like a boy's, with that candid expression some quite common men preserve to the end of their days by a rare internal gift of simplicity of heart and rectitude of soul. What induced him to accept me was a wonder. I had come out of a crack Australian clipper, where I had been third officer, and he seemed to have a prejudice against crack clippers as aristocratic and high-toned. He said to me, 'You know, in this ship you will have to work.' I said I had to work in every ship I had ever been in. 'Ah, but this is different, and you gentlemen out of them big ships; . . . but there! I dare say you will do. Join to-morrow.'

"I joined to-morrow. It was twenty-two years ago; and I was just twenty. How time passes! It was one of the happiest days of my life. Fancy! Second mate for the first time — a really responsible officer! I wouldn't have thrown up my new billet for a fortune. The mate looked me over carefully. He was also an old chap, but of another stamp. He had a Roman nose, a snow-white, long beard, and his name was Mahon, but he insisted that it should be pronounced Mann. He was well connected; yet there was something wrong with his luck, and he had never got on.

"As to the captain, he had been for years in coasters, then in the Mediterranean, and last in the West Indian trade. He had never been round the Capes. He could just write a kind of sketchy hand, and didn't care for writing at all. Both were thorough good seamen of course, and between those two old chaps I felt like a small boy between two grandfathers.

"The ship also was old. Her name was the *Judea.* Queer name, isn't it? She belonged to a man Wilmer, Wilcox — some name like that; but he has been bankrupt and dead these twenty years or more, and his name don't matter. She had been laid up in Shadwell basin for ever so long. You may imagine her state. She was all rust, dust, grime — soot aloft, dirt on deck. To me it was like coming out of a palace into a ruined cottage. She was about 400 tons, had a primitive windlass, wooden latches to the doors, not a bit of brass about her, and a big square stern. There was on it, below her name in big letters, a lot of scrollwork, with the gilt off, and some sort of a coat of arms, with the motto 'Do or Die' underneath. I remember it took my fancy immensely. There was a touch of romance in it, something that made me love the old thing — something that appealed to my youth!

"We left London in ballast — sand ballast — to load a cargo of coal in a northern port for Bankok. Bankok! I thrilled. I had been six years at sea, but had only seen Melbourne and Sydney, very good places, charming places in their way — but Bankok!

"We worked out of the Thames under canvas, with a North Sea pilot on board. His name was Jermyn, and he dodged all day long about the galley drying his handkerchief before the stove. Apparently he never slept. He was a dismal man, with a perpetual tear sparkling at the end of his nose, who either had been in trouble, or was in trouble, or expected to be in trouble – couldn't be happy unless something went wrong. He mistrusted my youth, my common-sense, and my seamanship, and made a point of showing it in a hundred little ways. I dare say he was right. It seems to me I knew very little then, and I know not much more now; but I cherish a hate for that Jermyn to this day.

"We were a week working up as far as Yarmouth Roads, and then we got into a gale – the famous October gale of twenty-two years ago. It was wind, lightning, sleet, snow, and a terrific sea. We were flying light, and you may imagine how bad it was when I tell you we had smashed bulwarks and a flooded deck. On the second night she shifted her ballast into the lee bow, and by that time we had been blown off somewhere on the Dogger Bank. There was nothing for it but go below with shovels and try to right her, and there we were in that vast hold, gloomy like a cavern, the tallow dips stuck and flickering on the beams, the gale howling above, the ship tossing about like mad on her side; there we all were, Jermyn, the captain, every one, hardly able to keep our feet, engaged on that gravedigger's work, and trying to toss shovelfuls of wet sand up to windward. At every tumble of the ship you could see vaguely in the dim light men falling down with a great flourish of shovels. One of the ship's boys (we had two), impressed by the weirdness of the scene, wept as if his heart would break. We could hear him blubbering somewhere in the shadows.

"On the third day the gale died out, and by-and-by a north-country tug picked us up. We took sixteen days in all to get from London to the Tyne! When we got into dock we had lost our turn for loading, and they hauled us off to a tier where we remained for a month. Mrs. Beard (the captain's name was Beard) came from Colchester to see the old man. She lived on board. The crew of runners had left, and there remained only the officers, one boy and the steward, a mulatto who answered to the name of Abraham. Mrs. Beard was an old woman, with a face all wrinkled and ruddy like a winter apple, and the figure of a young girl. She caught sight of me once, sewing on a button, and insisted on having my shirts to repair. This was something different from the captains' wives I had known on board crack clippers. When I brought her the shirts, she said: 'And the socks? They want mending, I am sure, and John's – Captain Beard's – things are all in order now. I would be glad of something to do.' Bless the old woman. She overhauled my outfit for me, and meantime I read for the first time *Sartor Resartus* and Burnaby's *Ride to Khiva.* I didn't understand much of the first then; but I remember I preferred the soldier to the philosopher at the time; a preference which life has only confirmed. One was a man, and the other was either more – or less. However, they are both dead and Mrs. Beard is dead, and youth, strength, genius, thoughts, achievements, simple hearts – all dies. . . . No matter.

"They loaded us at last. We shipped a crew. Eight able seamen and two boys. We hauled off one evening to the buoys at the dock-gates, ready to go out, and with a fair prospect of beginning the voyage next day. Mrs. Beard was to start for home by a late train. When the ship was fast we went to tea. We sat rather silent through the meal – Mahon, the old couple, and I. I finished first, and slipped away for a smoke, my cabin being in a deck-house just against the poop. It was high water, blowing fresh with a drizzle; the double dock-gates were opened, and the steam-colliers were going in and out in the darkness with their lights burning bright, a great splashing of propellers, rattling of winches, and a lot of hailing on the pier-heads. I watched the procession of headlights gliding high and of green lights gliding low in the night, when suddenly a red gleam flashed at me, vanished, came into view again, and remained. The fore-end of a steamer loomed up close. I shouted down the cabin. 'Come up, quick!' and then heard a startled voice saying afar in the dark, 'Stop her, sir.' A bell jingled. Another voice cried warningly, 'We are going right into that barque, sir.' The answer to this was a gruff 'All right,' and the next thing was a heavy crash as the steamer struck a glancing blow with the bluff of her bow about our fore-rigging. There was a moment of confusion, yelling, and running about. Steam roared. Then somebody was heard saying, 'All clear, sir.' . . . 'Are you all right?' asked the gruff voice. I had jumped forward to see the damage, and hailed back, 'I think so.' 'Easy astern,' said the gruff voice. A bell jingled. 'What steamer is that?' screamed Mahon. By that time she was no more to us than a bulky shadow manoeuvring a little way off. They shouted at us some name – a woman's name, Miranda or Melissa – or some such thing. 'This means another month in this beastly hole,' said Mahon to me, as we peered with lamps about the splintered bulwarks and broken braces. 'But where's the captain?'

"We had not heard or seen anything of him all that time. We went aft to look. A doleful voice arose hailing somewhere in the middle of the dock, '*Judea* ahoy!' . . . How the devil did he get there? . . . 'Hallo!' we shouted. 'I am adrift in our boat without oars,' he cried. A belated water-man offered his services, and Mahon struck a bargain with him for half-a-crown to tow our skipper alongside; but it was Mrs. Beard that came up the ladder first. They had been floating about the dock in that mizzly cold rain for nearly an hour. I was never so surprised in my life.

"It appears that when he heard my shout 'Come up' he understood at once what was the matter, caught up his wife, ran on deck, and across, and down into our boat, which was fast to the ladder. Not bad for a sixty-year-old. Just imagine that old fellow saving heroically in his arms that old woman – the woman of his life. He set her down on a thwart, and was ready to climb back on board when the painter came adrift somehow, and away they went together. Of course in the confusion we did not hear him shouting. He looked abashed. She said cheerfully, 'I suppose it does not matter my losing the train now?' 'No, Jenny – you go below and get warm,' he growled. Then to us: 'A sailor has no business with a wife – I say. There I was, out of the ship. Well, no harm done this time. Let's go and look at what that fool of a steamer smashed.'

"It wasn't much, but it delayed us three weeks. At the end of that time, the captain being engaged with his agents, I carried Mrs. Beard's bag to the railway-station and put her all comfy into a third-class carriage. She lowered the window to say, 'You are a good young man. If you see John — Captain Beard — without his muffler at night, just remind him from me to keep his throat well wrapped up.' 'Certainly, Mrs. Beard,' I said. 'You are a good young man; I noticed how attentive you are to John — to Captain—' The train pulled out suddenly; I took my cap off to the old woman: I never saw her again. . . . Pass the bottle.

"We went to sea next day. When we made that start for Bankok we had been already three months out of London. We had expected to be a fortnight or so — at the outside.

"It was January, and the weather was beautiful — the beautiful sunny winter weather that has more charm than in the summer-time, because it is unexpected, and crisp, and you know it won't, it can't, last long. It's like a windfall, like a godsend, like an unexpected piece of luck.

"It lasted all down the North Sea, all down Channel; and it lasted till we were three hundred miles or so to the westward of the Lizards: then the wind went round to the sou'west and began to pipe up. In two days it blew a gale. The *Judea,* hove to, wallowed on the Atlantic like an old candle-box. It blew day after day: it blew with spite, without interval, without mercy, without rest. The world was nothing but an immensity of great foaming waves rushing at us, under a sky low enough to touch with the hand and dirty like a smoked ceiling. In the stormy space surrounding us there was as much flying spray as air. Day after day and night after night there was nothing round the ship but the howl of the wind, the tumult of the sea, the noise of water pouring over her deck. There was no rest for her and no rest for us. She tossed, she pitched, she stood on her head, she sat on her tail, she rolled, she groaned, and we had to hold on while on deck and cling to our bunks when below, in a constant effort of body and worry of mind.

"One night Mahon spoke through the small window of my berth. It opened right into my very bed, and I was lying there sleepless, in my boots, feeling as though I had not slept for years, and could not if I tried. He said excitedly —

" 'You got the sounding-rod in here, Marlow? I can't get the pumps to suck. By God! it's no child's play.'

"I gave him the sounding-rod and lay down again, trying to think of various things — but I thought only of the pumps. When I came on deck they were still at it, and my watch relieved at the pumps. By the light of the lantern brought on deck to examine the sounding-rod I caught a glimpse of their weary, serious faces. We pumped all the four hours. We pumped all night, all day, all the week — watch and watch. She was working herself loose, and leaked badly — not enough to drown us at once, but enough to kill us with the work at the pumps. And while we pumped the ship was going from us piecemeal: the bulwarks went, the stanchions were torn out, the ventilators smashed, the cabin-door burst in.

There was not a dry spot in the ship. She was being gutted bit by bit. The long-boat changed, as if by magic, into matchwood where she stood in her gripes. I had lashed her myself, and was rather proud of my handiwork, which had withstood so long the malice of the sea. And we pumped. And there was no break in the weather. The sea was white like a sheet of foam, like a caldron of boiling milk; there was not a break in the clouds, no – not the size of a man's hand – no, not for so much as ten seconds. There was for us no sky, there were for us no stars, no sun, no universe – nothing but angry clouds and an infuriated sea. We pumped watch and watch, for dear life; and it seemed to last for months, for years, for all eternity, as though we had been dead and gone to a hell for sailors. We forgot the day of the week, the name of the month, what year it was, and whether we had ever been ashore. The sails blew away, she lay broadside on under a weather-cloth, the ocean poured over her, and we did not care. We turned those handles, and had the eyes of idiots. As soon as we had crawled on deck I used to take a round turn with a rope about the men, the pumps, and the mainmast, and we turned, we turned incessantly, with the water to our waists, to our necks, over our heads. It was all one. We had forgotten how it felt to be dry.

"And there was somewhere in me the thought: By Jove! this is the deuce of an adventure – something you read about; and it is my first voyage as second mate – and I am only twenty – and here I am lasting it out as well as any of these men, and keeping my chaps up to the mark. I was pleased. I would not have given up the experience for worlds. I had moments of exultation. Whenever the old dismantled craft pitched heavily with her counter high in the air, she seemed to me to throw up, like an appeal, like a defiance, like a cry to the clouds without mercy, the words written on her stern: '*Judea,* London. Do or Die.'

"O youth! The strength of it, the faith of it, the imagination of it! To me she was not an old rattletrap carting about the world a lot of coal for a freight – to me she was the endeavour, the test, the trial of life. I think of her with pleasure, with affection, with regret – as you would think of someone dead you have loved. I shall never forget her. . . . Pass the bottle.

"One night when tied to the mast, as I explained, we were pumping on, deafened with the wind, and without spirit enough in us to wish ourselves dead, a heavy sea crashed aboard and swept clean over us. As soon as I got my breath I shouted, as in duty bound, 'Keep on, boys!' when suddenly I felt something hard floating on deck strike the calf of my leg. I made a grab at it and missed. It was so dark we could not see each other's faces within a foot – you understand.

"After that thump the ship kept quiet for a while, and the thing, whatever it was, struck my leg again. This time I caught it – and it was a saucepan. At first, being stupid with fatigue and thinking of nothing but the pumps, I did not understand what I had in my hand. Suddenly it dawned upon me, and I shouted, 'Boys, the house on deck is gone. Leave this, and let's look for the cook.'

"There was a deck-house forward, which contained the galley, the cook's berth, and the quarters of the crew. As we had expected for days to see it swept away, the hands had been ordered to sleep in the cabin – the only safe place in the ship. The steward, Abraham, however, persisted in clinging to his berth, stupidly, like a mule – from sheer fright I believe, like an animal that won't leave a stable falling in an earthquake. So we went to look for him. It was chancing death, since once out of our lashings we were as exposed as if on a raft. But we went. The house was shattered as if a shell had exploded inside. Most of it had gone overboard – stove, men's quarters, and their property, all was gone; but two posts, holding a portion of the bulkhead to which Abraham's bunk was attached, remained as if by a miracle. We groped in the ruins and came upon this, and there he was, sitting in his bunk, surrounded by foam and wreckage, jabbering cheerfully to himself. He was out of his mind; completely and for ever mad, with this sudden shock coming upon the fag-end of his endurance. We snatched him up, lugged him aft, and pitched him head-first down the cabin companion. You understand there was no time to carry him down with infinite precautions and wait to see how he got on. Those below would pick him up at the bottom of the stairs all right. We were in a hurry to go back to the pumps. That business could not wait. A bad leak is an inhuman thing.

"One would think that the sole purpose of that fiendish gale had been to make a lunatic of that poor devil of a mulatto. It eased before morning, and next day the sky cleared, and as the sea went down the leak took up. When it came to bending a fresh set of sails the crew demanded to put back – and really there was nothing else to do. Boats gone, decks swept clean, cabin gutted, men without a stitch but what they stood in, stores spoiled, ships strained. We put her head for home, and – would you believe it? The wind came east right in our teeth. It blew fresh, it blew continuously. We had to beat up every inch of the way, but she did not leak so badly, the water keeping comparatively smooth. Two hours' pumping in every four is no joke – but it kept her afloat as far as Falmouth.

"The good people there live on casualties of the sea, and no doubt were glad to see us. A hungry crowd of shipwrights sharpened their chisels at the sight of that carcass of a ship. And, by Jove! they had pretty pickings off us before they were done. I fancy the owner was already in a tight place. There were delays. Then it was decided to take part of the cargo out and caulk her topsides. This was done, the repairs finished, cargo reshipped; a new crew came on board, and we went out – for Bankok. At the end of a week we were back again. The crew said they weren't going to Bankok – a hundred and fifty days' passage – in a something hooker that wanted pumping eight hours out of the twenty-four; and the nautical papers inserted again the little paragraph: '*Judea*. Barque. Tyne to Bankok; coals; put back to Falmouth leaky and with crew refusing duty.'

"There were more delays – more tinkering. The owner came down for a day, and said she was as right as a little fiddle. Poor old Captain Beard looked like the ghost of a Geordie skipper – through the worry and humiliation of it. Remember he was sixty, and it was his first command. Mahon said it was a foolish business, and would end badly. I loved the ship more than ever, and wanted awfully to get to Bankok. To Bankok! Magic name, blessed name. Mesopotamia wasn't a patch on it. Remember I was twenty, and it was my first second-mate's billet, and the East was waiting for me.

"We went out and anchored in the outer roads with a fresh crew – the third. She leaked worse than ever. It was as if those confounded shipwrights had actually made a hole in her. This time we did not even go outside. The crew simply refused to man the windlass.

"They towed us back to the inner harbour, and we became a fixture, a feature, an institution of the place. People pointed us out to visitors as 'That 'ere barque that's going to Bankok – has been here six months – put back three times.' On holidays the small boys pulling about in boats would hail, '*Judea,* ahoy!' and if a head showed above the rail shouted, 'Where you bound to? – Bankok?' and jeered. We were only three on board. The poor old skipper mooned in the cabin. Mahon undertook the cooking, and unexpectedly developed all a Frenchman's genius for preparing nice little messes. I looked languidly after the rigging. We became citizens of Falmouth. Every shopkeeper knew us. At the barber's or tobacconist's they asked familiarly, 'Do you think you will ever get to Bankok?' Meantime the owner, the underwriters, and the charterers squabbled amongst themselves in London, and our pay went on. . . . Pass the bottle.

"It was horrid. Morally it was worse than pumping for life. It seemed as though we had been forgotten by the world, belonged to nobody, would get nowhere; it seemed that, as if bewitched, we would have to live for ever and ever in that inner harbour, a derision and a byword to generations of long-shore loafers and dishonest boatmen. I obtained three months' pay and a five days' leave, and made a rush for London. It took me a day to get there and pretty well another to come back – but three months' pay went all the same. I don't know what I did with it. I went to a music-hall, I believe, lunched, dined, and supped in a swell place in Regent Street, and was back to time, with nothing but a complete set of Byron's works and a new railway rug to show for three months' work. The boat-man who pulled me off to the ship said: 'Hallo! I thought you had left the old thing. *She* will never get to Bankok.' 'That's all *you* know about it,' I said, scornfully – but I didn't like that prophecy at all.

"Suddenly a man, some kind of agent to somebody, appeared with full powers. He had grog-blossoms all over his face, an indomitable energy, and was a jolly soul. We leaped into life again. A hulk came alongside, took our cargo, and then we went into dry dock to get our copper stripped. No wonder she leaked. The poor thing, strained beyond endurance by the gale, had, as if in disgust, spat out all the oakum of her lower seams. She was recaulked, new coppered, and made as tight as a bottle. We went back to the hulk and reshipped our cargo.

"Then, on a fine moonlight night, all the rats left the ship.

"We had been infested with them. They had destroyed our sails, consumed more stores than the crew, affably shared our beds and our dangers, and now, when the ship was made seaworthy, concluded to clear out. I called Mahon to enjoy the spectacle. Rat after rat appeared on our rail, took a last look over his shoulder, and leaped with a hollow thud into the empty hulk. We tried to count them, but soon lost the tale. Mahon said: 'Well, well! don't talk to me about the intelligence of rats. They ought to have left before, when we had that narrow squeak from foundering. There you have the proof how silly is the superstition about them. They leave a good ship for an old rotten hulk, where there is nothing to eat, too, the fools! . . . I don't believe they know what is safe or what is good for them, any more than you or I.'

"And after some more talk we agreed that the wisdom of rats had been grossly overrated, being in fact no greater than that of men.

"The story of the ship was known, by this, all up the Channel from Land's End to the Forelands, and we could get no crew on the south coast. They sent us one all complete from Liverpool, and we left once more – for Bankok.

"We had fair breezes, smooth water right into the tropics, and the old *Judea* lumbered along in the sunshine. When she went eight knots everything cracked aloft, and we tied our caps to our heads; but mostly she strolled on at the rate of three miles an hour. What could you expect? She was tired – that old ship. Her youth was where mine is – where yours is – you fellows who listen to this yarn; and what friend would throw your years and your weariness in your face? We didn't grumble at her. To us aft, at least, it seemed as though we had been born in her, reared in her, had lived in her for ages, had never known any other ship. I would just as soon have abused the old village church at home for not being a cathedral.

"And for me there was also my youth to make me patient. There was all the East before me, and all life, and the thought that I had been tried in that ship and had come out pretty well. And I thought of men of old who, centuries ago, went that road in ships that sailed no better, to the land of palms, and spices, and yellow sands, and of brown nations ruled by kings more cruel than Nero the Roman, and more splendid than Solomon the Jew. The old bark lumbered on, heavy with her age and the burden of her cargo, while I lived the life of youth in ignorance and hope. She lumbered on through an interminable procession of days; and the fresh gilding flashed back at the setting sun, seemed to cry out over the darkening sea the words painted on her stern, '*Judea,* London. Do or Die.'

"Then we entered the Indian Ocean and steered northerly for Java Head. The winds were light. Weeks slipped by. She crawled on, do or die, and people at home began to think of posting us as overdue.

"One Saturday evening, I being off duty, the men asked me to give them an extra bucket of water or so – for washing clothes. As I did not wish to screw on the fresh-water pump so late, I went forward whistling, and with a key in my hand to unlock the forepeak scuttle, intending to serve the water out of a spare tank we kept there.

"The smell down below was as unexpected as it was frightful. One would have thought hundreds of paraffin-lamps had been flaring and smoking in that hole for days. I was glad to get out. The man with me coughed and said, 'Funny smell, sir.' I answered negligently, 'It's good for the health they say,' and walked aft.

"The first thing I did was to put my head down the square of the midship ventilator. As I lifted the lid a visible breath, something like a thin fog, a puff of faint haze, rose from the opening. The ascending air was hot, and had a heavy, sooty, paraffiny smell. I gave one sniff, and put down the lid gently. It was no use choking myself. The cargo was on fire.

"Next day she began to smoke in earnest. You see it was to be expected, for though the coal was of a safe kind, that cargo had been so handled, so broken up with handling, that it looked more like smithy coal than anything else. Then it had been wetted – more than once. It rained all the time we were taking it back from the hulk, and now with this long passage it got heated, and there was another case of spontaneous combustion.

"The captain called us into the cabin. He had a chart spread on the table, and looked unhappy. He said, 'The coast of West Australia is near, but I mean to proceed to our destination. It is the hurricane month, too; but we will just keep her head for Bankok, and fight the fire. No more puttting back anywhere, if we all get roasted. We will try first to stifle this 'ere damned combustion by want of air.'

"We tried. We battened down everything, and still she smoked. The smoke kept coming out through imperceptible crevices; it forced itself through bulkheads and covers; it oozed here and there and everywhere in slender threads, in an invisible film, in an incomprehensible manner. It made its way into the cabin, into the forecastle; it poisoned the sheltered places on the deck, it could be sniffed as high as the mainyard. It was clear that if the smoke came out the air came in. This was disheartening. This combustion refused to be stifled.

"We resolved to try water, and took the hatches off. Enormous volumes of smoke, whitish, yellowish, thick, greasy, misty, choking, ascended as high as the trucks. All hands cleared out aft. Then the poisonous cloud blew away, and we went back to work in a smoke that was no thicker now than that of an ordinary factory chimney.

"We rigged the force-pump, got the hose along, and by-and-by it burst. Well, it was as old as the ship – a prehistoric hose, and past repair. Then we pumped with the feeble head-pump, drew water with buckets, and in this way managed in time to pour lots of Indian Ocean into the main hatch. The bright stream flashed in sunshine, fell into a layer of white crawling smoke, and vanished on the black surface of coal. Steam ascended mingling with the smoke. We poured salt water as into a barrel without a bottom. It was our fate to pump in that ship, to pump out of her, to pump into her; and after keeping water out of her to save ourselves from being drowned, we frantically poured water into her to save ourselves from being burnt.

"And she crawled on, do or die, in the serene weather. The sky was a miracle of purity, a miracle of azure. The sea was polished, was blue, was pellucid, was sparkling like a precious stone, extending on all sides, all round to the horizon — as if the whole terrestrial globe had been one jewel, one colossal sapphire, a single gem fashioned into a planet. And on the lustre of the great calm waters the *Judea* glided imperceptibly, enveloped in languid and unclean vapours, in a lazy cloud that drifted to leeward, light and slow; a pestiferous cloud defiling the splendour of sea and sky.

"All this time of course we saw no fire. The cargo smouldered at the bottom somewhere. Once Mahon, as we were working side by side, said to me with a queer smile: 'Now, if she only would spring a tidy leak — like that time when we first left the Channel — it would put a stopper on this fire. Wouldn't it?' I remarked irrelevantly, 'Do you remember the rats?'

"We fought the fire and sailed the ship too as carefully as though nothing had been the matter. The steward cooked and attended on us. Of the other twelve men, eight worked while four rested. Everyone took his turn, captain included. There was equality, and if not exactly fraternity, then a deal of good feeling. Sometimes a man, as he dashed a bucketful of water down the hatchway, would yell out, 'Hurrah for Bankok!' and the rest laughed. But generally we were taciturn and serious — and thirsty. Oh! how thirsty! And we had to be careful with the water. Strict allowance. The ship smoked, the sun blazed. . . . Pass the bottle.

"We tried everything. We even made an attempt to dig down to the fire. No good, of course. No man could remain more than a minute below. Mahon, who went first, fainted there, and the man who went to fetch him out did likewise. We lugged them out on deck. Then I leaped down to show how easily it could be done. They had learned wisdom by that time, and contented themselves by fishing for me with a chainhook tied to a broom-handle, I believe. I did not offer to go and fetch up my shovel, which was left down below.

"Things began to look bad. We put the long-boat into the water. The second boat was ready to swing out. We had also another, a 14-foot thing, on davits aft, where it was quite safe.

"Then, behold, the smoke suddenly decreased. We redoubled our efforts to flood the bottom of the ship. In two days there was no smoke at all. Everybody was on the broad grin. This was on a Friday. On Saturday no work, but sailing the ship of course, was done. The men washed their clothes and their faces for the first time in a fortnight, and had a special dinner given them. They spoke of spontaneous combustion with contempt, and implied *they* were the boys to put out combustion. Somehow we all felt as though we each had inherited a large fortune. But a beastly smell of burning hung about the ship. Captain Beard had hollow eyes and sunken cheeks. I had never noticed so much before how twisted and bowed he was. He and Mahon prowled soberly about hatches and ventilators, sniffing. It struck me suddenly poor Mahon was a very, very old chap. As to me, I was as pleased and proud as though I had helped to win a great naval battle. O! Youth!

"The night was fine. In the morning a homeward-bound ship passed us hull down – the first we had seen for months; but we were nearing the land at last, Java Head being about 190 miles off, and nearly due north.

"Next day it was my watch on deck from eight to twelve. At breakfast the captain observed, 'It's wonderful how that smell hangs about the cabin.' About ten, the mate being on the poop, I stepped down on the main-deck for a moment. The carpenter's bench stood abaft the mainmast: I leaned against it sucking at my pipe, and the carpenter, a young chap, came to talk to me. He remarked. 'I think we have done very well, haven't we?' and then I perceived with annoyance the fool was trying to tilt the bench. I said curtly, 'Don't, Chips,' and immediately became aware of a queer sensation, of an absurd delusion, – I seemed somehow to be in the air. I heard all round me like a pent-up breath released – as if a thousand giants simultaneously had said Phoo! – and felt a dull concussion which made my ribs ache suddenly. No doubt about it – I was in the air, and my body was describing a short parabola. But short as it was, I had the time to think several thoughts in, as far as I can remember, the following order: 'This can't be the carpenter – What is it? – Some accident – Submarine volcano? – Coals, gas! – By Jove! we are being blown up – Everybody's dead – I am falling into the after hatch – I see fire in it.'

"The coal-dust suspended in the air of the hold had glowed dull-red at the moment of the explosion. In the twinkling of an eye, in an infinitesimal fraction of a second since the first tilt of the bench, I was sprawling full length on the cargo. I picked myself up and scrambled out. It was quick like a rebound. The deck was a wilderness of smashed timber, lying crosswise like trees in a wood after a hurricane; an immense curtain of soiled rags waved gently before me – it was the mainsail blown to strips. I thought, The masts will be toppling over directly; and to get out of the way bolted on all-fours towards the poop-ladder. The first person I saw was Mahon, with eyes like saucers, his mouth open, and the long white hair standing straight on end round his head like a silver halo. He was just about to go down when the sight of the main-deck stirring, heaving up, and changing into splinters before his eyes, petrified him on the top step. I stared at him in unbelief, and he stared at me with a queer kind of shocked curiosity. I did not know that I had no hair, no eyebrows, no eyelashes, that my young moustache was burnt off, that my face was black, one cheek laid open, my nose cut, and my chin bleeding. I had lost my cap, one of my slippers, and my shirt was torn to rags. Of all this I was not aware. I was amazed to see the ship still afloat, the poop-deck whole – and, most of all, to see anybody alive.

Also the peace of the sky and the serenity of the sea were distinctly surprising. I suppose I expected to see them convulsed with horror. . . . Pass the bottle.

"There was a voice hailing the ship from somewhere – in the air, in the sky – I couldn't tell. Presently I saw the captain – and he was mad. He asked me eagerly, 'Where's the cabin-table?' and to hear such a question was a frightful shock. I had just been blown up, you understand, and vibrated with that experience, – I wasn't quite sure whether I was alive. Mahon began to stamp with both feet and yelled at him, 'Good God! don't you see the deck's blown out of her?' I found my voice, and stammered out as if conscious of some gross neglect of duty, 'I don't know where the cabin-table is.' It was like an absurd dream.

"Do you know what he wanted next? Well, he wanted to trim the yards. Very placidly, and as if lost in thought, he insisted on having the foreyard squared. 'I don't know if there's anybody alive,' said Mahon, almost tearfully. 'Surely,' he said, gently, 'there will be enough left to square the foreyard.'

"The old chap, it seems, was in his own berth winding up the chronometers, when the shock sent him spinning. Immediately it occurred to him – as he said afterwards – that the ship had struck something, and ran out into the cabin. There, he saw, the cabin-table had vanished somewhere. The deck being blown up, it had fallen down into the lazarette of course. Where we had our breakfast that morning he saw only a great hole in the floor. This appeared to him so awfully mysterious, and impressed him so immensely, that what he saw and heard after he got on deck were mere trifles in comparison. And, mark, he noticed directly the wheel deserted and his barque off her course – and his only thought was to get that miserable, stripped, undecked, smouldering shell of a ship back again with her head pointing at her port of destination. Bankok! That's what he was after. I tell you this quiet, bowed, bandy-legged, almost deformed little man was immense in the singleness of his idea and in his placid ignorance of our agitation. He motioned us forward with a commanding gesture, and went to take the wheel himself.

"Yes; that was the first thing we did – trim the yards of that wreck! No one was killed, or even disabled, but everyone was more or less hurt. You should have seen them! Some were in rags, with black faces, like coal-heavers, like sweeps, and had bullet heads that seemed closely cropped, but were in fact singed to the skin. Others, of the watch below, awakened by being shot out from their collapsing bunks, shivered incessantly, and kept on groaning even as we went about our work. But they all worked. That crew of Liverpool hard cases had in them the right stuff. It's my experience they always have. It is the sea that gives it – the vastness, the loneliness surrounding their dark stolid souls. Ah! Well! we stumbled, we crept, we fell, we barked our shins on the wreckage, we hauled. The masts stood, but we did not know how much they might be charred down below. It was nearly calm, but a long swell ran from the west and made her roll. They might go at any moment. We looked at them with apprehension. One could not foresee which way they would fall.

"Then we retreated aft and looked about us. The deck was a tangle of planks on edge, of planks on end, of splinters, of ruined woodwork. The masts rose from that chaos like big trees above a matted undergrowth. The interstices of that mass of wreckage were full of something whitish, sluggish, stirring – of something that was like a greasy fog. The smoke of the invisible fire was coming up again, was trailing, like a poisonous thick mist in some valley choked with dead wood. Already lazy wisps were beginning to curl upwards amongst the mass of splinters. Here and there a piece of timber, stuck upright, resembled a post. Half of a fife-rail had been shot through the foresail, and the sky made a patch of glorious blue in the ignobly soiled canvas. A portion of several boards holding together had fallen across the rail, and one end protruded overboard, like a gangway leading upon nothing, like a gangway leading over the deep sea, leading to death – as if inviting us to walk the plank at once and be done with our ridiculous troubles. And still the air, the sky – a ghost, something invisible was hailing the ship.

"Someone had the sense to look over, and there was the helmsman, who had impulsively jumped overboard, anxious to come back. He yelled and swam lustily like a merman, keeping up with the ship. We threw him a rope, and presently he stood amongst us streaming with water and very crestfallen. The captain had surrendered the wheel, and apart, elbow on rail and chin in hand, gazed at the sea wistfully. We asked oursleves, What next? I thought, Now, this is something I like. This is great. I wonder what will happen. O youth!

"Suddenly Mahon sighted a steamer far astern. Captain Beard said, 'We may do something with her yet.' We hoisted two flags, which said in the international language of the sea, 'On fire. Want immediate assistance.' The steamer grew bigger rapidly, and by-and-by spoke with two flags on her foremast. 'I am coming to your assistance.'

"In half an hour she was abreast, to windward, within hail, and rolling slightly, with her engines stopped. We lost our composure, and yelled all together with excitement, 'We've been blown up.' A man in a white helmet, on the bridge, cried, 'Yes! All right! all right!' and he nodded his head, and smiled, and made soothing motions with his hand as though at a lot of frightened children. One of the boats dropped in the water, and walked towards us upon the sea with her long oars. Four Calashes pulled a swinging stroke. This was my first sight of Malay seamen. I've known them since, but what struck me then was their unconcern: they came alongside, and even the bowman standing up and holding to our main-chains with the boat-hook did not deign to lift his head for a glance. I thought people who had been blown up deserved more attention.

"A little man, dry like a chip and agile like a monkey, clambered up. It was the mate of the steamer. He gave one look, and cried, 'O boys – you had better quit.'

"We were silent. He talked apart with the captain for a time, – seemed to argue with him. Then they went away together to the steamer.

"When our skipper came back we learned that the steamer was the *Somerville,* Captain Nash, from West Australia to Singapore *via* Batavia with mails, and that the agreement was she should tow us to Anjer of Batavia, if possible, where we could extinguish the fire by scuttling, and then proceed on our voyage — to Bankok! The old man seemed excited. 'We will do it yet.' he said to Mahon, fiercely. He shook his fist at the sky. Nobody else said a word.

"At noon the steamer began to tow. She went ahead slim and high, and what was left of the *Judea* followed at the end of seventy fathom of tow-rope, — followed her swiftly like a cloud of smoke with mast-heads protruding above. We went aloft to furl the sails. We coughed on the yards, and were careful about the bunts. Do you see the lot of us there, putting a neat furl on the sails of that ship doomed to arrive nowhere? There was not a man who didn't think that at any moment the masts would topple over. From aloft we could not see the ship for smoke, and they worked carefully, passing the gaskets with even turns. 'Harbour furl — aloft there!' cried Mahon from below.

"You understand this? I don't think one of those chaps expected to get down in the usual way. When we did I heard them saying to each other, 'Well, I thought we would come down overboard, in a lump — sticks and all — blame if if I didn't.' 'That's what I was thinking to myself,' would answer wearily another battered and bandaged scarecrow. And, mind, these were men without the drilled-in habit of obedience. To an onlooker they would be a lot of profane scallywags without a redeeming point. What made them do it — what made them obey me when I, thinking consciously how fine it was, made them drop the bunt of the foresail twice to try and do it better? What? They had no professional reputation — no examples, no praise. It wasn't a sense of duty; they all knew well enough how to shirk, and laze, and dodge — when they had a mind to it — and mostly they had. Was it the two pounds ten a-month that sent them there? They didn't think their pay half good enough. No; it was something in them, something inborn and subtle and everlasting. I don't say positively that the crew of a French or German merchantman wouldn't have done it, but I doubt whether it would have been done in the same way. There was a completeness in it, something solid like a principle, and masterful like an instinct — a disclosure of something secret — of that hidden something, that gift of good or evil that makes racial difference, that shapes the fate of nations.

"It was that night at ten that, for the first time since we had been fighting it, we saw the fire. The speed of the towing had fanned the smouldering destruction. A blue gleam appeared forward, shining below the wreck of the deck. It wavered in patches, it seemed to stir and creep like the light of a glowworm. I saw it first, and told Mahon. 'Then the game's up,' he said. 'We had better stop this towing, or she will burst out suddenly fore and aft before we can clear out.' We set up a yell; rang bells to attract their attention; they towed on. At last Mahon and I had to crawl forward and cut the rope with an axe. There was no time to cast off the lashings. Red tongues could be seen licking the wilderness of splinters under our feet as we made our way back to the poop.

"Of course they very soon found out in the steamer that the rope was gone.

She gave a loud blast of her whistle, her lights were seen sweeping in a wide circle, she came up ranging close along-side, and stopped. We were all in a tight group on the poop looking at her. Every man had saved a little bundle or a bag. Suddenly a conical flame with a twisted top shot up forward and threw upon the black sea a circle of light, with the two vessels side by side and heaving gently in its centre. Captain Beard had been sitting on the gratings still and mute for hours, but now he rose slowly and advanced in front of us, to the mizzen-shrouds. Captain Nash hailed: 'Come along! Look sharp. I have mailbags on board. I will take you and your boats to Singapore.'

" 'Thank you! No!' said our skipper. 'We must see the last of the ship.'

" 'I can't stand by any longer,' shouted the other. 'Mails – you know.'

" 'Ay! ay! We are all right.'

" 'Very well! I'll report you in Singapore. . . . Good-bye!'

"He waved his hand. Our men dropped their bundles quietly. The steamer moved ahead, and passing out of the circle of light, vanished at once from our sight, dazzled by the fire which burned fiercely. And then I knew that I would see the East first as commander of a small boat. I thought it fine; and the fidelity to the old ship was fine. We should see the last of her. Oh, the glamour of youth! Oh, the fire of it, more dazzling than the flames of the burning ship, throwing a magic light on the wide earth, leaping audaciously to the sky, presently to be quenched by time, more cruel, more pitiless, more bitter than the sea – and like the flames of the burning ship surrounded by an impenetrable night.

. . .

"The old man warned us in his gentle and inflexible way that it was part of our duty to save for the underwriters as much as we could of the ship's gear. Accordingly we went to work aft, while she blazed forward to give us plenty of light. We lugged out a lot of rubbish. What didn't we save? An old barometer fixed with an absurd quantity of screws nearly cost me my life: a sudden rush of smoke came upon me, and I just got away in time. There were various stores, bolts of canvas, coils of rope; the poop looked like a marine bazaar, and the boats were lumbered to the gunwales. One would have thought the old man wanted to take as much as he could of his first command with him. He was very, very quiet, but off his balance evidently. Would you believe it? He wanted to take a length of old stream-cable and a kedge-anchor with him in the long-boat. We said, 'Ay, ay, sir,' deferentially, and on the quiet let the things slip overboard. The heavy medicine-chest went that way, two bags of green coffee, tins of paint – fancy, paint! – a whole lot of things. Then I was ordered with two hands into the boats to make a stowage and get them ready against the time it would be proper for us to leave the ship.

"We put everything straight, stepped the long-boat's mast for our skipper, who was to take charge of her, and I was not sorry to sit down for a moment. My face felt raw, every limb ached as if broken, I was aware of all my ribs, and would have sworn to a twist in the backbone. The boats, fast astern, lay in a deep shadow, and all around I could see the circle of the sea lighted by the fire. A gigantic flame arose forward straight and clear. It flared fierce, with noises like the whirr of wings, with rumbles as of thunder. There were cracks, detonations, and from the cone of flame the sparks flew upwards, as man is born to trouble, to leaky ships, and to ships that burn.

"What bothered me was that the ship, lying broadside to the swell and to such wind as there was – a mere breath – the boats would not keep astern where they were safe, but persisted, in a pig-headed way boats have, in getting under the counter and then swinging alongside. They were knocking about dangerously and coming near the flame, while the ship rolled on them, and, of course, there was always the danger of the masts going over the side at any moment. I and my two boat-keepers kept them off as best we could, with oars and boat-hooks; but to be constantly at it became exasperating, since there was no reason why we should not leave at once. We could not see those on board, nor could we imagine what caused the delay. The boat-keepers were swearing feebly, and I had not only my share of the work but also had to keep at it two men who showed a constant inclination to lay themselves down and let things slide.

"At last I hailed, 'On deck there,' and someone looked over. 'We're ready here,' I said. The head disappeared, and very soon popped up again. 'The captain says, All right, sir, and to keep the boats well clear of the ship.'

"Half an hour passed. Suddenly there was a frightful racket, rattle, clanking of chain, hiss of water, and millions of sparks flew up into the shivering column of smoke that stood leaning slightly above the ship. The cat-heads had burned away, and the two red-hot anchors had gone to the bottom, tearing out after them two hundred fathom of red-hot chain. The ship trembled, the mass of flame swayed as if ready to collapse, and the fore top-gallant-mast fell. It darted down like an arrow of fire, shot under, and instantly leaping up within an oar's-length of the boats, floated quietly, very black on the luminous sea. I hailed the deck again. After some time a man in an unexpectedly cheerful but also muffled tone, as though he had been trying to speak with his mouth shut, informed me, 'Coming directly, sir,' and vanished. For a long time I heard nothing but the whirr and roar of the fire. There were also whistling sounds. The boats jumped, tugged at the painters, ran at each other playfully, knocked their sides together, or, do what we would, swung in a bunch against the ship's side. I couldn't stand it any longer, and swarming up a rope, clambered aboard over the stern.

"It was as bright as day. Coming up like this, the sheet of fire facing me was a terrifying sight, and the heat seemed hardly bearable at first. On a settee cushion dragged out of the cabin Captain Beard, his legs drawn up and one arm under his head, slept with the light playing on him. Do you know what the rest were busy about? They were sitting on deck right aft, round an open case, eating bread and cheese and drinking bottled stout.

"On the background of flames twisting in fierce tongues above their heads they seemed at home like salamanders, and looked like a band of desperate pirates. The fire sparkled in the whites of their eyes, gleamed on patches of white skin seen through the torn shirts. Each had the marks as of a battle about him – bandaged heads, tied-up arms, a strip of dirty rag round a knee – and each man had a bottle between his legs and a chunk of cheese in his hand. Mahon got up. With his handsome and disreputable head, his hooked profile, his long white beard, and with an uncorked bottle in his hand, he resembled one of those reckless sea-robbers of old making merry amidst violence and disaster. 'The last meal on board,' he explained solemnly. 'We had nothing to eat all day, and it was no use leaving all this.' He flourished the bottle and indicated the sleeping skipper. 'He said he couldn't swallow anything, so I got him to lie down,' he went on; and as I started, 'I don't know whether you are aware, young fellow, the man had no sleep to speak of for days – and there will be dam' little sleep in the boats.' 'There will be no boats by-and-by if you fool about much longer,' I said indignantly. I walked up to the skipper and shook him by the shoulder. At last he opened his eyes, but did not move. 'Time to leave her, sir,' I said quietly.

"He got up painfully, looked at the flames, at the sea sparkling round the ship, and black, black as ink farther away; he looked at the stars shining dim through a thin veil of smoke in a sky black, black as Erebus.

" 'Youngest first,' he said.

"And the ordinary seaman, wiping his mouth with the back of his hand, got up, clambered over the taffrail, and vanished. Others followed. One, on the point of going over, stopped short to drain his bottle, and with a great swing of his arm flung it at the fire. 'Take this!' he cried.

"The skipper lingered disconsolately, and we left him to commune alone for a while with his first command. Then I went up again and brought him away at last. It was time. The ironwork on the poop was hot to the touch.

"Then the painter of the long-boat was cut, and the three boats, tied together, drifted clear of the ship. It was just sixteen hours after the explosion when we abandoned her. Mahon had charge of the second boat, and I had the smallest – the 14-foot thing. The long-boat would have taken the lot of us; but the skipper said we must save as much property as we could – for the underwriters – and so I got my first command. I had two men with me, a bag of biscuits, a few tins of meat, and a breaker of water. I was ordered to keep close to the long-boat, that in case of bad weather we might be taken into her.

"And do you know what I thought? I thought I would part company as soon as I could. I wanted to have my first command all to myself. I wasn't going to sail in a squadron if there were a chance for independent cruising. I would make land by myself. I would beat the other boats. Youth! All youth! The silly, charming, beautiful youth.

"But we did not make a start at once. We must see the last of the ship. And so the boats drifted about that night, heaving and setting on the swell. The men dozed, waked, sighed, groaned. I looked at the burning ship.

"Between the darkness of earth and heaven she was burning fiercely upon a disc of purple sea shot by the blood-red play of gleams; upon a disc of water glittering and sinister. A high, clear flame, an immense and lonely flame, ascended from the ocean, and from its summit the black smoke poured continuously at the sky. She burned furiously; mournful and imposing like a funeral pile kindled in the night, surrounded by the sea, watched over by the stars. A magnificent death had come like a grace, like a gift, like a reward to that old ship at the end of her laborious days. The surrender of her weary ghost to the keeping of stars and sea was stirring like the sight of a glorious triumph. The masts fell just before daybreak, and for a moment there was a burst and turmoil of sparks that seemed to fill with flying fire the night patient and watchful, the vast night lying silent upon the sea. At daylight she was only a charred shell, floating still under a cloud of smoke and bearing a glowing mass of coal within.

"Then the oars were got out, and the boats forming in a line moved round her remains as if in procession – the long-boat leading. As we pulled across her stern a slim dart of fire shot out viciously at us, and suddenly she went down, head first, in a great hiss of steam. The unconsumed stern was the last to sink; but the paint had gone, had cracked, had peeled off, and there were no letters, there was no word, no stubborn device that was like her soul, to flash at the rising sun her creed and her name.

"We made our way north. A breeze sprang up, and about noon all the boats came together for the last time. I had no mast or sail in mine, but I made a mast out of a spare oar and hoisted a boat-awning for a sail, with a boat-hook for a yard. She was certainly over-masted, but I had the satisfaction of knowing that with the wind aft I could beat the other two. I had to wait for them. Then we all had a look at the captain's chart and, after a sociable meal of hard bread and water, got our last instructions. These were simple: steer north, and keep together as much as possible. 'Be careful with that jury-rig, Marlow,' said the captain; and Mahon, as I sailed proudly past his boat, wrinkled his curved nose and hailed, 'You will sail that ship of yours under water, if you don't look out, young fellow.' He was a malicious old man – and may the deep sea where he sleeps now rock him gently, rock him tenderly to the end of time!

"Before sunset a thick rain-squall passed over the two boats, which were far astern, and that was the last I saw of them for a time. Next day I sat steering my cockle-shell – my first command – with nothing but water and sky around me. I did sight in the afternoon the upper sails of a ship far away, but said nothing, and my men did not notice her. You see I was afraid she might be homeward bound, and I had no mind to turn back from the portals of the East. I was steering for Java – another blessed name – like Bankok, you know. I steered many days.

"I need not tell you what it is to be knocking about in an open boat. I remember nights and days of calm, when we pulled, we pulled, and the boat seemed to stand still, as if bewitched within the circle of the sea horizon. I remember the heat, the deluge of rain-squalls that kept us bailing for dear life (but filled our water-cask), and I remember sixteen hours on end with a mouth dry as cinder and a steering-oar over the stern to keep my first command head on to a breaking sea. I did not know how good a man I was till then. I remember the drawn faces, the dejected figures of my two men, and I remember my youth and the feeling that will never come back any more – the feeling that I could last for ever, outlast the sea, the earth, and all men; the deceitful feeling that lures us on to joys, to perils, to love, to vain effort – to death; the triumphant conviction of strength, the heat of life in the handful of dust, the glow in the heart that with every year grows dim, grows cold, grows small, and expires – and expires, too soon, too soon – before life itself.

"And this is how I see the East. I have seen its secret places and have looked into its very soul; but now I see it always from a small boat, a high outline of mountains, blue and afar in the morning; like faint mist at noon; a jagged wall of purple at sunset. I have the feel of the oar in my hand, the vision of a scorching blue sea in my eyes. And I see a bay, a wide bay, smooth as glass and polished like ice, shimmering in the dark. A red light burns far off upon the gloom of the land, and the night is soft and warm. We drag at the oars with aching arms, and suddenly a puff of wind, a puff faint and tepid and laden with strange odours of blossoms, of aromatic wood, comes out of the still night – the first sigh of the East on my face. That I can never forget. It was impalpable and enslaving, like a charm, like a whispered promise of mysterious delight.

"We had been pulling this finishing spell for eleven hours. Two pulled, and he whose turn it was to rest sat at the tiller. We had made out the red light in that bay and steered for it, guessing it must mark some small coasting port. We passed two vessels, outlandish and high-sterned, sleeping at anchor, and, approaching the light, now very dim, ran the boat's nose against the end of a jutting wharf. We were blind with fatigue. My men dropped the oars and fell off the thwarts as if dead. I made fast to a pile. A current rippled softly. The scented obscurity of the shore was grouped into vast masses, a density of colossal clumps of vegetation, probably – mute and fantastic shapes. And at their foot the semicircle of a beach gleamed faintly, like an illusion. There was not a light, not a stir, not a sound. The mysterious East faced me, perfumed like a flower, silent like death, dark like a grave.

"And I sat weary beyond expression, exulting like a conqueror, sleepless and entranced as if before a profound, a fateful enigma.

"A splashing of oars, a measured dip reverberating on the level of water, intensified by the silence of the shore into loud claps, made me jump up. A boat, a European boat, was coming in. I invoked the name of the dead; I hailed: *Judea* ahoy! A thin shout answered.

"It was the captain. I had beaten the flagship by three hours, and I was glad to hear the old man's voice again, tremulous and tired. 'Is it you, Marlow?' 'Mind the end of that jetty, sir,' I cried.

"He approached cautiously, and brought up with the deep-sea lead-line which we had saved – for the underwriters. I eased my painter and fell alongside. He sat, a broken figure at the stern, wet with dew, his hands clasped in his lap. His men were asleep already. 'I had a terrible time of it,' he murmured. 'Mahon is behind – not very far.' We conversed in whispers, in low whispers, as if afraid to wake up the land. Guns, thunder, earthquakes would not have awakened the men just then.

"Looking round as we talked, I saw away at sea a bright light travelling in the night. 'There's a steamer passing the bay,' I said. She was not passing, she was entering, and she even came close and anchored. 'I wish,' said the old man, 'you would find out whether she is English. Perhaps they could give us a passage somewhere.' He seemed nervously anxious. So by dint of punching and kicking I started one of my men into a state of somnambulism, and giving him an oar, took another and pulled towards the lights of the steamer.

"There was a murmur of voices in her, metallic hollow clangs of the engine-room, footsteps on the deck. Her ports shone, round like dilated eyes. Shapes moved about, and there was a shadowy man high up on the bridge. He heard my oars.

"And then, before I could open my lips, the East spoke to me, but it was in a Western voice. A torrent of words was poured into the enigmatical, the fateful silence; outlandish, angry words, mixed with words and even whole sentences of good English, less strange but even more surprising. The voice swore and cursed violently; it riddled the solemn peace of the bay by a volley of abuse. It began by calling me Pig, and from that went crescendo into unmentionable adjectives – in English. The man up there raged aloud in two languages, and with a sincerity in his fury that almost convinced me I had, in some way, sinned against the harmony of the universe. I could hardly see him, but began to think he would work himself into a fit.

"Suddenly he ceased, and I could hear him snorting and blowing like a porpoise. I said –

" 'What steamer is this, pray?'

" 'Eh? What's this? And who are you?'

" 'Castaway crew of an English barque burnt at sea. We came here to-night. I am the second mate. The captain is in the long-boat, and wishes to know if you would give us a passage somewhere.'

" 'Oh, my goodness! I say. . . . This is the *Celestial* from Singapore on her return trip. I'll arrange with your captain in the morning, . . . and, . . . I say, . . . did you hear me just now?'

" 'I should think the whole bay heard you.'

" 'I thought you were a shore-boat. Now, look here – this infernal lazy scoundrel of a caretaker has gone to sleep again – curse him. The light is out, and I nearly ran foul of the end of this damned jetty. This is the third time he plays me this trick. Now, I ask you, can anybody stand this kind of thing? It's enough to drive a man out of his mind. I'll report him. . . . I'll get the Assistant Resident to give him the sack, by . . . ! See – there's no light. It's out, isn't it? I take you to witness the light's out. There should be a light, you know. A red light on the —'

" 'There was a light,' I said, mildly.

" 'But it's out, man! What's the use of talking like this? You can see for yourself it's out – don't you? If you had to take a valuable steamer along this God-forsaken coast you would want a light, too. I'll kick him from end to end of his miserable wharf. You'll see if I don't. I will —'

" 'So I may tell my captain you'll take us?' I broke in.

" 'Yes, I'll take you. Good-night.' he said, brusquely.

"I pulled back, made fast again to the jetty, and then went to sleep at last. I had faced the silence of the East. I had heard some of its language. But when I opened my eyes again the silence was as complete as though it had never been broken. I was lying in a flood of light, and the sky had never looked so far, so high, before. I opened my eyes and lay without moving.

"And then I saw the men of the East – they were looking at me. The whole length of the jetty was full of people. I saw brown, bronze, yellow faces, the black eyes, the glitter, the colour of an Eastern crowd. And all these beings stared without a murmur, without a sigh, without a movement. They stared down at the boats, at the sleeping men who at night had come to them from the sea. Nothing moved. The fronds of palms stood still against the sky. Not a branch stirred along the shore, and the brown roofs of hidden houses peeped through the green foliage, through the big leaves that hung shining and still like leaves forged of heavy metal. This was the East of the ancient navigators, so old, so mysterious, resplendent and sombre, living and unchanged, full of danger and promise. And these were the men. I sat up suddenly. A wave of movement passed through the crowd from end to end, passed along the heads, swayed the bodies, ran along the jetty like a ripple on the water, like a breath of wind on a field – and all was still again. I see it now – the wide sweep of the bay, the glittering sands, the wealth of green infinite and varied, the sea blue like the sea of a dream, the crowd of attentive faces, the blaze of vivid colour – the water reflecting it all, the curve of the shore, the jetty, the high-sterned outlandish craft floating still, and the three boats with the tired men from the West sleeping, unconscious of the land and the people and of the violence of sunshine. They slept thrown across the thwarts, curled on bottom-boards, in the careless attitudes of death. The head of the old skipper, leaning back in the stern of the long-boat, had fallen on his breast, and he looked as though he would never wake. Farther out old Mahon's face was upturned to the sky, with the long white beard spread out on his breast, as though he had been shot where he sat at the tiller; and a man, all in a heap in the bows of the boat, slept with both arms embracing the stemhead and with his cheek laid on the gunwale. The East looked at them without a sound.

"I have known its fascination since; I have seen the mysterious shores, the still water, the lands of brown nations, where a stealthy Nemesis lies in wait, pursues, overtakes so many of the conquering race, who are proud of their wisdom, of their knowledge, of their strength. But for me all the East is contained in that vision of my youth. It is all in that moment when I opened my young eyes on it. I came upon it from a tussle with the sea – and I was young – and I saw it looking at me. And this is all that is left of it! Only a moment; a moment of strength, of romance, of glamour – of youth! ... A flick of sunshine upon a strange shore, the time to remember, the time for a sigh, and – good-bye! – Night – Good-bye ...!"

He drank.

"Ah! The good old time – the good old time. Youth and the sea. Glamour and the sea! The good, strong sea, the salt, bitter sea, that could whisper to you and roar at you and knock your breath out of you."

He drank again.

"By all that's wonderful it is the sea, I believe, the sea itself – or is it youth alone? Who can tell? But you here – you all had something out of life: money, love – whatever one gets on shore – and, tell me, wasn't that the best time, that time when we were young at sea; young and had nothing, on the sea that gives nothing, except hard knocks – and sometimes a chance to feel your strength – that only – what you all regret?"

And we all nodded at him: the man of finance, the man of accounts, the man of law, we all nodded at him over the polished table that like a still sheet of brown water reflected our faces, lined, wrinkled; our faces marked by toil, by deceptions, by success, by love; our weary eyes looking still, looking always, looking anxiously for something out of life, that while it is expected is already gone – has passed unseen, in a sigh, in a flash – together with the youth, with the strength, with the romance of illusions.

THE SECRET SHARER

I

On my right hand there were lines of fishing stakes resembling a mysterious system of half-submerged bamboo fences, incomprehensible in its division of the domain of tropical fishes, and crazy of aspect as if abandoned forever by some nomad tribe of fishermen now gone to the other end of the ocean; for there was no sign of human habitation as far as the eye could reach. To the left a group of barren islets, suggesting ruins of stone walls, towers, and blockhouses, had its foundations set in a blue sea that itself looked solid, so still and stable did it lie below my feet; even the track of light from the westering sun shone smoothly, without that animated glitter which tells of an imperceptible ripple. And when I turned my head to take a parting glance at the tug which had just left us anchored outside the bar, I saw the straight line of the flat shore joined to the stable sea, edge to edge, with a perfect and unmarked closeness, in one leveled floor half brown, half blue under the enormous dome of the sky. Corresponding in their insignificance to the islets of the sea, two small clumps of trees, one on each side of the only fault in the impeccable joint, marked the mouth of the river Meinam we had just left on the first preparatory stage of our homeward journey; and, far back on the inland level, a larger and loftier mass, the grove surrounding the great Paknam pagoda, was the only thing on which the eye could rest from the vain task of exploring the monotonous sweep of the horizon. Here and there gleams as of a few scattered pieces of silver marked the windings of the great river; and on the nearest of them, just within the bar, the tug steaming right into the land became lost to my sight, hull and funnel and masts, as though the impassive earth had swallowed her up without an effort, without a tremor. My eye followed the light cloud of her smoke, now here, now there, above the plain, according to the devious curves of the stream, but always fainter and farther away, till I lost it at last behind the miter-shaped hill of the great pagoda. And then I was left alone with my ship, anchored at the head of the Gulf of Siam.

She floated at the starting point of a long journey, very still in an immense stillness, the shadows of her spars flung far to the eastward by the setting sun. At that moment I was alone on her decks. There was not a sound in her — and around us nothing moved, nothing lived, not a canoe on the water, not a bird in the air, not a cloud in the sky. In this breathless pause at the threshold of a long and arduous enterprise, the appointed task of both our existences to be carried out, far from all human eyes, with only sky and sea for spectators and for judges.

There must have been some glare in the air to interfere with one's sight, because it was only just before the sun left us that my roaming eyes made out beyond the highest ridges of the principal islet of the group something which did away with the solemnity of perfect solitude. The tide of darkness flowed on swiftly; and with tropical suddenness a swarm of stars came out above the shadowy earth, while I lingered yet, my hand resting lightly on my ship's rail as if on the shoulder of a trusted friend. But, with all that multitude of celestial bodies staring down at one, the comfort of quiet communion with her was gone for good. And there were also disturbing sounds by this time — voices, footsteps forward; the steward flitted along the main-deck, a busily ministering spirit; a hand bell tinkled urgently under the poop deck. . . .

I found my two officers waiting for me near the supper table, in the lighted cuddy. We sat down at once, and as I helped the chief mate, I said:

"Are you aware that there is a ship anchored inside the islands? I saw her mastheads above the ridge as the sun went down."

He raised sharply his simple face, overcharged by a terrible growth of whisker, and emitted his usual ejaculations: "Bless my soul, sir! You don't say so!"

My second mate was a round-cheeked, silent young man, grave beyond his years, I thought; but as our eyes happened to meet I detected a slight quiver on his lips. I looked down at once. It was not my part to encourage sneering on board my ship. It must be said, too, that I knew very little of my officers. In consequence of certain events of no particular significance, except to myself, I had been appointed to the command only a fortnight before. Neither did I know much of the hands forward. All these people had been together for eighteen months or so, and my position was that of the only stranger on board. I mention this because it has some bearing on what is to follow. But what I felt most was my being a stranger to the ship; and if all the truth must be told, I was somewhat of a stranger to myself. The youngest man on board (barring the second mate), and untried as yet by a position of the fullest responsibility, I was willing to take the adequacy of the others for granted. They had simply to be equal to their tasks; but I wondered how far I should turn out faithful to that ideal conception of one's own personality every man sets up for himself secretly.

Meantime the chief mate, with an almost visible effect of collaboration on the part of his round eyes and frightful whiskers, was trying to evolve a theory of the anchored ship. His dominant trait was to take all things into earnest consideration. He was of a painstaking turn of mind. As he used to say, he "liked to account to himself" for practically everything that came in his way, down to a miserable scorpion he had found in his cabin a week before. The why and the wherefore of that scorpion – how it got on board and came to select his room rather than the pantry (which was a dark place and more what a scorpion would be partial to), and how on earth it managed to drown itself in the inkwell of his writing desk – had exercised him infinitely. The ship within the islands was much more easily accounted for; and just as we were about to rise from table he made his pronouncement. She was, he doubted not, a ship from home lately arrived. Probably she drew too much water to cross the bar except at the top of spring tides. Therefore she went into that natural harbor to wait for a few days in preference to remaining in an open roadstead.

"That's so," confirmed the second mate, suddenly, in his slightly hoarse voice. "She draws over twenty feet. She's the Liverpool ship *Sephora* with a cargo of coal. Hundred and twenty-three days from Cardiff."

We looked at him in surprise.

"The tugboat skipper told me when he came on board for your letters, sir," explained the young man. "He expects to take her up the river the day after tomorrow."

After thus overwhelming us with the extent of his information he slipped out of the cabin. The mate observed regretfully that he "could not account for that young fellow's whims." What prevented him telling us all about it at once, he wanted to know.

I detained him as he was making a move. For the last two days the crew had had plenty of hard work, and the night before they had very little sleep. I felt painfully that I – a stranger – was doing something unusual when I directed him to let all hands turn in without setting an anchor watch. I proposed to keep on deck myself till one o'clock or thereabouts. I would get the second mate to relieve me at that hour.

"He will turn out the cook and the steward at four," I concluded, "and then give you a call. Of course at the slightest sign of any sort of wind we'll have the hands up and make a start at once."

He concealed his astonishment. "Very well, sir." Outside the cuddy he put his head in the second mate's door to inform him of my unheard-of caprice to take a five hours' anchor watch on myself. I heard the other raise his voice incredulously – "What? The Captain himself?" Then a few more murmurs, a door closed, then another. A few moments later I went on deck.

My strangeness, which had made me sleepless, had prompted that unconventional arrangement, as if I had expected in those solitary hours of the night to get on terms with the ship of which I knew nothing, manned by men of whom I knew very little more. Fast alongside a wharf, littered like any ship in port with a tangle of unrelated things, invaded by unrelated shore people, I had hardly seen her yet properly. Now, as she lay cleared for sea; the stretch of her main-deck seemed to me very fine under the stars. Very fine, very roomy for her size, and very inviting. I descended the poop and paced the waist, my mind picturing to myself the coming passage through the Malay Archipelago, down the Indian Ocean, and up the Atlantic. All its phases were familiar enough to me, every characteristic, all the alternatives which were likely to face me on the high seas – everything! . . . except the novel responsibility of command. But I took heart from the reasonable thought that the ship was like other ships, the men like other men, and that the sea was not likely to keep any special surprises expressly for my discomfiture.

Arrived at that comforting conclusion, I bethought myself of a cigar and went below to get it. All was still down there. Everybody at the after end of the ship was sleeping profoundly. I came out again on the quarterdeck, agreeably at ease in my sleeping suit on that warm breathless night, barefooted, a glowing cigar in my teeth, and, going forward, I was met by the profound silence of the fore end of the ship. Only as I passed the door of the forecastle I heard a deep, quiet, trustful sigh of some sleeper inside. And suddenly I rejoiced in the great security of the sea as compared with the unrest of the land, in my choice of that untempted life presenting no disquieting problems, invested with an elementary moral beauty by the absolute straightforwardness of its appeal and by the singleness of its purpose.

The riding light in the forerigging burned with a clear, untroubled, as if symbolic, flame, confident and bright in the mysterious shades of the night. Passing on my way aft along the other side of the ship, I observed that the rope side ladder, put over, no doubt, for the master of the tug when he came to fetch away our letters, had not been hauled in as it should have been. I became annoyed at this, for exactitude in some small matters is the very soul of discipline. Then I reflected that I had myself peremptorily dismissed my officers from duty, and by my own act had prevented the anchor watch being formally set and things properly attended to. I asked myself whether it was wise ever to interfere with the established routine of duties even from the kindest of motives. My action might have made me appear eccentric. Goodness only knew how that absurdly whiskered mate would "account" for my conduct, and what the whole ship thought of that informality of their new captain. I was vexed with myself.

Not from compunction certainly, but, as it were mechanically, I proceeded to get the ladder in myself. Now a side ladder of that sort is a light affair and comes in easily, yet my vigorous tug, which should have brought it flying on board, merely recoiled upon my body in a totally unexpected jerk. What the devil! . . . I was so astounded by the immovableness of the ladder that I remained stockstill, trying to account for it to myself like that imbecile mate of mine. In the end, of course, I put my head over the rail.

The side of the ship made an opaque belt of shadow on the darkling glassy shimmer of the sea. But I saw at once something elongated and pale floating very close to the ladder. Before I could form a guess a faint flash of phosphorescent light, which seemed to issue suddenly from the naked body of a man, flickered in the sleeping water with the elusive, silent play of summer lightning in a night sky. With a gasp I saw revealed to my stare a pair of feet, the long legs, a broad livid back immersed right up to the neck in a greenish cadaverous glow. One hand, awash, clutched the bottom rung of the ladder. He was complete but for the head. A headless corpse! The cigar dropped out of my gaping mouth with a tiny plop and a short hiss quite audible in the absolute stillness of all things under heaven. At that I suppose he raised up his face, dimly pale oval in the shadow of the ship's side. But even then I could only barely make out down there the shape of his black-haired head. However, it was enough for the horrid, frost-bound sensation which had gripped me about the chest to pass off. The moment of vain exclamations was past, too. I only climbed on the spare spar and leaned over the rail as far as I could, to bring my eyes nearer to that mystery floating alongside.

As he hung by the ladder, like a resting swimmer, the sea lightning played about his limbs at every stir; and he appeared in it ghastly, silvery, fishlike. He remained as mute as a fish, too. He made no motion to get out of the water, either. It was inconceivable that he should not attempt to come on board, and strangely troubling to suspect that perhaps he did not want to. And my first words were prompted by just that troubled incertitude.

"What's the matter?" I asked in my ordinary tone, speaking down to the face upturned exactly under mine.

"Cramp," it answered, no louder. Then slightly anxious, "I say, no need to call anyone."

"I was not going to," I said.

"Are you alone on deck?"

"Yes."

I had somehow the impression that he was on the point of letting go the ladder to swim away beyond my ken – mysterious as he came. But, for the moment, this being appearing as if he had risen from the bottom of the sea (it was certainly the nearest land to the ship) wanted only to know the time. I told him. And he, down there, tentatively:

"I suppose your captain's turned in?"

"I am sure he isn't," I said.

He seemed to struggle with himself, for I heard something like the low, bitter murmur of doubt. "What's the good?" His next words came out with a hesitating effort.

"Look here, my man. Could you call him out quietly?"

I thought the time had come to declare myself.

"*I* am the captain."

I heard a "By Jove!" whispered at the level of the water. The phosphorescence flashed in the swirl of the water all about his limbs, his other hand seized the ladder.

"My name's Leggatt."

The voice was calm and resolute. A good voice. The self-possession of that man had somehow induced a corresponding state in myself. It was very quietly that I remarked:

"You must be a good swimmer."

"Yes. I've been in the water practically since nine o'clock. The question for me now is whether I am to let go this ladder and go on swimming till I sink from exhaustion, or – to come on board here."

I felt this was no mere formula of desperate speech, but a real alternative in the view of a strong soul. I should have gathered from this that he was young; indeed, it is only the young who are ever confronted by such clear issues. But at the time it was pure intuition on my part. A mysterious communication was established already between us two – in the face of that silent, darkened tropical sea. I was young, too; young enough to make no comment. The man in the water began suddenly to climb up the ladder, and I hastened away from the rail to fetch some clothes. Before entering the cabin I stood still, listening in the lobby at the foot of the stairs. A faint snore came through the closed door of the chief mate's room. The second mate's door was on the hook, but the darkness in there was absolutely soundless. He, too, was young and could sleep like a stone. Remained the steward, but he was not likely to wake up before he was called. I got a sleeping suit out of my room and, coming back on deck, saw the naked man from the sea sitting on the main hatch, glimmering white in the darkness, his elbows on his knees and his head in his hands. In a moment he had concealed his damp body in a sleeping suit of the same gray-stripe pattern as the one I was wearing and followed me like my double on the poop. Together we moved right aft, barefooted, silent.

"What is it?" I asked in a deadened voice, taking the lighted lamp out of the binnacle, and raising it to his face.

"An ugly business."

He had rather regular features; a good mouth; light eyes under somewhat heavy, dark eyebrows; a smooth, square forehead; no growth on his cheeks; a small, brown mustache, and a well-shaped, round chin. His expression was concentrated, meditative, under the inspecting light of the lamp I held up to his face; such as a man thinking hard in solitude might wear. My sleeping suit was just right for his size. A well-knit young fellow of twenty-five at most. He caught his lower lip with the edge of white, even teeth.

"Yes," I said, replacing the lamp in the binnacle. The warm, heavy tropical night closed upon his head again.

"There's a ship over there," he murmured.

"Yes, I know. The *Sephora.* Did you know of us?"

"Hadn't the slightest idea. I am the mate of her —" He paused and corrected himself. "I should say I *was.*"

"Aha! Something wrong?"

"Yes. Very wrong indeed. I've killed a man."

"What do you mean? Just now?"

"No, on the passage. Weeks ago. Thirty-nine south. When I say a man —"

"Fit of temper," I suggested, confidently.

The shadowy, dark head, like mine, seemed to nod imperceptibly above the ghostly gray of my sleeping suit. It was, in the night, as though I had been faced by my own reflection in the depths of a somber and immense mirror.

"A pretty thing to have to own up to for a Conway boy," murmured my double, distinctly.

"You're a Conway boy?"

"I am," he said, as if startled. Then, slowly . . . "Perhaps you too —"

It was so; but being a couple of years older I had left before he joined. After a quick interchange of dates a silence fell; and I thought suddenly of my absurd mate with his terrific whiskers and the "Bless my soul – you don't say so" type of intellect. My double gave me an inkling of his thoughts by saying: "My father's a parson in Norfolk. Do you see me before a judge and jury on that charge? For myself I can't see the necessity. There are fellows that an angel from heaven — And I am not that. He was one of those creatures that are just simmering all the time with a silly sort of wickedness. Miserable devils that have no business to live at all. He wouldn't do his duty and wouldn't let anybody else do theirs. But what's the good of talking! You know well enought the sort of ill-conditioned snarling cur —"

He appealed to me as if our experiences had been as identical as our clothes. And I knew well enough the pestiferous danger of such a character where there are no means of legal repression. And I knew well enough also that my double there was no homicidal ruffian. I did not think of asking him for details, and he told me the story roughly in brusque, disconnected sentences. I needed no more. I saw it all going on as though I were myself inside that other sleeping suit.

"It happened while we were setting a reefed foresail, at dusk. Reefed foresail! You understand the sort of weather. The only sail we had left to keep the ship running; so you may guess what it had been like for days. Anxious sort of job, that. He gave me some of his cursed insolence at the sheet. I tell you I was overdone with this terrific weather that seemed to have no end to it. Terrific, I tell you – and a deep ship. I believe the fellow himself was half crazed with funk. It was no time for gentlemanly reproof, so I turned round and felled him like an ox. He up and at me. We closed just as an awful sea made for the ship. All hands saw it coming and took to the rigging, but I had him by the throat, and went on shaking him like a rat, the men above us yelling, 'Look out! look out!' Then a crash as if the sky had fallen on my head. They say that for over ten minutes hardly anything was to be seen of the ship—just the three masts and a bit of the forecastle head and of the poop all awash driving along in a smother of foam. It was a miracle that they found us, jammed together behind the forebitts. It's clear that I meant business, because I was holding him by the throat still when they picked us up. He was black in the face. It was too much for them. It seems they rushed us aft together, gripped as we were, screaming 'Murder!' like a lot of lunatics, and broke into the cuddy. And the ship running for her life, touch and go all the time, any minute her last in a sea fit to turn your hair gray only a-looking at it. I understand that the skipper, too, started raving like the rest of them. The man had been deprived of sleep for more than a week, and to have this sprung on him at the height of a furious gale nearly drove him out of his mind. I wonder they didn't fling me overboard after getting the carcass of their precious shipmate out of my fingers. They had rather a job to separate us, I've been told. A sufficiently fierce story to make an old judge and a respectable jury sit up a bit. The first thing I heard when I came to myself was the maddening howling of that endless gale, and on that the voice of the old man. He was hanging on to my bunk, staring into my face out of his sou'wester.

" 'Mr. Leggatt, you have killed a man. You can act no longer as chief mate of this ship.' "

His care to subdue his voice made it sound monotonous. He rested a hand on the end of the skylight to steady himself with, and all that time did not stir a limb, so far as I could see. "Nice little tale for a quiet tea party," he concluded in the same tone.

One of my hands, too, rested on the end of the skylight; neither did I stir a limb, so far as I knew. We stood less than a foot from each other. It occurred to me that if old "Bless my soul—you don't say so" were to put his head up the companion and catch sight of us, he would think he was seeing double, or imagine himself come upon a scene of weird witchcraft; the strange captain having a quiet confabulation by the wheel with his own gray ghost. I became very much concerned to prevent anything of the sort. I heard the other's soothing undertone.

"My father's a parson in Norfolk," it said. Evidently he had forgotten he had told me this important fact before. Truly a nice little tale.

"You had better slip down into my stateroom now," I said, moving off stealthily. My double followed my movements; our bare feet made no sound; I let him in, closed the door with care, and, after giving a call to the second mate, returned on deck for my relief.

"Not much sign of any wind yet," I remarked when he approached.

"No, sir. Not much," he assented, sleepily, in his hoarse voice, with just enough deference, no more, and barely suppressing a yawn.

"Well, that's all you have to look out for. You have got your orders."

"Yes, sir."

I paced a turn or two on the poop and saw him take up his position face forward with his elbow in the ratlines of the mizzen rigging before I went below. The mate's faint snoring was still going on peacefully. The cuddy lamp was burning over the table on which stood a vase with flowers, a polite attention from the ship's provision merchant – the last flowers we should see for the next three months at the very least. Two bunches of bananas hung from the beam symmetrically, one on each side of the rudder casing. Everything was as before in the ship – except that two of her captain's sleeping suits were simultaneously in use, one motionless in the cuddy, the other keeping very still in the captain's stateroom.

It must be explained here that my cabin had the form of the capital letter L, the door being within the angle and opening into the short part of the letter. A couch was to the left, the bed place to the right; my writing desk and the chronometers' table faced the door. But anyone opening it, unless he stepped right inside, had no view of what I call the long (or vertical) part of the letter. It contained some lockers surmounted by a bookcase; and a few clothes, a thick jacket or two, caps, oilskin coat, and such like, hung on hooks. There was at the bottom of that part a door opening into my bathroom, which could be entered also directly from the saloon. But that way was never used.

The mysterious arrival had discovered the advantage of this particular shape. Entering my room, lighted strongly by a big bulkhead lamp swung on gimbals above my writing desk, I did not see him anywhere till he stepped out quietly from behind the coats hung in the recessed part.

"I heard somebody moving about, and went in there at once," he whispered.

I, too, spoke under my breath.

"Nobody is likely to come in here without knocking and getting permission."

He nodded. His face was thin and the sunburn faded, as though he had been ill. And no wonder. He had been, I heard presently, kept under arrest in his cabin for nearly seven weeks. But there was nothing sickly in his eyes or in his expression. He was not a bit like me, really; yet, as we stood leaning over my bed place, whispering side by side, with our dark heads together and our backs to the door, anybody bold enough to open it stealthily would have been treated to the uncanny sight of a double captain busy talking in whispers with his other self.

"But all this doesn't tell me how you came to hang on to our side ladder," I inquired, in the hardly audible murmurs we used, after he had told me something more of the proceedings on board the *Sephora* once the bad weather was over.

"When we sighted Java Head I had had time to think all those matters out several times over. I had six weeks of doing nothing else, and with only an hour or so every evening for a tramp on the quarter-deck."

He whispered, his arms folded on the side of my bed place, staring through the open port. And I could imagine perfectly the manner of this thinking out — a stubborn if not a steadfast operation; something of which I should have been perfectly incapable.

"I reckoned it would be dark before we closed with the land," he continued, so low that I had to strain my hearing near as we were to each other, shoulder touching shoulder almost. "So I asked to speak to the old man. He always seemed very sick when he came to see me — as if he could not look me in the face. You know, that foresail saved the ship. She was too deep to have run long under bare poles. And it was I that managed to set it for him. Anyway, he came. When I had him in my cabin — he stood by the door looking at me as if I had the halter round my neck already — I asked him right away to leave my cabin door unlocked at night while the ship was going through Sunda Straits. There would be the Java coast within two or three miles, off Angier Point. I wanted nothing more. I've had a prize for swimming my second year in the Conway."

"I can believe it," I breathed out.

"God only knows why they locked me in every night. To see some of their faces you'd have thought they were afraid I'd go about at night strangling people. Am I a murdering brute? Do I look it? By Jove! If I had been he wouldn't have trusted himself like that into my room. You'll say I might have chucked him aside and bolted out, there and then — it was dark already. Well, no. And for the same reason I wouldn't think of trying to smash the door. There would have been a rush to stop me at the noise, and I did not mean to get into a confounded scrimmage. Somebody else might have got killed — for I would not have broken out only to get chucked back, and I did not want any more of that work. He refused, looking more sick than ever. He was afraid of the men, and also of that old second mate of his who had been sailing with him for years — a gray-headed old humbug; and his steward, too, had been with him devil knows how long — seventeen years or more — a dogmatic sort of loafer who hated me like poison, just because I was the chief mate. No chief mate ever made more than one voyage in the *Sephora,* you know. Those two old chaps ran the ship. Devil only knows what the skipper wasn't afraid of (all his nerve went to pieces altogether in that hellish spell of bad weather we had) — of what the law would do to him — of his wife, perhaps. Oh, yes! she's on board. Though I don't think she would have meddled. She would have been only too glad to have me out of the ship in any way. The 'brand of Cain' business, don't you see. That's all right. I was ready enough to go off wandering on the face of the earth — and that was price enough to pay for an Abel of that sort. Anyhow, he wouldn't listen to me. 'This thing must take its course. I represent the law here.' He was shaking like a leaf. 'So you won't?' 'No!' 'Then I hope you will be able to sleep on that,' I said, and turned my back on him. 'I wonder that *you* can,' cries he, and locks the door.

"Well after that, I couldn't. Not very well. That was three weeks ago. We have had a slow passage through the Java Sea; drifted about Carimata for ten days. When we anchored here they thought, I suppose, it was all right. The nearest land (and that's five miles) is the ship's destination; the consul would soon set about catching me; and there would have been no object in bolting to these islets there. I don't suppose there's a drop of water on them. I don't know how it was, but tonight that steward, after bringing me my supper, went out to let me eat it, and left the door unlocked. And I ate it — all there was, too. After I had finished I strolled out on the quarter-deck. I don't know that I meant to do anything. A breath of fresh air was all I wanted, I believe. Then a sudden temptation came over me. I kicked off my slippers and was in the water before I had made up my mind fairly. Somebody heard the splash and they raised an awful hullabaloo. 'He's gone! Lower the boats! He's committed suicide! No, he's swimming.' Certainly I was swimming. It's not so easy for a swimmer like me to commit suicide by drowning. I landed on the nearest islet before the boat left the ship's side. I heard them pulling about in the dark, hailing, and so on, but after a bit they gave up. Everything quieted down and the anchorage became as still as death. I sat down on a stone and began to think. I felt certain they would start searching for me at daylight. There was no place to hide on those stony things — and if there had been, what would have been the good? But now I was clear of that ship, I was not going back. So after a while I took off all my clothes, tied them up in a bundle with a stone inside, and dropped them in the deep water on the outer side of that islet. That was suicide enough for me. Let them think what they liked, but I didn't mean to drown myself. I meant to swim till I sank — but that's not the same thing. I struck out for another of these little islands, and it was from that one that I first saw your riding light. Something to swim for. I went on easily, and on the way I came upon a flat rock a foot or two above water. In the daytime, I dare say, you might make it out with a glass from your poop. I scrambled up on it and rested myself for a bit. Then I made another start. That last spell must have been over a mile."

His whisper was getting fainter and fainter, and all the time he stared straight out through the porthole, in which there was not even a star to be seen. I had not interrupted him. There was something that made comment impossible in his narrative, or perhaps in himself; a sort of feeling, a quality, which I can't find a name for. And when he ceased, all I found was a futile whisper: "So you swam for our light?"

"Yes — straight for it. It was something to swim for. I couldn't see any stars low down because the coast was in the way, and I couldn't see the land, either. The water was like glass. One might have been swimming in a confounded thousand-feet deep cistern with no place for scrambling out anywhere; but what I didn't like was the notion of swimming round and round like a crazed bullock before I gave out; and as I didn't mean to go back . . . No. Do you see me being hauled back, stark naked, off one of these little islands by the scruff of the neck and fighting like a wild beast? Somebody would have got killed for certain, and I did not want any of that. So I went on. Then your ladder —"

"Why didn't you hail the ship?" I asked, a little louder.

He touched my shoulder lightly. Lazy footsteps came right over our heads and stopped. The second mate had crossed from the other side of the poop and might have been hanging over the rail for all we knew.

"He couldn't hear us talking – could he?" My double breathed into my very ear, anxiously.

His anxiety was in answer, a sufficient answer, to the question I had put to him. An answer containing all the difficulty of that situation. I closed the porthole quietly, to make sure. A louder word might have been overheard.

"Who's that?" he whispered then.

"My second mate. But I don't know much more of the fellow than you do."

And I told him a little about myself. I had been appointed to take charge while I least expected anything of the sort, now quite a fortnight ago. I didn't know either the ship or the people. Hadn't had the time in port to look about me or size anybody up. And as to the crew, all they knew was that I was appointed to take the ship home. For the rest, I was almost as much of a stranger on board as himself, I said. And at the moment I felt it most acutely. I felt that it would take very little to make me a suspect person in the eyes of the ship's company.

He had turned about meantime; and we, the two strangers in the ship, faced each other in identical attitudes.

"Your ladder —" he murmured, after a silence. "Who'd have thought of finding a ladder hanging over at night in a ship anchored out here! I felt just then a very unpleasant faintness. After the life I've been leading for nine weeks, anybody would have got out of condition. I wasn't capable of swimming round as far as your rudder chains. And, lo and behold! there was a ladder to get hold of. After I gripped it I said to myself, 'What's the good?' When I saw a man's head looking over I thought I would swim away presently and leave him shouting – in whatever language it was. I didn't mind being looked at. I – I liked it. And then you speaking to me so quietly – as if you had expected me – made me hold on a little longer. It had been a confounded lonely time – I don't mean while swimming. I was glad to talk a little to somebody that didn't belong to the *Sephora*. As to asking for the captain, that was a mere impulse. It could have been no use, with all the ship knowing about me and the other people pretty certain to be round here in the morning. I don't know – I wanted to be seen, to talk with somebody, before I went on. I don't know what I would have said. . . . 'Fine night, isn't it?' or something of the sort."

"Do you think they will be round here presently?" I asked with some incredulity.

"Quite likely," he said, faintly.

He looked extremely haggard all of a sudden. His head rolled on his shoulders.

"H'm. We shall see then. Meantime get into that bed," I whispered. "Want help? There."

It was a rather high bed place with a set of drawers underneath. This amazing swimmer really needed the lift I gave him by seizing his leg. He tumbled in, rolled over on his back, and flung one arm across his eyes. And then, with his face nearly hidden, he must have looked exactly as I used to look in that bed. I gazed upon my other self for a while before drawing across carefully the two green serge curtains which ran on a brass rod. I thought for a moment of pinning them together for greater safety, but I sat down on the couch, and once there I felt unwilling to rise and hunt for a pin. I would do it in a moment. I was extremely tired, in a peculiarly intimate way, by the strain of stealthiness, by the effort of whispering and the general secrecy of this excitement. It was three o'clock by now and I had been on my feet since nine, but I was not sleepy; I could not have gone to sleep. I sat there, fagged out, looking at the curtains, trying to clear my mind of the confused sensation of being in two places at once, and greatly bothered by an exasperating knocking in my head. It was a relief to discover suddenly that it was not in my head at all, but on the outside of the door. Before I could collect myself the words "Come in" were out of my mouth, and the steward entered with a tray, bringing in my morning coffee. I had slept, after all, and I was so frightened that I shouted, "This way! I am here, steward," as though he had been miles away. He put down the tray on the table next the couch and only then said, very quietly, "I can see you are here, sir." I felt him give me a keen look, but I dared not meet his eyes just then. He must have wondered why I had drawn the curtains of my bed before going to sleep on the couch. He went out, hooking the door open as usual.

I heard the crew washing decks above me. I knew I would have been told at once if there had been any wind. Calm, I thought, and I was doubly vexed. Indeed, I felt dual more than ever. The steward reappeared suddenly in the doorway. I jumped up from the couch so quickly that he gave a start.

"What do you want here?"

"Close your port, sir – they are washing decks."

"It is closed," I said, reddening.

"Very well, sir." But he did not move from the doorway and returned my stare in an extraordinary, equivocal manner for a time. Then his eyes wavered, all his expression changed, and in a voice unusually gentle, almost coaxingly:

"May I come in to take the empty cup away, sir?"

"Of course!" I turned my back on him while he popped in and out. Then I unhooked and closed the door and even pushed the bolt. This sort of thing could not go on very long. The cabin was as hot as an oven, too. I took a peep at my double, and discovered that he had not moved, his arm was still over his eyes; but his chest heaved; his hair was wet; his chin glistened with perspiration. I reached over him and opened the port.

"I must show myself on deck," I reflected.

Of course, theoretically, I could do what I liked, with no one to say nay to me within the whole circle of the horizon; but to lock my cabin door and take the key away I did not dare. Directly I put my head out of the companion I saw the group of my two officers, the second mate barefooted, the chief mate in long India-rubber boots, near the break of the poop, and the steward halfway down the poop ladder talking to them eagerly. He happened to catch sight of me and dived, the second ran down on the main-deck shouting some order or other, and the chief mate came to meet me, touching his cap.

There was a sort of curiosity in his eye that I did not like. I don't know whether the steward had told them that I was "queer" only, or downright drunk, but I know the man meant to have a good look at me. I watched him coming with a smile which, as he got into point-blank range, took effect and froze his very whiskers. I did not give him time to open his lips.

"Square the yards by lifts and braces before the hands go to breakfast."

It was the first particular order I had given on board that ship; and I stayed on deck to see it executed, too. I had felt the need of asserting myself without loss of time. That sneering young cub got taken down a peg or two on that occasion, and I also seized the opportunity of having a good look at the face of every foremast man as they filed past me to go to the after braces. At breakfast time, eating nothing myself, I presided with such frigid dignity that the two mates were only too glad to escape from the cabin as soon as decency permitted; and all the time the dual working of my mind distracted me almost to the point of insanity. I was constantly watching myself, my secret self, as dependent on my actions as my own personality, sleeping in that bed, behind that door which faced me as I sat at the head of the table. It was very much like being mad, only it was worse because one was aware of it.

I had to shake him for a solid minute, but when at last he opened his eyes it was in the full possession of his senses, with an inquiring look.

"All's well so far," I whispered. "Now you must vanish into the bathroom."

He did so, as noiseless as a ghost, and then I rang for the steward, and facing him boldly, directed him to tidy up my stateroom while I was having my bath – "and be quick about it." As my tone admitted of no excuses, he said, "Yes, sir," and ran off to fetch his dustpan and brushes. I took a bath and did most of my dressing, splashing, and whistling softly for the steward's edification, while the secret sharer of my life stood drawn up bolt upright in that little space, his face looking very sunken in daylight, his eyelids lowered under the stern, dark line of his eyebrows drawn together by a slight frown.

When I left him there to go back to my room the steward was finishing dusting.

I sent for the mate and engaged him in some insignificant conversation. It was, as it were, trifling with the terrific character of his whiskers; but my object was to give him an opportunity for a good look at my cabin. And then I could at last shut, with a clear conscience, the door of my stateroom and get my double back into the recessed part. There was nothing else for it. He had to sit still on a small folding stool, half smothered by the heavy coats hanging there. We listened to the steward going into the bathroom out of the saloon, filling the water bottles there, scrubbing the bath, setting things to rights, whisk, bang, clatter – out again into the saloon – turn the key – click. Such was my scheme for keeping my second self invisible. Nothing better could be contrived under the circumstances. And there we sat; I at my writing desk ready to appear busy with some papers, he behind me out of sight of the door. It would not have been prudent to talk in daytime; and I could not have stood the excitement of that queer sense of whispering to myself. Now and then, glancing over my shoulder, I saw him far back there, sitting rigidly on the low stool, his bare feet close together, his arms folded, his head hanging on his breast – and perfectly still. Anybody would have taken him for me.

I was fascinated by it myself. Every moment I had to glance over my shoulder. I was looking at him when a voice outside the door said:

"Beg pardon, sir."

"Well!" . . . I kept my eyes on him, and so when the voice outside the door announced, "There's a ship's boat coming our way, sir," I saw him give a start – the first movement he had made for hours. But he did not raise his bowed head.

"All right. Get the ladder over."

I hesitated. Should I whisper something to him? But what? His immobility seemed to have been never disturbed. What could I tell him he did not know already? . . . Finally I went on deck.

II

The skipper of the *Sephora* had a thin red whisker all round his face, and the sort of complexion that goes with hair of that color; also the particular, rather smeary shade of blue in the eyes. He was not exactly a showy figure; his shoulders were high, his stature but middling – one leg slightly more bandy than the other. He shook hands, looking vaguely around. A spiritless tenacity was his main characteristic, I judged. I behaved with a politeness which seemed to disconcert him. Perhaps he was shy. He mumbled to me as if he were ashamed of what he was saying; gave his name (it was something like Archbold – but at this distance of years I hardly am sure), his ship's name, and a few other particulars of that sort, in the manner of a criminal making a reluctant and doleful confession. He had had terrible weather on the passage out – terrible – terrible – wife aboard, too.

By this time we were seated in the cabin and the steward brought in a tray with a bottle and glasses. "Thanks! No." Never took liquor. Would have some water, though. He drank two tumblerfuls. Terrible thirsty work. Ever since daylight had been exploring the islands round his ship.

"What was that for – fun?" I asked, with an appearance of polite interest.

"No!" He sighed. "Painful duty."

As he persisted in his mumbling and I wanted my double to hear every word, I hit upon the notion of informing him that I regretted to say I was hard of hearing.

"Such a young man, too!" he nodded, keeping his smeary blue, unintelligent eyes fastened upon me. "What was the cause of it – some disease?" he inquired, without the least sympathy and as if he thought that, if so, I'd got no more than I deserved.

"Yes; disease," I admitted in a cheerful tone which seemed to shock him. But my point was gained, because he had to raise his voice to give me his tale. It is not worth while to record that version. It was just over two months since all this had happened, and he had thought so much about it that he seemed completely muddled as to its bearings, but still immensely impressed.

"What would you think of such a thing happening on board your own ship? I've had the *Sephora* for these fifteen years. I am a well-known shipmaster."

He was densely distressed – and perhaps I should have sympathized with him if I had been able to detach my mental vision from the unsuspected sharer of my cabin as though he were my second self. There he was on the other side of the bulkhead, four or five feet from us, no more, as we sat in the saloon. I looked politely at Captain Archbold (if that was his name), but it was the other I saw, in a gray sleeping suit, seated on a low stool, his bare feet close together, his arms folded, and every word said between us falling into the ears of his dark head bowed on his chest.

"I have been at sea now, man and boy, for seven-and-thirty years, and I've never heard of such a thing happening in an English ship. And that it should be my ship. Wife on board, too."

I was hardly listening to him.

"Don't you think," I said, "that the heavy sea which, you told me, came aboard just then might have killed the man? I have seen the sheer weight of a sea kill a man very neatly, by simply breaking his neck."

"Good God!" he uttered, impressively, fixing his smeary blue eyes on me. "The sea! No man killed by the sea ever looked like that." He seemed positively scandalized at my suggestion. And as I gazed at him certainly not prepared for anything original on his part, he advanced his head close to mine and thrust his tongue out at me so suddenly that I couldn't help starting back.

After scoring over my calmness in this graphic way he nodded wisely. If I had seen the sight, he assured me, I would never forget it as long as I lived.

The weather was too bad to give the corpse a proper sea burial. So next day at dawn they took it up on the poop, covering its face with a bit of bunting; he read a short prayer, and then, just as it was, in its oilskins and long boots, they launched it amongst those mountainous seas that seemed ready every moment to swallow up the ship herself and the terrified lives on board of her.

"That reefed foresail saved you," I threw in.

"Under God – it did," he exclaimed fervently. "It was by a special mercy, I firmly believe, that it stood some of those hurricane squalls."

"It was the setting of that sail which –" I began.

"God's own hand in it," he interrupted me. "Nothing less could have done it. I don't mind telling you that I hardly dared give the order. It seemed impossible that we could touch anything without losing it, and then our last hope would have been gone."

The terror of that gale was on him yet. I let him go on for a bit, then said, casually – as if returning to a minor subject:

"You were very anxious to give up your mate to the shore people, I believe?"

He was. To the law. His obscure tenacity on that point had in it something incomprehensible and a little awful; something, as it were, mystical, quite apart from his anxiety that he should not be suspected of "countenancing any doings of that sort." Seven-and-thirty virtuous years at sea, of which over twenty of immaculate command, and the last fifteen in the *Sephora,* seemed to have laid him under some pitiless obligation.

"And you know," he went on, groping shame-facedly amongst his feelings, "I did not engage that young fellow. His people had some interest with my owners. I was in a way forced to take him on. He looked very smart, very gentlemanly, and all that. But do you know – I never liked him, somehow. I am a plain man. You see, he wasn't exactly the sort for the chief mate of a ship like the *Sephora.*"

I had become so connected in thoughts and impressions with the secret sharer of my cabin that I felt as if I, personally, were being given to understand that I, too, was not the sort that would have done for the chief mate of a ship like the *Sephora.* I had no doubt of it in my mind.

"Not at all the style of man. You understand," he insisted, superfluously, looking hard at me.

I smiled urbanely. He seemed at a loss for a while.

"I suppose I must report a suicide."

"Beg pardon?"

"Sui-cide! That's what I'll have to write to my owners directly I get in."

"Unless you manage to recover him before tomorrow," I assented, dispassionately. . . . "I mean, alive."

He mumbled something which I really did not catch, and I turned my ear to him in a puzzled manner. He fairly bawled:

"The land – I say, the mainland is at least seven miles off my anchorage."

"About that."

My lack of excitement, of curiosity, of surprise, of any sort of pronounced interest, began to arouse his distrust. But except for the felicitous pretense of deafness I had not tried to pretend anything. I had felt utterly incapable of playing the part of ignorance properly, and therefore was afraid to try. It is also certain that he had brought some ready-made suspicions with him, and that he viewed my politeness as a strange and unnatural phenomenon. And yet how else could I have received him? Not heartily! That was impossible for psychological reasons, which I need not state here. My only object was to keep off his inquiries. Surlily? Yes, but surliness might have provoked a point-blank question. From its novelty to him and from its nature, punctilious courtesy was the manner best calculated to restrain the man. But there was the danger of his breaking through my defense bluntly. I could not, I think, have met him by a direct lie, also for psychological (not moral) reasons. If he had only known how afraid I was of his putting my feeling of identity with the other to the test! But, strangely enough – (I thought of it only afterwards) – I believe that he was not a little disconcerted by the reverse side of that weird situation, by something in me that reminded him of the man he was seeking – suggested a mysterious similitude to the young fellow he had distrusted and disliked from the first.

However that might have been, the silence was not very prolonged. He took another oblique step.

"I reckon I had no more than a two-mile pull to your ship. Not a bit more."

"And quite enough, too, in this awful heat," I said.

Another pause full of mistrust followed. Necessity, they say, is mother of invention, but fear, too, is not barren of ingenious suggestions. And I was afraid he would ask me point-blank for news of my other self.

"Nice little saloon, isn't it?" I remarked, as if noticing for the first time the way his eyes roamed from one closed door to the other. "And very well fitted out, too. Here, for instance," I continued, reaching over the back of my seat negligently and flinging the door open, "is my bathroom."

He made an eager movement, but hardly gave it a glance. I got up, shut the door of the bathroom, and invited him to have a look round, as if I were very proud of my accommodation. He had to rise and be shown round, but he went through the business without any raptures whatever.

"And now we'll have a look at my stateroom," I declared, in a voice as loud as I dared to make it, crossing the cabin to the starboard side with purposely heavy steps.

He followed me in and gazed around. My intelligent double had vanished. I played my part.

"Very convenient – isn't it?"

"Very nice. Very comf . . ." He didn't finish and went out brusquely as if to escape from some unrighteous wiles of mine. But it was not to be. I had been too frightened not to feel vengeful; I felt I had him on the run, and I meant to keep him on the run. My polite insistence must have had something menacing in it, because he gave in suddenly. And I did not let him off a single item; mate's room, pantry, storerooms, the very sail locker which was also under the poop – he had to look into them all. When at last I showed him out on the quarter-deck he drew a long, spiritless sigh, and mumbled dismally that he must really be going back to his ship now. I desired my mate, who had joined us, to see to the captain's boat.

The man of whiskers gave a blast on the whistle which he used to wear hanging round his neck, and yelled, "*Sephora's* away!" My double down there in my cabin must have heard, and certainly could not feel more relieved than I. Four fellows came running out from somewhere forward and went over the side, while my own men, appearing on deck too, lined the rail. I escorted my visitor to the gangway ceremoniously, and nearly overdid it. He was a tenacious beast. On the very ladder he lingered, and in that unique, guiltily conscientious manner of sticking to the point:

"I say . . . you . . . you don't think that —"

I covered his voice loudly:

"Certainly not. . . . I am delighted. Good-by."

I had an idea of what he meant to say, and just saved myself by the privilege of defective hearing. He was too shaken generally to insist, but my mate, close witness of that parting, looked mystified and his face took on a thoughtful cast. As I did not want to appear as if I wished to avoid all communication with my officers, he had the opportunity to address me.

"Seems a very nice man. His boat's crew told our chaps a very extraordinary story, if what I am told by the steward is true. I suppose you had it from the captain, sir?"

"Yes. I had a story from the captain."

"A very horrible affair – isn't it, sir?"

"It is."

"Beats all these tales we hear about murders in Yankee ships."

"I don't think it beats them. I don't think it resembles them in the least."

"Bless my soul – you don't say so! But of course I've no acquaintance whatever with American ships, not I, so I couldn't go against your knowledge. It's horrible enough for me. . . . But the queerest part is that those fellows seemed to have some idea the man was hidden aboard here. They had really. Did you ever hear of such a thing?"

"Preposterous – isn't it?"

We were walking to and fro athwart the quarter-deck. No one of the crew forward could be seen (the day was Sunday), and the mate pursued:

"There was some little dispute about it. Our chaps took offense. 'As if we would harbor a thing like that,' they said. 'Wouldn't you like to look for him in our coalhole?' Quite a tiff. But they made it up in the end. I suppose he did drown himself. Don't you, sir?"

"I don't suppose anything."

"You have no doubt in the matter, sir?"

"None whatever."

I left him suddenly. I felt I was producing a bad impression, but with my double down there it was most trying to be on deck. And it was almost as trying to be below. Altogether a nerve-trying situation. But on the whole I felt less torn in two when I was with him. There was no one in the whole ship whom I dared take into my confidence. Since the hands had got to know his story, it would have been impossible to pass him off for anyone else, and an accidental discovery was to be dreaded now more than ever. . . .

The steward being engaged in laying the table for dinner, we could talk only with our eyes when I first went down. Later in the afternoon we had a cautious try at whispering. The Sunday quietness of the ship was against us; the stillness of air and water around her was against us; the elements, the men were against us – everything was against us in our secret partnership; time itself – for this could not go on forever. The very trust in Providence was, I suppose, denied to his guilt. Shall I confess that this thought cast me down very much? And as to the chapter of accidents which counts for so much in the book of success, I could only hope that it was closed. For what favorable accident could be expected?

"Did you hear everything?" were my first words as soon as we took up our position side by side, leaning over my bed place.

He had. And the proof of it was his earnest whisper, "The man told you he hardly dared to give the order."

I understood the reference to be to that saving foresail.

"Yes. He was afraid of it being lost in the setting."

"I assure you he never gave the order. He may think he did, but he never gave it. He stood there with me on the break of the poop after the main topsail blew away, and whimpered about our last hope – positively whimpered about it and nothing else – and the night coming on! To hear one's skipper go on like that in such weather was enough to drive any fellow out of his mind. It worked me up into a sort of desperation. I just took it into my own hands and went away from him, boiling, and —— But what's the use telling you? *You* know! . . . Do you think that if I had not been pretty fierce with them I should have got the men to do anything? Not It! The bo's'n perhaps? Perhaps! It wasn't a heavy sea – it was a sea gone mad! I suppose the end of the world will be something like that; and a man may have the heart to see it coming once and be done with it – but to have to face it day after day —— I don't blame anybody. I was precious little better than the rest. Only – I was an officer of that old coal wagon, anyhow ——"

"I quite understand," I conveyed that sincere assurance into his ear. He was out of breath with whispering; I could hear him pant slightly. It was all very simple. The same strung-up force which had given twenty-four men a chance, at least, for their lives, had, in a sort of recoil, crushed an unworthy mutinous existence.

But I had no leisure to weigh the merits of the matter – footsteps in the saloon, a heavy knock. "There's enough wind to get under way with, sir." Here was the call of a new claim upon my thoughts and even upon my feelings.

"Turn the hands up," I cried through the door. "I'll be on deck directly."

I was going out to make the acquaintance of my ship. Before I left the cabin our eyes met – the eyes of the only two strangers on board. I pointed to the recessed part where the little campstool awaited him and laid my finger on my lips. He made a gesture – somewhat vague – a little mysterious, accompanied by a faint smile, as if of regret.

This is not the place to enlarge upon the sensations of a man who feels for the first time a ship move under his feet to his own independent word. In my case they were not unalloyed. I was not wholly alone with my command; for there was that stranger in my cabin. Or rather, I was not completely and wholly with her. Part of me was absent. That mental feeling of being in two places at once affected me physically as if the mood of secrecy had penetrated my very soul. Before an hour had elapsed since the ship had begun to move, having occasion to ask the mate (he stood by my side) to take a compass bearing of the pagoda, I caught myself reaching up to his ear in whispers. I say I caught myself, but enough had escaped to startle the man. I can't describe it otherwise than by saying that he shied. A grave, preoccupied manner, as though he were in possession of some perplexing intelligence, did not leave him henceforth. A little later I moved away from the rail to look at the compass with such a stealthy gait that the helmsman noticed it – and I could not help noticing the unusual roundness of his eyes. These are trifling instances, though it's to no commander's advantage to be suspected of ludicrous eccentricities. But I was also more seriously affected. There are to a seaman certain words, gestures, that should in given conditions come as naturally, as instinctively as the winking of a menaced eye. A certain order should spring on to his lips without thinking; a certain sign should get itself made, so to speak, without reflection. But all unconscious alertness had abandoned me. I had to make an effort of will to recall myself back (from the cabin) to the conditions of the moment. I felt that I was appearing an irresolute commander to those people who were watching me more or less critically.

And, besides, there were the scares. On the second day out, for instance, coming off the deck in the afternoon (I had straw slippers on my bare feet) I stopped at the open pantry door and spoke to the steward. He was doing something there with his back to me. At the sound of my voice he nearly jumped out of his skin, as the saying is, and incidentally broke a cup.

"What on earth's the matter with you?" I asked, astonished.

He was extremely confused. "Beg your pardon, sir. I made sure you were in your cabin."

"You see I wasn't."

"No, sir. I could have sworn I had heard you moving in there not a moment ago. It's most extraordinary . . . very sorry, sir."

I passed on with an inward shudder. I was so identified with my secret double that I did not even mention the fact in those scanty, fearful whispers we exchanged. I suppose he had made some slight noise of some kind or other. It would have been miraculous if he hadn't at one time or another. And yet, haggard as he appeared, he looked always perfectly self-controlled, more than calm — almost invulnerable. On my suggestion he remained almost entirely in the bathroom, which, upon the whole, was the safest place. There could be really no shadow of an excuse for anyone ever wanting to go in there, once the steward had done with it. It was a very tiny place. Sometimes he reclined on the floor, his legs bent, his head sustained on one elbow. At others I would find him on the campstool, sitting in his gray sleeping suit and with his cropped dark hair like a patient, unmoved convict. At night I would smuggle him into my bed place, and we would whisper together, with the regular footfalls of the officer of the watch passing and repassing over our heads. It was an infinitely miserable time. It was lucky that some tins of fine preserves were stowed in a locker in my stateroom; hard bread I could always get hold of; and so he lived on stewed chicken, *pâté de foie gras,* asparagus, cooked oysters, sardines — on all sorts of abominable sham delicacies out of tins. My early-morning coffee he always drank; and it was all I dared do for him in that respect.

Every day there was the horrible maneuvering to go through so that my room and then the bathroom should be done in the usual way. I came to hate the sight of the steward, to abhor the voice of that harmless man. I felt that it was he who would bring on the disaster of discovery. It hung like a sword over our heads.

The fourth day out, I think (we were then working down the east side of the Gulf of Siam, tack for tack, in light winds and smooth water) — the fourth day, I say, of this miserable juggling with the unavoidable, as we sat at our evening meal, that man, whose slightest movement I dreaded, after putting down the dishes ran up on deck busily. This could not be dangerous. Presently he came down again; and then it appeared that he had remembered a coat of mine which I had thrown over a rail to dry after having been wetted in a shower which had passed over the ship in the afternoon. Sitting stolidly at the head of the table I became terrified at the sight of the garment on his arm. Of course he made for my door. There was no time to lose.

"Steward," I thundered. My nerves were so shaken that I could not govern my voice and conceal my agitation. This was the sort of thing that made my terrifically whiskered mate tap his forehead with his forefinger. I had detected him using that gesture while talking on deck with a confidential air to the carpenter. It was too far to hear a word, but I had no doubt that this pantomime could only refer to the strange new captain.

"Yes, sir," the pale-faced steward turned resignedly to me. It was this maddening course of being shouted at, checked without rhyme or reason, arbitrarily chased out of my cabin, suddenly called into it, sent flying out of his pantry on incomprehensible errands, that accounted for the growing wretchedness of his expression.

"Where are you going with that coat?"

"To your room, sir."

"Is there another shower coming?"

"I'm sure I don't know, sir. Shall I go up again and see, sir?"

"No! never mind."

My object was attained, as of course my other self in there would have heard everything that passed. During this interlude my two officers never raised their eyes off their respective plates; but the lip of that confounded cub, the second mate, quivered visibly.

I expected the steward to hook my coat on and come out at once. He was very slow about it; but I dominated my nervousness sufficiently not to shout after him. Suddenly I became aware (it could be heard plainly enough) that the fellow for some reason or other was opening the door of the bathroom. It was the end. The place was literally not big enough to swing a cat in. My voice died in my throat and I went stony all over. I expected to hear a yell of surprise and terror, and made a movement, but had not the strength to get on my legs. Everything remained still. Had my second self taken the poor wretch by the throat? I don't know what I could have done next moment if I had not seen the steward come out of my room, close the door, and then stand quietly by the sideboard.

"Saved," I thought. "But, no! Lost! Gone! He was gone!"

I laid my knife and fork down and leaned back in my chair. My head swam. After a while, when sufficiently recovered to speak in a steady voice, I instructed my mate to put the ship round at eight o'clock himself.

"I won't come on deck," I went on. "I think I'll turn in, and unless the wind shifts I don't want to be disturbed before midnight. I feel a bit seedy."

"You did look middling bad a little while ago," the chief mate remarked without showing any great concern.

They both went out, and I stared at the steward clearing the table. There was nothing to be read on that wretched man's face. But why did he avoid my eyes, I asked myself. Then I thought I should like to hear the sound of his voice.

"Steward!"

"Sir!" Startled as usual.

"Where did you hang up that coat?"

"In the bathroom, sir." The usual anxious tone. "It's not quite dry yet, sir."

For some time longer I sat in the cuddy. Had my double vanished as he had come? But of his coming there was an explanation, whereas his disappearance would be inexplicable. . . . I went slowly into my dark room, shut the door, lighted the lamp, and for a time dared not turn round. When at last I did I saw him standing bolt-upright in the narrow recessed part. It would not be true to say I had a shock, but an irresistible doubt of his bodily existence flitted through my mind. Can it be, I asked myself, that he is not visible to other eyes than mine? It was like being haunted. Motionless, with a grave face, he raised his hands slightly at me in a gesture which meant clearly, "Heavens! what a narrow escape!" Narrow indeed. I think I had come creeping quietly as near insanity as any man who has not actually gone over the border. That gesture restrained me, so to speak.

The mate with the terrific whiskers was now putting the ship on the other tack. In the moment of profound silence which follows upon the hands going to their stations I heard on the poop his raised voice: "Hard alee!" and the distant shout of the order repeated on the main-deck. The sails, in that light breeze, made but a faint fluttering noise. It ceased. The ship was coming round slowly: I held my breath in the renewed stillness of expectation; one wouldn't have thought that there was a single living soul on her decks. A sudden brisk shout, "Mainsail haul!" broke the spell, and in the noisy cries and rush overhead of the men running away with the main brace we two, down in my cabin, came together in our usual position by the bed place.

He did not wait for my question. "I heard him fumbling here and just managed to squat myself down in the bath," he whispered to me. "The fellow only opened the door and put his arm in to hang the coat up. All the same —"

"I never thought of that," I whispered back, even more appalled than before at the closeness of the shave, and marveling at that something unyielding in his character which was carrying him through so finely. There was no agitation in his whisper. Whoever was being driven distracted, it was not he. He was sane. And the proof of his sanity was continued when he took up the whispering again.

"It would never do for me to come to life again."

It was something that a ghost might have said. But what he was alluding to was his old captain's reluctant admission of the theory of suicide. It would obviously serve his turn – if I had understood at all the view which seemed to govern the unalterable purpose of his action.

"You must maroon me as soon as ever you can get amongst these islands off the Cambodge shore," he went on.

"Maroon you! We are not living in a boy's adventure tale," I protested. His scornful whispering took me up.

"We aren't indeed! There's nothing of a boy's tale in this. But there's nothing else for it. I want no more. You don't suppose I am afraid of what can be done to me? Prison or gallows or whatever they may please. But you don't see me coming back to explain such things to an old fellow in a wig and twelve respectable tradesmen, do you? What can they know whether I am guilty or not – or of *what* I am guilty, either? That's my affair. What does the Bible say? 'Driven off the face of the earth.' Very well, I am off the face of the earth now. As I came at night so I shall go."

"Impossible!" I murmured. "You can't."

"Can't? . . . Not naked like a soul on the Day of Judgment. I shall freeze on to this sleeping suit. The Last Day is not yet – and . . . you have understood thoroughly. Didn't you?"

I felt suddenly ashamed of myself. I may say truly that I understood – and my hesitation in letting that man swim away from my ship's side had been a mere sham sentiment, a sort of cowardice.

"It can't be done now till next night," I breathed out. "The ship is on the off-shore tack and the wind may fail us."

"As long as I know that you understand," he whispered. "But of course you do. It's a great satisfaction to have got somebody to understand. You seem to have been there on purpose." And in the same whisper, as if we two whenever we talked had to say things to each other which were not fit for the world to hear, he added, "It's very wonderful."

We remained side by side talking in our secret way – but sometimes silent or just exchanging a whispered word or two at long intervals. And as usual he stared through the port. A breath of wind came now and again into our faces. The ship might have been moored in dock, so gently and on an even keel she slipped through the water, that did not murmur even at our passage, shadowy and silent like a phantom sea.

At midnight I went on deck, and to my mate's great surprise put the ship round on the other tack. His terrible whiskers flitted round me in silent criticism. I certainly should not have done it if it had been only a question of getting out of that sleepy gulf as quickly as possible. I believe he told the second mate, who relieved him, that it was a great want of judgment. The other only yawned. That intolerable cub shuffled about so sleepily and lolled against the rails in such a slack, improper fashion that I came down on him sharply.

"Aren't you properly awake yet?"

"Yes, sir! I am awake."

"Well, then, be good enough to hold yourself as if you were. And keep a lookout. If there's any current we'll be closing with some islands before daylight."

The east side of the gulf is fringed with islands, some solitary, others in groups. On the blue background of the high coast they seem to float on silvery patches of calm water, arid and gray, or dark green and rounded like clumps of evergreen bushes, with the larger ones, a mile or two long, showing the outlines of ridges, ribs of gray rock under the dank mantle of matted leafage. Unknown to trade, to travel, almost to geography, the manner of life they harbor is an unsolved secret. There must be villages – settlements of fishermen at least – on the largest of them, and some communication with the world is probably kept up by native craft. But all that forenoon, as we headed for them, fanned along by the faintest of breezes, I saw no sign of man or canoe in the field of the telescope I kept on pointing at the scattered group.

At noon I gave no orders for a change of course, and the mate's whiskers became much concerned and seemed to be offering themselves unduly to my notice. At last I said:

"I am going to stand right in. Quite in — as far as I can take her."

The stare of extreme surprise imparted an air of ferocity also to his eyes, and he looked truly terrific for a moment.

"We're not doing well in the middle of the gulf," I continued, casually. "I am going to look for the land breezes tonight."

"Bless my soul! Do you mean, sir, in the dark amongst the lot of all them islands and reefs and shoals?"

"Well — if there are any regular land breezes at all on this coast one must get close inshore to find them, mustn't one?"

"Bless my soul!" he exclaimed again under his breath. All that afternoon he wore a dreamy, contemplative appearance which in him was a mark of perplexity. After dinner I went into my stateroom as if I meant to take some rest. There we two bent our dark heads over a half-unrolled chart lying on my bed.

"There," I said. "It's got to be Koh-ring. I've been looking at it ever since sunrise. It has got two hills and a low point. It must be inhabited. And on the coast opposite there is what looks like the mouth of a biggish river — with some towns, no doubt, not far up. It's the best chance for you that I can see."

"Anything. Koh-ring let it be."

He looked thoughtfully at the chart as if surveying chances and distances from a lofty height — and following with his eyes his own figure wandering on the blank land of Cochin-China, and then passing off that piece of paper clean out of sight into uncharted regions. And it was as if the ship had two captains to plan her course for her. I had been so worried and restless running up and down that I had not had the patience to dress that day. I had remained in my sleeping suit, with straw slippers and a soft floppy hat. The closeness of the heat in the gulf had been most oppressive, and the crew were used to seeing me wandering in that airy attire.

"She will clear the south point as she heads now," I whispered into his ear. "Goodness only knows when, though, but certainly after dark. I'll edge her in to half a mile, as far as I may be able to judge in the dark—"

"Be careful," he murmured, warningly — and I realized suddenly that all my future, the only future for which I was fit, would perhaps go irretrievably to pieces in any mishap to my first command.

I could not stop a moment longer in the room. I motioned him to get out of sight and made my way on the poop. That unplayful cub had the watch. I walked up and down for a while thinking things out, then beckoned him over.

"Send a couple of hands to open the two quarterdeck ports," I said, mildly.

He actually had the impudence, or else so forgot himself in his wonder at such an incomprehensible order, as to repeat:

"Open the quarter-deck ports! What for, sir?"

"The only reason you need concern yourself about is because I tell you to do so. Have them open wide and fastened properly."

He reddened and went off, but I believe made some jeering remark to the carpenter as to the sensible practice of ventilating a ship's quarter-deck. I know he popped into the mate's cabin to impart the fact to him because the whiskers came on deck, as it were by chance, and stole glances at me from below – for signs of lunacy or drunkenness, I suppose.

A little before supper, feeling more restless than ever, I rejoined, for a moment, my second self. And to find him sitting so quietly was surprising, like something against nature, inhuman.

I developed my plan in a hurried whisper.

"I shall stand in as close as I dare and then put her round. I will presently find means to smuggle you out of here into the sail locker, which communicates with the lobby. But there is an opening, a sort of square for hauling the sails out, which gives straight on the quarterdeck and which is never closed in fine weather, so as to give air to the sails. When the ship's way is deadened in stays and all the hands are aft at the main braces you will have a clear road to slip out and get overboard through the open quarter-deck port. I've had them both fastened up. Use a rope's end to lower yourself into the water so as to avoid a splash – you know. It could be heard and cause some beastly complication."

He kept silent for a while, then whispered, "I understand."

"I won't be there to see you go," I began with an effort. "The rest . . . I only hope I have understood, too."

"You have. From first to last" – and for the first time there seemed to be a faltering, something strained in his whisper. He caught hold of my arm, but the ringing of the supper bell made me start. He didn't though; he only released his grip.

After supper I didn't come below again till well past eight o'clock. The faint, steady breeze was loaded with dew; and the wet, darkened sails held all there was of propelling power in it. The night, clear and starry, sparkled darkly, and the opaque, lightless patches shifting slowly against the low stars were the drifting islets. On the port bow there was a big one more distant and shadowily imposing by the great space of sky it eclipsed.

On opening the door I had a back view of my very own self looking at a chart. He had come out of the recess and was standing near the table.

"Quite dark enough," I whispered.

He stepped back and leaned against my bed with a level, quiet glance. I sat on the couch. We had nothing to say to each other. Over our heads the officer of the watch moved here and there. Then I heard him move quickly. I knew what that meant. He was making for the companion; and presently his voice was outside my door.

"We are drawing in pretty fast, sir. Land looks rather close."

"Very well," I answered. "I am coming on deck directly."

I waited till he was gone out of the cuddy, then rose. My double moved too. The time had come to exchange our last whispers, for neither of us was ever to hear each other's natural voice.

"Look here!" I opened a drawer and took out three sovereigns. "Take this anyhow. I've got six and I'd give you the lot, only I must keep a little money to buy some fruit and vegetables for the crew from native boats as we go through Sunda Straits."

He shook his head.

"Take it," I urged him, whispering desperately. "No one can tell what —"

He smiled and slapped meaningly the only pocket of the sleeping jacket. It was not safe, certainly. But I produced a large old silk handkerchief of mine, and tying the three pieces of gold in a corner, pressed it on him. He was touched, I supposed, because he took it at last and tied it quickly round his waist under the jacket, on his bare skin.

Our eyes met; several seconds elapsed, till, our glances still mingled, I extended my hand and turned the lamp out. Then I passed through the cuddy, leaving the door of my room wide open. . . . "Steward!"

He was still lingering in the pantry in the greatness of his zeal, giving a rub-up to a plated cruet stand the last thing before going to bed. Being careful not to wake up the mate, whose room was opposite, I spoke in an undertone.

He looked round anxiously. "Sir!"

"Can you get me a little hot water from the galley?"

"I am afraid, sir, the galley fire's been out for some time now."

"Go and see."

He flew up the stairs.

"Now," I whispered, loudly, into the saloon — too loudly, perhaps, but I was afraid I couldn't make a sound. He was by my side in an instant — the double captain slipped past the stairs — through a tiny dark passage . . . a sliding door. We were in the sail locker, scrambling on our knees over the sails. A sudden thought struck me. I saw myself wandering barefooted, bareheaded, the sun beating on my dark poll. I snatched off my floppy hat and tried hurriedly in the dark to ram it on my other self. He dodged and fended off silently. I wonder what he thought had come to me before he understood and suddenly desisted. Our hands met gropingly, lingered united in a steady, motionless clasp for a second. . . . No word was breathed by either of us when they separated.

I was standing quietly by the pantry door when the steward returned.

"Sorry, sir. Kettle barely warm. Shall I light the spirit lamp?"

"Never mind."

I came out on deck slowly. It was now a matter of conscience to shave the land as close as possible – for now he must go overboard whenever the ship was put in stays. Must! There could be no going back for him. After a moment I walked over the leeward and my heart flew into my mouth at the nearness of the land on the bow. Under any other circumstances I would not have held on a minute longer. The second mate had followed me anxiously.

I looked on till I felt I could command my voice.

"She will weather," I said then in a quiet tone.

"Are you going to try that, sir?" he stammered out incredulously.

I took no notice of him and raised my tone just enough to be heard by the helmsman.

"Keep her good full."

"Good full, sir."

The wind fanned my cheek, the sails slept, the world was silent. The strain of watching the dark loom of the land grow bigger and denser was too much for me. I had shut my eyes – because the ship must go closer. She must! The stillness was intolerable. Were we standing still?

When I opened my eyes the second view started my heart with a thump. The black southern hill of Koh-ring seemed to hang right over the ship like a towering fragment of the ever-lasting night. On that enormous mass of blackness there was not a gleam to be seen, not a sound to be heard. It was gliding irresistibly towards us and yet seemed already within reach of the hand. I saw the vague figures of the watch grouped in the waist, gazing in awed silence.

"Are you going on, sir?" inquired an unsteady voice at my elbow.

I ignored it. I had to go on.

"Keep her full. Don't check her way. That won't do now," I said, warningly.

"I can't see the sails very well," the helmsman answered me, in strange, quavering tones.

Was she close enough? Already she was, I won't say in the shadow of the land, but in the very blackness of it, already swallowed up as it were, gone too close to be recalled, gone from me altogether.

"Give the mate a call," I said to the young man who stood at my elbow as still as death. "And turn all hands up."

My tone had a borrowed loudness reverberated from the height of the land. Several voices cried out together; "We are all on deck, sir."

Then stillness again, with the great shadow gliding closer, towering higher, without a light, without a sound. Such a hush had fallen on the ship that she might have been a bark of the dead floating in slowly under the very gate of Erebus.

"My God! Where are we?"

It was the mate moaning at my elbow. He was thunderstruck, and as it were deprived of the moral support of his whiskers. He clapped his hands and absolutely cried out, "Lost!"

"Be quiet," I said, sternly.

He lowered his tone, but I saw the shadowy gesture of his despair. "What are we doing here?"

"Looking for the land wind."

He made as if to tear his hair, and addressed me recklessly.

"She will never get out. You have done it, sir. I knew it'd end in something like this. She will never weather, and you are too close now to stay. She'll drift ashore before she's round. O my God!"

I caught his arm as he was raising it to batter his poor devoted head, and shook it violently.

"She's ashore already," he wailed, trying to tear himself away.

"Is she? . . . Keep good full there!"

"Good full, sir," cried the helmsman in a frightened, thin, childlike voice.

I hadn't let go the mate's arm and went on shaking it. "Ready about, do you hear? You go forward" – shake – "and stop there" – shake – "and hold your noise" – shake – "and see these head-sheets properly overhauled" – shake, shake – shake.

And all the time I dared not look towards the land lest my heart should fail me. I released my grip at last and he ran forward as if fleeing for dear life.

I wondered what my double there in the sail locker thought of this commotion. He was able to hear everything – and perhaps he was able to understand why, on my conscience, it had to be thus close – no less. My first order "Hard alee!" re-echoed ominously under the towering shadow of Koh-ring as if I had shouted in a mountain gorge. And then I watched the land intently. In that smooth water and light wind it was impossible to feel the ship coming-to. No! I could not feel her. And my second self was making now ready to ship out and lower himself overboard. Perhaps he was gone already . . . ?

The great black mass brooding over our very mastheads began to pivot away from the ship's side silently. And now I forgot the secret stranger ready to depart, and remembered only that I was a total stranger to the ship. I did not know her. Would she do it? How was she to be handled?

I swung the mainyard and waited helplessly. She was perhaps stopped, and her very fate hung in the balance, with the black mass of Koh-ring like the gate of the everlasting night towering over her taffrail. What would she do now? Had she way on her yet? I stepped to the side swiftly, and on the shadowy water I could see nothing except a faint phosphorescent flash revealing the glassy smoothness of the sleeping surface. It was impossible to tell – and I had not learned yet the feel of my ship. Was she moving? What I needed was something easily seen, a piece of paper, which I could throw overboard and watch. I had nothing on me. To run down for it I didn't dare. There was no time. All at once my strained, yearning stare distinguished a white object floating within a yard of the ship's side. White on the black water. A phosphorescent flash passed under it. What was that thing? . . . I recognized my own floppy hat. It must have fallen off his head . . . and he didn't bother. Now I had what I wanted – the saving mark for my eyes. But I hardly thought of my other self, now gone from the ship, to be hidden forever from all friendly faces, to be a fugitive and a vagabond on the earth, with no brand of the curse on his sane forehead to stay a slaying hand . . . too proud to explain.

And I watched the hat – the expression of my sudden pity for his mere flesh. It had been meant to save his homeless head from the dangers of the sun. And now – behold – it was saving the ship, by serving me for a mark to help out the ignorance of my strangeness. Ha! It was drifting forward, warning me just in time that the ship had gathered sternway.

"Shift the helm," I said in a low voice to the seaman standing still like a statue.

The man's eyes glistened wildly in the binnacle light as he jumped round to the other side and spun round the wheel.

I walked to the break of the poop. On the overshadowed deck all hands stood by the forebraces waiting for my order. The stars ahead seemed to be gliding from right to left. And all was so still in the world that I heard the quiet remark, "She's round," passed in a tone of intense relief between two seamen.

"Let go and haul."

The foreyards ran round with a great noise, amidst cheery cries. And now the frightful whiskers made themselves heard giving various orders. Already the ship was drawing ahead. And I was alone with her. Nothing! no one in the world should stand now between us, throwing a shadow on the way of silent knowledge and mute affection, the perfect communion of a seaman with his first command.

Walking to the taffrail, I was in time to make out, on the very edge of a darkness thrown by a towering black mass like the very gateway of Erebus – yes, I was in time to catch an evanescent glimpse of my white hat left behind to mark the spot where the secret sharer of my cabin and of my thoughts, as though he were my second self, had lowered himself into the water to take his punishment: a free man, a proud swimmer striking out for a new destiny.

ANTON CHEKHOV 1860–1904

A doctor by profession, Chekhov trained himself to look at human experience clinically, without betraying in obvious ways his strong emotional involvement with the people he observed. Yet he was a man of great passion who felt in his own life the extremes of ecstasy and despair. As a long-time sufferer from tuberculosis (from which he died at forty-four) he also knew the strange states of consciousness — of delirium, euphoria, and vast depression — typical of that disease. The result in his writing is a cool view of extraordinary experience: obsessed, maddened, or profoundly miserable characters are set in relief by the matter-of-factness of the narration. Chekhov feels deeply for these characters but he wants to show them as they really exist: living in worlds too taken up with individual concerns to pay attention to their agony. In the work of Tolstoy and Dostoyevsky, Chekhov's older contemporaries, the extreme emotion of characters carries the world around them toward a quasi-religious pitch of intensity; but in Chekhov's the sufferer or the ecstatic produces *no* effect on his environment — being always seen as queerly apart from the everyday, unmelodramatic life that Chekhov's cool narration establishes. Thus Iona's misery is finally communicable only to his horse, and Jakob's long-repressed sadness at human mortality can only be expressed on his fiddle when he is alone, and can be bequeathed only bizarrely: by leaving the fiddle to a man he detests, who plays its beautiful sad notes for the sentimental indulgence of businessmen.

Outside of Russia Chekhov has been best known for the four plays that have become great classics of twentieth-century drama: *The Seagull, Uncle Vanya, Three Sisters,* and *The Cherry Orchard.* In all of these plays the characters are sympathetically seen as caught in a web of relationships in which their passions, oddities, and traditional allegiances are irrelevant. They call out beautifully and movingly, but nobody except the audience leaves his own little world long enough to listen. Events go their own way without respect to the characters' desires or aspirations.

One can see how appropriate the drama was for this vision of reality: people pour out their private concerns to others on the stage who either ignore them or appropriate them into their own concerns. In productions of his plays, Chekhov always insisted on realistic costumes and sets. Against these his characters revealed the styles of their illusions about themselves and their roles in the world.

But despite his affinity for the theater, Chekhov came to it only late in his life, after he had long been famous in Russia for his short stories. As a student he wrote short comic sketches for Moscow newspapers, thereby supporting a desperately poor household consisting of his parents and five brothers and sisters. His father had failed as a grocer in Taganrog, a town in southern Russia, and had fled from his creditors to the obscurity of Moscow's slums. His wife and children moved to a different quarter of the city, and much of the burden of their support then fell on Chekhov. As a writer for the newspapers Chekhov developed a reporter's knack of catching moods in a few words and an ability to spot character-revealing detail. These qualities he developed in the more self-contained form of the short story; and though as he grew more famous he could afford to write longer stories that did not fit the newspaper format, in general his finest works are no more than about fifteen pages.

Chekhov's fame as a short-story writer brought him enough money to buy his family a small house and some land in the countryside outside Moscow. He participated in rural life as a landowner and as a doctor, and he made use of his observations in his stories and later in his plays. As his tuberculosis grew worse he was forced to leave the severe climate of Moscow and take up residence in Yalta. His last years were brightened to some extent by his marriage to one of the actresses in the Moscow company that produced his plays, but there was inevitably some strain introduced into the marriage by his enforced residence in Yalta while his wife was acting in Moscow. The accounts of his last days in a German health resort under the care of German doctors (whom he despised) reveal the cynical yet compassionate sensibility that informs all of his writing. He was given a great public funeral in Moscow, which by one of those peculiar ironies of history was conducted as Chekhov might have imagined it in fiction. The corpse arrived in a box labelled "Lard." After that was straightened out, most of the procession that had assembled to honor the great writer mistakenly followed to the graveyard the cortege of a general that happened to be passing by.

MISERY

"To Whom Shall I Tell My Grief?"

The twilight of evening. Big flakes of wet snow are whirling lazily about the street lamps, which have just been lighted, and lying in a thin soft layer on roofs, horses' backs, shoulders, caps. Iona Potapov, the sledge-driver, is all white like a ghost. He sits on the box without stirring, bent as double as the living body can be bent. If a regular snowdrift fell on him it seems as though even then he would not think it necessary to shake it off. . . . His little mare is white and motionless too. Her stillness, the angularity of her lines, and the stick-like straightness of her legs make her look like a halfpenny gingerbread horse. She is probably lost in thought. Anyone who has been torn away from the plough, from the familiar gray landscapes, and cast into this slough, full of monstrous lights, of unceasing uproar and hurrying people, is bound to think.

It is a long time since Iona and his nag have budged. They came out of the yard before dinner-time and not a single fare yet. But now the shades of evening are falling on the town. The pale light of the street lamps changes to a vivid color, and the bustle of the street grows noisier.

"Sledge to Vyborgskaya!" Iona hears. "Sledge!"

Iona starts, and through his snow-plastered eyelashes sees an officer in a military overcoat with a hood over his head.

"To Vyborgskaya," repeats the officer. "Are you asleep? To Vyborgskaya!"

In token of assent Iona gives a tug at the reins which sends cakes of snow flying from the horse's back and shoulders. The officer gets into the sledge. The sledge-driver clicks to the horse, cranes his neck like a swan, rises in his seat, and more from habit than necessity brandishes his whip. The mare cranes her neck, too, crooks her stick-like legs, and hesitatingly sets off. . . .

"Where are you shoving, you devil?" Iona immediately hears shouts from the dark mass shifting to and fro before him. "Where the devil are you going? Keep to the r-right!"

"You don't know how to drive! Keep to the right," says the officer angrily.

A coachman driving a carriage swears at him; a pedestrian crossing the road and brushing the horse's nose with his shoulder looks at him angrily and shakes the snow off his sleeve. Iona fidgets on the box as though he were sitting on thorns, jerks his elbows, and turns his eyes about like one possessed, as though he did not know where he was or why he was there.

"What rascals they all are!" says the officer jocosely. "They are simply doing their best to run up against you or fall under the horse's feet. They must be doing it on purpose."

Iona looks at his fare and moves his lips. . . . Apparently he means to say something, but nothing comes but a sniff.

"What?" inquires the officer.

Iona gives a wry smile, and straining his throat, brings out huskily: "My son . . . er . . . my son died this week, sir."

"H'm! What did he die of?"

Iona turns his whole body round to his fare, and says:

"Who can tell! It must have been from fever. . . . He lay three days in the hospital and then he died. . . . God's will."

"Turn round, you devil!" comes out of the darkness. "Have you gone cracked, you old dog? Look where you are going!"

"Drive on! drive on! . . ." says the officer. "We shan't get there till tomorrow going on like this. Hurry up!"

The sledge-driver cranes his neck again, rises in his seat, and with heavy grace swings his whip. Several times he looks round at the officer, but the latter keeps his eyes shut and is apparently disinclined to listen. Putting his fare down at Vyborgskaya, Iona stops by a restaurant, and again sits huddled up on the box. . . . Again the wet snow paints him and his horse white. One hour passes, and then another. . . .

Three young men, two tall and thin, one short and hunchbacked, come up, railing at each other and loudly stamping on the pavement with their goloshes.

"Cabby, to the Police Bridge!" the hunchback cries in a cracked voice. "The three of us, . . . twenty kopecks!"

Iona tugs at the reins and clicks to his horse. Twenty kopecks is not a fair price, but he has no thoughts for that. Whether it is a rouble or whether it is five kopecks does not matter to him now so long as he has a fare. . . . The three young men, shoving each other and using bad language, go up to the sledge, and all three try to sit down at once. The question remains to be settled: Which are to sit down and which one is to stand? After a long altercation, ill-temper, and abuse, they come to the conclusion that the hunchback must stand because he is the shortest.

"Well, drive on," says the hunchback in his cracked voice, settling himself and breathing down Iona's neck. "Cut along! What a cap you've got, my friend! You wouldn't find a worse one in all Petersburg. . . "

"He-he! . . . he-he! . . ." laughs Iona. "It's nothing to boast of!"

"Well, then, nothing to boast of, drive on! Are you going to drive like this all the way? Eh? Shall I give you one in the neck?"

"My head aches," says one of the tall ones. "At the Dukmasovs' yesterday Vaska and I drank four bottles of brandy between us."

"I can't make out why you talk such stuff," says the other tall one angrily. "You lie like a brute."

"Strike me dead, it's the truth! . . ."

"It's about as true as that a louse coughs."

"He-he!" grins Iona. "Me-er-ry gentlemen!"

"Tfoo! the devil take you!" cries the hunchback indignantly. "Will you get on, you old plague, or won't you? Is that the way to drive? Give her one with the whip. Hang it all, give it her well."

Iona feels behind his back the jolting person and quivering voice of the hunchback. He hears abuse addressed to him, he sees people, and the feeling of loneliness begins little by little to be less heavy on his heart. The hunchback swears at him, till he chokes over some elaborately whimsical string of epithets and is overpowered by his cough. His tall companions begin talking of a certain Nadyezhda Petrovna. Iona looks round at them. Waiting till there is a brief pause, he looks round once more and says:

"This week . . . er . . . my . . . er . . . son died!"

"We shall all die, . . ." says the hunchback with a sigh, wiping his lips after coughing. "Come, drive on! drive on! My friends, I simply cannot stand crawling like this! When will he get us there?"

"Well, you give him a little encouragement . . . one in the neck!"

"Do you hear, you old plague? I'll make you smart. If one stands on ceremony with fellows like you one may as well walk. Do you hear, you old dragon? Or don't you care a hang what we say?"

And Iona hears rather than feels a slap on the back of his neck.

"He-he! . . ." he laughs. "Merry gentlemen. . . . God give you health!"

"Cabman, are you married?" asks one of the tall ones.

"I? He-he! Me-er-ry gentlemen. The only wife for me now is the damp earth. . . . He-ho-ho! . . . The grave that is! . . . Here my son's dead and I am alive. . . . It's a strange thing, death has come in at the wrong door. . . . Instead of coming for me it went for my son. . . ."

And Iona turns round to tell them how his son died, but at that point the hunchback gives a faint sigh and announces that, thank God! they have arrived at last. After taking his twenty kopecks, Iona gazes for a long while after the revelers, who disappear into a dark entry. Again he is alone and again there is silence for him. . . . The misery which has been for a brief space eased comes back again and tears his heart more cruelly than ever. With a look of anxiety and suffering Iona's eyes stray restlessly among the crowds moving to and fro on both sides of the street: can he not find among those thousands someone who will listen to him? But the crowds flit by heedless of him and his misery. . . . His misery is immense, beyond all bounds. If Iona's heart were to burst and his misery to flow out, it would flood the whole world, it seems, but yet it is not seen. It has found a hiding-place in such an insignificant shell that one would not have found it with a candle by daylight. . . .

Iona sees a house-porter with a parcel and makes up his mind to address him.

"What time will it be, friend?" he asks.

"Going on for ten. . . . Why have you stopped here? Drive on!"

Iona drives a few paces away, bends himself double, and gives himself up to his misery. He feels it is no good to appeal to people. But before five minutes have passed he draws himself up, shakes his head as though he feels a sharp pain, and tugs at the reins. . . . He can bear it no longer.

"Back to the yard!" he thinks. "To the yard!"

And his little mare, as though she knew his thoughts, falls to trotting. An hour and a half later Iona is sitting by a big dirty stove. On the stove, on the floor, and on the benches are people snoring. The air is full of smells and stuffiness. Iona looks at the sleeping figures, scratches himself, and regrets that he has come home so early. . . .

"I have not earned enough to pay for the oats, even," he thinks. "That's why I am so miserable. A man who knows how to do his work, . . . who has had enough to eat, and whose horse has had enough to eat, is always at ease. . . ."

In one of the corners a young cabman gets up, clears his throat sleepily, and makes for the waterbucket.

"Want a drink?" Iona asks him.

"Seems so."

"May it do you good. . . . But my son is dead, mate. . . . Do you hear? This week in the hospital. . . . It's queer business. . . ."

Iona looks to see the effect produced by his words, but he sees nothing. The young man has covered his head over and is already asleep. The old man sighs and scratches himself. . . . Just as the young man had been thirsty for water, he thirsts for speech. His son will soon have been dead a week, and he has not really talked to anybody yet. . . . He wants to talk of it properly, with deliberation. . . . He wants to tell how his son was taken ill, how he suffered, what he said before he died, how he died. . . . He wants to describe the funeral, and how he went to the hospital to get his son's clothes. He still has his daughter Anisya in the country. . . . And he wants to talk about her too. . . . Yes, he has plenty to talk about now. His listener ought to sigh and exclaim and lament. . . . It would be even better to talk to women. Though they are silly creatures, they blubber at the first word.

"Let's go out and have a look at the mare," Iona thinks. "There is always time for sleep. . . . You'll have sleep enough, no fear. . . ."

He puts on his coat and goes into the stables where his mare is standing. He thinks about oats, about hay, about the weather.... He cannot think about his son when he is alone.... To talk about him with someone is possible, but to think of him and picture him is insufferable anguish....

"Are you munching?" Iona asks his mare, seeing her shining eyes. "There, munch away, munch away.... Since we have not earned enough for oats, we will eat hay.... Yes,... I have grown too old to drive.... My son ought to be driving, not I.... He was a real cabman.... He ought to have lived...."

Iona is silent for a while, and then he goes on:

"That's how it is, old girl.... Kuzma Ionitch is gone.... He said good-by to me.... He went and died for no reason.... Now, suppose you had a little colt, and you were own mother to that little colt.... And all at once that same little colt went and died.... You'd be sorry, wouldn't you?..."

The little mare munches, listens, and breathes on her master's hands. Iona is carried away and tells her all about it.

ROTHSCHILD'S FIDDLE

The town was small – no better than a village – and it was inhabited almost entirely by old people who died so seldom that it was positively painful. In the hospital, and even in the prison, coffins were required very seldom. In one word, business was bad. If Yakob Ivanof had been coffin-maker in the government town, he would probably have owned his own house, and called himself Yakob Matvieitch; but, as it was, he was known only by the name of Yakob, with the street nickname given for some obscure reason of "Bronza"; and lived as poorly as a simple peasant in a little, ancient cabin with only one room; and in this room lived he, Marfa, the stove, a double bed, the coffins, a joiner's bench, and all the domestic utensils.

Yet Yakob made admirable coffins, durable and good. For peasants and petty tradespeople he made them all of one size, taking himself as model; and this method never failed him, for though he was seventy years of age, there was not a taller or stouter man in the town, not even in the prison. For women and for men of good birth he made his coffins to measure, using for this purpose an iron yardwand. Orders for children's coffins he accepted very unwillingly, made them without measurement, as if in contempt, and every time when paid for his work exclaimed:

"Thanks. But I confess I don't care much for wasting time on trifles."

In addition to coffin-making Yakob drew a small income from his skill with the fiddle. At weddings in the town there usually played a Jewish orchestra, the conductor of which was the tinsmith Moses Ilitch Shakhkes, who kept more than half the takings for himself. As Yakob played very well upon the fiddle, being particularly skilful with Russian songs, Shakhkes sometimes employed him in the orchestra, paying him fifty kopecks a day, exclusive of gifts from the guests. When Bronza sat in the orchestra he perspired and his face grew purple; it was always hot, the smell of garlic was suffocating; the fiddle whined, at his right ear snored the double-bass, at his left wept the flute, played by a lanky, red-haired Jew with a whole network of red and blue veins upon his face, who bore the same surname as the famous millionaire Rothschild. And even the merriest tunes this accursed Jew managed to play sadly. Without any tangible cause Yakob had become slowly penetrated with hatred and contempt for Jews, and especially for Rothschild; he began with irritation, then swore at him, and once even was about to hit him; but Rothschild flared up, and, looking at him furiously, said:

"If it were not that I respect you for your talents, I should send you flying out of the window."

Then he began to cry. So Bronza was employed in the orchestra very seldom, and only in cases of extreme need when one of the Jews was absent.

Yakob had never been in a good humour. He was always overwhelmed by the sense of the losses which he suffered. For instance, on Sundays and saints' days it was a sin to work, Monday was a tiresome day – and so on; so that in one way or another, there were about two hundred days in the year when he was compelled to sit with his hands idle. That was one loss! If anyone in the town got married without music, or if Shakhkes did not employ Yakob, that was another loss. The Inspector of Police was ill for two years, and Yakob waited with impatience for his death, yet in the end the Inspector transferred himself to the government town for the purpose of treatment, where he got worse and died. There was another loss, a loss at the very least of ten roubles, as the Inspector's coffin would have been an expensive one lined with brocade. Regrets for his losses generally overtook Yakob at night; he lay in bed with the fiddle beside him, and, with his head full of such speculations, would take the bow, the fiddle giving out through the darkness a melancholy sound which made Yakob feel better.

On the sixth of May last year Marfa was suddenly taken ill. She breathed heavily, drank much water and staggered. Yet next morning she lighted the stove, and even went for water. Towards evening she lay down. All day Yakob had played on the fiddle, and when it grew dark he took the book in which every day he inscribed his losses, and from want of something better to do, began to add them up. The total amounted to more than a thousand roubles. The thought of such losses so horrified him that he threw the book on the floor and stamped his feet. Then he took up the book, snapped his fingers, and sighed heavily. His face was purple, and wet with perspiration. He reflected that if this thousand roubles had been lodged in the bank the interest per annum would have amounted to at least forty roubles. That meant that the forty roubles were also a loss. In one word, wherever you turn, everywhere you meet with loss, and profits none.

"Yakob," cried Marfa unexpectedly, "I am dying."

He glanced at his wife. Her face was red from fever and unusually clear and joyful; and Bronza, who was accustomed to see her pale, timid, and unhappy-looking, felt confused. It seemed as if she were indeed dying, and were happy in the knowledge that she was leaving for ever the cabin, the coffins, and Yakob. And now she looked at the ceiling and twitched her lips, as if she had seen Death her deliverer, and were whispering with him.

Morning came; through the window might be seen the rising of the sun. Looking at his old wife, Yakob somehow remembered that all his life he had never treated her kindly, never caressed her, never pitied her, never thought of buying her a kerchief for her head, never carried away from the weddings a piece of tasty food, but only roared at her, abused her for his losses, and rushed at her with shut fists. True, he had never beaten her, but he had often frightened her out of her life and left her rooted to the ground with terror. Yes, and he had forbidden her to drink tea, as the losses without that were great enough; so she drank always hot water. And now, beginning to understand why she had such a strange, enraptured face, he felt uncomfortable.

When the sun had risen high he borrowed a cart from a neighbour, and brought Marfa to the hospital. There were not many patients there, and he had to wait only three hours. To his joy he was received not by the doctor but by his assistant, Maxim Nikolaitch, an old man of whom it was said that, although he was drunken and quarrelsome, he knew more than the doctor.

"May your health be good!" said Yakob, leading the old woman into the dispensary. "Forgive me, Maxim Nikolaitch, for troubling you with my empty affairs. But there, you can see for yourself my object is ill. The companion of my life, as they say, excuse the expression . . ."

Contracting his grey brows and smoothing his whiskers, the assistant began to examine the old woman, who sat on the tabouret, bent, skinny, sharp-nosed, and with open mouth so that she resembled a bird that is about to drink.

"So . . ." said the assistant slowly, and then sighed. "Influenza and may be a bit of a fever. There is typhus now in the town . . . What can I do? She is an old woman, glory be to God. . . . How old?"

"Sixty-nine years, Maxim Nikolaitch."

"An old woman. It's high time for her."

"Of course! Your remark is very just," said Yakob, smiling out of politeness. "And I am sincerely grateful for your kindness; but allow me to make one remark; every insect is fond of life."

The assistant replied in a tone which implied that upon him alone depended her life or death. "I will tell you what you'll do, friend; put on her head a cold compress, and give her these powders twice a day. And good-bye to you."

By the expression of the assistant's face, Yakob saw that it was a bad business, and that no powders would make it any better; it was quite plain to him that Marfa was beyond repair, and would assuredly die, if not to-day then to-morrow. He touched the assistant on the arm, blinked his eyes, and said in a whisper:

"Yes, Maxim Nikolaitch, but you will let her blood."

"I have no time, no time, friend. Take your old woman, and God be with you!"

"Do me this one kindness!" implored Yakob. "You yourself know that if she merely had her stomach out of order, or some internal organ wrong, then powders and mixtures would cure; but she has caught cold. In cases of cold the first thing is to bleed the patient."

But the assistant had already called for the next patient, and into the dispensary came a peasant woman with a little boy.

"Be off!" he said to Yakob, with a frown.

"At least try the effect of leeches. I will pray God eternally for you."

The assistant lost his temper, and roared:

"Not another word."

Yakob also lost his temper, and grew purple in the face; but he said nothing more and took Marfa under his arm and led her out of the room. As soon as he had got her into the cart, he looked angrily and contemptuously at the hospital and said:

"What an artist! He will let the blood of a rich man, but for a poor man grudges even a leech. Herod!"

When they arrived home, and entered the cabin, Marfa stood for a moment holding on to the stove. She was afraid that if she were to lie down Yakob would begin to complain about his losses, and abuse her for lying in bed and doing no work. And Yakob looked at her with tedium in his soul and remembered that to-morrow was John the Baptist, and the day after Nikolai the Miracle-worker, and then came Sunday, and after that Monday – another idle day. For four days no work could be done, and Marfa would be sure to die on one of these days. Her coffin must be made to-day. He took the iron yardwand, went up to the old woman and took her measure. After that she lay down, and Yakob crossed himself, and began to make a coffin.

When the work was finished, Bronza put on his spectacles and wrote in his book of losses:

"Marfa Ivanova's coffin – 2 roubles, 40 kopecks."

And he sighed. All the time Marfa had lain silently with her eyes closed. Towards evening, when it was growing dark, she called her husband:

"Rememberest, Yakob?" she said, looking at him joyfully. "Rememberest, fifty years ago God gave us a baby with yellow hair. Thou and I then sat every day by the river . . . under the willow . . . and sang songs." And laughing bitterly she added: "The child died."

"That is all imagination," said Yakob.

Later on came the priest, administered to Marfa the Sacrament and extreme unction. Marfa began to mutter something incomprehensible, and towards morning, died.

The old-women neighbours washed her, wrapped her in her winding sheet, and laid her out. To avoid having to pay the deacon's fee, Yakob himself read the psalms; and escaped a fee also at the graveyard, as the watchman there was his godfather. Four peasants carried the coffin free, out of respect for the deceased. After the coffin walked a procession of old women, beggars, and two cripples. The peasants on the road crossed themselves piously. And Yakob was very satisfied that everything passed off in honour, order, and cheapness, without offence to anyone. When saying good-bye for the last time to Marfa, he tapped the coffin with his fingers, and thought "An excellent piece of work."

But while he was returning from the graveyard he was overcome with extreme weariness. He felt unwell, he breathed feverishly and heavily, he could hardly stand on his feet. His brain was full of unaccustomed thoughts. He remembered again that he had never taken pity on Marfa and never caressed her. The fifty-two years during which they had lived in the same cabin stretched back to eternity, yet in the whole of that eternity he had never thought of her, never paid any attention to her, but treated her as if she were a cat or a dog. Yet every day she had lighted the stove, boiled and baked, fetched water, chopped wood, slept with him on the same bed; and when he returned drunk from weddings, she had taken his fiddle respectfully, and hung it on the wall, and put him to bed – all this silently with a timid, worried expression on her face. And now he felt that he could take pity on her, and would like to buy her a present, but it was too late. . . .

Towards Yakob smiling and bowing came Rothschild.

"I was looking for you, uncle," he said. "Moses Ilitch sends his compliments, and asks you to come across to him at once."

Yakob felt inclined to cry.

"Begone!" he shouted, and continued his path.

"You can't mean that," cried Rothschild in alarm, running after him. "Moses Ilitch will take offence! He wants you at once."

The way in which the Jew puffed and blinked, and the multitude of his red freckles awoke in Yakob disgust. He felt disgust, too, for his green frock-coat, with its black patches, and his whole fragile, delicate figure.

"What do you mean by coming after me, garlic?" he shouted. "Keep off!"

The Jew also grew angry, and cried:

"If you don't take care to be a little politer I will send you flying over the fence."

"Out of my sight!" roared Yakob, rushing on him with clenched fists. "Out of my sight, abortion, or I will beat the soul out of your cursed body! I have no peace with Jews."

Rothschild was frozen with terror; he squatted down and waved his arms above his head, as if warding off blows, and then jumped up and ran for his life. While running he hopped, and flourished his hands; and the twitching of his long, fleshless spine could plainly be seen. The boys in the street were delighted with the incident, and rushed after him, crying, "Jew! Jew!" The dogs pursued him with loud barks. Someone laughed, then someone whistled, and the dogs barked louder and louder. Then, it must have been, a dog bit Rothschild, for there rang out a sickly, despairing cry.

Yakob walked past the common, and then along the outskirts of the town; and the street boys cried, "Bronza! Bronza!" With a piping note snipe flew around him, and ducks quacked. The sun baked everything, and from the water came scintillations so bright that it was painful to look at. Yakob walked along the path by the side of the river, and watched a stout, red-cheeked lady come out of the bathing-place. Not far from the bathing-place sat a group of boys catching crabs with meat; and seeing him they cried maliciously, "Bronza! Bronza!" And at this moment before him rose a thick old willow with an immense hollow in it, and on it a raven's nest.... And suddenly in Yakob's mind awoke the memory of the child with the yellow hair of whom Marfa had spoken.... Yes, it was the same willow, green, silent, sad.... How it had aged, poor thing!

He sat underneath it, and began to remember. On the other bank, where was now a flooded meadow, there then stood a great birch forest, and farther away, where the now bare hill glimmered on the horizon, was an old pine wood. Up and down the river went barges. But now everything was flat and smooth; on the opposite bank stood only a single birch, young and shapely, like a girl; and on the river were only ducks and geese where once had floated barges. It seemed that since those days even the geese had become smaller. Yakob closed his eyes, and in imagination saw flying towards him an immense flock of white geese.

He began to wonder how it was that in the last forty or fifty years of his life he had never been near the river, or if he had, had never noticed it. Yet it was a respectable river, and by no means contemptible; it would have been possible to fish in it, and the fish might have been sold to tradesmen, officials, and the attendant at the railway station buffet, and the money could have been lodged in the bank; he might have used it for rowing from country-house to country-house and playing on the fiddle, and everyone would have paid him money; he might even have tried to act as bargee – it would have been better than making coffins; he might have kept geese, killed them and sent them to Moscow in the winter-time – from the feathers alone he would have made as much as ten roubles a year. But he had yawned away his life, and done nothing. What losses! Akh, what losses! and if he had done all together – caught fish, played on the fiddle, acted as bargee, and kept geese – what a sum he would have amassed! But he had never even dreamed of this; life had passed without profits, without any satisfaction; everything had passed away unnoticed; before him nothing remained. But look backward – nothing but losses, such losses that to think of them it makes the blood run cold. And why cannot a man live without these losses? Why had the birch wood and the pine forest both been cut down? Why is the common pasture unused? Why do people do exactly what they ought not to do? Why did he all his life scream, roar, clench his fists, insult his wife? For what imaginable purpose did he frighten and insult the Jew? Why, indeed, do people prevent one another living in peace? All these are also losses! Terrible losses! If it were not for hatred and malice people would draw from one another incalculable profits.

Evening and night, twinkled in Yakob's brain the willow, the fish, the dead geese, Marfa with her profile like that of a bird about to drink, the pale, pitiable face of Rothschild, and an army of snouts thrusting themselves out of the darkness and muttering about losses. He shifted from side to side, and five times in the night rose from his bed and played on the fiddle.

In the morning he rose with an effort and went to the hospital. The same Maxim Nikolaitch ordered him to bind his head with a cold compress, and gave him powders; and by the expression of his face and by his tone Yakob saw that it was a bad business, and that no powders would make it any better. But upon his way home he reflected that from death at least there would be one profit; it would no longer be necessary to eat, to drink, to pay taxes, or to injure others; and as a man lies in his grave not one year, but hundreds and thousands of years, the profit was enormous. The life of man was, in short, a loss, and only his death a profit. Yet this consideration, though entirely just, was offensive and bitter; for why in this world is it so ordered that life, which is given to a man only once, passes by without profit?

He did not regret dying, but as soon as he arrived home and saw his fiddle, his heart fell, and he felt sorry. The fiddle could not be taken to the grave; it must remain an orphan, and the same thing would happen with it as had happened with the birchwood and the pineforest. Everything in this world decayed, and would decay! Yakob went to the door of the hut and sat upon the threshold stone, pressing his fiddle to his shoulder. Still thinking of life, full of decay and full of losses, he began to play, and as the tune poured out plaintively and touchingly, the tears flowed down his cheeks. And the harder he thought, the sadder was the song of the fiddle.

The latch creaked twice, and in the wicket door appeared Rothschild. The first half of the yard he crossed boldly, but seeing Yakob, he stopped short, shrivelled up, and apparently from fright began to make signs as if he wished to tell the time with his fingers.

"Come on, don't be afraid," said Yakob kindly, beckoning him. "Come!"

With a look of distrust and terror Rothschild drew near and stopped about two yards away.

"Don't beat me, Yakob, it is not my fault!" he said, with a bow. "Moses Ilitch has sent me again. 'Don't be afraid!' he said, 'go to Yakob again and tell him that without him we cannot possibly get on.' The wedding is on Wednesday. Shapovaloff's daughter is marrying a wealthy man. . . . It will be a first-class wedding," added the Jew, blinking one eye.

"I cannot go," answered Yakob, breathing heavily. "I am ill, brother."

And again he took his bow, and the tears burst from his eyes and fell upon the fiddle. Rothschild listened attentively, standing by his side with arms folded upon his chest. The distrustful, terrified expression upon his face little by little changed into a look of suffering and grief, he rolled his eyes as if in an ecstacy of torment, and ejaculated "Wachchch!" And the tears slowly rolled down his cheeks and made little black patches on his green frock-coat.

All day long Yakob lay in bed and worried. With evening came the priest, and, confessing him, asked whether he had any particular sin which he would like to confess; and Yakob exerted his fading memory, and remembering Marfa's unhappy face, and the Jew's despairing cry when he was bitten by the dog, said in a hardly audible voice:

"Give the fiddle to Rothschild."

And now in the town everyone asks: Where did Rothschild get such an excellent fiddle? Did he buy it or steal it . . . or did he get it in pledge? Long ago he abandoned his flute, and now plays on the fiddle only. From beneath his bow issue the same mournful sounds as formerly came from the flute; but when he tries to repeat the tune that Yakob played when he sat on the threshold stone, the fiddle emits sounds so passionately sad and full of grief that the listeners weep; and he himself rolls his eyes and ejaculates "Wachchch!" . . . But this new song so pleases everyone in the town that wealthy traders and officials never fail to engage Rothschild for their social gatherings, and even force him to play it as many as ten times.

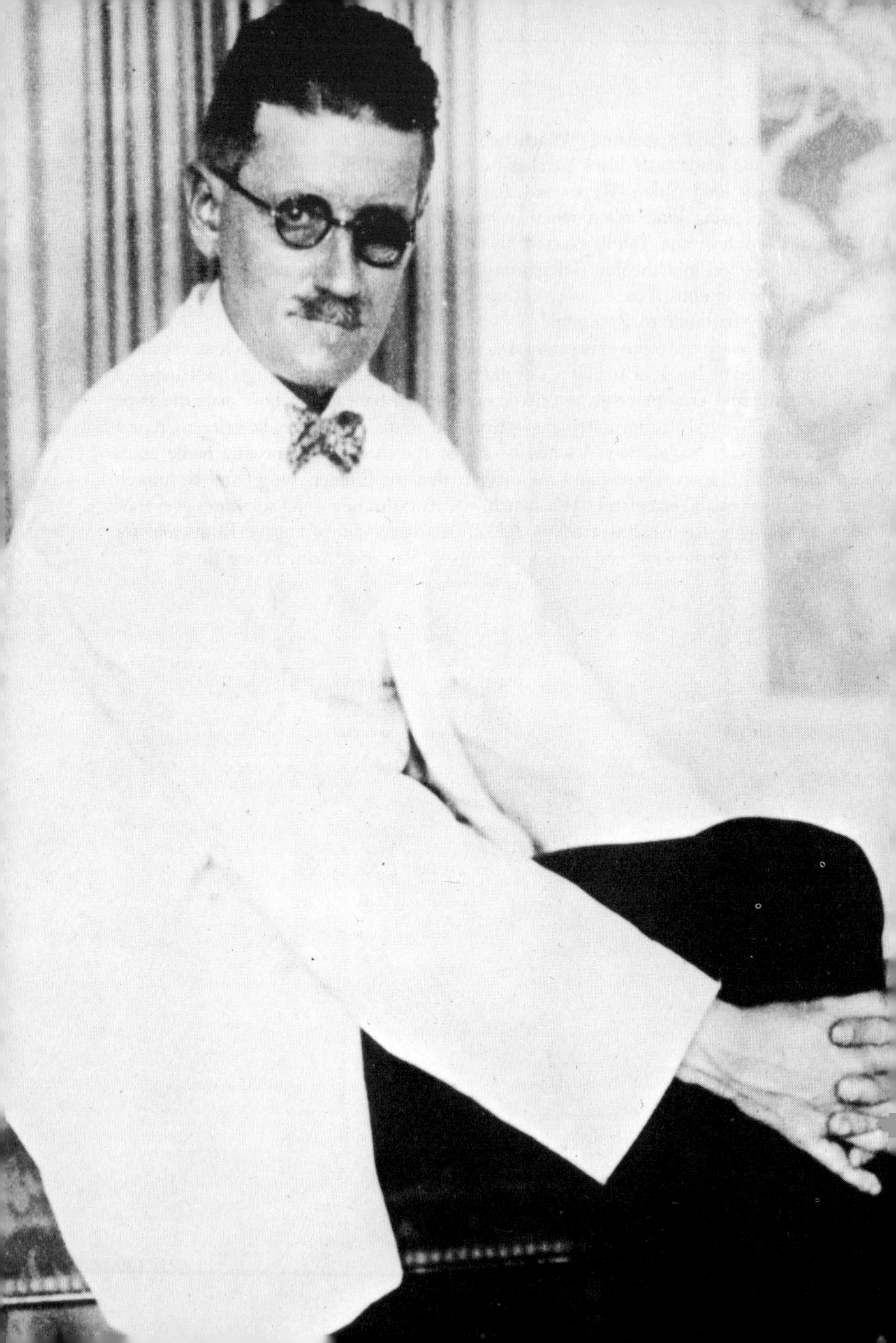

JAMES JOYCE 1882–1941

For Joyce the city of Dublin was a microcosm of Western Civilization: its classic eighteenth-century architecture bathed in popular sentimental songs of lost loves and lost causes; Bishop Berkeley, Dean Swift, and Shelley still present — along with the Holy Roman Catholic Church, the hated authority of the British Empire, the ghosts of Irish martyrs, and the wishful vision of a pure Gaelic heritage. Of course all cities have histories, but most also have such an active present that history is more or less left to the contemplative citizenry, becoming apparent to the masses only on ceremonial occasions. What Joyce observed was that the Dublin in which he was born and raised was a city with no present: that is, with no special mission in the modern world. Instead, everyone seemed to be endlessly engaged in making the past part of their current lives. The boy in "Araby," imagining himself on a holy crusade to a fabulous Eastern land on behalf of his beloved Lady, is just acting out on an adolescent level what all his elders are doing in other ways. Gretta in "The Dead" is lost in a reverie of lost love in the West country, Miss Ivors in visions of ancient Ireland revived, others in the transporting songs of the music halls and the Italian opera.

Though fascinated by this timeless microcosm, Joyce found that he could not live in it. The collection from which these stories are taken, *Dubliners* (1912), shows the city as paralyzed, and in his autobiographical first novel, *A Portrait of the Artist as a Young Man* (1916), he presents the flight of Stephen Dedalus to Paris. Though in *Ulysses* (1922) Stephen is back in Dublin, except for short periods Joyce himself never returned. Imaginatively he kept Dublin as the subject of all his work, but he himself found it necessary to remain an exile, living in France and Italy, living apart from the city he portrayed with great specificity in his fiction. He was often in need, supporting his wife and children by giving English lessons and soliciting funds from friends who believed in his work.

More than any other modern writer, he believed in an ideal of the completely detached artist — a kind of god who presides over his characters without any comment except that made by the characters' speech and a precise arrangement of detail. From the chaste artistry of *Dubliners* Joyce expanded his fiction to include more exuberant forms of Dublin life – the comic and the bawdy being especially evident (and shocking to some readers) in *Ulysses* and in his last novel *Finnegans Wake* (1939).

ARABY

North Richmond Street, being blind, was a quiet street except at the hour when the Christian Brothers' School set the boys free. An uninhabited house of two storeys stood at the blind end, detached from its neighbours in a square ground. The other houses of the street, conscious of decent lives within them, gazed at one another with brown imperturbable faces.

The former tenant of our house, a priest, had died in the back drawing-room. Air, musty from having been long enclosed, hung in all the rooms, and the waste room behind the kitchen was littered with old useless papers. Among these I found a few paper-covered books, the pages of which were curled and damp: *The Abbot,* by Walter Scott, *The Devout Communicant* and *The Memoirs of Vidocq.* I liked the last best because its leaves were yellow. The wild garden behind the house contained a central apple-tree and a few straggling bushes under one of which I found the late tenant's rusty bicycle-pump. He had been a very charitable priest; in his will he had left all his money to institutions and the furniture of his house to his sister.

When the short days of winter came dusk fell before we had well eaten our dinners. When we met in the street the houses had grown sombre. The space of sky above us was the colour of ever-changing violet and towards it the lamps of the street lifted their feeble lanterns. The cold air stung us and we played till our bodies glowed. Our shouts echoed in the silent street. The career of our play brought us through the dark muddy lanes behind the houses where we ran the gantlet of the rough tribes from the cottages, to the back doors of the dark dripping gardens where odours arose from the ashpits, to the dark odorous stables where a coachman smoothed and combed the horse or shook music from the buckled harness. When we returned to the street light from the kitchen windows had filled the areas. If my uncle was seen turning the corner we hid in the shadow until we had seen him safely housed. Or if Mangan's sister came out on the doorstep to call her brother in to his tea we watched her from our shadow peer up and down the street. We waited to see whether she would remain or go in and, if she remained, we left our shadow and walked up to Mangan's steps resignedly.

She was waiting for us, her figure defined by the light from the half-opened door. Her brother always teased her before he obeyed and I stood by the railings looking at her. Her dress swung as she moved her body and the soft rope of her hair tossed from side to side.

Every morning I lay on the floor in the front parlour watching her door. The blind was pulled down to within an inch of the sash so that I could not be seen. When she came out on the doorstep my heart leaped. I ran to the hall, seized my books and followed her. I kept her brown figure always in my eye and, when we came near the point at which our ways diverged, I quickened my pace and passed her. This happened morning after morning. I had never spoken to her, except for a few casual words, and yet her name was like a summons to all my foolish blood.

Her image accompanied me even in places the most hostile to romance. On Saturday evenings when my aunt went marketing I had to go to carry some of the parcels. We walked through the flaring streets, jostled by drunken men and bargaining women, amid the curses of labourers, the shrill litanies of shop-boys who stood on guard by the barrels of pigs' cheeks, the nasal chanting of street-singers, who sang a *come-all-you* about O'Donovan Rossa, or a ballad about the troubles in our native land. These noises converged in a single sensation of life for me: I imagined that I bore my chalice safely through a throng of foes. Her name sprang to my lips at moments in strange prayers and praises which I myself did not understand. My eyes were often full of tears (I could not tell why) and at times a flood from my heart seemed to pour itself out into my bosom. I thought little of the future. I did not know whether I would ever speak to her or not or, if I spoke to her, how I could tell her of my confused adoration. But my body was like a harp and her words and gestures were like fingers running upon the wires.

One evening I went into the back drawing-room in which the priest had died. It was a dark rainy evening and there was no sound in the house. Through one of the broken panes I heard the rain impinge upon the earth, the fine incessant needles of water playing in the sodden beds. Some distant lamp or lighted window gleamed below me. I was thankful that I could see so little. All my senses seemed to desire to veil themselves and, feeling that I was about to slip from them, I pressed the palms of my hands together until they trembled, murmuring: *O love! O love!* many times.

At last she spoke to me. When she addressed the first words to me I was so confused that I did not know what to answer. She asked me was I going to *Araby*. I forget whether I answered yes or no. It would be a splendid bazaar, she said; she would love to go.

–And why can't you? I asked.

While she spoke she turned a silver bracelet round and round her wrist. She could not go, she said, because there would be a retreat that week in her convent.

Her brother and two other boys were fighting for their caps and I was alone at the railings. She held one of the spikes, bowing her head towards me. The light from the lamp opposite our door caught the white curve of her neck, lit up her hair that rested there and, falling, lit up the hand upon the railing. It fell over one side of her dress and caught the white border of a petticoat, just visible as she stood at ease.

–It's well for you, she said.

–If I go, I said, I will bring you something.

What innumerable follies laid waste my waking and sleeping thoughts after that evening! I wished to annihilate the tedious intervening days. I chafed against the work of school. At night in my bedroom and by day in the classroom her image came between me and the page I strove to read. The syllables of the word *Araby* were called to me through the silence in which my soul luxuriated and cast an Eastern enchantment over me. I asked for leave to go to the bazaar on Saturday night. My aunt was surprised and hoped it was not some Freemason affair. I answered few questions in class. I watched my master's face pass from amiability to sternness; he hoped I was not beginning to idle. I could not call my wandering thoughts together. I had hardly any patience with the serious work of life which, now that it stood between me and my desire, seemed to me child's play, ugly monotonous child's play.

On Saturday morning I reminded my uncle that I wished to go to the bazaar in the evening. He was fussing at the hall-stand, looking for the hat-brush, and answered me curtly:

–Yes, boy, I know.

As he was in the hall I could not go into the front parlour and lie at the window. I left the house in bad humour and walked slowly towards the school. The air was pitilessly raw and already my heart misgave me.

When I came home to dinner my uncle had not yet been home. Still it was early. I sat staring at the clock for some time and, when its ticking began to irritate me, I left the room. I mounted the staircase and gained the upper part of the house. The high cold empty gloomy rooms liberated me and I went from room to room singing. From the front window I saw my companions playing below in the street. Their cries reached me weakened and indistinct and, leaning my forehead against the cool glass, I looked over at the dark house where she lived. I may have stood there for an hour, seeing nothing but the brown-clad figure cast by my imagination, touched discreetly by the lamplight at the curved neck, at the hand upon the railings and at the border below the dress.

When I came downstairs again I found Mrs Mercer sitting at the fire. She was an old garrulous woman, a pawnbroker's widow, who collected used stamps for some pious purpose. I had to endure the gossip of the tea-table. The meal was prolonged beyond an hour and still my uncle did not come. Mrs Mercer stood up to go: she was sorry she couldn't wait any longer, but it was after eight o'clock and she did not like to be out late, as the night air was bad for her. When she had gone I began to walk up and down the room, clenching my fists. My aunt said:

—I'm afraid you may put off your bazaar for this night of Our Lord.

At nine o'clock I heard my uncle's latchkey in the halldoor. I heard him talking to himself and heard the hallstand rocking when it had received the weight of his overcoat. I could interpret these signs. When he was midway through his dinner I asked him to give me the money to go to the bazaar. He had forgotten.

—The people are in bed and after their first sleep now, he said.

I did not smile. My aunt said to him energetically:

—Can't you give him the money and let him go? You've kept him late enough as it is.

My uncle said he was very sorry he had forgotten. He said he believed in the old saying: *All work and no play makes Jack a dull boy.* He asked me where I was going and, when I had told him a second time he asked me did I know *The Arab's Farewell to his Steed.* When I left the kitchen he was about to recite the opening lines of the piece to my aunt.

I held a florin tightly in my hand as I strode down Buckingham Street towards the station. The sight of the streets thronged with buyers and glaring with gas recalled to me the purpose of my journey. I took my seat in a third-class carriage of a deserted train. After an intolerable delay the train moved out of the station slowly. It crept onward among ruinous houses and over the twinkling river. At Westland Row Station a crowd of people pressed to the carriage doors; but the porters moved them back, saying that it was a special train for the bazaar. I remained alone in the bare carriage. In a few minutes the train drew up beside an improvised wooden platform. I passed out on to the road and saw by the lighted dial of a clock that it was ten minutes to ten. In front of me was a large building which displayed the magical name.

I could not find any sixpenny entrance and, fearing that the bazaar would be closed, I passed in quickly through a turnstile, handing a shilling to a weary-looking man. I found myself in a big hall girdled at half its height by a gallery. Nearly all the stalls were closed and the greater part of the hall was in darkness. I recognized a silence like that which pervades a church after a service. I walked into the centre of the bazaar timidly. A few people were gathered about the stalls which were still open. Before a curtain, over which the words *Café Chantant* were written in coloured lamps, two men were counting money on a salver. I listened to the fall of the coins.

Remembering with difficulty why I had come I went over to one of the stalls and examined porcelain vases and flowered tea-sets. At the door of the stall a young lady was talking and laughing with two young gentlemen. I remarked their English accents and listened vaguely to their conversation.

—O, I never said such a thing!

–O, but you did!

–O, but I didn't!

–Didn't she say that?

–Yes. I heard her.

–O, there's a . . . fib!

Observing me the young lady came over and asked me did I wish to buy anything. The tone of her voice was not encouraging; she seemed to have spoken to me out of a sense of duty. I looked humbly at the great jars that stood like eastern guards at either side of the dark entrance to the stall and murmured:

–No, thank you.

The young lady changed the position of one of the vases and went back to the two young men. They began to talk of the same subject. Once or twice the young lady glanced at me over her shoulder.

I lingered before her stall, though I knew my stay was useless, to make my interest in her wares seem the more real. Then I turned away slowly and walked down the middle of the bazaar. I allowed the two pennies to fall against the sixpence in my pocket. I heard a voice call from one end of the gallery that the light was out. The upper part of the hall was now completely dark.

Gazing up into the darkness I saw myself as a creature driven and derided by vanity; and my eyes burned with anguish and anger.

THE DEAD

Lily, the caretaker's daughter, was literally run off her feet. Hardly had she brought one gentleman into the little pantry behind the office on the ground floor and helped him off with his overcoat than the wheezy hall-door bell clanged again and she had to scamper along the bare hallway to let in another guest. It was well for her she had not to attend to the ladies also. But Miss Kate and Miss Julia had thought of that and had converted the bathroom upstairs into a ladies' dressing-room. Miss Kate and Miss Julia were there, gossiping and laughing and fussing, walking after each other to the head of the stairs, peering down over the banisters and calling down to Lily to ask her who had come.

It was always a great affair, the Misses Morkan's annual dance. Everybody who knew them came to it, members of the family, old friends of the family, the members of Julia's choir, any of Kate's pupils that were grown up enough and even some of Mary Jane's pupils too. Never once had it fallen flat. For years and years it had gone off in splendid style as long as anyone could remember; ever since Kate and Julia, after the death of their brother Pat, had left the house in Stoney Batter and taken Mary Jane, their only niece, to live with them in the dark gaunt house on Usher's Island, the upper part of which they had rented from Mr Fulham, the cornfactor on the ground floor. That was a good thirty years ago if it was a day. Mary Jane, who was then a little girl in short clothes, was now the main prop of the household for she had the organ in Haddington Road. She had been through the Academy and gave a pupils' concert every year in the upper room of the Antient Concert Rooms. Many of her pupils belonged to better-class families on the Kingstown and Dalkey line. Old as they were, her aunts also did their share. Julia, though she was quite grey, was still the leading soprano in Adam and Eve's, and Kate, being too feeble to go about much, gave music lessons to beginners on the old square piano in the back room. Lily, the caretaker's daughter, did housemaid's work for them. Though their life was modest they believed in eating well; the best of everything: diamond-bone sirloins, three-shilling tea and the best bottled stout. But Lily seldom made a mistake in the orders so that she got on well with her three mistresses. They were fussy, that was all. But the only thing they would not stand was back answers.

Of course they had good reason to be fussy on such a night. And then it was long after ten o'clock and yet there was no sign of Gabriel and his wife. Besides they were dreadfully afraid that Freddy Malins might turn up screwed. They would not wish for worlds that any of Mary Jane's pupils should see him under the influence; and when he was like that it was sometimes very hard to manage him. Freddy Malins always came late but they wondered what could be keeping Gabriel: and that was what brought them every two minutes to the banisters to ask Lily had Gabriel or Freddy come.

—O, Mr Conroy, said Lily to Gabriel when she opened the door for him, Miss Kate and Miss Julia thought you were never coming. Good-night, Mrs Conroy.

—I'll engage they did, said Gabriel, but they forget that my wife here takes three mortal hours to dress herself.

He stood on the mat, scraping the snow from his goloshes, while Lily led his wife to the foot of the stairs and called out:

—Miss Kate, here's Mrs Conroy.

Kate and Julia came toddling down the dark stairs at once. Both of them kissed Gabriel's wife, said she must be perished alive and asked was Gabriel with her.

—Here I am as right as the mail, Aunt Kate! Go on up. I'll follow, called out Gabriel from the dark.

He continued scraping his feet vigorously while the three women went upstairs, laughing, to the ladies' dressing-room. A light fringe of snow lay like a cape on the shoulders of his overcoat and like toecaps on the toes of his goloshes; and, as the buttons of his overcoat slipped with a squeaking noise through the snow-stiffened frieze, a cold fragrant air from out-of-doors escaped from crevices and folds.

—Is it snowing again, Mr Conroy? asked Lily.

She had preceded him into the pantry to help him off with his overcoat. Gabriel smiled at the three syllables she had given his surname and glanced at her. She was a slim, growing girl, pale in complexion and with hay-coloured hair. The gas in the pantry made her look still paler. Gabriel had known her when she was a child and used to sit on the lowest step nursing a rag doll.

—Yes, Lily, he answered, and I think we're in for a night of it.

He looked up at the pantry ceiling, which was shaking with the stamping and shuffling of feet on the floor above, listened for a moment to the piano and then glanced at the girl, who was folding his overcoat carefully at the end of a shelf.

—Tell me, Lily, he said in a friendly tone, do you still go to school?

—O no, sir, she answered. I'm done schooling this year and more.

—O, then, said Gabriel gaily, I suppose we'll be going to your wedding one of these fine days with your young man, eh?

The girl glanced back at him over her shoulder and said with great bitterness:

—The men that is now is only all palaver and what they can get out of you.

Gabriel coloured as if he felt he had made a mistake and, without looking at her, kicked off his goloshes and flicked actively with his muffler at his patent-leather shoes.

He was a stout tallish young man. The high colour of his cheeks pushed upwards even to his forehead where it scattered itself in a few formless patches of pale red; and on his hairless face there scintillated restlessly the polished lenses and the bright gilt rims of the glasses which screened his delicate and restless eyes. His glossy black hair was parted in the middle and brushed in a long curve behind his ears where it curled slightly beneath the groove left by his hat.

When he had flicked lustre into his shoes he stood up and pulled his waistcoat down more tightly on his plump body. Then he took a coin rapidly from his pocket.

—O Lily, he said, thrusting it into her hands, it's Christmas-time, isn't it? Just . . . here's a little. . . .

He walked rapidly towards the door.

—O no, sir! cried the girl, following him. Really, sir, I wouldn't take it.

—Christmas-time! Christmas-time! said Gabriel, almost trotting to the stairs and waving his hand to her in deprecation.

The girl, seeing that he had gained the stairs, called out after him:

—Well, thank you, sir.

He waited outside the drawing-room door until the waltz should finish, listening to the skirts that swept against it and to the shuffling of feet. He was still discomposed by the girl's bitter and sudden retort. It had cast a gloom over him which he tried to dispel by arranging his cuffs and the bows of his tie. Then he took from his waistcoat pocket a little paper and glanced at the headings he had made for his speech. He was undecided about the lines from Robert Browning for he feared they would be above the heads of his hearers. Some quotation that they could recognize from Shakespeare or from the Melodies would be better. The indelicate clacking of the men's heels and the shuffling of their soles reminded him that their grade of culture differed from his. He would only make himself ridiculous by quoting poetry to them which they could not understand. They would think that he was airing his superior education. He would fail with them just as he had failed with the girl in the pantry. He had taken up a wrong tone. His whole speech was a mistake from first to last, an utter failure.

Just then his aunts and his wife came out of the ladies' dressing-room. His aunts were two small plainly dressed old women. Aunt Julia was an inch or so the taller. Her hair, drawn low over the tops of her ears, was grey; and grey also, with darker shadows, was her large flaccid face. Though she was stout in build and stood erect her slow eyes and parted lips gave her the appearance of a woman who did not know where she was or where she was going. Aunt Kate was more vivacious. Her face, healthier than her sister's, was all puckers and creases, like a shrivelled red apple, and her hair, braided in the same old-fashioned way, had not lost its ripe nut colour.

The both kissed Gabriel frankly. He was their favourite nephew, the son of their dead elder sister, Ellen, who had married T. J. Conroy of the Port and Docks.

—Gretta tells me you're not going to take a cab back to Monkstown to-night, Gabriel, said Aunt Kate.

—No, said Gabriel, turning to his wife, we had quite enough of that last year, hadn't we. Don't you remember, Aunt Kate, what a cold Gretta got out of it? Cab windows rattling all the way, and the east wind blowing in after we passed Merion. Very jolly it was. Gretta caught a dreadful cold.

Aunt Kate frowned severely and nodded her head at every word.

—Quite right, Gabriel, quite right, she said. You can't be too careful.

—But as for Gretta there, said Gabriel, she'd walk home in the snow if she were let.

Mrs Conroy laughed.

—Don't mind him, Aunt Kate, she said. He's really an awful bother, what with green shades for Tom's eyes at night and making him do the dumb-bells, and forcing Eva to eat the stirabout. The poor child! And she simply hates the sight of it! . . . O, but you'll never guess what he makes me wear now!

She broke out into a peal of laughter and glanced at her husband, whose admiring and happy eyes had been wandering from her dress to her face and hair. The two aunts laughed heartily too, for Gabriel's solicitude was a standing joke with them.

—Goloshes! said Mrs Conroy. That's the latest. Whenever it's wet underfoot I must put on my goloshes. To-night even he wanted me to put them on, but I wouldn't. The next thing he'll buy me will be a diving suit.

Gabriel laughed nervously and patted his tie reassuringly while Aunt Kate nearly doubled herself, so heartily did she enjoy the joke. The smile soon faded from Aunt Julia's face and her mirthless eyes were directed towards her nephew's face. After a pause she asked:

—And what are goloshes, Gabriel?

—Goloshes, Julia! exclaimed her sister. Goodness me, don't you know what goloshes are? You wear them over your . . . over your boots, Gretta, isn't it?

—Yes, said Mrs Conroy. Guttapercha things. We both have a pair now. Gabriel says everyone wears them on the continent.

—O, on the continent, murmured Aunt Julia, nodding her head slowly.

Gabriel knitted his brows and said, as if he were slightly angered:

—It's nothing very wonderful but Gretta thinks it very funny because she says the word reminds her of Christy Minstrels.

—But tell me, Gabriel, said Aunt Kate, with brisk tact. Of course, you've seen about the room. Gretta was saying . . .

—O, the room is all right, replied Gabriel. I've taken one in the Gresham.

—To be sure, said Aunt Kate, by far the best thing to do. And the children, Gretta, you're not anxious about them?

—O, for one night, said Mrs Conroy. Besides, Bessie will look after them.

—To be sure, said Aunt Kate again. What a comfort it is to have a girl like that, one you can depend on! There's that Lily, I'm sure I don't know what has come over her lately. She's not the girl she was at all.

Gabriel was about to ask his aunt some questions on this point but she broke off suddenly to gaze after her sister who had wandered down the stairs and was craning her neck over the banisters.

–Now, I ask you, she said, almost testily, where is Julia going? Julia! Julia! Where are you going?

Julia, who had gone halfway down one flight, came back and announced blandly:

–Here's Freddy.

At the same moment a clapping of hands and a final flourish of the pianist told that the waltz had ended. The drawing-room door was open from within and some couples came out. Aunt Kate drew Gabriel aside hurriedly and whispered into his ear:

–Slip down, Gabriel, like a good fellow and see if he's all right, and don't let him up if he's screwed. I'm sure he's screwed. I'm sure he is.

Gabriel went to the stairs and listened over the banisters. He could hear two persons talking in the pantry. Then he recognized Freddy Malins' laugh. He went down the stairs noisily.

–It's such a relief, said Aunt Kate to Mrs Conroy, that Gabriel is here. I always feel easier in my mind when he's here. . . . Julia, there's Miss Daly and Miss Power will take some refreshment. Thanks for your beautiful waltz, Miss Daly. It made lovely time.

A tall wizen-faced man, with a stiff grizzled moustache and swarthy skin, who was passing out with his partner said:

–And may we have some refreshment, too, Miss Morkan?

–Julia, said Aunt Kate summarily, and here's Mr Browne and Miss Furlong. Take them in, Julia, with Miss Daly and Miss Power.

–I'm the man for the ladies, said Mr Browne, pursing his lips until his moustache bristled and smiling in all his wrinkles. You know, Miss Morkan, the reason they are so fond of me is –

He did not finish his sentence, but, seeing that Aunt Kate was out of earshot, at once led the three young ladies into the back room. The middle of the room was occupied by two square tables placed end to end, and on these Aunt Julia and the caretaker were straightening and smoothing a large cloth. On the sideboard were arrayed dishes and plates, and glasses and bundles of knives and forks and spoons. The top of the closed square piano served also as a sideboard for viands and sweets. At a smaller sideboard in one corner two young men were standing, drinking hop-bitters.

Mr Browne led his charges thither and invited them all, in jest, to some ladies' punch, hot, strong and sweet. As they said they never took anything strong he opened three bottles of lemonade for them. Then he asked one of the young men to move aside, and, taking hold of the decanter, filled out for himself a goodly measure of whisky. The young men eyed him respectfully while he took a trial sip.

—God help me, he said, smiling, it's the doctor's orders.

His wizened face broke into a broader smile, and the three young ladies laughed in musical echo to his pleasantry, swaying their bodies to and fro, with nervous jerks of their shoulders. The boldest said:

—O, now, Mr Browne, I'm sure the doctor never ordered anything of the kind.

Mr Browne took another sip of his whisky and said, with sidling mimicry:

—Well, you see, I'm like the famous Mrs Cassidy, who is reported to have said: *Now, Mary Grimes, if I don't take it, make me take it, for I feel I want it.*

His hot face had leaned forward a little too confidentially and he had assumed a very low Dublin accent so that the young ladies, with one instinct, received his speech in silence. Miss Furlong, who was one of Mary Jane's pupils, asked Miss Daly what was the name of the pretty waltz she had played; and Mr Browne, seeing that he was ignored, turned promptly to the two young men who were more appreciative.

A red-faced young woman, dressed in pansy, came into the room, excitedly clapping her hands and crying:

—Quadrilles! Quadrilles!

Close on her heels came Aunt Kate, crying:

—Two gentlemen and three ladies, Mary Jane!

—O, here's Mr Bergin and Mr Kerrigan, said Mary Jane. Mr Kerrigan, will you take Miss Power? Miss Furlong, may I get you a partner, Mr Bergin. O, that'll just do now.

—Three ladies, Mary Jane, said Aunt Kate.

The two young gentlemen asked the ladies if they might have the pleasure, and Mary Jane turned to Miss Daly.

—O, Miss Daly, you're really awfully good, after playing for the last two dances, but really we're so short of ladies to-night.

—I don't mind in the least, Miss Morkan.

—But I've a nice partner for you, Mr Bartell D'Arcy, the tenor. I'll get him to sing later on. All Dublin is raving about him.

—Lovely voice, lovely voice! said Aunt Kate.

As the piano had twice begun the prelude to the first figure Mary Jane led her recruits quickly from the room. They had hardly gone when Aunt Julia wandered slowly into the room, looking behind her at something.

—What is the matter, Julia? asked Aunt Kate anxiously. Who is it?

Julia, who was carrying in a column of table-napkins, turned to her sister and said, simply, as if the question had surprised her:

—It's only Freddy, Kate, and Gabriel with him.

In fact right behind her Gabriel could be seen piloting Freddy Malins across the landing. The latter, a young man of about forty, was of Gabriel's size and build, with very round shoulders. His face was fleshy and pallid, touched with colour only at the thick hanging lobes of his ears and at the wide wings of his nose. He had coarse features, a blunt nose, a convex and receding brow, tumid and protruded lips. His heavy-lidded eyes and the disorder of his scanty hair made him look sleepy. He was laughing heartily in a high key at a story which he had been telling Gabriel on the stairs and at the same time rubbing the knuckles of his left fist backwards and forwards into his left eye.

—Good-evening, Freddy, said Aunt Julia.

Freddy Malins bade the Misses Morkan good-evening in what seemed an offhand fashion by reason of the habitual catch in his voice and then, seeing that Mr Browne was grinning at him from the sideboard, crossed the room on rather shaky legs and began to repeat in an undertone the story he had just told to Gabriel.

—He's not so bad, is he? said Aunt Kate to Gabriel.

Gabriel's brows were dark but he raised them quickly and answered:

—O no, hardly noticeable.

—Now, isn't he a terrible fellow! she said. And his poor mother made him take the pledge on New Year's Eve. But come on, Gabriel, into the drawing-room.

Before leaving the room with Gabriel she signalled to Mr Browne by frowning and shaking her forefinger in warning to and fro. Mr Browne nodded in answer and, when she had gone, said to Freddy Malins:

—Now, then, Teddy, I'm going to fill you out a good glass of lemonade just to buck you up.

Freddy Malins, who was nearing the climax of his story, waved the offer aside impatiently but Mr Browne, having first called Freddy Malins' attention to a disarray in his dress, filled out and handed him a full glass of lemonade. Freddy Malins' left hand accepted the glass mechanically, his right hand being engaged in the mechanical readjustment of his dress. Mr Browne, whose face was once more wrinkling with mirth, poured out for himself a glass of whisky while Freddy Malins exploded, before he had well reached the climax of his story, in a kink of high-pitched bronchitic laughter and, setting down his untasted and overflowing glass, began to rub the knuckles of his left fist backwards and forwards into his left eye, repeating words of his phrase as well as his fit of laughter would allow him.

• • •

Gabriel could not listen while Mary Jane was playing her Academy piece, full of runs and difficult passages, to the hushed drawing-room. He liked music but the piece she was playing had no melody for him and he doubted whether it had any melody for the other listeners, though they had begged Mary Jane to play something. Four young men, who had come from the refreshment-room to stand in the doorway at the sound of the piano, had gone away quietly in couples after a few minutes. The only persons who seemed to follow the music were Mary Jane herself, her hands racing along the key-board or lifted from it at the pauses like those of a priestess in momentary imprecation, and Aunt Kate standing at her elbow to turn the page.

Gabriel's eyes, irritated by the floor, which glittered with beeswax under the heavy chandelier, wandered to the wall above the piano. A picture of the balcony scene in *Romeo and Juliet* hung there and beside it was a picture of the two murdered princes in the Tower which Aunt Julia had worked in red, blue and brown wools when she was a girl. Probably in the school they had gone to as girls that kind of work had been taught, for one year his mother had worked for him as a birthday present a waistcoat of purple tabinet, with little foxes' heads upon it, lined with brown satin and having round mulberry buttons. It was strange that his mother had had no musical talent though Aunt Kate used to call her the brains carrier of the Morkan family. Both she and Julia had always seemed a little proud of their serious and matronly sister. Her photograph stood before the pierglass. She held an open book on her knees and was pointing out something in it to Constantine who, dressed in a man-o'-war suit, lay at her feet. It was she who had chosen the names for her sons for she was very sensible of the dignity of family life. Thanks to her, Constantine was now senior curate in Balbriggan and, thanks to her, Gabriel himself had taken his degree in the Royal University. A shadow passed over his face as he remembered her sullen opposition to his marriage. Some slighting phrases she had used still rankled in his memory; she had once spoken of Gretta as being country cute and that was not true of Gretta at all. It was Gretta who had nursed her during all her last long illness in their house at Monkstown.

He knew that Mary Jane must be near the end of her piece for she was playing again the opening melody with runs of scales after every bar and while he waited for the end the resentment died down in his heart. The piece ended with a trill of octaves in treble and a final deep octave in the bass. Great applause greeted Mary Jane as, blushing and rolling up her music nervously, she escaped from the room. The most vigorous clapping came from the four young men in the doorway who had gone away to the refreshment-room at the beginning of the piece but had come back when the piano had stopped.

Lancers were arranged. Gabriel found himself partnered with Miss Ivors. She was a frank-mannered talkative young lady, with a freckled face and prominent brown eyes. She did not wear a low-cut bodice and the large brooch which was fixed in the front of her collar bore on it an Irish device.

When they had taken their places she said abruptly:

—I have a crow to pluck with you.

—With me? said Gabriel.

She nodded her head gravely.

—What is it? asked Gabriel, smiling at her solemn manner.

—Who is G. C.? answered Miss Ivors, turning her eyes upon him.

Gabriel coloured and was about to knit his brows, as if he did not understand, when she said bluntly:

–O, innocent Amy! I have found out that you write for *The Daily Express*. Now, aren't you ashamed of yourself?

–Why should I be ashamed of myself? asked Gabriel, blinking his eyes and trying to smile.

–Well, I'm ashamed of you, said Miss Ivors frankly. To say you'd write for a rag like that. I didn't think you were a West Briton.

A look of perplexity appeared on Gabriel's face. It was true that he wrote a literary column every Wednesday in *The Daily Express*, for which he was paid fifteen shillings. But that did not make him a West Briton surely. The books he received for review were almost more welcome than the paltry cheque. He loved to feel the covers and turn over the pages of newly printed books. Nearly every day when his teaching in the college was ended he used to wander down the quays to the second-hand booksellers, to Hickey's on Bachelor's Walk, to Webbs' or Massey's on Aston's Quay, or to O'Clohissey's in the by-street. He did not know how to meet her charge. He wanted to say that literature was above politics. But they were friends of many years' standing and their careers had been parallel, first at the University and then as teachers: he could not risk a grandiose phrase with her. He continued blinking his eyes and trying to smile and murmured lamely that he saw nothing political in writing reviews of books.

When their turn to cross had come he was still perplexed and inattentive. Miss Ivors promptly took his hand in a warm grasp and said in a soft friendly tone:

–Of course, I was only joking. Come, we cross now.

When they were together again she spoke of the University question and Gabriel felt more at ease. A friend of hers had shown her his review of Browning's poems. That was how she had found out the secret: but she liked the review immensely. Then she said suddenly:

–O, Mr Conroy, will you come for an excursion to the Aran Isles this summer? We're going to stay there a whole month. It will be splendid out in the Atlantic. You ought to come. Mr Clancy is coming, and Mr Kilkelly and Kathleen Kearney. It would be splendid for Gretta too if she'd come. She's from Connacht, isn't she?

–Her people are, said Gabriel shortly.

–But you will come, won't you? said Miss Ivors, laying her warm hand eagerly on his arm.

–The fact is, said Gabriel, I have already arranged to go –

–Go where? asked Miss Ivors.

–Well, you know, every year I go for a cycling tour with some fellows and so –

–But where? asked Miss Ivors.

—Well, we usually go to France or Belgium or perhaps Germany, said Gabriel awkwardly.

—And why do you go to France or Belgium, said Miss Ivors, instead of visiting your own land?

—Well, said Gabriel, it's partly to keep in touch with the languages and partly for a change.

—And haven't you your own language to keep in touch with – Irish? asked Miss Ivors.

—Well, said Gabriel, if it comes to that, you know, Irish is not my language.

Their neighbours had turned to listen to the cross-examination. Gabriel glanced right and left nervously and tried to keep his good humour under the ordeal which was making a blush invade his forehead.

—And haven't you your own land to visit, continued Miss Ivors, that you know nothing of, your own people, and your own country?

—O, to tell you the truth, retorted Gabriel suddenly, I'm sick of my own country, sick of it!

—Why? asked Miss Ivors.

Gabriel did not answer for his retort had heated him.

—Why? repeated Miss Ivors.

They had to go visiting together and, as he had not answered her, Miss Ivors said warmly:

—Of course, you've no answer.

Gabriel tried to cover his agitation by taking part in the dance with great energy. He avoided her eyes for he had seen a sour expression on her face. But when they met in the long chain he was surprised to feel his hand firmly pressed. She looked at him from under her brows for a moment quizzically until he smiled. Then, just as the chain was about to start again, she stood on tiptoe and whispered into his ear:

—West Briton!

When the lancers were over Gabriel went away to a remote corner of the room where Freddy Malins' mother was sitting. She was a stout feeble old woman with white hair. Her voice had a catch in it like her son's and she stuttered slightly. She had been told that Freddy had come and that he was nearly all right. Gabriel asked her whether she had had a good crossing. She lived with her married daughter in Glasgow and came to Dublin on a visit once a year. She answered placidly that she had had a beautiful crossing and that the captain had been most attentive to her. She spoke also of the beautiful house her daughter kept in Glasgow, and of all the nice friends they had there. While her tongue rambled on Gabriel tried to banish from his mind all memory of the unpleasant incident with Miss Ivors. Of course the girl or woman, or whatever she was, was an enthusiast but there was a time for all things. Perhaps he ought not to have answered her like that.

But she had no right to call him a West Briton before people, even in joke. She had tried to make him ridiculous before people, heckling him and staring at him with her rabbit's eyes.

He saw his wife making her way towards him through the waltzing couples. When she reached him she said into his ear:

–Gabriel, Aunt Kate wants to know won't you carve the goose as usual. Miss Daly will carve the ham and I'll do the pudding.

–All right, said Gabriel.

–She's sending in the younger ones first as soon as this waltz is over so that we'll have the table to ourselves.

–Were you dancing? asked Gabriel.

–Of course I was. Didn't you see me? What words had you with Molly Ivors?

–No words. Why? Did she say so?

–Something like that. I'm trying to get that Mr D'Arcy to sing. He's full of conceit, I think.

–There were no words, said Gabriel moodily, only she wanted me to go for a trip to the west of Ireland and I said I wouldn't.

His wife clasped her hands excitedly and gave a little jump.

–O, do go, Gabriel, she cried. I'd love to see Galway again.

–You can go if you like, said Gabriel coldly.

She looked at him for a moment, then turned to Mrs Malins and said:

–There's a nice husband for you, Mrs Malins.

While she was threading her way back across the room Mrs Malins, without adverting to the interruption, went on to tell Gabriel what beautiful places there were in Scotland and beautiful scenery. Her son-in-law brought them every year to the lakes and they used to go fishing. Her son-in-law was a splendid fisher. One day he caught a fish, a beautiful big big fish, and the man in the hotel boiled it for their dinner.

Gabriel hardly heard what she said. Now that supper was coming near he began to think again about his speech and about the quotation. When he saw Freddy Malins coming across the room to visit his mother Gabriel left the chair free for him and retired into the embrasure of the window. The room had already cleared and from the back room came the clatter of plates and knives. Those who still remained in the drawing-room seemed tired of dancing and were conversing quietly in little groups. Gabriel's warm trembling fingers tapped the cold pane of the window. How cool it must be outside! How pleasant it would be to walk out alone, first along by the river and then through the park! The snow would be lying on the branches of the trees and forming a bright cap on the top of the Wellington Monument. How much more pleasant it would be there than at the supper-table!

He ran over the headings of his speech: Irish hospitality, sad memories, the

Three Graces, Paris, the quotation from Browning. He repeated to himself a phrase he had written in his review: *One feels that one is listening to a thought-tormented music.* Miss Ivors had praised the review. Was she sincere? Had she really any life of her own behind all her propagandism? There had never been ill-feeling between them until that night. It unnerved him to think that she would be at the supper-table; looking up at him while he spoke with her critical quizzing eyes. Perhaps she would not be sorry to see him fail in his speech. An idea came into his mind and gave him courage. He would say, alluding to Aunt Kate and Aunt Julia: *Ladies and Gentlemen, the generation which is now on the wane among us may have had its faults but for my part I think it had certain qualities of hospitality, of humour, of humanity, which the new and very serious and hypereducated generation that is growing up around us seems to me to lack.* Very good: that was one for Miss Ivors. What did he care that his aunts were only two ignorant old women?

A murmur in the room attracted his attention. Mr Browne was advancing from the door, gallantly escorting Aunt Julia, who leaned upon his arm, smiling and hanging her head. An irregular musketry of applause escorted her also as far as the piano and then, as Mary Jane seated herself on the stool, and Aunt Julia, no longer smiling, half turned so as to pitch her voice fairly into the room, gradually ceased. Gabriel recognized the prelude. It was that of an old song of Aunt Julia's — *Arrayed for the Bridal.* Her voice, strong and clear in tone, attacked with great spirit the runs which embellish the air and though she sang very rapidly she did not miss even the smallest of the grace notes. To follow the voice, without looking at the singer's face, was to feel and share the excitement of swift and secure flight. Gabriel applauded loudly with all the others at the close of the song and loud applause was borne in from the invisible supper-table. It sounded so genuine that a little colour struggled into Aunt Julia's face as she bent to replace in the music-stand the old leather-bound song-book that had her initials on the cover. Freddy Malins, who had listened with his head perched sideways to hear her better, was still applauding when every one else had ceased and talking animatedly to his mother who nodded her head gravely and slowly in acquiescence. At last, when he could clap no more, he stood up suddenly and hurried across the room to Aunt Julia whose hand he seized and held in both his hands, shaking it when words failed him or the catch in his voice proved too much for him.

—I was just telling my mother, he said, I never heard you sing so well, never. No, I never heard your voice so good as it is to-night. Now! Would you believe that now? That's the truth. Upon my word and honour that's the truth. I never heard your voice sound so fresh and so . . . so clear and fresh, never.

Aunt Julia smiled broadly and murmured something about compliments as she released her hand from his grasp. Mr Browne extended his open hand towards her and said to those who were near him in the manner of a showman introducing a prodigy to an audience:

—Miss Julia Morkan, my latest discovery!

He was laughing very heartily at this himself when Freddy Malins turned to him and said:

—Well, Browne, if you're serious you might make a worse discovery. All I can say is I never heard her sing half so well as long as I am coming here. And that's the honest truth.

—Neither did I, said Mr Browne. I think her voice has greatly improved.

Aunt Julia shrugged her shoulders and said with meek pride:

—Thirty years ago I hadn't a bad voice as voices go.

—I often told Julia, said Aunt Kate emphatically, that she was simply thrown away in that choir. But she never would be said by me.

She turned as if to appeal to the good sense of the others against a refractory child while Aunt Julia gazed in front of her, a vague smile or reminiscence playing on her face.

—No, continued Aunt Kate, she wouldn't be said or led by anyone, slaving there in that choir night and day, night and day. Six o'clock on Christmas morning! And all for what?

—Well, isn't it for the honour of God, Aunt Kate? asked Mary Jane, twisting round on the piano-stool and smiling.

Aunt Kate turned fiercely on her niece and said:

—I know all about the honour of God, Mary Jane, but I think it's not at all honourable for the pope to turn out the women out of the choirs that have slaved there all their lives and put little whipper-snappers of boys over their heads. I suppose it is for the good of the Church if the pope does it. But it's not just, Mary Jane, and it's not right.

She had worked herself into a passion and would have continued in defence of her sister for it was a sore subject with her but Mary Jane, seeing that all the dancers had come back, intervened pacifically:

—Now, Aunt Kate, you're giving scandal to Mr Browne who is of the other persuasion.

Aunt Kate turned to Mr Browne, who was grinning at this allusion to his religion, and said hastily:

—O, I don't question the pope's being right. I'm only a stupid old woman and I wouldn't presume to do such a thing. But there's such a thing as common everyday politeness and gratitude. And if I were in Julia's place I'd tell that Father Healy straight up to his face . . .

—And besides, Aunt Kate, said Mary Jane, we really are all hungry and when we are hungry we are all very quarrelsome.

—And when we are thirsty we are also quarrelsome, added Mr. Browne.

—So that we had better go to supper, said Mary Jane, and finish the discussion afterwards.

On the landing outside the drawing-room Gabriel found his wife and Mary

Jane trying to persuade Miss Ivors to stay for supper. But Miss Ivors, who had put on her hat and was buttoning her cloak, would not stay. She did not feel in the least hungry and she had already overstayed her time.

–But only for ten minutes, Molly, said Mrs Conroy. That won't delay you.

–To take a pick itself, said Mary Jane, after all your dancing.

–I really couldn't, said Miss Ivors.

–I am afraid you didn't enjoy yourself at all, said Mary Jane hopelessly.

–Ever so much, I assure you, said Miss Ivors, but you really must let me run off now.

–But how can you get home? asked Mrs Conroy.

–O, it's only two steps up the quay.

Gabriel hesitated a moment and said:

–If you will allow me, Miss Ivors, I'll see you home if you really are obliged to go.

But Miss Ivors broke away from them.

–I won't hear of it, she cried. For goodness sake go in to your suppers and don't mind me. I'm quite well able to take care of myself.

–Well, you're the comical girl, Molly, said Mrs Conroy frankly.

–*Beannacht libh,* cried Miss Ivors, with a laugh, as she ran down the staircase.

Mary Jane gazed after her, a moody puzzled expression on her face, while Mrs Conroy leaned over the banisters to listen for the hall-door. Gabriel asked himself was he the cause of her abrupt departure. But she did not seem to be in ill humour: she had gone away laughing. He stared blankly down the staircase.

At that moment Aunt Kate came toddling out of the supper-room, almost wringing her hands in despair.

–Where is Gabriel? she cried. Where on earth is Gabriel? There's everyone waiting in there, stage to let, and nobody to carve the goose!

–Here I am, Aunt Kate! cried Gabriel, with sudden animation, ready to carve a flock of geese, if necessary.

A fat brown goose lay at one end of the table and at the other end, on a bed of creased paper strewn with sprigs of parsley, lay a great ham, stripped of its outer skin and peppered over with crust crumbs, a neat paper frill round its shin and beside this was a round of spiced beef. Between these rival ends ran parallel lines of side-dishes: two little minsters of jelly, red and yellow; a shallow dish full of blocks of blancmange and red jam, a large green leaf-shaped dish with a stalk-shaped handle, on which lay bunches of purple raisins and peeled almonds, a companion dish on which lay a solid rectangle of Smyrna figs, a dish of custard topped with grated nutmeg, a small bowl full of chocolates and sweets wrapped in gold and silver papers and a glass vase in which stood some tall celery stalks. In the centre of the table there stood, as sentries to a fruit-stand which upheld a pyramid of oranges and American apples, two squat old-fashioned decanters of cut glass, one containing port and the other dark sherry. On the closed square piano a pudding in a huge yellow dish lay in waiting and behind it were three squads of bottles of stout and ale and minerals, drawn up according to the colours of their uniforms, the first two black, with brown and red labels, the third and smallest squad white, with transverse green sashes.

Gabriel took his seat boldly at the head of the table and, having looked to the edge of the carver, plunged his fork firmly into the goose. He felt quite at ease now for he was an expert carver and liked nothing better than to find himself at the head of a well-laden table.

–Miss Furlong, what shall I send you? he asked. A wing or a slice of the breast?

–Just a small slice of the breast.

–Miss Higgins, what for you?

–O, anything at all, Mr Conroy.

While Gabriel and Miss Daly exchanged plates of goose and plates of ham and spiced beef Lily went from guest to guest with a dish of hot floury potatoes wrapped in a white napkin. This was Mary Jane's idea and she had also suggested apple sauce for the goose but Aunt Kate had said that plain roast goose without apple sauce had always been good enough for her and she hoped she might never eat worse. Mary Jane waited on her pupils and saw that they got the best slices and Aunt Kate and Aunt Julia opened and carried across from the piano bottles of stout and ale for the gentlemen and bottles of minerals for the ladies. There was a great deal of confusion and laughter and noise, the noise of orders and counter-orders, of knives and forks, of corks and glass-stoppers. Gabriel began to carve second helpings as soon as he had finished the first round without serving himself. Everyone protested loudly so that he compromised by taking a long draught of stout for he had found the carving hot work. Mary Jane settled down quietly to her supper but Aunt Kate and Aunt Julia were still toddling round the table, walking on each other's heels, getting in each other's way and giving each other unheeded orders. Mr Browne begged of them to sit down and eat their suppers and so did Gabriel but they said there was time enough so that, at last, Freddy Malins stood up and, capturing Aunt Kate, plumped her down on her chair amid general laughter.

When everyone had been well served Gabriel said, smiling:

–Now, if anyone wants a little more of what vulgar people call stuffing let him or her speak.

A chorus of voices invited him to begin his own supper and Lily came forward with three potatoes which she had reserved for him.

–Very well, said Gabriel amiably, as he took another preparatory draught, kindly forget my existence, ladies and gentlemen, for a few minutes.

He set to his supper and took no part in the conversation with which the table covered Lily's removal of the plates. The subject of talk was the opera company which was then at the Theatre Royal. Mr Bartell D'Arcy, the tenor, a dark-complexioned young man with a smart moustache, praised very highly the leading contralto of the company but Miss Furlong thought she had a rather vulgar style of production. Freddy Malins said there was a negro chieftain singing in the second part of the Gaiety pantomime who had one of the finest tenor voices he had ever heard.

–Have you heard him? he asked Mr Bartell D'Arcy across the table.

–No, answered Mr Bartell D'Arcy carelessly.

–Because, Freddy Malins explained, now I'd be curious to hear your opinion of him. I think he has a grand voice.

–It takes Teddy to find out the really good things, said Mr Browne familiarly to the table.

–And why couldn't he have a voice too? asked Freddy Malins sharply. Is it because he's only a black?

Nobody answered this question and Mary Jane led the table back to the legitimate opera. One of her pupils had given her a pass for *Mignon.* Of course it was very fine, she said, but it made her think of poor Georgina Burns. Mr Browne could go back farther still, to the old Italian companies that used to come to Dublin – Tietjens, Ilma de Murzka, Campanini, the great Trebelli, Giuglini, Ravelli, Aramburo. Those were the days, he said, when there was something like singing to be heard in Dublin. He told too of how the top gallery of the old Royal used to be packed night after night, of how one night an Italian tenor had sung five encores to *Let Me Like a Soldier Fall,* introducing a high C every time, and of how the gallery boys would sometimes in their enthusiasm unyoke the horses from the carriage of some great *prima donna* and pull her themselves through the streets to her hotel. Why did they never play the grand old operas now, he asked, *Dinorah, Lucrezia Borgia?* Because they could not get the voices to sing them: that was why.

–O, well, said Mr Bartell D'Arcy, I presume there are as good singers to-day as there were then.

–Where are they? asked Mr Browne defiantly.

–In London, Paris, Milan, said Mr Bartell D'Arcy warmly. I suppose Caruso, for example, is quite good, if not better than any of the men you have mentioned.

–Maybe so, said Mr Browne. But I may tell you I doubt it strongly.

–O, I'd give anything to hear Caruso sing, said Mary Jane.

–For me, said Aunt Kate, who had been picking a bone, there was only one tenor. To please me, I mean. But I suppose none of you ever heard of him.

–Who was he, Miss Morkan? asked Mr Bartell D'Arcy politely.

–His name, said Aunt Kate, was Parkinson. I heard him when he was in his prime and I think he had then the purest tenor voice that was ever put into a man's throat.

–Strange, said Mr Bartell D'Arcy. I never even heard of him.

—Yes, yes, Miss Morkan is right, said Mr Browne. I remember hearing of old Parkinson but he's too far back for me.

—A beautiful pure sweet mellow English tenor, said Aunt Kate with enthusiasm.

Gabriel having finished, the huge pudding was transferred to the table. The clatter of forks and spoons began again. Gabriel's wife served out spoonfuls of the pudding and passed the plates down the table. Midway down they were held up by Mary Jane, who replenished them with raspberry or orange jelly or with blancmange and jam. The pudding was of Aunt Julia's making and she received praises for it from all quarters. She herself said that it was not quite brown enough.

—Well, I hope, Miss Morkan, said Mr Browne, that I'm brown enough for you because, you know, I'm all brown.

All the gentlemen, except Gabriel, ate some of the pudding out of compliment to Aunt Julia. As Gabriel never ate sweets the celery had been left for him. Freddy Malins also took a stalk of celery and ate it with his pudding. He had been told that celery was a capital thing for the blood and he was just then under doctor's care. Mrs Malins, who had been silent all through the supper, said that her son was going down to Mount Melleray in a week or so. The table then spoke of Mount Melleray, how bracing the air was down there, how hospitable the monks were and how they never asked for a penny-piece from their guests.

—And do you mean to say, asked Mr Browne incredulously, that a chap can go down there and put up there as if it were a hotel and live on the fat of the land and then come away without paying a farthing?

—O, most people give some donation to the monastery when they leave, said Mary Jane.

—I wish we had an institution like that in our Church, said Mr Browne candidly.

He was astonished to hear that the monks never spoke, got up at two in the morning and slept in their coffins. He asked what they did it for.

—That's the rule of the order, said Aunt Kate firmly.

—Yes, but why? asked Mr Browne.

Aunt Kate repeated that it was the rule, that was all. Mr Browne still seemed not to understand. Freddy Malins explained to him, as best he could, that the monks were trying to make up for the sins committed by all the sinners in the outside world. The explanation was not very clear for Mr Browne grinned and said:

—I like that idea very much but wouldn't a comfortable spring bed do them as well as a coffin?

—The coffin, said Mary Jane, is to remind them of their last end.

As the subject had grown lugubrious it was buried in a silence of the table during which Mrs Malins could be heard saying to her neighbour in an indistinct undertone:

—They are very good men, the monks, very pious men.

The raisins and almonds and figs and apples and oranges and chocolates and sweets were now passed about the table and Aunt Julia invited all the guests to have either port or sherry. At first Mr Bartell D'Arcy refused to take either but one of his neighbours nudged him and whispered something to him upon which he allowed his glass to be filled. Gradually as the last glasses were being filled the conversation ceased. A pause followed, broken only by the noise of the wine and by unsettlings of chairs. The Misses Morkan, all three, looked down at the tablecloth. Some one coughed once or twice and then a few gentlemen patted the table gently as a signal for silence. The silence came and Gabriel pushed back his chair and stood up.

The patting at once grew louder in encouragement and then ceased altogether. Gabriel leaned his ten trembling fingers on the tablecloth and smiled nervously at the company. Meeting a row of upturned faces he raised his eyes to the chandelier. The piano was playing a waltz tune and he could hear the skirts sweeping against the drawing-room door. People, perhaps, were standing in the snow on the quay outside, gazing up at the lighted windows and listening to the waltz music. The air was pure there. In the distance lay the park where the trees were weighted with snow. The Wellington Monument wore a gleaming cap of snow that flashed westward over the white field of Fifteen Acres.

He began:

–Ladies and Gentlemen.

–It has fallen to my lot this evening, as in years past, to perform a very pleasing task but a task for which I am afraid my poor powers as a speaker are all too inadequate.

–No, no! said Mr Browne.

–But, however that may be, I can only ask you to-night to take the will for the deed and to lend me your attention for a few moments while I endeavour to express to you in words what my feelings are on this occasion.

–Ladies and Gentlemen. It is not the first time that we have gathered together under this hospitable roof, around this hospitable board. It is not the first time that we have been the recipients – or perhaps, I had better say, the victims – of the hospitality of certain good ladies.

He made a circle in the air with his arm and paused. Every one laughed or smiled at Aunt Kate and Aunt Julia and Mary Jane who all turned crimson with pleasure. Gabriel went on more boldly:

–I feel more strongly with every recurring year that our country has no tradition which does it so much honour and which it should guard so jealously as that of its hospitality. It is a tradition that is unique as far as my experience goes (and I have visited not a few places abroad) among the modern nations. Some would say, perhaps, that with us it is rather a failing than anything to be boasted of. But granted even that, it is, to my mind, a princely failing, and one that I trust will long be cultivated among us. Of one thing, at least, I am sure. As long as this one roof shelters the good ladies aforesaid – and I wish from my heart it may do so for many and many a long year to come – the tradition of genuine warm-hearted courteous Irish hospitality, which our forefathers have handed down to us and which we in turn must hand down to our descendants, is still alive among us.

A hearty murmur of assent ran round the table. It shot through Gabriel's mind that Miss Ivors was not there and that she had gone away discourteously: and he said with confidence in himself:

–Ladies and Gentlemen.

–A new generation is growing up in our midst, a generation actuated by new ideas and new principles. It is serious and enthusiastic for these new ideas and its enthusiasm, even when it is misdirected, is, I believe, in the main sincere. But we are living in a sceptical and, if I may use the phrase, a thought-tormented age: and sometimes I fear that this new generation, educated or hypereducated as it is, will lack those qualities of humanity, of hospitality, of kindly humour which belonged to an older day. Listening to-night to the names of all those great singers of the past it seemed to me, I must confess, that we were living in a less spacious age. Those days might, without exaggeration, be called spacious days: and if they are gone beyond recall let us hope, at least, that in gatherings such as this we shall still speak of them with pride and affection, still cherish in our hearts the memory of those dead and gone great ones whose fame the world will not willingly let die.

–Hear, hear! said Mr Browne loudly.

–But yet, continued Gabriel, his voice falling into a softer inflection, there are always in gatherings such as this sadder thoughts that will recur to our minds: thoughts of the past, of youth, of changes, of absent faces that we miss here to-night. Our path through life is strewn with many such sad memories: and were we to brood upon them always we could not find the heart to go on bravely with our work among the living. We have all of us living duties and living affections which claim, and rightly claim, our strenuous endeavours.

–Therefore, I will not linger on the past. I will not let any gloomy moralizing intrude upon us here to-night. Here we are gathered together for a brief moment from the bustle and rush of our everyday routine. We are met here as friends, in the spirit of good-fellowship, as colleagues, also to a certain extent, in the true spirit of *camaraderie,* and as the guests of – what shall I call them? – the Three Graces of the Dublin musical world.

The table burst into applause and laughter at this sally. Aunt Julia vainly asked each of her neighbours in turn to tell her what Gabriel had said.

–He says we are the Three Graces, Aunt Julia, said Mary Jane.

Aunt Julia did not understand but she looked up, smiling, at Gabriel, who continued in the same vein:

–Ladies and Gentlemen.

–I will not attempt to play to-night the part that Paris played on another occasion.

I will not attempt to choose between them. The task would be an invidious one and one beyond my poor powers. For when I view them in turn, whether it be our chief hostess herself, whose good heart, whose too good heart, has become a byword with all who know her, or her sister, who seems to be gifted with perennial youth and whose singing must have been a surprise and a revelation to us all to-night, or, last but not least, when I consider our youngest hostess, talented, cheerful, hard-working and the best of nieces, I confess, Ladies and Gentlemen, that I do not know to which of them I should award the prize.

Gabriel glanced down at his aunts and, seeing the large smile on Aunt Julia's face and the tears which had risen to Aunt Kate's eyes, hastened to his close. He raised his glass of port gallantly, while every member of the company fingered a glass expectantly, and said loudly:

–Let us toast them all three together. Let us drink to their health, wealth, long life, happiness and prosperity and may they long continue to hold the proud and self-won position which they hold in their profession and the position of honour and affection which they hold in our hearts.

All the guests stood up, glass in hand, and, turning towards the three seated ladies, sang in unison, with Mr Browne as leader:

For they are jolly gay fellows,
For they are jolly gay fellows,
Which nobody can deny.

Aunt Kate was making frank use of her handkerchief and even Aunt Julia seemed moved. Freddy Malins beat time with his pudding-fork and the singers turned towards one another, as if in melodious conference, while they sang, with emphasis:

Unless he tells a lie,
Unless he tells a lie.

Then, turning once more towards their hostesses, they sang:

For they are jolly gay fellows,
For they are jolly gay fellows,
For they are jolly gay fellows,
Which nobody can deny.

The acclamation which followed was taken up beyond the door of the supper-room by many of the other guests and renewed time after time, Freddy Malins acting as officer with his fork on high.

. . .

The piercing morning air came into the hall where they were standing so that Aunt Kate said:

–Close the door, somebody. Mrs Malins will get her death of cold.

–Browne is out there, Aunt Kate, said Mary Jane.

–Browne is everywhere, said Aunt Kate, lowering her voice.

Mary Jane laughed at her tone.

–Really, she said archly, he is very attentive.

–He has been laid on here like the gas, said Aunt Kate in the same tone, all during the Christmas.

She laughed herself this time good-humouredly and then added quickly:

–But tell him to come in, Mary Jane, and close the door. I hope to goodness he didn't hear me.

At that moment the hall-door was opened and Mr Browne came in from the doorstep, laughing as if his heart would break. He was dressed in a long green overcoat with mock astrakhan cuffs and collar and wore on his head an oval fur cap. He pointed down the snow-covered quay from where the sound of shrill prolonged whistling was borne in.

–Teddy will have all the cabs in Dublin out, he said.

Gabriel advanced from the little pantry behind the office, struggling into his overcoat and, looking round the hall, said:

–Gretta not down yet?

–She's getting on her things, Gabriel, said Aunt Kate.

–Who's playing up there? asked Gabriel.

–Nobody. They're all gone.

–O no, Aunt Kate, said Mary Jane. Bartell D'Arcy and Miss O'Callaghan aren't gone yet.

–Someone is strumming at the piano, anyhow, said Gabriel.

Mary Jane glanced at Gabriel and Mr Browne and said with a shiver:

–It makes me feel cold to look at you two gentlemen muffled up like that. I wouldn't like to face your journey home at this hour.

–I'd like nothing better this minute, said Mr Browne stoutly, than a rattling fine walk in the country or a fast drive with a good spanking goer between the shafts.

–We used to have a very good horse and trap at home, said Aunt Julia sadly.

–The never-to-be-forgotten Johnny, said Mary Jane, laughing.

Aunt Kate and Gabriel laughed too.

–Why, what was wonderful about Johnny? asked Mr Browne.

–The late lamented Patrick Morkan, our grandfather, that is, explained Gabriel, commonly known in his later years as the old gentleman, was a glue-boiler.

–O, now, Gabriel, said Aunt Kate, laughing, he had a starch mill.

–Well, glue or starch, said Gabriel, the old gentleman had a horse by the name of Johnny. And Johnny used to work in the old gentleman's mill, walking round and round in order to drive the mill. That was all very well; but now comes the tragic part about Johnny. One fine day the old gentleman thought he'd like to drive out with the quality to a military review in the park.

—The Lord have mercy on his soul, said Aunt Kate compassionately.

—Amen, said Gabriel. So the old gentleman, as I said, harnessed Johnny and put on his very best tall hat and his very best stock collar and drove out in grand style from his ancestral mansion somewhere near Back Lane, I think.

Every one laughed, even Mrs Malins, at Gabriel's manner and Aunt Kate said:

—O now, Gabriel, he didn't live in Back Lane, really. Only the mill was there.

—Out from the mansion of his forefathers, continued Gabriel, he drove with Johnny. And everything went on beautifully until Johnny came in sight of King Billy's statue: and whether he fell in love with the horse King Billy sits on or whether he thought he was back again in the mill, anyhow he began to walk around the statue.

Gabriel paced in a circle round the hall in his goloshes amid the laughter of the others.

—Round and round he went, said Gabriel, and the old gentleman, who was a very pompous old gentleman, was highly indignant. *Go on, sir! What do you mean, sir? Johnny! Johnny! Most extraordinary conduct! Can't understand the horse!*

The peals of laughter which followed Gabriel's imitation of the incident were interrupted by a resounding knock at the hall-door. Mary Jane ran to open it and let in Freddy Malins. Freddy Malins, with his hat well back on his head and his shoulders humped with cold, was puffing and steaming after his exertions.

—I could only get one cab, he said.

—O, we'll find another along the quay, said Gabriel.

—Yes, said Aunt Kate. Better not keep Mrs Malins standing in the draught.

Mrs Malins was helped down the front steps by her son and Mr Browne and, after many manoeuvers, hoisted into the cab. Freddy Malins clambered in after her and spent a long time settling her on the seat, Mr Browne helping him with advice. At last she was settled comfortably and Freddy Malins invited Mr Browne into the cab. There was a good deal of confused talk, and then Mr Browne got into the cab. The cabman settled his rug over his knees, and bent down for the address. The confusion grew greater and the cabman was directed differently by Freddy Malins and Mr Browne, each of whom had his head out through a window of the cab. The difficulty was to know where to drop Mr Browne along the route and Aunt Kate, Aunt Julia and Mary Jane helped the discussion from the doorstep with cross-directions and contradictions and abundance of laughter. As for Freddy Malins he was speechless with laughter. He popped his head in and out of the window every moment, to the great danger of his hat, and told his mother how the discussion was progressing till at last Mr Browne shouted to the bewildered cabman above the din of everybody's laughter:

—Do you know Trinity College?

—Yes, sir, said the cabman.

—Well, drive bang up against Trinity College gates, said Mr Browne, and then we'll tell you where to go. You understand now?

—Yes, sir, said the cabman.

—Make like a bird for Trinity College.

—Right, sir, cried the cabman.

The horse was whipped up and the cab rattled off along the quay amid a chorus of laughter and adieus.

Gabriel had not gone to the door with the others. He was in a dark part of the hall gazing up the staircase. A woman was standing near the top of the first flight, in the shadow also. He could not see her face but he could see the terracotta and salmonpink panels of her skirt which the shadow made appear black and white. It was his wife. She was leaning on the banisters, listening to something. Gabriel was surprised at her stillness and strained his ear to listen also. But he could hear little save the noise of laughter and dispute on the front steps, a few chords struck on the piano and a few notes of a man's voice singing.

He stood still in the gloom of the hall, trying to catch the air that the voice was singing and gazing up at his wife. There was grace and mystery in her attitude as if she were a symbol of something. He asked himself what is a woman standing on the stairs in the shadow, listening to distant music, a symbol of. If he were a painter he would paint her in that attitude. Her blue felt hat would show off the bronze of her hair against the darkness and the dark panels of her skirt would show off the light ones. *Distant Music* he would call the picture if he were a painter.

The half-door was closed; and Aunt Kate, Aunt Julia and Mary Jane came down the hall, still laughing.

—Well, isn't Freddy terrible? said Mary Jane. He's really terrible.

Gabriel said nothing but pointed up the stairs towards where his wife was standing. Now that the hall-door was closed the voice and the piano could be heard more clearly. Gabriel held up his hand for them to be silent. The song seemed to be in the old Irish tonality and the singer seemed uncertain both of his words and of his voice. The voice, made plaintive by distance and by the singer's hoarseness, faintly illuminated the cadence of the air with words expressing grief:

O, the rain falls on my heavy locks
And the dew wets my skin,
My babe lies cold . . .

—O, exclaimed Mary Jane. It's Bartell D'Arcy singing and he wouldn't sing all the night. O, I'll get him to sing a song before he goes.

—O do, Mary Jane, said Aunt Kate.

Mary Jane brushed past the others and ran to the staircase but before she reached it the singing stopped and the piano was closed abruptly.

—O, what a pity! she cried. Is he coming down, Gretta?

Gabriel heard his wife answer yes and saw her come down towards them. A few steps behind her were Mr Bartell D'Arcy and Miss O'Callaghan.

–O, Mr D'Arcy, cried Mary Jane, it's downright mean of you to break off like that when we were all in raptures listening to you.

–I have been at him all the evening, said Miss O'Callaghan, and Mrs Conroy too and he told us he had a dreadful cold and couldn't sing.

–O, Mr D'Arcy, said Aunt Kate, now that was a great fib to tell.

–Can't you see that I'm as hoarse as a crow? said Mr D'Arcy roughly.

He went into the pantry hastily and put on his overcoat. The others, taken aback by his rude speech, could find nothing to say. Aunt Kate wrinkled her brows and made signs to the others to drop the subject. Mr D'Arcy stood swathing his neck carefully and frowning.

–It's the weather, said Aunt Julia, after a pause.

–Yes, everybody has colds, said Aunt Kate readily, everybody.

–They say, said Mary Jane, we haven't had snow like it for thirty years; and I read this morning in the newspapers that the snow is general all over Ireland.

–I love the look of snow, said Aunt Julia sadly.

–So do I, said Miss O'Callaghan. I think Christmas is never really Christmas unless we have the snow on the ground.

–But poor Mr D'Arcy doesn't like the snow, said Aunt Kate, smiling.

Mr D'Arcy came from the pantry, fully swathed and buttoned, and in a repentant tone told them the history of his cold. Everyone gave him advice and said it was a great pity and urged him to be very careful of his throat in the night air. Gabriel watched his wife who did not join in the conversation. She was standing right under the dusty fanlight and the flame of the gas lit up the rich bronze of her hair which he had seen her drying at the fire a few days before. She was in the same attitude and seemed unaware of the talk about her. At last she turned towards them and Gabriel saw that there was colour on her cheeks and that her eyes were shining. A sudden tide of joy went leaping out of his heart.

–Mr D'Arcy, she said, what is the name of that song you were singing?

–It's called *The Lass of Aughrim,* said Mr D'Arcy, but I couldn't remember it properly. Why? Do you know it?

–*The Lass of Aughrim,* she repeated. I couldn't think of the name.

–It's a very nice air, said Mary Jane. I'm sorry you were not in voice to-night.

–Now, Mary Jane, said Aunt Kate, don't annoy Mr D'Arcy. I won't have him annoyed.

Seeing that all were ready to start she shepherded them to the door where good-night was said:

–Well, good-night, Aunt Kate, and thanks for the pleasant evening.

–Good-night, Gabriel. Good-night, Gretta!

–Good-night, Aunt Kate, and thanks ever so much. Good-night, Aunt Julia.

–O, good-night, Gretta, I didn't see you.

–Good-night, Mr D'Arcy. Good-night, Miss O'Callaghan.

–Good-night, Miss Morkan.

–Good-night, again.

–Good-night, all. Safe home.

–Good-night. Good-night.

The morning was still dark. A dull yellow light brooded over the houses and the river; and the sky seemed to be descending. It was slushy underfoot; and only streaks and patches of snow lay on the roofs, on the parapets of the quay and on the area railings. The lamps were still burning redly in the murky air and, across the river, the palace of the Four Courts stood out menacingly against the heavy sky.

She was walking on before him with Mr Bartell D'Arcy, her shoes in a brown parcel tucked under one arm and her hands holding her skirt up from the slush. She had no longer any grace of attitude but Gabriel's eyes were still bright with happiness. The blood went bounding along his veins; and the thoughts went rioting through his brain, proud, joyful, tender, valorous.

She was walking on before him so lightly and so erect that he longed to run after her noiselessly, catch her by the shoulders and say something foolish and affectionate into her ear. She seemed to him so frail that he longed to defend her against something and then to be alone with her. Moments of their secret life together burst like stars upon his memory. A heliotrope envelope was lying beside his breakfast-cup and he was caressing it with his hand. Birds were twittering in the ivy and the sunny web of the curtain was shimmering along the floor: he could not eat for happiness. They were standing on the crowded platform and he was placing a ticket inside the warm palm of her glove. He was standing with her in the cold, looking in through a grated window at a man making bottles in a roaring furnace. It was very cold. Her face, fragrant in the cold air, was quite close to his; and suddenly she called out to the man at the furnace:

–Is the fire hot, sir?

But the man could not hear her with the noise of the furnace. It was just as well. He might have answered rudely.

A wave of yet more tender joy escaped from his heart and went coursing in warm flood along his arteries. Like the tender fires of stars moments of their life together, that no one knew of or would ever know of, broke upon and illumined his memory. He longed to recall to her those moments, to make her forget the years of their dull existence together and remember only their moments of ecstasy. For the years, he felt, had not quenched his soul or hers. Their children, his writing, her household cares had not quenched all their souls' tender fire. In one letter that he had written to her then he had said: *Why is it that words like these seem to me so dull and cold? Is it because there is no word tender enough to be your name?*

Like distant music these words that he had written years before were borne towards him from the past. He longed to be alone with her. When the others had gone away, when he and she were in their room in the hotel, then they would be along together. He would call her softly:

–Gretta!

Perhaps she would not hear at once: she would be undressing. Then something in his voice would strike her. She would turn and look at him. . . .

At the corner of Winetavern Street they met a cab. He was glad of its rattling noise as it saved him from conversation. She was looking out of the window and seemed tired. The others spoke only a few words, pointing out some building or street. The horse galloped along wearily under the murky morning sky, dragging his old rattling box after his heels, and Gabriel was again in a cab with her, galloping to catch the boat, galloping to their honeymoon.

As the cab drove across O'Connell Bridge Miss O'Callaghan said:

–They say you never cross O'Connell Bridge without seeing a white horse.

–I see a white man this time, said Gabriel.

–Where? asked Mr Bartell D'Arcy.

Gabriel pointed to the statue, on which lay patches of snow. Then he nodded familiarly to it and waved his hand.

–Good-night, Dan, he said gaily.

When the cab drew up before the hotel Gabriel jumped out and, in spite of Mr Bartell D'Arcy's protest, paid the driver. He gave the man a shilling over his fare. The man saluted and said:

–A prosperous New Year to you, sir.

–The same to you, said Gabriel cordially.

She leaned for a moment on his arm in getting out of the cab and while standing at the curbstone, bidding the others good-night. She leaned lightly on his arm, as lightly as when she had danced with him a few hours before. He had felt proud and happy then, happy that she was his, proud of her grace and wifely carriage. But now, after the kindling again of so many memories, the first touch of her body, musical and strange and perfumed, sent through him a keen pang of lust. Under cover of her silence he pressed her arm closely to his side; and, as they stood at the hotel door, he felt that they had escaped from their lives and duties, escaped from home and friends and run away together with wild and radiant hearts to a new adventure.

An old man was dozing in a great hooded chair in the hall. He lit a candle in the office and went before them to the stairs. They followed him in silence, their feet falling in soft thuds on the thickly carpeted stairs. She mounted the stairs behind the porter, her head bowed in the ascent, her frail shoulders curved as with a burden, her skirt girt tightly about her. He could have flung his arms about her hips and held her still for his arms were trembling with desire to seize her and only the stress of his nails against the palms of his hands held the wild impulse of his body in check. The porter halted on the stairs to settle his guttering candle. They halted too on the steps below him. In the silence Gabriel could hear the falling of the molten wax into the tray and the thumping of his own heart against his ribs.

The porter led them along a corridor and opened a door. Then he set his unstable candle down on a toilet-table and asked at what hour they were to be called in the morning.

–Eight, said Gabriel.

The porter pointed to the tap of the electric-light and began a muttered apology but Gabriel cut him short.

–We don't want any light. We have light enough from the street. And I say, he added, pointing to the candle, you might remove that handsome article, like a good man.

The porter took up his candle again, but slowly for he was surprised by such a novel idea. Then he mumbled good-night and went out. Gabriel shot the lock to.

A ghostly light from the street lamp lay in a long shaft from one window to the door. Gabriel threw his overcoat and hat on a couch and crossed the room towards the window. He looked down into the street in order that his emotion might calm a little. Then he turned and leaned against a chest of drawers with his back to the light. She had taken off her hat and cloak and was standing before a large swinging mirror, unhooking her waist. Gabriel paused for a few moments, watching her, and then said:

–Gretta!

She turned away from the mirror slowly and walked along the shaft of light towards him. Her face looked so serious and weary that the words would not pass Gabriel's lips. No, it was not the moment yet.

–You looked tired, he said.

–I am a little, she answered.

–You don't feel ill or weak?

–No, tired: that's all.

She went on to the window and stood there, looking out. Gabriel waited again and then, fearing that diffidence was about to conquer him, he said abruptly:

–By the way, Gretta!

–What is it?

–You know that poor fellow Malins? he said quickly.

–Yes. What about him?

–Well, poor fellow, he's a decent sort of chap after all, continued Gabriel in a false voice. He gave me back that sovereign I lent him and I didn't expect it really. It's a pity he wouldn't keep away from that Browne, because he's not a bad fellow at heart.

He was trembling now with annoyance. Why did she seem so abstracted? He did not know how he could begin. Was she annoyed, too, about something? If she would only turn to him or come to him of her own accord! To take her as she was would be brutal. No, he must see some ardour in her eyes first. He longed to be master of her strange mood.

—When did you lend him the pound? she asked, after a pause.

Gabriel strove to restrain himself from breaking out into brutal language about the sottish Malins and his pound. He longed to cry to her from his soul, to crush her body against his, to overmaster her. But he said:

—O, at Christmas, when he opened that little Christmas-card shop in Henry Street.

He was in such a fever of rage and desire that he did not hear her come from the window. She stood before him for an instant, looking at him strangely. Then, suddenly raising herself on tiptoe and resting her hands lightly on his shoulders, she kissed him.

—You are a very generous person, Gabriel, she said.

Gabriel, trembling with delight at her sudden kiss and at the quaintness of her phrase, put his hands on her hair and began smoothing it back, scarcely touching it with his fingers. The washing had made it fine and brilliant. His heart was brimming over with happiness. Just when he was wishing for it she had come to him of her own accord. Perhaps her thoughts had been running with his. Perhaps she had felt the impetuous desire that was in him and then the yielding mood had come upon her. Now that she had fallen to him so easily he wondered why he had been so diffident.

He stood, holding her head between his hands. Then, slipping one arm swiftly about her body and drawing her towards him, he said softly:

—Gretta dear, what are you thinking about?

She did not answer nor yield wholly to his arm. He said again, softly:

—Tell me what it is, Gretta. I think I know what is the matter. Do I know?

She did not answer at once. Then she said in an outburst of tears:

—O, I am thinking about that song, *The Lass of Aughrim.*

She broke loose from him and ran to the bed and, throwing her arms across the bed-rail, hid her face. Gabriel stood stock-still for a moment in astonishment and then followed her. As he passed in the way of the cheval-glass he caught sight of himself in full length, his broad, well-filled shirt-front, the face whose expression always puzzled him when he saw it in a mirror and his glimmering gilt-rimmed eyeglasses. He halted a few paces from her and said:

—What about the song? Why does that make you cry?

She raised her head from her arms and dried her eyes with the back of her hand like a child. A kinder note than he had intended went into his voice.

—Why, Gretta? he asked.

—I am thinking about a person long ago who used to sing that song.

–And who was the person long ago? asked Gabriel, smiling.

–It was a person I used to know in Galway when I was living with my grandmother, she said.

The smile passed away from Gabriel's face. A dull anger began to gather again at the back of his mind and the dull fires of his lust began to glow angrily in his veins.

–Someone you were in love with? he asked ironically.

–It was a young boy I used to know, she answered, named Michael Furey. He used to sing that song, *The Lass of Aughrim.* He was very delicate.

Gabriel was silent. He did not wish her to think that he was interested in this delicate boy.

–I can see him so plainly, she said after a moment. Such eyes as he had: big dark eyes! And such an expression in them–an expression!

–O then, you were in love with him? said Gabriel.

–I used to go out walking with him, she said, when I was in Galway.

A thought flew across Gabriel's mind.

–Perhaps that was why you wanted to go to Galway with that Ivors girl? he said coldly.

She looked at him and asked in surprise:

–What for?

Her eyes made Gabriel feel awkward. He shrugged his shoulders and said:

–How do I know? To see him perhaps.

She looked away from him along the shaft of light towards the window in silence.

–He is dead, she said at length. He died when he was only seventeen. Isn't it a terrible thing to die so young as that?

–What was he? asked Gabriel, still ironically.

–He was in the gasworks, she said.

Gabriel felt humiliated by the failure of his irony and by the evocation of this figure from the dead, a boy in the gas works. While he had been full of memories of their secret life together, full of tenderness and joy and desire, she had been comparing him in her mind with another. A shameful consciousness of his own person assailed him. He saw himself as a ludicrous figure, acting as a pennyboy for his aunts, a nervous well-meaning sentimentalist, orating to vulgarians and idealizing his own clownish lusts, the pitiable fatuous fellow he had caught a glimpse of in the mirror. Instinctively he turned his back more to the light lest she might see the shame that burned upon his forehead.

He tried to keep up his tone of cold interrogation but his voice when he spoke was humble and indifferent.

–I suppose you were in love with this Michael Furey, Gretta, he said.

–I was great with him at that time, she said.

Her voice was veiled and sad. Gabriel, feeling now how vain it would be to try to lead her whither he had purposed, caressed one of her hands and said, also sadly:

—And what did he die of so young, Gretta? Consumption, was it?

—I think he died for me, she answered.

A vague terror seized Gabriel at this answer as if, at that hour when he had hoped to triumph, some impalpable and vindictive being was coming against him, gathering forces against him in its vague world. But he shook himself free of it with an effort of reason and continued to caress her hand. He did not question her again for he felt that she would tell him of herself. Her hand was warm and moist: it did not respond to his touch but he continued to caress it just as he had caressed her first letter to him that spring morning.

—It was in the winter, she said, about the beginning of the winter when I was going to leave my grandmother's and come up here to the convent. And he was ill at the time in his lodgings in Galway and wouldn't be let out and his people in Oughterard were written to. He was in decline, they said, or something like that. I never knew rightly.

She paused for a moment and sighed.

—Poor fellow, she said. He was very fond of me and he was such a gentle boy. We used to go out together, walking, you know, Gabriel, like the way they do in the country. He was going to study singing only for his health. He had a very good voice, poor Michael Furey.

—Well; and then? asked Gabriel.

—And then when it came to the time for me to leave Galway and come up to the convent he was much worse and I wouldn't be let see him so I wrote a letter saying I was going up to Dublin and would be back in the summer and hoping he would be better then.

She paused for a moment to get her voice under control and then went on:

—Then the night before I left I was in my grandmother's house in Nuns' Island, packing up, and I heard gravel thrown up against the window. The window was so wet I couldn't see so I ran downstairs as I was and slipped out the back into the garden and there was the poor fellow at the end of the garden, shivering.

—And did you not tell him to go back? asked Gabriel.

—I implored of him to go home at once and told him he would get his death in the rain. But he said he did not want to live. I can see his eyes as well as well! He was standing at the end of the wall where there was a tree.

—And did he go home? asked Gabriel.

—Yes, he went home. And when I was only a week in the convent he died and he was buried in Oughterard where his people came from. O, the day I heard that, that he was dead!

She stopped, choking with sobs, and overcome by emotion, flung herself face downward on the bed, sobbing in the quilt. Gabriel held her hand for a moment longer, irresolutely, and then, shy of intruding on her grief, let it fall gently and walked quietly to the window.

She was fast asleep.

Gabriel, leaning on his elbow, looked for a few moments unresentfully on her tangled hair and half-open mouth, listening to her deep-drawn breath. So she had had that romance in her life: a man had died for her sake. It hardly pained him now to think how poor a part he, her husband, had played in her life. He watched her while she slept as though he and she had never lived together as man and wife. His curious eyes rested long upon her face and on her hair: and, as he thought of what she must have been then, in that time of her first girlish beauty, a strange friendly pity for her entered his soul. He did not like to say even to himself that her face was no longer beautiful but he knew that it was no longer the face for which Michael Furey had braved death.

Perhaps she had not told him all the story. His eyes moved to the chair over which she had thrown some of her clothes. A petticoat string dangled to the floor. One boot stood up-right, its limp upper fallen down: the fellow of it lay upon its side. He wondered at his riot of emotions of an hour before. From what had it proceeded? From his aunt's supper, from his own foolish speech, from the wine and dancing, the merry-making when saying good-night in the hall, the pleasure of the walk along the river in the snow. Poor Aunt Julia! She, too, would soon be a shade with the shade of Patrick Morkan and his horse. He had caught that haggard look upon her face for a moment when she was singing *Arrayed for the Bridal.* Soon, perhaps, he would be sitting in that same drawing-room, dressed in black, his silk hat on his knees. The blinds would be drawn down and Aunt Kate would be sitting beside him, crying and blowing her nose and telling him how Julia had died. He would cast about in his mind for some words that might console her, and would find only lame and useless ones. Yes, yes: that would happen very soon.

The air of the room chilled his shoulders. He stretched himself cautiously along under the sheets and lay down beside his wife. One by one they were all becoming shades. Better pass boldly into that other world, in the full glory of some passion, than fade and wither dismally with age. He thought of how she who lay beside him had locked in her heart for so many years that image of her lover's eyes when he had told her that he did not wish to live.

Generous tears filled Gabriel's eyes. He had never felt like that himself towards any woman but he knew that such a feeling must be love. The tears gathered more thickly in his eyes and in the partial darkness he imagined he saw the form of a young man standing under a dripping tree. Other forms were near. His soul had approached that region where dwell the vast hosts of the dead. He was conscious of, but could not apprehend, their wayward and flickering existence. His own identity was fading out into a grey impalpable world: the solid world itself which these dead had one time reared and lived in was dissolving and dwindling.

A few light taps upon the pane made him turn to the window. It had begun to snow again. He watched sleepily the flakes, silver and dark, falling obliquely against the lamplight. The time had come for him to set out on his journey westward. Yes, the newspapers were right: snow was general all over Ireland. It was falling on every part of the dark central plain, on the treeless hills, falling softly upon the Bog of Allen and, farther westward, softly falling into the dark mutinous Shannon waves. It was falling, too, upon every part of the lonely churchyard on the hill where Michael Furey lay buried. It lay thickly drifted on the crooked crosses and headstones, on the spears of the little gate, on the barren thorns. His soul swooned slowly as he heard the snow falling faintly through the universe and faintly falling, like the descent of their last end, upon all the living and the dead.

D. H. LAWRENCE 1885–1930

The coal-mining industry in Lawrence's native Nottinghamshire, England, became for him a symbol of blight in the modern world. Becoming increasingly mechanical to meet the growing need for fuel in industrialized England, coal mining seemed to him not only to corrupt the earth from which it took the coal but also to insinuate a pervasive blackness into the people who lived nearby. Lawrence watched his father, a miner, succumb to the dirt and ugliness of the mine and to its dehumanizing force. Used like a machine, his father gradually lost his capacity for life: his marriage became a mockery of what had once been a vital relationship, and Lawrence's mother, a strong long-suffering woman (rather like the main character in "Odour of Chrysanthemums") in effect turned to her son for salvation. She determined that Lawrence should be educated and escape his father's fate; and indeed he did attend the university and qualify as a biology teacher in a boys' school near London. But Mrs. Lawrence's influence on her son ran much deeper than his choice of a career; his love for her made him extraordinarily sensitive to the nuances of relationships between men and women, and especially aware of the eternal struggle between the desire to possess and be possessed by someone else and the need to be free.

As he stayed by his mother in her agonizing last stages of cancer, Lawrence felt part of himself die too. After her death he grew dangerously ill, but at the crisis he willed to live, to confront in his writing the forces that acted so powerfully within him. Lawrence was then twenty-seven and the author of two not-very-remarkable novels. With a characteristic burst of exuberance he gave up school teaching, extricated himself from a stagnant affair with his childhood sweetheart, and carried away to Italy the unhappily married wife of his former professor of French, Frieda von Richthofen Weekley.

This scandalous elopment was romantic, brave, and artistically liberating for Lawrence. In six months of hard work in Italy he completed the final version of *Sons and Lovers* (1913), his first novel to show the mark of genius. More major fiction followed, and though his relationship with Frieda was more than usually turbulent, it sustained him; eventually they married and remained together until Lawrence died of tuberculosis at forty-five.

World War I (in which Lawrence did not serve because of his poor health) profoundly depressed him. It seemed to him that all the inhumanity of modern industrial civilization had been let loose, and that the England that survived the war was a spiritual wasteland. After the war Lawrence and Frieda left England and roamed the world, seeking in the rituals of primitive peoples a means of asserting a mystical connection between man and the earth. As might be expected, their quest brought as much disappointment as success, but it did keep in the forefront of Lawrence's consciousness the special need of modern man to wrestle with the forces that insulate him from his fellow men, that lock him into habits and patterns of living which twist and atrophy the essential self. Having turned away from an acceptance of his own death, Lawrence sought to portray characters discovering a way out of their special deadness. An uninhibited acceptance of one's physical being, love that does not smother, exuberance, and a refusal to let mechanism penetrate the personality were the essential qualities to be sought – in fact they constitute a kind of map of his greatest novel, *Women in Love* (1920). But always in Lawrence – perhaps because he constantly lived with a fatal disease – is the sense that the quest for life is so perilous that at any moment what has been repressed may explode into murder and self-destruction (as in "The Prussian Officer"), or (as in Lawrence's life) one's vital energies may fail and surrender the fort to death.

THE PRUSSIAN OFFICER

I

They had marched more than thirty kilometres since dawn, along the white, hot road where occasional thickets of trees threw a moment of shade, then out into the glare again. On either hand, the valley, wide and shallow, glittered with heat; dark green patches of rye, pale young corn, fallow and meadow and black pine woods spread in a dull, hot diagram under a glistening sky. But right in front the mountains ranged across, pale blue and very still, snow gleaming gently out of the deep atmosphere. And towards the mountains, on and on, the regiment marched between the rye fields and the meadows, between the scraggy fruit trees set regularly on either side the high road. The burnished, dark green rye threw off a suffocating heat, the mountains drew gradually nearer and more distinct. While the feet of the soldiers grew hotter, sweat ran through their hair under their helmets, and their knapsacks could burn no more in contact with their shoulders, but seemed instead to give off a cold, prickly sensation.

He walked on and on in silence, staring at the mountains ahead, that rose sheer out of the land, and stood fold behind fold, half earth, half heaven, the heaven, the barrier with slits of soft snow, in the pale, bluish peaks.

He could now walk almost without pain. At the start, he had determined not to limp. It had made him sick to take the first steps, and during the first mile or so, he had compressed his breath, and the cold drops of sweat had stood on his forehead. But he had walked it off. What were they after all but bruises! He had looked at them, as he was getting up: deep bruises on the backs of his thighs. And since he had made his first step in the morning, he had been conscious of them, till now he had a tight, hot place in his chest, with suppressing the pain, and holding himself in. There seemed no air when he breathed. But he walked almost lightly.

The Captain's hand had trembled at taking his coffee at dawn: his orderly saw it again. And he saw the fine figure of the Captain wheeling on horseback at the farm-house ahead, a handsome figure in pale blue uniform with facings of scarlet, and the metal gleaming on the black helmet and the sword-scabbard, and dark streaks of sweat coming on the silky bay horse. The orderly felt he was connected with that figure moving so suddenly on horseback: he followed it like a shadow, mute and inevitable and damned by it. And the officer was always aware of the tramp of the company behind, the march of his orderly among the men.

The Captain was a tall man of about forty, grey at the temples. He had a handsome, finely knit figure, and was one of the best horsemen in the West. His orderly, having to rub him down, admired the amazing riding-muscles of his loins.

For the rest, the orderly scarcely noticed the officer any more than he noticed himself. It was rarely he saw his master's face: he did not look at it. The Captain had reddish-brown, stiff hair, that he wore short upon his skull. His moustache was also cut short and bristly over a full, brutal mouth. His face was rather rugged, the cheeks thin. Perhaps the man was the more handsome for the deep lines in his face, the irritable tension of his brow, which gave him the look of a man who fights with life. His fair eyebrows stood bushy over light blue eyes that were always flashing with cold fire.

He was a Prussian aristocrat, haughty and overbearing. But his mother had been a Polish Countess. Having made too many gambling debts when he was young, he had ruined his prospects in the Army, and remained an infantry captain. He had never married: his position did not allow of it, and no woman had ever moved him to it. His time he spent riding – occasionally he rode one of his own horses at the races – and at the officers' club. Now and then he took himself a mistress. But after such an event, he returned to duty with his brow still more tense, his eyes still more hostile and irritable. With the men, however, he was merely impersonal, though a devil when roused; so that, on the whole, they feared him, but had no great aversion from him. They accepted him as the inevitable.

To his orderly he was at first cold and just and indifferent: he did not fuss over trifles. So that his servant knew practically nothing about him, except just what orders he would give, and how he wanted them obeyed. That was quite simple. Then the change gradually came.

The orderly was a youth of about twenty-two, of medium height, and well built. He had strong, heavy limbs, was swarthy, with a soft, black, young moustache. There was something altogether warm and young about him. He had firmly marked eyebrows over dark, expressionless eyes, that seemed never to have thought, only to have received life direct through his senses, and acted straight from instinct.

Gradually the officer had become aware of his servant's young, vigorous, unconscious presence about him. He could not get away from the sense of the youth's person, while he was in attendance. It was like a warm flame upon the older man's tense, rigid body, that had become almost unliving, fixed. There was something so free and self-contained about him, and something in the young fellow's movement, that made the officer aware of him. And this irritated the Prussian.

He did not choose to be touched into life by his servant. He might easily have changed his man, but he did not. He now very rarely looked direct at his orderly, but kept his face averted, as if to avoid seeing him. And yet as the young soldier moved unthinking about the apartment, the elder watched him, and would notice the movement of his strong young shoulders under the blue cloth, the bend of his neck. And it irritated him. To see the soldier's young, brown, shapely peasant's hand grasp the loaf or the wine-bottle sent a flash of hate or of anger through the elder man's blood. It was not that the youth was clumsy: it was rather the blind, instinctive sureness of movement of an unhampered young animal that irritated the officer to such a degree.

Once, when a bottle of wine had gone over, and the red gushed out on to the tablecloth, the officer had started up with an oath, and his eyes, bluey like fire, had held those of the confused youth for a moment. It was a shock for the young soldier. He felt something sink deeper, deeper into his soul, where nothing had ever gone before. It left him rather blank and wondering. Some of his natural completeness in himself was gone, a little uneasiness took its place. And from that time an undiscovered feeling had held between the two men.

Henceforward the orderly was afraid of really meeting his master. His subconsciousness remembered those steely blue eyes and the harsh brows, and did not intend to meet them again. So he always stared past his master, and avoided him. Also, in a little anxiety, he waited for the three months to have gone, when his time would be up. He began to feel a constraint in the Captain's presence, and the soldier even more than the officer wanted to be left alone, in his neutrality as servant.

He had served the Captain for more than a year, and knew his duty. This he performed easily, as if it were natural to him. The officer and his commands he took for granted, as he took the sun and the rain, and he served as a matter of course. It did not implicate him personally.

But now if he were going to be forced into a personal interchange with his master he would be like a wild thing caught, he felt he must get away.

But the influence of the young soldier's being had penetrated through the officer's stiffened discipline, and perturbed the man in him. He, however, was a gentleman, with long, fine hands and cultivated movements, and was not going to allow such a thing as the stirring of his innate self. He was a man of passionate temper, who had always kept himself suppressed. Occasionally there had been a duel, an outburst before the soldiers. He knew himself to be always on the point of breaking out. But he kept himself hard to the idea of the Service. Whereas the young soldier seemed to live out his warm, full nature, to give it off in his very movements, which had a certain zest, such as wild animals have in free movement. And this irritated the officer more and more.

In spite of himself, the Captain could not regain his neutrality of feeling towards his orderly. Nor could he leave the man alone. In spite of himself, he watched him, gave him sharp orders, tried to take up as much of his time as possible. Sometimes he flew into a rage with the young soldier, and bullied him. Then the orderly shut himself off, as it were out of earshot, and waited, with sullen, flushed face, for the end of the noise. The words never pierced to his intelligence, he made himself, protectively, impervious to the feelings of his master.

He had a scar on his left thumb, a deep seam going across the knuckle. The officer had long suffered from it, and wanted to do something to it. Still it was there, ugly and brutal on the young, brown hand. At last the Captain's reserve gave way. One day, as the orderly was smoothing out the tablecloth, the officer pinned down his thumb with a pencil, asking:

"How did you come by that?"

The young man winced and drew back at attention.

"A wood axe, Herr Hauptmann," he answered.

The officer waited for further explanation. None came. The orderly went about his duties. The elder man was sullenly angry. His servant avoided him. And the next day he had to use all his will-power to avoid seeing the scarred thumb. He wanted to get hold of it and— A hot flame ran in his blood.

He knew his servant would soon be free, and would be glad. As yet, the soldier had held himself off from the elder man. The Captain grew madly irritable. He could not rest when the soldier was away, and when he was present, he glared at him with tormented eyes. He hated those fine, black brows over the unmeaning, dark eyes, he was infuriated by the free movement of the handsome limbs, which no military discipline could make stiff. And he became harsh and cruelly bullying, using contempt and satire. The young soldier only grew more mute and expressionless.

"What cattle were you bred by, that you can't keep straight eyes? Look me in the eyes when I speak to you."

And the soldier turned his dark eyes to the other's face, but there was no sight in them: he stared with the slightest possible cast, holding back his sight, perceiving the blue of his master's eyes, but receiving no look from them. And the elder man went pale, and his reddish eyebrows twitched. He gave his order, barrenly.

Once he flung a heavy military glove into the young soldier's face. Then he had the satisfaction of seeing the black eyes flare up into his own, like a blaze when straw is thrown on a fire. And he had laughed with a little tremor and a sneer.

But there were only two months more. The youth instinctively tried to keep himself intact: he tried to serve the officer as if the latter were an abstract authority and not a man. All his instinct was to avoid personal contact, even definite hate. But in spite of himself the hate grew, responsive to the officer's passion. However, he put it in the background. When he had left the Army he could dare acknowledge it. By nature he was active, and had many friends. He thought what amazing good fellows they were. But, without knowing it, he was alone. Now this solitariness was intensified. It would carry him through his term. But the officer seemed to be going irritably insane, and the youth was deeply frightened.

The soldier had a sweetheart, a girl from the mountains, independent and primitive. The two walked together, rather silently. He went with her, not to talk, but to have his arm round her, and for the physical contact. This eased him, made it easier for him to ignore the Captain; for he could rest with her held fast against his chest. And she, in some unspoken fashion, was there for him. They loved each other.

The Captain perceived it, and was mad with irritation. He kept the young man engaged all the evenings long, and took pleasure in the dark look that came on his face. Occasionally, the eyes of the two men met, those of the younger sullen and dark, doggedly unalterable, those of the elder sneering with restless contempt.

The officer tried hard not to admit the passion that had got hold of him. He would not know that his feeling for his orderly was anything but that of a man incensed by his stupid, perverse servant. So, keeping quite justified and conventional in his consciousness, he let the other thing run on. His nerves, however, were suffering. At last he slung the end of a belt in his servant's face. When he saw the youth start back, the pain-tears in his eyes and the blood on his mouth, he had felt at once a thrill of deep pleasure and of shame.

But this, he acknowledged to himself was a thing he had never done before. The fellow was too exasperating. His own nerves must be going to pieces. He went away for some days with a woman.

It was a mockery of pleasure. He simply did not want the woman. But he stayed on for his time. At the end of it, he came back in an agony of irritation, torment, and misery. He rode all the evening, then came straight in to supper. His orderly was out. The officer sat with his long, fine hands lying on the table, perfectly still, and all his blood seemed to be corroding.

At last his servant entered. He watched the strong, easy young figure, the fine eyebrows, the thick black hair. In a week's time the youth had got back his old well-being. The hands of the officer twitched and seemed to be full of mad flame. The young man stood at attention, unmoving, shut off.

The meal went in silence. But the orderly seemed eager. He made a clatter with the dishes.

"Are you in a hurry?" asked the officer, watching the intent, warm face of his servant. The other did not reply.

"Will you answer my question?" said the Captain.

"Yes, sir," replied the orderly, standing with his pile of deep Army plates. The Captain waited, looked at him, then asked again:

"Are you in a hurry?"

"Yes, sir," came the answer, that sent a flash through the listener.

"For what?"

"I was going out, sir."

"I want you this evening."

There was a moment's hesitation. The officer had a curious stiffness of countenance.

"Yes, sir," replied the servant, in his throat.

"I want you to-morrow evening also – in fact, you may consider your evenings occupied, unless I give you leave."

The mouth with the young moustache set close.

"Yes, sir," answered the orderly, loosening his lips for a moment.

He again turned to the door.

"And why have you a piece of pencil in your ear?"

The orderly hesitated, then continued on his way without answering. He set the plates in a pile outside the door, took the stump of pencil from his ear, and put it in his pocket. He had been copying a verse for his sweetheart's birthday card. He returned to finish clearing the table. The officer's eyes were dancing, he had a little, eager smile.

"Why have you a piece of pencil in your ear?" he asked.

The orderly took his hands full of dishes. His master was standing near the great green stove, a little smile on his face, his chin thrust forward. When the young soldier saw him his heart suddenly ran hot. He felt blind. Instead of answering, he turned dazedly to the door. As he was crouching to set down the dishes, he was pitched forward by a kick from behind. The pots went in a stream down the stairs, he clung to the pillar of the banisters. And as he was rising he was kicked heavily again, and again, so that he clung sickly to the post for some moments. His master had gone swiftly into the room and closed the door. The maidservant downstairs looked up the staircase and made a mocking face at the crockery disaster.

The officer's heart was plunging. He poured himself a glass of wine, part of which he spilled on the floor, and gulped the remainder, leaning against the cool, green stove. He heard his man collecting the dishes from the stairs. Pale, as if intoxicated, he waited. The servant entered again. The Captain's heart gave a pang, as of pleasure, seeing the young fellow bewildered and uncertain on his feet, with pain.

"Schöner!" he said.

The soldier was a little slower in coming to attention.

"Yes, sir!"

The youth stood before him, with pathetic young moustache, and fine eyebrows very distinct on his forehead of dark marble.

"I asked you a question."

"Yes, sir."

The officer's tone bit like acid.

"Why had you a pencil in your ear?"

Again the servant's heart ran hot, and he could not breathe. With dark, strained eyes, he looked at the officer, as if fascinated. And he stood there sturdily planted, unconscious. The withering smile came into the Captain's eyes, and he lifted his foot.

"I – I forgot it – sir," panted the soldier, his dark eyes fixed on the other man's dancing blue ones.

"What was it doing there?"

He saw the young man's breast heaving as he made an effort for words.

"I had been writing."

"Writing what?"

Again the soldier looked him up and down. The officer could hear him panting. The smile came into the blue eyes. The soldier worked his dry throat, but could not speak. Suddenly the smile lit like a flame on the officer's face, and a kick came heavily against the orderly's thigh. The youth moved a pace sideways. His face went dead, with two black, staring eyes.

"Well?" said the officer.

The orderly's mouth had gone dry, and his tongue rubbed in it as on dry brown-paper. He worked his throat. The officer raised his foot. The servant went stiff.

"Some poetry, sir," came the crackling, unrecognizable sound of his voice.

"Poetry, what poetry?" asked the Captain, with a sickly smile.

Again there was the working in the throat. The Captain's heart had suddenly gone down heavily, and he stood sick and tired.

"For my girl, sir," he heard the dry, inhuman sound.

"Oh!" he said, turning away. "Clear the table."

"Click!" went the soldier's throat; then again, "click!" and then the half-articulate: "Yes, sir."

The young soldier was gone, looking old, and walking heavily.

The officer, left alone, held himself rigid, to prevent himself from thinking. His instinct warned him that he must not think. Deep inside him was the intense gratification of his passion, still working powerfully. Then there was a counter-action, a horrible breaking down of something inside him, a whole agony of reaction. He stood there for an hour motionless, a chaos of sensations, but rigid with a will to keep blank his consciousness, to prevent his mind grasping. And he held himself so until the worst of the stress had passed, when he began to drink, drank himself to an intoxication, till he slept obliterated. When he woke in the morning he was shaken to the base of his nature. But he had fought off the realization of what he had done. He had prevented his mind from taking it in, had suppressed it along with his instincts, and the conscious man had nothing to do with it. He felt only as after a bout of intoxication, weak, but the affair itself all dim and not to be recovered. Of the drunkenness of his passion he successfully refused remembrance. And when his orderly appeared with coffee, the officer assumed the same self he had had the morning before. He refused the event of the past night – denied it had even been – and was successful in his denial. He had not done any such thing – not he himself. Whatever there might be lay at the door of a stupid, insubordinate servant.

The orderly had gone about in a stupor all the evening. He drank some beer because he was parched, but not much, the alcohol made his feeling come back, and he could not bear it. He was dulled, as if nine-tenths of the ordinary man in him were inert. He crawled about disfigured. Still, when he thought of the kicks, he went sick, and when he thought of the threat of more kicking, in the room afterwards, his heart went hot and faint, and he panted, remembering the one that had come. He had been forced to say, "For my girl." He was much too done even to want to cry. His mouth hung slightly open, like an idiot's. He felt vacant, and wasted. So, he wandered at his work, painfully, and very slowly and clumsily, fumbling blindly with the brushes, and finding it difficult, when he sat down, to summon the energy to move again. His limbs, his jaw, were slack and nerveless. But he was very tired. He got to bed at last and slept inert, relaxed, in a sleep that was rather stupor than slumber, a dead night of stupefaction shot through with gleams of anguish.

In the morning were the manoeuvers. But he woke even before the bugle sounded. The painful ache in his chest, the dryness in his throat, the awful steady feeling of misery made his eyes come awake and dreary at once. He knew, without thinking, what had happened. And he knew that the day had come again, when he must go on with his round. The last bit of darkness was being pushed out of the room. He would have to move his inert body and go on. He was so young, and had known so little trouble, that he was bewildered. He only wished it would stay night, so that he could lie still, covered up by the darkness. And yet nothing would prevent the day from coming, nothing would save him from having to get up and saddle the Captain's horse, and make the Captain's coffee. It was there, inevitable. And then, he thought, it was impossible. Yet they would not leave him free. He must go and take the coffee to the Captain. He was too stunned to understand it. He only knew it was inevitable – inevitable, however long he lay inert.

At last, after heaving at himself, for he seemed to be a mass of inertia, he got up. But he had to force every one of his movements from behind, with his will. He felt lost, and dazed, and helpless. Then he clutched hold of the bed, the pain was so keen. And looking at his thighs, he saw the darker bruises on his swarthy flesh and he knew that, if he pressed one of his fingers on one of the bruises, he should faint. But he did not want to faint – he did not want anybody to know. No one should ever know. It was between him and the Captain. There were only the two people in the world now – himself and the Captain.

Slowly, economically, he got dressed and forced himself to walk. Everything was obscure, except just what he had his hands on. But he managed to get through his work. The very pain revived his dull senses. The worst remained yet. He took the tray and went up to the Captain's room. The officer, pale and heavy, sat at the table. The orderly, as he saluted, felt himself put out of existence. He stood still for a moment submitting to his own nullification – then he gathered himself, seemed to regain himself, and then the Captain began to grow vague, unreal, and the younger soldier's heart beat up. He clung to this situation – that the Captain did not exist – so that he himself might live. But when he saw his officer's hand tremble as he took the coffee, he felt everything falling shattered. And he went away, feeling as if he himself were coming to pieces, disintegrated. And when the Captain was there on horseback, giving orders, while he himself stood, with rifle and knapsack, sick with pain, he felt as if he must shut his eyes – as if he must shut his eyes on everything. It was only the long agony of marching with a parched throat that filled him with one single, sleep-heavy intention: to save himself.

II

He was getting used even to his parched throat. That the snowy peaks were radiant among the sky, that the whity-green glacier-river twisted through its pale shoals, in the valley below, seemed almost supernatural. But he was going mad with fever and thirst. He plodded on uncomplaining. He did not want to speak, not to anybody. There were two gulls, like flakes of water and snow, over the river. The scent of green rye soaked in sunshine came like a sickness. And the march continued, monotonously, almost like a bad sleep.

At the next farm-house, which stood low and broad near the high road, tubs of water had been put out. The soldiers clustered round to drink. They took off their helmets, and the steam mounted from their wet hair. The Captain sat on horseback, watching. He needed to see his orderly. His helmet threw a dark shadow over his light, fierce eyes, but his moustache and mouth and chin were distinct in the sunshine. The orderly must move under the presence of the figure of the horseman. It was not that he was afraid, or cowed. It was as if he was disembowelled, made empty, like an empty shell. He felt himself as nothing, a shadow creeping under the sunshine. And, thirsty as he was, he could scarcely drink, feeling the Captain near him. He would not take off his helmet to wipe his wet hair. He wanted to stay in shadow, not to be forced into consciousness. Starting, he saw the light heel of the officer prick the belly of the horse; the Captain cantered away, and he himself could relapse into vacancy.

Nothing, however, could give him back his living place in the hot, bright morning.

He felt like a gap among it all. Whereas the Captain was prouder, overriding. A hot flash went through the young servant's body. The Captain was firmer and prouder with life, he himself was empty as a shadow. Again the flash went through him, dazing him out. But his heart ran a little firmer.

The company turned up the hill, to make a loop for the return. Below, from among the trees, the farmbell clanged. He saw the labourers, mowing barefoot at the thick grass, leave off their work and go downhill, their scythes hanging over their shoulders, like long, bright claws curving down behind them. They seemed like dream-people, as if they had no relation to himself. He felt as in a blackish dream: as if all the other things were there and had form, but he himself was only a consciousness, a gap that could think and perceive.

The soldiers were tramping silently up the glaring hillside. Gradually his head began to revolve, slowly, rhythmically. Sometimes it was dark before his eyes, as if he saw this world through a smoked glass, frail shadows and unreal. It gave him a pain in his head to walk.

The air was too scented, it gave no breath. All the lush green-stuff seemed to be issuing its sap, till the air was deathly, sickly with the smell of greenness. There was the perfume of clover, like pure honey and bees. Then there grew a faint acrid tang – they were near the beeches; and then a queer clattering noise, and a suffocating, hideous smell; they were passing a flock of sheep, a shepherd in a black smock, holding his crook. Why should the sheep huddle together under this fierce sun? He felt that the shepherd would not see him, though he could see the shepherd.

At last there was the halt. They stacked rifles in a conical stack, put down their kit in a scattered circle around it, and dispersed a little, sitting on a small knoll high on the hillside. The chatter began. The soldiers were steaming with heat, but were lively. He sat still, seeing the blue mountains rising upon the land, twenty kilometres away. There was a blue fold in the ranges, then out of that, at the foot, the broad, pale bed of the river, stretches of whity-green water between pinkish-grey shoals among the dark pine woods. There it was, spread out a long way off. And it seemed to come downhill, the river. There was a raft being steered, a mile away. It was a strange country. Nearer, a red-roofed, broad farm with white base and square dots of windows crouched beside the wall of beech foliage on the wood's edge. There were long strips of rye and clover and pale green corn. And just at his feet, below the knoll, was a darkish bog, where globe flowers stood breathless still on their slim stalks. And some of the pale gold bubbles were burst, and a broken fragment hung in the air. He thought he was going to sleep.

Suddenly something moved into his coloured mirage before his eyes. The Captain, a small, light-blue and scarlet figure, was trotting evenly between the strips of corn, along the level brow of the hill. And the man making flag-signals was coming on. Proud and sure moved the horseman's figure, the quick, bright thing, in which was concentrated all the light of this morning, which for the rest lay a fragile, shining shadow. Submissive, apathetic, the young soldier sat and stared. But as the horse slowed to a walk, coming up the last steep path, the great flash flared over the body and soul of the orderly. He sat waiting. The back of his head felt as if it were weighted with a heavy piece of fire. He did not want to eat. His hands trembled slightly as he moved them. Meanwhile the officer on horseback was approaching slowly and proudly. The tension grew in the orderly's soul. Then again, seeing the Captain ease himself on the saddle, the flash blazed through him.

The Captain looked at the patch of light blue and scarlet, and dark heads, scattered closely on the hillside. It pleased him. The command pleased him. And he was feeling proud. His orderly was among them in common subjection. The officer rose a little on his stirrups to look. The young soldier sat with averted, dumb face. The Captain relaxed on his seat. His slim-legged, beautiful horse, brown as a beech nut, walked proudly uphill. The Captain passed into the zone of the company's atmosphere: a hot smell of men, of sweat, of leather. He knew it very well. After a word with the lieutenant, he went a few paces higher, and sat there, a dominant figure, his sweat-marked horse swishing its tail, while he looked down on his men, on his orderly, a nonentity among the crowd.

The young soldier's heart was like fire in his chest, and he breathed with difficulty. The officer, looking downhill, saw three of the young soldiers, two pails of water between them, staggering across a sunny green field. A table had been set up under a tree, and there the slim lieutenant stood, importantly busy. Then the Captain summoned himself to an act of courage. He called his orderly.

The flame leapt into the soldier's throat as he heard the command, and he rose blindly, stifled. He saluted, standing below the officer. He did not look up. But there was the flicker in the Captain's voice.

"Go to the inn and fetch me . . ." the officer gave his commands. "Quick!" he added.

At the last word, the heart of the servant leapt with a flash, and he felt the strength come over his body. But he turned in mechanical obedience, and set off at a heavy run downhill, looking almost like a bear, his trousers bagging over his military boots. And the officer watched this blind, plunging run all the way.

But it was only the outside of the orderly's body that was obeying so humbly and mechanically. Inside had gradually accumulated a core into which all the energy of that young life was compact and concentrated. He executed his commission, and plodded quickly back uphill. There was a pain in his head, as he walked, that made him twist his features unknowingly. But hard there in the centre of his chest was himself, himself, firm, and not to be plucked to pieces.

The captain had gone up into the wood. The orderly plodded through the hot, powerfully smelling zone of the company's atmosphere. He had a curious mass of energy inside him now. The Captain was less real than himself. He approached the green entrance to the wood. There, in the half-shade, he saw the horse standing, the sunshine and the flickering shadow of leaves dancing over his brown body.

There was a clearing where timber had lately been felled. Here, in the gold-green shade beside the brilliant cup of sunshine, stood two figures, blue and pink, the bits of pink showing out plainly. The Captain was talking to his lieutenant.

The orderly stood on the edge of the bright clearing, where great trunks of trees, stripped and glistening, lay stretched like naked, brown-skinned bodies. Chips of wood littered the trampled floor, like splashed light, and the bases of the felled trees stood here and there, with their raw, level tops. Beyond was the brilliant, sunlit green of a beech.

"Then I will ride forward," the orderly heard his Captain say. The lieutenant saluted and strode away. He himself went forward. A hot flash passed through his belly, as he tramped towards his officer.

The Captain watched the rather heavy figure of the young soldier stumble forward, and his veins, too, ran hot. This was to be man to man between them. He yielded before the solid, stumbling figure with bent head. The orderly stooped and put the food on a level-sawn tree-base. The Captain watched the glistening, sun-inflamed, naked hands. He wanted to speak to the young soldier, but could not. The servant propped a bottle against his thigh, pressed open the cork, and poured out the beer into the mug. He kept his head bent. The Captain accepted the mug.

"Ho!" he said, as if amiably.

The flame sprang out of the orderly's heart, nearly suffocating him.

"Yes, sir," he replied, between shut teeth.

And he heard the sound of the Captain's drinking, and he clenched his fists, such a strong torment came into his wrists. Then came the faint clang of the closing of the pot-lid. He looked up. The Captain was watching him. He glanced swiftly away. Then he saw the officer stoop and take a piece of bread from the tree-base. Again the flash of flame went through the young soldier, seeing the stiff body stoop beneath him, and his hands jerked. He looked away. He could feel the officer was nervous. The bread fell as it was being broken. The officer ate the other piece. The two men stood tense and still, the master laboriously chewing his bread, the servant staring with averted face, his fist clenched.

Then the young soldier started. The officer had pressed open the lid of the mug again. The orderly watched the lid of the mug, and the white hand that clenched the handle, as if he were fascinated. It was raised. The youth followed it with his eyes. And then he saw the thin, strong throat of the elder man moving up and down as he drank, the strong jaw working. And the instinct which had been jerking at the young man's wrists suddenly jerked free. He jumped, feeling as if it were rent in two by a strong flame.

The spur of the officer caught in a tree-root, he went down backwards with a crash, the middle of his back thudding sickeningly against a sharp-edged tree-base, the pot flying away. And in a second the orderly, with serious, earnest young face, and underlip between his teeth, had got his knee in the officer's chest and was pressing the chin backward over the farther edge of the tree-stump, pressing, with all his heart behind in a passion of relief, the tension of his wrists exquisite with relief. And with the base of his palms he shoved at the chin, with all his might. And it was pleasant, too, to have that chin, that hard jaw already slightly rough with beard, in his hands. He did not relax one hair's breadth, but, all the force of all his blood exulting in his thrust, he shoved back the head of the other man, till there was a little "cluck" and a crunching sensation. Then he felt as if his head went to vapour. Heavy convulsions shook the body of the officer, frightening and horrifying the young soldier. Yet it pleased him, too, to repress them. It pleased him to keep his hands pressing back the chin, to feel the chest of the other man yield in expiration to the weight of his strong, young knees, to feel the hard twitchings of the prostrate body jerking his own whole frame, which was pressed down on it.

But it went still. He could look into the nostrils of the other man, the eyes he could scarcely see. How curiously the mouth was pushed out, exaggerating the full lips, and the moustache bristling up from them. Then, with a start, he noticed the nostrils gradually filled with blood. The red brimmed, hesitated, ran over, and went in a thin trickle down the face to the eyes.

It shocked and distressed him. Slowly, he got up. The body twitched and sprawled there, inert. He stood and looked at it in silence. It was a pity *it* was broken. It represented more than the thing which had kicked and bullied him. He was afraid to look at the eyes. They were hideous now, only the whites showing, and the blood running to them. The face of the orderly was drawn with horror at the sight. Well, it was so. In his heart he was satisfied. He had hated the face of the Captain. It was extinguished now. There was a heavy relief in the orderly's soul. That was as it should be. But he could not bear to see the long, military body lying broken over the tree-base, the fine fingers crisped. He wanted to hide it away.

Quickly, busily, he gathered it up and pushed it under the felled tree trunks, which rested their beautiful, smooth length either end on logs. The face was horrible with blood. He covered it with the helmet. Then he pushed the limbs straight and decent, and brushed the dead leaves off the fine cloth of the uniform. So, it lay quite still in the shadow under there. A little strip of sunshine ran along the breast, from a chink between the logs. The orderly sat by it for a few moments. Here his own life also ended.

Then, through his daze, he heard the lieutenant, in a loud voice, explaining to the men outside the wood, that they were to suppose the bridge on the river below was held by the enemy. Now they were to march to the attack in such and such a manner. The lieutenant had no gift of expression. The orderly, listening from habit, got muddled. And when the lieutenant began it all again he ceased to hear.

He knew he must go. He stood up. It surprised him that the leaves were glittering in the sun, and the chips of wood reflecting white from the ground. For him a change had come over the world. But for the rest it had not – all seemed the same. Only he had left it. And he could not go back. It was his duty to return with the beer-pot and the bottle. He could not. He had left all that. The lieutenant was still hoarsely explaining. He must go, or they would overtake him. And he could not bear contact with anyone now.

He drew his fingers over his eyes, trying to find out where he was. Then he turned away. He saw the horse standing in the path. He went up to it and mounted. It hurt him to sit in the saddle. The pain of keeping his seat occupied him as they cantered through the wood. He would not have minded anything, but he could not get away from the sense of being divided from the others. The path led out of the trees. On the edge of the wood he pulled up and stood watching. There in the spacious sunshine of the valley soldiers were moving in a little swarm. Every now and then, a man harrowing on a strip of fallow shouted to his oxen, at the turn. The village and the white-towered church was small in the sunshine. And he no longer belonged to it – he sat there, beyond, like a man outside in the dark. He had gone out from everyday life into the unknown, and he could not, he even did not want to go back.

Turning from the sun-blazing valley, he rode deep into the wood. Tree-trunks, like people standing grey and still, took no notice as he went. A doe, herself a moving bit of sunshine and shadow, went running through the flecked shade. There were bright green rents in the foliage. Then it was all pine wood, dark and cool. And he was sick with pain, he had an intolerable great pulse in his head, and he was sick. He had never been ill in his life. He felt lost, quite dazed with all this.

Trying to get down from the horse, he fell, astonished at the pain and his lack of balance. The horse shifted uneasily. He jerked its bridle and sent it cantering jerkily away. It was his last connection with the rest of things.

But he only wanted to lie down and not be disturbed. Stumbling through the trees, he came on a quiet place where beeches and pine trees grew on a slope. Immediately he had lain down and closed his eyes, his consciousness went racing on without him. A big pulse of sickness beat in him as if it throbbed through the whole earth. He was burning with dry heat. But he was too busy, too tearingly active in the incoherent race of delirium to observe.

III

He came to with a start. His mouth was dry and hard, his heart beat heavily, but he had not the energy to get up. His heart beat heavily. Where was he? – the barracks – at home? There was something knocking. And, making an effort, he looked round – trees, and litter of greenery, and reddish, bright, still pieces of sunshine on the floor. He did not believe he was himself, he did not believe what he saw. Something was knocking. He made a struggle towards consciousness, but relapsed. Then he struggled again. And gradually his surroundings fell into relationship with himself. He knew, and a great pang of fear went through his heart. Somebody was knocking. He could see the heavy, black rags of a fir tree overhead. Then everything went black. Yet he did not believe he had closed his eyes. He had not. Out of the blackness sight slowly emerged again. And someone was knocking. Quickly, he saw the blood-disfigured face of his Captain, which he hated. And he held himself still with horror. Yet, deep inside him, he knew that it was so, the Captain should be dead. But the physical delirium got hold of him. Someone was knocking. He lay perfectly still, as if dead, with fear. And he went unconscious.

When he opened his eyes again, he started, seeing something creeping swiftly up a tree-trunk. It was a little bird. And the bird was whistling overhead. Tap-tap-tap – it was the small, quick bird rapping the tree-trunk with its beak, as if its head were a little round hammer. He watched it curiously. It shifted sharply, in its creeping fashion. Then, like a mouse, it slid down the bare trunk. Its swift creeping sent a flash of revulsion through him. He raised his head. It felt a great weight. Then, the little bird ran out of the shadow across a still patch of sunshine, its little head bobbing swiftly, its white legs twinkling brightly for a moment. How neat it was in its build, so compact, with pieces of white on its wings. There were several of them. They were so pretty – but they crept like swift, erratic mice, running here and there among the beech-mast.

He lay down again exhausted, and his consciousness lapsed. He had a horror of the little creeping birds. All his blood seemed to be darting and creeping in his head. And yet he could not move.

He came to with a further ache of exhaustion. There was the pain in his head, and the horrible sickness, and his inability to move. He had never been ill in his life. He did not know where he was or what he was. Probably he had got sunstroke. Or what else? – he had silenced the Captain for ever – some time ago – oh, a long time ago. There had been blood on his face, and his eyes had turned upwards. It was all right, somehow. It was peace. But now he had got beyond himself. He had never been here before. Was it life, or not life? He was by himself. They were in a big, bright place, those others, and he was outside. The town, all the country, a big bright place of light: and he was outside, here, in the darkened open beyond, where each thing existed alone. But they would all have to come out there sometime, those others. Little, and left behind him, they all were. There had been father and mother and sweetheart. What did they all matter? This was the open land.

He sat up. Something scuffled. It was a little, brown squirrel running in lovely, undulating bounds over the floor, its red tail completing the undulation of its body – and then, as it sat up, furling and unfurling. He watched it, pleased. It ran on again, friskily, enjoying itself. It flew wildly at another squirrel, and they were chasing each other, and making little scolding, chattering noises. The soldier wanted to speak to them. But only a hoarse sound came out of his throat. The squirrels burst away – they flew up the trees. And then he saw the one peeping round at him, half-way up a tree-trunk. A start of fear went through him, though, in so far as he was conscious, he was amused. It still stayed, its little, keen face staring at him half-way up the tree-trunk, its little ears pricked up, its clawey little hands clinging to the bark, its white breast reared. He started from it in panic.

Struggling to his feet, he lurched away. He went on walking, walking, looking for something – for a drink. His brain felt hot and inflamed for want of water. He stumbled on. Then he did not know anything. He went unconscious as he walked. Yet he stumbled on, his mouth open.

When, to his dumb wonder, he opened his eyes on the world again, he no longer tried to remember what it was. There was thick, golden light behind golden-green glitterings, and tall, grey-purple shafts, and darknesses further off, surrounding him, growing deeper. He was conscious of a sense of arrival. He was amid the reality, on the real, dark bottom. But there was the thirst burning in his brain. He felt lighter not so heavy. He supposed it was newness. The air was muttering with thunder. He thought he was walking wonderfully swiftly and was coming straight to relief – or was it to water?

Suddenly he stood still with fear. There was a tremendous flare of gold, immense – just a few dark trunks like bars between him and it. All the young level wheat was burnished gold glaring on its silky green. A woman, full-skirted, a black cloth on her head for head-dress, was passing like a block of shadow through the glistening, green corn, into the full glare. There was a farm, too, pale blue in shadow, and the timber black. There was a church spire, nearly fused away in the gold. The woman moved on, away from him. He had no language with which to speak to her. She was the bright, solid unreality. She would make a noise of words that would confuse him, and her eyes would look at him without seeing him. She was crossing there to the other side. He stood against a tree.

When at last he turned, looking down the long, bare grove whose flat bed was already filling dark, he saw the mountains in a wonder-light, not far away, and radiant. Behind the soft, grey ridge of the nearest range the further mountains stood golden and pale grey, the snow all radiant like pure, soft gold. So still, gleaming in the sky, fashioned pure out of the ore of the sky, they shone in their silence. He stood and looked at them, his face illuminated. And like the golden, lustrous gleaming of the snow he felt his own thirst bright in him. He stood and gazed, leaning against a tree. And then everything slid away into space.

During the night the lightning fluttered perpetually, making the whole sky white. He must have walked again. The world hung livid round him for moments, fields a level sheen of grey-green light, trees in dark bulk, and the range of clouds black across a white sky. Then the darkness fell like a shutter, and the night was whole. A faint flutter of a half-revealed world, that could not quite leap out of the darkness! – Then there again stood a sweep of pallor for the land, dark shapes looming, a range of clouds hanging overhead. The world was a ghostly shadow, thrown for a moment upon the pure darkness, which returned ever whole and complete.

And the mere delirium of sickness and fever went on inside him — his brain opening and shutting like the night — then sometimes convulsions of terror from something with great eyes that stared round a tree — then the long agony of the march, and the sun decomposing his blood — then the pang of hate for the Captain, followed by a pang of tenderness and ease. But everything was distorted, born of an ache and resolving into an ache.

In the morning he came definitely awake. Then his brain flamed with the sole horror of thirstiness! The sun was on his face, the dew was steaming from his wet clothes. Like one possessed, he got up. There, straight in front of him, blue and cool and tender, the mountains ranged across the pale edge of the morning sky. He wanted them — he wanted them alone — he wanted to leave himself and be identified with them. They did not move, they were still and soft, with white, gentle markings of snow. He stood still, mad with suffering, his hands crisping and clutching. Then he was twisting in a paroxysm on the grass.

He lay still, in a kind of dream of anguish. His thirst seemed to have separated itself from him, and to stand apart, a single demand. Then the pain he felt was another single self. Then there was the clog of his body, another separate thing. He was divided among all kinds of separate beings. There was some strange, agonized connection between them, but they were drawing further apart. Then they would all split. The sun, drilling down on him, was drilling through the bond. Then they would all fall, fall through the everlasting lapse of space. Then again, his consciousness reasserted itself. He roused on to his elbow and stared at the gleaming mountains. There they ranked, all still and wonderful between earth and heaven. He stared till his eyes went black, and the mountains, as they stood in their beauty, so clean and cool, seemed to have it, that which was lost in him.

IV

When the soldiers found him, three hours later, he was lying with his face over his arm, his black hair giving off heat under the sun. But he was still alive. Seeing the open, black mouth the young soldiers dropped him in horror.

He died in the hospital at night, without having seen again.

The doctors saw the bruises on his legs, behind, and were silent.

The bodies of the two men lay together, side by side, in the mortuary, the one white and slender, but laid rigidly at rest, the other looking as if every moment it must rouse into life again, so young and unused, from a slumber.

ODOUR OF CHRYSANTHEMUMS

I

The small locomotive engine, Number 4, came clanking, stumbling down from Selston with seven full wagons. It appeared round the corner with loud threats of speed, but the colt that it startled from among the gorse, which still flickered indistinctly in the raw afternoon, out-distanced it at a canter. A woman, walking up the railway line to Underwood, drew back into the hedge, held her basket aside, and watched the footplate of the engine advancing. The trucks thumped heavily past, one by one, with slow inevitable movement, as she stood insignificantly trapped between the jolting black wagons and the hedge; then they curved away towards the coppice where the withered oak leaves dropped noiselessly, while the birds, pulling at the scarlet hips beside the track, made off into the dusk that had already crept into the spinney. In the open, the smoke from the engine sank and cleaved to the rough grass. The fields were dreary and forsaken, and in the marshy strip that led to the whimsey, a reedy pit-pond, the fowls had already abandoned their run along the alders, to roost in the tarred fowl-house. The pit-bank loomed up beyond the pond, flames like red sores licking its ashy sides, in the afternoon's stagnant light. Just beyond rose the tapering chimneys and the clumsy black headstocks of Brinsley Colliery. The two wheels were spinning fast up against the sky, and the winding engine rapped out its little spasms. The miners were being turned up.

The engine whistled as it came into the wide bay of railway lines beside the colliery, where rows of trucks stood in harbour.

Miners, single, trailing and in groups, passed like shadows diverging home. At the edge of the ribbed level of sidings squat a low cottage, three steps down from the cinder track. A large bony vine clutched at the house, as if to claw down the tiled roof. Round the bricked yard grew a few wintry primroses. Beyond, the long garden sloped down to a bush-covered brook course. There were some twiggy apple trees, winter-crack trees, and ragged cabbages. Beside the path hung dishevelled pink chrysanthemums, like pink cloths hung on bushes. A woman came stooping out of the felt-covered fowl-house, half-way down the garden. She closed and padlocked the door, then drew herself erect, having brushed some bits from her white apron.

She was a tall woman of imperious mien, handsome, with definite black eyebrows. Her smooth black hair was parted exactly. For a few moments she stood steadily watching the miners as they passed along the railway: then she turned towards the brook course. Her face was calm and set, her mouth was closed with disillusionment. After a moment she called:

"John!" There was no answer. She waited, and then said distinctly:

"Where are you?"

"Here!" replied a child's sulky voice from among the bushes. The woman looked piercingly through the dusk.

"Are you at that brook?" she asked sternly.

For answer the child showed himself before the raspberry-canes that rose like whips. He was a small, sturdy boy of five. He stood quite still, defiantly.

"Oh!" said the mother, conciliated. "I thought you were down at that wet brook – and you remember what I told you —"

The boy did not move or answer.

"Come, come on in," she said more gently, "it's getting dark. There's your grandfather's engine coming down the line!"

The lad advanced slowly, with resentful, taciturn movement. He was dressed in trousers and waistcoat of cloth that was too thick and hard for the size of the garments. They were evidently cut down from a man's clothes.

As they went slowly towards the house he tore at the ragged wisps of chrysanthemums and dropped the petals in handfuls along the path.

"Don't do that – it does look nasty," said his mother. He refrained, and she, suddenly pitiful, broke off a twig with three or four wan flowers and held them against her face. When mother and son reached the yard her hand hesitated, and instead of laying the flower aside, she pushed it in her apron-band. The mother and son stood at the foot of the three steps looking across the bay of lines at the passing home of the miners. The trundle of the small train was imminent. Suddenly the engine loomed past the house and came to a stop opposite the gate.

The engine-driver, a short man with round grey beard, leaned out of the cab high above the woman.

"Have you got a cup of tea?" he said in a cheery, hearty fashion.

It was her father. She went in, saying she would mash. Directly, she returned.

"I didn't come to see you on Sunday," began the little grey-bearded man.

"I didn't expect you," said his daughter.

The engine-driver winced; then, reassuming his cheery, airy manner, he said:

"Oh, have you heard then? Well, and what do you think — ?"

"I think it is soon enough," she replied.

At her brief censure the little man made an impatient gesture, and said coaxingly, yet with dangerous coldness:

"Well, what's a man to do? It's no sort of life for a man of my years, to sit at my own hearth like a stranger. And if I'm going to marry again it may as well be soon as late – what does it matter to anybody?"

The woman did not reply, but turned and went into the house. The man in the engine-cab stood assertive, till she returned with a cup of tea and a piece of bread and butter on a plate. She went up the steps and stood near the footplate of the hissing engine.

"You needn't 'a' brought me bread an' butter," said her father. "But a cup of tea" – he sipped appreciatively – "it's very nice." He sipped for a moment or two, then: "I hear as Walter's got another bout on," he said.

"When hasn't he?" said the woman bitterly.

"I heerd tell of him in the 'Lord Nelson' braggin' as he was going to spend that b— afore he went: half a sovereign that was."

"When?" asked the woman.

"A' Sat'day night – I know that's true."

"Very likely," she laughed bitterly. "He gives me twenty-three shillings."

"Aye, it's a nice thing, when a man can do nothing with his money but make a beast of himself!" said the grey-whiskered man. The woman turned her head away. Her father swallowed the last of his tea and handed her the cup.

"Aye," he sighed, wiping his mouth. "It's a settler, it is —"

He put his hand on the lever. The little engine strained and groaned, and the train rumbled towards the crossing. The woman again looked across the metals. Darkness was settling over the spaces of the railway and trucks: the miners, in grey sombre groups, were still passing home. The winding engine pulsed hurriedly, with brief pauses. Elizabeth Bates looked at the dreary flow of men, then she went indoors. Her husband did not come.

The kitchen was small and full of firelight; red coals piled glowing up the chimney mouth. All the life of the room seemed in the white, warm hearth and the steel fender reflecting the red fire. The cloth was laid for tea; cups glinted in the shadows. At the back, where the lowest stairs protruded into the room, the boy sat struggling with a knife and a piece of white wood. He was almost hidden in the shadow. It was half-past four. They had but to await the father's coming to begin tea. As the mother watched her son's sullen little struggle with the wood, she saw herself in his silence and pertinacity; she saw the father in her child's indifference to all but himself. She seemed to be occupied by her husband. He had probably gone past his home, slung past his own door, to drink before he came in, while his dinner spoiled and wasted in waiting. She glanced at the clock, then took the potatoes to strain them in the yard. The garden and fields beyond the brook were closed in uncertain darkness. When she rose with the saucepan, leaving the drain steaming into the night behind her, she saw the yellow lamps were lit along the high road that went up the hill away beyond the space of the railway lines and the field.

Then again she watched the men trooping home, fewer now and fewer.

Indoors the fire was sinking and the room was dark red. The woman put her saucepan on the hob, and set a batter-pudding near the mouth of the oven. Then she stood unmoving. Directly, gratefully, came quick young steps to the door. Someone hung on the latch a moment, then a little girl entered and began pulling off her outdoor things, dragging a mass of curls, just ripening from gold to brown, over her eyes with her hat.

Her mother chid her for coming late from school, and said she would have to keep her at home the dark winter days.

"Why, mother, it's hardly a bit dark yet. The lamp's not lighted, and my father's not home."

"No, he isn't. But it's a quarter to five! Did you see anything of him?"

The child became serious. She looked at her mother with large, wistful blue eyes.

"No, mother, I've never seen him. Why? Has he come up an' gone past, to Old Brinsley? He hasn't, mother, 'cos I never saw him."

"He'd watch that," said the mother bitterly, "he'd take care as you didn't see him. But you may depend upon it, he's seated in the 'Prince o' Wales.' He wouldn't be this late."

The girl looked at her mother piteously.

"Let's have our teas, mother, should we?" said she.

The mother called John to table. She opened the door once more and looked out across the darkness of the lines. All was deserted: she could not hear the winding-engines.

"Perhaps," she said to herself, "he's stopped to get some ripping done."

They sat down to tea. John, at the end of the table near the door, was almost lost in the darkness. Their faces were hidden from each other. The girl crouched against the fender slowly moving a thick piece of bread before the fire. The lad, his face a dusky mark on the shadow, sat watching her who was transfigured in the red glow.

"I do think it's beautiful to look in the fire," said the child.

"Do you?" said her mother. "Why?"

"It's so red, and full of little caves – and it feels so nice, and you can fair smell it."

"It'll want mending directly," replied her mother, "and then if your father comes he'll carry on and say there never is a fire when a man comes home sweating from the pit. A public-house is always warm enough."

There was silence till the boy said complainingly: "Make haste, our Annie."

"Well, I am doing! I can't make the fire do it no faster, can I?"

"She keeps wafflin' it about so's to make 'er slow," grumbled the boy.

"Don't have such an evil imagination, child," replied the mother.

Soon the room was busy in the darkness with the crisp sound of crunching. The mother ate very little. She drank her tea determinedly, and sat thinking. When she rose her anger was evident in the stern unbending of her head. She looked at the pudding in the fender, and broke out:

"It is a scandalous thing as a man can't even come home to his dinner! If it's crozzled up to a cinder I don't see why I should care. Past his very door he goes to get to a public-house, and here I sit with his dinner waiting for him —"

She went out. As she dropped piece after piece of coal on the red fire, the shadows fell on the walls, till the room was almost in total darkness.

"I canna see," grumbled John. In spite of herself, the mother laughed.

"You know the way to your mouth," she said. She set the dust-pan outside the door. When she came again like a shadow on the hearth, the lad repeated, complaining sulkily:

"I canna see."

"Good gracious!" cried the mother irritably, "you're as bad as your father if it's a bit dusk!"

Nevertheless, she took a paper spill from a sheaf on the mantelpiece and proceeded to light the lamp that hung from the ceiling in the middle of the room. As she reached up, her figure displayed itself just rounding with maternity.

"Oh, mother — !" exclaimed the girl.

"What?" said the woman, suspended in the act of putting the lampglass over the flame. The copper reflector shone handsomely on her, as she stood with uplifted arm, turning to face her daughter.

"You've got a flower in your apron!" said the child, in a little rapture at this unusual event.

"Goodness me!" exclaimed the woman, relieved. "One would think the house was afire." She replaced the glass and waited a moment before turning up the wick. A pale shadow was seen floating vaguely on the floor.

"Let me smell!" said the child, still rapturously, coming forward and putting her face to her mother's waist.

"Go along, silly!" said the mother, turning up the lamp. The light revealed their suspense so that the woman felt it almost unbearable. Annie was still bending at her waist. Irritably, the mother took the flowers out from her apron-band.

"Oh, mother – don't take them out!" Annie cried, catching her hand and trying to replace the sprig.

"Such nonsense!" said the mother, turning away. The child put the pale chrysanthemums to her lips, murmuring:

"Don't they smell beautiful!"

Her mother gave a short laugh.

"No," she said, "not to me. It was chrysanthemums when I married him, and chrysanthemums when you were born, and the first time they ever brought him home drunk, he'd got brown chrysanthemums in his button-hole."

She looked at the children. Their eyes and their parted lips were wondering. The mother sat rocking in silence for some time. Then she looked at the clock.

"Twenty minutes to six!" In a tone of fine bitter carelessness she continued: "Eh, he'll not come now till they bring him. There he'll stick! But he needn't come rolling in here in his pit-dirt, for *I* won't wash him. He can lie on the floor — Eh, what a fool I've been, what a fool! And this is what I came here for, to this dirty hole, rats and all, for him to slink past his very door. Twice last week – he's begun now —"

She silenced herself, and rose to clear the table.

While for an hour or more the children played, subduedly intent, fertile of imagination, united in fear of the mother's wrath, and in dread of their father's home-coming, Mrs. Bates sat in her rockingchair making a 'singlet' of thick cream-coloured flannel, which gave a dull wounded sound as she tore off the grey edge. She worked at her sewing with energy, listening to the children, and her anger wearied itself, lay down to rest, opening its eyes from time to time and steadily watching, its ears raised to listen. Sometimes even her anger quailed and shrank, and the mother suspended her sewing, tracing the footsteps that thudded along the sleepers outside; she would lift her head sharply to bid the children 'hush,' but she recovered herself in time, and the footsteps went past the gate, and the children were not flung out of their play-world.

But at last Annie sighed, and gave in. She glanced at her wagon of slippers, and loathed the game. She turned plaintively to her mother.

"Mother!" – but she was inarticulate.

John crept out like a frog from under the sofa. His mother glanced up.

"Yes," she said, "just look at those shirt-sleeves!"

The boy held them out to survey them, saying nothing. Then somebody called in a hoarse voice away down the line, and suspense bristled in the room, till two people had gone by outside, talking.

"It is time for bed," said the mother.

"My father hasn't come," wailed Annie plaintively. But her mother was primed with courage.

"Never mind. They'll bring him when he does come – like a log." She meant there would be no scene. "And he may sleep on the floor till he wakes himself. I know he'll not go to work to-morrow after this!"

The children had their hands and faces wiped with a flannel. They were very quiet. When they had put on their night-dresses, they said their prayers, the boy mumbling. The mother looked down at them, at the brown silken bush of intertwining curls in the nape of the girl's neck, at the little black head of the lad, and her heart burst with anger at their father, who caused all three such distress. The children hid their faces in her skirts for comfort.

When Mrs. Bates came down, the room was strangely empty, with a tension of expectancy. She took up her sewing and stitched for some time without raising her head. Meantime her anger was tinged with fear.

II

The clock struck eight and she rose suddenly, dropping her sewing on her chair. She went to the stair-foot door, opened it, listening. Then she went out, locking the door behind her.

Something scuffled in the yard, and she started, though she knew it was only the rats with which the place was over-run. The night was very dark. In the great bay of railway lines, bulked with trucks, there was no trace of light, only away back she could see a few yellow lamps at the pit-top, and the red smear of the burning pit-bank on the night. She hurried along the edge of the track, then, crossing the converging lines, came to the stile by the white gates, whence she emerged on the road. Then the fear which had led her shrank. People were walking up to New Brinsley; she saw the light in the houses; twenty yards farther on were the broad windows of the 'Prince of Wales,' very warm and bright, and the loud voices of men could be heard distinctly. What a fool she had been to imagine that anything had happened to him! He was merely drinking over there at the 'Prince of Wales.' She faltered. She had never yet been to fetch him, and she never would go. So she continued her walk towards the long straggling line of houses, standing back on the highway. She entered a passage between the dwellings.

"Mr. Rigley? – Yes! Did you want him? No, he's not in at this minute."

The raw-boned woman leaned forward from her dark scullery and peered at the other, upon whom fell a dim light through the blind of the kitchen window.

"Is it Mrs. Bates?" she asked in a tone tinged with respect.

"Yes. I wondered if your Master was at home. Mine hasn't come yet."

"'Asn't 'e! Oh Jack's been 'ome an' 'ad 'is dinner an' gone out. 'E's just gone for 'alf an hour afore bed-time. Did you call at the 'Prince of Wales'?"

"No —"

"No, you didn't like —! It's not very nice." The other woman was indulgent. There was an awkward pause. "Jack never said nothink about – about your Master," she said.

"No! – I expect he's stuck in there!"

Elizabeth Bates said this bitterly, and with recklessness. She knew that the woman across the yard was standing at her door listening, but she did not care. As she turned:

"Stop a minute! I'll just go an' ask Jack if 'e knows anythink," said Mrs. Rigley.

"Oh no – I wouldn't like to put —!"

"Yes, I will, if you'll just step inside an' see as th' childer doesn't come downstairs and set themselves afire."

Elizabeth Bates, murmuring a remonstrance, stepped inside. The other woman apologised for the state of the room.

The kitchen needed apology. There were little frocks and trousers and childish undergarments on the squab and on the floor, and a litter of playthings everywhere.

On the black American cloth of the table were pieces of bread and cake, crusts, slops, and a teapot with cold tea.

"Eh, ours is just as bad," said Elizabeth Bates, looking at the woman, not at the house. Mrs. Rigley put a shawl over her head and hurried out, saying:

"I shanna be a minute."

The other sat, noting with faint disapproval the general untidiness of the room. Then she fell to counting the shoes of various sizes scattered over the floor. There were twelve. She sighed and said to herself: "No wonder!" – glancing at the litter. There came the scratching of two pairs of feet on the yard, and the Rigleys entered. Elizabeth Bates rose. Rigley was a big man, with very large bones. His head looked particularly bony. Across his temple was a blue scar, caused by a wound got in the pit, a wound in which the coal-dust remained blue like tattooing.

" 'Asna 'e come whoam yit?" asked the man, without any form of greeting, but with deference and sympathy. "I couldna say wheer he is – 'e's non ower theer!" – he jerked his head to signify the 'Prince of Wales.'

" 'E's 'appen gone up to th' 'Yew,' " said Mrs. Rigley.

There was another pause. Rigley had evidently something to get off his mind:

"Ah left 'im finishin' a stint," he began. "Loose-all 'ad bin gone about ten minutes when we com'n away, an' I shouted: 'Are ter comin', Walt?' an' 'e said: 'Go on, Ah shanna be but a'ef a minnit,' so we com'n ter th' bottom, me an' Bowers, thinkin' as 'e wor just behint, an' 'ud come up i' th' next bantle —"

He stood perplexed, as if answering a charge of deserting his mate. Elizabeth Bates, now again certain of disaster, hastened to reassure him:

"I expect 'e's gone up to th' 'Yew Tree', as you say. It's not the first time. I've fretted myself into a fever before now. He'll come home when they carry him."

"Ay, isn't it too bad!" deplored the other woman.

"I'll just step up to Dick's an' see if 'e *is* theer," offered the man, afraid of appearing alarmed, afraid of taking liberties.

"Oh, I wouldn't think of bothering you that far," said Elizabeth Bates, with emphasis, but he knew she was glad of his offer.

As they stumbled up the entry, Elizabeth Bates heard Rigley's wife run across the yard and open her neighbor's door. At this, suddenly all the blood in her body seemed to switch away from her heart.

"Mind!" warned Rigley. "Ah've said many a time as Ah'd fill up them ruts in this entry, sumb'dy 'll be breakin' their legs yit."

She recovered herself and walked quickly along with the miner.

"I don't like leaving the children in bed, and nobody in the house," she said.

"No, you dunna!" he replied courteously. They were soon at the gate of the cottage.

"Well, I shanna be many minnits. Dunna you be frettin' now, 'e'll be all right," said the butty.

"Thank you very much, Mr. Rigley," she replied.

"You're welcome!" he stammered, moving away. "I shanna be many minnits."

The house was quiet. Elizabeth Bates took off her hat and shawl, and rolled back the rug. When she had finished, she sat down. It was a few minutes past nine. She was startled by the rapid chuff of the winding-engine at the pit, and the sharp whirr of the brakes on the rope as it descended. Again she felt the painful sweep of her blood, and she put her hand to her side, saying aloud: "Good gracious! – it's only the nine o'clock deputy going down," rebuking herself.

She sat still, listening. Half an hour of this, and she was wearied out.

"What am I working myself up like this for?" she said pitiably to herself, "I s'll only be doing myself some damage."

She took out her sewing again.

At a quarter to ten there were footsteps. One person! She watched for the door to open. It was an elderly woman, in a black bonnet and a black woollen shawl – his mother. She was about sixty years old, pale, with blue eyes, and her face all wrinkled and lamentable. She shut the door and turned to her daughter-in-law peevishly.

"Eh, Lizzie, whatever shall we do, whatever shall we do!" she cried.

Elizabeth drew back a little, sharply.

"What is it, mother?" she said.

The elder woman seated herself on the sofa.

"I don't know, child, I can't tell you!" – she shook her head slowly. Elizabeth sat watching her, anxious and vexed.

"I don't know," replied the grandmother, sighing very deeply. "There's no end to my troubles, there isn't. The things I've gone through, I'm sure it's enough —!" She wept without wiping her eyes, the tears running.

"But, mother," interrupted Elizabeth, "what do you mean? What is it?"

The grandmother slowly wiped her eyes. The fountains of her tears were stopped by Elizabeth's directness. She wiped her eyes slowly.

"Poor child! Eh, you poor thing!" she moaned. "I don't know what we're going to do, I don't – and you as you are – it's a thing, it is indeed!"

Elizabeth waited.

"Is he dead?" she asked, and at the words her heart swung violently, though she felt a slight flush of shame at the ultimate extravagance of the question. Her words suficiently frightened the old lady, almost brought her to herself.

"Don't say so, Elizabeth! We'll hope it's not as bad as that; no, may the Lord spare us that, Elizabeth. Jack Rigley came just as I was sittin' down to a glass afore going to bed, an' 'e said: ''Appen you'll go down th' line, Mrs. Bates. Walt's had an accident. 'Appen you'll go an' sit wi' 'er till we can get him home.' I hadn't time to ask him a word afore he was gone. An' I put my bonnet on an' come straight down, Lizzie. I thought to myself: 'Eh, that poor blessed child, if anybody should come an' tell her sudden, there's no knowin' what'll 'appen to 'er.' You mustn't let it upset you, Lizzie – or you know what to expect. How long is it, six months – or is it five, Lizzie? Ay!" – the old woman shook her head – "time slips on, it slips on! Ay!"

Elizabeth's thoughts were busy elsewhere. If he was killed – would she be able to manage on the little pension and what she could earn? – she counted up rapidly. If he was hurt – they wouldn't take him to the hospital – how tiresome he would be to nurse! – but perhaps she'd be able to get him away from the drink and his hateful ways. She would – while he was ill. The tears offered to come to her eyes at the picture. But what sentimental luxury was this she was beginning? She turned to consider the children. At any rate she was absolutely necessary for them. They were her business.

"Ay!" repeated the old woman, "it seems but a week or two since he brought me his first wages. Ay – he was a good lad, Elizabeth, he was, in his way. I don't know why he got to be such a trouble, I don't. He was a happy lad at home, only full of spirits. But there's no mistake he's been a handful of trouble, he has! I hope the Lord'll spare him to mend his ways. I hope so, I hope so. You've had a sight o' trouble with him, Elizabeth, you have indeed. But he was a jolly enough lad wi' me, he was, I can assure you. I don't know how it is. . . ."

The old woman continued to muse aloud, a monotonous irritating sound, while Elizabeth thought concentratedly, startled once, when she heard the winding-engine chuff quickly, and the brakes skirr with a shriek. Then she heard the engine more slowly, and the brakes made no sound. The old woman did not notice. Elizabeth waited in suspense. The mother-in-law talked, with lapses into silence.

"But he wasn't your son, Lizzie, an' it makes a difference. Whatever he was, I remember him when he was little, an' I learned to understand him and to make allowances. You've got to make allowances for them —"

It was half-past ten, and the old woman was saying: "But it's trouble from beginning to end; you're never too old for trouble, never too old for that —" when the gate banged back, and there were heavy feet on the steps.

"I'll go, Lizzie, let me go," cried the old woman, rising. But Elizabeth was at the door. It was a man in pit-clothes.

"They're bringin' 'im, Missis," he said. Elizabeth's heart halted a moment. Then it surged on again, almost suffocating her.

"Is he – is it bad?" she asked.

The man turned away, looking at the darkness:

"The doctor says 'e'd been dead hours. 'E saw 'im i' th' lampcabin."

The old woman, who stood just behind Elizabeth, dropped into a chair, and folded her hands, crying: "Oh, my boy, my boy!"

"Hush!" said Elizabeth, with a sharp twitch of a frown. "Be still, mother, don't waken th' children: I wouldn't have them down for anything!"

The old woman moaned softly, rocking herself. The man was drawing away. Elizabeth took a step forward.

"How was it?" she asked.

"Well, I couldn't say for sure," the man replied, very ill at ease. " 'E wor finishin' a stint an' th' butties 'ad gone, an' a lot o' stuff come down atop 'n 'im."

"And crushed him?" cried the widow, with a shudder.

"No," said the man, "it fell at th' back of 'im. 'E wor under th' face, an' it niver touched 'im. It shut 'im in. It seems 'e wor smothered."

Elizabeth shrank back. She heard the old woman behind her cry:

"What? – what did 'e say it was?"

The man replied, more loudly: " 'E wor smothered!"

Then the old woman wailed aloud, and this relieved Elizabeth.

"Oh, mother," she said, putting her hand on the old woman, "don't waken th' children, don't waken th' children."

She wept a little, unknowing, while the old mother rocked herself and moaned. Elizabeth remembered that they were bringing him home, and she must be ready. "They'll lay him in the parlour," she said to herself, standing a moment pale and perplexed.

Then she lighted a candle and went into the tiny room. The air was cold and damp, but she could not make a fire, there was no fireplace. She set down the candle and looked round. The candlelight glittered on the lustre-glasses, on the two vases that held some of the pink chrysanthemums, and on the dark mahogany. There was a cold, deathly smell of chrysanthemums in the room. Elizabeth stood looking at the flowers. She turned away, and calculated whether there would be room to lay him on the floor, between the couch and the chiffonier. She pushed the chairs aside. There would be room to lay him down and to step around him. Then she fetched the old red tablecloth, and another old cloth, spreading them down to save her bit of carpet. She shivered on leaving the parlour; so, from the dresser drawer she took a clean shirt and put it at the fire to air. All the time her mother-in-law was rocking herself in the chair and moaning.

"You'll have to move from there, mother," said Elizabeth. "They'll be bringing him in. Come in the rocker."

The old mother rose mechanically, and seated herself by the fire, continuing to lament. Elizabeth went into the pantry for another candle, and there, in the little pent-house under the naked tiles, she heard them coming. She stood still in the pantry doorway, listening. She heard them pass the end of the house, and come awkwardly down the three steps, a jumble of shuffling footsteps and muttering voices. The old woman was silent. The men were in the yard.

Then Elizabeth heard Matthews, the manager of the pit, say: "You go in first, Jim. Mind!"

The door came open, and the two women saw a collier backing into the room, holding one end of a stretcher, on which they could see the nailed pit-boots of the dead man. The two carriers halted, the man at the head stooping to the lintel of the door.

"Wheer will you have him?" asked the manager, a short, white-bearded man.

Elizabeth roused herself and came from the pantry carrying the unlighted candle.

"In the parlour," she said.

"In there, Jim!" pointed the manager, and the carriers backed round into the tiny room. The coat with which they had covered the body fell off as they awkwardly turned through the two doorways, and the women saw their man, naked to the waist, lying stripped for work. The old woman began to moan in a low voice of horror.

"Lay th' stretcher at th' side," snapped the manager, "an' put 'im on th' cloths. Mind now, mind! Look you now —!"

One of the men had knocked off a vase of chrysanthemums. He stared awkwardly, then they set down the stretcher. Elizabeth did not look at her husband. As soon as she could get in the room, she went and picked up the broken vase and the flowers.

"Wait a minute!" she said.

The three men waited in silence while she mopped up the water with a duster.

"Eh, what a job, what a job, to be sure!" the manager was saying, rubbing his brow with trouble and perplexity. "Never knew such a thing in my life, never! He'd no busines to ha' been left. I never knew such a thing in my life! Fell over him clean as a whistle, an' shut him in. Not four foot of space, there wasn't – yet it scarce bruised him."

He looked down at the dead man, lying prone, half naked, all grimed with coal-dust.

"'Sphyxiated,' the doctor said. It *is* the most terrible job I've ever known. Seems as if it was done o' purpose. Clean over him, an' shut 'im in, like a mouse-trap" – he made a sharp, descending gesture with his hand.

The colliers standing by jerked aside their heads in hopeless comment.

The horror of the thing bristled upon them all.

Then they heard the girl's voice upstairs calling shrilly: "Mother, mother – who is it? Mother, who is it?"

Elizabeth hurried to the foot of the stairs and opened the door:

"Go to sleep!" she commanded sharply. "What are you shouting about? Go to sleep at once – there's nothing —"

Then she began to mount the stairs. They could hear her on the boards, and on the plaster floor of the little bedroom. They could hear her distinctly:

"What's the matter now? – what's the matter with you, silly thing?" – her voice was much agitated, with an unreal gentleness.

"I thought it was some men come," said the plaintive voice of the child. "Has he come?"

"Yes, they've brought him. There's nothing to make a fuss about. Go to sleep now, like a good child."

They could hear her voice in the bedroom, they waited whilst she covered the children under the bedclothes.

"Is he drunk?" asked the girl, timidly, faintly.

"No! No – he's not! He – he's asleep."

"Is he asleep downstairs?"

"Yes – and don't make a noise."

There was silence for a moment, then the men heard the frightened child again:

"What's that noise?"

"It's nothing, I tell you, what are you bothering for?"

The noise was the grandmother moaning. She was oblivious of everything, sitting on her chair rocking and moaning. The manager put his hand on her arm and bade her "Sh – sh!!"

The old woman opened her eyes and looked at him. She was shocked by this interruption, and seemed to wonder.

"What time is it?" the plaintive thin voice of the child, sinking back unhappily into sleep, asked this last question.

"Ten o'clock," answered the mother more softly. Then she must have bent down and kissed the children.

Matthews beckoned to the men to come away. They put on their caps and took up the stretcher. Stepping over the body, they tiptoed out of the house. None of them spoke till they were far from the wakeful children.

When Elizabeth came down she found her mother alone on the parlour floor, leaning over the dead man, the tears dropping on him.

"We must lay him out," the wife said. She put on the kettle, then returning knelt at the feet, and began to unfasten the knotted leather laces. The room was clammy and dim with only one candle, so that she had to bend her face almost to the floor. At last she got off the heavy boots and put them away.

"You must help me now," she whispered to the old woman. Together they stripped the man.

When they arose, saw him lying in the naïve dignity of death, the women stood arrested in fear and respect. For a few moments they remained still, looking down, the old mother whimpering. Elizabeth felt countermanded. She saw him, how utterly inviolable he lay in himself. She had nothing to do with him. She could not accept it. Stooping, she laid her hand on him, in claim. He was still warm, for the mine was hot where he had died. His mother had his face between her hands, and was murmuring incoherently. The old tears fell in succession as drops from wet leaves; the mother was not weeping, merely her tears flowed. Elizabeth embraced the body of her husband, with cheek and lips. She seemed to be listening, inquiring, trying to get some connection. But she could not. She was driven away. He was impregnable.

She rose, went into the kitchen, where she poured warm water into a bowl, brought soap and flannel and a soft towel.

"I must wash him," she said.

Then the old mother rose stiffly, and watched Elizabeth as she carefully washed his face, carefully brushing the big blond moustache from his mouth with the flannel. She was afraid with a bottomless fear, so she ministered to him. The old woman, jealous, said:

"Let me wipe him!" – and she kneeled on the other side drying slowly as Elizabeth washed, her big black bonnet sometimes brushing the dark head of her daughter-in-law. They worked thus in silence for a long time. They never forgot it was death, and the touch of the man's dead body gave them strange emotions, different in each of the women; a great dread possessed them both, the mother felt the lie was given to her womb, she was denied; the wife felt the utter isolation of the human soul, the child within her was a weight apart from her.

At last it was finished. He was a man of handsome body, and his face showed no traces of drink. He was blond, full-fleshed, with fine limbs. But he was dead.

"Bless him," whispered his mother, looking always at his face, and speaking out of sheer terror. "Dear lad – bless him!" She spoke in a faint, sibilant ecstasy of fear and mother love.

Elizabeth sank down again to the floor, and put her face against his neck, and trembled and shuddered. But she had to draw away again. He was dead, and her living flesh had no place against his. A great dread and weariness held her: she was so unavailing. Her life was gone like this.

"White as milk he is, clear as a twelve-month baby, bless him, the darling!" the old mother murmured to herself. "Not a mark on him, clear and clean and white, beautiful as ever a child was made," she murmured with pride. Elizabeth kept her face hidden.

"He went peaceful, Lizzie – peaceful as sleep. Isn't he beautiful, the lamb? Ay – he must ha' made his peace, Lizzie. 'Appen he made it all right, Lizzie, shut in there. He'd have time. He wouldn't look like this if he hadn't made his peace. The lamb, the dear lamb. Eh, but he had a hearty laugh. I loved to hear it. He had the heartiest laugh, Lizzie, as a lad —"

Elizabeth looked up. The man's mouth was fallen back, slightly open under the cover of the moustache. The eyes, half shut, did not show glazed in the obscurity. Life with its smoky burning gone from him, had left him apart and utterly alien to her. And she knew what a stranger he was to her. In her womb was ice of fear, because of this separate stranger with whom she had been living as one flesh. Was this what it all meant – utter, intact separateness, obscured by heat of living? In dread she turned her face away. The fact was too deadly. There had been nothing between them, and yet they had come together, exchanging their nakedness repeatedly. Each time he had taken her, they had been two isolated beings, far apart as now. He was no more responsible than she. The child was like ice in her womb. For as she looked at the dead man, her mind, cold and detached, said clearly: "Who am I? What have I been doing? I have been fighting a husband who did not exist. *He* existed all the time. What wrong have I done? What was that I have been living with? There lies the reality, this man." And her soul died in her for fear: she knew she had never seen him, he had never seen her, they had met in the dark and had fought in the dark, not knowing whom they met nor whom they fought. And now she saw, and turned silent in seeing. For she had been wrong. She had said he was something he was not; she had felt familiar with him. Whereas he was apart all the while, living as she never lived, feeling as she never felt.

In fear and shame she looked at his naked body, that she had known falsely. And he was the father of her children. Her soul was torn from her body and stood apart. She looked at his naked body and was ashamed, as if she had denied it. After all, it was itself. It seemed awful to her. She looked at his face, and she turned her own face to the wall. For his look was other than hers, his way was not her way. She had denied him what he was – she saw it now. She had refused him as himself. And this had been her life, and his life. She was grateful to death, which restored the truth. And she knew she was not dead.

And all the while her heart was bursting with grief and pity for him. What had he suffered? What stretch of horror for this helpless man! She was rigid with agony. She had not been able to help him. He had been cruelly injured, this naked man, this other being, and she could make no reparation. There were the children – but the children belonged to life. This dead man had nothing to do with them. He and she were only channels through which life had flowed to issue in the children. She was a mother – but how awful she knew it now to have been a wife. And he, dead now, how awful he must have felt it to be a husband. She felt that in the next world he would be a stranger to her. If they met there, in the beyond, they would only be ashamed of what had been before. The children had come, for some mysterious reason, out of both of them. But the children did not unite them. Now he was dead, she knew how eternally he was apart from her, how eternally he had nothing more to do with her. She saw this episode of her life closed. They had denied each other in life. Now he had withdrawn. An anguish came over her. It was finished then: it had become hopeless between them long before he died. Yet he had been her husband. But how little!

"Have you got his shirt, 'Lizabeth?"

Elizabeth turned without answering, though she strove to weep and behave as her mother-in-law expected. But she could not, she was silenced. She went into the kitchen and returned with the garment.

"It is aired," she said, grasping the cotton shirt here and there to try. She was almost ashamed to handle him; what right had she or anyone to lay hands on him; but her touch was humble on his body. It was hard work to clothe him. He was so heavy and inert. A terrible dread gripped her all the while: that he could be so heavy and utterly inert, unresponsive, apart. The horror of the distance between them was almost too much for her – it was so infinite a gap she must look across.

At last it was finished. They covered him with a sheet and left him lying, with his face bound. And she fastened the door of the little parlour, lest the children should see what was lying there. Then, with peace sunk heavy on her heart, she went about making tidy the kitchen. She knew she submitted to life, which was her immediate master. But from death, her ultimate master, she winced with fear and shame.

ERNEST HEMINGWAY 1899–1961

Certainly as much as any other writer in this book, Hemingway lived the life he wrote about. The Michigan woods, the Italian front in World War I, Paris in the twenties, big-game hunting in Africa, bullfighting in Spain, the Spanish Civil War, the rough life of the Caribbean Sea – not only was he there but he was actively engaged in it all. The relation of Hemingway's books to his life is thus in one sense like Conrad's in that what he wrote about was a real-life version of the kind of exploits found in boys' adventure stories. And like Conrad, Hemingway sought to portray the significance of exciting adventures rather than portraying merely the excitement itself. But there the similarity between the two writers ends: for Hemingway is unlike Conrad in insisting that the significance of an event can be conveyed only by a scrupulous report of real details – not attitudes or feelings but facts. For Hemingway the only way to express how a man felt is to describe what he did, how he did it, what he said, what happened. Appeals to the reader's compassion, admiration, and awe seemed to him a bad writer's fakery. There is no need for us to determine whether he or Conrad was right, for they were interested in describing different things: Conrad in states of perception that reveal, or distort, or possibly just miss the essence of experience, and Hemingway in experience so realistically reported that it conveys to the reader in the only possible way what it meant and how it felt in the living.

Hemingway killed himself with a shotgun in his house in the wild and beautiful Idaho mountains. Though ill (but he had been ill many times before) and threatened by weakness and loss of control at that time, he was at the apex of success, both monetarily and professionally: the book he had recently finished, *A Moveable Feast* (1964), is a fine series of acid sketches based on his life in Paris and is perhaps even at the level of his best novels (*The Sun Also Rises,* 1926, and *A Farewell to Arms,* 1929). He seems to have felt that he no longer had the energy to go on creating himself, holding back by discipline and honor the chaos that threatened to annihilate the self.

It is both sad and revealing that Hemingway should die by suicide, for in his writing he sought to capture those extraordinarily intense moments in which one is most aware of death. As a boy he learned from his father (who himself committed suicide) the exhilaration of surviving in the Michigan woods and of hunting right, with respect for the hunted. Later he found equivalent moments that contained a confrontation with death: in war, bullfighting, deep-sea fishing. The pressure of non-life, of potential chaos, is keenly felt in the stories here. Though we never learn what Nick's history is, he is clearly engaged in a great effort of self-reconstruction. He ritualistically insists that all the details of his journey into the woods be perfect, as if one false move would destroy the communion that is being established between him and nature. And then there is the swamp, deep and dark, where the big ones are. It fascinates Nick, but he stops short, cautiously satisfied with his reestablishment of a former self, unwilling at the moment to risk more: "In the swamp fishing was a tragic adventure. Nick did not want it." But the challenge of the swamp remains; it lingers in his mind, as his last sentence makes clear: "There were plenty of days coming when he could fish the swamp."

Norman Mailer insightfully sums up this special kind of energy in Hemingway's fiction and in his life. "It is possible," Mailer says, "that Hemingway lived every day in the style of the suicide. What a great dread is that. It is the dread that sits in the silences of his short declarative sentences. At any instant, by any failure in magic, by a mean defeat, or by a moment of cowardice, Hemingway could be thrust back again into the agonizing demands of courage." ("Punching Papa," in *Cannibals and Christians.*)

BIG TWO-HEARTED RIVER: PART I

The train went on up the track out of sight, around one of the hills of burnt timber. Nick sat down on the bundle of canvas and bedding the baggage man had pitched out of the door of the baggage car. There was no town, nothing but the rails and the burned-over country. The thirteen saloons that had lined the one street of Seney had not left a trace. The foundations of the Mansion House hotel stuck up above the ground. The stone was chipped and split by the fire. It was all that was left of the town of Seney. Even the surface had been burned off the ground.

Nick looked at the burned-over stretch of hillside, where he had expected to find the scattered houses of the town and then walked down the railroad track to the bridge over the river. The river was there. It swirled against the log spiles of the bridge. Nick looked down into the clear, brown water, colored from the pebbly bottom, and watched the trout keeping themselves steady in the current with wavering fins. As he watched them they changed their positions by quick angles, only to hold steady in the fast water again. Nick watched them a long time.

He watched them holding themselves with their noses into the current, many trout in deep, fast moving water, slightly distorted as he watched far down through the glassy convex surface of the pool, its surface pushing and swelling smooth against the resistance of the log-driven piles of the bridge. At the bottom of the pool were the big trout. Nick did not see them at first. Then he saw them at the bottom of the pool, big trout looking to hold themselves on the gravel bottom in a varying mist of gravel and sand, raised in spurts by the current.

Nick looked down into the pool from the bridge. It was a hot day. A kingfisher flew up the stream. It was a long time since Nick had looked into a stream and seen trout. They were very satisfactory. As the shadow of the kingfisher moved up the stream, a big trout shot upstream in a long angle, only his shadow marking the angle, then lost his shadow as he came through the surface of the water, caught the sun, and then, as he went back into the stream under the surface, his shadow seemed to float down the stream with the current, unresisting, to his post under the bridge where he tightened facing up into the current.

Nick's heart tightened as the trout moved. He felt all the old feeling.

He turned and looked down the stream. It stretched away, pebbly-bottomed with shallows and big boulders and a deep pool as it curved away around the foot of a bluff.

Nick walked back up the ties to where his pack lay in the cinders beside the railway track. He was happy. He adjusted the pack harness around the bundle, pulling straps tight, slung the pack on his back, got his arms through the shoulder straps and took some of the pull off his shoulders by leaning his forehead against the wide band of the tumpline. Still, it was too heavy. It was much too heavy. He had his leather rod-case in his hand and leaning forward to keep the weight of the pack high on his shoulders he walked along the road that paralleled the railway track, leaving the burned town behind in the heat, and then turned off around a hill with a high, fire-scarred hill on either side onto a road that went back into the country. He walked along the road feeling the ache from the pull of the heavy pack. The road climbed steadily. It was hard work walking up-hill. His muscles ached and the day was hot, but Nick felt happy. He felt he had left everything behind, the need for thinking, the need to write, other needs. It was all back of him.

From the time he had gotten down off the train and the baggage man had thrown his pack out of the open car door things had been different. Seney was burned, the country was burned over and changed, but it did not matter. It could not all be burned. He knew that. He hiked along the road, sweating in the sun, climbing to cross the range of hills that separated the railway from the pine plains.

The road ran on, dipping occasionally, but always climbing. Nick went on up. Finally the road after going parallel to the burnt hillside reached the top. Nick leaned back against a stump and slipped out of the pack harness. Ahead of him, as far as he could see, was the pine plain. The burned country stopped off at the left with the range of hills. On ahead islands of dark pine trees rose out of the plain. Far off to the left was the line of the river. Nick followed it with his eye and caught glints of the water in the sun.

There was nothing but the pine plain ahead of him, until the far blue hills that marked the Lake Superior height of land. He could hardly see them, faint and far away in the heat-light over the plain. If he looked too steadily they were gone. But if he only half-looked they were there, the far-off hills of the height of land.

Nick sat down against the charred stump and smoked a cigarette. His pack balanced on the top of the stump, harness holding ready, a hollow molded in it from his back. Nick sat smoking, looking out over the country. He did not need to get his map out. He knew where he was from the position of the river.

As he smoked, his legs stretched out in front of him, he noticed a grasshopper walk along the ground and up onto his woolen sock. The grasshopper was black. As he had walked along the road, climbing, he had started many grasshoppers from the dust. They were all black. They were not the big grasshoppers with yellow and black or red and black wings whirring out from their black wing sheathing as they fly up. These were just ordinary hoppers, but all a sooty black in color. Nick had wondered about them as he walked, without really thinking about them. Now, as he watched the black hopper that was nibbling at the wool of his sock with its fourway lip, he realized that they had all turned black from living in the burned-over land. He realized that the fire must have come the year before, but the grasshoppers were all black now. He wondered how long they would stay that way.

Carefully he reached his hand down and took hold of the hopper by the wings. He turned him up, all his legs walking in the air, and looked at his jointed belly. Yes, it was black too, iridescent where the back and head were dusty.

"Go on, hopper," Nick said, speaking out loud for the first time. "Fly away somewhere."

He tossed the grasshopper up into the air and watched him sail away to a charcoal stump across the road.

Nick stood up. He leaned his back against the weight of his pack where it rested upright on the stump and got his arms through the shoulder straps. He stood with the pack on his back on the brow of the hill looking out across the country, toward the distant river and then struck down the hillside away from the road. Underfoot the ground was good walking. Two hundred yards down the hillside the fire line stopped. Then it was sweet fern, growing ankle high, to walk through, and clumps of jack pines; a long undulating country with frequent rises and descents, sandy underfoot and the country alive again.

Nick kept his direction by the sun. He knew where he wanted to strike the river and he kept on through the pine plain, mounting small rises to see other rises ahead of him and sometimes from the top of a rise a great solid island of pines off to his right or his left. He broke off some sprigs of the heathery sweet fern, and put them under his pack straps. The chafing crushed it and he smelled it as he walked.

He was tired and very hot, walking across the uneven, shadeless pine plain. At any time he knew he could strike the river by turning off to his left. It could not be more than a mile away. But he kept on toward the north to hit the river as far upstream as he could go in one day's walking.

For some time as he walked Nick had been in sight of one of the big islands of pine standing out above the rolling high ground he was crossing. He dipped down and then as he came slowly up to the crest of the bridge he turned and made toward the pine trees.

There was no underbrush in the island of pine trees. The trunks of the trees went straight up or slanted toward each other. The trunks were straight and brown without branches. The branches were high above. Some interlocked to make a solid shadow on the brown forest floor. Around the grove of trees was a bare space. It was brown and soft underfoot as Nick walked on it. This was the over-lapping of the pine needle floor, extending out beyond the width of the high branches. The trees had grown tall and the branches moved high, leaving in the sun this bare space they had once covered with shadow. Sharp at the edge of this extension of the forest floor commenced the sweet fern.

Nick slipped off his pack and lay down in the shade. He lay on his back and looked up into the pine trees. His neck and back and the small of his back rested as he stretched. The earth felt good against his back. He looked up at the sky, through the branches, and then shut his eyes. He opened them and looked up again. There was a wind high up in the branches. He shut his eyes again and went to sleep.

Nick woke stiff and cramped. The sun was nearly down. His pack was heavy and the straps painful as he lifted it on. He leaned over with the pack on and picked up the leather rod-case and started out from the pine trees across the sweet fern swale, toward the river. He knew it could not be more than a mile.

He came down a hillside covered with stumps into a meadow. At the edge of the meadow flowed the river. Nick was glad to get to the river. He walked upstream through the meadow. His trousers were soaked with the dew as he walked. After the hot day, the dew had come quickly and heavily. The river made no sound. It was too fast and smooth. At the edge of the meadow, before he mounted to a piece of high ground to make camp, Nick looked down the river at the trout rising. They were rising to insects come from the swamp on the other side of the stream when the sun went down. The trout jumped out of water to take them. While Nick walked through the little stretch of meadow alongside the stream, trout had jumped high out of water. Now as he looked down the river, the insects must be settling on the surface, for the trout were feeding steadily all down the stream. As far down the long stretch as he could see, the trout were rising, making circles all down the surface of the water, as though it were starting to rain.

The ground rose, wooded and sandy, to overlook the meadow, the stretch of river and the swamp. Nick dropped his pack and rod-case and looked for a level piece of ground. He was very hungry and he wanted to make his camp before he cooked. Between two jack pines, the ground was quite level. He took the ax out of the pack and chopped out two projecting roots. That leveled a piece of ground large enough to sleep on. He smoothed out the sandy soil with his hand and pulled the sweet fern bushes by their roots. His hands smelled good from the sweet fern. He smoothed the uprooted earth. He did not want anything making lumps under the blankets. When he had the ground smooth, he spread his three blankets. One he folded double, next to the ground. The other two he spread on top.

With the ax he slit off a bright slab of pine from one of the stumps and split it into pegs for the tent. He wanted them long and solid to hold in the ground. With the tent unpacked and spread on the ground, the pack, leaning against a jack pine, looked much smaller. Nick tied the rope that served the tent for a ridge-pole to the trunk of one of the pine trees and pulled the tent up off the ground with the other end of the rope and tied it to the other pine. The tent hung on the rope like a canvas blanket on a clothesline. Nick poked a pole he had cut up under the back peak of the canvas and then made it a tent by pegging out the sides. He pegged the side out taut and drove the pegs deep, hitting them down into the ground with the flat of the ax until the rope loops were buried and the canvas was drum tight.

Across the open mouth of the tent Nick fixed cheesecloth to keep out mosquitoes. He crawled inside under the mosquito bar with various things from the pack to put at the head of the bed under the slant of the canvas. Inside the tent the light came through the brown canvas. It smelled pleasantly of canvas. Already there was something mysterious and homelike. Nick was happy as he crawled inside the tent. He had not been unhappy all day. This was different though. Now things were done. There had been this to do. Now it was done. It had been a hard trip. He was very tired. That was done. He had made his camp. He was settled. Nothing could touch him. It was a good place to camp. He was there, in the good place. He was in his home where he had made it. Now he was hungry.

He came out, crawling under the cheesecloth. It was quite dark outside. It was lighter in the tent.

Nick went over to the pack and found, with his fingers, a long nail in a paper sack of nails, in the bottom of the pack. He drove it into the pine tree, holding it close and hitting it gently with the flat of the ax. He hung the pack up on the nail. All his supplies were in the pack. They were off the ground and sheltered now.

Nick was hungry. He did not believe he had ever been hungrier. He opened and emptied a can of pork and beans and a can of spaghetti into the frying pan.

"I've got a right to eat this kind of stuff, if I'm willing to carry it," Nick said. His voice sounded strange in the darkening woods. He did not speak again.

He started a fire with some chunks of pine he got with the ax from a stump. Over the fire he stuck a wire grill, pushing the four legs down into the ground with his boot. Nick put the frying pan on the grill over the flames. He was hungrier. The beans and spaghetti warmed. Nick stirred them and mixed them together. They began to bubble, making little bubbles that rose with difficulty to the surface. There was a good smell. Nick got out a bottle of tomato catchup and cut four slices of bread. The little bubbles were coming faster now. Nick sat down beside the fire and lifted the frying pan off. He poured about half the contents out into the tin plate. It spread slowly on the plate. Nick knew it was too hot. He poured on some tomato catchup. He knew the beans and spaghetti were still too hot. He looked at the fire, then at the tent, he was not going to spoil it all by burning his tongue. For years he had never enjoyed fried bananas because he had never been able to wait for them to cool. His tongue was very sensitive. He was very hungry. Across the river in the swamp, in the almost dark, he saw a mist rising. He looked at the tent once more. All right. He took a full spoonful from the plate.

"Chrise," Nick said, "Geezus Chrise," he said happily.

He ate the whole plateful before he remembered the bread. Nick finished the second plateful with the bread, mopping the plate shiny. He had not eaten since a cup of coffee and a ham sandwich in the station restaurant at St. Ignace. It had been a very fine experience. He had been that hungry before, but had not been able to satisfy it. He could have made camp hours before if he had wanted to. There were plenty of good places to camp on the river. But this was good.

Nick tucked two big chips of pine under the grill. The fire flared up. He had forgotten to get water for the coffee. Out of the pack he got a folding canvas bucket and walked down the hill, across the edge of the meadow, to the stream. The other bank was in the white mist. The grass was wet and cold as he knelt on the bank and dipped the canvas bucket into the stream. It bellied and pulled hard in the current. The water was ice cold. Nick rinsed the bucket and carried it full up to the camp. Up away from the stream it was not so cold.

Nick drove another big nail and hung up the bucket full of water. He dipped the coffee pot half full, put some more chips under the grill onto the fire and put the pot on. He could not remember which way he made coffee. He could remember an argument about it with Hopkins, but not which side he had taken. He decided to bring it to a boil. He remembered now that was Hopkins's way. He had once argued about everything with Hopkins. While he waited for the coffee to boil, he opened a small can of apricots. He liked to open cans. He emptied the can of apricots out into a tin cup. While he watched the coffee on the fire, he drank the juice syrup of the apricots, carefully at first to keep from spilling, then meditatively, sucking the apricots down. They were better than fresh apricots.

The coffee boiled as he watched. The lid came up and coffee and grounds ran down the side of the pot. Nick took it off the grill. It was a triumph for Hopkins. He put sugar in the empty apricot cup and poured some of the coffee out to cool. It was too hot to pour and he used his hat to hold the handle of the coffee pot. He would not let it steep in the pot at all. Not the first cup. It should be straight Hopkins all the way. Hop deserved that. He was a very serious coffee drinker. He was the most serious man Nick had ever known. Not heavy, serious. That was a long time ago. Hopkins spoke without moving his lips. He had played polo. He made millions of dollars in Texas. He had borrowed carfare to go to Chicago, when the wire came that his first big well had come in. He could have wired for money. That would have been too slow. They called Hop's girl the Blonde Venus. Hop did not mind because she was not his real girl. Hopkins said very confidently that none of them would make fun of his real girl. He was right. Hopkins went away when the telegram came. That was on the Black River. It took eight days for the telegram to reach him. Hopkins gave away his .22 caliber

Colt automatic pistol to Nick. He gave his camera to Bill. It was to remember him always by. They were all going fishing again next summer. The Hop Head was rich. He would get a yacht and they would all cruise along the north shore of Lake Superior. He was excited but serious. They said good-bye and all felt bad. It broke up the trip. They never saw Hopkins again. That was a long time ago on the Black River.

Nick drank the coffee, the coffee according to Hopkins. The coffee was bitter. Nick laughed. It made a good ending to the story. His mind was starting to work. He knew he could choke it because he was tired enough. He spilled the coffee out of the pot and shook the grounds loose into the fire. He lit a cigarette and went inside the tent. He took off his shoes and trousers, sitting on the blankets, rolled the shoes up inside the trousers for a pillow and got in between the blankets.

Out through the front of the tent he watched the glow of the fire, when the night wind blew on it. It was a quiet night. The swamp was perfectly quiet. Nick stretched under the blanket comfortably. A mosquito hummed close to his ear. Nick sat up and lit a match. The mosquito was on the canvas, over his head. Nick moved the match quickly up to it. The mosquito made a satisfactory hiss in the flame. The match went out. Nick lay down again under the blanket. He turned on his side and shut his eyes. He was sleepy. He felt sleep coming. He curled up under the blanket and went to sleep.

BIG TWO-HEARTED RIVER: PART II

In the morning the sun was up and the tent was starting to get hot. Nick crawled out under the mosquito netting stretched across the mouth of the tent, to look at the morning. The grass was wet on his hands as he came out. He held his trousers and his shoes in his hands. The sun was just up over the hill. There was the meadow, the river and the swamp. There were birch trees in the green of the swamp on the other side of the river.

The river was clear and smoothly fast in the early morning. Down about two hundred yards were three logs all the way across the stream. They made the water smooth and deep above them. As Nick watched, a mink crossed the river on the logs and went into the swamp. Nick was excited. He was excited by the early morning and the river. He was really too hurried to eat breakfast, but he knew he must. He built a little fire and put on the coffee pot.

While the water was heating in the pot he took an empty bottle and went down over the edge of the high ground to the meadow. The meadow was wet with dew and Nick wanted to catch grasshoppers for bait before the sun dried the grass. He found plenty of good grasshoppers. They were at the base of the grass stems. Sometimes they clung to a grass stem. They were cold and wet with the dew, and could not jump until the sun warmed them. Nick picked them up, taking only the medium-sized brown ones, and put them into the bottle. He turned over a log and just under the shelter of the edge were several hundred hoppers. It was a grasshopper lodging house. Nick put about fifty of the medium browns into the bottle. While he was picking up the hoppers the others warmed in the sun and commenced to hop away. They flew when they hopped. At first they made one flight and stayed stiff when they landed, as though they were dead.

Nick knew that by the time he was through with breakfast they would be as lively as ever. Without dew in the grass it would take him all day to catch a bottle full of good grasshoppers and he would have to crush many of them, slamming at them with his hat. He washed his hands at the stream. He was excited to be near it. Then he walked up to the tent. The hoppers were already jumping stiffly in the grass. In the bottle, warmed by the sun, they were jumping in a mass. Nick put in a pine stick as a cork. It plugged the mouth of the bottle enough, so the hoppers could not get out and left plenty of air passage.

He had rolled the log back and knew he could get grasshoppers there every morning.

Nick laid the bottle full of jumping grasshoppers against a pine trunk. Rapidly he mixed some buckwheat flour with water and stirred it smooth, one cup of flour, one cup of water. He put a handful of coffee in the pot and dipped a lump of grease out of a can and slid it sputtering across the hot skillet. On the smoking skillet he poured smoothly the buckwheat batter. It spread like lava, the grease spitting sharply. Around the edges the buckwheat cake began to firm, then brown, then crisp. The surface was bubbling slowly to porousness. Nick pushed under the browned under surface with a fresh pine chip. He shook the skillet sideways and the cake was loose on the surface. I won't try and flop it, he thought. He slid the chip of clean wood all the way under the cake, and flopped it over onto its face. It sputtered in the pan.

When it was cooked Nick regreased the skillet. He used all the batter. It made another big flap jack and one smaller one.

Nick ate a big flapjack and a smaller one, covered with apple butter. He put apple butter on the third cake, folded it over twice, wrapped it in oiled paper and put it in his shirt pocket. He put the apple butter jar back in the pack and cut bread for two sandwiches.

In the pack he found a big onion. He sliced it in two and peeled the silky outer skin. Then he cut one half into slices and made onion sandwiches. He wrapped them in oiled paper and buttoned them in the other pocket of his khaki shirt. He turned the skillet upside down on the grill, drank the coffee, sweetened and yellow brown with the condensed milk in it, and tidied up the camp. It was a good camp.

Nick took his fly rod out of the leather rod-case, jointed it, and shoved the rod-case back into the tent. He put on the reel and threaded the line through the guides. He had to hold it from hand to hand, as he threaded it, or it would slip back through its own weight. It was a heavy, double tapered fly line. Nick had paid eight dollars for it a long time ago. It was made heavy to lift back in the air and come forward flat and heavy and straight to make it possible to cast a fly which has no weight. Nick opened the aluminum leader box. The leaders were coiled between the damp flannel pads. Nick had wet the pads at the water cooler on the train up to St. Ignace. In the damp pads the gut leaders had softened and Nick unrolled one and tied it by a loop at the end to the heavy fly line. He fastened a hook on the end of the leader. It was a small hook; very thin and springy.

Nick took it from his hook book, sitting with the rod across his lap. He tested the knot and the spring of the rod by pulling the line taut. It was a good feeling. He was careful not to let the hook bite into his finger.

He started down to the stream, holding his rod, the bottle of grasshoppers hung from his neck by a thong tied in half hitches around the neck of the bottle. His landing net hung by a hook from his belt. Over his shoulder was a long flour sack tied at each corner into an ear. The cord went over his shoulder. The sack flapped against his legs.

Nick felt awkward and professionally happy with all his equipment hanging from him. The grasshopper bottle swung against his chest. In his shirt the breast pockets bulged against him with the lunch and his fly book.

He stepped into the stream. It was a shock. His trousers clung tight to his legs. His shoes felt the gravel. The water was a rising cold shock.

Rushing, the current sucked against his legs. Where he stepped in, the water was over his knees. He waded with the current. The gravel slid under his shoes. He looked down at the swirl of water below each leg and tipped up the bottle to get a grasshopper.

The first grasshopper gave a jump in the neck of the bottle and went out into the water. He was sucked under in the whirl by Nick's right leg and came to the surface a little way down stream. He floated rapidly, kicking. In a quick circle, breaking the smooth surface of the water, he disappeared. A trout had taken him.

Another hopper poked his face out of the bottle. His antennae wavered. He was getting his front legs out of the bottle to jump. Nick took him by the head and held him while he threaded the slim hook under his chin, down through his thorax and into the last segments of his abdomen. The grasshopper took hold of the hook with his front feet, spitting tobacco juice on it. Nick dropped him into the water.

Holding the rod in his right hand he let out line against the pull of the grasshopper in the current. He stripped off line from the reel with his left hand and let it run free. He could see the hopper in the little waves of the current. It went out of sight.

There was a tug on the line. Nick pulled against the taut line. It was his first strike. Holding the now living rod across the current, he brought in the line with his left hand. The rod bent in jerks, the trout pumping against the current. Nick knew it was a small one. He lifted the rod straight up in the air. It bowed with the pull.

He saw the trout in the water jerking with his head and body against the shifting tangent of the line in the stream.

Nick took the line in his left hand and pulled the trout, thumping tiredly against the current, to the surface. His back was mottled the clear, water-over-gravel color, his side flashing in the sun. The rod under his right arm, Nick stooped, dipping his right hand into the current. He held the trout, never still, with his moist right hand, while he unhooked the barb from his mouth, then dropped him back into the stream.

He hung unsteadily in the current, then settled to the bottom beside a stone. Nick reached down his hand to touch him, his arm to the elbow under water.

The trout was steady in the moving stream, resting on the gravel, beside a stone. As Nick's fingers touched him, touched his smooth, cool, underwater feeling he was gone, gone in a shadow across the bottom of the stream.

He's all right, Nick thought. He was only tired.

He had wet his hand before he touched the trout, so he would not disturb the delicate mucus that covered him. If a trout was touched with a dry hand, a white fungus attacked the unprotected spot. Years before when he had fished crowded streams, with fly fishermen ahead of him and behind him, Nick had again and again come on dead trout, furry with white fungus, drifted against a rock, or floating belly up in some pool. Nick did not like to fish with other men on the river. Unless they were of your party, they spoiled it.

He wallowed down the stream, above his knees in the current, through the fifty yards of shallow water above the pile of logs that crossed the stream. He did not rebait his hook and held it in his hand as he waded. He was certain he could catch small trout in the shallows, but he did not want them. There would be no big trout in the shallows this time of day.

Now the water deepened up his thighs sharply and coldly. Ahead was the smooth dammed-back flood of water above the logs. The water was smooth and dark; on the left, the lower edge of the meadow; on the right the swamp.

Nick leaned back against the current and took a hopper from the bottle. He threaded the hopper on the hook and spat on him for good luck. Then he pulled several yards of line from the reel and tossed the hopper out ahead onto the fast, dark water. It floated down towards the logs, then the weight of the line pulled the bait under the surface. Nick held the rod in his right hand, letting the line run out through his fingers.

There was a long tug. Nick struck and the rod came alive and dangerous, bent double, the line tightening, coming out of water, tightening, all in a heavy, dangerous, steady pull. Nick felt the moment when the leader would break if the strain increased and let the line go.

The reel ratcheted into a mechanical shriek as the line went out in a rush. Too fast. Nick could not check it, the line rushing out, the reel note rising as the line ran out.

With the core of the reel showing, his heart feeling stopped with the excitement, leaning back against the current that mounted icily his thighs, Nick thumbed the reel hard with his left hand. It was awkward getting his thumb inside the fly reel frame.

As he put on pressure the line tightened into sudden hardness and beyond the logs a huge trout went high out of water. As he jumped, Nick lowered the tip of the rod. But he felt, as he dropped the tip to ease the strain, the moment when the strain was too great; the hardness too tight. Of course, the leader had broken. There was no mistaking the feeling when all spring left the line and it became dry and hard. Then it went slack.

His mouth dry, his heart down, Nick reeled in. He had never seen so big a trout. There was a heaviness, a power not to be held, and then the bulk of him, as he jumped. He looked as broad as a salmon.

Nick's hand was shaky. He reeled in slowly. The thrill had been too much. He felt, vaguely, a little sick, as though it would be better to sit down.

The leader had broken where the hook was tied to it. Nick took it in his hand. He thought of the trout somewhere on the bottom, holding himself steady over the gravel, far down below the light, under the logs, with the hook in his jaw. Nick knew the trout's teeth would cut through the snell of the hook. The hook would imbed itself in his jaw. He'd bet the trout was angry. Anything that size would be angry. That was a trout. He had been solidly hooked. Solid as a rock. He felt like a rock, too, before he started off. By God, he was a big one. By God, he was the biggest one I ever heard of.

Nick climbed out onto the meadow and stood, water running down his trousers and out of his shoes, his shoes squlchy. He went over and sat on the logs. He did not want to rush his sensations any.

He wriggled his toes in the water, in his shoes, and got out a cigarette from his breast pocket. He lit it and tossed the match into the fast water below the logs. A tiny trout rose at the match, as it swung around in the fast current. Nick laughed. He would finish the cigarette.

He sat on the logs, smoking, drying in the sun, the sun warm on his back, the river shallow ahead entering the woods, curving into the woods, shallows, light glittering, big water-smooth rocks, cedars along the bank and white birches, the logs warm in the sun, smooth to sit on, without bark, gray to the touch; slowly the feeling of disappointment left him. It went away slowly, the feeling of disappointment that came sharply after the thrill that made his shoulders ache. It was all right now. His rod lying out on the logs, Nick tied a new hook on the leader, pulling the gut tight until it grimped into itself in a hard knot.

He baited up, then picked up the rod and walked to the far end of the logs to get into the water, where it was not too deep. Under and beyond the logs was a deep pool. Nick walked around the shallow shelf near the swamp shore until he came out on the shallow bed of the stream.

On the left, where the meadow ended and the woods began, a great elm tree was uprooted. Gone over in a storm, it lay back into the woods, its roots clotted with dirt, grass growing in them, rising a solid bank beside the stream. The river cut to the edge of the uprooted tree. From where Nick stood he could see deep channels, like ruts, cut in the shallow bed of the stream by the flow of the current. Pebbly where he stood and pebbly and full of boulders beyond; where it curved near the tree roots, the bed of the stream was marly and between the ruts of deep water green weed fronds swung in the current.

Nick swung the rod back over his shoulder and forward, and the line, curving forward, laid the grasshopper down on one of the deep channels in the weeds. A trout struck and Nick hooked him.

Holding the rod far out toward the uprooted tree and sloshing backward in the current, Nick worked the trout, plunging, the rod bending alive, out of the danger of the weeds into the open river. Holding the rod, pumping alive against the current, Nick brought the trout in. He rushed, but always came, the spring of the rod yielding to the rushes, sometimes jerking under the water, but always bringing him in. Nick eased downstream with the rushes. The rod above his head he led the trout over the net, then lifted.

The trout hung heavy in the net, mottled trout back and silver sides in the meshes. Nick unhooked him; heavy sides, good to hold, big undershot jaw, and slipped him, heaving and big sliding, into the long sack that hung from his shoulders in the water.

Nick spread the mouth of the sack against the current and it filled, heavy with water. He held it up, the bottom in the stream, and the water poured out through the sides. Inside at the bottom was the big trout, alive in the water.

Nick moved downstream. The sack out ahead of him sunk heavy in the water, pulling from his shoulders.

It was getting hot, the sun hot on the back of his neck.

Nick had one good trout. He did not care about getting many trout. Now the stream was shallow and wide. There were trees along both banks. The trees of the left bank made short shadows on the current in the forenoon sun. Nick knew there were trout in each shadow. In the afternoon, after the sun had crossed toward the hills, the trout would be in the cool shadows on the other side of the stream.

The very biggest ones would lie up close to the bank. You could always pick them up there on the Black. When the sun was down they all moved out into the current. Just when the sun made the water blinding in the glare before it went down, you were liable to strike a big trout anywhere in the current. It was almost impossible to fish then, the surface of the water was blinding as a mirror in the sun. Of course, you could fish upstream, but a stream like the Black, or this, you had to wallow against the current and in a deep place, the water piled up on you. It was no fun to fish upstream with this much current.

Nick moved along through the shallow stretch watching the banks for deep holes. A beech tree grew close beside the river, so that the branches hung down into the water. The stream went back in under the leaves. There were always trout in a place like that.

Nick did not care about fishing that hole. He was sure he would get hooked in the branches.

It looked deep though. He dropped the grasshopper so the current took it under water, back in under the overhanging branch. The line pulled hard and Nick struck. The trout threshed heavily, half out of water in the leaves and branches. The line was caught. Nick pulled hard and the trout was off. He reeled in and holding the hook in his hand, walked down the stream.

Ahead, close to the left bank, was a big log. Nick saw it was hollow; pointing up river the current entered it smoothly, only a little ripple spread each side of the log. The water was deepening. The top of the hollow log was gray and dry. It was partly in the shadow.

Nick took the cork out of the grasshopper bottle and a hopper clung to it. He picked him off, hooked him and tossed him out. He held the rod far out so that the hopper on the water moved into the current flowing into the hollow log. Nick lowered the rod and the hopper floated in. There was a heavy strike. Nick swung the rod against the pull. It felt as though he were hooked into the log itself, except for the live feeling.

He tried to force the fish out into the current. It came, heavily.

The line went slack and Nick thought the trout was gone. Then he saw him, very near, in the current, shaking his head, trying to get the hook out. His mouth was clamped shut. He was fighting the hook in the clear flowing current.

Looping in the line with his left hand, Nick swung the rod to make the line taut and tried to lead the trout toward the net, but he was gone, out of sight, the line pumping. Nick fought him against the current, letting him thump in the water against the spring of the rod. He shifted the rod to his left hand, worked the trout upstream, holding his weight, fighting on the rod, and then let him down into the net. He lifted him clear of the water, a heavy half circle in the net, the net dripping, unhooked him and slid him into the sack.

He spread the mouth of the sack and looked down in at the two big trout alive in the water.

Through the deepening water, Nick waded over to the hollow log. He took the sack off, over his head, the trout flopping as it came out of water, and hung it so the trout were deep in the water. The he pulled himself up on the log and sat, the water from his trouser and boots running down into the stream. He laid his rod down, moved along to the shady end of the log and took the sandwiches out of his pocket. He dipped the sandwiches in the cold water. The current carried away the crumbs. He ate the sandwiches and dipped his hat full of water to drink, the water running out through his hat just ahead of his drinking.

It was cool in the shade, sitting on the log. He took a cigarette out and struck a match to light it. The match sunk into the gray wood, making a tiny furrow. Nick leaned over the side of the log, found a hard place and lit the match. He sat smoking and watching the river.

Ahead the river narrowed and went into a swamp. The river became smooth and deep and the swamp looked solid with cedar trees, their trunks close together, their branches solid. It would not be possible to walk through a swamp like that. The branches grew so low. You would have to keep almost level with the ground to move at all. You could not crash through the branches. That must by why the animals that lived in swamps were built the way they were, Nick thought.

He wished he had brought something to read. He felt like reading. He did not feel like going on into the swamp. He looked down the river. A big cedar slanted all the way across the stream. Beyond that the river went into the swamp.

Nick did not want to go in there now. He felt a reaction against deep wading with the water deepening up under his armpits, to hook big trout in places impossible to land them. In the swamp the banks were bare, the big cedars came together overhead, the sun did not come through, except in patches; in the fast deep water, in the half light, the fishing would be tragic. In the swamp fishing was a tragic adventure. Nick did not want it. He did not want to go down the stream any further today.

He took out his knife, opened it and stuck it in the log. Then he pulled up the sack, reached into it and brought out one of the trout. Holding him near the tail, hard to hold, alive, in his hand, he whacked him against the log. The trout quivered, rigid. Nick laid him on the log in the shade and broke the neck of the other fish the same way. He laid them side by side on the log. They were fine trout.

Nick cleaned them, slitting them from the vent to the tip of the jaw. All the insides and the gills and tongue came out in one piece. They were both males; long gray-white strips of milt, smooth and clean. All the insides clean and compact, coming out all together. Nick tossed the offal ashore for the minks to find.

He washed the trout in the stream. When he held them back up in the water they looked like live fish. Their color was not gone yet. He washed his hands and dried them on the log. Then he laid the trout on the sack spread out on the log, rolled them up in it, tied the bundle and put it in the landing net. His knife was still standing, blade stuck in the log. He cleaned it on the wood and put it in his pocket.

Nick stood up on the log, holding his rod, the landing net hanging heavy, then stepped into the water and splashed ashore. He climbed the bank and cut up into the woods, toward the high ground. He was going back to camp. He looked back. The river just showed through the trees. There were plenty of days coming when he could fish the swamp.

WILLIAM FAULKNER 1897–1962

The oldest of the southern writers in this book (Richard Wright, Carson McCullers, Flannery O'Connor, and James Alan McPherson are the others), Faulkner more than any of them set out to make the modern South in all its complexity the subject of his fiction. In the South's history, in its heat, its chivalric code (set side-by-side with carpetbagging trickery), its racism violently and guiltily maintained, its corruption of the land, Faulkner saw the terms of modern life. He invented a mythical county, Yoknapatawpha, Mississippi, that is a distillation of the culture he perceived around him. As he wrote stories and novels about Yoknapatawpha in the thirties and forties, the county became peopled with families whose past was known, whose adventures intersected with others', whose imaginary land could be mapped. But Faulkner never attempted to create a saga that had to be read sequentially: none of his novels and stories depends on another – though obviously the more the reader knows the richer his experience.

Faulkner grew up listening to tales. His father's house was the center for relatives who enjoyed exhibiting their story-telling talents. They talked about local happenings, but especially about their family's past. And indeed there was much romance in that past. Before the Civil War Faulkner's grandfather had made a fortune in various enterprises and had established himself as one of the great men in Mississippi. The Civil War helped to confirm his dedication to aristocratic values: honor, loyalty, manliness, the duty to lead. A colonel in the Confederate army, he on two occasions shot down plotters against his life. (He was finally killed, long after the war, in a similar attack.)

Faulkner's father inherited a much diminished fortune and a far quieter life from Colonel Faulkner: for a while the president of a local bank, he later became the treasurer of the University of Mississippi. In World War I Faulkner joined the British air force, and upon his return he attended the university for a short time; but he had no taste for academic subjects, preferring the passionate (and often high-spirited and comic) life of the common people in the town. For a while he thought of himself mainly as a poet, but partly under the influence of

Sherwood Anderson, whom he knew in New Orleans in the mid-twenties, he began to combine his gift for telling a good tale, his keen ear for all kinds of speech, and his ability to sustain a mood of passionate intensity into increasingly fine fiction. In 1929 he published *The Sound and the Fury,* a novel of extraordinary virtuosity and brilliance — certainly the most original and perhaps the best American novel of the twentieth century. During the thirties he wrote his other great novels — *As I Lay Dying* (1930), *Light in August* (1932), and *Absalom! Absalom!* (1936) — as well as many fine short stories.

So well does Faulkner present the tensions that exist in his Mississippi that the very atmosphere of his fiction is charged with them. In the "bloody twilight" of "Dry September" the human voice of the barber doubting that Will Mayes could have committed the crime is heard against other stupid, insistent, and finally engulfing voices of the town. Out of the speakers' various twisted and misdirected values arises an inevitable community violence, one that cannot be checked either by the barber's horror or by Will's moving expression of frightened bewilderment. Afterwards the consequences linger in the suffocating air — a common guilt that cannot be denied, nor accepted either, without terrible personal distortion.

Though of course Faulkner himself was a white man who had necessarily to understand the black experience from the outside, he was extremely sensitive to relations between the races. In a South that seemed to him remarkable for having sold out its proclaimed values, he saw many blacks — like the chief character of "Pantaloon in Black" — as forging the only honest terms by which one can live. And from the point of view of the southern whites, he recognized the guilt epitomized by generations of slavery as a fundamental source of a curse on the South.

Like Hemingway, Faulkner's major work was behind him before World War II, though it was in the fifties that the two writers shared the world's recognition of their pre-eminence. Faulkner's acceptance speech for the Nobel Prize for Literature in 1950 is a notable assertion of human values in the postwar era.

DRY SEPTEMBER

I

Through the bloody September twilight, aftermath of sixty-two rainless days, it had gone like a fire in dry grass — the rumor, the story, whatever it was. Something about Miss Minnie Cooper and a Negro. Attacked, insulted, frightened: none of them, gathered in the barber shop on that Saturday evening where the ceiling fan stirred, without freshening it, the vitiated air, sending back upon them, in recurrent surges of stale pomade and lotion, their own stale breath and odors, knew exactly what had happened.

"Except it wasn't Will Mayes," a barber said. He was a man of middle age; a thin, sand-colored man with a mild face, who was shaving a client. "I know Will Mayes. He's a good nigger. And I know Miss Minnie Cooper, too."

"What do you know about her?" a second barber said.

"Who is she?" the client said. "A young girl?"

"No," the barber said. "She's about forty, I reckon. She aint married. That's why I dont believe — "

"Believe, hell!" a hulking youth in a sweat-stained silk shirt said. "Wont you take a white woman's word before a nigger's?"

"I dont believe Will Mayes did it," the barber said. "I know Will Mayes."

"Maybe you know who did it, then. Maybe you already got him out of town, you damn niggerlover."

"I dont believe anybody did anything. I dont believe anything happened. I leave it to you fellows if them ladies that get old without getting married dont have notions that a man cant — "

"Then you are a hell of a white man," the client said. He moved under the cloth. The youth had sprung to his feet.

"You dont?" he said. "Do you accuse a white woman of lying?"

The barber held the razor poised above the half-risen client. He did not look around.

"It's this durn weather," another said. "It's enough to make a man do anything. Even to her."

Nobody laughed. The barber said in his mild, stubborn tone: "I aint accusing nobody of nothing. I just know and you fellows know how a woman that never — "

"You damn niggerlover!" the youth said.

"Shut up, Butch," another said. "We'll get the facts in plenty of time to act."

"Who is? Who's getting them?" the youth said. "Facts, hell! I — "

"You're a fine white man," the client said. "Aint you?" In his frothy beard he looked like a desert rat in the moving pictures. "You can tell them, Jack," he said to the youth. "If there aint any white mèn in this town you can count on me, even if I aint only a drummer and a stranger."

"That's right, boys," the barber said. "Find out the truth first. I know Will Mayes."

"Well, by God!" the youth shouted. "To think that a white man in this town — "

"Shut up, Butch," the second speaker said. "We got plenty of time."

The client sat up. He looked at the speaker. "Do you claim that anything excuses a nigger attacking a white woman?' Do you mean to tell me you are a white man and you'll stand for it? You better go back North where you came from. The South dont want your kind here."

"North what?" the second said. "I was born and raised in this town."

"Well, by God!" the youth said. He looked about with a strained, baffled gaze, as if he was trying to remember what it was he wanted to say or to do. He drew his sleeve across his sweating face. "Damn if I'm going to let a white woman — "

"You tell them, Jack," the drummer said. "By God, if they — "

The screen door crashed open. A man stood in the floor, his feet apart and his heavy-set body poised easily. His white shirt was open at the throat; he wore a felt hat. His hot, bold glance swept the group. His name was McLendon. He had commanded troops at the front in France and had been decorated for valor.

"Well," he said, "are you going to sit there and let a black son rape a white woman on the streets of Jefferson?"

Butch sprang up again. The silk of his shirt clung flat to his heavy shoulders. At each armpit was a dark halfmoon. "That's what I been telling them! That's what I — "

"Did it really happen?" a third said. "This aint the first man scare she ever had, like Hawkshaw says. Wasn't there something about a man on the kitchen roof, watching her undress, about a year ago?"

"What?" the client said. "What's that?" The barber had been slowly forcing him back into the chair; he arrested himself reclining, his head lifted, the barber still pressing him down.

McLendon whirled on the third speaker. "Happen? What the hell difference does it make? Are you going to let the black sons get away with it until one really does it?"

"That's what I'm telling them!" Butch shouted. He cursed, long and steady, pointless.

"Here, here," a fourth said. "Not so loud. Dont talk so loud."

"Sure," McLendon said; "no talking necessary at all. I've done my talking. Who's with me?" He poised on the balls of his feet, roving his gaze.

The barber held the drummer's face down, the razor poised. "Find out the facts first, boys. I know Willy Mayes. It wasn't him. Let's get the sheriff and do this thing right."

McLendon whirled upon him his furious, rigid face. The barber did not look away. They looked like men of different races. The other barbers had ceased also above their prone clients. "You mean to tell me," McLendon said, "that you'd take a nigger's word before a white woman's? Why, you damn niggerloving – "

The third speaker rose and grasped McLendon's arm; he too had been a soldier. "Now, now. Let's figure this thing out. Who knows anything about what really happened?"

"Figure out hell!" McLendon jerked his arm free. "All that're with me get up from there. The ones that aint – " He roved his gaze, dragging his sleeve across his face.

Three men rose. The drummer in the chair sat up. "Here," he said, jerking at the cloth about his neck; "get this rag off me. I'm with him. I dont live here, but by God, if our mothers and wives and sisters – " He smeared the cloth over his face and flung it to the floor. McLendon stood in the floor and cursed the others. Another rose and moved toward him. The remainder sat uncomfortable, not looking at one another, then one by one they rose and joined him.

The barber picked the cloth from the floor. He began to fold it neatly. "Boys, dont do that. Will Mayes never done it. I know."

"Come on," McLendon said. He whirled. From his hip pocket protruded the butt of a heavy automatic pistol. They went out. The screen door crashed behind them reverberant in the dead air.

The barber wiped the razor carefully and swiftly, and put it away, and ran to the rear, and took his hat from the wall. "I'll be back as soon as I can," he said to the other barbers. "I cant let – " He went out, running. The two other barbers followed him to the door and caught it on the rebound, leaning out and looking up the street after him. The air was flat and dead. It had a metallic taste at the base of the tongue.

"What can he do?" the first said. The second one was saying "Jees Christ, Jees Christ" under his breath. "I'd just as lief be Will Mayes as Hawk, if he gets McLendon riled."

"Jees Christ, Jees Christ," the second whispered.

"You reckon he really done it to her?" the first said.

II

She was thirty-eight or thirty-nine. She lived in a small frame house with her invalid mother and a thin, sallow, unflagging aunt, where each morning between ten and eleven she would appear on the porch in a lace-trimmed boudoir cap, to sit swinging in the porch swing until noon. After dinner she lay down for a while, until the afternoon began to cool. Then, in one of the three or four new voile dresses which she had each summer, she would go downtown to spend the afternoon in the stores with the other ladies, where they would handle the goods and haggle over the prices in cold, immediate voices, without any intention of buying.

She was of comfortable people — not the best in Jefferson, but good people enough — and she was still on the slender side of ordinary looking, with a bright, faintly haggard manner and dress. When she was young she had had a slender, nervous body and a sort of hard vivacity which had enabled her for a time to ride upon the crest of the town's social life as exemplified by the high school party and church social period of her contemporaries while still children enough to be unclass-conscious.

She was the last to realize that she was losing ground; that those among whom she had been a little brighter and louder flame than any other were beginning to learn the pleasure of snobbery — male — and retaliation — female. That was when her face began to wear that bright, haggard look. She still carried it to parties on shadowy porticoes and summer lawns, like a mask or a flag, with that bafflement of furious repudiation of truth in her eyes. One evening at a party she heard a boy and two girls, all schoolmates, talking. She never accepted another invitation.

She watched the girls with whom she had grown up as they married and got homes and children, but no man ever called on her steadily until the children of the other girls had been calling her "aunty" for several years, the while their mothers told them in bright voices about how popular Aunt Minnie had been as a girl. Then the town began to see her driving on Sunday afternoons with the cashier in the bank. He was a widower of about forty — a high-colored man, smelling always faintly of the barber shop or of whisky. He owned the first automobile in town, a red runabout; Minnie had the first motoring bonnet and veil the town ever saw. Then the town began to say: "Poor Minnie." "But she is old enough to take care of herself," others said. That was when she began to ask her old schoolmates that their children call her "cousin" instead of "aunty."

It was twelve years now since she had been relegated into adultery by public opinion, and eight years since the cashier had gone to a Memphis bank, returning for one day each Christmas, which he spent at an annual bachelors' party at a hunting club on the river. From behind their curtains the neighbors would see the party pass, and during the over-the-way Christmas day visiting they would tell her about him, about how well he looked, and how they heard that he was prospering in the city, watching with bright, secret eyes her haggard, bright face. Usually by that hour there would be the scent of whisky on her breath. It was supplied her by a youth, a clerk at the soda fountain: "Sure; I buy it for the old gal. I reckon she's entitled to a little fun."

Her mother kept to her room altogether now; the gaunt aunt ran the house. Against that background Minnie's bright dresses, her idle and empty days, had a quality of furious unreality. She went out in the evenings only with women now, neighbors, to the moving pictures. Each afternoon she dressed in one of the new dresses and went downtown alone, where her young "cousins" were already strolling in the late afternoons with their delicate, silken heads and thin, awkward arms and conscious hips, clinging to one another or shrieking and giggling with paired boys in the soda fountain when she passed and went on along the serried store fronts, in the doors of which the sitting and lounging men did not even follow her with their eyes any more.

III

The barber went swiftly up the street where the sparse lights, insect-swirled, glared in rigid and violent suspension in the lifeless air. The day had died in a pall of dust; above the darkened square, shrouded by the spent dust, the sky was as clear as the inside of a brass bell. Below the east was a rumor of the twice-waxed moon.

When he overtook them McLendon and three others were getting into a car parked in an alley. McLendon stooped his thick head, peering out beneath the top. "Changed your mind, did you?" he said. "Damn good thing; by God, tomorrow when this town hears about how you talked tonight — "

"Now, now," the other ex-soldier said. "Hawkshaw's all right. Come on, Hawk; jump in."

"Will Mayes never done it, boys," the barber said. "If anybody done it. Why, you all know well as I do there aint any town where they got better niggers than us. And you know how a lady will kind of think things about men when there aint any reason to, and Miss Minnie anyway — "

"Sure, sure," the soldier said. "We're just going to talk to him a little; that's all."

"Talk hell!" Butch said. "When we're through with the — "

"Shut up, for God's sake!" the soldier said. "Do you want everybody in town — "

"Tell them, by God!" McLendon said. "Tell everyone of the sons that'll let a white woman — "

"Let's go; let's go: here's the other car." The second car slid squealing out of a cloud of dust at the alley mouth. McLendon started his car and took the lead. Dust lay like fog in the street. The street lights hung nimbused as in water. They drove on out of town.

A rutted lane turned at right angles. Dust hung above it too, and above all the land. The dark bulk of the ice plant, where the Negro Mayes was night watchman, rose against the sky. "Better stop here, hadn't we?" the soldier said. McLendon did not reply. He hurled the car up and slammed to a stop, the headlights glaring on the blank wall.

"Listen here, boys," the barber said; "if he's here, dont that prove he never done it? Dont it? If it was him, he would run. Dont you see he would?" The second car came up and stopped. McLendon got down; Butch sprang down beside him. "Listen, boys," the barber said.

"Cut the lights off!" McLendon said. The breathless dark rushed down. There was no sound in it save their lungs as they sought air in the parched dust in which for two months they had lived; then the diminishing crunch of McLendon's and Butch's feet, and a moment later McLendon's voice:

"Will! . . . Will!"

Below the east the wan hemorrhage of the moon increased. It heaved above the ridge, silvering the air, the dust, so that they seemed to breathe, live, in a bowl of molten lead. There was no sound of nightbird nor insect, no sound save their breathing and a faint ticking of contracting metal about the cars. Where their bodies touched one another they seemed to sweat dryly, for no more moisture came. "Christ!" a voice said; "let's get out of here."

But they didn't move until vague noises began to grow out of the darkness ahead; then they got out and waited tensely in the breathless dark. There was another sound: a blow, a hissing expulsion of breath and McLendon cursing in undertone. They stood a moment longer, then they ran forward. They ran in a stumbling clump, as though they were fleeing something. "Kill him, kill the son," a voice whispered. McLendon flung them back.

"Not here," he said. "Get him into the car." "Kill him, kill the black son!" the voice murmured. They dragged the Negro to the car. The barber had waited beside the car. He could feel himself sweating and he knew he was going to be sick at the stomach.

"What is it, captains?" the Negro said. "I aint done nothing. 'Fore God, Mr John." Someone produced handcuffs. They worked busily about the Negro as though he were a post, quiet, intent, getting in one another's way. He submitted to the handcuffs, looking swiftly and constantly from dim face to dim face. "Who's here, captains?" he said, leaning to peer into the faces until they could feel his breath and smell his sweaty reek. He spoke a name or two. "What you all say I done, Mr John?"

McLendon jerked the car door open. "Get in!" he said.

The Negro did not move. "What you all going to do with me, Mr John?

I aint done nothing. White folks, captains, I aint done nothing: I swear 'fore God." He called another name.

"Get in!" McLendon said. He struck the Negro. The others expelled their breath in a dry hissing and struck him with random blows and he whirled and cursed them, and swept his manacled hands across their faces and slashed the barber upon the mouth, and the barber struck him also. "Get him in there," McLendon said. They pushed at him. He ceased struggling and got in and sat quietly as the others took their places. He sat between the barber and the soldier, drawing his limbs in so as not to touch them, his eyes going swiftly and constantly from face to face. Butch clung to the running board. The car moved on. The barber nursed his mouth with his handkerchief.

"What's the matter, Hawk?" the soldier said.

"Nothing," the barber said. They regained the highroad and turned away from town. The second car dropped back out of the dust. They went on, gaining speed; the final fringe of houses dropped behind.

"Goddamn, he stinks!" the soldier said.

"We'll fix that," the drummer in front beside McLendon said. On the running board Butch cursed into the hot rush of air. The barber leaned suddenly forward and touched McLendon's arm.

"Let me out, John," he said.

"Jump out, niggerlover," McLendon said without turning his head. He drove swiftly. Behind them the sourceless lights of the second car glared in the dust. Presently McLendon turned into a narrow road. It was rutted with disuse. It led back to an abandoned brick kiln – a series of reddish mounds and weed- and vine-choked vats without bottom. It had been used for pasture once, until one day the owner missed one of his mules. Although he prodded carefully in the vats with a long pole, he could not even find the bottom of them.

"John," the barber said.

"Jump out, then," McLendon said, hurling the car along the ruts. Beside the barber the Negro spoke:

"Mr Henry."

The barber sat forward. The narrow tunnel of the road rushed up and past. Their motion was like an extinct furnace blast: cooler, but utterly dead. The car bounded from rut to rut.

"Mr Henry," the Negro said.

The barber began to tug furiously at the door. "Look out, there!" the soldier said, but the barber had already kicked the door open and swung onto the running board. The soldier leaned across the Negro and grasped at him, but he had already jumped. The car went on without checking speed.

The impetus hurled him crashing through dust-sheathed weeds, into the ditch. Dust puffed about him, and in a thin, vicious crackling of sapless stems he lay choking and retching until the second car passed and died away. Then he rose and limped on until he reached the highroad and turned toward town, brushing at his clothes with his hands. The moon was higher, riding high and clear of the dust at last, and after a while the town began to glare beneath the dust. He went on, limping. Presently he heard cars and the glow of them grew in the dust behind him and he left the road and crouched again in the weeds until they passed. McLendon's car came last now. There were four people in it and Butch was not on the running board.

They went on; the dust swallowed them; the glare and the sound died away. The dust of them hung for a while, but soon the eternal dust absorbed it again. The barber climbed back onto the road and limped on toward town.

IV

As she dressed for supper on that Saturday evening, her own flesh felt like fever. Her hands trembled among the hooks and eyes, and her eyes had a feverish look, and her hair swirled crisp and crackling under the comb. While she was still dressing the friends called for her and sat while she donned her sheerest underthings and stockings and a new voile dress. "Do you feel strong enough to go out?" they said, their eyes bright too, with a dark glitter. "When you have had time to get over the shock, you must tell us what happened. What he said and did; everything."

In the leafed darkness, as they walked toward the square, she began to breathe deeply, something like a swimmer preparing to dive, until she ceased trembling, the four of them walking slowly because of the terrible heat and out of solicitude for her. But as they neared the square she began to tremble again, walking with her head up, her hands clenched at her sides, their voices about her murmurous, also with that feverish, glittering quality of their eyes.

They entered the square, she in the center of the group, fragile in her fresh dress. She was trembling worse. She walked slower and slower, as children eat ice cream, her head up and her eyes bright in the haggard banner of her face, passing the hotel and the coatless drummers in chairs along the curb looking around at her: "That's the one: see? The one in pink in the middle." "Is that her? What did they do with the nigger? Did they – ?" "Sure. He's all right." "All right, is he?" "Sure. He went on a little trip." Then the drug store, where even the young men lounging in the doorway tipped their hats and followed with their eyes the motion of her hips and legs when she passed.

They went on, passing the lifted hats of the gentlemen, the suddenly ceased voices, deferent, protective. "Do you see?" the friends said. Their voices sounded like long, hovering sighs of hissing exultation. "There's not a Negro on the square. Not one."

They reached the picture show. It was like a miniature fairyland with its lighted lobby and colored lithographs of life caught in its terrible and beautiful mutations. Her lips began to tingle. In the dark, when the picture began, it would be all right; she could hold back the laughing so it would not waste away so fast and so soon. So she hurried on before the turning faces, the undertones of low astonishment, and they took their accustomed places where she could see the aisle against the silver glare and the young men and girls coming in two and two against it.

The lights flicked away; the screen glowed silver, and soon life began to unfold, beautiful and passionate and sad, while still the young men and girls entered, scented and sibilant in the half dark, their paired backs in silhouette delicate and sleek, their slim, quick bodies awkward, divinely young, while beyond them the silver dream accumulated inevitably on and on. She began to laugh. In trying to suppress it, it made more noise than ever; heads began to turn. Still laughing, her friends raised her and led her out, and she stood at the curb, laughing on a high, sustained note, until the taxi came up and they helped her in.

They removed the pink voile and the sheer underthings and the stockings, and put her to bed, and cracked ice for her temples, and sent for the doctor. He was hard to locate, so they ministered to her with hushed ejaculations, renewing the ice and fanning her. While the ice was fresh and cold she stopped laughing and lay still for a time, moaning only a little. But soon the laughing welled again and her voice rose screaming.

"Shhhhhhhhhhh! Shhhhhhhhhhhhhh!" they said, freshening the icepack, smoothing her hair, examining it for gray; "poor girl!" Then to one another: "Do you suppose anything really happened?" their eyes darkly aglitter, secret and passionate. "Shhhhhhhhhh! Poor girl! Poor Minnie!"

V

It was midnight when McLendon drove up to his neat new house. It was trim and fresh as a birdcage and almost as small, with its clean, green-and-white paint. He locked the car and mounted the porch and entered. His wife rose from a chair beside the reading lamp. McLendon stopped in the floor and stared at her until she looked down.

"Look at that clock," he said, lifting his arm, pointing. She stood before him, her face lowered, a magazine in her hands. Her face was pale, strained, and weary-looking. "Haven't I told you about sitting up like this, waiting to see when I come in?"

"John," she said. She laid the magazine down. Poised on the balls of his feet, he glared at her with his hot eyes, his sweating face.

"Didn't I tell you?" He went toward her. She looked up then. He caught her shoulder. She stood passive, looking at him.

"Don't, John. I couldn't sleep . . . The heat; something. Please, John. You're hurting me."

"Didn't I tell you?" He released her and half struck, half flung her across the chair, and she lay there and watched him quietly as he left the room.

He went on through the house, ripping off his shirt, and on the dark, screened porch at the rear he stood and mopped his head and shoulders with the shirt and flung it away. He took the pistol from his hip and laid it on the table beside the bed, and sat on the bed and removed his shoes, and rose and slipped his trousers off. He was sweating again already, and he stooped and hunted furiously for the shirt. At last he found it and wiped his body again, and, with his body pressed against the dusty screen, he stood panting. There was no movement, no sound, not even an insect. The dark world seemed to lie stricken beneath the cold moon and the lidless stars

PANTALOON IN BLACK

I

He stood in the worn, faded clean overalls which Mannie herself had washed only a week ago, and heard the first clod strike the pine box. Soon he had one of the shovels himself, which in his hands (he was better than six feet and weighed better than two hundred pounds) resembled the toy shovel a child plays with at the shore, its half cubic foot of flung dirt no more than the light gout of sand the child's shovel would have flung. Another member of his sawmill gang touched his arm and said, "Lemme have hit, Rider." He didn't even falter. He released one hand in midstroke and flung it backward, striking the other across the chest, jolting him back a step, and restored the hand to the moving shovel, flinging the dirt with that effortless fury so that the mound seemed to be rising of its own volition, not built up from above but thrusting visibly upward out of the earth itself, until at last the grave, save for its rawness, resembled any other marked off without order about the barren plot by shards of pottery and broken bottles and old brick and other objects insignificant to sight but actually of a profound meaning and fatal to touch, which no white man could have read. Then he straightened up and with one hand flung the shovel quivering upright in the mound like a javelin and turned and began to walk away, walking on even when an old woman came out of the meagre clump of his kin and friends and a few old people who had known him and his dead wife both since they were born, and grasped his forearm. She was his aunt. She had raised him. He could not remember his parents at all.

"Whar you gwine?" she said.

"Ah'm goan home," he said.

"You dont wants ter go back dar by yoself," she said. "You needs to eat. You come on home and eat."

"Ah'm goan home," he repeated, walking out from under her hand, his forearm like iron, as if the weight on it were no more than that of a fly, the other members of the mill gang whose head he was giving way quietly to let him pass. But before he reached the fence one of them overtook him; he did not need to be told it was his aunt's messenger.

"Wait, Rider," the other said. "We gots a jug in de bushes — " Then the other said what he had not intended to say, what he had never conceived of himself saying in circumstances like these, even though everybody knew it — the dead who either will not or cannot quit the earth yet although the flesh they once lived in has been returned to it, let the preachers tell and reiterate and affirm how they left it not only without regret but with joy, mounting toward glory: "You dont wants ter go back dar. She be wawkin yit."

He didn't pause, glancing down at the other, his eyes red at the inner corners in his high, slightly backtilted head. "Lemme lone, Acey," he said. "Doan mess wid me now," and went on, stepping over the three-strand wire fence without even breaking his stride, and crossed the road and entered the woods. It was middle dusk when he emerged from them and crossed the last field, stepping over that fence too in one stride, into the lane. It was empty at this hour of Sunday evening — no family in wagon, no rider, no walkers churchward to speak to him and carefully refrain from looking after him when he had passed — the pale, powder-light, powder-dry dust of August from which the long week's marks of hoof and wheel had been blotted by the strolling and unhurried Sunday shoes, with somewhere beneath them, vanished but not gone, fixed and held in the annealing dust, the narrow, splay-toed prints of his wife's bare feet where on Saturday afternoons she would walk to the commissary to buy their next week's supplies while he took his bath; himself, his own prints, setting the period now as he strode on, moving almost as fast as a smaller man could have trotted, his body breasting the air her body had vacated, his eyes touching the objects — post and tree and field and house and hill — her eyes had lost.

The house was the last one in the lane, not his but rented from Carothers Edmonds, the local white land-owner. But the rent was paid promptly in advance, and even in just six months he had refloored the porch and rebuilt and roofed the kitchen, doing the work himself on Saturday afternoon and Sunday with his wife helping him, and bought the stove. Because he made good money: sawmilling ever since he began to get his growth at fifteen and sixteen and now, at twenty-four, head of the timber gang itself because the gang he headed moved a third again as much timber between sunup and sundown as any other moved, handling himself at times out of the vanity of his own strength logs which ordinarily two men would have handled with canthooks; never without work even in the old days when he had not actually needed the money, when a lot of what he wanted, needed perhaps, didn't cost money — the women bright and dark and for all purposes nameless he didn't need to buy and it didn't matter to him what he wore and there was always food for him at any hour of day or night in the house of his aunt who didn't even want to take the two dollars he gave her each Saturday — so there had been only the Saturday and Sunday dice and whiskey that had to be paid for until that day six months ago when he saw Mannie, whom he had known all his life, for the first time and said to himself: "Ah'm thu wid all dat," and they married and he rented the cabin from Carothers Edmonds and built a fire on the hearth on their wedding night as the tale told how Uncle Lucas Beauchamp, Edmonds' oldest tenant, had done on his forty-five years ago and which had burned ever since; and he would rise and dress and eat his breakfast by lamplight to walk the four miles to the mill by sunup, and exactly one hour after sundown he would enter the house again, five days a week, until Saturday. Then the first hour would not have passed noon when he would mount the steps and knock, not on post or doorframe but on the underside of the gallery roof itself, and enter and ring the bright cascade of silver dollars onto the scrubbed table in the kitchen where his dinner simmered on the stove and the galvanised tub of hot water and the baking powder can of soft soap and the towel made of scalded flour sacks sewn together and his clean overalls and shirt waited, and Mannie would gather up the money and walk the half-mile to the commissary and buy their next week's supplies and bank the rest of the money in Edmonds' safe and return and they would eat once again without haste or hurry after five days – the sidemeat, the greens, the cornbread, the buttermilk from the well-house, the cake which she baked every Saturday now that she had a stove to bake in.

But when he put his hand on the gate it seemed to him suddenly that there was nothing beyond it. The house had never been his anyway, but now even the new planks and sills and shingles, the hearth and stove and bed, were all a part of the memory of somebody else, so that he stopped in the half-open gate and said aloud, as though he had gone to sleep in one place and then waked suddenly to find himself in another: "Whut's Ah doin hyar?" before he went on. Then he saw the dog. He had forgotten it. He remembered neither seeing nor hearing it since it began to howl just before dawn yesterday – a big dog, a hound with a strain of mastiff from somewhere (he had told Mannie a month after they married: "Ah needs a big dawg. You's de onliest least thing whut ever kep up wid me one day, leff alone fo weeks.") coming out from beneath the gallery and approaching, not running but seeming rather to drift across the dusk until it stood lightly against his leg, its head raised until the tips of his fingers just touched it, facing the house and making no sound; whereupon, as if the animal controlled it, had lain guardian before it during his absence and only this instant relinquished, the shell of planks and shingles facing him solidified, filled, and for the moment he believed that he could not possibly enter it. "But Ah needs to eat," he said. "Us bofe needs to eat," he said, moving on though the dog did not follow until he turned and cursed it. "Come on hyar!" he said. "Whut you skeered of? She lacked you too, same as me," and they mounted the steps and crossed the porch and entered the house – the dusk-filled single room where all those six months were now crammed and crowded into one instant of time until there was no space left for air to breathe, crammed and crowded about the hearth where the fire which was to have lasted to the end of them, before which in the days before he was able to buy the stove he would enter after his four-mile walk from the mill and find her, the shape of her narrow back and haunches squatting, one narrow spread hand shielding her face from the blaze over which the other hand held the skillet, had already fallen to a dry, light soilure of dead ashes when the sun rose yesterday – and himself standing there while the last of light died about the strong and indomitable beating of his heart and the deep steady arch and collapse of his chest which walking fast over the rough going of woods and fields had not increased and standing still in the quiet and fading room had not slowed down.

Then the dog left him. The light pressure went off his flank; he heard the click and hiss of its claws on the wooden floor as it surged away and he thought at first that it was fleeing. But it stopped just outside the front door, where he could see it now, and the upfling of its head as the howl began, and then he saw her too. She was standing in the kitchen door, looking at him. He didn't move. He didn't breathe nor speak until he knew his voice would be all right, his face fixed too not to alarm her. "Mannie," he said. "Hit's awright. Ah aint afraid." Then he took a step toward her, slow, not even raising his hand yet, and stopped. Then he took another step. But this time as soon as he moved she began to fade. He stopped at once, not breathing again, motionless, willing his eyes to see that she had stopped too. But she had not stopped. She was fading, going. "Wait." he said, talking as sweet as he had ever heard his voice speak to a woman: "Den lemme go wid you, honey." But she was going. She was going fast now, he could actually feel between them the insuperable barrier of that very strength which could handle alone a log which would have taken any two other men to handle, of the blood and bones and flesh too strong, invincible for life, having learned at least once with his own eyes how tough, even in sudden and violent death, not a young man's bones and flesh perhaps but the will of that bone and flesh to remain alive, actually was.

Then she was gone. He walked through the door where she had been standing, and went to the stove. He did not light the lamp. He needed no light. He had set the stove up himself and built the shelves for the dishes, from among which he took two plates by feel and from the pot sitting cold on the cold stove he ladled onto the plates the food which his aunt had brought yesterday and of which he had eaten yesterday though now he did not remember when he had eaten it nor what it was, and carried the plates to the scrubbed bare table beneath the single small fading window and drew two chairs up and sat down, waiting again until he knew his voice would be what he wanted it to be. "Come on hyar, now," he said roughly. "Come on hyar and eat yo supper. Ah aint gonter have no – " and ceased, looking down at his plate, breathing the strong, deep pants, his chest arching and collapsing until he stopped it presently and held himself motionless for perhaps a half minute, and raised a spoonful of the cold and glutinous peas to his mouth. The congealed and lifeless mass seemed to bounce on contact with his lips. Not even warmed from mouth-heat, peas and spoon spattered and rang upon the plate; his chair crashed backward and he was standing, feeling the muscles of his jaw beginning to drag his mouth open, tugging upward the top half of his head. But he stopped that too before it became sound, holding himself again while he rapidly scraped the food from his plate onto the other and took it up and left the kitchen, crossed the other room and the gallery and set the plate on the bottom step and went on toward the gate.

The dog was not there, but it overtook him within the first half mile. There was a moon then, their two shadows flitting broken and intermittent among the trees or slanted long and intact across the slope of pasture or old abandoned fields upon the hills, the man moving almost as fast as a horse could have moved over that ground, altering his course each time a lighted window came in sight, the dog trotting at heel while their shadows shortened to the moon's curve until at last they trod them and the last far lamp had vanished and the shadows began to lengthen on the other hand, keeping to heel even when a rabbit burst from almost beneath the man's foot, then lying in the gray of dawn beside the man's prone body, beside the labored heave and collapse of the chest, the loud harsh snoring which sounded not like groans of pain but like someone engaged without arms in prolonged single combat.

When he reached the mill there was nobody there but the fireman – an older man just turning from the woodpile, watching quietly as he crossed the clearing, striding as if he were going to walk not only through the boiler shed but through (or over) the boiler too, the overalls which had been clean yesterday now draggled and soiled and drenched to the knees with dew, the cloth cap flung onto the side of his head, hanging peak downward over his ear as he always wore it, the whites of his eyes rimmed with red and with something urgent and strained about them. "Whar yo bucket?" he said. But before the fireman could answer he had stepped past him and lifted the polished lard pail down from a nail in a post. "Ah just wants a biscuit," he said.

"Eat hit all," the fireman said. "Ah'll eat outen de yuthers' buckets at dinner. Den you gawn home and go to bed. You dont looks good."

"Ah aint come hyar to look," he said, sitting on the ground, his back against the post, the open pail between his knees, cramming the food into his mouth with his hands, wolfing it – peas again, also gelid and cold, a fragment of yesterday's Sunday fried chicken, a few rough chunks of this morning's fried sidemeat, a biscuit the size of a child's cap – indiscriminate, tasteless. The rest of the crew was gathering now, with voices and sounds of movement outside the boiler shed; presently the white foreman rode into the clearing on a horse. He did not look up, setting the empty pail aside, rising, looking at no one, and went to the branch and lay on his stomach and lowered his face to the water, drawing the water into himself with the same deep, strong, troubled inhalations that he had snored with, or as when he had stood in the empty house at dusk yesterday, trying to get air.

Then the trucks were rolling. The air pulsed with the rapid beating of the exhaust and the whine and clang of the saw, the trucks rolling one by one up to the skidway, he mounting the trucks in turn, to stand balanced on the load he freed, knocking the chocks out and casting loose the shackle chains and with his cant-hook squaring the sticks of cypress and gum and oak one by one to the incline and holding them until the next two men of his gang were ready to receive and guide them, until the discharge of each truck became one long rumbling roar punctuated by grunting shouts and, as the morning grew and the sweat came, chanted phrases of song tossed back and forth. He did not sing with them. He rarely ever did, and this morning might have been no different from any other – himself man-height again above the heads which carefully refrained from looking at him, stripped to the waist now, the shirt removed and the overalls knotted about his hips by the suspender straps, his upper body bare except for the handkerchief about his neck and the cap clapped and clinging somehow over his right ear, the mounting sun sweat-glinted steel-blue on the midnight-colored bunch and slip of muscles until the whistle blew for noon and he said to the two men at the head of the skidway: "Look out. Git out de way," and rode the log down the incline, balanced erect upon it in short rapid backward-running steps above the headlong thunder.

His aunt's husband was waiting for him – an old man, as tall as he was, but lean, almost frail, carrying a tin pail in one hand and a covered plate in the other; they too sat in the shade beside the branch a short distance from where the others were opening their dinner pails. The bucket contained a fruit jar of buttermilk packed in a clean damp towsack. The covered dish was a peach pie, still warm. "She baked hit fer you dis mawin," the uncle said. "She say fer you to come home." He didn't answer, bent forward a little, his elbows on his knees, holding the pie in both hands, wolfing at it, the syrupy filling smearing and trickling down his chin, blinking rapidly as he chewed, the whites of his eyes covered a little more by the creeping red. "Ah went to yo house last night, but you want dar. She sont me. She wants you to come home. She kept de lamp burnin all last night fer you."

"Ah'm awright," he said.

"You aint awright. De Lawd guv, and He tuck away. Put yo faith and trust in Him. And she kin help you."

"Whut faith and trust?" he said. "Whut Mannie ever done ter Him? Whut He wanter come messin wid me and —"

"Hush!" the old man said. "Hush!"

Then the trucks were rolling again. Then he could stop needing to invent to himself reasons for his breathing, until after a while he began to believe he had forgot about breathing since now he could not hear it himself above the steady thunder of the rolling logs; whereupon as soon as he found himself believing he had forgotten it, he knew that he had not, so that instead of tipping the final log onto the skidway he stood up and cast his cant-hook away as if it were a burnt match and in the dying reverberation of the last log's rumbling descent he vaulted down between the two slanted tracks of the skid, facing the log which still lay on the truck. He had done it before – taken a log from the truck onto his hands, balanced, and turned with it and tossed it onto the skidway, but never with a stick of this size, so that in a complete cessation of all sound save the pulse of the exhaust and the light free-running whine of the disengaged saw since every eye there, even that of the white foreman, was upon him, he nudged the log to the edge of the truckframe and squatted and set his palms against the underside of it. For a time there was no movement at all. It was as if the unrational and inanimate wood had invested, mesmerised the man with some of its own primal inertia. Then a voice said quietly: "He got hit. Hit's off de truck," and they saw the crack and gap of air, watching the infinitesimal straightening of the braced legs until the knees locked, the movement mounting infinitesimally through the belly's insuck, the arch of the chest, the neck cords, lifting the lip from the white clench of teeth in passing, drawing the whole head backward and only the bloodshot fixity of the eyes impervious to it, moving on up the arms and the straightening elbows until the balanced log was higher than his head. "Only he aint gonter turn wid dat un," the same voice said. "And when he try to put hit back on de truck, hit gonter kill him." But none of them moved. Then – there was no gathering of supreme effort – the log seemed to leap suddenly backward over his head of its own volition, spinning, crashing and thundering down the incline; he turned and stepped over the slanting track in one stride and walked through them as they gave way and went on across the clearing toward the woods even though the foreman called after him: "Rider!" and again: "You, Rider!"

At sundown he and the dog were in the river swamp four miles away – another clearing, itself not much larger than a room, a hut, a hovel partly of planks and partly of canvas, an unshaven white man standing in the door beside which a shotgun leaned, watching him as he approached, his hand extended with four silver dollars on the palm. "Ah wants a jug," he said.

"A jug?" the white man said. "You mean a pint. This is Monday. Aint you all running this week?"

"Ah laid off," he said. "Whar's my jug?" waiting, looking at nothing apparently, blinking his bloodshot eyes rapidly in his high, slightly back-tilted head, then turning, the jug hanging from his crooked middle finger against his leg, at which moment the white man looked suddenly and sharply at his eyes as though seeing them for the first time – the eyes which had been strained and urgent this morning and which now seemed to be without vision too and in which no white showed at all – and said,

"Here. Gimme that jug. You dont need no gallon. I'm going to give you that pint, give it to you. Then you get out of here and stay out. Dont come back until — " Then the white man reached and grasped the jug, whereupon the other swung it behind him, sweeping his other arm up and out so that it struck the white man across the chest.

"Look out, white folks," he said. "Hit's mine. Ah done paid you."

The white man cursed him. "No you aint. Here's your money. Put that jug down, nigger."

"Hit's mine," he said, his voice quiet, gentle even, his face quiet save for the rapid blinking of the red eyes. "Ah done paid for hit," turning on, turning his back on the man and the gun both, and recrossed the clearing to where the dog waited beside the path to come to heel again. They moved rapidly on between the close walls of impenetrable cane-stalks which gave a sort of blondness to the twilight and possessed something of that oppression, that lack of room to breathe in, which the walls of his house had had. But this time, instead of fleeing it, he stopped and raised the jug and drew the cob stopper from the fierce duskreek of uncured alcohol and drank, gulping the liquid solid and cold as ice water, without either taste or heat until he lowered the jug and the air got in. "Hah," he said. "Dat's right. Try me. Try me, big boy. Ah gots something hyar now dat kin whup you."

And, once free of the bottom's unbreathing blackness, there was the moon again, his long shadow and that of the lifted jug slanting away as he drank and then held the jug poised, gulping the silver air into his throat until he could breathe again, speaking to the jug: "Come on now. You always claim you's a better man den me. Come on now. Prove it." He drank again, swallowing the chill liquid tamed of taste or heat either while the swallowing lasted, feeling it flow solid and cold with fire, past then enveloping the strong steady panting of his lungs until they too ran suddenly free as his moving body ran in the silver solid wall of air he breasted. And he was all right, his striding shadow and the trotting one of the dog travelling swift as those of two clouds along the hill; the long cast of his motionless shadow and that of the lifted jug slanting across the slope as he watched the frail figure of his aunt's husband toiling up the hill.

"Dey tole me at de mill you was gone," the old man said. "Ah knowed whar to look. Come home, son. Dat ar cant help you."

"Hit done awready hope me," he said. "Ah'm awready home. Ah'm snakebit now and pizen cant hawm me."

"Den stop and see her. Leff her look at you. Dat's all she axes: just leff her look at you — " But he was already moving. "Wait!" the old man cried. "Wait!"

"You cant keep up," he said, speaking into the silver air, breasting aside the silver solid air which began to flow past him almost as fast as it would have flowed past a moving horse. The faint frail voice was already lost in the night's infinitude, his shadow and that of the dog scudding the free miles, the deep strong panting of his chest running free as air now because he was all right.

Then, drinking, he discovered suddenly that no more of the liquid was entering his mouth. Swallowing, it was no longer passing down his throat, his throat and mouth filled now with a solid and unmoving column which without reflex or revulsion sprang, columnar and intact and still retaining the mold of his gullet, outward glinting in the moonlight, splintering, vanishing into the myriad murmur of the dewed grass. He drank again. Again his throat merely filled solidly until two icy rills ran from his mouthcorners; again the intact column sprang silvering, glinting, shivering, while he panted the chill of air into his throat, the jug poised before his mouth while he spoke to it: "Awright. Ah'm ghy try you again. Soon as you makes up yo mind to stay whar I puts you, Ah'll leff you alone." He drank, filling his gullet for the third time and lowered the jug one instant ahead of the bright intact repetition, panting, indrawing the cool of air until he could breathe. He stoppered the cob carefully back into the jug and stood, panting, blinking, the long cast of his solitary shadow slanting away across the hill and beyond, across the mazy infinitude of all the night-bound earth. "Awright," he said. "Ah just misread de sign wrong. Hit's done done me all de help Ah needs. Ah'm awright now. Ah doan needs no mo of hit."

He could see the lamp in the window as he crossed the pasture, passing the black-and-silver yawn of the sandy ditch where he had played as a boy with empty snuff-tins and rusted harness-buckles and fragments of trace-chains and now and then an actual wheel, passing the garden patch where he had hoed in the spring days while his aunt stood sentry over him from the kitchen window, crossing the grassless yard in whose dust he had sprawled and crept before he learned to walk. He entered the house, the room, the light itself, and stopped in the door, his head back-tilted a little as if he could not see, the jug hanging from his crooked finger, against his leg. "Unc Alec say you wanter see me," he said.

"Not just to see you," his aunt said. "To come home, whar we kin help you."

"Ah'm awright," he said. "Ah doan needs no help."

"No," she said. She rose from the chair and came and grasped his arm as she had grasped it yesterday at the grave. Again, as on yesterday, the forearm was like iron under her hand. "No! When Alec come back and tole me how you had wawked off de mill and de sun not half down, Ah knowed why and whar. And dat cant help you."

"Hit done awready hope me. Ah'm awright now."

"Dont lie to me," she said. "You aint never lied to me. Dont lie to me now."

Then he said it. It was his own voice, without either grief or amazement, speaking quietly out of the tremendous panting of his chest which in a moment now would begin to strain at the walls of this room too. But he would be gone in a moment.

"Nome," he said. "Hit aint done me no good."

"And hit cant! Cant nothing help you but Him! Ax Him! Tole Him about hit! He wants to hyar you and help you!"

"Efn He God, Ah dont needs to tole Him. Efn He God, He awready know hit. Awright. Hyar Ah is. Leff Him come down hyar and do me some good."

"On yo knees!" she cried. "On yo knees and ax Him!" But it was not his knees on the floor, it was his feet. And for a space he could hear her feet too on the planks of the hall behind him and her voice crying after him from the door: "Spoot! Spoot!" — crying after him across the moon-dappled yard the name he had gone by in his childhood and adolescence, before the men he worked with and the bright dark nameless women he had taken in course and forgotten until he saw Mannie that day and said, "Ah'm thu wid all dat," began to call him Rider.

It was just after midnight when he reached the mill. The dog was gone now. This time he could not remember when nor where. At first he seemed to remember hurling the empty jug at it. But later the jug was still in his hand and it was not empty, although each time he drank now the two icy runnels streamed from his mouth-corners, sopping his shirt and overalls until he walked constantly in the fierce chill of the liquid tamed now of flavor and heat and odor too even when the swallowing ceased. "Sides that," he said, "Ah wouldn't thow nothin at him. Ah mout kick him efn he needed hit and was close enough. But Ah wouldn't ruint no dog chunkin hit."

The jug was still in his hand when he entered the clearing and paused among the mute soaring of the moon-blond lumber-stacks. He stood in the middle now of the unimpeded shadow which he was treading again as he had trod it last night, swaying a little, blinking about at the stacked lumber, the skidway, the piled logs waiting for tomorrow, the boiler-shed all quiet and blanched in the moon. And then it was all right. He was moving again. But he was not moving, he was drinking, the liquid cold and swift and tasteless and requiring no swallowing, so that he could not tell if it were going down inside or outside. But it was all right. And now he was moving, the jug gone now and he didn't know the when or where of that either. He crossed the clearing and entered the boiler shed and went on through it, crossing the junctureless backloop of time's trepan, to the door of the tool-room, the faint glow of the lantern beyond the plank-joints, the surge and fall of living shadow, the mutter of voices, the mute click and scutter of the dice, his hand loud on the barred door, his voice loud too: "Open hit. Hit's me. Ah'm snakebit and bound to die."

Then he was through the door and inside the tool-room. They were the same faces — three members of his timber gang, three or four others of the mill crew, the white night-watchman with the heavy pistol in his hip pocket and the small heap of coins and worn bills on the floor before him, one who was called Rider and was Rider standing above the squatting circle, swaying a little, blinking, the dead muscles of his face shaped into smiling while the white man stared up at him. "Make room, gamblers," he said. "Make room. Ah'm snakebit and de pizen cant hawm me."

"You're drunk," the white man said. "Get out of here. One of you niggers open the door and get him out of here."

"Dass awright, boss-man," he said, his voice equable, his face still fixed in the faint rigid smiling beneath the blinking of the red eyes; "Ah aint drunk. Ah just cant wawk straight fer dis yar money weighin me down."

Now he was kneeling too, the other six dollars of his last week's pay on the floor before him, blinking, still smiling at the face of the white man opposite, then, still smiling, he watched the dice pass from hand to hand around the circle as the white man covered the bets, watching the soiled and palm-worn money in front of the white man gradually and steadily increase, watching the white man cast and win two doubled bets in succession then lose one for twenty-five cents, the dice coming to him at last, the cupped snug clicking of them in his fist. He spun a coin into the center.

"Shoots a dollar," he said, and cast, and watched the white man pick up the dice and flip them back to him. "Ah lets hit lay," he said. "Ah'm snakebit. Ah kin pass wid anything," and cast, and this time one of the negroes flipped the dice back. "Ah lets hit lay," he said, and cast, and moved as the white man moved, catching the white man's wrist before his hand reached the dice, the two of them squatting, facing each other above the dice and the money, his left hand grasping the white man's wrist, his face still fixed in the rigid and deadened smiling, his voice equable, almost deferential: "Ah kin pass even wid miss-outs. But dese hyar yuther boys — " until the white man's hand sprang open and the second pair of dice clattered onto the floor beside the first two and the white man wrenched free and sprang up and back and reached the hand backward toward the pocket where the pistol was.

The razor hung between his shoulder-blades from a loop of cotton string round his neck inside his shirt. The same motion of the hand which brought the razor forward over his shoulder flipped the blade open and freed it from the cord, the blade opening on until the back edge of it lay across the knuckles of his fist, his thumb pressing the handle into his closing fingers, so that in the second before the half-drawn pistol exploded he actually struck at the white man's throat not with the blade but with a sweeping blow of his fist, following through in the same motion so that not even the first jet of blood touched his hand or arm.

II

After it was over — it didn't take long; they found the prisoner on the following day, hanging from the bell-rope in a negro schoolhouse about two miles from the sawmill, and the coroner had pronounced his verdict of death at the hands of a person or persons unknown and surrendered the body to its next of kin all within five minutes — the sheriff's deputy who had been officially in charge of the business was telling his wife about it. They were in the kitchen. His wife was cooking supper. The deputy had been out of bed and in motion ever since the jail delivery shortly before midnight of yesterday and had covered considerable ground since, and he was spent now from lack of sleep and hurried food at hurried and curious hours and, sitting in a chair beside the stove, a little hysterical too.

"Them damn niggers," he said. "I swear to godfrey, it's a wonder we have as little trouble with them as we do. Because why? Because they aint human. They look like a man and they walk on their hind legs like a man, and they can talk and you can understand them and you think they are understanding you, at least now and then. But when it comes to the normal human feelings and sentiments of human beings, they might just as well be a damn herd of wild buffaloes. Now you take this one today — "

"I wish you would," his wife said harshly. She was a stout woman, handsome once, graying now and with a neck definitely too short, who looked not harried at all but composed in fact, only choleric. Also, she had attended a club rook-party that afternoon and had won the first, the fifty-cent, prize until another member had insisted on a recount of the scores and the ultimate throwing out of one entire game. "Take him out of my kitchen, anyway. You sheriffs! Sitting around that courthouse all day long, talking. It's no wonder two or three men can walk in and take prisoners out from under your very noses. They would take your chairs and desks and window sills too if you ever got your feet and backsides off of them that long."

"It's more of them Birdsongs than just two or three," the deputy said. "There's forty-two active votes in that connection. Me and Maydew taken the poll-list and counted them one day. But listen – " The wife turned from the stove, carrying a dish. The deputy snatched his feet rapidly out of the way as she passed him, passed almost over him, and went into the dining room. The deputy raised his voice a little to carry the increased distance: "His wife dies on him. All right. But does he grieve? He's the biggest and busiest man at the funeral. Grabs a shovel before they even got the box into the grave they tell me, and starts throwing dirt onto her faster than a slip scraper could have done it. But that's all right – " His wife came back. He moved his feet again and altered his voice again to the altered range: " – maybe that's how he felt about her. There aint any law against a man rushing his wife into the ground, provided he never had nothing to do with rushing her to the cemetery too. But here the next day he's the first man back at work except the fireman, getting back to the mill before the fireman had his fire going, let alone steam up; five minutes earlier and he could even have helped the fireman wake Birdsong up so Birdsong could go home and go back to bed again, or he could even have cut Birdsong's throat then and saved everybody trouble.

"So he comes to work, the first man on the job, when McAndrews and everybody else expected him to take the day off since even a nigger couldn't want no better excuse for a holiday than he had just buried his wife, when a white man would have took the day off out of pure respect no matter how he felt about his wife, when even a little child would have had sense enough to take a day off when he would still get paid for it too. But not him. The first man there, jumping from one log truck to another before the starting whistle quit blowing even, snatching up ten-foot cypress logs by himself and throwing them around like matches. And then, when everybody had finally decided that that's the way to take him, the way he wants to be took, he walks off the job in the middle of the afternoon without by-your-leave or much obliged or goodbye to McAndrews or nobody else, gets himself a whole gallon of bust-skull white-mule whisky, comes straight back to the mill and to the same crap game where Birdsong has been running crooked dice on them mill niggers for fifteen years, goes straight to the same game where he has been peacefully losing a probably steady average ninety-nine percent of his pay ever since he got big enough to read the spots on them miss-out dice, and cuts Birdsong's throat clean to the neckbone five minutes later." The wife passed him again and went to the dining room. Again he drew his feet back and raised his voice:

"So me and Maydew go out there. Not that we expected to do any good, as he had probably passed Jackson, Tennessee, about daylight; and besides, the simplest way to find him would be just to stay close behind them Birdsong boys. Of course there wouldn't be nothing hardly worth bringing back to town after they did find him, but it would close the case. So it's just by the merest chance that we go by his house; I dont even remember why we went now, but we did; and there he is. Sitting behind the barred front door with a open razor on one knee and a loaded shotgun on the other? No. He was asleep. A big pot of field peas et clean empty on the stove, and him laying in the back yard asleep in the broad sun with just his head under the edge of the porch in the shade and a dog that looked like a cross between a bear and a Polled Angus steer yelling fire and murder from the back door. And we wake him and he sets up and says, 'Awright, white folks. Ah done it. Jest dont lock me up,' and Maydew says, 'Mr Birdsong's kinfolks aint going to lock you up neither. You'll have plenty of fresh air when they get hold of you,' and he says, 'Ah done it. Jest dont lock me up' — advising, instructing the sheriff not to lock him up; he done it all right and it's too bad but it aint convenient for him to be cut off from the fresh air at the moment. So we loaded him into the car, when here come the old woman — his ma or aunt or something — panting up the road at a dog-trot, wanting to come with us too, and Maydew trying to explain to her what would maybe happen to her too if them Birdsong kin catches us before we can get him locked up, only she is coming anyway, and like Maydew says, her being in the car too might be a good thing if the Birdsongs did happen to run into us, because after all interference with the law cant be condoned even if the Birdsong connection did carry that beat for Maydew last summer.

"So we brought her along too and got him to town and into the jail all right and turned him over to Ketcham and Ketcham taken him on up stairs and the old woman coming too, right on up to the cell, telling Ketcham, 'Ah tried to raise him right. He was a good boy. He aint never been in no trouble till now. He will suffer for what he done. But dont let the white folks get him,' until Ketcham says, 'You and him ought to thought of that before he started barbering white men without using no lather first.' So he locked them both up in the cell because he felt like Maydew did, that her being in there with him might be a good influence on the Birdsong boys if anything started if he should happen to be running for sheriff or something when Maydew's term was up. So Ketcham come on back down stairs and pretty soon the chain gang come in and went on up to the bull pen and he thought things had settled down for a while when all of a sudden he begun to hear the yelling, not howling: yelling, though there wasn't no words in it, and he grabbed his pistol and run back up stairs to the bull pen where the chain gang was and Ketcham could see into the cell where the old woman was kind of squinched down in one corner and where that nigger had done tore that iron cot clean out of the floor it was bolted to and was standing in the middle of the cell, holding the cot over his head like it was a baby's cradle, yelling, and says to the old woman, 'Ah aint goan hurt you,' and throws the cot against the wall and comes and grabs holt of the steel barred door and rips it out of the wall, bricks hinges and all, and walks out of the cell toting the door over his head like it was a gauze window-screen, hollering, "It's awright. It's awright. Ah aint trying to git away.'

"Of course Ketcham could have shot him right there, but like he said, if it wasn't going to be the law, then them Birdsong boys ought to have the first lick at him. So Ketcham dont shoot. Instead, he jumps in behind where them chain gang niggers was kind of backed off from the steel door, hollering, 'Grab him! Throw him down!' except the niggers hung back at first too until Ketcham gets in where he can kick the ones he can reach, batting at the others with the flat of the pistol until they rush him. And Ketcham says that for a full minute that nigger would grab them as they come in and fling them clean across the room like they was rag dolls, saying, 'Ah aint trying to git out. Ah aint trying to git out,' until at last they pulled him down – a big mass of nigger heads and arms and legs boiling around on the floor and even then Ketcham says every now and then a nigger would come flying out and go sailing through the air across the room, spraddled out like a flying squirrel and with his eyes sticking out like car headlights, until at last they had him down and Ketcham went in and begun peeling away niggers until he could see him laying there under the pile of them, laughing, with tears big as glass marbles running across his face and down past his ears and making a kind of popping sound on the floor like somebody dropping bird eggs, laughing and laughing and saying, 'Hit look lack Ah just cant quit thinking. Look lack Ah just cant quit.' And what do you think of that?"

"I think if you eat any supper in this house you'll do it in the next five minutes," his wife said from the dining room. "I'm going to clear this table then and I'm going to the picture show."

VLADIMIR NABOKOV b. 1899

Nabokov was born and brought up in a rich, privileged, cultured world that has no counterpart today – certainly not in Russia and not really anywhere else either. A broad country estate on which the young Nabokov studied nature and became a lepidopterist (an expert on butterflies); French and English governesses; annual luxurious pilgrimages to the French Riviera – the life of the European high bourgeoisie of a vanished era was Nabokov's. It was all destroyed by World War I and the Bolshevik Revolution. At nineteen Nabokov became a permanent exile from his country, with memories of childhood that seemed as much the stuff of fairy tales as of reality. After his exile from Russia he entered Trinity College, Cambridge, England, taking a first-class degree in modern languages in 1922, the same year in which his beloved and admired father was assassinated by two Russian monarchist gunmen. Now the head of his family, he moved to Berlin, where there was a large group of Russian émigrés from whose constant political discussion and intrigue Nabokov remained somewhat detached. In Berlin and later in Paris he supported himself in various ways – coaching tennis, teaching languages, making up chess problems for magazines – but he never deviated from his main objective of becoming a major writer. During the thirties he produced a steady stream of articles, poems, stories, and novels written mostly in Russian but also in German, French, and English. The finest is *Dar,* or in the English translation *The Gift,* written in 1938, just before he was to undergo yet another exile when Hitler overran France. Nabokov with his wife and son escaped to America, and in the next twenty years he not only became an American citizen but an American writer as well. He embraced the country – its special kind of English, its movies, highways, motels, colleges, butterflies – and the results are apparent in his two best novels written in English: *Lolita* (1955), which at last brought him enough money so he could devote himself exclusively to writing, and *Pale Fire* (1962). Since 1960 Nabokov has lived most of the year in Montreux, Switzerland, retaining both his citizenship and an affectionate attachment to the United States.

The narrators of these two stories are haunted. Ghosts from the past stalk them, and in one sense they write to assert that now: Central Park, New York, 1943, or now: Boston, 1948, is real, and what happened in France or Russia years ago is just a memory. But *just* a memory? To these narrators memory, the recapturing of the past, is the supreme creative act that alone reveals the meaning of otherwise chaotic and bizarre experience. Perhaps like Nabokov himself, remembering not only his bygone youth but a different civilization, the narrators are not exempt from nostalgia. A mark of their toughness and reliability – and Nabokov's – is that their nostalgia does not consist of a longing to *return* to the past; indeed, except for certain isolated moments that stick in the memory like the frozen life of a snapshot, their past was not especially pleasant, was, in fact, always a disappointment. Thus in "First Love," nothing comes of the boy's "first love" except the beautiful memory that is this story. The tension in the stories is not between a nostalgically recollected past and the present, but between the beautiful patterns that imagination can impose upon experience and the disorganized (maybe even hostile) nature of experience itself.

One of the most useful approaches to Nabokov is through identifying different kinds of time in his stories. There is always the sought-after stillness of a picture postcard: frozen time in which the narrator can arrange himself in perfect harmony with a setting that he knows will not change. Unfortunately, however, such stillness is not to be found in the real world; the tick of the clock, the turning of the earth, destroys it – carrying the boy from his first love, the newly married husband from his bride. What remains possible, though, is an apparently only second-best kind of time, a mixture of ideal and real time, memory, which also must be sought but is at least achievable in the real world (in Central Park, 1943, or Boston, 1948). The narrator in effect asks us to join him in establishing memory against the rapidly moving time-stream without. If he and we succeed, the result is a story whose subject is the destruction of ideal time by real time (often imaged by a train moving relentlessly through a landscape of pictures merely glimpsed).

The relationships among the ideal, real, and the part-ideal, part-real times are very delicate, and if the narrator is to do what he sets out to do – create a story – he has to maintain a constructive tension among them. A difficult job, for he is never a dispassionate observer but someone who as he writes is tempted to leap into his story and to substitute his life *then* for his life *now*.

Precariousness is a condition of life in Nabokov's stories, and another way of approaching the stories is to look at what *threatens* the narrator – both in the past that he describes and in his present effort of reconstruction. The major threats are the relentless passage of time itself and the failure of memory ("I cannot recall the dog's name and this bothers me," the narrator of "First Love" says); but there are subtler threats as well. One certainly is the possibility that man's surroundings may be totally irrelevant to his personality. When the narrator of "That in Aleppo Once . . ." walks out of the railroad station to find the train with his wife on it gone, what he sees is not a correlative of his grief and panic — some indication that physical reality is in harmony with his sensibility — but the blank inhuman irrelevance of "naked indifferent rails and a lone piece of orange peel."

Another threat to Nabokov's narrators is the presence of competing story-tellers who want to make their own fiction out of events in the narrator's life. What annoys the narrator of "That in Aleppo Once . . ." as much as the loss of his wife is her maddening habit of putting him into a hundred different stories and scattering them throughout Europe. As his title indicates, the narrator wants to think of himself as a kind of deceived Othello; and it is specially galling for him to face the fact that not only may he have unknowingly played his marriage according to his wife's script, but that now this story he is telling, *his* story, has to compete with all of hers. The threat is double: to his understanding of what happened, and to his art.

Sometimes the competition with the rival story-teller is not so direct: the narrator has just a vague feeling that, despite the form that he is trying to impose on his experience, it all really happened like a myth. In short, the narrator's view of himself as a human being who has willed his actions may be illusory; he may actually have been a puppet acting out an age-old drama and failing to perceive the determining pattern behind what happened. As the narrator of "That in Aleppo Once . . ." says of a carriage ride that seems ominously beyond his control, "What was driving us was something more than a booted and buckled fool."

In general, then, the precariousness that charges Nabokov's fiction is generated by a multitude of threats to all that is superbly human: time sweeping experience before it: art turning out to be self-satisfying dreams; language to be a mere game, like chess; the world to be unresponsive to human sensibility; and Fate, not man's will, dictating our lives. These narrators, both very human, are haunted by these possibilities, and they wistfully set out to express what it feels like to live with them.

FIRST LOVE

I

In the early years of this century, a travel agency on Nevski Avenue displayed a three-foot-long model of an oak-brown international sleeping car. In delicate verisimilitude it completely outranked the painted tin of my clockwork trains. Unfortunately it was not for sale. One could make out the blue upholstery inside, the embossed leather lining of the compartment walls, their polished panels, inset mirrors, tulip-shaped reading lamps, and other maddening details. Spacious windows alternated with narrower ones, single or geminate, and some of these were of frosted glass. In a few of the compartments, the beds had been made.

The then great and glamorous Nord Express (it was never the same after World War I), consisting solely of such international cars and running but twice a week, connected St. Petersburg with Paris. I would have said: directly with Paris, had passengers not been obliged to change from one train to a superficially similar one at the Russo-German frontier (Verzhbolovo-Eydtkuhnen), where the ample and lazy Russian sixty-and-a-half-inch gauge was replaced by the fifty-six-and-a-half-inch standard of Europe and coal succeeded birch logs.

In the far end of my mind I can unravel, I think, at least five such journeys to Paris, with the Riviera or Biarritz as their ultimate destination. In 1909, the year I now single out, my two small sisters had been left at home with nurses and aunts. Wearing gloves and a traveling cap, my father sat reading a book in the compartment he shared with our tutor. My brother and I were separated from them by a washroom. My mother and her maid occupied a compartment adjacent to ours. The odd one of our party, my father's valet, Osip (whom, a decade later, the pedantic Bolsheviks were to shoot, because he appropriated our bicycles instead of turning them over to the nation), had a stranger for companion.

In April of that year, Peary had reached the North Pole. In May, Chaliapin had sung in Paris. In June, bothered by rumors of new and better Zeppelins, the United States War Department had told reporters of plans for an aerial Navy.

In July, Blériot had flown from Calais to Dover (with a little additional loop when he lost his bearings). It was late August now. The firs and marshes of northwestern Russia sped by, and on the following day gave way to German pine barrens and heather.

At a collapsible table, my mother and I played a card game called *durachki.* Although it was still broad daylight, our cards, a glass, and on a different plane the locks of a suitcase were reflected in the window. Through forest and field, and in sudden ravines, and among scuttling cottages, those discarnate gamblers kept steadily playing on for steadily sparkling stakes.

"*Ne budet-li, tï ved' ustal* [Haven't you had enough, aren't you tired]?" my mother would ask, and then would be lost in thought as she slowly shuffled the cards. The door of the compartment was open and I could see the corridor window, where the wires – six thin black wires – were doing their best to slant up, to ascend skywards, despite the lightning blows dealt them by one telegraph pole after another; but just as all six, in a triumphant swoop of pathetic elation, were about to reach the top of the window, a particularly vicious blow would bring them down, as low as they had ever been, and they would have to start all over again.

When, on such journeys as these, the train changed its pace to a dignified amble and all but grazed house fronts and shop signs, as we passed through some big German town, I used to feel a twofold excitement, which terminal stations could not provide. I saw a city with its toylike trams, linden trees, and brick walls enter the compartment, hobnob with the mirrors, and fill to the brim the windows on the corridor side. This informal contact between train and city was one part of the thrill. The other was putting myself in the place of some passer-by who, I imagined, was moved as I would be moved myself to see the long, romantic, auburn cars, with their intervestibular connecting curtains as black as bat wings and their metal lettering copper-bright in the low sun, unhurriedly negotiate an iron bridge across an everyday thoroughfare and then turn, with all windows suddenly ablaze, around a last block of houses.

There were drawbacks to those optical amalgamations. The wide-windowed dining car, a vista of chaste bottles of mineral water, miter-folded napkins, and dummy chocolate bars (whose wrappers – Cailler, Kohler, and so forth – enclosed nothing but wood) would be perceived at first as a cool haven beyond a consecution of reeling blue corridors; but as the meal progressed toward its fatal last course, one would keep catching the car in the act of being recklessly sheathed, lurching waiters and all, in the landscape, while the landscape itself went through a complex system of motion, the day-time moon stubbornly keeping abreast of one's plate, the distant meadows opening fanwise, the near trees sweeping up on invisible swings toward the track, a parallel rail line all at once committing suicide by anastomosis, a bank of nictitating grass rising, rising, rising, until the little witness of mixed velocities was made to disgorge his portion of *omelette aux confitures de fraises.*

It was at night, however, that the *Compagnie Internationale des Wagons-Lits et des Grands Express Européens* lived up to the magic of its name. From my bed under my brother's bunk (Was he asleep? Was he there at all?), in the semidarkness of our compartment, I watched things, and parts of things, and shadows, and sections of shadows cautiously moving about and getting nowhere. The woodwork gently creaked and crackled. Near the door that led to the toilet, a dim garment on a peg and, higher up, the tassel of the blue, bivalved night light swung rhythmically. It was hard to correlate those halting approaches, that hooded stealth, with the headlong rush of the outside night, which I knew *was* rushing by, spark-streaked, illegible.

I would put myself to sleep by the simple act of identifying myself with the engine driver. A sense of drowsy well-being invaded my veins as soon as I had everything nicely arranged – the carefree passengers in their rooms enjoying the ride I was giving them, smoking, exchanging knowing smiles, nodding, dozing; the waiters and cooks and train guards (whom I had to place somewhere) carousing in the diner; and myself, goggled and begrimed, peering out of the engine cab at the tapering track, at the ruby or emerald point in the black distance. And then, in my sleep, I would see something totally different – a glass marble rolling under a grand piano or a toy engine lying on its side with its wheels still working gamely.

A change in the speed of the train sometimes interrupted the current of my sleep. Slow lights were stalking by; each, in passing, investigated the same chink, and then a luminous compass measured the shadows. Presently, the train stopped with a long-drawn Westinghousian sigh. Something (my brother's spectacles, as it proved next day) fell from above. It was marvelously exciting to move to the foot of one's bed, with part of the bedclothes following, in order to undo cautiously the catch of the window shade, which could be made to slide only halfway up, impeded as it was by the edge of the upper berth.

Like moons around Jupiter, pale moths revolved about a lone lamp. A dismembered newspaper stirred on a bench. Somewhere on the train one could hear muffled voices, somebody's comfortable cough. There was nothing particularly interesting in the portion of station platform before me, and still I could not tear myself away from it until it departed of its own accord.

Next morning, wet fields with misshapen willows along the radius of a ditch or a row of poplars afar, traversed by a horizontal band of milky-white mist, told one that the train was spinning through Belgium. It reached Paris at 4 P.M.; and even if the stay was only an overnight one, I had always time to purchase something – say, a little brass *Tour Eiffel,* rather roughly coated with silver paint – before we boarded at noon on the following day the Sud Express, which, on its way to Madrid, dropped us around 10 P.M. at the La Négresse station of Biarritz, a few miles from the Spanish frontier.

II

Biarritz still retained its quiddity in those days. Dusty blackberry bushes and weedy *terrains à vendre* bordered the road that led to our villa. The Carlton was still being built. Some thirty-six years had to elapse before Brigadier General Samuel McCroskey would occupy the royal suite of the Hotel du Palais, which stands on the site of a former palace, where, in the sixties, that incredibly agile medium, Daniel Home, is said to have been caught stroking with his bare foot (in imitation of a ghost hand) the kind, trustful face of Empress Eugénie. On the promenade near the Casino, an elderly flower girl, with carbon eyebrows and a painted smile, nimbly slipped the plump torus of a carnation into the buttonhole of an intercepted stroller whose left jowl accentuated its royal fold as he glanced down sideways at the coy insertion of the flower.

Along the back line of the *plage,* various seaside chairs and stools supported the parents of straw-hatted children who were playing in front on the sand. I could be seen on my knees trying to set a found comb aflame by means of a magnifying glass. Men sported white trousers that to the eye of today would look as if they had comically shrunk in the washing; ladies wore, that particular season, light coats with silk-faced lapels, hats with big crowns and wide brims, dense embroidered white veils, frill-fronted blouses, frills at their wrists, frills on their parasols. The breeze salted one's lips. At a tremendous pace a stray golden-orange butterfly came dashing across the palpitating *plage.*

Additional movement and sound were provided by vendors hawking *cacahuètes,* sugared violets, pistachio ice cream of a heavenly green, cachou pellets, and huge convex pieces of dry, gritty, waferlike stuff that came from a red barrel. With a distinctness that no later superpositions have dimmed, I see that waffleman stomp along through deep mealy sand, with the heavy cask on his bent back. When called, he would sling it off his shoulder by a twist of its strap, bang it down on the sand in a Tower of Pisa position, wipe his face with his sleeve, and proceed to manipulate a kind of arrow-and-dial arrangement with numbers on the lid of the cask. The arrow rasped and whirred around. Luck was supposed to fix the size of a sou's worth of wafer. The bigger the piece, the more I was sorry for him.

The process of bathing took place on another part of the beach. Professional bathers, burly Basques in black bathing suits, were there to help ladies and children enjoy the terrors of the surf. Such a *baigneur* would place you with your back to the incoming wave and hold you by the hand as the rising, rotating mass of foamy, green water violently descended upon you from behind, knocking you off your feet with one mighty wallop. After a dozen of these tumbles, the *baigneur,* glistening like a seal, would lead his panting, shivering, moistly snuffling charge landward, to the flat foreshore, where an unforgettable old woman with gray hairs on her chin promptly chose a bathing robe from several hanging on a clothesline.

In the security of a little cabin, one would be helped by yet another attendant to peel off one's soggy, sand-heavy bathing suit. It would plop onto the boards, and, still shivering, one would step out of it and trample on its bluish, diffuse stripes. The cabin smelt of pine. The attendant, a hunchback with beaming wrinkles, brought a basin of steaming-hot water, in which one immersed one's feet. From him I learned, and have preserved ever since in a glass cell of my memory, that "butterfly" in the Basque language is *misericoletea* – or at least it sounded so (among the seven words I have found in dictionaries the closest approach is *micheletea*).

III

On the browner and wetter part of the *plage,* that part which at low tide yielded the best mud for castles, I found myself digging, one day, side by side with a little French girl called Colette.

She would be ten in November, I had been ten in April. Attention was drawn to a jagged bit of violet mussel shell upon which she had stepped with the bare sole of her narrow long-toed foot. No, I was not English. Her greenish eyes seemed flecked with the overflow of the freckles that covered her sharp-featured face. She wore what might now be termed a playsuit, consisting of a blue jersey with rolled-up sleeves and blue knitted shorts. I had taken her at first for a boy and then had been puzzled by the bracelet on her thin wrist and the corkscrew brown curls dangling from under her sailor cap.

She spoke in birdlike bursts of rapid twitter, mixing governess English and Parisian French. Two years before, on the same *plage,* I had been much attached to the lovely, sun-tanned little daughter of a Serbian physician; but when I met Colette, I knew at once that this was the real thing. Colette seemed to me so much stranger than all my other chance playmates at Biarritz! I somehow acquired the feeling that she was less happy than I, less loved. A bruise on her delicate, downy forearm gave rise to awful conjectures. "He pinches as bad as my mummy," she said, speaking of a crab. I evolved various schemes to save her from her parents, who were *"des bourgeois de Paris"* as I heard somebody tell my mother with a slight shrug. I interpreted the disdain in my own fashion, as I knew that those people had come all the way from Paris in their blue-and-yellow limousine (a fashionable adventure in those days) but had drably sent Colette with her dog and governess by an ordinary coach train. The dog was a female fox terrier with bells on her collar and a most waggly behind. From sheer exuberance, she would lap up salt water out of Colette's toy pail. I remember the sail, the sunset, and the lighthouse pictured on that pail, but I cannot recall the dog's name, and this bothers me.

During the two months of our stay at Biarritz, my passion for Colette all but surpassed my passion for butterflies. Since my parents were not keen to meet hers, I saw her only on the beach; but I thought of her constantly. If I noticed she had been crying, I felt a surge of helpless anguish that brought tears to my own eyes. I could not destroy the mosquitoes that had left their bites on her frail neck, but I could, and did, have a successful fist fight with a red-haired boy who had been rude to her. She used to give me warm handfuls of hard candy. One day, as we were bending together over a starfish, and Colette's ringlets were tickling my ear, she suddenly turned toward me and kissed me on the cheek. So great was my emotion that all I could think of saying was, "You little monkey."

I had a gold coin that I assumed would pay for our elopement. Where did I want to take her? Spain? America? The mountains above Pau? *"Là-bas, là-bas, dans la montagne,"* as I had heard Carmen sing at the opera. One strange night, I lay awake, listening to the recurrent thud of the ocean and planning our flight. The ocean seemed to rise and grope in the darkness and then heavily fall on its face.

Of our actual getaway, I have little to report. My memory retains a glimpse of her obediently putting on rope-soled canvas shoes, on the lee side of a flapping tent, while I stuffed a folding butterfly net into a brown paper bag. The next glimpse is of our evading pursuit by entering a pitch-dark *cinéma* near the Casino (which, of course, was absolutely out of bounds). There we sat, holding hands across the dog, which now and then gently jingled in Colette's lap, and were shown a jerky, drizzly, but highly exciting bullfight at St. Sebástian. My final glimpse is of myself being led along the promenade by my tutor. His long legs move with a kind of ominous briskness and I can see the muscles of his grimly set jaw working under the tight skin. My bespectacled brother, aged nine, whom he happens to hold with his other hand, keeps trotting out forward to peer at me with awed curiosity, like a little owl.

Among the trivial souvenirs acquired at Biarritz before leaving, my favorite was not the small bull of black stone and not the sonorous sea shell but something which now seems almost symbolic – a meerschaum penholder with a tiny peephole of crystal in its ornamental part. One held it quite close to one's eye, screwing up the other, and when one had got rid of the shimmer of one's own lashes, a miraculous photographic view of the bay and of the line of cliffs ending in a lighthouse could be seen inside.

And now a delightful thing happens. The process of recreating that penholder and the microcosm in its eyelet stimulates my memory to a last effort. I try again to recall the name of Colette's dog – and, sure enough, along those remote beaches, over the glossy evening sands of the past, where each footprint slowly fills up with sunset water, here it comes, here it comes, echoing and vibrating: Floss, Floss, Floss!

Colette was back in Paris by the time we stopped there for a day before continuing our homeward journey; and there, in a fawn park under a cold blue sky, I saw her (by arrangement between our mentors, I believe) for the last time. She carried a hoop and a short stick to drive it with, and everything about her was extremely proper and stylish in an autumnal, Parisian, *tenue-de-ville-pour-fillettes* way. She took from her governess and slipped into my brother's hand a farewell present, a box of sugar-coated almonds, meant, I knew, solely for me; and instantly she was off, tap-tapping her glinting hoop through light and shade, around and around a fountain choked with dead leaves near which I stood. The leaves mingle in my memory with the leather of her shoes and gloves, and there was, I remember, some detail in her attire (perhaps a ribbon on her Scottish cap, or the pattern of her stockings) that reminded me then of the rainbow spiral in a glass marble. I still seem to be holding that wisp of iridescence, not knowing exactly where to fit it, while she runs with her hoop ever faster around me and finally dissolves among the slender shadows cast on the graveled path by the interlaced arches of its low looped fence.

"THAT IN ALEPPO ONCE . . ."

Dear V. – Among other things, this is to tell you that at last I am here, in the country whither so many sunsets have led. One of the first persons I saw was our good old Gleb Alexandrovich Gekko gloomily crossing Columbus Avenue in quest of the *petit café du coin* which none of us three will ever visit again. He seemed to think that somehow or other you were betraying our national literature, and he gave me your address with a deprecatory shake of his gray head, as if you did not deserve the treat of hearing from me.

I have a story for you. Which reminds me – I mean putting it like this reminds me – of the days when we wrote our first udder-warm bubbling verse, and all things, a rose, a puddle, a lighted window, cried out to us: "I'm a rhyme!" Yes, this is a most useful universe. We play, we die: *ig-rhyme, umi rhyme.* And the sonorous souls of Russian verbs lend a meaning to the wild gesticulation of trees or to some discarded newspaper sliding and pausing, and shuffling again, with abortive flaps and apterous jerks along an endless wind-swept embankment. But just now I am not a poet. I come to you like that gushing lady in Chekhov who was dying to be described.

I married, let me see, about a month after you left France and a few weeks before the gentle Germans roared into Paris. Although I can produce documentary proofs of matrimony, I am positive now that my wife never existed. You may know her name from some other source, but that does not matter: it is the name of an illusion. Therefore, I am able to speak of her with as much detachment as I would of a character in a story (one of your stories, to be precise).

It was love at first touch rather than at first sight, for I had met her several times before without experiencing any special emotions; but one night, as I was seeing her home, something quaint she had said made me stoop with a laugh and lightly kiss her on the hair – and of course we all know of that blinding blast which is caused by merely picking up a small doll from the floor of a carefully abandoned house: the soldier involved hears nothing; for him it is but an ecstatic soundless and boundless expansion of what had been during his life a pin point of light in the dark center of his being. And really, the reason we think of death in celestial terms is that the visible firmament, especially at night (above our blacked-out Paris with the gaunt arches of its Boulevard Exelmans and the ceaseless Alpine gurgle of desolate latrines), is the most adequate and ever-present symbol of that vast silent explosion.

But I cannot discern her. She remains as nebulous as my best poem — the one you made such gruesome fun of in the *Literaturnïe Zapiski*. When I want to imagine her, I have to cling mentally to a tiny brown birthmark on her downy forearm, as one concentrates upon a punctuation mark in an illegible sentence. Perhaps, had she used a greater amount of make-up or used it more constantly, I might have visualized her face today, or at least the delicate transverse furrows of dry, hot rouged lips; but I fail, I fail — although I still feel their elusive touch now and then in the blindman's buff of my senses, in that sobbing sort of dream when she and I clumsily clutch at each other through a heart-breaking mist and I cannot see the color of her eyes for the blank luster of brimming tears drowning their irises.

She was much younger than I — not as much younger as was Nathalie of the lovely bare shoulders and long earrings in relation to swarthy Pushkin; but still there was a sufficient margin for that kind of retrospective romanticism which finds pleasure in imitating the destiny of a unique genius (down to the jealousy, down to the filth, down to the stab of seeing her almond-shaped eyes turn to her blond Cassio behind her peacock-feathered fan) even if one cannot imitate his verse. She liked mine though, and would scarcely have yawned as the other was wont to do every time her husband's poem happened to exceed the length of a sonnet. If she has remained a phantom to me, I may have been one to her: I suppose she had been solely attracted by the obscurity of my poetry; then tore a hole through its veil and saw a stranger's unlovable face.

As you know, I had been for some time planning to follow the example of your fortunate flight. She described to me an uncle of hers who lived, she said, in New York: he had taught riding at a Southern college and had wound up by marrying a wealthy American woman; they had a little daughter born deaf. She said she had lost their address long ago, but a few days later it miraculously turned up, and we wrote a dramatic letter to which we never received any reply. This did not much matter, as I had already obtained a sound affidavit from Professor Lomchenko of Chicago; but little else had been done in the way of getting the necessary papers, when the invasion began, whereas I foresaw that if we stayed on in Paris some helpful compatriot of mine would sooner or later point out to the interested party sundry passages in one of my books where I argued that, with all her many black sins, Germany was still bound to remain forever and ever the laughing stock of the world.

So we started upon our disastrous honeymoon. Crushed and jolted amid the apocalyptic exodus, waiting for unscheduled trains that were bound for unknown destinations, walking through the stale stage setting of abstract towns, living in a permanent twilight of physical exhaustion, we fled; and the farther we fled, the clearer it became that what was driving us on was something more than a booted and buckled fool with his assortment of variously propelled junk – something of which he was a mere symbol, something monstrous and impalpable, a timeless and faceless mass of immemorial horror that still keeps coming at me from behind even here, in the green vacuum of Central Park.

Oh, she bore it gamely enough – with a kind of dazed cheerfulness. Once, however, quite suddenly she started to sob in a sympathetic railway carriage. "The dog," she said, "the dog we left. I cannot forget the poor dog." The honesty of her grief shocked me, as we had never had any dog. "I know," she said, "but I tried to imagine we had actually bought that setter. And just think, he would be now whining behind a locked door." There had never been any talk of buying a setter.

I should also not like to forget a certain stretch of highroad and the sight of a family of refugees (two women, a child) whose old father, or grandfather, had died on the way. The sky was a chaos of black and flesh-colored clouds with an ugly sunburst beyond a hooded hill, and the dead man was lying on his back under a dusty plane tree. With a stick and their hands the women had tried to dig a roadside grave, but the soil was too hard; they had given it up and were sitting side by side, among the anemic poppies, a little apart from the corpse and its upturned beard. But the little boy was still scratching and scraping and tugging until he tumbled a flat stone and forgot the object of his solemn exertions as he crouched on his haunches, his thin, eloquent neck showing all its vertebrae to the headsman, and watched with surprise and delight thousands of minute brown ants seething, zigzagging, dispersing, heading for places of safety in the Gard, and the Aude, and the Drome, and the Var, and the Basses-Pyrénées – we two paused only in Pau.

Spain proved too difficult and we decided to move on to Nice. At a place called Faugères (a ten-minute stop) I squeezed out of the train to buy some food. When a couple of minutes later I came back, the train was gone, and the muddled old man responsible for the atrocious void that faced me (coal dust glittering in the heat between naked indifferent rails, and a lone piece of orange peel) brutally told me that, anyway, I had had no right to get out.

In a better world I could have had my wife located and told what to do (I had both tickets and most of the money); as it was, my nightmare struggle with the telephone proved futile, so I dismissed the whole series of diminutive voices barking at me from afar, sent two or three telegrams which are probably on their way only now, and late in the evening took the next local to Montpellier, farther than which her train would not stumble. Not finding her there, I had to choose between two alternatives: going on because she might have boarded the Marseilles train which I had just missed, or going back because she might have returned to Faugères. I forgot now what tangle of reasoning led me to Marseilles and Nice.

Beyond such routine action as forwarding false data to a few unlikely places, the police did nothing to help: one man bellowed at me for being a nuisance; another sidetracked the question by doubting the authenticity of my marriage certificate because it was stamped on what he contended to be the wrong side; a third, a fat *commissaire* with liquid brown eyes confessed that he wrote poetry in his spare time. I looked up various acquaintances among the numerous Russians domiciled or stranded in Nice. I heard those among them who chanced to have Jewish blood talk of their doomed kinsmen crammed into hell-bound trains; and my own plight, by contrast, acquired a commonplace air of irreality while I sat in some crowded café with the milky blue sea in front of me and a shell-hollow murmur behind telling and retelling the tale of massacre and misery, and the gray paradise beyond the ocean, and the ways and whims of harsh consuls.

A week after my arrival an indolent plain-clothes man called upon me and took me down a crooked and smelly street to a black-stained house with the word "hotel" almost erased by dirt and time; there, he said, my wife had been found. The girl he produced was an absolute stranger, of course; but my friend Holmes kept on trying for some time to make her and me confess we were married, while her taciturn and muscular bedfellow stood by and listened, his bare arms crossed on his striped chest.

When at length I got rid of those people and had wandered back to my neighborhood, I happened to pass by a compact queue waiting at the entrance of a food store; and there, at the very end, was my wife, straining on tiptoe to catch a glimpse of what exactly was being sold. I think the first thing she said to me was that she hoped it was oranges.

Her tale seemed a trifle hazy, but perfectly banal. She had returned to Faugères and gone straight to the Commissariat instead of making inquiries at the station, where I had left a message for her. A party of refugees suggested that she join them; she spent the night in a bicycle shop with no bicycles, on the floor, together with three elderly women who lay, she said, like three logs in a row. Next day she realized that she had not enough money to reach Nice. Eventually she borrowed some from one of the log-women. She got into the wrong train, however, and traveled to a town the name of which she could not remember. She had arrived at Nice two days ago and had found some friends at the Russian church. They had told her I was somewhere around, looking for her, and would surely turn up soon.

Some time later, as I sat on the edge of the only chair in my garret and held her by her slender young hips (she was combing her soft hair and tossing her head back with every stroke), her dim smile changed all at once into an odd quiver and she placed one hand on my shoulder, staring down at me as if I were a reflection in a pool, which she had noticed for the first time.

"I've been lying to you, dear," she said. "*Ya lgunia.* I stayed for several nights in Montpellier with a brute of a man I met on the train. I did not want it at all. He sold hair lotions."

The time, the place, the torture. Her fan, her gloves, her mask. I spent that night and many others getting it out of her bit by bit, but not getting it all. I was under the strange delusion that first I must find out every detail, reconstruct every minute, and only then decide whether I could bear it. But the limit of desired knowledge was unattainable, nor could I ever foretell the approximate point after which I might imagine myself satiated, because of course the denominator of every fraction of knowledge was potentially as infinite as the number of intervals between the fractions themselves.

Oh, the first time she had been too tired to mind, and the next had not minded because she was sure I had deserted her; and she apparently considered that such explanations ought to be a kind of consolation prize for me instead of the nonsense and agony they really were. It went on like that for eons, she breaking down every now and then, but soon rallying again, answering my unprintable questions in a breathless whisper or trying with a pitiful smile to wriggle into the semisecurity of irrelevant commentaries, and I crushing and crushing the mad molar till my jaw almost burst with pain, a flaming pain which seemed somehow preferable to the dull, humming ache of humble endurance.

And mark, in between the periods of this inquest, we were trying to get from reluctant authorities certain papers which in their turn would make it lawful to apply for a third kind which would serve as a stepping-stone towards a permit enabling the holder to apply for yet other papers which might or might not give him the means of discovering how and why it had happened. For even if I could imagine the accursed recurrent scene, I failed to link up its sharp-angled grotesque shadows with the dim limbs of my wife as she shook and rattled and dissolved in my violent grasp.

So nothing remained but to torture each other, to wait for hours on end in the Prefecture, filling forms, conferring with friends who had already probed the innermost viscera of all visas, pleading with secretaries, and filling forms again, with the result that her lusty and versatile traveling salesman became blended in a ghastly mix-up with rat-whiskered snarling officials, rotting bundles of obsolete records, the reek of violet ink, bribes slipped under gangrenous blotting paper, fat flies tickling moist necks with their rapid cold padded feet, new-laid clumsy concave photographs of your six subhuman doubles, the tragic eyes and patient politeness of petitioners born in Slutzk, Starodub, or Bobruisk, the funnels and pulleys of the Holy Inquisition, the awful smile of the bald man with the glasses, who had been told that his passport could not be found.

I confess that one evening, after a particularly abominable day, I sank down on a stone bench weeping and cursing a mock world where millions of lives were being juggled by the clammy hands of consuls and *commissaires.* I noticed she was crying too, and then I told her that nothing would really have mattered the way it mattered now, had she not gone and done what she did.

"You will think me crazy," she said with a vehemence that, for a second, almost made a real person of her, "but I didn't — I swear that I didn't. Perhaps I live several lives at once. Perhaps I wanted to test you. Perhaps this bench is a dream and we are in Saratov or on some star."

It would be tedious to niggle the different stages through which I passed before accepting finally the first version of her delay. I did not talk to her and was a good deal alone. She would glimmer and fade, and reappear with some trifle she thought I would appreciate — a handful of cherries, three precious cigarettes or the like — treating me with the unruffled mute sweetness of a nurse that trips from and to a gruff convalescent. I ceased visiting most of our mutual friends because they had lost all interest in my passport affairs and seemed to have turned vaguely inimical. I composed several poems. I drank all the wine I could get. I clasped her one day to my groaning breast, and we went for a week to Caboule and lay on the round pink pebbles of the narrow beach. Strange to say, the happier our new relations seemed, the stronger I felt an undercurrent of poignant sadness, but I kept telling myself that this was an intrinsic feature of all true bliss.

In the meantime, something had shifted in the moving pattern of our fates and at last I emerged from a dark and hot office with a couple of plump *visas de sortie* cupped in my trembling hands. Into these the U.S.A. serum was duly injected, and I dashed to Marseilles and managed to get tickets for the very next boat. I returned and tramped up the stairs. I saw a rose in a glass on the table — the sugar pink of its obvious beauty, the parasitic air bubbles clinging to its stem. Her two spare dresses were gone, her comb was gone, her checkered coat was gone, and so was the mauve hairband with a mauve bow that had been her hat. There was no note pinned to the pillow, nothing at all in the room to enlighten me, for of course the rose was merely what French rhymsters call *une cheville.*

I went to the Veretennikovs, who could tell me nothing; to the Hellmans, who refused to say anything; and to the Elagins, who were not sure whether to tell me or not. Finally the old lady — and you know what Anna Vladimirovna is like at crucial moments — asked for her rubber-tipped cane, heavily but energetically dislodged her bulk from her favorite armchair, and took me into the garden. There she informed me that, being twice my age, she had the right to say I was a bully and a cad.

You must imagine the scene: the tiny graveled garden with its blue Arabian Nights jar and solitary cypress; the cracked terrace where the old lady's father had dozed with a rug on his knees when he retired from his Novgorod governorship to spend a few last evenings in Nice; the pale-green sky; a whiff of vanilla in the deepening dusk; the crickets emitting their metallic trill pitched at two octaves above middle C; and Anna Vladimirovna, the folds of her cheeks jerkily dangling as she flung at me a motherly but quite undeserved insult.

During several preceding weeks, my dear V., every time she had visited by herself the three or four families we both knew, my ghostly wife had filled the eager ears of all those kind people with an extraordinary story. To wit: that she had madly fallen in love with a young Frenchman who could give her a turreted home and a crested name; that she had implored me for a divorce and I had refused; that in fact I had said I would rather shoot her and myself than sail to New York alone; that she had said her father in a similar case had acted like a gentleman; that I had answered I did not give a hoot for her *cocu de père.*

There were loads of other preposterous details of the kind – but they all hung together in such a remarkable fashion that no wonder the old lady made me swear I would not seek to pursue the lovers with a cocked pistol. They had gone, she said, to a château in Lozère. I inquired whether she had ever set eyes upon the man. No, but she had been shown his picture. As I was about to leave, Anna Vladimirovna, who had slightly relaxed and had even given me her five fingers to kiss, suddenly flared up again, struck the gravel with her cane, and said in her deep strong voice: "But one thing I shall never forgive you – her dog, that poor beast which you hanged with your own hands before leaving Paris."

Whether the gentleman of leisure had changed into a traveling salesman, or whether the metamorphosis had been reversed, or whether again he was neither the one nor the other, but the nondescript Russian who had courted her before our marriage – all this was absolutely inessential. She had gone. That was the end. I should have been a fool had I begun the nightmare business of searching and waiting for her all over again.

On the fourth morning of a long and dismal sea voyage, I met on the deck a solemn but pleasant old doctor with whom I had played chess in Paris. He asked me whether my wife was very much incommoded by the rough seas. I answered that I had sailed alone; whereupon he looked taken aback and then said he had seen her a couple of days before going on board, namely in Marseilles, walking, rather aimlessly he thought, along the embankment. She said that I would presently join her with bag and tickets.

This is, I gather, the point of the whole story – although if you write it, you had better not make him a doctor, as that kind of thing has been overdone. It was at that moment that I suddenly knew for certain that she had never existed at all. I shall tell you another thing. When I arrived I hastened to satisfy a certain morbid curiosity: I went to the address she had given me once; it proved to be an anonymous gap between two office buildings; I looked for her uncle's name in the directory; it was not there; I made some inquiries, and Gekko, who knows everything, informed me that the man and his horsey wife existed all right, but had moved to San Francisco after their deaf little girl had died.

Viewing the past graphically, I see our mangled romance engulfed in a deep valley of mist between the crags of two matter-of-fact mountains: life had been real before, life will be real from now on, I hope. Not tomorrow, though. Perhaps after tomorrow. You, happy mortal, with your lovely family (how is Ines? how are the twins?) and your diversified work (how are the lichens?), can hardly be expected to puzzle out my misfortune in terms of human communion, but you may clarify things for me through the prism of your art.

Yet the pity of it. Curse your art, I am hideously unhappy. She keeps on walking to and fro where the brown nets are spread to dry on the hot stone slabs and the dappled light of the water plays on the side of a moored fishing boat. Somewhere, somehow, I have made some fatal mistake. There are tiny pale bits of broken fish scales glistening here and there in the brown meshes. It may all end in *Aleppo* if I am not careful. Spare me, V.: you would load your dice with an unbearable implication if you took that for a title.

JORGE LUIS BORGES b. 1899

Besides having been born in the same year, Borges shares with Nabokov a vast learning in all languages and literatures. He grew up in Buenos Aires, reading in his father's well-stocked library, continued his education in Spain and Switzerland, and then returned to Argentina to become a librarian himself. But as opposed to Nabokov's pixyish way with his erudition, Borges is deeply mystical: reality for him approaches that vertiginous simultaneity that he describes in Funes's perception of three wine glasses on a table: "Funes saw all the shoots, clusters, and grapes of the vine. He remembered the shapes of the clouds in the south at dawn on the 30th of April of 1882, and he could compare them in his recollection with the marbled grain in the design of a leather-bound book which he had seen only once."

Borges's vision of experience, in which imaginary animals from Old Norse myths exist alongside precisely observed details of contemporary Buenos Aires, probably owes a lot to the fact that after years of failing sight he went totally blind in 1957. His way of writing is like Hladik's in "The Secret Miracle": he imagines a story all at once, as in a flash of revelation rather than as a sequence of sentences, holding the story as an entity in his mind while he makes mental revisions, only then releasing it so as to speak to the ordinary world of time. This method of imagining reinforces Borges's constant subject, which is the variety of human perceptions under different conditions, in different states of mind. Thus it is as real for Borges's characters to see God in a tiny letter on a page in an atlas as it is for them to observe the shadow of a bee on a wall or feel a drop of water on one's forehead. And the connections among such perceptions may be equally surprising, since relationships are not limited to the usual cause-and-effect connections that depend upon ordinary assumptions about time and space.

Borges's labyrinthine landscape of the imagination was largely unknown outside of Argentina until 1961, the year in which he shared the International Publishers' Prize with Samuel Beckett. Since then, with Borges's collaboration, several collections of his works have been translated into English, and his stature as a writer is now internationally recognized. He has made a number of public appearances in the United States and charmed audiences with his gentle, low-keyed brilliance. Politically, for many years he had difficulties in his own country: his opposition to Nazi influence in Argentina just before and during World War II put him at odds with the government, and when after the war Perón became dictator he rewarded Borges's outspoken dissent by demoting him from librarian to chicken inspector.

THE SECRET MIRACLE

And God had him die for a hundred years and then revived him and said:

"How long have you been here?"

"A day or a part of a day," he answered.

– *Koran, II, 261*

The night of March 14, 1943, in an apartment in the Zeltnergasse of Prague, Jaromir Hladik, the author of the unfinished drama entitled *The Enemies,* of *Vindication of Eternity* and of a study of the indirect Jewish sources of Jakob Böhme, had a dream of a long game of chess. The players were not two persons, but two illustrious families; the game had been going on for centuries. Nobody could remember what the stakes were, but it was rumored that they were enormous, perhaps infinite; the chessmen and the board were in a secret tower. Jaromir (in his dream) was the first-born of one of the contending families. The clock struck the hour for the game, which could not be postponed. The dreamer raced over the sands of a rainy desert, and was unable to recall either the pieces or the rules of chess. At that moment he awoke. The clangor of the rain and of the terrible clocks ceased. A rhythmic, unanimous noise, punctuated by shouts of command, arose from the Zeltnergasse. It was dawn, and the armored vanguard of the Third Reich was entering Prague.

On the nineteenth the authorities received a denunciation; that same nineteenth, toward evening, Jaromir Hladik was arrested. He was taken to an aseptic, white barracks on the opposite bank of the Moldau. He was unable to refute a single one of the Gestapo's charges; his mother's family name was Jaroslavski, he was of Jewish blood, his study on Böhme had a marked Jewish emphasis, his signature had been one more on the protest against the *Anschluss.* In 1928 he had translated the *Sepher Yezirah* for the publishing house of Hermann Barsdorf. The fulsome catalogue of the firm had exaggerated, for publicity purposes, the translator's reputation, and the catalogue had been examined by Julius Rothe, one of the officials who held Hladik's fate in his hands. There is not a person who, except in the field of his own specialization, is not credulous; two or three adjectives in Gothic type were enough to persuade Julius Rothe of Hladik's importance, and he ordered him sentenced to death *pour encourager les autres.* The execution was set for March 29th, at 9:00 A.M. This delay (whose importance the reader will grasp later) was owing to the desire on the authorities' part to proceed impersonally and slowly, after the manner of vegetables and plants.

Hladik's first reaction was mere terror. He felt he would not have shrunk from the gallows, the block, or the knife, but that death by a firing squad was unbearable. In vain he tried to convince himself that the plain, unvarnished fact of dying was the fearsome thing, not the attendant circumstances. He never wearied of conjuring up these circumstances, senselessly trying to exhaust all their possible variations. He infinitely anticipated the process of his dying, from the sleepless dawn to the mysterious volley. Before the day set by Julius Rothe he died hundreds of deaths in courtyards whose forms and angles strained geometrical probabilities, machine-gunned by variable soldiers in changing numbers, who at times killed him from a distance, at others from close by. He faced these imaginary executions with real terror (perhaps with real bravery); each simulacrum lasted a few seconds. When the circle was closed, Jaromir returned once more and interminably to the tremulous vespers of his death. Then he reflected that reality does not usually coincide with our anticipation of it; with a logic of his own he inferred that to foresee a circumstantial detail is to prevent its happening. Trusting in this weak magic, he invented, *so that they would not happen,* the most gruesome details. Finally, as was natural, he came to fear that they were prophetic. Miserable in the night, he endeavored to find some way to hold fast to the fleeting substance of time. He knew that it was rushing headlong toward the dawn of the twenty-ninth. He reasoned aloud: "I am now in the night of the twenty-second; while this night lasts (and for six nights more), I am invulnerable, immortal." The nights of sleep seemed to him deep, dark pools in which he could submerge himself. There were moments when he longed impatiently for the final burst of fire that would free him, for better or for worse, from the vain compulsion of his imaginings. On the twenty-eighth, as the last sunset was reverberating from the high barred windows, the thought of his drama, *The Enemies,* deflected him from these abject considerations.

Hladik had rounded forty. Aside from a few friendships and many habits, the problematic exercise of literature constituted his life. Like all writers, he measured the achievements of others by what they had accomplished, asking of them that they measure him by what he envisaged or planned. All the books he had published had left him with a complex feeling of repentance. His studies of the work of Böhme, of Ibn Ezra, and of Fludd had been characterized essentially by mere application; his translation of the *Sepher Yezirah,* by carelessness, fatigue, and conjecture. *Vindication of Eternity* perhaps had fewer shortcomings. The first volume gave a history of man's various concepts of eternity, from the immutable Being of Parmenides to the modifiable Past of Hinton. The second denied (with Francis

Bradley) that all the events of the universe make up a temporal series, arguing that the number of man's possible experiences is not infinite, and that a single "repetition" suffices to prove that time is a fallacy . . . Unfortunately, the arguments that demonstrate this fallacy are equally fallacious. Hladik was in the habit of going over them with a kind of contemptuous perplexity. He had also composed a series of Expressionist poems; to the poet's chagrin they had been included in an anthology published in 1924, and no subsequent anthology but inherited them. From all this equivocal, uninspired past Hladik had hoped to redeem himself with his drama in verse, *The Enemies.* (Hladik felt the verse form to be essential because it makes it impossible for the spectators to lose sight of irreality, one of art's requisites.)

The drama observed the unities of time, place, and action. The scene was laid in Hradčany, in the library of Baron von Roemerstadt, on one of the last afternoons of the nineteenth century. In the first scene of the first act a strange man visits Roemerstadt. (A clock was striking seven, the vehemence of the setting sun's rays glorified the windows, a passionate, familiar Hungarian music floated in the air.) This visit is followed by others; Roemerstadt does not know the people who are importuning him, but he has the uncomfortable feeling that he has seen them somewhere, perhaps in a dream. They all fawn upon him, but it is apparent — first to the audience and then to the Baron — that they are secret enemies, in league to ruin him. Roemerstadt succeeds in checking or evading their involved schemings. In the dialogue mention is made of his sweetheart, Julia von Weidenau, and a certain Jaroslav Kubin, who at one time pressed his attentions on her. Kubin has now lost his mind, and believes himself to be Roemerstadt. The dangers increase; Roemerstadt, at the end of the second act, is forced to kill one of the conspirators. The third and final act opens. The incoherencies gradually increase; actors who had seemed out of the play reappear; the man Roemerstadt killed returns for a moment. Someone points out that evening has not fallen; the clock strikes seven, the high windows reverberate in the western sun, the air carries an impassioned Hungarian melody. The first actor comes on and repeats the lines he had spoken in the first scene of the first act. Roemerstadt speaks to him without surprise; the audience understands that Roemerstadt is the miserable Jaroslav Kubin. The drama has never taken place; it is the circular delirium that Kubin lives and relives endlessly.

Hladik had never asked himself whether this tragicomedy of errors was preposterous or admirable, well thought out or slipshod. He felt that the plot I have just sketched was best contrived to cover up his defects and point up his abilities and held the possibility of allowing him to redeem (symbolically) the meaning of his life. He had finished the first act and one or two scenes of the third; the metrical nature of the work made it possible for him to keep working it over, changing the hexameters, without the manuscript in front of him. He thought how he still had two acts to do, and that he was going to die very soon. He spoke with God in the darkness: "If in some fashion I exist, if I am not one of Your repetitions and mistakes, I exist as the author of *The Enemies.* To finish this drama, which can justify me and justify You, I need another year. Grant me these days, You to whom the centuries and time belong." This was the last night, the most dreadful of all, but ten minutes later sleep flooded over him like a dark water.

Toward dawn he dreamed that he had concealed himself in one of the naves of the Clementine Library. A librarian wearing dark glasses asked him: "What are you looking for?" Hladik answered: "I am looking for God." The librarian said to him: "God is in one of the letters on one of the pages of one of the four hundred thousand volumes of the Clementine. My fathers and the fathers of my fathers have searched for this letter; I have grown blind seeking it." He removed his glasses, and Hladik saw his eyes, which were dead. A reader came in to return an atlas. "This atlas is worthless," he said, and handed it to Hladik, who opened it at random. He saw a map of India as in a daze. Suddenly sure of himself, he touched one of the tiniest letters. A ubiquitous voice said to him: "The time of your labor has been granted." At this point Hladik awoke.

He remembered that men's dreams belong to God, and that Maimonides had written that the words heard in a dream are divine when they are distinct and clear and the person uttering them cannot be seen. He dressed: two soldiers came into the cell and ordered him to follow them.

From behind the door, Hladik had envisaged a labyrinth of passageways, stairs, and separate buildings. The reality was less spectacular: they descended to an inner court by a narrow iron stairway. Several soldiers – some with uniform unbuttoned – were examining a motorcycle and discussing it. The sergeant looked at the clock; it was 8:44. They had to wait until it struck nine. Hladik, more insignificant than pitiable, sat down on a pile of wood. He noticed that the soldiers' eyes avoided his. To ease his wait, the sergeant handed him a cigarette. Hladik did not smoke; he accepted it out of politeness or humility. As he lighted it, he noticed that his hands were shaking. The day was clouding over; the soldiers spoke in a low voice as though he were already dead. Vainly he tried to recall the woman of whom Julia von Weidenau was the symbol.

The squad formed and stood at attention. Hladik, standing against the barracks wall, waited for the volley. Someone pointed out that the wall was going to be stained with blood; the victim was ordered to step forward a few paces. Incongruously, this reminded Hladik of the fumbling preparations of photographers. A big drop of rain struck one of Hladik's temples and rolled slowly down his cheek; the sergeant shouted the final order.

The physical universe came to a halt.

The guns converged on Hladik, but the men who were to kill him stood motionless. The sergeant's arm eternized an unfinished gesture. On a paving stone of the courtyard a bee cast an unchanging shadow. The wind had ceased, as in a picture. Hladik attempted a cry, a word, a movement of the hand. He realized that he was paralyzed. Not a sound reached him from the halted world. He thought: "I am in hell, I am dead." He thought: "I am mad." He thought: "Time has stopped." Then he reflected that if that was the case, his mind would have stopped too. He wanted to test this; he repeated (without moving his lips) Vergil's mysterious fourth Eclogue. He imagined that the now remote soldiers must be sharing his anxiety; he longed to be able to communicate with them. It astonished him not to feel the least fatigue, not even the numbness of his protracted immobility. After an indeterminate time he fell asleep. When he awoke the world continued motionless and mute. The drop of water still clung to his cheek, the shadow of the bee to the stone. The smoke from the cigarette he had thrown away had not dispersed. Another "day" went by before Hladik understood.

He had asked God for a whole year to finish his work; His omnipotence had granted it. God had worked a secret miracle for him; German lead would kill him at the set hour, but in his mind a year would go by between the order and its execution. From perplexity he passed to stupor, from stupor to resignation, from resignation to sudden gratitude.

He had no document but his memory; the training he had acquired with each added hexameter gave him a discipline unsuspected by those who set down and forget temporary, incomplete paragraphs. He was not working for posterity or even for God, whose literary tastes were unknown to him. Meticulously, motionlessly, secretely, he wrought in time his lofty, invisible labyrinth. He worked the third act over twice. He eliminated certain symbols as over-obvious, such as the repeated striking of the clock, the music. Nothing hurried him. He omitted, he condensed, he amplified. In certain instances he came back to the original version. He came to feel an affection for the courtyard, the barracks; one of the faces before him modified his conception of Roemerstadt's character. He discovered that the wearying cacophonies that bothered Flaubert so much are mere visual superstitions, weakness and limitation of the written word, not the spoken . . . He concluded his drama. He had only the problem of a single phrase. He found it. The drop of water slid down his cheek. He opened his mouth in a maddened cry, moved his face, dropped under the quadruple blast.

Jaromir Hladik died on March 29, at 9:02 A.M.

FUNES, THE MEMORIOUS

I remember him (I scarcely have the right to use this ghostly verb; only one man on earth deserved the right, and he is dead), I remember him with a dark passionflower in his hand, looking at it as no one has ever looked at such a flower, though they might look from the twilight of day until the twilight of night, for a whole life long. I remember him, his face immobile and Indian-like, and singularly *remote,* behind his cigarette. I remember (I believe) the strong delicate fingers of the plainsman who can braid leather. I remember, near those hands, a vessel in which to make maté tea, bearing the arms of the Banda Oriental; I remember, in the window of the house, a yellow rush mat, and beyond, a vague marshy landscape. I remember clearly his voice, the deliberate, resentful, nasal voice of the old eastern shore man, without the Italianate sibilants of today. I did not see him more than three times; the last time, in 1887. . . .

That all those who knew him should write something about him seems to me a very felicitous idea; my testimony may perhaps be the briefest and without doubt the poorest, and it will not be the least impartial. The deplorable fact of my being an Argentinian will hinder me from falling into a dithyramb – an obligatory form in the Uruguay, when the theme is an Uruguayan.

Littérateur, slicker, Buenos Airean: Funes did not use these insulting phrases, but I am sufficiently aware that for him I represented these unfortunate categories. Pedro Leandro Ipuche has written that Funes was a precursor of the superman, "an untamed and vernacular Zarathustra"; I do not doubt it, but one must not forget, either, that he was a countryman from the town of Fray Bentos, with certain incurable limitations.

My first recollection of Funes is quite clear, I see him at dusk, sometime in March or February of the year '84. That year, my father had taken me to spend the summer at Fray Bentos. I was on my way back from the farm at San Francisco with my cousin Bernardo Haedo. We came back singing, on horseback; and this last fact was not the only reason for my joy. After a sultry day, an enormous slate-gray storm had obscured the sky. It was driven on by a wind from the south; the trees were already tossing like madmen; and I had the apprehension (the secret hope) that the elemental downpour would catch us out in the open. We were running a kind of race with the tempest. We rode into a narrow lane which wound down between two enormously high brick footpaths. It had grown black of a sudden; I now heard rapid, almost secret steps above; I raised my eyes and saw a boy running along the narrow, cracked path as if he were running along a narrow, broken wall. I remember the loose trousers, tight at the bottom, the hemp sandals; I remember the cigarette in the hard visage, standing out against the by now limitless darkness. Bernardo unexpectedly yelled to him: "What's the time, Ireneo?" Without looking up, without stopping, Ireneo replied: "In ten minutes it will be eight o'clock, child Bernardo Juan Francisco." The voice was sharp, mocking.

I am so absent-minded that the dialogue which I have just cited would not have penetrated my attention if it had not been repeated by my cousin, who was stimulated, I think, by a certain local pride and by a desire to show himself indifferent to the other's three-sided reply.

He told me that the boy above us in the pass was a certain Ireneo Funes, renowned for a number of eccentricities, such as that of having nothing to do with people and of always knowing the time, like a watch. He added that Ireneo was the son of María Clementina Funes, an ironing woman in the town, and that his father, some people said, was an "Englishman" named O'Connor, a doctor in the salting fields, though some said the father was a horse-breaker, or scout, from the province of El Salto. Ireneo lived with his mother, at the edge of the country house of the Laurels.

In the years '85 and '86 we spent the summer in the city of Montevideo. We returned to Fray Bentos in '87. As was natural, I inquired after all my acquaintances, and finally, about "the chronometer Funes." I was told that he had been thrown by a wild horse at the San Francisco ranch, and that he had been hopelessly crippled. I remember the impression of uneasy magic which the news provoked in me: the only time I had seen him we were on horseback, coming from San Francisco, and he was in a high place; from the lips of my cousin Bernardo the affair sounded like a dream elaborated with elements out of the past. They told me that Ireneo did not move now from his cot, but remained with his eyes fixed on the backyard fig tree, or on a cobweb. At sunset he allowed himself to be brought to the window. He carried pride to the extreme of pretending that the blow which had befallen him was a good thing.... Twice I saw him behind the iron grate which sternly delineated his eternal imprisonment: unmoving, once, his eyes closed; unmoving also, another time, absorbed in the contemplation of a sweet-smelling sprig of lavender cotton.

At the time I had begun, not without some ostentation, the methodical study of Latin. My valise contained the *De viris illustribus* of Lhomond, the *Thesaurus* of Quicherat, Caesar's *Commentaries,* and an odd-numbered volume of the *Historia Naturalis* of Pliny, which exceeded (and still exceeds) my modest talents as a Latinist.

Everything is noised around in a small town; Ireneo, at his small farm on the outskirts, was not long in learning of the arrival of these anomalous books. He sent me a flowery, ceremonious letter, in which he recalled our encounter, unfortunately brief, "on the seventh day of February of the year '84," and alluded to the glorious services which Don Gregorio Haedo, my uncle, dead the same year, "had rendered to the Two Fatherlands in the glorious campaign of Ituzaingó," and he solicited the loan of any one of the volumes, to be accompanied by a dictionary "for the better intelligence of the original text, for I do not know Latin as yet." He promised to return them in good condition, almost immediately. The letter was perfect, very nicely constructed; the orthography was of the type sponsored by Andrés Bello: *i* for *y*, *j* for *g*. At first I naturally suspected a jest. My cousins assured me it was not so, that these were the ways of Ireneo. I did not know whether to attribute to impudence, ignorance, or stupidity, the idea that the difficult Latin required no other instrument than a dictionary; in order fully to undeceive him I sent the *Gradus ad Parnassum* of Quicherat, and the Pliny.

On February 14, I received a telegram from Buenos Aires telling me to return immediately, for my father was "in no way well." God forgive me, but the prestige of being the recipient of an urgent telegram, the desire to point out to all of Fray Bentos the contradiction between the negative form of the news and the positive adverb, the temptation to dramatize my sorrow as I feigned a virile stoicism, all no doubt distracted me from the possibility of anguish. As I packed my valise, I noted that I was missing the *Gradus* and the volume of the *Historia Naturalis*. The "Saturn" was to weigh anchor on the morning of the next day; that night, after supper, I made my way to the house of Funes. Outside, I was surprised to find the night no less oppressive than the day.

Ireneo's mother received me at the modest ranch.

She told me that Ireneo was in the back room and that I should not be disturbed to find him in the dark, for he knew how to pass the dead hours without lighting the candle. I crossed the cobblestone patio, the small corridor; I came to the second patio. A great vine covered everything, so that the darkness seemed complete. Of a sudden I heard the high-pitched, mocking voice of Ireneo. The voice spoke in Latin; the voice (which came out of the obscurity) was reading, with obvious delight, a treatise or prayer or incantation. The Roman syllables resounded in the earthen patio; my suspicion made them seem undecipherable, interminable; afterward, in the enormous dialogue of that night, I learned that they made up the first paragraph of the twenty-fourth chapter of the seventh book of the *Historia Naturalis*. The subject of this chapter is memory; the last words are *ut nihil non iisdem verbis redderetur auditum.*

Without the least change in his voice, Ireneo bade me come in. He was lying on the cot, smoking. It seems to me that I did not see his face until dawn; I seem to recall the momentary glow of the cigarette. The room smelled vaguely of dampness. I sat down, and repeated the story of the telegram and my father's illness.

I come now to the most difficult point in my narrative. For the entire story has no other point (the reader might as well know it by now) than this dialogue of almost a half-century ago. I shall not attempt to reproduce his words, now irrecoverable. I prefer truthfully to make a résumé of the many things Ireneo told me. The indirect style is remote and weak; I know that I sacrifice the effectiveness of my narrative; but let my readers imagine the nebulous sentences which clouded that night.

Ireneo began by enumerating, in Latin and Spanish, the cases of prodigious memory cited in the *Historia Naturalis:* Cyrus, king of the Persians, who could call every soldier in his armies by name; Mithridates Eupator, who administered justice in the twenty-two languages of his empire; Simonides, inventor of mnemotechny; Metrodorus, who practiced the art of repeating faithfully what he heard once. With evident good faith Funes marveled that such things should be considered marvelous. He told me that previous to the rainy afternoon when the blue-tinted horse threw him, he had been – like any Christian – blind, deaf, mute, somnambulistic, memoryless. (I tried to remind him of his precise perception of time, his memory for proper names; he paid no attention to me.) For nineteen years, he said, he had lived like a person in a dream: he looked without seeing, heard without hearing, forgot everything – almost everything. On falling from the horse, he lost consciousness; when he recovered it, the present was almost intolerable it was so rich and bright; the same was true of the most ancient and most trivial memories. A little later he realized that he was crippled. This fact scarcely interested him. He reasoned (or felt) that immobility was a minimum price to pay. And now, his perception and his memory were infallible.

We, in a glance, perceive three wine glasses on the table; Funes saw all the shoots, clusters, and grapes of the vine. He remembered the shapes of the clouds in the south at dawn on the 30th of April of 1882, and he could compare them in his recollection with the marbled grain in the design of a leather-bound book which he had seen only once, and with the lines in the spray which an oar raised in the Río Negro on the eve of the battle of the Quebracho. These recollections were not simple; each visual image was linked to muscular sensations, thermal sensations, etc. He could reconstruct all his dreams, all his fancies. Two or three times he had reconstructed an entire day. He told me: *I have more memories in myself alone than all men have had since the world was a world.* And again: *My dreams are like your vigils.* And again, toward dawn: *My memory, sir, is like a garbage disposal.*

A circumference on a blackboard, a rectangular triangle, a rhomb, are forms which we can fully intuit; the same held true with Ireneo for the tempestuous mane of a stallion, a herd of cattle in a pass, the ever-changing flame or the innumerable ash, the many faces of a dead man during the course of a protracted wake. He could perceive I do not know how many stars in the sky.

These things he told me; neither then nor at any time later did they seem doubtful. In those days neither the cinema nor the phonograph yet existed;

nevertheless, it seems strange, almost incredible, that no one should have experimented on Funes. The truth is that we all live by leaving behind; no doubt we all profoundly know that we are immortal and that sooner or later every man will do all things and know everything.

The voice of Funes, out of the darkness, continued. He told me that toward 1886 he had devised a new system of enumeration and that in a very few days he had gone beyond twenty-four thousand. He had not written it down, for what he once meditated would not be erased. The first stimulus to his work, I believe, had been his discontent with the fact that "thirty-three Uruguayans" required two symbols and three words, rather than a single word and a single symbol. Later he applied his extravagant principle to the other numbers. In place of seven thousand thirteen, he would say (for example) *Máximo Perez;* in place of seven thouand fourteen, *The Train;* other numbers were *Luis Melián Lafinur, Olimar, Brimstone, Clubs, The Whale, Gas, The Caldron, Napoleon, Augustin de Vedia.* In lieu of five hundred, he would say *nine.* Each word had a particular sign, a species of mark; the last were very complicated. . . . I attempted to explain that this rhapsody of unconnected terms was precisely the contrary of a system of enumeration. I said that to say three hundred and sixty-five was to say three hundreds, six tens, five units: an analysis which does not exist in such numbers as *The Negro Timoteo* or *The Flesh Blanket.* Funes did not understand me, or did not wish to understand me.

Locke, in the seventeenth century, postulated (and rejected) an impossible idiom in which each individual object, each stone, each bird and branch had an individual name; Funes had once projected an analogous idiom, but he had renounced it as being too general, too ambiguous. In effect, Funes not only remembered every leaf on every tree of every wood, but even every one of the times he had perceived or imagined it. He determined to reduce all of his past experience to some seventy thousand recollections, which he would later define numerically. Two considerations dissuaded him: the thought that the task was interminable and the thought that it was useless. He knew that at the hour of his death he would scarcely have finished classifying even all the memories of his childhood.

The two projects I have indicated (an infinite vocabulary for the natural series of numbers, and a usable mental catalogue of all the images of memory) are lacking in sense, but they reveal a certain stammering greatness. They allow us to make out dimly, or to infer, the dizzying world of Funes. He was, let us not forget, almost incapable of general, platonic ideas. It was not only difficult for him to understand that the generic term *dog* embraced so many unlike specimens of differing sizes and different forms; he was disturbed by the fact that a dog at three-fourteen (seen in profile) should have the same name as the dog at three-fifteen (seen from the front). His own face in the mirror, his own hands, surprised him on every occasion. Swift writes that the emperor of Lilliput could discern the movement of the minute hand; Funes could continuously make out the tranquil advances of corruption, of caries, of fatigue. He noted the progress of death, of moisture. He was the solitary and lucid spectator of a multiform world which was instantaneously and almost intolerably exact. Babylon, London, and New York have overawed the imagination of men with their ferocious splendor; no one, in those populous towers or upon those surging avenues, has felt the heat and pressure of a reality as indefatigable as that which day and night converged upon the unfortunate Ireneo in his humble South American farmhouse. It was very difficult for him to sleep. To sleep is to be abstracted from the world; Funes, on his back in his cot, in the shadows, imagined every crevice and every molding of the various houses which surrounded him. (I repeat, the least important of his recollections was more minutely precise and more lively than our perception of a physical pleasure or a physical torment.) Toward the east, in a section which was not yet cut into blocks of homes, there were some new unknown houses. Funes imagined them black, compact, made of a single obscurity; he would turn his face in this direction in order to sleep. He would also imagine himself at the bottom of the river, being rocked and annihilated by the current.

Without effort, he had learned English, French, Portuguese, Latin. I suspect, nevertheless, that he was not very capable of thought. To think is to forget a difference, to generalize, to abstract. In the overly replete world of Funes there were nothing but details, almost contiguous details.

The equivocal clarity of dawn penetrated along the earthen patio.

Then it was that I saw the face of the voice which had spoken all through the night. Ireneo was nineteen years old; he had been born in 1868; he seemed as monumental as bronze, more ancient than Egypt, anterior to the prophecies and the pyramids. It occurred to me that each one of my words (each one of my gestures) would live on in his implacable memory; I was benumbed by the fear of multiplying superfluous gestures.

Ireneo Funes died in 1889, of a pulmonary congestion.

RICHARD WRIGHT 1908–1960

Wright was born in the Deep South, indeed in the *bottom* South, the son of a sharecropper on a plantation in Natchez, Mississippi. After years of disastrous crop failures, his father deserted the family, and his mother, a trained grade-school teacher, had to move from place to place working as a maid.

When Wright graduated (as valedictorian) from an all-black grammar school he had not had a single complete year of schooling in any one place. At that point, the end of his formal schooling, his chances of rising from the kinds of jobs he had to take – yard boy, brass polisher, porter – were infinitesimal. And to think of acquiring the learning, the training, or even the time to be a writer seemed pure fantasy. Furthermore, Wright knew at first hand what happened to "uppity" blacks in Mississippi: his uncle was murdered, a friend's brother castrated for being less than respectful. It was at this time that the dominant theme of Wright's fiction was being forged: the passionate necessity of escape from an atmosphere charged with fear – to someplace, anyplace, even if there was no basis for imagining what that place might be.

For Wright, the place was Chicago, hardly a paradise in the Depression, but there he managed to support himself meagerly by selling quarter-a-week insurance to poor people, sending a little money home to his mother, then crippled, and spending long hours reading in the public library. He was especially attracted to the naturalist school of writers (Dreiser, for example) who portrayed environment and social conditions as determining personality. Theirs was a good influence on him because through them he learned to give his cry of rage the solid specification needed to make it available to readers. Wright learned how to portray not only the suffering individual but also the reality of the world that stifled and oppressed him.

In 1938 *Story Magazine* awarded Wright a $500 prize for his first book, a collection of stories entitled *Uncle Tom's Children.* From that time on his success as a writer was assured. He began to turn his attention from the plight of the rural southern black to that of the black exploited in the ghettos of Chicago and New York. His great story "The Man Who Lived Underground" is on one level an elaborate metaphor of the urban black's relation to the city. Though a member of the Communist Party during the Depression, Wright saw too deeply into the individual to represent blacks as being simply victims of capitalism. In the late thirties he wrote a novel, *Lawd Today,* about the entrapment of a black postal worker in suffocating life in Chicago, but he seems to have withheld publication (the novel was finally published posthumously) because it developed into a far more complicated portrait than the Party line demanded.

Native Son (1940) established Wright as a major literary figure. It makes clear what had previously been powerfully implicit in his fiction: that violence is the only possible act that allows the black to break out of the stereotype forced on him by society. The murder in the novel forces two kinds of recognitions: for white society, the recognition that without terrible consequences its fear and guilt about blacks cannot be quieted by a system of oppression; for the hero, Bigger Thomas, a new awareness that he is a human being who can will himself into life.

After the war, Wright became increasingly committed to these essentially existential perceptions and, dissatisfied with the mechanical explanations of Communism, he moved to France and joined the circle of French Existentialists led by Sartre. Still he remained dedicated to the cause of blacks in America. Not only was the vision of rage and violence in his fiction prophetic of many aspects of Black Power today, but Wright also worked directly for causes that are now recognized as crucial: he studied African culture and fostered an awareness of the role of African history in the black experience in America; and in *White Man, Listen* (1957) he collected a series of his lectures demanding that emerging black nations be allowed to develop their own cultures free of white colonialism.

BIG BOY LEAVES HOME

I

Yo mama don wear no drawers . . .

Clearly, the voice rose out of the woods, and died away. Like an echo another voice caught it up:

Ah seena when she pulled em off . . .

Another, shrill, cracking, adolescent:

N she washed 'em in alcohol . . .

Then a quartet of voices, blending in harmony, floated high above the tree tops:

N she hung 'em out in the hall . . .

Laughing easily, four black boys came out of the woods into cleared pasture. They walked lollingly in bare feet, beating tangled vines and bushes with long sticks.

"Ah wished Ah knowed some mo lines t tha song."

"Me too."

"Yeah, when yuh gits t where she hangs em out in the hall yuh has t stop."

"Shucks, whut goes wid *hall?*"

"Call."

"Fall."

"Wall."

"Quall."

They threw themselves on the grass, laughing.

"Big Boy?"

"Huh?"

"Yuh know one thing?"

"Whut?"

"Yuh sho is crazy!"

"Crazy?"

"Yeah, yuh crazys a bed-bug!"
"Crazy bout whut?"
"Man, whoever hearda *quall?"*
"Yuh said yuh wanted something to go wid *hall,* didnt yuh?"
"Yeah, but whuts a *quall?"*
"Nigger, a *qualls* a *quall."*

They laughed easily, catching and pulling long green blades of grass with their toes.

"Waal, ef a *qualls* a *quall,* whut IS a *quall?"*
"Oh, Ah know."
"Whut?"
"Tha ol song goes something like this:

Yo mama don wear no drawers,
Ah seena when she pulled em off,
N she washed em in alcohol,
N she hung em out in the hall,
N then she put em back on her QUALL!"

They laughed again. Their shoulders were flat to the earth, their knees propped up, and their faces square to the sun.

"Big Boy, yuhs CRAZY!"
"Don ax me nothin else."
"Nigger, yuhs CRAZY!"

They fell silent, smiling, drooping the lids of their eyes softly against the sunlight.

"Man, don the groun feel warm?"
"Jus lika bed."
"Jeeesus, Ah could stay here ferever."
"Me too."
"Ah kin feel tha ol sun goin all thu me."
"Feels like mah bones is warm."

In the distance a train whistled mournfully.

"There goes number fo!"
"Hittin on all six!"
"Highballin it down the line!"
"Boun fer up Noth, Lawd, boun fer up Noth!"

They began to chant, pounding bare heels in the grass.

Dis train boun fo Glory
Dis train, Oh Hallelujah
Dis train boun fo Glory
Dis train, Oh Hallelujah

Dis train boun fo Glory
Ef yuh ride no need fer fret er worry
Dis train, Oh Hallelujah
Dis train . . .

Dis train don carry no gambler
Dis train, Oh Hallelujah
Dis train don carry no gambler
Dis train, Oh Hallelujah
Dis train don carry no gambler
No fo day creeper er midnight rambler
Dis train, Oh Hallelujah
Dis train . . .

When the song ended they burst out laughing, thinking of a train bound for Glory.

"Gee, thas a good ol song!"

"Huuuuummmmmmmmman . . ."

"What?"

"Geeee whiiiiiiz . . ."

"Whut?"

"Somebody don let win! Das whut!"

Buck, Bobo and Lester jumped up. Big Boy stayed on the ground, feigning sleep.

"Jeeesus, tha sho stinks!"

"Big Boy!"

Big Boy feigned to snore.

"Big Boy!"

Big Boy stirred as though in sleep.

"Big Boy!"

"Hunh?"

"Yuh rotten inside!"

"Rotten?"

"Lawd cant yuh smell it?"

"Smell whut?"

"Nigger, yuh mus gotta bad col!"

"Smell whut?"

"NIGGER, YUH BROKE WIN!"

Big Boy laughed and fell back on the grass, closing his eyes.

"The hen whut cackles is the hen whut laid the egg."

"We ain no hens."

"Yuh cackled, didnt yuh?"

The three moved off with noses turned up.

"C mon!"

"Where yuh-all goin?"

"T the creek fer a swim."

"Yeah, les swim."

"Naw buddy naw!" said Big Boy, slapping the air with a scornful palm.

"Aw, c mon! Don be a heel!"

"N git *lynched?* Hell naw!"

"He ain gonna see us."

"How yuh know?"

"Cause he ain."

"Yuh-all go on. Ahma stay right here," said Big Boy.

"Hell, let im stay! C mon, les go," said Buck.

The three walked off, swishing at grass and bushes with sticks. Big Boy looked lazily at their backs.

"Hey!"

Walking on, they glanced over their shoulders.

"Hey, niggers!"

"C mon!"

Big Boy grunted, picked up his stick, pulled to his feet, and stumbled off.

"Wait!"

"C mon!"

He ran, caught up with them, leaped upon their backs, bearing them to the ground.

"Quit, Big Boy!"

"Gawddam, nigger!"

"Git t hell offa me!"

Big Boy sprawled in the grass beside them, laughing and pounding his heels in the ground.

"Nigger, whut yuh think we is, hosses?"

"How come yuh awways hoppin on us?"

"Lissen, wes goona double-team on yuh one of these days n beat yo ol ass good."

Big Boy smiled.

"Sho nough?"

"Yeah, don yuh like it?"

"We gonna beat yuh sos yuh cant walk!"

"N dare yuh t do nothin erbout it!"

Big Boy bared his teeth.

"C mon! Try it now!"

The three circled around him.

"Say, Buck, yuh grab his feets!"

"N yuh git his head, Lester!"

"N Bobo, yuh berhin n grab his arms!"

Keeping more than arm's length, they circled round and round Big Boy.

"C mon!" said Big Boy, feinting at one and then the other.

Round and round they circled, but could not seem to get any closer. Big Boy stopped and braced his hands on his hips.

"Is all three of yuh-all scareda me?"

"Les git im some other time," said Bobo, grinning.

"Yeah, we kin ketch yuh when yuh ain thinkin," said Lester.

"We kin trick yuh," said Buck.

They laughed and walked together.

Big Boy belched.

"Ahm hongry," he said.

"Me too."

"Ah wished Ah hada big hot pota belly-busters!"

"Cooked wid some good ol salty ribs . . ."

"N some good ol egg cornbread . . ."

"N some buttermilk . . ."

"N some hot peach cobbler swimmin in juice . . ."

"Nigger, hush!"

They began to chant, emphasizing the rhythm by cutting at grass with sticks.

Bye n bye
Ah wanna piece of pie
Pies too sweet
Ah wanna piece of meat
Meats too red
Ah wanna piece of bread
Breads too brown
Ah wanna go t town
Towns too far
Ah wanna ketch a car
Cars too fas
Ah fall n break mah ass
Ahll understan it better bye n bye . . .

They climbed over a barbed-wire fence and entered a stretch of thick woods. Big Boy was whistling softly, his eyes half-closed.

"LES GIT IM!"

Buck, Lester, and Bobo whirled, grabbed Big Boy about the neck, arms, and legs, bearing him to the ground. He grunted and kicked wildly as he went back into weeds.

"Hol im tight!"

"Git his arms! Git his arms!"

"Set on his legs so he cant kick!"

Big Boy puffed heavily, trying to get loose.

"WE GOT YUH NOW, GAWDDAMMIT, WE GOT YUH NOW!"

"Thas a Gawddam lie!" said Big Boy. He kicked, twisted, and clutched for a hold on one and then the other.

"Say, yuh-all hep me hol his arms!" said Bobo.

"Aw, we got this bastard now!" said Lester.

"Thas a Gawddam lie!" said Big Boy again.

"Say, yuh-all hep me hol his arms!" called Bobo.

Big Boy managed to encircle the neck of Bobo with his left arm. He tightened his elbow scissors-like and hissed through his teeth:

"Yuh got me, ain yuh?"

"Hol im!"

"Les beat this bastard's ass!"

"Say hep me hol his *arms!* Hes got aholda mah *neck!*" cried Bobo.

Big Boy squeezed Bobo's neck and twisted his head to the ground.

"Yuh got me, ain yuh?"

"Quit, Big Boy, yuh chokin me; yuh hurtin mah neck!" cried Bobo.

"Turn me loose!" said Big Boy.

"Ah ain got yuh! Its the others whut got yuh!" pleaded Bobo.

"Tell them others t git t hell offa me or Ahma break yo neck," said Big Boy.

"Ssssay, yyuh-all gggit ooooffa Bbig Boy. Hhhes got me," gurgled Bobo.

"Cant yuh hol im?"

"Nnaw, hhes ggot mmah nneck . . ."

Big Boy squeezed tighter.

"N Ahma break it too less yuh tell em t git t hell offa me!"

"Ttturn mmmeee llloose," panted Bobo, tears gushing.

"Cant yuh hol im, Bobo?" asked Buck.

"Nnaw, yuh-all tturn im lloose; hhhes got mah nnneck . . ."

"Grab his neck, Bobo . . ."

"Ah cant; yugurgur . . ."

To save Bobo, Lester and Buck got up and ran to a safe distance. Big Boy released Bobo, who staggered to his feet, slobbering and trying to stretch a crick out of his neck.

"Shucks, nigger, yuh almos broke mah neck," whimpered Bobo.

"Ahm goona break yo ass nex time," said Big Boy.

"Ef Bobo coulda hel yuh we woulda had yuh," yelled Lester.

"Ah wuznt gonna let im do that," said Big Boy.

They walked together again, swishing sticks.

"Yuh see," began Big Boy, "when a ganga guys jump on yuh, all yuh gotta do is jus put the heat on one of them n make im tell the others t let up, see?"

"Gee, thas a good idee!"
"Yeah, thas a good idee!"
"But yuh almos broke mah neck, man," said Bobo.
"Ahma smart nigger," said Big Boy, thrusting out his chest.

II

They came to the swimming hole.
"Ah ain goin in," said Bobo.
"Done got scared?" asked Big Boy.
"Naw, Ah ain scared . . ."
"How come yuh ain goin in?"
"Yuh know ol man Harvey don erllow no niggers t swim in this hole."
"N just las year he took a shot at Bob fer swimmin in here," said Lester.
"Shucks, ol man Harvey ain studyin bout us niggers," said Big Boy.
"Hes at home thinkin about his jelly-roll," said Buck.
They laughed.
"Buck, yo mins lowern a snakes belly," said Lester.
"Ol man Harveys too doggone ol t think erbout jelly-roll," said Big Boy.
"Hes dried up; all the saps done lef im," said Bobo.
"C mon, les go!" said Big Boy.
Bobo pointed.
"See tha sign over yonder?"
"Yeah."
"Whut it say?"
"NO TRESPASSIN," read Lester.
"Know whut tha mean?"
"Mean ain no dogs n niggers erllowed," said Buck.
"Waal, wes here now," said Big Boy. "Ef he ketched us even like this thered be trouble, so we just as waal go on in . . ."
"Ahm wid the nex one!"
"Ahll go ef anybody else goes!"
Big Boy looked carefully in all directions. Seeing nobody, he began jerking off his overalls.
"LAS ONE INS A OL DEAD DOG!"
"THAS YO MA!"
"THAS YO PA!"
"THAS BOTH YO MA N YO PA!"
They jerked off their clothes and threw them in a pile under a tree. Thirty seconds later they stood, black and naked, on the edge of the hole under a sloping embankment. Gingerly Big Boy touched the water with his foot.

"Man, this waters col," he said.

"Ahm gonna put mah cloes back on," said Bobo, withdrawing his foot.

Big Boy grabbed him about the waist.

"Like hell yuh is!"

"Git outta the way, nigger!" Bobo yelled.

"Thrown im in!" said Lester.

"Duck im!"

Bobo crouched, spread his legs, and braced himself against Big Boy's body. Locked in each other's arms, they tussled on the edge of the hole, neither able to throw the other.

"C mon, les me n yuh push em in."

"O.K."

Laughing, Lester and Buck gave the two locked bodies a running push. Big Boy and Bobo splashed, sending up silver spray in the sunlight. When Big Boy's head came up he yelled:

"Yuh bastard!"

"Tha wuz yo ma yuh pushed!" said Bobo, shaking his head to clear the water from his eyes.

They did a surface dive, came up and struck out across the creek. The muddy water foamed. They swam back, waded into shallow water, breathing heavily and blinking eyes.

"C mon in!"

"Man, the waters fine!"

Lester and Buck hesitated.

"Les wet em," Big Boy whispered to Bobo.

Before Lester and Buck could back away, they were dripping wet from handsful of scooped water.

"Hey, quit!"

"Gawddam, nigger! Tha waters col!"

"C mon in!" called Big Boy.

"We jus as waal go on in now," said Buck.

"Look n see ef anybodys comin."

Kneeling, they squinted among the trees.

"Ain nobody."

"C mon, les go."

They waded in slowly, pausing each few steps to catch their breath. A desperate water battle began. Closing eyes and backing away, they shunted water into one another's faces with the flat palms of hands.

"Hey, cut it out!"

"Yeah, Ahm bout drownin!"

They came together in water up to their navels, blowing and blinking. Big Boy ducked, upsetting Bobo.

"Look out, nigger!"

"Don holler so loud!"

"Yeah, they kin hear yo ol big mouth a mile erway."

"This waters too col fer me."

"Thas cause it rained yistiddy."

They swam across and back again.

"Ah wish we hada bigger place t swim in."

"The white folks got plenty swimmin pools n we ain got none."

"Ah useta swim in the ol Missippi when we lived in Vicksburg."

Big Boy put his head under the water and blew his breath. A sound came like that of a hippopotamus.

"C mon, les be hippos."

Each went to a corner of the creek and put his mouth just below the surface and blew like a hippopotamus. Tiring, they came and sat under the embankment.

"Look like Ah gotta chill."

"Me too."

"Les stay here n dry off."

"Jeeesus, Ahm col!"

They kept still in the sun, suppressing shivers. After some of the water had dried off their bodies they began to talk through clattering teeth.

"Whut would yuh do ef ol man Harveyd come erlong right now?"

"Run like hell!"

"Man, Ahd run so fas hed thinka black streaka lightnin shot pass im."

"But spose he hada gun?"

"Aw, nigger, shut up!"

They were silent. They ran their hands over wet, trembling legs, brushing water away. Then their eyes watched the sun sparkling on the restless creek.

Far away a train whistled.

"There goes number seven!"

"Heading fer up Noth!"

"Blazin it down the line!"

"Lawd, Ahm goin Noth some day."

"Me too, man."

"They say colored folks up Noth is got ekual rights."

They grew pensive. A black winged butterfly hovered at the water's edge. A bee droned. From somewhere came the sweet scent of honeysuckles. Dimly they could hear sparrows twittering in the woods. They rolled from side to side, letting sunshine dry their skins and warm their blood. They plucked blades of grass and chewed them.

"Oh!"

They looked up, their lips parting.

"Oh!"

A white woman, poised on the edge of the opposite embankment, stood directly in front of them, her hat in her hand and her hair lit by the sun.

"Its a woman!" whispered Big Boy in an underbreath. "A *white* woman!"

They stared, their hands instinctively covering their groins. Then they scrambled to their feet. The white woman backed slowly out of sight. They stood for a moment, looking at one another.

"Les git outta here!" Big Boy whispered.

"Wait till she goes erway."

"Les run, theyll ketch us here naked like this!"

"Mabbe theres a man wid her."

"C mon, les git our cloes," said Big Boy.

They waited a moment longer, listening.

"Whut t hell! Ahma git mah cloes," said Big Boy.

Grabbing at short tufts of grass, he climbed the embankment.

"Don run out there now!"

"C mon back, fool!"

Bobo hesitated. He looked at Big Boy, and then at Buck and Lester.

"Ahm goin wid Big Boy n git mah cloes," he said.

"Don run out there naked like tha, fool!" said Buck, "Yuh don know whos out there!"

Big Boy was climbing over the edge of the embankment.

"C mon," he whispered.

Bobo climbed after. Twenty-five feet away the woman stood. She had one hand over her mouth. Hanging by fingers, Buck and Lester peeped over the edge.

"C mon back; that womans scared," said Lester.

Big Boy stopped, puzzled. He looked at the woman. He looked at the bundle of clothes. Then he looked at Buck and Lester.

"C mon, les git our cloes!"

He made a step.

"Jim!" the woman screamed.

Big Boy stopped and looked around. His hands hung loosely at his sides. The woman, her eyes wide, her hand over her mouth, backed away to the tree where their clothes lay in a heap.

"Big Boy, come back n wait till shes gone!"

Bobo ran to Big Boy's side.

"Les go home! Theyll ketch us here," he urged.

Big Boy's throat felt tight.

"Lady, we wanna git our cloes," he said.

Buck and Lester climbed the embankment and stood indecisively. Big Boy ran toward the tree.

"Jim!" the woman screamed. "Jim! Jim!"

Black and naked, Big Boy stopped three feet from her.

"We wanna git our cloes," he said again, his words coming mechanically.

He made a motion.

"You go away! You go away! I tell you, you go away!"

Big Boy stopped again, afraid. Bobo ran and snatched the clothes. Buck and Lester tried to grab theirs out of his hands.

"You go away! You go away! You go away!" the woman screamed.

"Les go!" said Bobo, running toward the woods.

CRACK!

Lester grunted, stiffened, and pitched forward. His forehead struck a toe of the woman's shoes.

Bobo stopped, clutching the clothes. Buck whirled. Big Boy stared at Lester, his lips moving.

"Hes gotta gun; hes gotta gun!" yelled Buck, running wildly.

CRACK!

Buck stopped at the edge of the embankment, his head jerked backward, his body arched stiffly to one side; he toppled headlong, sending up a shower of bright spray to the sunlight. The creek bubbled.

Big Boy and Bobo backed away, their eyes fastened fearfully on a white man who was running toward them. He had a rifle and wore an army officer's uniform. He ran to the woman's side and grabbed her hand.

"You hurt, Bertha, you hurt?"

She stared at him and did not answer.

The man turned quickly. His face was red. He raised the rifle and pointed it at Bobo. Bobo ran back, holding the clothes in front of his chest.

"Don shoot me, Mistah, don shoot me . . ."

Big Boy lunged for the rifle, grabbing the barrel.

"You black sonofabitch!"

Big Boy clung desperately.

"Let go, you black bastard!"

The barrel pointed skyward.

CRACK!

The white man, taller and heavier, flung Big Boy to the ground. Bobo dropped the clothes, ran up, and jumped onto the white man's back.

"You black sonsofbitches!"

The white man released the rifle, jerked Bobo to the ground, and began to batter the naked boy with his fists. Then Big Boy swung, striking the man in the mouth with the barrel. His teeth caved in and he fell, dazed. Bobo was on his feet.

"C mon, Big Boy, les go!"

Breathing hard, the white man got up and faced Big Boy. His lips were trembling, his neck and chin wet with blood. He spoke quietly.

"Give me that gun, boy!"

Big Boy leveled the rifle and backed away.

The white man advanced.

"Boy, I say give me that gun!"

Bobo had the clothes in his arms.

"Run, Big Boy, run!"

The man came at Big Boy.

"Ahll kill yuh; Ahll kill yuh!" said Big Boy.

His fingers fumbled for the trigger.

The man stopped, blinked, spat blood. His eyes were bewildered. His face whitened. Suddenly, he lunged for the rifle, his hands outstretched.

CRACK!

He fell forward on his face.

"Jim!"

Big Boy and Bobo turned in surprise to look at the woman.

"Jim!" she screamed again, and fell weakly at the foot of the tree.

Big Boy dropped the rifle, his eyes wide. He looked around. Bobo was crying and clutching the clothes.

"Big Boy, Big Boy . . ."

Big Boy looked at the rifle, started to pick it up, but didn't. He seemed at a loss. He looked at Lester, then at the white man; his eyes followed a thin stream of blood that seeped to the ground.

"Yuh done killed him," mumbled Bobo.

"Les go home!"

Naked, they turned and ran toward the woods. When they reached the barbed-wire fence they stopped.

"Les git our cloes on," said Big Boy.

They slipped quickly into overalls. Bobo held Lester's and Buck's clothes.

"Whut we gonna do wid these?"

Big Boy stared. His hands twitched.

"Leave em."

They climbed the fence and ran through the woods. Vines and leaves switched their faces. Once Bobo tripped and fell.

"C mon!" said Big Boy.

Bobo started crying, blood streaming from his scratches.

"Ahm scared!"

"C mon! Don cry! We wanna git hom fo they ketches us!"

"Ahm scared!" said Bobo again, his eyes full of tears.

Big Boy grabbed his hand and dragged him along.

"C mon!"

III

They stopped when they got to the end of the woods. They could see the open road leading home, home to ma and pa. But they hung back, afraid. The thick shadows cast from the trees were friendly and sheltering. But the wide glare of sun stretching out over the fields was pitiless. They crouched behind an old log.

"We gotta git home," said Big Boy.

"They's gonna lynch us," said Bobo, half-questioningly.

Big Boy did not answer.

"Theys gonna lynch us," said Bobo again.

Big Boy shuddered.

"Hush!" he said. He did not want to think of it. He could not think of it; there was but one thought, and he clung to that one blindly. He had to get home, home to ma and pa.

Their heads jerked up. Their ears had caught the rhythmic jingle of a wagon. They fell to the ground and clung flat to the side of a log. Over the crest of the hill came the top of a hat. A white face. Then shoulders in a blue shirt. A wagon drawn by two horses pulled into full view.

Big Boy and Bobo held their breath, waiting. Their eyes followed the wagon till it was lost in dust around a bend in the road.

"We gotta git home," said Big Boy.

"Ahm scared," said Bobo.

"C mon! Les keep t the fields."

They ran till they came to the cornfields. Then they went slower, for last year's corn stubbles bruised their feet.

They came in sight of a brickyard.

"Wait a minute," gasped Big Boy.

They stopped.

"Ahm goin on t mah home n yuh better go on t yos."

Bobo's eyes grew round.

"Ahm scared!"

"Yuh better go on!"

"Lemme go wid yuh; they'll ketch me . . ."

"Ef yuh kin git home mabbe yo folks kin hep yuh t git erway."

Big Boy started off. Bobo grabbed him.

"Lemme go wid yuh!"

Big Boy shook free.

"Ef yuh stay here theys gonna lynch yuh!" he yelled, running.

After he had gone about twenty-five yards he turned and looked; Bobo was flying through the woods like the wind.

Big Boy slowed when he came to the railroad. He wondered if he ought to go through the streets or down the track. He decided on the tracks. He could dodge a train better than a mob.

He trotted along the ties, looking ahead and back. His cheek itched, and he felt it. His hand came away smeared with blood. He wiped it nervously on his overalls.

When he came to his back fence he heaved himself over. He landed among a flock of startled chickens. A bantam rooster tried to spur him. He slipped and fell in front of the kitchen steps, grunting heavily. The ground was slick with greasy dishwater.

Panting, he stumbled through the doorway.

"Lawd, Big Boy, whuts wrong wid yuh?"

His mother stood gaping in the middle of the floor. Big Boy flopped wordlessly onto a stool, almost toppling over. Pots simmered on the stove. The kitchen smelled of food cooking.

"Whuts the matter, Big Boy?"

Mutely, he looked at her. Then he burst into tears. She came and felt the scratches on his face.

"Whut happened t yuh, Big Boy? Somebody been botherin yuh?"

"They after me, Ma! They after me . . ."

"Who!"

"Ah . . . Ah . . . We . . ."

"Big Boy, whuts wrong wid yuh?"

"He killed Lester n Buck," he muttered simply.

"Killed!"

"Yessum."

"Lester n Buck!"

"Yessum, Ma!"

"How killed?"

"He shot em, Ma!"

"Lawd Gawd in Heaven, have mercy on us all! This is mo trouble, mo trouble," she moaned, wringing her hands.

"N Ah killed im, Ma . . ."

She stared, trying to understand.

"Whut happened, Big Boy?"

"We tried t git our cloes from the tree . . ."

"Whut tree?"

"We wuz swimmin, Ma. N the white woman . . ."

"*White* woman? . . ."

"Yessum. She wuz at the swimmin hole . . ."

"Lawd have mercy! Ah knowed yuh boys wuz gonna keep on till yuh got into somethin like this!"

She ran into the hall.

"Lucy!"

"Mam?"

"C mere!"

"Mam?"

"C mere, Ah say!"

"Whutcha wan, Ma? Ahm sewin."

"Chile, will yuh c mere like Ah ast yuh?"

Lucy came to the door holding an unfinished apron in her hands. When she saw Big Boy's face she looked wildly at her mother.

"Whuts the matter?"

"Wheres Pa?"

"Hes out front, Ah reckon."

"Git im, quick!"

"Whuts the matter, Ma?"

"Go git yo Pa, Ah say!"

Lucy ran out. The mother sank into a chair, holding a dish rag. Suddenly, she sat up.

"Big Boy, Ah thought yuh wuz at school?"

Big Boy looked at the floor.

"How come yuh didnt go t school?"

"We went t the woods."

She sighed.

"Ah done done all Ah kin fer yuh, Big Boy. Only Gawd kin hep yuh now."

"Ma, don let em git me; don let em git me . . ."

His father came into the doorway. He stared at Big Boy, then at his wife.

"Whuts Big Boy inter now?" he asked sternly.

"Saul, Big Boys done gone n got inter trouble wid the white folks."

The old man's mouth dropped, and he looked from one to the other.

"Saul, we gotta git im erway from here."

"Open yo mouth n talk! Whut yuh been doin?" The old man gripped Big Boy's shoulders and peered at the scratches on his face.

"Me n Lester n Buck n Bobo wuz out on ol man Harveys place swimmin . . ."

"Saul, its a *white* woman!"

Big Boy winced. The old man compressed his lips and stared at his wife. Lucy gaped at her brother as though she had never seen him before.

"Whut happened? Cant yuh-all talk?" the old man thundered, with a certain helplessness in his voice.

"We wuz swimmin," Big Boy began, "n then a white woman comes up t the hole. We got up right erway t git our cloes sos we could git erway, n she started screamin. Our cloes wuz right by the tree where she wuz standing, n when we started to git em she jus screamed. We tol her we wanted our cloes . . . Yuh see, Pa, she wuz standin right *by* our cloes; n when we went t git em she jus screamed . . . Bobo got the cloes, n then he shot Lester . . ."

"*Who* shot Lester?"

"The white man."

"Whut white man?"

"Ah dunno, Pa. He wuz a soljer, n he had a rifle."

"A *soljer?*"

"Yessuh, Pa. A soljer."

The old man frowned.

"N then whut yuh-all do?"

"Waal, Buck said, 'Hes gotta gun!' N we started runnin. N then he shot Buck, n he fell in the swimmin hole. We didnt see im no mo . . . He wuz close on us then. He looked at the white woman n then he started to shoot Bobo. Ah grabbed the gun, n we started fightin. Bobo jumped on his back. He started beatin Bobo. Then Ah hit im wid the gun. Then he started at me n Ah shot im. Then we run . . ."

"Who seen?"

"Nobody."

"Wheres Bobo?"

"He went home."

"Anybody run after yuh-all?"

"Nawsuh."

"Yuh see anybody?"

"Nawsuh. Nobody but a white man. But he didnt see us."

"How long fo yuh-all lef the swimmin hole?"

"Little while ergo."

The old man nervously brushed his hand across his eyes and walked to the door. His lips moved, but no words came.

"Saul, whut we gonna do?"

"Lucy," began the old man, "go t Brother Sanders n tell im Ah said c mere; n go t Brother Jenkins n tell im Ah said c mere; n go t Elder Peters n tell im Ah said c mere. N don say nothin t nobody but whut Ah tol yuh. N when yuh git thu come straight back. Now go!"

Lucy dropped her apron across the back of a chair and ran down the steps. The mother bent over, crying and praying. The old man walked slowly over to Big Boy.

"Big Boy?"

Big Boy swallowed.

"Ahm talkin t yuh!"

"Yessuh."

"How come yuh didnt go t school this mawnin?"

"We went t the woods."

"Didnt yo ma send yuh t school?"

"Yessuh."

"How come yuh didnt go?"

"We went t the woods."

"Don yuh know thas wrong?"

"Yessuh."

"How come yuh go?"

Big Boy looked at his fingers, knotted them, and squirmed in his seat.

"AHM TALKIN T YUH!"

His wife straightened up and said reprovingly:

"Saul!"

The old man desisted, yanking nervously at the shoulder straps of his overalls.

"How long wuz the woman there?"

"Not long."

"Wuz she young?"

"Yessuh. Lika gal."

"Did yuh-all say anythin t her?"

"Nawsuh. We jus said we wanted our cloes."

"N whut she say?"

"Nothin, Pa. She jus backed erway t the tree n screamed."

The old man stared, his lips trying to form a question.

"Big Boy, did yuh-all bother her?"

"Nawsuh, Pa. We didnt *touch* her."

"How long fo the white man come up?"

"Right erway."

"Whut he say?"

"Nothin. He jus cussed us."

Abruptly the old man left the kitchen.

"Ma, cant Ah go fo they ketches me?"

"Sauls doin whut he kin."

"Ma, Ma, Ah don wan em t ketch me . . ."

"Sauls doin whut he kin. Nobody but the good Lawd kin hep us now."

The old man came back with a shotgun and leaned it in a corner. Fascinatedly, Big Boy looked at it.

There was a knock at the front door.

"Liza, see whos there."

She went. They were silent, listening. They could hear her talking.

"Whos there?"

"Me."

"Who?"

"Me, Brother Sanders."

"C mon in. Sauls waitin fer yuh."

Sanders paused in the doorway, smiling.

"Yuh sent fer me, Brother Morrison?"

"Brother Sanders, wes in deep trouble here."

Sanders came all the way into the kitchen.

"Yeah?"

"Big Boy done gone n killed a white man."

Sanders stopped short, then came forward, his face thrust out, his mouth open. His lips moved several times before he could speak.

"A *white* man?"

"They gonna kill me; they gonna kill me!" Big Boy cried, running to the old man.

"Saul, cant we git im erway somewhere?"

"Here now, take it easy; take it easy," said Sanders, holding Big Boy's wrists.

"They gonna kill me; they gonna lynch me!"

Big Boy slipped to the floor. They lifted him to a stool. His mother held him closely, pressing his head to her bosom.

"Whut we gonna do?" asked Sanders.

"Ah done sent fer Brother Jenkins n Elder Peters."

Sanders leaned his shoulders against the wall. Then, as the full meaning of it all came to him, he exclaimed:

"Theys gonna git a mob! . . ." His voice broke off and his eyes fell on the shotgun.

Feet came pounding on the steps. They turned toward the door. Lucy ran in crying. Jenkins followed. The old man met him in the middle of the room, taking his hand.

"Wes in bad trouble here, Brother Jenkins. Big Boy's done gone n killed a white man. Yuh-alls gotta hep me . . ."

Jenkins looked hard at Big Boy.

"Elder Peters says hes comin," said Lucy.

"When all this happen?" asked Jenkins.

"Near bout a hour ergo, now," said the old man.

"Whut we gonna do?" asked Jenkins.

"Ah wanna wait till Elder Peters come," said the old man helplessly.

"But we gotta work fas ef we gonna do anythin," said Sanders.

"Well git in trouble jus standin here like this."

Big Boy pulled away from his mother.

"Pa, lemme go now, Lemme go now!"

"Be still, Big Boy!"

"Where kin yuh go?"

"Ah could ketch a freight!"

"Thas *sho* death!" said Jenkins. "Theyll be watchin em all!"

"Kin yuh-all hep me wid some money?" the old man asked.

They shook their heads.

"Saul, whut kin we do? Big Boy cant stay here."

There was another knock at the door.

The old man backed stealthily to the shotgun.

"Lucy go!"

Lucy looked at him, hesitating.

"Ah better go," said Jenkins.

It was Elder Peters. He came in hurriedly.

"Good evenin, everybody!"

"How yuh, Elder?"

"Good evenin."

"How yuh today?"

Peters looked around the crowded kitchen.

"Whuts the matter?"

"Elder, wes in deep trouble," began the old man. "Big Boy n some mo boys . . ."

". . . Lester n Buck n Bobo . . ."

". . . wuz over on ol man Harveys place swimmin . . ."

"N he don like us niggers *none,*" said Peters emphatically. He widened his legs and put his thumbs in the armholes of his vest.

". . . n some white woman . . ."

"Yeah?" said Peters, coming closer.

". . . comes erlong n the boys tries t git their cloes where they don lef em under a tree. Waal, she started screamin n all, see? Reckon she thought the boys wuz after her. Then a white man in a soljers suit shoots two of em . . ."

". . . Lester n Buck . . ."

"Huummm," said Peters. "Tha wuz ol man Harveys son."

"Harveys son?"

"Yuh mean the one tha wuz in the Army?"

"Yuh mean Jim?"

"Yeah," said Peters. "The papers said he wuz here fer a vacation from his regiment. N tha woman the boys saw wuz jus erbout his wife . . ."

They stared at Peters. Now that they knew what white person had been killed, their fears became definite.

"N whut else happened?"

"Big Boy shot the man . . ."

"Harveys *son?*"

"He had t, Elder. He wuz gonna shoot im ef he didnt . . ."

"Lawd!" said Peters. He looked around and put his hat back on.

"How long ergo wuz this?"

"Mighty near an hour, now, Ah reckon."

"Do the white folks know yit?"

"Don know, Elder."

"Yuh-all better git this boy outta here right now," said Peters. "Cause ef yuh don theres gonna be a lynchin . . ."

"Where kin Ah go, Elder?" Big Boy ran up to him.

They crowded around Peters. He stood with his legs wide apart, looking up at the ceiling.

"Mabbe we kin hide im in the church till he kin git erway," said Jenkins.

Peters' lips flexed.

"Naw, Brother, thall never do! Theyll git im there sho. N anyhow, ef they ketch im there itll ruin us all. We gotta git the boy outta town . . ."

Sanders went up to the old man.

"Lissen," he said in a whisper. "Mah son, Will, the one whut drives fer the Magnolia Express Company, is taking a truck o goods t Chicawgo in the mawnin. If we kin hide Big Boy somewhere till then, we kin put im on the truck . . ."

"Pa, please, lemme go wid Will when he goes in the mawnin," Big Boy begged.

The old man stared at Sanders.

"Yuh reckon thas safe?"

"Its the only thing yuh *kin* do," said Peters.

"But where we gonna hide im till then?"

"Whut time yo boy leavin out in the mawnin?"

"At six."

They were quiet, thinking. The water kettle on the stove sang.

"Pa, Ah knows where Will passes erlong wid the truck out on Bullards Road. Ah kin hide in one of them ol kilns . . ."

"Where?"

"In one of them kilns we built . . ."

"But theyll git yuh there," wailed the mother.

"But there ain no place else fer im t go."

"Theres some holes big ernough fer me t git in n stay till Will comes erlong," said Big Boy. "Please, Pa, lemme go fo they ketches me . . ."

"Let im go!"

"Please, Pa . . ."

The old man breathed heavily.

"Lucy, git his things!"

"Saul, theyll git im out there!" wailed the mother, grabbing Big Boy.

Peters pulled her away.

"Sister Morrison, ef yuh don let im go n git erway from here hes gonna be caught shos theres a Gawd in Heaven!"

Lucy came running with Big Boy's shoes and pulled them on his feet. The old man thrust a battered hat on his head. The mother went to the stove and dumped the skillet of corn pone into her apron. She wrapped it, and unbuttoning Big Boy's overalls, pushed it into his bosom.

"Heres somethin fer yuh t eat; n pray, Big Boy, cause thas all anybody kin do now . . ."

Big Boy pulled to the door, his mother clinging to him.

"Let im go, Sister Morrison!"

"Run fas, Big Boy!"

Big Boy raced across the yard, scattering the chickens. He paused at the fence and hollered back:

"Tell Bobo where Ahm hidin n tell im t c mon!"

IV

He made for the railroad, running straight toward the sunset. He held his left hand tightly over his heart, holding the hot pone of corn bread there. At times he stumbled over the ties, for his shoes were tight and hurt his feet. His throat burned from thirst; he had had no water since noon.

He veered off the track and trotted over the crest of a hill, following Bullard's Road. His feet slipped and slid in the dust. He kept his eyes straight ahead, fearing every clump of shrubbery, every tree. He wished it were night. If he could only get to the kilns without meeting anyone. Suddenly a thought came to him like a blow. He recalled hearing the old folks tell tales of bloodhounds, and fear made him run slower. None of them had thought of that. Spose blood-houns wuz put on his trail? Lawd! Spose a whole pack of em, foamin n howlin, tore im t pieces? He went limp and his feet dragged. Yeah, thas whut they wuz gonna send after im, blood-houns! N then thered be no way fer im t dodge! Why hadnt Pa let im take tha shotgun? He stopped. He oughta go back n git tha shotgun. And then when the mob came he would take some with him.

In the distance he heard the approach of a train. It jarred him back to a sharp sense of danger. He ran again, his big shoes sopping up and down in the dust. He was tired and his lungs were bursting from running. He wet his lips, wanting water. As he turned from the road across a plowed field he heard the train roaring at his heels. He ran faster, gripped in terror.

He was nearly there now. He could see the black clay on the sloping hillside. Once inside a kiln he would be safe. For a little while, at least. He thought of the shotgun again. If he only had something! Someone to talk to . . . Thas right! Bobo! Bobod be wid im. Hed almost fergot Bobo. Bobod bringa gun; he knowed he would. N tergether they could kill the whole mob. Then in the mawning theyd git inter Will's truck n go far erway, t Chicawgo . . .

He slowed to a walk, looking back and ahead. A light wind skipped over the grass. A beetle lit on his cheek and he brushed it off. Behind the dark pines hung a red sun. Two bats flapped against that sun. He shivered, for he was growing cold; the sweat on his body was drying.

He stopped at the foot of the hill, trying to choose between two patches of black kilns high above him. He went to the left, for there lay the ones he, Bobo, Lester, and Buck had dug only last week. He looked around again; the landscape was bare. He climbed the embankment and stood before a row of black pits sinking four and five feet deep into the earth. He went to the largest and peered in. He stiffened when his ears caught the sound of a whir. He ran back a few steps and poised on his toes. Six foot of snake slid out of the pit and went into coil. Big Boy looked around wildly for a stick. He ran down the slope, peering into the grass. He stumbled over a tree limb. He picked it up and tested it by striking it against the ground.

Warily, he crept back up the slope, his stick poised. When about seven feet from the snake he stopped and waved the stick. The coil grew tighter, the whir sounded louder, and a flat head reared to strike. He went to the right, and the flat head followed him, the blue-black tongue darting forth; he went to the left, and the flat head followed him there too.

He stopped, teeth clenched. He had to kill this snake. Jus had t kill im! This wuz the safest pit on the hillside. He waved the stick again, looking at the snake before, thinking of a mob behind. The flat head reared higher. With stick over shoulder, he jumped in, swinging. The stick sang through the air, catching the snake on the side of the head, sweeping him out of coil. There was a brown writhing mass. Then Big Boy was upon him, pounding blows home, one on top of the other. He fought viciously, his eyes red, his teeth bared in a snarl. He beat till the snake lay still; then he stomped it with his heel, grinding its head into the dirt.

He stopped, limp, wet. The corners of his lips were white with spittle. He spat and shuddered.

Cautiously, he went to the hole and peered. He longed for a match. He imagined whole nests of them in there waiting. He put the stick into the hole and waved it around. Stooping, he peered again. It mus be awright. He looked over the hillside, his eyes coming back to the dead snake. Then he got to his knees and backed slowly into the hole.

When inside he felt there must be snakes all about him, ready to strike. It seemed he could see and feel them there, waiting tensely in coil. In the dark he imagined long white fangs ready to sink into his neck, his side, his legs. He wanted to come out, but kept still. Shucks, he told himself, ef there wuz any snakes in here they sho woulda done bit me by now. Some of his fear left, and he relaxed.

With elbows on ground and chin on palms, he settled. The clay was cold to his knees and thighs, but his bosom was kept warm by the hot pone of corn bread. His thirst returned and he longed for a drink. He was hungry, too. But he did not want to eat the corn pone. Naw, not now. Mabbe after erwhile, after Bobo came. Then theyd both eat the corn pone.

The view from his hole was fringed by the long tufts of grass. He could see all the way to Bullard's Road, and even beyond. The wind was blowing, and in the east the first touch of dusk was rising. Every now and then a bird floated past, a spot of wheeling black printed against the sky. Big Boy sighed, shifted his weight, and chewed at a blade of grass. A wasp droned. He heard number nine, far away and mournful.

The train made him remember how they had dug these kilns on long hot summer days, how they had made boilers out of big tin cans, filled them with water, fixed stoppers for steam, cemented them in holes with wet clay, and built fires under them. He recalled how they had danced and yelled when a stopper blew out of a boiler, letting out a big spout of steam and a shrill whistle. There were times when they had the whole hillside blazing and smoking. Yeah, yuh see, Big Boy wuz Casey Jones n wuz speedin it down the gleamin rails of the Southern Pacific. Bobo had number two on the Santa Fe. Buck wuz on the Illinoy Central. Lester the Nickel Plate. Lawd, how they shelved the wood in! The boiling water would almost jar the cans loose from the clay. More and more pine-knots and dry leaves would be piled under the cans. Flames would grow so tall they would have to shield their eyes. Sweat would pour off their faces. Then, suddenly, a peg would shoot high into the air, and

Pssseeeezzzzzzzzzzzzzzzzzzz . . .

Big Boy sighed and stretched out his arm, quenching the flames and scattering the smoke. Why didnt Bobo c mon? He looked over the fields; there was nothing but dying sunlight. His mind drifted back to the kilns. He remembered the day when Buck, jealous of his winning, had tried to smash his kiln. Yeah, that ol sonofabitch! Naw, Lawd! He didnt go t say tha! Whut wuz he thinkin erbout? Cussin the dead! Yeah, po ol Buck wuz dead now. N Lester too. Yeah, it wuz awright fer Buck t smash his kiln. Sho. N he wished he hadnt socked ol Buck so hard tha day. He wuz sorry fer Buck now. N he sho wished he hadnt cussed po ol Bucks ma, neither. Tha wuz sinful! Mabbe Gawd would git im fer tha? But he didnt go t do it! Po Buck! Po Lester! Hed never treat anybody like tha ergin, never . . .

Dusk was slowly deepening. Somewhere, he could not tell exactly where, a cricket took up a fitful song. The air was growing soft and heavy. He looked over the fields, longing for Bobo . . .

He shifted his body to ease the cold damp of the ground, and thought back over the day. Yeah, hed been dam right erbout not wantin t go swimmin. N ef hed followed his right min hed neverve gon n got inter all this trouble. At first hed said naw. But shucks, somehow hed just went on wid the res. Yeah, he shoulda went on t school tha mawnin, like Ma told im t do. But, hell, who wouldnt git tireda awways drivin a guy t school! Tha wuz the big trou awways drivin a guy t school. He wouldnt be in all this trouble now ef it wuznt fer that Gawddam school! Impatiently, he took the grass out of his mouth and threw it away, demolishing the little red school house . . .

Yeah, ef they had all kept still n quiet when tha ol white woman showed-up, mabbe shedve went on off. But yuh never kin tell erbout these white folks. Mabbe she wouldntve went. Mabbe tha white man woulda killed all of em! All *fo* of em! Yeah, yuh never kin tell erbout white folks. Then, ergin, mabbe tha white woman woulda went on off n laffed. Yeah, mabbe tha white man woulda said: *Yuh nigger bastards git t hell outta here! Yuh know Gawddam well yuh don berlong here!* N then they woulda grabbed their cloes n run like all hell . . . He blinked the white man away. Where wuz Bobo? Why didnt he hurry up n c mon?

He jerked another blade and chewed. Yeah, ef pa had only let im have tha shotgun! He could stan off a whole mob wid a shotgun. He looked at the ground as he turned a shotgun over his hands. Then he leveled it at an advancing white man. *Boooom!* The man curled up. Another came. He reloaded quickly, and let him have what the other had got. He too curled up. Then another came. He got the same medicine. Then the whole mob swirled around him, and he blazed away, getting as many as he could. They closed in; but, by Gawd, he had done his part, hadnt he? N the newspapersd say: NIGGER KILLS DOZEN OF MOB BEFO LYNCHED! Er mabbe theyd say: TRAPPED NIGGER SLAYS TWENTY BEFO KILLED! He smiled a little. Tha wouldnt be so bad, would it? Blinking the newspaper away, he looked over the fields. Where wuz Bobo? Why didnt he hurry up n c mon?

He shifted, trying to get a crick out of his legs. Shucks, he wuz gittin tireda this. N it wuz almos dark now. Yeah, there wuz a little bittie star way over yonder in the eas. Mabbe tha white man wuznt dead? Mabbe they wuznt even lookin fer im? Mabbe he could go back home now? Naw, better wait erwhile. Thad be bes. But, Lawd, ef he only had some water! He could hardly swallow, his throat was so dry. Gawddam them white folks! Thas all they wuz good fer, t run a nigger down lika rabbit! Yeah, they git yuh in a corner n then they let yuh have it. A thousan of em! He shivered, for the cold of the clay was chilling his bones. Lawd, spose they foun im here in this hole? N wid nobody t hep im? . . . But ain no use in thinking erbout tha; wait till trouble come fo yuh start fightin it. But ef tha mob came one by one hed wipe em all out. Clean up the whole bunch. He caught one by the neck and choked him long and hard, choked him till his tongue and eyes popped out. Then he jumped upon his chest and stomped him like he had stomped that snake. When he had finished with one, another came. He choked him too. Choked till he sank slowly to the ground, gasping . . .

"Hoalo!"

Big Boy snatched his fingers from the white man's neck and looked over the fields. He saw nobody. Had someone spied him? He was sure that somebody had hollered. His heart pounded. But, shucks, nobody couldnt see im here in this hole . . . But mabbe theyd seen im when he wuz comin n had laid low n wuz now closin in on im! Praps they wuz signalin fer the others? Yeah, they wuz creepin up on im! Mabbe he oughta git up n run . . . Oh! Mabbe tha wuz Bobo! Yeah, Bobo! He oughta clim out n see ef Bobo wuz lookin fer im . . . He stiffened.

"Hoalo!"

"Hoalo!"

"Wheres yuh?"

"Over here on Bullards Road!"

"C mon over!"

"Awright!"

He heard footsteps. Then voices came again, low and far away this time.

"Seen anybody?"

"Naw. Yuh?"

"Naw."

"Yuh reckon they got erway?"

"Ah dunno. Its hard t tell."

"Gawddam them sonofabitchin niggers!"

"We oughta kill ever black bastard in this country!"

"Waal, Jim got two of em, anyhow."

"But Bertha said there wuz *fo!*"

"Where in hell they hidin?"

"She said one of em wuz named Big Boy, or somethin like tha."

"We went t his shack lookin fer im."

"Yeah?"

"But we didnt fin im."

"These niggers stick tergether; they don never tell on each other."

"We looked all thu the shack n couldnt fin hide ner hair of im. Then we drove the ol woman n man out n set the shack on fire . . ."

"Jeesus! Ah wished Ah coulda been there!"

"Yuh shoulda heard the ol nigger woman howl . . ."

"Hoalo!"

"C mon over!"

Big Boy eased to the edge and peeped. He saw a white man with a gun slung over his shoulder running down the slope. Wuz they gonna search the hill? Lawd, there wuz no way fer im t git erway now; he wuz caught! He shoulda knowed theyd git im here. N he didnt hava thing, notta thing t fight wid. Yeah, soon as the blood-houns came theyd fin im. Lawd, have mercy! Theyd lynch im right here on the hill . . . Theyd git im n tie im t a stake n burn im erlive! Lawd! Nobody but the good Lawd could hep im now, nobody . . .

He heard more feet running. He nestled deeper. His chest ached. Nobody but the good Lawd could hep now. They wuz crowdin all round im n when they hada big crowd theyd close in on im. Then itd be over . . . The good Lawd would have t hep im, cause nobody could hep im now, nobody . . .

And then he went numb when he remembered Bobo. Spose Bobod come now? Hed be caught sho! Both of em would be caught! They'd make Bobo tell where he wuz! Bobo oughta not try to come now. Somebody oughta tell im . . . But there wuz nobody; there wuz no way . . .

He eased slowly back to the opening. There was a large group of men. More were coming. Many had guns. Some had coils of rope slung over shoulders.

"Ah tell yuh they still here, somewhere . . ."

"But we looked all over!"

"What t hell! Wouldnt do t let em git erway!"

"Naw. Ef they git erway notta woman in this town would be safe."

"Say, whuts tha yuh got?"

"Er pillar."

"Fer whut?"

"Feathers, fool!"

"Chris! Thisll be hot ef we kin ketch them niggers!"

"Ol Anderson said he wuz gonna bringa barrela tar!"

"Ah got some gasoline in mah car ef yuh need it."

Big Boy had no feelings now. He was waiting. He did not wonder if they were coming after him. He just waited. He did not wonder about Bobo. He rested his cheek against the cold clay, waiting.

A dog barked. He stiffened. It barked again. He balled himself into a knot at the bottom of the hole, waiting. Then he heard the patter of dog feet.

"Look!"

"Whuts he got?"

"Its a snake!"

"Yeah, the dogs foun a snake!"

"Gee, its a big one!"

"Shucks, Ah wish he could fin one of them sonofabitchin niggers!"

The voices sank to low murmurs. Then he heard number twelve, its bell tolling and whistle crying as it slid along the rails. He flattened himself against the clay. Someone was singing:

"We'll hang ever nigger t a sour apple tree . . ."

When the song ended there was hard laughter. From the other side of the hill he heard the dog barking furiously. He listened. There was more than one dog now. There were many and they were barking their throats out.

"Hush, Ah hear them dogs!"

"When theys barkin like tha theys foun somethin!"

"Here they come over the hill!"

"WE GOT IM! WE GOT IM!"

There came a roar. Tha mus be Bobo; tha mus be Bobo . . . In spite of his fear, Big Boy looked. The road, and half of the hillside across the road, were covered with men. A few were at the top of the hill, stenciled against the sky. He could see dark forms moving up the slopes. They were yelling.

"By Gawd, we got im!"

"C mon!"

"Where is he?"
"Theyre bringin im over the hill!"
"Ah got a rope fer im!"
"Say, somebody go n git the others!"
"Where is he? Cant we see im, Mister?"
"They say Berthas comin, too."
"Jack! Jack! Don leave me! Ah wanna see im!"
"Theyre bringin im over the hill, sweetheart!"
"AH WANNA BE THE FIRS T PUT A ROPE ON THA BLACK BASTARDS NECK!"
"Les start the fire!"
"Heat the tar!"
"Ah got some chains t chain im."
"Bring im over this way!"
"Chris, Ah wished Ah hada drink . . ."

Big Boy saw men moving over the hill. Among them was a long dark spot. Tha mus be Bobo; tha mus be Bobo theys carryin . . . They'll git im here. He oughta git up n run. He clamped his teeth and ran his hand across his forehead, bringing it away wet. He tried to swallow, but could not; his throat was dry.

They had started the song again:

"We'll hang ever nigger t a sour apple tree . . ."

There were women singing now. Their voices made the song round and full. Song waves rolled over the top of pine trees. The sky sagged low, heavy with clouds. Wind was rising. Sometimes cricket cries cut surprisingly across the mob song. A dog had gone to the utmost top of the hill. At each lull of the song his howl floated full into the night.

Big Boy shrank when he saw the first tall flame light the hillside. Would they see im here? Then he remembered you could not see into the dark if you were standing in the light. As flames leaped higher he saw two men rolling a barrel up the slope.

"Say, gimme a han here, will yuh?"
"Awright, heave!"
"C mon! Straight up! Git t the other end!"
"Ah got the feathers here in this pillar!"
"BRING SOME MO WOOD!"

Big Boy could see the barrel surrounded by flames. The mob fell back, forming a dark circle. Theyd fin im here! He had a wild impuse to climb out and fly across the hills. But his legs would not move. He stared hard, trying to find Bobo. His eyes played over a long dark spot near the fire. Fanned by wind, flames leaped higher. He jumped. That dark spot had moved. Lawd, thas Bobo; thas Bobo . . .

He smelt the scent of tar, faint at first, then stronger. The wind brought it full into his face, then blew it away. His eyes burned and he rubbed them with his knuckles. He sneezed.

"LES GIT SOURVINEERS!"

He saw the mob close in around the fire. Their faces were hard and sharp in the light of the flames. More men and women were coming over the hill. The long dark spot was smudged out.

"Everbody git back!"

"Look! Hes gotta finger!"

"C MON! GIT THE GALS BACK FROM THE FIRE!"

"Hes got one of his ears, see?"

"Whuts the matter!"

"A woman fell out! Fainted, Ah reckon . . ."

The stench of tar permeated the hillside. The sky was black and the wind was blowing hard.

"HURRY UP N BURN THE NIGGER FO IT RAINS!"

Big Boy saw the mob fall back, leaving a small knot of men about the fire. Then, for the first time, he had a full glimpse of Bobo. A black body flashed in the light. Bobo was struggling, twisting; they were binding his arms and legs.

When he saw them tilt the barrel he stiffened. A scream quivered. He knew the tar was on Bobo. The mob fell back. He saw a tar-drenched body glistening and turning.

"THE BASTARDS GOT IT!"

There was a sudden quiet. Then he shrank violently as the wind carried, like a flurry of snow, a widening spiral of white feathers into the night. The flames leaped tall as the trees. The scream came again. Big Boy trembled and looked. The mob was running down the slopes, leaving the fire clear. Then he saw a writhing white mass cradled in yellow flame, and heard screams, one on top of the other, each shriller and shorter than the last. The mob was quiet now, standing still, looking up the slopes at the writhing white mass gradually growing black, growing black in a cradle of yellow flame.

"PO ON MO GAS!"

"Gimme a lif, will yuh!"

Two men were struggling, carrying between them a heavy can. They set it down, tilted it, leaving it so that the gas would trickle down to the hollowed earth around the fire.

Big Boy slid back into the hole, his face buried in clay. He had no feelings now, no fears. He was numb, empty, as though all blood had been drawn from him. Then his muscles flexed taut when he heard a faint patter. A tiny stream of cold water seeped to his knees, making him push back to a drier spot. He looked up; rain was beating in the grass.

"Its rainin!"

"C mon, les git t town!"

"... don worry, when the fire git thu wid im hell be gone..."

"Wait, Charles! Don leave me; its slippery here..."

"Ahll take some of yuh ladies back in mah car..."

Big Boy heard the dogs barking again, this time closer. Running feet pounded past. Cold water chilled his ankles. He could hear raindrops steadily hissing.

Now a dog was barking at the mouth of the hole, barking furiously, sensing a presence there. He balled himself into a knot and clung to the bottom, his knees and shins buried in water. The bark came louder. He heard paws scraping and felt the hot scent of dog breath on his face. Green eyes glowed and drew nearer as the barking, muffled by the closeness of the hole, beat upon his eardrums. Backing till his shoulders pressed against the clay, he held his breath. He pushed out his hands, his fingers stiff. The dog yawped louder, advancing, his bark rising sharp and thin. Big Boy rose to his knees, his hands before him. Then he flattened out still more against the bottom, breathing lungsful of hot dog scent, breathing it slowly, hard, but evenly. The dog came closer, bringing hotter dog scent. Big Boy could go back no more. His knees were slipping and slopping in the water. He braced himself, ready. Then, he never exactly knew how – he never knew whether he had lunged or the dog had lunged – they were together, rolling in the water. The green eyes were beneath him, between his legs. Dognails bit into his arms. His knees slipped backward and he landed full on the dog; the dog's breath left in a heavy gasp. Instinctively, he fumbled for the throat as he felt the dog twisting between his knees. The dog snarled, long and low, as though gathering strength. Big Boy's hands traveled swiftly over the dog's back, groping for the throat. He felt dognails again and saw green eyes, but his fingers had found the throat. He choked, feeling his fingers sink; he choked, throwing back his head and stiffening his arms. He felt the dog's body heave, felt dognails digging into his loins. With strength flowing from fear, he closed his fingers, pushing his full weight on the dog's throat. The dog heaved again, and lay still... Big Boy heard the sound of his own breathing filling the hole, and heard shouts and footsteps above him going past.

For a long, long time he held the dog, held it long after the last footstep had died out, long after the rain had stopped.

V

Morning found him still on his knees in a puddle of rainwater, staring at the stiff body of a dog. As the air brightened he came to himself slowly. He held still for a long time, as though waking from a dream, as though trying to remember.

The chug of a truck came over the hill. He tried to crawl to the opening. His knees were stiff and a thousand needle-like pains shot from the bottom of his feet to the calves of his legs. Giddiness made his eyes blur. He pulled up and looked. Through brackish light he saw Will's truck standing some twenty-five yards away, the engine running. Will stood on the runningboard, looking over the slopes of the hill.

Big Boy scuffled out, falling weakly in the wet grass. He tried to call to Will, but his dry throat would make no sound. He tried again.

"Will!"

Will heard, answering:

"Big Boy, c mon!"

He tried to run, and fell. Will came, meeting him in the tall grass.

"C mon," Will said, catching his arm.

They struggled to the truck.

"Hurry up!" said Will, pushing him onto the runningboard.

Will pushed back a square trapdoor which swung above the back of the driver's seat. Big Boy pulled through, landing with a thud on the bottom. On hands and knees he looked around in the semi-darkness.

"Wheres Bobo?"

Big Boy stared.

"Wheres Bobo?"

"They got im."

"When?"

"Las night."

"The mob?"

Big Boy pointed in the direction of a charred sapling on the slope of the opposite hill. Will looked. The trapdoor fell. The engine purred, the gears whined, and the truck lurched forward over the muddy road, sending Big Boy on his side.

For a while he lay as he had fallen, on his side, too weak to move. As he felt the truck swing around a curve he straightened up and rested his back against a stack of wooden boxes. Slowly, he began to make out objects in the darkness. Through two long cracks fell thin blades of daylight. The floor was of smooth steel, and cold to his thighs. Splinters and bits of sawdust danced with the rumble of the truck. Each time they swung around a curve he was pulled over the floor; he grabbed at corners of boxes to steady himself. Once he heard the crow of a rooster. It made him think of home, of ma and pa. He thought he remembered hearing somewhere that the house had burned, but could not remember where . . . It all seemed unreal now.

He was tired. He dozed, swaying with the lurch. Then he jumped awake. The truck was running smoothly, on gravel. Far away he heard two short blasts from the Buckeye Lumber Mill. Unconsciously, the thought sang through his mind: Its six erclock . . .

The trapdoor swung in. Will spoke through a corner of his mouth.

"How yuh comin?"

"Awright."

"How they git Bobo?"

"He wuz comin over the hill."

"Whut they do?"

"They burnt im . . . Will, Ah wan some water; mah throats like fire . . ."

"Well git some when we pass a fillin station."

Big Boy leaned back and dozed. He jerked awake when the truck stopped. He heard Will get out. He wanted to peep through the trapdoor, but was afraid. For a moment, the wild fear he had known in the hole came back. Spose theyd search n fin im? He quieted when he heard Will's footstep on the runningboard. The trapdoor pushed in. Will's hat came through, dripping.

"Take it, quick!"

Big Boy grabbed, spilling water into his face. The truck lurched. He drank. Hard cold lumps of brick rolled into his hot stomach. A dull pain made him bend over. His intestines seemed to be drawing into a tight knot. After a bit it eased, and he sat up, breathing softly.

The truck swerved. He blinked his eyes. The blades of daylight had turned brightly golden. The sun had risen.

The truck sped over the asphalt miles, sped northward,. jolting him, shaking out of his bosom the crumbs of corn bread, making them dance with the splinters and sawdust in the golden blades of sunshine.

He turned on his side and slept.

THE MAN WHO LIVED UNDERGROUND

I've got to hide, he told himself. His chest heaved as he waited, crouching in a dark corner of the vestibule. He was tired of running and dodging. Either he had to find a place to hide, or he had to surrender. A police car swished by through the rain, its siren rising sharply. They're looking for me all over . . . He crept to the door and squinted through the fogged plate glass. He stiffened as the siren rose and died in the distance. Yes, he had to hide, but where? He gritted his teeth. Then a sudden movement in the street caught his attention. A throng of tiny columns of water snaked into the air from the perforations of a manhole cover. The columns stopped abruptly, as though the perforations had become clogged; a gray spout of sewer water jutted up from underground and lifted the circular metal cover, juggled it for a moment, then let it fall with a clang.

He hatched a tentative plan: he would wait until the siren sounded far off, then he would go out. He smoked and waited, tense. At last the siren gave him his signal; it wailed, dying, going away from him. He stepped to the sidewalk, then paused and looked curiously at the open manhole, half expecting the cover to leap up again. He went to the center of the street and stooped and peered into the hole, but could see nothing. Water rustled in the black depths.

He started with terror; the siren sounded so near that he had the idea that he had been dreaming and had awakened to find the car upon him. He dropped instinctively to his knees and his hands grasped the rim of the manhole. The siren seemed to hoot directly above him and with a wild gasp of exertion he snatched the cover far enough off to admit his body. He swung his legs over the opening and lowered himself into watery darkness. He hung for an eternal moment to the rim by his finger tips, then he felt rough metal prongs and at once he knew that sewer workmen used these ridges to lower themselves into manholes. Fist over fist, he let his body sink until he could feel no more prongs. He swayed in dank space; the siren seemed to howl at the very rim of the manhole. He dropped and was washed violently into an ocean of warm, leaping water. His head was battered against a wall and he wondered if this were death. Frenziedly his fingers clawed and sank into a crevice. He steadied himself and measured the strength of the current with his own muscular tension. He stood slowly in water that dashed past his knees with fearful velocity.

He heard a prolonged scream of brakes and the siren broke off. Oh, God! They had found him! Looming above his head in the rain a white face hovered over the hole. "How did this damn thing get off?" he heard a policeman ask. He saw the steel cover move slowly until the hole looked like a quarter moon turned black. "Give me a hand here," someone called. The cover clanged into place, muffling the sights and sounds of the upper world. Knee-deep in the pulsing current, he breathed with aching chest, filling his lungs with the hot stench of yeasty rot.

From the perforations of the manhole cover, delicate lances of hazy violet sifted down and wove a mottled pattern upon the surface of the streaking current. His lips parted as a car swept past along the wet pavement overhead, its heavy rumble soon dying out, like the hum of a plane speeding through a dense cloud. He had never thought that cars could sound like that; everything seemed strange and unreal under here. He stood in darkness for a long time, knee-deep in rustling water, musing.

The odor of rot had become so general that he no longer smelled it. He got his cigarettes, but discovered that his matches were wet. He searched and found a dry folder in the pocket of his shirt and managed to strike one; it flared weirdly in the wet gloom, glowing greenishly, turning red, orange, then yellow. He lit a crumpled cigarette; then, by the flickering light of the match, he looked for support so that he would not have to keep his muscles flexed against the pouring water. His pupils narrowed and he saw to either side of him two steaming walls that rose and curved inward some six feet above his head to form a dripping, mouse-colored dome. The bottom of the sewer was a sloping V-trough. To the left, the sewer vanished in ashen fog. To the right was a steep down-curve into which water plunged.

He saw now that had he not regained his feet in time, he would have been swept to death, or had he entered any other manhole he would have probably drowned. Above the rush of the current he heard sharper juttings of water; tiny streams were spewing into the sewer from smaller conduits. The match died; he struck another and saw a mass of debris sweep past him and clog the throat of the down-curve. At once the water began rising rapidly. Could he climb out before he drowned? A long hiss sounded and the debris was sucked from sight; the current lowered. He understood now what had made the water toss the manhole cover; the down-curve had become temporarily obstructed and the perforations had become clogged.

He was in danger; he might slide into a down-curve; he might wander with a lighted match into a pocket of gas and blow himself up; or he might contract some horrible disease . . . Though he wanted to leave, an irrational impulse held him rooted. To the left, the convex ceiling swooped to a height of less than five feet. With cigarette slanting from pursed lips, he waded with taut muscles, his feet sloshing over the slimy bottom, his shoes sinking into spongy slop, the slate-colored water cracking in creamy foam against his knees. Pressing his flat left palm against the lowered ceiling, he struck another match and saw a metal pole nestling in a niche of the wall. Yes, some sewer workman had left it. He reached for it, then jerked his head away as a whisper of scurrying life whisked past and was still. He held the match close and saw a huge rat, wet with slime, blinking beady eyes and baring tiny fangs. The light blinded the rat and the frizzled head moved aimlessly. He grabbed the pole and let it fly against the rat's soft body; there was shrill piping and the grizzly body splashed into the dun-colored water and was snatched out of sight, spinning in the scuttling stream.

He swallowed and pushed on, following the curve of the misty cavern, sounding the water with the pole. By the faint light of another manhole cover he saw, amid loose wet brick, a hole with walls of damp earth leading into blackness. Gingerly he poked the pole into it; it was hollow and went beyond the length of the pole. He shoved the pole before him, hoisted himself upward, got to his hands and knees, and crawled. After a few yards he paused, struck to wonderment by the silence; it seemed that he had traveled a million miles away from the world. As he inched forward again he could sense the bottom of the dirt tunnel becoming dry and lowering slightly. Slowly he rose and to his astonishment he stood erect. He could not hear the rustling of the water now and he felt confoundingly alone, yet lured by the darkness and silence.

He crept a long way, then stopped, curious, afraid. He put his right foot forward and it dangled in space; he drew back in fear. He thrust the pole outward and it swung in emptiness. He trembled, imagining the earth crumbling and burying him alive. He scratched a match and saw that the dirt floor sheered away steeply and widened into a sort of cave some five feet below him. An old sewer, he muttered. He cocked his head, hearing a feathery cadence which he could not identify. The match ceased to burn.

Using the pole as a kind of ladder, he slid down and stood in darkness. The air was a little fresher and he could still hear vague noises. Where was he? He felt suddenly that someone was standing near him and he turned sharply, but there was only darkness. He poked cautiously and felt a brick wall; he followed it and the strange sounds grew louder. He ought to get out of here. This was crazy. He could not remain here for any length of time; there was no food and no place to sleep. But the faint sounds tantalized him; they were strange but familiar. Was it a motor? A baby crying? Music? A siren? He groped on, and the sounds came so clearly that he could feel the pitch and timbre of human voices. Yes, singing! That was it! He listened with open mouth. It was a church service. Enchanted, he groped toward the waves of melody.

Jesus, take me to your home above
And fold me in the bosom of Thy love...

The singing was on the other side of the brick wall. Excited, he wanted to watch the service without being seen. Whose church was it? He knew most of the churches in this area above ground, but the singing sounded too strange and detached for him to guess. He looked to the left, to the right, down to the black dirt, then upward and was startled to see a bright sliver of light slicing the darkness like the blade of a razor. He struck one of his two remaining matches and saw rusty pipes running along an old concrete ceiling. Photographically he located the exact position of the pipes in his mind. The match flame sank and he sprang upward; his hands clutched a pipe. He swung his legs and tossed his body onto the bed of pipes and they creaked, swaying up and down; he thought that the tier was about to crash, but nothing happened. He edged to the crevice and saw a segment of black men and women, dressed in white robes, singing, holding tattered songbooks in their black palms. His first impulse was to laugh, but he checked himself.

What was he doing? He was crushed with a sense of guilt. Would God strike him dead for that? The singing swept on and he shook his head, disagreeing in spite of himself. They oughtn't to do that, he thought. But he could think of no reason *why* they should not do it. Just singing with the air of the sewer blowing in on them . . . He felt that he was gazing upon something abysmally obscene, yet he could not bring himself to leave.

After a long time he grew numb and dropped to the dirt. Pain throbbed in his legs and a deeper pain, induced by the sight of those black people groveling and begging for something they could never get, churned in him. A vague conviction made him feel that those people should stand unrepentant and yield no quarter in singing and praying, yet *he* had run away from the police, had pleaded with them to believe in *his* innocence. He shook his head, bewildered.

How long had he been down here? He did not know. This was a new kind of living for him; the intensity of feelings he had experienced when looking at the church people sing made him certain that he had been down here a long time, but his mind told him that the time must have been short. In this darkness the only notion he had of time was when a match flared and measured time by its fleeting light. He groped back through the hole toward the sewer and the waves of song subsided and finally he could not hear them at all. He came to where the earth hole ended and he heard the noise of the current and time lived again for him, measuring the moments by the wash of the water.

The rain must have slackened, for the flow of water had lessened and came only to his ankles. Ought he to go up into the streets and take his chances on hiding somewhere else? But they would surely catch him. The mere thought of dodging and running again from the police made him tense. No, he would stay and plot how to elude them. But what could he do down here? He walked forward into the sewer and came to another manhole cover; he stood beneath it, debating. Fine pencils of gold spilled suddenly from the little circles in the manhole cover and trembled on the surface of the current. Yes, street lamps . . . It must be night . . .

He went forward for about a quarter of an hour, wading aimlessly, poking the pole carefully before him. Then he stopped, his eyes fixed and intent. What's that? A strangely familiar image attracted and repelled him. Lit by the yellow stems from another manhole cover was a tiny nude body of a baby snagged by debris and half-submerged in water. Thinking that the baby was alive, he moved impulsively to save it, but his roused feelings told him that it was dead, cold, nothing, the same nothingness he had felt while watching the men and women singing in the church. Water blossomed about the tiny legs, the tiny arms, the tiny head, and rushed onward. The eyes were closed, as though in sleep; the fists were clenched, as though in protest; and the mouth gaped black in a soundless cry.

He straightened and drew in his breath, feeling that he had been staring for all eternity at the ripples of veined water skimming impersonally over the shriveled limbs. He felt as condemned as when the policemen had accused him. Involuntarily he lifted his hand to brush the vision away, but his arm fell listlessly to his side. Then he acted; he closed his eyes and reached forward slowly with the soggy shoe of his right foot and shoved the dead baby from where it had been lodged. He kept his eyes closed, seeing the little body twisting in the current as it floated from sight. He opened his eyes, shivered, placed his knuckles in the sockets, hearing the water speed in the somber shadows.

He tramped on, sensing at times a sudden quickening in the current as he passed some conduit whose waters were swelling the stream that slid by his feet. A few minutes later he was standing under another manhole cover, listening to the faint rumble of noises above ground. Streetcars and trucks, he mused. He looked down and saw a stagnant pool of gray-green sludge; at intervals a balloon pocket rose from the scum, glistening a bluish-purple, and burst. Then another. He turned, shook his head, and tramped back to the dirt cave by the church, his lips quivering.

Back in the cave, he sat and leaned his back against a dirt wall. His body was trembling slightly. Finally his senses quieted and he slept. When he awakened he felt stiff and cold. He had to leave this foul place, but leaving meant facing those policemen who had wrongly accused him. No, he could not go back aboveground. He remembered the beating they had given him and how he had signed his name to a confession, a confession which he had not even read. He had been too tired when they had shouted at him, demanding that he sign his name; he had signed it to end his pain.

He stood and groped about in the darkness. The church singing had stopped. How long had he slept? He did not know. But he felt refreshed and hungry. He doubled his fist nervously, realizing that he could not make a decision. As he walked about he stumbled over an old rusty iron pipe. He picked it up and felt a jagged edge. Yes, there was a brick wall and he could dig into it. What would he find? Smiling, he groped to the brick wall, sat, and began digging idly into damp cement. I can't make any noise, he cautioned himself. As time passed he grew thirsty, but there was no water. He had to kill time or go aboveground. The cement came out of the wall easily; he extracted four bricks and felt a soft draft blowing into his face. He stopped, afraid. What was beyond? He waited a long time and nothing happened; then he began digging again, soundlessly, slowly; he enlarged the hole and crawled through into a dark room and collided with another wall. He felt his way to the right; the wall ended and his fingers toyed in space, like the antennae of an insect.

He fumbled on and his feet struck something hollow, like wood. What's this? He felt with his fingers. Steps . . . He stooped and pulled off his shoes and mounted the stairs and saw a yellow chink of light shining and heard a low voice speaking. He placed his eye to a keyhole and saw the nude waxen figure of a man stretched out upon a white table. The voice, low-pitched and vibrant, mumbled indistinguishable words, neither rising nor falling. He craned his neck and squinted to see the man who was talking, but he could not locate him. Above the naked figure was suspended a huge glass container filled with a blood-red liquid from which a white rubber tube dangled. He crouched closer to the door and saw the tip end of a black object lined with pink satin. A coffin, he breathed. This is an undertaker's establishment . . . A fine-spun lace of ice covered his body and he shuddered. A throaty chuckle sounded in the depths of the yellow room.

He turned to leave. Three steps down it occurred to him that a light switch should be nearby; he felt along the wall, found an electric button, pressed it, and a blinding glare smote his pupils so hard that he was sightless, defenseless. His pupils contracted and he wrinkled his nostrils at a peculiar odor. At once he knew that he had been dimly aware of this odor in the darkness, but the light had brought it sharply to his attention. Some kind of stuff they use to embalm, he thought. He went down the steps and saw piles of lumber, coffins, and a long workbench. In one corner was a tool chest. Yes, he could use tools, could tunnel through walls with them. He lifted the lid of the chest and saw nails, a hammer, a crowbar, a screwdriver, a light bulb, and a long length of electric wire. Good! He would lug these back to his cave.

He was about to hoist the chest to his shoulders when he discovered a door behind the furnace. Where did it lead? He tried to open it and found it securely bolted. Using the crowbar so as to make no sound, he pried the door open; it swung on creaking hinges, outward. Fresh air came to his face and he caught the faint roar of faraway sound. Easy now, he told himself. He widened the door and a lump of coal rattled toward him. A coalbin . . . Evidently the door led into another basement. The roaring noise was louder now, but he could not identify it. Where was he? He groped slowly over the coal pile, then ranged in darkness over a gritty floor. The roaring noise seemed to come from above him, then below. His fingers followed a wall until he touched a wooden ridge. A door, he breathed.

The noise died to a low pitch; he felt his skin prickle. It seemed that he was playing a game with an unseen person whose intelligence outstripped his. He put his ear to the flat surface of the door. Yes, voices . . . Was this a prize fight stadium?

The sound of the voices came near and sharp, but he could not tell if they were joyous or despairing. He twisted the knob until he heard a soft click and felt the springy weight of the door swinging toward him. He was afraid to open it, yet captured by curiosity and wonder. He jerked the door wide and saw on the far side of the basement a furnace glowing red. Ten feet away was still another door, half ajar. He crossed and peered through the door into an empty, high-ceilinged corridor that terminated in a dark complex of shadow. The belling voices rolled about him and his eagerness mounted. He stepped into the corridor and the voices swelled louder. He crept on and came to a narrow stairway leading circularly upward; there was no question but that he was going to ascend those stairs.

Mounting the spiraled staircase, he heard the voices roll in a steady wave, then leap to crescendo, only to die away, but always remaining audible. Ahead of him glowed red letters: E-X-I-T. At the top of the steps he paused in front of a black curtain that fluttered uncertainly. He parted the folds and looked into a convex depth that gleamed with clusters of shimmering lights. Sprawled below him was a stretch of human faces, tilted upward, chanting, whistling, screaming, laughing. Dangling before the faces, high upon a screen of silver, were jerking shadows. A movie, he said with slow laughter breaking from his lips.

He stood in a box in the reserved section of a movie house and the impulse he had had to tell the people in the church to stop their singing seized him. These people were laughing at their lives, he thought with amazement. They were shouting and yelling at the animated shadows of themselves. His compassion fired his imagination and he stepped out of the box, walked out upon thin air, walked on down to the audience; and, hovering in the air just above them, he stretched out his hand to touch them . . . His tension snapped and he found himself back in the box, looking down into the sea of faces. No; it could not be done; he could not awaken them. He sighed. Yes, these people were children, sleeping in their living, awake in their dying.

He turned away, parted the black curtain, and looked out. He saw no one. He started down the white stone steps and when he reached the bottom he saw a man in trim blue uniform coming toward him. So used had he become to being underground that he thought that he could walk past the man, as though he were a ghost. But the man stopped. And he stopped.

"Looking for the men's room, sir?" the man asked, and, without waiting for an answer, he turned and pointed. "This way, sir. The first door to your right."

He watched the man turn and walk up the steps and go out of sight. Then he laughed. What a funny fellow! He went back to the basement and stood in the red darkness, watching the glowing embers in the furnace. He went to the sink and turned the faucet and the water flowed in a smooth silent stream that looked like a spout of blood. He brushed the mad image from his mind and began to wash his hands leisurely, looking about for the usual bar of soap. He found one and rubbed it in his palms until a rich lather bloomed in his cupped fingers, like a scarlet sponge. He scrubbed and rinsed his hands meticulously, then hunted for a towel; there was none. He shut off the water, pulled off his shirt, dried his hands on it; when he put it on again he was grateful for the cool dampness that came to his skin.

Yes, he was thirsty; he turned on the faucet again, bowled his fingers and when the water bubbled over the brim of his cupped palms, he drank in long, slow swallows. His bladder grew tight; he shut off the water, faced the wall, bent his head, and watched a red stream strike the floor. His nostrils wrinkled against acrid wisps of vapor; though he had tramped in the waters of the sewer, he stepped back from the wall so that his shoes, wet with sewer slime, would not touch his urine.

He heard footsteps and crawled quickly into the coalbin. Lumps rattled noisily. The footsteps came into the basement and stopped. Who was it? Had someone heard him and come down to investigate? He waited, crouching, sweating. For a long time there was silence, then he heard the clang of metal and a brighter glow lit the room. Somebody's tending the furnace, he thought. Footsteps came closer and he stiffened. Looming before him was a white face lined with coal dust, the face of an old man with watery blue eyes. Highlights spotted his gaunt cheekbones, and he held a huge shovel. There was a screechy scrape of metal against stone, and the old man lifted a shovelful of coal and went from sight.

The room dimmed momentarily, then a yellow glare came as coal flared at the furnace door. Six times the old man came to the bin and went to the furnace with shovels of coal, but not once did he lift his eyes. Finally he dropped the shovel, mopped his face with a dirty handkerchief, and sighed: "Wheeew!" He turned slowly and trudged out of the basement, his footsteps dying away.

He stood, and lumps of coal clattered down the pile. He stepped from the bin and was startled to see the shadowy outline of an electric bulb hanging above his head. Why had not the old man turned it on? Oh, yes . . . He understood. The old man had worked here for so long that he had no need for light; he had learned a way of seeing in his dark world, like those sightless worms that inch along underground by a sense of touch.

His eyes fell upon a lunch pail and he was afraid to hope that it was full. He picked it up; it was heavy. He opened it. *Sandwiches!* He looked guiltily around; he was alone. He searched farther and found a folder of matches and a half-empty tin of tobacco; he put them eagerly into his pocket and clicked off the light. With the lunch pail under his arm, he went through the door, groped over the pile of coal, and stood again in the lighted basement of the undertaking establishment. I've got to get those tools, he told himself. And turn off that light. He tiptoed back up the steps and switched off the light; the invisible voice still droned on behind the door. He crept down and, seeing with his fingers, opened the lunch pail and tore off a piece of paper bag and brought out the tin and spilled grains of tobacco into the makeshift concave. He rolled it and wet it with spittle, then inserted one end into his mouth and lit it: he sucked smoke that bit his lungs. The nicotine reached his brain, went out along his arms to his finger tips, down to his stomach, and over all the tired nerves of his body.

He carted the tools to the hole he had made in the wall. Would the noise of the falling chest betray him? But he would have to take a chance; he had to have those tools. He lifted the chest and shoved it; it hit the dirt on the other side of the wall with a loud clatter. He waited, listening; nothing happened. Head first, he slithered through and stood in the cave. He grinned, filled with a cunning idea. Yes, he would now go back into the basement of the undertaking establishment and crouch behind the coal pile and dig another hole. Sure! Fumbling, he opened the tool chest and extracted a crowbar, a screwdriver, and a hammer; he fastened them securely about his person.

With another lumpish cigarette in his flexed lips, he crawled back through the hole and over the coal pile and sat, facing the brick wall. He jabbed with the crowbar and the cement sheered away; quicker than he thought, a brick came loose. He worked an hour; the other bricks did not come easily. He sighed, weak from effort. I ought to rest a little, he thought. I'm hungry. He felt his way back to the cave and stumbled along the wall till he came to the tool chest. He sat upon it, opened the lunch pail, and took out two thick sandwiches. He smelled them. Pork chops . . . His mouth watered. He closed his eyes and devoured a sandwich, savoring the smooth rye bread and juicy meat. He ate rapidly, gulping down lumpy mouthfuls that made him long for water. He ate the other sandwich and found an apple and gobbled that up too, sucking the core till the last trace of flavor was drained from it. Then, like a dog, he ground the meat bones with his teeth, enjoying the salty, tangy marrow. He finished and stretched out full length on the ground and went to sleep. . . .

. . . His body was washed by cold water that gradually turned warm and he was buoyed upon a stream and swept out to sea where waves rolled gently and suddenly he found himself walking upon the water how strange and delightful to walk upon the water and he came upon a nude woman holding a nude baby in her arms and the woman was sinking into the water holding the baby above her head and screaming *help* and he ran over the water to the woman and he reached her just before she went down and he took the baby from her hands and stood watching the breaking bubbles where the woman sank and he called *lady* and still no answer yes dive down there and rescue that woman but he could not take this baby with him and he stooped and laid the baby tenderly upon the surface of the water expecting it to sink but it floated and he leaped into the water and held his breath and strained his eyes to see through the gloomy volume of water but there was no woman and he opened his mouth and called *lady* and the water bubbled and his chest ached and his arms were tired but he could not see the woman and he called again *lady lady* and his feet touched sand at the bottom of the sea and his chest felt as though it would burst and he bent his knees and propelled himself upward and water rushed past him and his head bobbed out and he breathed deeply and looked around where was the baby the baby was gone and he rushed over the water looking for the baby calling *where is it* and the empty sky and sea threw back his voice *where is it* and he began to doubt that he could stand upon the water and then he was sinking and as he struggled the water rushed him downward spinning dizzily and he opened his mouth to call for help and water surged into his lungs and he choked . . .

He groaned and leaped erect in the dark, his eyes wide. The images of terror that thronged his brain would not let him sleep. He rose, made sure that the tools were hitched to his belt, and groped his way to the coal pile and found the rectangular gap from which he had taken the bricks. He took out the crowbar and hacked. Then dread paralyzed him. How long had he slept? Was it day or night now? He had to be careful. Someone might hear him if it were day. He hewed softly for hours at the cement, working silently. Faintly quivering in the air above him was the dim sound of yelling voices. Crazy people, he muttered. They're still there in that movie . . .

Having rested, he found the digging much easier. He soon had a dozen bricks out. His spirits rose. He took out another brick and his fingers fluttered in space. Good! What lay ahead of him? Another basement? He made the hole larger, climbed through, walked over an uneven floor and felt a metal surface. He lighted a match and saw that he was standing behind a furnace in a basement; before him, on the far side of the room, was a door. He crossed and opened it; it was full of odds and ends. Daylight spilled from a window above his head.

Then he was aware of a soft, continuous tapping. What was it? A clock? No, it was louder than a clock and more irregular. He placed an old empty box beneath the window, stood upon it, and looked into an areaway. He eased the window up and crawled through; the sound of the tapping came clearly now. He glanced about; he was alone. Then he looked upward at a series of window ledges. The tapping identified itself. That's a typewriter, he said to himself. It seemed to be coming from just above. He grasped the ridges of a rain pipe and lifted himself upward; through a half-inch opening of window he saw a doorknob about three feet away. No, it was not a doorknob; it was a small circular disk made of stainless steel with many fine markings upon it. He held his breath; an eerie white hand, seemingly detached from its arm, touched the metal knob and whirled it, first to the left, then to the right. It's a safe! . . . Suddenly he could see the dial no more; a huge metal door swung slowly toward him and he was looking into a safe filled with green wads of paper money, rows of coins wrapped in brown paper, and glass jars and boxes of various sizes. His heart quickened. Good Lord! The white hand went in and out of the safe, taking wads of bills and cylinders of coins. The hand vanished and he heard the muffled click of the big door as it closed.

Only the steel dial was visible now. The typewriter still tapped in his ears, but he could not see it. He blinked, wondering if what he had seen was real. There was more money in that safe than he had seen in all his life.

As he clung to the rain pipe, a daring idea came to him and he pulled the screwdriver from his belt. If the white hand twirled that dial again, he would be able to see how far to left and right it spun and he would have the combination! His blood tingled. I can scratch the numbers right here, he thought. Holding the pipe with one hand, he made the sharp edge of the screwdriver bite into the brick wall. Yes, he could do it. Now, he was set. Now, he had a reason for staying here in the underground. He waited for a long time, but the white hand did not return. Goddamn! Had he been more alert, he could have counted the twirls and he would have had the combination. He got down and stood in the areaway, sunk in reflection.

How could he get into that room? He climbed back into the basement and saw wooden steps leading upward. Was that the room where the safe stood? Fearing that the dial was now being twirled, he clambered through the window, hoisted himself up the rain pipe, and peered; he saw only the naked gleam of the steel dial. He got down and doubled his fists. Well, he would explore the basement. He returned to the basement room and mounted the steps to the door and squinted through the keyhole; all was dark, but the tapping was still somewhere near, still faint and directionless. He pushed the door in; along one wall of a room was a table piled with radios and electrical equipment. A radio shop, he muttered.

Well, he could rig up a radio in his cave. He found a sack, slid the radio into it, and slung it across his back. Closing the door, he went down the steps and stood again in the basement, disappointed. He had not solved the problem of the steel dial and he was irked. He set the radio on the floor and again hoisted himself through the window and up the rain pipe and squinted; the metal door was swinging shut. Goddamn! He's worked the combination again. If I had been patient, I'd have had it! How could he get into that room? He *had* to get into it. He could jimmy the window, but it would be much better if he could get in without any traces. To the right of him, he calculated, should be the basement of the building that held the safe; therefore, if he dug a hole right *here,* he ought to reach his goal.

He began a quiet scraping; it was hard work, for the bricks were not damp. He eventually got one out and lowered it softly to the floor. He had to be careful; perhaps people were beyond this wall. He extracted a second layer of brick and found still another. He gritted his teeth, ready to quit. I'll dig one more, he resolved. When the next brick came out he felt air blowing into his face. He waited to be challenged, but nothing happened.

He enlarged the hole and pulled himself through and stood in quiet darkness. He scratched a match to flame and saw steps; he mounted and peered through a keyhole: Darkness . . . He strained to hear the typewriter, but there was only silence. Maybe the office had closed? He twisted the knob and swung the door in; a frigid blast made him shiver. In the shadows before him were halves and quarters of hogs and lambs and steers hanging from metal hooks on the low ceiling, red meat encased in folds of cold white fat. Fronting him was frost-coated glass from behind which came indistinguishable sounds. The odor of fresh raw meat sickened him and he backed away. A meat market, he whispered.

He ducked his head, suddenly blinded by light. He narrowed his eyes; the red-white rows of meat were drenched in yellow glare. A man wearing a crimson spotted jacket came in and took down a bloody meat cleaver. He eased the door to, holding it ajar just enough to watch the man, hoping that the darkness in which he stood would keep him from being seen. The man took down a hunk of steer and placed it upon a bloody wooden block and bent forward and whacked with the cleaver. The man's face was hard, square, grim; a jet of mustache smudged his upper lip and a glistening cowlick of hair fell over his left eye. Each time he lifted the cleaver and brought it down upon the meat, he let out a short, deep-chested grunt. After he had cut the meat, he wiped blood off the wooden block with a sticky wad of gunny sack and hung the cleaver upon a hook. His face was proud as he placed the chunk of meat in the crook of his elbow and left.

The door slammed and the light went off; once more he stood in shadow. His tension ebbed. From behind the frosted glass he heard the man's voice: "Forty-eight cents a pound, ma'am." He shuddered, feeling that there was something he had to do. But what? He stared fixedly at the cleaver, then he sneezed and was terrified for fear that the man had heard him. But the door did not open. He took down the cleaver and examined the sharp edge smeared with cold blood. Behind the ice-coated glass a cash register rang with a vibrating, musical tinkle.

Absent-mindedly holding the meat cleaver, he rubbed the glass with his thumb and cleared a spot that enabled him to see into the front of the store. The shop was empty, save for the man who was now putting on his hat and coat. Beyond the front window a wan sun shone in the streets; people passed and now and then a fragment of laughter or the whir of a speeding auto came to him. He peered closer and saw on the right counter of the shop a mosquito netting covering pears, grapes, lemons, oranges, bananas, peaches, and plums. His stomach contracted.

The man clicked out the light and he gritted his teeth, muttering, Don't lock the icebox door . . . The man went through the door of the shop and locked it from the outside. Thank God! Now, he would eat some more! He waited, trembling. The sun died and its rays lingered on in the sky, turning the streets to dusk. He opened the door and stepped inside the shop. In reverse letters across the front window was: NICK'S FRUITS AND MEATS. He laughed, picked up a soft ripe yellow pear and bit into it; juice squirted; his mouth ached as his saliva glands reacted to the acid of the fruit. He ate three pears, gobbled six bananas, and made away with several oranges, taking a bite out of their tops and holding them to his lips and squeezing them as he hungrily sucked the juice.

He found a faucet, turned it on, laid the cleaver aside, pursed his lips under the stream until his stomach felt about to burst. He straightened and belched, feeling satisfied for the first time since he had been underground. He sat upon the floor, rolled and lit a cigarette, his bloodshot eyes squinting against the film of drifting smoke. He watched a patch of sky turn red, then purple; night fell and he lit another cigarette, brooding. Some part of him was trying to remember the world he had left, and another part of him did not want to remember it. Sprawling before him in his mind was his wife, Mrs. Wooten for whom he worked, the three policemen who had picked him up . . . He possessed them now more completely than he had ever possessed them when he had lived aboveground. How this had come about he could not say, but he had no desire to go back to them. He laughed, crushed the cigarette, and stood up.

He went to the front door and gazed out. Emotionally he hovered between the world aboveground and the world underground. He longed to go out, but sober judgment urged him to remain here. Then impulsively he pried the lock loose with one swift twist of the crowbar; the door swung outward. Through the twilight he saw a white man and a white woman coming toward him. He held himself tense, waiting for them to pass; but they came directly to the door and confronted him.

"I want to buy a pound of grapes," the woman said.

Terrified, he stepped back into the store. The white man stood to one side and the woman entered.

"Give me a pound of dark ones," the woman said.

The white man came slowly forward, blinking his eyes.

"Where's Nick?" the man asked.

"Were you just closing?" the woman asked.

"Yes, ma'am," he mumbled. For a second he did not breathe, then he mumbled again: "Yes, ma'am."

"I'm sorry," the woman said.

The street lamps came on, lighting the store somewhat. Ought he run? But that would raise an alarm. He moved slowly, dreamily, to a counter and lifted up a bunch of grapes and showed them to the woman.

"Fine," the woman said. "But isn't that more than a pound?"

He did not answer. The man was staring at him intently.

"Put them in a bag for me," the woman said, fumbling with her purse.

"Yes, ma'am."

He saw a pile of paper bags under a narrow ledge; he opened one and put the grapes in.

"Thanks," the woman said, taking the bag and placing a dime in his dark palm.

"Where's Nick?" the man asked again. "At supper?"

"Sir? Yes, sir," he breathed.

They left the store and he stood trembling in the doorway. When they were out of sight, he burst out laughing and crying. A trolley car rolled noisily past and he controlled himself quickly. He flung the dime to the pavement with a gesture of contempt and stepped into the warm night air. A few shy stars trembled above him. The look of things was beautiful, yet he felt a lurking threat. He went to an unattended newsstand and looked at a stack of papers. He saw a headline: HUNT NEGRO FOR MURDER.

He felt that someone had slipped up on him from behind and was stripping off his clothes; he looked about wildly, went quickly back into the store, picked up the meat cleaver where he had left it near the sink, then made his way through the icebox to the basement. He stood for a long time, breathing heavily. They know I didn't do anything, he muttered. But how could he prove it? He had signed a confession. Though innocent, he felt guilty, condemned. He struck a match and held it near the steel blade, fascinated and repelled by the dried blotches of blood. Then his fingers gripped the handle of the cleaver with all the strength of his body, he wanted to fling the cleaver from him, but he could not. The match flame wavered and fled; he struggled through the hole and put the cleaver in the sack with the radio. He was determined to keep it, for what purpose he did not know.

He was about to leave when he remembered the safe. Where was it? He wanted to give up, but felt that he ought to make one more try. Opposite the last hole he had dug, he tunneled again, plying the crowbar. Once he was so exhausted that he lay on the concrete floor and panted. Finally he made another hole. He wriggled through and his nostrils filled with the fresh smell of coal. He struck a match; yes, the usual steps led upward. He tiptoed to a door and eased it open. A fair-haired white girl stood in front of a steel cabinet, her blue eyes wide upon him. She turned chalky and gave a high-pitched scream. He bounded down the steps and raced to his hole and clambered through, replacing the bricks with nervous haste. He paused, hearing loud voices.

"What's the matter, Alice?"

"A man . . ."

"What man? Where?"

"A man was at that door . . ."

"Oh, nonsense!"

"He was looking at me through the door!"

"Aw, you're dreaming."

"I *did* see a man!"

The girl was crying now.

"There's nobody here."

Another man's voice sounded.

"What is it, Bob?"

"Alice says she saw a man in here, in that door!"

"Let's take a look."

He waited, poised for flight. Footsteps descended the stairs.

"There's nobody down here."

"The window's locked."

"And there's no door."

"You ought to fire that dame."

"Oh, I don't know. Women are that way."

"She's too hysterical."

The men laughed. Footsteps sounded again on the stairs. A door slammed. He sighed, relieved that he had escaped. But he had not done what he had set out to do; his glimpse of the room had been too brief to determine if the safe was there. He had to know. Boldly he groped through the hole once more; he reached the steps and pulled off his shoes and tip-toed up and peered through the keyhole. His head accidentally touched the door and it swung silently in a fraction of an inch; he saw the girl bent over the cabinet, her back to him. Beyond her was the safe. He crept back down the steps, thinking exultingly: I found it!

Now he had to get the combination. Even if the window in the areaway was locked and bolted, he could gain entrance when the office closed. He scoured through the holes he had dug and stood again in the basement where he had left the radio and the cleaver. Again he crawled out of the window and lifted himself up the rain pipe and peered. The steel dial showed lonely and bright, reflecting the yellow glow of an unseen light. Resigned to a long wait, he sat and leaned against the wall. From far off came the faint sounds of life aboveground; once he looked with a baffled expression at the dark sky. Frequently he rose and climbed the pipe to see the white hand spin the dial, but nothing happened. He bit his lip with impatience. It was not the money that was luring him, but the mere fact that he could get it with impunity. Was the hand now twirling the dial? He rose and looked, but the white hand was not in sight.

Perhaps it would be better to watch continuously? Yes; he clung to the pipe and watched the dial until his eyes thickened with tears. Exhausted, he stood again in the areaway. He heard a door being shut and he clawed up the pipe and looked. He jerked tense as a vague figure passed in front of him. He stared unblinkingly, hugging the pipe with one hand and holding the screwdriver with the other, ready to etch the combination upon the wall. His ears caught: *Dong . . . Dong . . . Dong . . .Dong . . . Dong . . . Dong . . . Dong . . .* Seven o'clock, he whispered. Maybe they were closing now? What kind of a store would be open as late as this? he wondered. Did anyone live in the rear? Was there a night watchman? Perhaps the safe was *already* locked for the night! Goddamn! While he had been eating in that shop, they had locked up everything . . . Then, just as he was about to give up, the white hand touched the dial and turned it once to the right and stopped at six. With quivering fingers, he etched 1–R–6 upon the brick wall with the tip of the screwdriver. The hand twirled the dial twice to the left and stopped at two, and he engraved 2–L–2 upon the wall. The dial was spun four times to the right and stopped at six again; he wrote 4–R–6. The dial rotated three times to the left and was centered straight up and down; he wrote 3–L–0. The door swung open and again he saw the piles of green money and the rows of wrapped coins. I got it, he said grimly.

Then he was stone still, astonished. There were two hands now. A right hand lifted a wad of green bills and deftly slipped it up the sleeve of a left arm. The hands trembled; again the right hand slipped a packet of bills up the left sleeve. He's stealing, he said to himself. He grew indignant, as if the money belonged to him. Though *he* had planned to steal the money, he despised and pitied the man. He felt that his stealing the money and the man's stealing were two entirely different things. He wanted to steal the money merely for the sensation involved in getting it, and he had no intention whatever of spending a penny of it; but he knew that the man who was now stealing it was going to spend it, perhaps for pleasure. The huge steel door closed with a soft click.

Though angry, he was somewhat satisfied. The office would close soon. I'll clean the place out, he mused. He imagined the entire office staff cringing with fear; the police would question everyone for a crime they had not committed, just as they had questioned him. And they would have no idea of how the money had been stolen until they discovered the holes he had tunneled in the walls of the basements. He lowered himself and laughed mischievously, with the abandoned glee of an adolescent.

He flattened himself against the wall as the window above him closed with rasping sound. He looked; somebody was bolting the window securely with a metal screen. That won't help you, he snickered to himself. He clung to the rain pipe until the yellow light in the office went out. He went back into the basement, picked up the sack containing the radio and cleaver, and crawled through the two holes he had dug and groped his way into the basement of the building that held the safe. He moved in slow motion, breathing softly. Be careful now, he told himself. There might be a night watchman . . . In his memory was the combination written in bold white characters as upon a blackboard. Eel-like he squeezed through the last hole and crept up the steps and put his hand on the knob and pushed the door in about three inches. Then his courage ebbed; his imagination wove dangers for him.

Perhaps the night watchman was waiting in there, ready to shoot. He dangled his cap on a forefinger and poked it past the jamb of the door. If anyone fired, they would hit his cap; but nothing happened. He widened the door, holding the crowbar high above his head, ready to beat off an assailant. He stood like that for five minutes; the rumble of a streetcar brought him to himself. He entered the room. Moonlight floated in from a side window. He confronted the safe, then checked himself. Better take a look around first . . . He stepped about and found a closed door. Was the night watchman in there? He opened it and saw a washbowl, a faucet, and a commode. To the left was still another door that opened into a huge dark room that seemed empty; on the far side of that room he made out the shadow of still another door. Nobody's here, he told himself.

He turned back to the safe and fingered the dial; it spun with ease. He laughed and twirled it just for fun. Get to work, he told himself. He turned the dial to the figures he saw on the blackboard of his memory; it was so easy that he felt that the safe had not been locked at all. The heavy door eased loose and he caught hold of the handle and pulled hard, but the door swung open with a slow momentum of its own. Breathless, he gaped at wads of green bills, rows of wrapped coins, curious glass jars full of white pellets, and many oblong green metal boxes. He glanced guiltily over his shoulder; it seemed impossible that someone should not call to him to stop.

They'll be surprised in the morning, he thought. He opened the top of the sack and lifted a wad of compactly tied bills; the money was crisp and new. He admired the smooth, cleancut edges. The fellows in Washington sure know how to make this stuff, he mused. He rubbed the money with his fingers, as though expecting it to reveal hidden qualities. He lifted the wad to his nose and smelled the fresh odor of ink. Just like any other paper, he mumbled. He dropped the wad into the sack and picked up another. Holding the bag, he thought and laughed.

There was in him no sense of possessiveness; he was intrigued with the form and color of the money, with the manifold reactions which he knew that men aboveground held toward it. The sack was one-third full when it occurred to him to examine the denominations of the bills; without realizing it, he had put many wads of one-dollar bills into the sack. Aw, nuts, he said in disgust. Take the big ones . . . He dumped the one-dollar bills onto the floor and swept all the hundred-dollar bills he could find into the sack, then he raked in rolls of coins with crooked fingers.

He walked to a desk upon which sat a typewriter, the same machine which the blond girl had used. He was fascinated by it; never in his life had he used one of them. It was a queer instrument of business, something beyond the rim of his life. Whenever he had been in an office where a girl was typing, he had almost always spoken in whispers. Remembering vaguely what he had seen others do, he inserted a sheet of paper into the machine; it went in lopsided and he did not know how to straighten it. Spelling in a soft diffident voice, he pecked out his name on the keys: *freddaniels.* He looked at it and laughed. He would learn to type correctly one of these days.

Yes, he would take the typewriter too. He lifted the machine and placed it atop the bulk of money in the sack. He did not feel that he was stealing, for the cleaver, the radio, the money, and the typewriter were all on the same level of value, all meant the same thing to him. They were the serious toys of the men who lived in the dead world of sunshine and rain he had left, the world that had condemned him, branded him guilty.

But what kind of a place is this? He wondered. What was in that dark room to his rear? He felt for his matches and found that he had only one left. He leaned the sack against the safe and groped forward into the room, encountering smooth, metallic objects that felt like machines. Baffled, he touched a wall and tried vainly to locate an electric switch. Well, he *had* to strike his last match. He knelt and struck it, cupping the flame near the floor with his palms. The place seemed to be a factory, with benches and tables. There were bulbs with green shades spaced about the tables; he turned on a light and twisted it low so that the glare was limited. He saw a half-filled packet of cigarettes and appropriated it. There were stools at the benches and he concluded that men worked here at some trade. He wandered and found a few half-used folders of matches. If only he could find more cigarettes! But there were none.

But what kind of a place was this? On a bench he saw a pad of paper captioned: PEER'S – MANUFACTURING JEWELERS. His lips formed an "O," then he snapped off the light and ran back to the safe and lifted one of the glass jars and stared at the tiny white pellets. Gingerly he picked up one and found that it was wrapped in tissue paper. He peeled the paper and saw a glittering stone that looked like glass, glinting white and blue sparks. Diamonds, he breathed.

Roughly he tore the paper from the pellets and soon his palm quivered with precious fire. Trembling, he took all four glass jars from the safe and put them into the sack. He grabbed one of the metal boxes, shook it, and heard a tinny rattle. He pried off the lid with the screwdriver. Rings! Hundreds of them . . . Were they worth anything? He scooped up a handful and jets of fire shot fitfully from the stones. These are diamonds too, he said. He pried open another box. Watches! A chorus of soft, metallic ticking filled his ears. For a moment he could not move, then he dumped all the boxes into the sack.

He shut the safe door, then stood looking around, anxious not to overlook anything. Oh! He had seen a door in the room where the machines were. What was in there? More valuables? He re-entered the room, crossed the floor, and stood undecided before the door. He finally caught hold of the knob and pushed the door in; the room beyond was dark. He advanced cautiously inside and ran his fingers along the wall for the usual switch, then he was stark still. *Something had moved in the room!* What was it? Ought he to creep out, taking the rings and diamonds and money? Why risk what he already had? He waited and the ensuing silence gave him confidence to explore further. Dare he strike a match? Would not a match flame make him a good target? He tensed again as he heard a faint sigh; he was now convinced that there was something alive near him, something that lived and breathed. On tiptoe he felt slowly along the wall, hoping that he would not collide with anything. Luck was with him; he found the light switch.

No; don't turn the light on . . . Then suddenly he realized that he did not know in what direction the door was. Goddamn! He had to turn the light on or strike a match. He fingered the switch for a long time, then thought of an idea. He knelt upon the floor, reached his arm up to the switch and flicked the button, hoping that if anyone shot, the bullet would go above his head. The moment the light came on he narrowed his eyes to see quickly. He sucked in his breath and his body gave a violent twitch and was still. In front of him, so close that it made him want to bound up and scream, was a human face.

He was afraid to move lest he touch the man. If the man had opened his eyes at that moment, there was no telling what he might have done. The man – long and rawboned – was stretched out on his back upon a little cot, sleeping in his clothes, his head cushioned by a dirty pillow; his face, clouded by a dark stubble of beard, looked straight up to the ceiling. The man sighed, and he grew tense to defend himself; the man mumbled and turned his face away from the light. I've got to turn off that light, he thought. Just as he was about to rise, he saw a gun and cartridge belt on the floor at the man's side. Yes, he would take the gun and cartridge belt, not to use them, but just to keep them, as one takes a memento from a country fair. He picked them up and was about to click off the light when his eyes fell upon a photograph perched upon a chair near the man's head; it was the picture of a woman, smiling, shown against a background of open fields; at the woman's side were two young children, a boy and a girl. He smiled indulgently; he could send a bullet into that man's brain and time would be over for him . . .

He clicked off the light and crept silently back into the room where the safe stood; he fastened the cartridge belt about him and adjusted the holster at his right hip. He strutted about the room on tiptoe, lolling his head nonchalantly, then paused, abruptly pulled the gun, and pointed it with grim face toward an imaginary foe. "Boom!" he whispered fiercely. Then he bent forward with silent laughter. That's just like they do it in the movies, he said.

He contemplated his loot for a long time, then got a towel from the washroom and tied the sack securely. When he looked up he was momentarily frightened by his shadow looming on the wall before him. He lifted the sack, dragged it down the basement steps, lugged it across the basement, gasping for breath. After he had struggled through the hole, he clumsily replaced the bricks, then tussled with the sack until he got it to the cave. He stood in the dark, wet with sweat, brooding about the diamonds, the rings, the watches, the money; he remembered the singing in the church, the people yelling in the movie, the dead baby, the nude man stretched out upon the white table . . . He saw these items hovering before his eyes and felt that some dim meaning linked them together, that some magical relationship made them kin. He stared with vacant eyes, convinced that all of these images, with their tongueless reality, were striving to tell him something . . .

Later, seeing with his fingers, he untied the sack and set each item neatly upon the dirt floor. Exploring, he took the bulb, the socket, and the wire out of the tool chest; he was elated to find a double socket at one end of the wire. He crammed the stuff into his pockets and hoisted himself upon the rusty pipes and squinted into the church; it was dim and empty. Somewhere in this wall were live electric wires; but where? He lowered himself, groped and tapped the wall with the butt of the screwdriver; listening vainly for hollow sounds. I'll just take a chance and dig, he said.

For an hour he tried to dislodge a brick, and when he struck a match, he found that he had dug a depth of only an inch! No use in digging here, he sighed. By the flickering light of a match, he looked upward, then lowered his eyes, only to glance up again, startled. Directly above his head, beyond the pipes, was a wealth of electric wiring. I'll be damned, he snickered.

He got an old dull knife from the chest and, seeing again with his fingers, separated the two strands of wire and cut away the insulation. Twice he received a slight shock. He scraped the wiring clean and managed to join the two twin ends, then screwed in the bulb. The sudden illumination blinded him and he shut his lids to kill the pain in his eyeballs. I've got that much done, he thought jubilantly.

He placed the bulb on the dirt floor and the light cast a blatant glare on the bleak clay walls. Next he plugged one end of the wire that dangled from the radio into the light socket and bent down and switched on the button; almost at once there was the harsh sound of static, but no words or music. Why won't it work? he wondered. Had he damaged the mechanism in any way? Maybe it needed grounding? Yes . . . He rummaged in the tool chest and found another length of wire, fastened it to the ground of the radio, and then tied the opposite end to a pipe. Rising and growing distinct, a slow strain of music entranced him with its measured sound. He sat upon the chest, deliriously happy.

Later he searched again in the chest and found a half-gallon can of glue; he opened it and smelled a sharp odor. Then he recalled that he had not even looked at the money. He took a wad of green bills and weighed it in his palm, then broke the seal and held one of the bills up to the light and studied it closely. *The United States of America will pay to the bearer on demand one hundred dollars,* he read in slow speech; then: *This note is legal tender for all debts, public and private. . . .* He broke into a musing laugh, feeling that he was reading of the doings of people who lived on some far-off planet. He turned the bill over and saw on the other side of it a delicately beautiful building gleaming with paint and set amidst green grass. He had no desire whatever to count the money; it was what it stood for — the various currents of life swirling aboveground — that captivated him. Next he opened the rolls of coins and let them slide from their paper wrappings to the ground; the bright, new gleaming pennies and nickles and dimes piled high at his feet, a glowing mound of shimmering copper and silver. He sifted them through his fingers, listening to their tinkle as they struck the conical heap.

Oh, yes! He had forgotten. He would now write his name on the typewriter.

He inserted a piece of paper and poised his fingers to write. But what was his name? He stared, trying to remember. He stood and glared about the dirt cave, his name on the tip of his lips. But it would not come to him. Why was he here? Yes, he had been running away from the police. But why? His mind was blank. He bit his lips and sat again, feeling a vague terror. But why worry? He laughed, then pecked slowly: *itwasalonghotday*. He was determined to type the sentence without making any mistakes. How did one make capital letters? He experimented and luckily discovered how to lock the machine for capital letters and then shift it back to lower case. Next he discovered how to make spaces, then he wrote neatly and correctly: *It was a long hot day*. Just why he selected that sentence he did not know; it was merely the ritual of performing the thing that appealed to him. He took the sheet out of the machine and looked around with stiff neck and hard eyes and spoke to an imaginary person:

"Yes, I'll have the contracts ready tomorrow."

He laughed. That's just the way they talk, he said. He grew weary of the game and pushed the machine aside. His eyes fell upon the can of glue, and a mischievous idea bloomed in him, filling him with nervous eagerness. He leaped up and opened the can of glue, then broke the seals on all the wads of money. I'm going to have some wallpaper, he said with a luxurious, physical laugh that made him bend at the knees. He took the towel with which he had tied the sack and balled it into a swab and dipped it into the can of glue and dabbed glue onto the wall; then he pasted one green bill by the side of another. He stepped back and cocked his head. Jesus! That's funny . . . He slapped his thighs and guffawed. He had triumphed over the world aboveground! He was free! If only people could see this! He wanted to run from this cave and yell his discovery to the world.

He swabbed all the dirt walls of the cave and pasted them with green bills; when he had finished the walls blazed with a yellow-green fire. Yes, this room would be his hide-out; between him and the world that had branded him guilty would stand this mocking symbol. He had not stolen the money; he had simply picked it up, just as a man would pick up firewood in a forest. And that was how the world aboveground now seemed to him, a wild forest filled with death.

The walls of money finally palled on him and he looked about for new interests to feed his emotions. The cleaver! He drove a nail into the wall and hung the bloody cleaver upon it. Still another idea welled up. He pried open the metal boxes and lined them side by side on the dirt floor. He grinned at the gold and fire. From one box he lifted up a fistful of ticking gold watches and dangled them by their gleaming chains. He stared with an idle smile, then began to wind them up; he did not attempt to set them at any given hour, for there was no time for him now. He took a fistful of nails and drove them into the papered walls and hung the watches upon them, letting them swing down by their glittering chains, trembling and ticking busily against the backdrop of green with the lemon sheen of the electric light shining upon the metal watch casings, converting the golden disks into blobs of liquid yellow. Hardly had he hung up the last watch than the idea extended itself; he took more nails from the chest and drove them into the green paper and took the boxes of rings and went from nail to nail and hung up the golden bands. The blue and white sparks from the stones filled the cave with brittle laughter, as though enjoying his hilarious secret. People certainly can do some funny things, he said to himself.

He sat upon the tool chest, alternately laughing and shaking his head soberly. Hours later he became conscious of the gun sagging at his hip and he pulled it from the holster. He had seen men fire guns in movies, but somehow his life had never led him into contact with firearms. A desire to feel the sensation others felt in firing came over him. But someone might hear . . . Well, what if they did? They would not know where the shot had come from. Not in their wildest notions would they think that it had come from under the streets! He tightened his fingers on the trigger; there was a deafening report and it seemed that the entire underground had caved in upon his eardrums; and in the same instant there flashed an orange-blue spurt of flame that died quickly but lingered on as a vivid after-image. He smelled the acrid stench of burnt powder filling his lungs and he dropped the gun abruptly.

The intensity of his feelings died and he hung the gun and cartridge belt upon the wall. Next he lifted the jars of diamonds and turned them bottom upward, dumping the white pellets upon the ground. One by one he picked them up and peeled the tissue paper from them and piled them in a neat heap. He wiped his sweaty hands on his trousers, lit a cigarette, and commenced playing another game. He imagined that he was a rich man who lived aboveground in the obscene sunshine and he was strolling through a park of a summer morning, smiling, nodding to his neighbors, sucking an after-breakfast cigar. Many times he crossed the floor of the cave, avoiding the diamonds with his feet, yet subtly gauging his footsteps so that his shoes, wet with sewer slime, would strike the diamonds at some undetermined moment. After twenty minutes of sauntering, his right foot smashed into the heap and diamonds lay scattered in all directions, glinting with a million tiny chuckles of icy laughter. Oh, shucks, he mumbled in mock regret, intrigued by the damage he had wrought. He continued walking, ignoring the brittle fire. He felt that he had a glorious victory locked in his heart.

He stooped and flung the diamonds more evenly over the floor and they showered rich sparks, collaborating with him. He went over the floor and trampled the stones just deeply enough for them to be faintly visible, as though they were set deliberately in the prongs of a thousand rings. A ghostly light bathed the cave. He sat on the chest and frowned. Maybe *any*thing's right, he mumbled. Yes, if the world as men had made it was right, then anything else was right, any act a man took to satisy himself, murder, theft, torture.

He straightened with a start. What was happening to him? He was drawn to these crazy thoughts, yet they made him feel vaguely guilty. He would stretch out upon the ground, then get up; he would want to crawl again through the holes he had dug, but would restrain himself; he would think of going again up into the streets, but fear would hold him still. He stood in the middle of the cave, surrounded by green walls and a laughing floor, trembling. He was going to do something, but what? Yes, he was afraid of himself, afraid of doing some nameless thing.

To control himself, he turned on the radio. A melancholy piece of music rose. Brooding over the diamonds on the floor was like looking up into a sky full of restless stars; then the illusion turned into its opposite: he was high up in the air looking down at the twinkling lights of a sprawling city. The music ended and a man recited news events. In the same attitude in which he had contemplated the city, so now, as he heard the cultivated tone, he looked down upon land and sea as men fought, as cities were razed, as planes scattered death upon open towns, as long lines of trenches wavered and broke. He heard the names of generals and the names of mountains and the names of countries and the names and numbers of divisions that were in action on different battle fronts. He saw black smoke billowing from the stacks of warships as they neared each other over wastes of water and he heard their huge thunder as red-hot shells screamed across the surface of night seas. He saw hundreds of planes wheeling and droning in the sky and heard the clatter of machine guns as they fought each other and he saw planes falling in plumes of smoke and blaze of fire. He saw steel tanks rumbling across fields of ripe wheat to meet other tanks and there was a loud clang of steel as numberless tanks collided. He saw troops with fixed bayonets charging in waves against other troops who held fixed bayonets and men groaned as steel ripped into their bodies and they went down to die . . . The voice of the radio faded and he was staring at the diamonds on the floor at his feet.

He shut off the radio, fighting an irrational compulsion to act. He walked aimlessly about the cave, touching the walls with his finger tips. Suddenly he stood still. *What was the matter with him?* Yes, he knew . . . It was these walls; these crazy walls were filling him with a wild urge to climb out into the dark sunshine aboveground. Quickly he doused the light to banish the shouting walls, then sat again upon the tool chest. Yes, he was trapped. His muscles were flexed taut and sweat ran down his face. He knew now that he could not stay here and he could not go out. He lit a cigarette with shaking fingers; the match flame revealed the green-papered walls with militant distinctness; the purple on the gun barrel glinted like a threat; the meat cleaver brooded with its eloquent splotches of blood; the mound of silver and copper smoldered angrily; the diamonds winked at him from the floor; and the gold watches ticked and trembled, crowning time the king of consciousness, defining the limits of living . . . The match blaze died and he bolted from where he stood and collided brutally with the nails upon the walls. The spell was broken. He shuddered, feeling that, in spite of his fear, sooner or later he would go up into that dead sunshine and somehow say something to somebody about all this.

He sat again upon the tool chest. Fatigue weighed upon his forehead and eyes. Minutes passed and he relaxed. He dozed, but his imagination was alert. He saw himself rising, wading again in the sweeping water of the sewer; he came to a manhole and climbed out and was amazed to discover that he had hoisted himself into a room filled with armed policemen who were watching him intently. He jumped awake in the dark; he had not moved. He sighed, closed his eyes, and slept again; this time his imagination designed a scheme of protection for him. His dreaming made him feel that he was standing in a room watching over his own nude body lying stiff and cold upon a white table. At the far end of the room he saw a crowd of people huddled in a corner, afraid of his body. Though lying dead upon the table he was standing in some mysterious way at his side, warding off the people, guarding his body, and laughing to himself as he observed the situation. They're scared of me, he thought.

He awakened with a start, leaped to his feet, and stood in the center of the black cave. It was a full minute before he moved again. He hovered between sleeping and waking, unprotected, a prey of wild fears. He could neither see nor hear. One part of him was asleep; his blood coursed slowly and his flesh was numb. On the other hand he was roused to a strange, high pitch of tension. He lifted his fingers to his face, as though about to weep. Gradually his hands lowered and he struck a match, looking about, expecting to see a door through which he could walk to safety; but there was no door, only the green walls and the moving floor. The match flame died and it was dark again.

Five minutes later he was still standing when the thought came to him that he had been asleep. Yes . . . But he was not yet fully awake; he was still queerly blind and deaf. How long had he slept? Where was he? Then suddenly he recalled the green-papered walls of the cave and in the same instant he heard loud singing coming from the church beyond the wall. Yes, they woke me up, he muttered. He hoisted himself and lay atop the bed of pipes and brought his face to the narrow slit. Men and women stood here and there between pews. A song ended and a young black girl tossed back her head and closed her eyes and broke plaintively into another hymn:

Glad, glad, glad, oh, so glad
I got Jesus in my soul . . .

Those few words were all she sang, but what her words did not say, her emotions said as she repeated the lines, varying the mood and tempo, making her tone express meanings which her conscious mind did not know. Another woman melted her voice with the girl's, and then an old man's voice merged with that of the two women. Soon the entire congregation was singing:

Glad, glad, glad, oh, so glad
I got Jesus in my soul . . .

They're wrong, he whispered in the lyric darkness. He felt that their search for a happiness they could never find made them feel that they had committed some dreadful offense which they could not remember or understand. He was now in possession of the feeling that had gripped him when he had first come into the underground. It came to him in a series of questions: Why was this sense of guilt so seemingly innate, so easy to come by, to think, to feel, so verily physical? It seemed that when one felt this guilt one was retracing in one's feelings a faint pattern designed long before; it seemed that one was always trying to remember a gigantic shock that had left a haunting impression upon one's body which one could not forget or shake off, but which had been forgotten by the conscious mind, creating in one's life a state of eternal anxiety.

He had to tear himself away from this; he got down from the pipes. His nerves were so taut that he seemed to feel his brain pushing through his skull. He felt that he had to do something, but he could not figure out what it was. Yet he knew that if he stood here until he made up his mind, he would never move. He crawled through the hole he had made in the brick wall and the exertion afforded him respite from tension. When he entered the basement of the radio store, he stopped in fear, hearing loud voices.

"Come on, boy! Tell us what you did with the radio!"

"Mister, I didn't steal the radio! I swear!"

He heard a dull thumping sound and he imagined a boy being struck violently.

"Please, mister!"

"Did you take it to a pawn shop?"

"No, sir! I didn't steal the radio! I got a radio at home," the boy's voice pleaded hysterically. "Go to my home and look!"

There came to his ears the sound of another blow. It was so funny that he had to clap his hand over his mouth to keep from laughing out loud. They're beating some poor boy, he whispered to himself, shaking his head. He felt a sort of distant pity for the boy and wondered if he ought to bring back the radio and leave it in the basement. No. Perhaps it was a good thing that they were beating the boy; perhaps the beating would bring to the boy's attention, for the first time in his life, the secret of his existence, the guilt that he could never get rid of.

Smiling, he scampered over a coal pile and stood again in the basement of the building where he had stolen the money and jewelry. He lifted himself into the areaway, climbed the rain pipe, and squinted through a two-inch opening of window. The guilty familiarity of what he saw made his muscles tighten. Framed before him in a bright tableau of daylight was the night watchman sitting upon the edge of a chair, stripped to the waist, his head sagging forward, his eyes red and puffy. The watchman's face and shoulders were stippled with red and black welts. Back of the watchman stood the safe, the steel door wide open showing the empty vault. Yes, they think he did it, he mused.

Footsteps sounded in the room and a man in a blue suit passed in front of him, then another, then still another. Policemen, he breathed. Yes, they were trying to make the watchman confess, just as they had once made him confess to a crime he had not done. He stared into the room, trying to recall something. Oh . . . Those were the same policemen who had beaten him, had made him sign that paper when he had been too tired and sick to care. Now, they were doing the same thing to the watchman. His heart pounded as he saw one of the policemen shake a finger into the watchman's face.

"Why don't you admit it's an inside job, Thompson?" the policeman said.

"I've told you all I know," the watchman mumbled through swollen lips.

"But nobody was here but you!" the policeman shouted.

"I was sleeping," the watchman said. "It was wrong, but I was sleeping all that night!"

"Stop telling us that lie!"

"It's the truth!"

"When did you get the combination?"

"I don't know how to open the safe," the watchman said.

He clung to the rain pipe, tense; he wanted to laugh, but he controlled himself. He felt a great sense of power; yes, he could go back to the cave, rip the money off the walls, pick up the diamonds and rings, and bring them here and write a note, telling them where to look for their foolish toys. No . . . What good would that do? It was not worth the effort. The watchman was guilty; although he was not guilty of the crime of which he had been accused, he was guilty, had always been guilty. The only thing that worried him was that the man who had been really stealing was not being accused. But he consoled himself: they'll catch him sometime during his life.

He saw one of the policemen slap the watchman across the mouth.

"Come clean, you bastard!"

"I've told you all I know," the watchman mumbled like a child.

One of the police went to the rear of the watchman's chair and jerked it from under him; the watchman pitched forward upon his face.

"Get up!" a policeman said.

Trembling, the watchman pulled himself up and sat limply again in the chair.

"Now, are you going to talk?"

"I've told you all I know," the watchman gasped.

"Where did you hide the stuff?"

"I didn't take it!"

"Thompson, your brains are in your feet," one of the policemen said. "We're going to string you up and get them back into your skull."

He watched the policemen clamp handcuffs on the watchman's wrists and ankles; then they lifted the watchman and swung him upside-down and hoisted his feet to the edge of a door. The watchman hung, head down, his eyes bulging. They're crazy, he whispered to himself as he clung to the ridges of the pipe.

"You going to talk?" a policeman shouted into the watchman's ear.

He heard the watchman groan.

"We'll let you hang there till you talk, see?"

He saw the watchman close his eyes.

"Let's take 'im down. He passed out," a policeman said.

He grinned as he watched them take the body down and dump it carelessly upon the floor. The policeman took off the handcuffs.

"Let 'im come to. Let's get a smoke," a policeman said.

The three policemen left the scope of his vision. A door slammed. He had an impulse to yell to the watchman that he could escape through the hole in the basement and live with him in the cave. But he wouldn't understand, he told himself. After a moment he saw the watchman rise and stand, swaying from weakness. He stumbled across the room to a desk, opened a drawer, and took out a gun. He's going to kill himself, he thought, intent, eager, detached, yearning to see the end of the man's actions. As the watchman stared vaguely about he lifted the gun to his temple; he stood like that for some minutes, biting his lips until a line of blood etched its way down a corner of his chin. No, he oughtn't do that, he said to himself in a mood of pity.

"Don't!" he half whispered and half yelled.

The watchman looked wildly about; he had heard him. But it did not help; there was a loud report and the watchman's head jerked violently and he fell like a log and lay prone, the gun clattering over the floor.

The three policemen came running into the room with drawn guns. One of the policemen knelt and rolled the watchman's body over and stared at a ragged, scarlet hole in the temple.

"Our hunch was right," the kneeling policeman said. "He was guilty, all right."

"Well, this ends the case," another policeman said.

"He knew he was licked," the third one said with grim satisfaction.

He eased down the rain pipe, crawled back through the holes he had made, and went back into his cave. A fever burned in his bones. He had to act, yet he was afraid. His eyes stared in the darkness as though propped open by invisible hands, as though they had become lidless. His muscles were rigid and he stood for what seemed to him a thousand years.

When he moved again his actions were informed with precision, his muscular system reinforced from a reservoir of energy. He crawled through the hole of earth, dropped into the gray sewer current, and sloshed ahead. When his right foot went forward at a street intersection, he fell backward and shot down into water. In a spasm of terror his right hand grabbed the concrete ledge of a down-curve and he felt the streaking water tugging violently at his body. The current reached his neck and for a moment he was still. He knew if he moved clumsily he would be sucked under. He held onto the ledge with both hands and slowly pulled himself up. He sighed, standing once more in the sweeping water, thankful that he had missed death.

He waded on through sludge, moving with care, until he came to a web of light sifting down from a manhole cover. He saw steel hooks running up the side of the sewer wall; he caught hold and lifted himself and put his shoulder to the cover and moved it an inch. A crash of sound came to him as he looked into a hot glare of sunshine through which blurred shapes moved. Fear scalded him and he dropped back into the pallid current and stood paralyzed in the shadows. A heavy car rumbled past overhead, jarring the pavement, warning him to stay in his world of dark light, knocking the cover back into place with an imperious clang.

He did not know how much fear he felt, for fear claimed him completely; yet it was not a fear of the police or of people, but a cold dread at the thought of the actions he knew he would perform if he went out into that cruel sunshine. His mind said no; his body said yes; and his mind could not understand his feelings. A low whine broke from him and he was in the act of uncoiling. He climbed upward and heard the faint honking of auto horns. Like a frantic cat clutching a rag, he clung to the steel prongs and heaved his shoulder against the cover and pushed it off halfway. For a split second his eyes were drowned in the terror of yellow light and he was in a deeper darkness than he had ever known in the underground.

Partly out of the hole, he blinked, regaining enough sight to make out meaningful forms. An odd thing was happening: No one was rushing forward to challenge him. He had imagined the moment of his emergence as a desperate tussle with men who wanted to cart him off to be killed; instead, life froze about him as the traffic stopped. He pushed the cover aside, stood, swaying in a world so fragile that he expected it to collapse and drop him into some deep void. But nobody seemed to pay him heed. The cars were now swerving to shun him and the gaping hole.

"Why in hell don't you put up a red light, dummy?" a raucous voice yelled.

He understood; they thought that he was a sewer workman. He walked toward the sidewalk, weaving unsteadily through the moving traffic.

"Look where you're going, nigger!"

"That's right! Stay there and get killed!"

"You blind, you bastard?"

"Go home and sleep your drunk off!"

A policeman stood at the curb, looking in the opposite direction. When he passed the policeman, he feared that he would be grabbed, but nothing happened.

Where was he? Was this real? He wanted to look about to get his bearings, but felt that something awful would happen to him if he did. He wandered into a spacious doorway of a store that sold men's clothing and saw his reflection in a long mirror: his cheekbones protruded from a hairy black face; his greasy cap was perched askew upon his head and his eyes were red and glassy. His shirt and trousers were caked with mud and hung loosely. His hands were gummed with a black stickiness. He threw back his head and laughed so loudly that passers-by stopped and stared.

He ambled on down the sidewalk, not having the merest notion of where he was going. Yet, sleeping within him, was the drive to go somewhere and say something to somebody. Half an hour later his ears caught the sound of spirited singing.

The Lamb, the Lamb, the Lamb
I hear thy voice a-calling
The Lamb, the Lamb, the Lamb
I feel thy grace a-falling

A church! He exclaimed. He broke into a run and came to brick steps leading downward to a subbasement. This is it! The church into which he had peered. Yes, he was going in and tell them. What? He did not know; but, once face to face with them, he would think of what to say. Must be Sunday, he mused. He ran down the steps and jerked the door open; the church was crowded and a deluge of song swept over him.

The Lamb, the Lamb, the Lamb
Tell me again your story
The Lamb, the Lamb, the Lamb
Flood my soul with your glory

He stared at the singing faces with a trembling smile.

"Say!" he shouted.

Many turned to look at him, but the song rolled on. His arm was jerked violently.

"I'm sorry, Brother, but you can't do that in here," a man said.

"But, mister!"

"You can't act rowdy in God's house," the man said.

"He's filthy," another man said.

"But I want to tell 'em," he said loudly.

"He stinks," someone muttered.

The song had stopped, but at once another one began.

Oh, wondrous sight upon the cross
Vision sweet and divine
Oh, wondrous sight upon the cross
Full of such love sublime

He attempted to twist away, but other hands grabbed him and rushed him into the doorway.

"Let me alone!" he screamed, struggling.

"Get out!"

"He's drunk," somebody said. "He ought to be ashamed!"

"He acts crazy!"

He felt that he was failing and he grew frantic.

"But, mister, let me tell – "

"Get away from this door, or I'll call the police!"

He stared, his trembling smile fading in a sense of wonderment.

"The police," he repeated vacantly.

"Now, get!"

He was pushed toward the brick steps and the door banged shut. The waves of song came.

Oh, wondrous sight, wondrous sight
Lift my heavy heart above
Oh, wondrous sight, wondrous sight
Fill my weary soul with love

He was smiling again now. Yes, the police . . . That was it! Why had he not thought of it before? The idea had been deep down in him, and only now did it assume supreme importance. He looked up and saw a street sign: COURT STREET – HARTSDALE AVENUE. He turned and walked northward, his mind filled with the image of the police station. Yes, that was where they had beaten him, accused him, and had made him sign a confession of his guilt. He would go there and clear up everything, make a statement. What statement? He did not know. He was the statement, and since it was all so clear to him, surely he would be able to make it clear to others.

He came to the corner of Hartsdale Avenue and turned westward. Yeah, there's the station . . . A policeman came down the steps and walked past him without a glance. He mounted the stone steps and went through the door, paused; he was in a hallway where several policemen were standing, talking, smoking. One turned to him.

"What do you want, boy?"

He looked at the policeman and laughed.

"What in hell are you laughing about?" the policeman asked.

He stopped laughing and stared. His whole being was full of what he wanted to say to them, but he could not say it.

"Are you looking for the Desk Sergeant?"

"Yes, sir," he said quickly; then: "Oh, no, sir."

"Well, make up your mind, now."

Four policemen grouped themselves around him.

"I'm looking for the men," he said.

"What men?"

Peculiarly, at that moment he could not remember the names of the policemen; he recalled their beating him, the confession he had signed, and how he had run away from them. He saw the cave next to the church, the money on the walls, the guns, the rings, the cleaver, the watches, and the diamonds on the floor.

"They brought me here," he began.

"When?"

His mind flew back over the blur of the time lived in the underground blackness. He had no idea of how much time had elapsed, but the intensity of what had happened to him told him that it could not have transpired in a short space of time, yet his mind told him that time must have been brief.

"It was a long time ago." He spoke like a child relating a dimly remembered dream. "It was a long time," he repeated, following the promptings of his emotions. "They beat me . . . I was scared . . . I ran away."

A policeman raised a finger to his temple and made a derisive circle.

"Nuts," the policeman said.

"Do you know what place this is, boy?"

"Yes, sir. The police station," he answered sturdily, almost proudly.

"Well, who do you want to see?"

"The men," he said again, feeling that surely they knew the men. "You know the men," he said in a hurt tone.

"What's your name?"

He opened his lips to answer and no words came. He had forgotten. But what did it matter if he had? It was not important.

"Where do you live?"

Where did he live? It had been so long ago since he had lived up here in this strange world that he felt it was foolish even to try to remember. Then for a moment the old mood that had dominated him in the underground surged back. He leaned forward and spoke eagerly.

"They said I killed the woman."

"What woman?" a policeman asked.

"And I signed a paper that said I was guilty," he went on, ignoring their questions. "Then I ran off . . ."

"Did you run off from an institution?"

"No, sir," he said, blinking and shaking his head. "I came from under the ground. I pushed off the manhole cover and climbed out . . ."

"All right, now," a policeman said, placing an arm about his shoulder. "We'll send you to the psycho and you'll be taken care of."

"Maybe he's a Fifth Columnist!" a policeman shouted.

There was laughter and, despite his anxiety, he joined in. But the laughter lasted so long that it irked him.

"I got to find those men," he protested mildly.

"Say, boy, what have you been drinking?"

"Water," he said. "I got some water in a basement."

"Were the men you ran away from dressed in white, boy?"

"No, sir," he said brightly. "They were men like you."

An elderly policeman caught hold of his arm.

"Try and think hard. Where did they pick you up?"

He knitted his brows in an effort to remember, but he was blank inside. The policeman stood before him demanding logical answers and he could no longer think with his mind; he thought with his feelings and no words came.

"I was guilty," he said. "Oh, no, sir. I wasn't then, I mean, mister!"

"Aw, talk sense. Now, where did they pick you up?"

He felt challenged and his mind began reconstructing events in reverse; his feelings ranged back over the long hours and he saw the cave, the sewer, the bloody room where it was said that a woman had been killed.

"Oh, yes, sir," he said, smiling. "I was coming from Mrs. Wooten's."

"Who is she?"

"I work for her."

"Where does she live?"

"Next door to Mrs. Peabody, the woman who was killed."

The policemen were very quiet now, looking at him intently.

"What do you know about Mrs. Peabody's death, boy?"

"Nothing, sir. But they said I killed her. But it doesn't make any difference. I'm guilty!"

"What are you talking about, boy?"

His smile faded and he was possessed with memories of the underground; he saw the cave next to the church and his lips moved to speak. But how could he say it? The distance between what he felt and what these men meant was vast. Something told him, as he stood there looking into their faces, that he would never be able to tell them, that they would never believe him even if he told them.

"All the people I saw was guilty," he began slowly.

"Aw, nuts," a policeman muttered.

"Say," another policeman said, "that Peabody woman was killed over on Winewood. That's Number Ten's beat."

"Where's Number Ten?" a policeman asked.

"Upstairs in the swing room," someone answered.

"Take this boy up, Sam," a policeman ordered.

"O.K. Come along, boy."

An elderly policeman caught hold of his arm and led him up a flight of wooden stairs, down a long hall, and to a door.

"Squad Ten!" the policeman called through the door.

"What?" a gruff voice answered.

"Someone to see you!"

"About what?"

The old policeman pushed the door in and then shoved him into the room.

He stared, his lips open, his heart barely beating. Before him were the three policemen who had picked him up and had beaten him to extract the confession. They were seated about a small table, playing cards. The air was blue with smoke and sunshine poured through a high window, lighting up fantastic smoke shapes. He saw one of the policemen look up; the policeman's face was tired and a cigarette dropped limply from one corner of his mouth and both of his fat, puffy eyes were squinting and his hands gripped his cards.

"Lawson!" the man exclaimed.

The moment the man's name sounded he remembered the names of all of them: Lawson, Murphy, and Johnson. How simple it was. He waited, smiling, wondering how they would react when they knew that he had come back.

"Looking for me?" the man who had been called Lawson mumbled, sorting his cards. "For what?"

So far only Murphy, the red-headed one, had recognized him.

"Don't you-all remember me?" he blurted, running to the table.

All three of the policemen were looking at him now. Lawson, who seemed the leader, jumped to his feet.

"Where in hell have you been?"

"Do you know 'im, Lawson?" the old policeman asked.

"Huh?" Lawson frowned. "Oh, yes. I'll handle 'im." The old policeman left the room and Lawson crossed to the door and turned the key in the lock. "Come here, boy," he ordered in a cold tone.

He did not move; he looked from face to face. Yes, he would tell them about his cave.

"He looks batty to me," Johnson said, the one who had not spoken before.

"Why in hell did you come back here?" Lawson said.

"I – I just didn't want to run away no more," he said. "I'm all right, now." He paused; the men's attitude puzzled him.

"You've been hiding, huh?" Lawson asked in a tone that denoted that he had not heard his previous words. "You told us you were sick, and when we left you in the room, you jumped out of the window and ran away."

Panic filled him. Yes, they were indifferent to what he would say! They were waiting for him to speak and they would laugh at him. He had to rescue himself from this bog; he had to force the reality of himself upon them.

"Mister, I took a sackful of money and pasted it on the walls . . ." he began.

"I'll be damned," Lawson said.

"Listen," said Murphy, "let me tell you something for your own good. We don't want you, see? You're free, free as air. Now go home and forget it. It was all a mistake. We caught the guy who did the Peabody job. He wasn't colored at all. He was an Eyetalian."

"Shut up!" Lawson yelled. "Have you no sense!"

"But I want to tell 'im," Murphy said.

"We can't let this crazy fool go," Lawson exploded. "He acts nuts, but this may be a stunt . . ."

"I was down in the basement," he began in a childlike tone, as though repeating a lesson learned by heart; "and I went into a movie . . ." His voice failed. He was getting ahead of his story. First, he ought to tell them about the singing in the church, but what words could he use? He looked at them appealingly. "I went into a shop and took a sackful of money and diamonds and watches and rings . . . I didn't steal 'em, I'll give 'em all back. I just took 'em to play with . . ." He paused, stunned by their disbelieving eyes.

Lawson lit a cigarette and looked at him coldly.

"What did you do with the money?" he asked in a quiet, waiting voice.

"I pasted the hundred-dollar bills on the walls."

"What walls?" Lawson asked.

"The walls of the dirt room," he said, smiling, "the room next to the church. I hung up the rings and the watches and I stamped the diamonds into the dirt . . ." He saw that they were not understanding what he was saying. He grew frantic to make them believe, his voice tumbled on eagerly. "I saw a dead baby and a dead man . . ."

"Aw, you're nuts," Lawson snarled, shoving him into a chair.

"But mister . . ."

"Johnson, where's the paper he signed?" Lawson asked.

"What paper?"

"The confession, fool!"

Johnson pulled out his billfold and extracted a crumpled piece of paper.

"Yes, sir, mister," he said, stretching forth his hand. "That's the paper I signed . . ."

Lawson slapped him and he would have toppled had his chair not struck a wall behind him. Lawson scratched a match and held the paper over the flame; the confession burned down to Lawson's fingertips.

He stared, thunderstruck; the sun of the underground was fleeting and the terrible darkness of the day stood before him. They did not believe him, but he *had* to make them believe him!

"But mister . . ."

"It's going to be all right, boy," Lawson said with a quiet, soothing laugh. "I've burned your confession, see? You didn't sign anything." Lawson came close to him with the black ashes cupped in his palm. "You don't remember a thing about this, do you?"

"Don't you-all be scared of me," he pleaded, sensing their uneasiness. "I'll sign another paper, if you want me to. I'll show you the cave."

"What's your game, boy?" Lawson asked suddenly.

"What are you trying to find out?" Johnson asked.

"Who sent you here?" Murphy demanded.

"Nobody sent me, mister," he said. "I just want to show you the room . . ."

"Aw, he's plumb bats," Murphy said. "Let's ship 'im to the psycho."

"No," Lawson said. "He's playing a game and I wish to God I knew what it was."

There flashed through his mind a definite way to make them believe him; he rose from the chair with nervous excitement.

"Mister, I saw the night watchman blow his brains out because you accused him of stealing," he told them. "But he didn't steal the money and diamonds. I took 'em."

Tigerishly Lawson grabbed his collar and lifted him bodily.

"Who told you about that?"

"Don't get excited, Lawson," Johnson said. "He read about it in the papers."

Lawson flung him away.

"He couldn't have," Lawson said, pulling papers from his pocket. "I haven't turned in the reports yet."

"Then how *did* he find out?" Murphy asked.

"Let's get out of here," Lawson said with quick resolution. "Listen, boy, we're going to take you to a nice, quiet place, see?"

"Yes, sir," he said. "And I'll show you the underground."

"Goddamn," Lawson muttered, fastening the gun at his hip. He narrowed his eyes at Johnson and Murphy. "Listen," he spoke just above a whisper, "say nothing about this, you hear?"

"O.K.," Johnson said.

"Sure," Murphy said.

Lawson unlocked the door and Johnson and Murphy led him down the stairs. The hallway was crowded with policemen.

"What have you got there, Lawson?"

"What did he do, Lawson?"

"He's psycho, ain't he, Lawson?"

Lawson did not answer; Johnson and Murphy led him to the car parked at the curb, pushed him into the back seat. Lawson got behind the steering wheel and the car rolled forward.

"What's up, Lawson?" Murphy asked.

"Listen," Lawson began slowly, "we tell the papers that he spilled about the Peabody job, then he escapes. The Wop is caught and we tell the papers that we steered them wrong to trap the real guy, see? Now this dope shows up and acts nuts. If we let him go, he'll squeal that we framed him, see?"

"I'm all right, mister," he said, feeling Murphy's and Johnson's arm locked rigidly into his. "I'm guilty . . . I'll show you everything in the underground. I laughed and laughed . . ."

"Shut that fool up!" Lawson ordered.

Johnson tapped him across the head with a blackjack and he fell back against the seat cushion, dazed.

"Yes, sir," he mumbled. "I'm all right."

The car sped along Hartsdale Avenue, then swung onto Pine Street and rolled to State Street, then turned south. It slowed to a stop, turned in the middle of a block, and headed north again.

"You're going around in circles, Lawson," Murphy said.

Lawson did not answer; he was hunched over the steering wheel. Finally he pulled the car to a stop at a curb.

"Say, boy, tell us the truth," Lawson asked quietly. "Where did you hide?"

"I didn't hide, mister."

The three policemen were staring at him now; he felt that for the first time they were willing to understand him.

"Then what happened?"

"Mister, when I looked through all of those holes and saw how people were living, I loved 'em . . ."

"Cut out that crazy talk!" Lawson snapped. "Who sent you back here?"

"Nobody, mister."

"Maybe he's talking straight," Johnson ventured.

"All right," Lawson said. "Nobody hid you. Now, tell us *where* you hid."

"I went underground . . ."

"What goddamn underground do you keep talking about?"

"I just went . . ." He paused and looked into the street, then pointed to a manhole cover. "I went down in there and stayed."

"In the *sewer?*"

"Yes, sir."

The policemen burst into a sudden laugh and ended quickly. Lawson swung the car around and drove to Woodside Avenue; he brought the car to a stop in front of a tall apartment building.

"What're we going to do, Lawson?" Murphy asked.

"I'm taking him up to my place," Lawson said. "We've got to wait until night. There's nothing we can do now."

They took him out of the car and led him into a vestibule.

"Take the steps," Lawson muttered.

They led him up four flights of stairs and into the living room of a small apartment. Johnson and Murphy let go of his arms and he stood uncertainly in the middle of the room.

"Now, listen, boy," Lawson began, "forget those wild lies you've been telling us. Where did you hide?"

"I just went underground, like I told you."

The room rocked with laughter. Lawson went to a cabinet and got a bottle of whisky; he placed glasses for Johnson and Murphy. The three of them drank.

He felt that he could not explain himself to them. He tried to muster all the sprawling images that floated in him; the images stood out sharply in his mind, but he could not make them have the meaning for others that they had for him. He felt so helpless that he began to cry.

"He's nuts, all right," Johnson said. "All nuts cry like that."

Murphy crossed the room and slapped him.

"Stop that raving!"

A sense of excitement flooded him; he ran to Murphy and grabbed his arm.

"Let me show you the cave," he said. "Come on, and you'll see!"

Before he knew it a sharp blow had clipped him on the chin; darkness covered his eyes. He dimly felt himself being lifted and laid out on the sofa. He heard low voices and struggled to rise, but hard hands held him down. His brain was clearing now. He pulled to a sitting posture and stared with glazed eyes. It had grown dark. How long had he been out?

"Say, boy," Lawson said soothingly, "will you show us the underground?"

His eyes shone and his heart swelled with gratitude. Lawson believed him! He rose, glad; he grabbed Lawson's arm, making the policeman spill whisky from the glass to his shirt.

"Take it easy, goddammit," Lawson said.

"Yes, sir."

"O.K. We'll take you down. But you'd better be telling us the truth, you hear?"

He clapped his hands in wild joy.

"I'll show you everything!"

He had triumphed at last! He would now do what he had felt was compelling him all along. At last he would be free of his burden.

"Take 'im down," Lawson ordered.

They led him down to the vestibule; when he reached the sidewalk he saw that it was night and a fine rain was falling.

"It's just like when I went down," he told them.

"What?" Lawson asked.

"The rain," he said, sweeping his arm in a wide arc. "It was raining when I went down. The rain made the water rise and lift the cover off."

"Cut it out," Lawson snapped.

They did not believe him now, but they would. A mood of high selflessness throbbed in him. He could barely contain his rising spirits. They would see what he had seen; they would feel what he had felt. He would lead them through all the holes he had dug and . . . He wanted to make a hymn, prance about in physical ecstasy, throw his arm about the policemen in fellowship.

"Get into the car," Lawson ordered.

He climbed in and Johnson and Murphy sat at either side of him; Lawson slid behind the steering wheel and started the motor.

"Now, tell us where to go," Lawson said.

"It's right around the corner from where the lady was killed," he said.

The car rolled slowly and he closed his eyes, remembering the song he had heard in the church, the song that had wrought him to such a high pitch of terror and pity. He sang softly, lolling his head:

Glad, glad, glad, oh, so glad
I got Jesus in my soul . . .

"Mister," he said, stopping his song, "you ought to see how funny the rings look on the wall." He giggled. "I fired a pistol, too. Just once, to see how it felt."

"What do you suppose he's suffering from?" Johnson asked.

"Delusions of grandeur, maybe," Murphy said.

"Maybe it's because he lives in a white man's world," Lawson said.

"Say, boy, what did you eat down there?" Murphy asked, prodding Johnson anticipatorily with his elbow.

"Pears, oranges, bananas, and pork chops," he said.

The car filled with laughter.

"You didn't eat any watermelon?" Lawson asked, smiling.

"No, sir," he answered calmly. "I didn't see any."

The three policemen roared harder and louder.

"Boy, you're sure some case," Murphy said, shaking his head in wonder.

The car pulled to a curb.

"All right, boy," Lawson said. "Tell us where to go."

He peered through the rain and saw where he had gone down. The streets, save for a few dim lamps glowing softly through the rain, were dark and empty.

"Right there, mister," he said, pointing.

"Come on; let's take a look," Lawson said.

"Well, suppose he did hide down there," Johnson said, "what is that supposed to prove?"

"I don't believe he hid down there," Murphy said.

"It won't hurt to look," Lawson said. "Leave things to me."

Lawson got out of the car and looked up and down the street.

He was eager to show them the cave now. If he could show them what he had seen, then they would feel what he had felt and they in turn would show it to others and those others would feel as they had felt, and soon everybody would be governed by the same impulse of pity.

"Take 'im out," Lawson ordered.

Johnson and Murphy opened the door and pushed him out; he stood trembling in the rain, smiling. Again Lawson looked up and down the street; no one was in sight. The rain came down hard, slanting like black wires across the wind-swept air.

"All right," Lawson said. "Show us."

He walked to the center of the street, stopped and inserted a finger in one of the tiny holes of the cover and tugged, but he was too weak to budge it.

"Did you really go down in there, boy?" Lawson asked; there was a doubt in his voice.

"Yes, sir. Just a minute. I'll show you."

"Help 'im get that damn thing off," Lawson said.

Johnson stepped forward and lifted the cover; it clanged against the wet pavement. The hole gaped round and black.

"I went down in there," he announced with pride.

Lawson gazed at him for a long time without speaking, then he reached his right hand to his holster and drew his gun.

"Mister, I got a gun just like that down there," he said, laughing and looking into Lawson's face. "I fired it once then hung it on the wall. I'll show you."

"Show us how you went down," Lawson said quietly.

"I'll go down first, mister, and then you-all can come after me, hear?" he spoke like a little boy playing a game.

"Sure, sure," Lawson said soothingly. "Go ahead. We'll come."

He looked brightly at the policemen; he was bursting with happiness. He bent down and placed his hands on the rim of the hole and sat on the edge, his feet dangling into watery darkness. He heard the familiar drone of the gray current. He lowered his body and hung for a moment by his fingers, then he went downward on the steel prongs, hand over hand, until he reached the last rung. He dropped and his feet hit the water and he felt the stiff current trying to suck him away. He balanced himself quickly and looked back upward at the policemen.

"Come on, you-all!" he yelled, casting his voice above the rustling at his feet.

The vague forms that towered above him in the rain did not move. He laughed, feeling that they doubted him. But, once they saw the things he had done, they would never doubt again.

"Come on! The cave isn't far!" he yelled. "But be careful when your feet hit the water, because the current's pretty rough down here!"

Lawson still held the gun. Murphy and Johnson looked at Lawson quizzically.

"What are we going to do, Lawson?" Murphy asked.

"We are not going to follow that crazy nigger down into that sewer, are we?" Johnson asked.

"Come on, you-all!" he begged in a shout.

He saw Lawson raise the gun and point it directly at him. Lawson's face twitched, as though he were hesitating.

Then there was a thunderous report and a streak of fire ripped through his chest. He was hurled into the water, flat on his back. He looked in amazement at the blurred white faces looming above him. They shot me, he said to himself. The water flowed past him, blossoming in foam about his arms, his legs, and his head. His jaw sagged and his mouth gaped soundless. A vast pain gripped his head and gradually squeezed out consciousness. As from a great distance he heard hollow voices.

"What did you shoot him for, Lawson?"

"I had to."

"Why?"

"You've got to shoot his kind. They'd wreck things."

As though in a deep dream, he heard a metallic clank; they had replaced the manhole cover, shutting out forever the sound of wind and rain. From overhead came the muffled roar of a powerful motor and the swish of a speeding car. He felt the strong tide pushing him slowly into the middle of the sewer, turning him about. For a split second there hovered before his eyes the glittering cave, the shouting walls, and the laughing floor . . . Then his mouth was full of thick, bitter water. The current spun him around. He sighed and closed his eyes, a whirling object rushing alone in the darkness, veering, tossing, lost in the heart of the earth.

BERNARD MALAMUD b. 1914

Malamud catches the essence of the streets of his native Brooklyn — the voices, accents, turns of phrase, that reveal people's ethnic identity and, at the same time, their special individuality. When Malamud was a boy his parents worked long hours and he was allowed to roam the streets, dreaming and observing. What he saw and heard appears constantly in his fiction, the background against which his characters play out their lives; and the sensibility through which the reader perceives this background is often that of a boy — a good, kind, somewhat lonely boy who watches adults at various sorts of joy, nastiness, and violence.

One of Malamud's finest talents is his ability to portray the relationships that developed in the big city ghettos between the Jews who were gradually moving out during the twenties and thirties and the blacks who were moving up from the South to take their place in the old tenement houses. In "Black is My Favorite Color" Nat Lime's sweet but uncomprehending attempt to love blacks more than he loves whites exposes a wide range of emotion, from the comic insistence of Charity Sweetness on eating her hard-boiled eggs in the toilet to the deeply felt cry of Ornita rejecting Nat: "I got troubles enough of my own." To this Brooklyn of racial intermixing, Malamud brought a compassionate Yiddish sense of humor — a conviction that do what you will the absurd will happen to you — and a tragic feel for human suffering, the literary representation of which he found in Dostoyevsky. The blacks he portrays are, of course, seen from a Jewish point of view, and it is this fact that constitutes the central irony in "Angel Levine"; nevertheless, even though Malamud's assertion that blacks are in a sense his own people produces ironies, his is a supreme act of human and artistic sympathy that reveals a relationship between the races.

Malamud began writing in high school, went to C.C.N.Y., graduating in 1936, and, after doing various jobs to support himself during the Depression, earned an M.A. in English from Columbia in 1942. He taught English in Oregon (a fictionalized version of his experience there is *A New Life,* 1961), and more recently at Bennington. With the publication of *The Assistant* in 1957, his reputation as a writer was assured. His short stories are collected in *The Magic Barrel* (1958) and *Idiots First* (1963). *The Fixer* (1966) won the National Book Award and the Pulitzer Prize. His recent novel, *The Tenants* (1971), is an extended treatment of black-Jewish relationships.

ANGEL LEVINE

Manischevitz, a tailor, in his fifty-first year suffered many reverses and indignities. Previously a man of comfortable means, he overnight lost all he had, when his establishment caught fire and, after a metal container of cleaning fluid exploded, burned to the ground. Although Manischevitz was insured against fire, damage suits by two customers who had been hurt in the flames deprived him of every penny he had collected. At almost the same time, his son, of much promise, was killed in the war, and his daughter, without so much as a word of warning, married a lout and disappeared with him as off the face of the earth. Thereafter Manischevitz was victimized by excruciating backaches and found himself unable to work even as a presser — the only kind of work available to him — for more than an hour or two daily, because beyond that the pain from standing became maddening. His Fanny, a good wife and mother, who had taken in washing and sewing, began before his eyes to waste away. Suffering shortness of breath, she at last became seriously ill and took to her bed. The doctor, a former customer of Manischevitz, who out of pity treated them, at first had difficulty diagnosing her ailment but later put it down as hardening of the arteries at an advanced stage. He took Manischevitz aside, prescribed complete rest for her, and in whispers gave him to know there was little hope.

Throughout his trials Manischevitz had remained somewhat stoic, almost unbelieving that all this had descended upon his head, as if it were happening, let us say, to an acquaintance or some distant relative; it was in sheer quantity of woe incomprehensible. It was also ridiculous, unjust, and because he had always been a religious man, it was in a way an affront to God. Manischevitz believed this in all his suffering. When his burden had grown too crushingly heavy to be borne he prayed in his chair with shut hollow eyes: "My dear God, sweetheart, did I deserve that this should happen to me?" Then recognizing the worthlessness of it, he put aside the complaint and prayed humbly for assistance: "Give Fanny back her health, and to me for myself that I shouldn't feel pain in every step. Help now or tomorrow is too late. This I don't have to tell you." And Manischevitz wept.

Manischevitz's flat, which he had moved into after the disastrous fire, was a meager one, furnished with a few sticks of chairs, a table, and bed, in one of the poorer sections of the city. There were three rooms: a small, poorly-papered living room; an apology for a kitchen, with a wooden icebox; and the comparatively large bedroom where Fanny lay in a sagging secondhand bed, gasping for breath. The bedroom was the warmest room of the house and it was here, after his outburst to God, that Manischevitz, by the light of two small bulbs overhead, sat reading his Jewish newspaper. He was not truly reading, because his thoughts were everywhere; however the print offered a convenient resting place for his eyes, and a word or two, when he permitted himself to comprehend them, had the momentary effect of helping him forget his troubles. After a short while he discovered, to his surprise, that he was actively scanning the news, searching for an item of great interest to him. Exactly what he thought he would read he couldn't say — until he realized, with some astonishment, that he was expecting to discover something about himself. Manischevitz put his paper down and looked up with the distinct impression that someone had entered the apartment, though he could not remember having heard the sound of the door opening. He looked around: the room was very still, Fanny sleeping, for once, quietly. Half-frightened, he watched her until he was satisfied she wasn't dead; then, still disturbed by the thought of an unannounced visitor, he stumbled into the living room and there had the shock of his life, for at the table sat a Negro reading a newspaper he had folded up to fit into one hand.

"What do you want here?" Manischevitz asked in fright.

The Negro put down the paper and glanced up with a gentle expression. "Good evening." He seemed not to be sure of himself, as if he had got into the wrong house. He was a large man, bonily built, with a heavy head covered by a hard derby, which he made no attempt to remove. His eyes seemed sad, but his lips, above which he wore a slight mustache, sought to smile; he was not otherwise prepossessing. The cuffs of his sleeves, Manischevitz noted, were frayed to the lining and the dark suit was badly fitted. He had very large feet. Recovering from his fright, Manischevitz guessed he had left the door open and was being visited by a case worker from the Welfare Department — some came at night — for he had recently applied for relief. Therefore he lowered himself into a chair opposite the Negro, trying, before the man's uncertain smile, to feel comfortable. The former tailor sat stiffly but patiently at the table, waiting for the investigator to take out his pad and pencil and begin asking questions; but before long he became convinced the man intended to do nothing of the sort.

"Who are you?" Manischevitz at last asked uneasily

"If I may, insofar as one is able to, identify myself, I bear the name of Alexander Levine."

In spite of all his troubles Manischevitz felt a smile growing on his lips. "You said Levine?" he politely inquired.

The Negro nodded. "That is exactly right."

Carrying the jest farther, Manischevitz asked, "You are maybe Jewish?"

"All my life I was, willingly."

The tailor hesitated. He had heard of black Jews but had never met one. It gave an unusual sensation.

Recognizing in afterthought something odd about the tense of Levine's remark, he said doubtfully, "You ain't Jewish anymore?"

Levine at this point removed his hat, revealing a very white part in his black hair, but quickly replaced it. He replied, "I have recently been disincarnated into an angel. As such, I offer you my humble assistance, if to offer is within my province and ability – in the best sense." He lowered his eyes in apology. "Which calls for added explanation: I am what I am granted to be, and at present the completion is in the future."

"What kind of angel is this?" Manischevitz gravely asked.

"A bona fide angel of God, within prescribed limitations," answered Levine, "not to be confused with the members of any particular sect, order, or organization here on earth operating under a similar name."

Manischevitz was thoroughly disturbed. He had been expecting something but not this. What sort of mockery was it – provided Levine was an angel – of a faithful servant who had from childhood lived in the synagogues, always concerned with the word of God?

To test Levine he asked, "Then where are your wings?"

The Negro blushed as well as he was able. Manischevitz understood this from his changed expression. "Under certain circumstances we lose privileges and prerogatives upon returning to earth, no matter for what purpose, or endeavoring to assist whosoever."

"So tell me," Manischevitz said triumphantly, "how did you get here?"

"I was transmitted."

Still troubled, the tailor said, "If you are a Jew, say the blessing for bread."

Levine recited it in sonorous Hebrew.

Although moved by the familiar words Manischevitz still felt doubt that he was dealing with an angel.

"If you are an angel," he demanded somewhat angrily, "give me the proof."

Levine wet his lips. "Frankly, I cannot perform either miracles or near miracles, due to the fact that I am in a condition of probation. How long that will persist or even consist, I admit, depends on the outcome."

Manischevitz racked his brains for some means of causing Levine positively to reveal his true identity, when the Negro spoke again:

"It was given me to understand that both your wife and you require assistance of a salubrious nature?"

The tailor could not rid himself of the feeling that he was the butt of a jokester. Is this what a Jewish angel looks like? he asked himself. This I am not convinced.

He asked a last question. "So if God sends to me an angel, why a black? Why not a white that there are so many of them?"

"It was my turn to go next," Levine explained.

Manischevitz could not be persuaded. "I think you are a faker."

Levine slowly rose. His eyes showed disappointment and worry. "Mr. Manischevitz," he said tonelessly, "if you should desire me to be of assistance to you any time in the near future, or possibly before, I can be found" – he glanced at his fingernails – "in Harlem."

He was by then gone.

The next day Manischevitz felt some relief from his backache and was able to work four hours at pressing. The day after, he put in six hours; and the third day four again. Fanny sat up a little and asked for some halvah to suck. But on the fourth day the stabbing, breaking ache afflicted his back, and Fanny again lay supine, breathing with blue-lipped difficulty.

Manischevitz was profoundly disappointed at the return of his active pain and suffering. He had hoped for a longer interval of easement, long enough to have some thought other than of himself and his troubles. Day by day, hour by hour, minute after minute, he lived in pain, pain his only memory, questioning the necessity of it, inveighing against it, also, though with affection, against God. Why *so much,* Gottenyu? If He wanted to teach His servant a lesson for some reason, some cause – the nature of His nature – to teach him, say, for reasons of his weakness, his pride, perhaps, during his years of prosperity, his frequent neglect of God – to give him a little lesson, why then any of the tragedies that had happened to him, any *one* would have sufficed to chasten him. But *all together* – the loss of both his children, his means of livelihood, Fanny's health and his – that was too much to ask one frail-boned man to endure. Who, after all, was Manischevitz that he had been given so much to suffer? A tailor. Certainly not a man of talent. Upon him suffering was largely wasted. It went nowhere, into nothing: into more suffering. His pain did not earn him bread, nor fill the cracks in the wall, nor lift, in the middle of the night, the kitchen table; only lay upon him, sleepless, so sharply, oppressively, that he could many times have cried out yet not heard himself through this thickness of misery.

In this mood he gave no thought to Mr. Alexander Levine, but at moments when the pain waivered, slightly diminishing, he sometimes wondered if he had been mistaken to dismiss him. A black Jew and angel to boot – very hard to believe, but suppose he *had* been sent to succor him, and he, Manischevitz, was in his blindness too blind to comprehend? It was this thought that put him on the knife-point of agony.

Therefore the tailor, after much self-questioning and continuing doubt, decided he would seek the self-styled angel in Harlem. Of course he had great difficulty, because he had not asked for specific directions, and movement was tedious to him. The subway took him to 116th Street, and from there he wandered in the dark world. It was vast and its lights lit nothing. Everywhere were shadows, often moving. Manischevitz hobbled along with the aid of a cane, and not knowing where to seek in the blackened tenement buildings, looked fruitlessly through store windows. In the stores he saw people and *everybody* was black. It was an amazing thing to observe. When he was too tired, too unhappy to go farther, Manischevitz stopped in front of a tailor's store. Out of familiarity with the appearance of it, with some sadness he entered. The tailor, an old skinny Negro with a mop of woolly gray hair, was sitting cross-legged on his workbench, sewing a pair of full-dress pants that had a razor slit all the way down the seat.

"You'll excuse me, please, gentleman," said Manischevitz, admiring the tailor's deft, thimbled fingerwork, "but you know maybe somebody by the name Alexander Levine?"

The tailor, who Manischevitz thought, seemed a little antagonistic to him, scratched his scalp.

"Cain't say I ever heared dat name."

"Alex-ander Lev-ine," Manischevitz repeated it.

The man shook his head. "Cain't say I heared."

About to depart, Manischevitz remembered to say: "He is an angel, maybe."

"Oh *him,*" said the tailor clucking. "He hang out in dat honky tonk down here a ways." He pointed with his skinny finger and returned to the pants.

Manischevitz crossed the street against a red light and was almost run down by a taxi. On the block after the next, the sixth store from the corner was a cabaret, and the name in sparkling lights was Bella's. Ashamed to go in, Manischevitz gazed through the neon-lit window, and when the dancing couples had parted and drifted away, he discovered at a table on the side, towards the rear, Levine.

He was sitting alone, a cigarette butt hanging from the corner of his mouth, playing solitaire with a dirty pack of cards, and Manischevitz felt a touch of pity for him, for Levine had deteriorated in appearance. His derby was dented and had a gray smudge on the side. His ill-fitting suit was shabbier, as if he had been sleeping in it. His shoes and trouser cuffs were muddy, and his face was covered with an impenetrable stubble the color of licorice. Manischevitz, though deeply disappointed, was about to enter, when a big-breasted Negress in a purple evening gown appeared before Levine's table, and with much laughter through many white teeth, broke into a vigorous shimmy. Levine looked straight at Manischevitz with a haunted expression, but the tailor was too paralyzed to move or acknowledge it. As Bella's gyrations continued, Levine rose, his eyes lit in excitement. She embraced him with vigor, both his hands clasped around her big restless buttocks and they tangoed together across the floor, loudly applauded by the noisy customers. She seemed to have lifted Levine off his feet and his large shoes hung limp as they danced. They slid past the windows where Manischevitz, white-faced, stood staring in. Levine winked slyly and the tailor left for home.

• • •

Fanny lay at death's door. Through shrunken lips she muttered concerning her childhood, the sorrows of the marriage bed, the loss of her children, yet wept to live. Manischevitz tried not to listen, but even without ears he would have heard. It was not a gift. The doctor panted up the stairs, a broad but bland, unshaven man (it was Sunday), and soon shook his head. A day at most, or two. He left at once, not without pity, to spare himself Manischevitz's multiplied sorrow; the man who never stopped hurting. He would someday get him into a public home.

Manischevitz visited a synagogue and there spoke to God, but God had absented himself. The tailor searched his heart and found no hope. When she died he would live dead. He considered taking his life although he knew he wouldn't. Yet it was something to consider. Considering, you existed. He railed against God – Can you love a rock, a broom, an emptiness? Baring his chest, he smote the naked bones, cursing himself for having believed.

Asleep in a chair that afternoon, he dreamed of Levine. He was standing before a faded mirror, preening small decaying opalescent wings. "This means," mumbled Manischevitz, as he broke out of sleep, "that it is possible he could be an angel." Begging a neighbor lady to look in on Fanny and occasionally wet her lips with a few drops of water, he drew on his thin coat, gripped his walking stick, exchanged some pennies for a subway token, and rode to Harlem. He knew this act was the last desperate one of his woe: to go without belief, seeking a black magician to restore his wife to invalidism. Yet if there was no choice, he did at least what was chosen.

He hobbled to Bella's but the place had changed hands. It was now, as he breathed, a synagogue in a store. In the front, towards him, were several rows of empty wooden benches. In the rear stood the Ark, its portals of rough wood covered with rainbows of sequins; under it a long table on which lay the sacred scroll unrolled, illuminated by the dim light from a bulb on a chain overhead. Around the table, as if frozen to it and the scroll, which they all touched with their fingers, sat four Negroes wearing skullcaps. Now as they read the Holy Word, Manischevitz could, through the plate glass window, hear the singsong chant of their voices. One of them was old, with a gray beard. One was bubble-eyed. One was humpbacked. The fourth was a boy, no older than thirteen. Their heads moved in rhythmic swaying. Touched by this sight from his childhood and youth, Manischevitz entered and stood silent in the rear.

"Neshoma," said bubble eyes, pointing to the word with a stubby finger. "Now what dat mean?"

"That's the word that means soul," said the boy. He wore glasses.

"Let's git on wid de commentary," said the old man.

"Ain't necessary," said the humpback. "Souls is immaterial substance. That's all. The soul is derived in that manner. The immateriality is derived from the substance, and they both, causally an' otherwise, derived from the soul. There can be no higher."

"That's the highest."

"Over de top."

"Wait a minute," said bubble eyes. "I don't see what is dat immaterial substance. How come de one gits hitched up to de odder?" He addressed the humpback.

"Ask me something hard. Because it is substanceless immateriality. It couldn't be closer together, like all the parts of the body under one skin – closer."

"Hear now," said the old man.

"All you done is switched de words."

"It's the primum mobile, the substanceless substance from which comes all things that were incepted in the idea – you, me and everything and body else."

"Now how did all dat happen? Make it sound simple."

"It de speerit," said the old man. "On de face of de water moved de speerit. An' dat was good. It say so in de Book. From de speerit ariz de man."

"But now listen here. How come it become substance if it all de time a spirit?"

"God alone done dat."

"Holy! Holy! Praise His Name."

"But has dis spirit got some kind of a shade or color?" asked bubble eyes, deadpan.

"Man of course not. A spirit is a spirit."

"Then how come we is colored?" he said with a triumphant glare.

"Ain't got nothing to do wid dat."

"I still like to know."

"God put the spirit in all things," answered the boy. "He put it in the green leaves and the yellow flowers. He put it with the gold in the fishes and the blue in the sky. That's how come it came to us."

"Amen."

"Praise Lawd and utter loud His speechless name."

"Blow de bugle till it bust the sky."

They fell silent, intent upon the next word. Manischevitz approached them.

"You'll excuse me," he said. "I am looking for Alexander Levine. You know him maybe?"

"That's the angel," said the boy.

"Oh, *him,*" snuffed bubble eyes.

"You'll find him at Bella's. It's the establishment right across the street," the humpback said.

Manischevitz said he was sorry that he could not stay, thanked them, and limped across the street. It was already night. The city was dark and he could barely find his way.

But Bella's was bursting with the blues. Through the window Manischevitz recognized the dancing crowd and among them sought Levine. He was sitting loose-lipped at Bella's side table. They were tippling from an almost empty whiskey fifth. Levine had shed his old clothes, wore a shiny new checkered suit, pearl-gray derby, cigar, and big, two-tone button shoes. To the tailor's dismay, a drunken look had settled upon his formerly dignified face. He leaned toward Bella, tickled her ear lobe with his pinky, while whispering words that sent her into gales of raucous laughter. She fondled his knee.

Manischevitz, girding himself, pushed open the door and was not welcomed.

"This place reserved."

"Beat it, pale puss."

"Exit, Yankel, Semitic trash."

But he moved towards the table where Levine sat, the crowd breaking before him as he hobbled forward.

"Mr. Levine," he spoke in a trembly voice. "Is here Manischevitz."

Levine glared blearily. "Speak yo' piece, son."

Manischevitz shuddered. His back plagued him. Cold tremors tormented his crooked legs. He looked around, everybody was all ears.

"You'll excuse me. I would like to talk to you in a private place."

"Speak, Ah is a private pusson."

Bella laughed piercingly. "Stop it, boy, you killin' me."

Manischevitz, no end disturbed, considered fleeing but Levine addressed him:

"Kindly state the pu'pose of yo' communication with yo's truly."

The tailor wet cracked lips. "You are Jewish. This I am sure."

Levine rose, nostrils flaring. "Anythin' else yo' got to say?"

Manischevitz's tongue lay like stone.

"Speak now or fo'ever hold off."

Tears blinded the tailor's eyes. Was ever man so tried? Should he say he believed a half-drunken Negro to be an angel?

The silence slowly petrified.

Manischevitz was recalling scenes of his youth as a wheel in his mind whirred: believe, do not, yes, no, yes, no. The pointer pointed to yes, to between yes and no, to no, no it was yes. He sighed. It moved but one had still to make a choice.

"I think you are an angel from God." He said it in a broken voice, thinking, If you said it it was said. If you believed it you must say it. If you believed, you believed.

The hush broke. Everybody talked but the music began and they went on dancing. Bella, grown bored, picked up the cards and dealt herself a hand.

Levine burst into tears. "How you have humiliated me."

Manischevitz apologized.

"Wait'll I freshen up." Levine went to the men's room and returned in his old clothes.

No one said goodbye as they left.

They rode to the flat via subway. As they walked up the stairs Manischevitz pointed with his cane at his door.

"That's all been taken care of," Levine said. "You best go in while I take off."

Disappointed that it was so soon over but torn by curiosity, Manischevitz followed the angel up three flights to the roof. When he got there the door was already padlocked.

Luckily he could see through a small broken window. He heard an odd noise, as though of a whirring of wings, and when he strained for a wider view, could have sworn he saw a dark figure borne aloft on a pair of magnificent black wings.

A feather drifted down. Manischevitz gasped as it turned white, but it was only snowing.

He rushed downstairs. In the flat Fanny wielded a dust mop under the bed and then upon the cobwebs on the wall.

"A wonderful thing, Fanny," Manischevitz said. "Believe me, there are Jews everywhere."

BLACK IS MY FAVORITE COLOR

Charity Sweetness sits in the toilet eating her two hard-boiled eggs while I'm having my ham sandwich and coffee in the kitchen. That's how it goes only don't get the idea of ghettoes. If there's a ghetto I'm the one that's in it. She's my cleaning woman from Father Divine and comes in once a week to my small three-room apartment on my day off from the liquor store. "Peace," she says to me, "Father reached on down and took me right up in Heaven." She's a small person with a flat body, frizzy hair, and a quiet face that the light shines out of, and Mama had such eyes before she died. The first time Charity Sweetness came in to clean, a little more than a year and a half, I made the mistake to ask her to sit down at the kitchen table with me and eat her lunch. I was still feeling not so hot after Ornita left but I'm the kind of a man – Nat Lime, forty-four, a bachelor with a daily growing bald spot on the back of my head, and I could lose frankly fifteen pounds – who enjoys company so long as he has it. So she cooked up her two hardboiled eggs and sat down and took a small bite out of one of them. But after a minute she stopped chewing and she got up and carried the eggs in a cup in the bathroom, and since then she eats there. I said to her more than once, "Okay, Charity Sweetness, so have it your way, eat the eggs in the kitchen by yourself and I'll eat when you're done," but she smiles absent-minded, and eats in the toilet. It's my fate with colored people.

Although black is still my favorite color you wouldn't know it from my luck except in short quantities even though I do all right in the liquor store business in Harlem, on Eighth Avenue between 110th and 111th. I speak with respect. A large part of my life I've had dealings with Negro people, most on a business basis but sometimes for friendly reasons with genuine feeling on both sides. I'm drawn to them. At this time of my life I should have one or two good colored friends but the fault isn't necessarily mine. If they knew what was in my heart towards them, but how can you tell that to anybody nowadays? I've tried more than once but the language of the heart either is a dead language or else nobody understands it the way you speak it. Very few. What I'm saying is, personally for me there's only one human color and that's the color of blood. I like a black person if not because he's black, then because I'm white. It comes to the same thing. If I wasn't white my first choice would be black. I'm satisfied to be white because I have no other choice. Anyway, I got an eye for color. I appreciate. Who wants everybody to be the same? Maybe it's like some kind of a talent. Nat Lime might be a liquor dealer in Harlem, but once in the jungle in New Guinea in the Second War, I got the idea when I shot at a running Jap and missed him, that I had some kind of a talent, though maybe it's the kind where you have a marvelous idea now and then but in the end what do they come to? After all, it's a strange world.

Where Charity Sweetness eats her eggs makes me think about Buster Wilson when we were both boys in the Williamsburg section of Brooklyn. There was this long block of run-down dirty frame houses in the middle of a not-so-hot white neighborhood full of pushcarts. The Negro houses looked to me like they had been born and died there, dead not long after the beginning of the world. I lived on the next street. My father was a cutter with arthritis in both hands, big red knuckles and swollen fingers so he didn't cut, and my mother was the one who went to work. She sold paper bags from a second-hand pushcart in Ellery Street. We didn't starve but nobody ate chicken unless we were sick or the chicken was. This was my first acquaintance with a lot of black people and I used to poke around on their poor block. I think I thought, brother, if there can be like this, what can't there be? I mean I caught an early idea what life was about. Anyway I met Buster Wilson there. He used to play marbles by himself. I sat on the curb across the street, watching him shoot one marble lefty and the other one righty. The hand that won picked up the marbles. It wasn't so much of a game but he didn't ask me to come over. My idea was to be friendly, only he never encouraged, he discouraged. Why did I pick him out for a friend? Maybe because I had no others then, we were new in the neighborhood, from Manhattan. Also I liked his type. Buster did everything alone. He was a skinny kid and his brothers' clothes hung on him like worn-out potato sacks. He was a beanpole boy, about twelve, and I was then ten. His arms and legs were burnt out matchsticks. He always wore a brown wool sweater, one arm half unraveled, the other went down to the wrist. His long and narrow head had a white part cut straight in the short woolly hair, maybe with a ruler there, by his father, a barber but too drunk to stay a barber. In those days though I had little myself I was old enough to know who was better off, and the whole block of colored houses made me feel bad in the daylight. But I went there as much as I could because the street was full of life. In the night it looked different, it's hard to tell a cripple in the dark. Sometimes I was afraid to walk by the houses when they were dark and quiet. I was afraid there were people looking at me that I couldn't see. I liked it better when they had parties at night and everybody had a good time. The musicians played their banjos and saxophones and the houses shook with the music and laughing. The young girls, with their pretty dresses and ribbons in their hair, caught me in my throat when I saw them through the windows.

But with the parties came drinking and fights. Sundays were bad days after the Saturday night parties. I remember once that Buster's father, also long and loose, always wearing a dirty gray Homburg hat, chased another black man in the street with a half-inch chisel. The other one, maybe five feet high, lost his shoe and when they wrestled on the ground he was already bleeding through his suit, a thick red blood smearing the sidewalk. I was frightened by the blood and wanted to pour it back in the man who was bleeding from the chisel. On another time Buster's father was playing in a crap game with two big bouncy red dice, in the back of an alley between two middle houses. Then about six men started fist-fighting there, and they ran out of the alley and hit each other in the street. The neighbors, including children, came out and watched, everybody afraid but nobody moving to do anything. I saw the same thing near my store in Harlem, years later, a big crowd watching two men in the street, their breaths hanging in the air on a winter night, murdering each other with switch knives, but nobody moved to call a cop. I didn't either. Anyway, I was just a young kid but I still remember how the cops drove up in a police paddy wagon and broke up the fight by hitting everybody they could hit with big nightsticks. This was in the days before LaGuardia. Most of the fighters were knocked out cold, only one or two got away. Buster's father started to run back in his house but a cop ran after him and cracked him on his Homburg hat with a club, right on the front porch. Then the Negro men were lifted up by the cops, one at the arms and the other at the feet, and they heaved them in the paddy wagon. Buster's father hit the back of the wagon and fell, with his nose spouting very red blood, on top of three other men. I personally couldn't stand it, I was scared of the human race so I ran home, but I remember Buster watching without any expression in his eyes. I stole an extra fifteen cents from my mother's pocketbook and I ran back and asked Buster if he wanted to go to the movies. I would pay. He said yes. This was the first time he talked to me.

So we went more than once to the movies. But we never got to be friends. Maybe because it was a one-way proposition – from me to him. Which includes my invitations to go with me, my (poor mother's) movie money, Hershey chocolate bars, watermelon slices, even my best Nick Carter and Merriwell books that I spent hours picking up in the junk shops, and that he never gave me back. Once he let me go in his house to get a match so we could smoke some butts we found, but it smelled so heavy, so impossible, I died till I got out of there. What I saw in the way of furniture I won't mention – the best was falling apart in pieces. Maybe we went to the movies all together five or six matinees that spring and in the summertime, but when the shows were over he usually walked home by himself.

"Why don't you wait for me, Buster?" I said. "We're both going in the same direction."

But he was walking ahead and didn't hear me. Anyway he didn't answer.

One day when I wasn't expecting it he hit me in the teeth. I felt like crying but not because of the pain. I spit blood and said, "What did you hit me for? What did I do to you?"

"Because you a Jew bastard. Take your Jew movies and your Jew candy and shove them up your Jew ass."

And he ran away.

I thought to myself how was I to know he didn't like the movies. When I was a man I thought, you can't force it.

Years later, in the prime of my life, I met Mrs. Ornita Harris. She was standing by herself under an open umbrella at the bus stop, crosstown 110th, and I picked up her green glove that she had dropped on the wet sidewalk. It was in the end of November. Before I could ask her was it hers, she grabbed the glove out of my hand, closed her umbrella, and stepped in the bus. I got on right after her.

I was annoyed so I said, "If you'll pardon me, Miss, there's no law that you have to say thanks, but at least don't make a criminal out of me."

"Well, I'm sorry," she said, "but I don't like white men trying to do me favors."

I tipped my hat and that was that. In ten minutes I got off the bus but she was already gone.

Who expected to see her again but I did. She came into my store about a week later for a bottle of scotch.

"I would offer you a discount," I told her, "but I know you don't like a certain kind of a favor and I'm not looking for a slap in the face."

Then she recognized me and got a little embarrassed.

"I'm sorry I misunderstood you that day."

"So mistakes happen."

The result was she took the discount. I gave her a dollar off.

She used to come in about every two weeks for a fifth of Haig and Haig. Sometimes I waited on her, sometimes my helpers, Jimmy or Mason, also colored, but I said to give the discount. They both looked at me but I had nothing to be ashamed. In the spring when she came in we used to talk once in a while. She was a slim woman, dark but not the most dark, about thirty years I would say, also well built, with a combination nice legs and a good-size bosom that I like. Her face was pretty, with big eyes and high cheek bones, but lips a little thick and nose a little broad. Sometimes she didn't feel like talking, she paid for the bottle, less discount, and walked out. Her eyes were tired and she didn't look to me like a happy woman.

I found out her husband was once a window cleaner on the big buildings, but one day his safety belt broke and he fell fifteen stories. After the funeral she got a job as a manicurist in a Times Square barber shop. I told her I was a bachelor and lived with my mother in a small three-room apartment on West Eighty-third near Broadway. My mother had cancer, and Ornita said she was very sorry.

One night in July we went out together. How that happened I'm still not so sure. I guess I asked her and she didn't say no. Where do you go out with a Negro woman? We went to the Village. We had a good dinner and walked in Washington Square Park. It was a hot night. Nobody was surprised when they saw us, nobody looked at us like we were against the law. If they looked maybe they saw my new lightweight suit that I bought yesterday and my shiny bald spot when we walked under a lamp, also how pretty she was for a man of my type. We went in a movie on West Eighth Street. I didn't want to go in but she said she had heard about the picture. We went in like strangers and we came out like strangers. I wondered what was in her mind and I thought to myself, whatever is in there it's not a certain white man that I know. All night long we went together like we were chained. After the movie she wouldn't let me take her back to Harlem. When I put her in a taxi she asked me, "Why did we bother?"

For the steak, I wanted to say. Instead I said, "You're worth the bother."

"Thanks anyway."

Kiddo, I thought to myself after the taxi left, you just found out what's what, now the best thing is forget her.

It's easy to say. In August we went out the second time. That was the night she wore a purple dress and I thought to myself, my God, what colors. Who paints that picture paints a masterpiece. Everybody looked at us but I had pleasure. That night when she took off her dress it was in a furnished room I had the sense to rent a few days before. With my sick mother, I couldn't ask her to come to my apartment, and she didn't want me to go home with her where she lived with her brother's family on West 115th near Lenox Avenue. Under her purple dress she wore a black slip, and when she took that off she had white underwear. When she took off the white underwear she was black again. But I know where the next white was, if you want to call it white. And that was the night I think I fell in love with her, the first time in my life though I have liked one or two nice girls I used to go with when I was a boy. It was a serious proposition. I'm the kind of a man when I think of love I'm thinking of marriage. I guess that's why I am a bachelor.

That same week I had a holdup in my place, two big men — both black — with revolvers. One got excited when I rang open the cash register so he could take the money and he hit me over the ear with his gun. I stayed in the hospital a couple of weeks. Otherwise I was insured. Ornita came to see me. She sat on a chair without talking much. Finally I saw she was uncomfortable so I suggested she ought to go home.

"I'm sorry it happened," she said.

"Don't talk like it's your fault."

When I got out of the hospital my mother was dead. She was a wonderful person. My father died when I was thirteen and all by herself she kept the family alive and together. I sat shive for a week and remembered how she sold paper bags on her pushcart. I remembered her life and what she tried to teach me. Nathan, she said, if you ever forget you are a Jew a goy will remind you. Mama, I said, rest in peace on this subject. But if I do something you don't like, remember, on earth it's harder than where you are. Then when my week of mourning was finished, one night I said, "Ornita, let's get married. We're both honest people and if you love me like I love you it won't be such a bad time. If you don't like New York I'll sell out here and we'll move someplace else. Maybe to San Francisco where nobody knows us. I was there for a week in the Second War and I saw white and colored living together."

"Nat," she answered me, "I like you but I'd be afraid. My husband woulda killed me."

"Your husband is dead."

"Not in my memory."

"In that case I'll wait."

"Do you know what it'd be like — I mean the life we could expect?"

"Ornita," I said, "I'm the kind of a man, if he picks his own way of life he's satisfied."

"What about children? Were you looking forward to half-Jewish polka dots?"

"I was looking forward to children."

"I can't," she said.

Can't is can't. I saw she was afraid and the best thing was not to push. Sometimes when we met she was so nervous that whatever we did she couldn't enjoy it. At the same time I still thought I had a chance. We were together more and more. I got rid of my furnished room and she came to my apartment — I gave away Mama's bed and bought a new one. She stayed with me all day on Sundays. When she wasn't so nervous she was affectionate, and if I know what love is, I had it. We went out a couple of times a week, the same way — usually I met her in Times Square and sent her home in a taxi, but I talked more about marriage and she talked less against it. One night she told me she was still trying to convince herself but she was almost convinced. I took an inventory of my liquor stock so I could put the store up for sale.

Ornita knew what I was doing. One day she quit her job, the next day she took it back. She also went away a week to visit her sister in Philadelphia for a little rest. She came back tired but said maybe. Maybe is maybe so I'll wait. The way she said it it was closer to yes. That was the winter two years ago. When she was in Philadelphia I called up a friend of mine from the Army, now CPA, and told him I would appreciate an invitation for an evening. He knew why. His wife said yes right away. When Ornita came back we went there. The wife made a fine dinner. It wasn't a bad time and they told us to come again. Ornita had a few drinks. She looked relaxed, wonderful. Later, because of a twenty-four hour taxi strike I had to take her home on the subway. When we got to the 116th Street station she told me to stay on the train, and she would walk the couple of blocks to her house. I didn't like a woman walking alone on the streets at that time of the night. She said she never had any trouble but I insisted nothing doing. I said I would walk to her stoop with her and when she went upstairs I would go back to the subway.

On the way there, on 115th in the middle of the block before Lenox, we were stopped by three men — maybe they were boys. One had a black hat with a half-inch brim, one a green cloth hat, and the third wore a black leather cap. The green hat was wearing a short coat and the other two had long ones. It was under a street light but the leather cap snapped a six-inch switchblade open in the light.

"What you doin' with this white son of a bitch?" he said to Ornita.

"I'm minding my own business," she answered him, "and I wish you would too."

"Boys," I said, "we're all brothers. I'm a reliable merchant in the neighborhood. This young lady is my dear friend. We don't want any trouble. Please let us pass."

"You talk like a Jew landlord," said the green hat. "Fifty a week for a single room."

"No charge fo' the rats," said the half-inch brim.

"Believe me, I'm no landlord. My store is 'Nathan's Liquors' between Hundred Tenth and Eleventh. I also have two colored clerks, Mason and Jimmy, and they will tell you I pay good wages as well as I give discounts to certain customers."

"Shut your mouth, Jewboy," said the leather cap, and he moved the knife back and forth in front of my coat button. "No more black pussy for you."

"Speak with respect about this lady, please."

I got slapped on my mouth.

"That ain't no lady," said the long face in the half-inch brim, "that's black pussy. She deserve to have evvy bit of her hair shave off. How you like to have evvy bit of your hair shave off, black pussy?"

"Please leave me and this gentleman alone or I'm gonna scream long and loud. That's my house three doors down."

They slapped her. I never heard such a scream. Like her husband was falling fifteen stories.

I hit the one that slapped her and the next I knew I was lying in the gutter with a pain in my head. I thought, goodbye, Nat, they'll stab me for sure, but all they did was take my wallet and run in three different directions.

Ornita walked back with me to the subway and she wouldn't let me go home with her again.

"Just get home safely."

She looked terrible. Her face was gray and I still remembered her scream. It was a terrible winter night, very cold February, and it took me an hour and ten minutes to get home. I felt bad for leaving her but what could I do?

We had a date downtown the next night but she didn't show up, the first time.

In the morning I called her in her place of business.

"For God's sake, Ornita, if we got married and moved away we wouldn't have that kind of trouble that we had. We wouldn't come in that neighborhood any more."

"Yes, we would. I have family there and don't want to move anyplace else. The truth of it is I can't marry you, Nat. I got troubles enough of my own."

"I coulda sworn you love me."

"Maybe I do but I can't marry you."

"For God's sake, why?"

"I got enough trouble of my own."

I went that night in a cab to her brother's house to see her. He was a quiet man with a thin mustache. "She gone," he said, "left for a long visit to some close relatives in the South. She said to tell you she appreciate your intentions but didn't think it will work out."

"Thank you kindly," I said.

Don't ask me how I got home.

Once on Eighth Avenue, a couple of blocks from my store, I saw a blind man with a white cane tapping on the sidewalk. I figured we were going in the same direction so I took his arm.

"I can tell you're white," he said.

A heavy colored woman with a full shopping bag rushed after us.

"Never mind," she said, "I know where he live."

She pushed me with her shoulder and I hurt my leg on the fire hydrant.

That's how it is. I give my heart and they kick me in my teeth.

"Charity Sweetness – you hear me? – come out of that goddamn toilet!"

SAUL BELLOW b. 1915

Though born in Canada, Bellow grew up in Chicago, and it is life there – from the immigrant Jewish community in which he lived as a young man during the Depression to the intellectual life of the university (where he was a student and is now a professor) – that forms the basis of his fiction. He was first widely recognized for his autobiographical novel *The Adventures of Augie March* (1953). The young Augie is typical of Bellow's sensitive characters with elaborate inner lives who get involved with events that are too much for them to control; their good intentions, their illusions about themselves, are out of line with the way things really happen. They are misunderstood, cheated – or, most interesting of all, co-opted by the fantasies of others. However powerful their own dreams, they find, like the hero of Bellow's novel *Mr. Sammler's Planet* (1969), that modern life on *this* planet moves according to some unpredictable logic that frustrates their hopes. They then either give in rather grumblingly, as the father-to-be does here, to immediate satisfactions within what they recognize as long-term disaster, or are forced to invent still more elaborate visions of themselves to try to accommodate reality.

In his early fiction, of which "A Father-to-Be" is an excellent example, Bellow tended to reign in his characters' fabrication of wish-fulfilling lives for themselves. There is more or less an equality between the keenly observed details of life and the characters' fancies. In *Augie March* the "feel" of Chicago in the Depression is very real, and quite as intense as Augie's imagination of himself. Later, however, Bellow consciously abandoned the ideal of a tightly made fiction and allowed fantasy-building to dominate. Hattie, in "Leaving the Yellow House," bursts out into drunken (and touchingly fruitless) will-writing; and she is sensationally outdone by the character Herzog in the 1964 novel that bears his name. Overwhelmed by learning, as well as the usual desires for small sensual pleasures, Herzog explodes in magnificent flights of *chutzpah*, which are, if anything, less realized in his life than Hattie's modest hopes are in hers.

A FATHER-TO-BE

The strangest notions had a way of forcing themselves into Rogin's mind. Just thirty-one and passable-looking, with short black hair, small eyes, but a high, open forehead, he was a research chemist, and his mind was generally serious and dependable. But on a snowy Sunday evening while this stocky man, buttoned to the chin in a Burberry coat and walking in his preposterous gait – feet turned outwards – was going towards the subway, he fell into a peculiar state.

He was on his way to have supper with his fiancée. She had phoned him a short while ago and said, "You'd better pick up a few things on the way."

"What do we need?"

"Some roast beef, for one thing. I bought a quarter of a pound coming home from my aunt's."

"Why a quarter of a pound, Joan?" said Rogin, deeply annoyed. "That's just about enough for one good sandwich."

"So you have to stop at a delicatessen. I had no more money."

He was about to ask, "What happened to the thirty dollars I gave you on Wednesday?" but he knew that would not be right.

"I had to give Phyllis money for the cleaning woman," said Joan.

Phyllis, Joan's cousin, was a young divorcée, extremely wealthy. The two women shared an apartment.

"Roast beef," he said, "and what else?"

"Some shampoo, sweetheart. We've used up all the shampoo. And hurry, darling, I've missed you all day."

"And I've missed you," said Rogin, but to tell the truth he had been worrying most of the time. He had a younger brother whom he was putting through college. And his mother, whose annuity wasn't quite enough in these days of inflation and high taxes, needed money, too. Joan had debts he was helping her to pay, for she wasn't working. She was looking for something suitable to do. Beautiful, well educated, aristocratic in her attitude, she couldn't clerk in a dime store; she couldn't model clothes (Rogin thought this made girls vain and stiff, and he didn't want her to); she couldn't be a waitress or a cashier. What could she be? Well, something would turn up, and meantime Rogin hesitated to complain. He paid her bills – the dentist, the department store, the osteopath, the doctor, the psychiatrist. At Christmas, Rogin almost went mad. Joan bought him a velvet smoking jacket with frog fasteners, a beautiful pipe, and a pouch. She bought Phyllis a garnet brooch, an Italian silk umbrella, and a gold cigarette holder. For other friends, she bought Dutch pewter and Swedish glassware. Before she was through, she had spent five hundred dollars of Rogin's money. He loved her too much to show his suffering. He believed she had a far better nature than his. She didn't worry about money. She had a marvellous character, always cheerful, and she really didn't need a psychiatrist at all. She went to one because Phyllis did and it made her curious. She tried too much to keep up with her cousin, whose father had made millions in the rug business.

While the woman in the drugstore was wrapping the shampoo bottle, a clear idea suddenly arose in Rogin's thoughts: Money surrounds you in life as the earth does in death. Superimposition is the universal law. Who is free? No one is free. Who has no burdens? Everyone is under pressure. The very rocks, the waters of the earth, beasts, men, children – everyone has some weight to carry. This idea was extremely clear to him at first. Soon it became rather vague, but it had a great effect nevertheless, as if someone had given him a valuable gift. (Not like the velvet smoking jacket he couldn't bring himself to wear, or the pipe it choked him to smoke.) The notion that all were under pressure and affliction, instead of saddening him, had the opposite influence. It put him in a wonderful mood. It was extraordinary how happy he became and, in addition, clear-sighted. His eyes all at once were open to what was around him. He saw with delight how the druggist and the woman who wrapped the shampoo bottle were smiling and flirting, how the lines of worry in her face went over into lines of cheer and the druggist's receding gums did not hinder his kidding and friendliness. And in the delicatessen, also, it was amazing how much Rogin noted and what happiness it gave him simply to be there.

Delicatessens on Sunday night, when all other stores are shut, will overcharge you ferociously, and Rogin would normally have been on guard, but he was not tonight, or scarcely so. Smells of pickle, sausage, mustard, and smoked fish overjoyed him. He pitied the people who would buy the chicken salad and chopped herring; they could do it only because their sight was too dim to see what they were getting – the fat flakes of pepper on the chicken, the soppy herring, mostly vinegar-soaked stale bread. Who would buy them? Late risers, people living alone, waking up in the darkness of the afternoon, finding their refrigerators empty, or people whose gaze was turned inwards. The roast beef looked not bad, and Rogin ordered a pound.

While the storekeeper was slicing the meat, he yelled at a Puerto Rican kid who was reaching for a bag of chocolate cookies, "Hey, you want to pull me down the whole display on yourself? You, *chico,* wait a half a minute." This storekeeper, though he looked like one of Pancho Villa's bandits, the kind that smeared their enemies with syrup and staked them down on anthills, a man with toadlike eyes and stout hands made to clasp pistols hung around his belly, was not so bad. He was a New York man, thought Rogin – who was from Albany himself – a New York man toughened by every abuse of the city, trained to suspect everyone. But in his own realm, on the board behind the counter, there was justice. Even clemency.

The Puerto Rican kid wore a complete cowboy outfit – a green hat with white braid, guns, chaps, spurs, boots, and gauntlets – but he couldn't speak any English. Rogin unhooked the cellophane bag of hard circular cookies and gave it to him. The boy tore the cellophane with his teeth and began to chew one of those dry chocolate discs. Rogin recognized his state – the energetic dream of childhood. Once, he, too, had found these dry biscuits delicious. It would have bored him now to eat one.

What else would Joan like? Rogin thought fondly. Some strawberries? "Give me some frozen strawberries. No, raspberries, she likes those better. And heavy cream. And some rolls, cream cheese, and some of those rubber-looking gherkins."

"What rubber?"

"Those, deep green, with eyes. Some ice cream might be in order, too."

He tried to think of a compliment, a good comparison, an endearment, for Joan when she'd open the door. What about her complexion? There was really nothing to compare her sweet, small, daring, shapely, timid, defiant, loving face to. How difficult she was, and how beautiful!

As Rogin went down into the stony, odorous, metallic, captive air of the subway, he was diverted by an unusual confession made by a man to his friend. These were two very tall men, shapeless in their winter clothes, as if their coats concealed suits of chain mail.

"So, how long have you known me?" said one.

"Twelve years."

"Well, I have an admission to make," he said. "I've decided that I might as well. For years I've been a heavy drinker. You didn't know. Practically an alcoholic."

But his friend was not surprised, and he answered immediately, "Yes, I did know."

"You knew? Impossible! How could you?"

Why, thought Rogin, as if it could be a secret! Look at that long, austere, alcohol-washed face, that drink-ruined nose, the skin by his ears like turkey wattles, and those whisky-saddened eyes.

"Well, I did know, though."

"You couldn't have. I can't believe it." He was upset, and his friend didn't seem to want to soothe him. "But it's all right now," he said. "I've been going to a doctor and taking pills, a new revolutionary Danish discovery. It's a miracle. I'm beginning to believe they can cure you of anything and everything. You can't beat the Danes in science. They do everything. They turned a man into a woman."

"That isn't how they stop you from drinking, is it?"

"No. I hope not. This is only like aspirin. It's super-aspirin. They call it the aspirin of the future. But if you use it, you have to stop drinking."

Rogin's illuminated mind asked of itself while the human tides of the subway swayed back and forth, and cars linked and transparent like fish bladders raced under the streets: How come he thought nobody would know what everybody couldn't help knowing? And, as a chemist, he asked himself what kind of compound this new Danish drug might be, and started thinking about various inventions of his own, synthetic albumen, a cigarette that lit itself, a cheaper motor fuel. Ye gods, but he needed money! As never before. What was to be done? His mother was growing more and more difficult. On Friday night, she had neglected to cut up his meat for him, and he was hurt. She had sat at the table motionless, with her long-suffering face, severe, and let him cut his own meat, a thing she almost never did. She had always spoiled him and made his brother envy him. But what she expected now! Oh, Lord, how he had to pay, and it had never even occurred to him formerly that these things might have a price.

Seated, one of the passengers, Rogin recovered his calm, happy, even clairvoyant state of mind. To think of money was to think as the world wanted you to think; then you'd never be your own master. When people said they wouldn't do something for love or money, they meant that love and money were opposite passions and one the enemy of the other. He went on to reflect how little people knew about this, how they slept through life, how small a light the light of consciousness was. Rogin's clean, snub-nosed face shone while his heart was torn with joy at these deeper thoughts of our ignorance. You might take this drunkard as an example, who for long years thought his closest friends never suspected he drank. Rogin looked up and down the aisle for this remarkable knightly symbol, but he was gone.

However, there was no lack of things to see. There was a small girl with a new white muff; into the muff a doll's head was sewn, and the child was happy and affectionately vain of it, while her old man, stout and grim, with a huge scowling nose, kept picking her up and resettling her in the seat, as if he were trying to change her into something else. Then another child, led by her mother, boarded the car, and this other child carried the very same doll-faced muff, and this greatly annoyed both parents. The woman, who looked like a difficult, contentious woman, took her daughter away. It seemed to Rogin that each child was in love with its own muff and didn't even see the other, but it was one of his foibles to think he understood the hearts of little children.

A foreign family next engaged his attention. They looked like Central Americans to him. On one side the mother, quite old, dark-faced, white-haired, and worn out; on the other a son with the whitened, porous hands of a dishwasher. But what was the dwarf who sat between them – a son or a daughter? The hair was long and wavy and the cheeks smooth, but the shirt and tie were masculine. The overcoat was feminine, but the shoes – the shoes were a puzzle. A pair of brown oxfords with an outer seam like a man's, but Baby Louis heels like a woman's – a plain toe like a man's, but a strap across the instep like a woman's. No stockings. That didn't help much. The dwarf's fingers were beringed, but without a wedding band. There were small grim dents in the cheeks. The eyes were puffy and concealed, but Rogin did not doubt that they could reveal strange things if they chose and that this was a creature of remarkable understanding. He had for many years owned De la Mare's "Memoirs of a Midget." Now he took a resolve; he would read it. As soon as he had decided, he was free from his consuming curiosity as to the dwarf's sex and was able to look at the person who sat beside him.

Thoughts very often grow fertile in the subway, because of the motion, the great company, the subtlety of the rider's state as he rattles under streets and rivers, under the foundations of great buildings, and Rogin's mind had already been strangely stimulated. Clasping the bag of groceries from which there rose odors of bread and pickle spice, he was following a train of reflections, first about the chemistry of sex determination, the X and Y chromosomes, hereditary linkages, the uterus, afterwards about his brother as a tax exemption. He recalled two dreams of the night before. In one, an undertaker had offered to cut his hair, and he had refused. In another, he had been carrying a woman on his head. Sad dreams, both! Very sad! Which was the woman – Joan or Mother? And the undertaker – his lawyer? He gave a deep sigh, and by force of habit began to put together his synthetic albumen that was to revolutionize the entire egg industry.

Meanwhile, he had not interrupted his examination of the passengers and had fallen into a study of the man next to him. This was a man whom he had never in his life seen before but with whom he now suddenly felt linked through all existence. He was middle-aged, sturdy, with clear skin and blue eyes. His hands were clean, well-formed, but Rogin did not approve of them. The coat he wore was a fairly expensive blue check such as Rogin would never have chosen for himself. He would not have worn blue suède shoes, either, or such a faultless hat, a cumbersome felt animal of a hat encircled by a high, fat ribbon. There are all kinds of dandies, not all of them are of the flaunting kind; some are dandies of respectability, and Rogin's fellow-passenger was one of these. His straight-nosed profile was handsome, yet he had betrayed his gift, for he was flat-looking. But in his flat way he seemed to warn people that he wanted no difficulties with them, he wanted nothing to do with them. Wearing such blue suède shoes, he could not afford to have people treading on his feet, and he seemed to draw about himself a circle of privilege, notifying all others to mind their own business and let him read his paper. He was holding a *Tribune,* and perhaps it would be overstatement to say that he was reading. He was holding it.

His clear skin and blue eyes, his straight and purely Roman nose – even the way he sat – all strongly suggested one person to Rogin: Joan. He tried to escape the comparison, but it couldn't be helped. This man not only looked like Joan's father, whom Rogin detested; he looked like Joan herself. Forty years hence, a son of hers, provided she had one, might be like this. A son of hers? Of such a son, he himself, Rogin, would be the father. Lacking in dominant traits as compared with Joan, his heritage would not appear. Probably the child would resemble her. Yes, think forty years ahead, and a man like this, who sat by him knee to knee in the hurtling car among their fellow-creatures, unconscious participants in a sort of great carnival of transit – such a man would carry forwards what had been Rogin.

This was why he felt bound to him through all existence. What were forty years reckoned against eternity! Forty years were gone, and he was gazing at his own son. Here he was. Rogin was frightened and moved. "My son! My son!" he said to himself, and the pity of it almost made him burst into tears. The holy and frightful work of the masters of life and death brought this about. We were their instruments. We worked towards ends we thought were our own. But no! The whole thing was so unjust. To suffer, to labour, to toil and force your way through the spikes of life, to crawl through its darkest caverns, to push through the worst, to struggle under the weight of economy, to make money – only to become the father of a fourth-rate man of the world like this, so flat-looking, with his ordinary, clean, rosy, uninteresting, self-satisfied, fundamentally bourgeois face. What a curse to have a dull son! A son like this, who could never understand his father. They had absolutely nothing, but nothing, in common, he and this neat, chubby, blue-eyed man. He was so pleased, thought Rogin, with all he owned and all he did and all he was that he could hardly unfasten his lip. Look at that lip, sticking up at the tip like a little thorn or egg tooth. He wouldn't give anyone the time of day. Would this perhaps be general forty years from now? Would personalities be chillier as the world aged and grew colder? The inhumanity of the next generation incensed Rogin. Father and son had no sign to make to each other. Terrible! Inhuman! What a vision of existence it gave him. Man's personal aims were nothing, illusion. The life force occupied each of us in turn in its progress towards its own fulfilment, trampling on our individual humanity, using us for its own ends like mere dinosaurs or bees, exploiting love heartlessly, making us engage in the social process, labour, struggle for money, and submit to the law of pressure, the universal law of layers, superimposition!

What the blazes am I getting into? Rogin thought. To be the father of a throwback to *her* father. The image of this white-haired, gross, peevish old man with his ugly selfish blue eyes revolted Rogin. This was how his grandson would look.

Joan, with whom Rogin was now more and more displeased, could not help that. For her, it was inevitable. But did it have to be inevitable for him? Well, then, Rogin, you fool, don't be a damned instrument. Get out of the way!

But it was too late for this, because he had already experienced the sensation of sitting next to his own son, his son and Joan's. He kept staring at him, waiting for him to say something, but the presumptive son remained coldly silent though he must have been aware of Rogin's scrutiny. They even got out at the same stop – Sheridan Square. When they stepped to the platform, the man, without even looking at Rogin, went away in a different direction in his detestable blue-checked coat, with his rosy, nasty face.

The whole thing upset Rogin very badly. When he approached Joan's door and heard Phyllis's little dog Henri barking even before he could knock, his face was very tense. "I won't be used," he declared to himself. "I have my own right to exist." Joan had better watch out. She had a light way of bypassing grave questions he had given earnest thought to. She always assumed no really disturbing thing would happen. He could not afford the luxury of such a carefree, debonair attitude himself, because he had to work hard and earn money so that disturbing things would *not* happen. Well, at the moment this situation could not be helped, and he really did not mind the money if he could feel that she was not necessarily the mother of such a son as his subway son or entirely the daughter of that awful, obscene father of hers. After all, Rogin was not himself so much like either of his parents, and quite different from his brother.

Joan came to the door, wearing one of Phyllis's expensive housecoats. It suited her very well. At first sight of her happy face, Rogin was brushed by the shadow of resemblance; the touch of it was extremely light, almost figmentary, but it made his flesh tremble.

She began to kiss him, saying, "Oh, my baby. You're covered with snow. Why didn't you wear your hat? It's all over its little head" – her favorite third-person endearment.

"Well, let me put down this bag of stuff. Let me take off my coat," grumbled Rogin, and escaped from her embrace. Why couldn't she wait making up to him? "It's so hot in here. My face is burning. Why do you keep the place at this temperature? And that damned dog keeps barking. If you didn't keep it cooped up, it wouldn't be so spoiled and noisy. Why doesn't anybody ever walk him?"

"Oh, it's not really so hot here! You've just come in from the cold. Don't you think this housecoat fits me better than Phyllis? Especially across the hips. She thinks so, too. She may sell it to me."

"I hope not," Rogin almost exclaimed.

She brought a towel to dry the melting snow from his short, black hair. The flurry of rubbing excited Henri intolerably, and Joan locked him up in the bedroom, where he jumped persistently against the door with a rhythmic sound of claws on the wood.

Joan said, "Did you bring the shampoo?"

"Here it is."

"Then I'll wash your hair before dinner. Come."

"I don't want it washed."

"Oh, come on," she said, laughing.

Her lack of consciousness of guilt amazed him. He did not see how it could be. And the carpeted, furnished, lamplit, curtained room seemed to stand against his vision. So that he felt accusing and angry, his spirit sore and bitter, but it did not seem fitting to say why. Indeed, he began to worry lest the reason for it all slip away from him.

They took off his coat and his shirt in the bathroom, and she filled the sink. Rogin was full of his troubled emotions; now that his chest was bare he could feel them even more distinctly inside, and he said to himself, "I'll have a thing or two to tell her pretty soon. I'm not letting them get away with it. 'Do you think,' he was going to tell her, 'that I alone was made to carry the burden of the whole world on me? Do you think I was born just to be taken advantage of and sacrificed? Do you think I'm just a natural resource, like a coal mine, or oil well, or fishery, or the like? Remember, that I'm a man is no reason why I should be loaded down. I have a soul in me no bigger or stronger than yours. Take away the externals, like the muscles, deeper voice, and so forth, and what remains? A pair of spirits, practically alike. So why shouldn't there also be equality? I can't always be the strong one.' "

"Sit here," said Joan, bringing up a kitchen stool to the sink. "Your hair's gotten all matted."

He sat with his breast against the cool enamel, his chin on the edge of the basin, the green, hot, radiant water reflecting the glass and the tile, and the sweet, cool, fragrant juice of the shampoo poured on his head. She began to wash him.

"You have the healthiest-looking scalp," she said. "It's all pink."

He answered, "Well, it should be white. There must be something wrong with me."

"But there's absolutely nothing wrong with you," she said, and pressed against him from behind, surrounding him, pouring the water gently over him until it seemed to him that the water came from within him, it was the warm fluid of his own secret loving spirit overflowing into the sink, green and foaming, and the words he had rehearsed he forgot, and his anger at his son-to-be disappeared altogether, and he sighed, and said to her from the water-filled hollow of the sink, "You always have such wonderful ideas, Joan. You know? You have a kind of instinct, a regular gift."

LEAVING THE YELLOW HOUSE

The neighbors – there were in all six white people who lived at Sego Desert Lake – told one another that old Hattie could no longer make it alone. The desert life, even with a forced-air furnace in the house and butane gas brought from town in a truck, was still too difficult for her. There were older women in the county. Twenty miles away was Amy Walters, the gold miner's widow. But she was a hardier old girl. Every day of the year she took a bath in the lake. And Amy was crazy about money and knew how to manage it, as Hattie did not. Hattie was not exactly a drunkard, but she hit the bottle pretty hard, and now she was in trouble and there was a limit to the help she could expect from even the best of neighbors.

They were fond of her, though. You couldn't help being fond of Hattie. She was big and cheerful, puffy, comic, boastful, with a big round back and stiff, rather long legs. Before the century began she had graduated from finishing school and studied the organ in Paris. But now she didn't know a note from a skillet; she had tantrums when she played canasta. And all that remained of her fine fair hair was frizzled along her forehead in small grey curls. Her forehead was not much wrinkled, but the skin was bluish, the color of skim milk. She walked with long strides in spite of the heaviness of her hips, pushing on, round-backed, with her shoulders and showing the flat rubber bottoms of her shoes.

Once a week, in the same cheerful, plugging but absent way, she took off her short skirt and the dirty aviator's jacket with the wool collar and put on a girdle, a dress and high-heeled shoes. When she stood on these heels her fat old body trembled. She wore a big brown Rembrandt-like tam with a ten-cent-store brooch, eyelike, carefully centered. She drew a straight line with lipstick on her mouth, leaving part of the upper lip pale. At the wheel of her old turret-shaped car, she drove, seemingly methodical but speeding dangerously, across forty miles of mountainous desert to buy frozen meat pies and whiskey. She went to the Laundromat and the hairdresser, and then had lunch with two Martinis at the Arlington. Afterwards she would often visit Marian Nabot's Silvermine Hotel at Miller Street near skid row and pass the rest of the day gossiping and drinking with her cronies, old divorcées like herself who had settled in the West. Hattie never gambled any more and she didn't care for the movies, and at five o'clock she drove back at the same speed, calmly, partly blinded by the smoke of her cigarette. She was a tough-looking smoker. The fixed cigarette gave her a watering eye.

The Rolfes and the Paces were her only white neighbors at Sego Desert Lake. There was Sam Jervis too, but he was only an old gandy walker who did odd jobs in her garden, and she did not count him. Nor did she count among her neighbors Darly, the dudes' cowboy who worked for the Paces, nor Swede, the telegrapher. Pace had a guest ranch, and Rolfe and his wife were rich and had retired. Thus there were three good houses at the Lake, Hattie's yellow house, Pace's and the Rolfes'. All the rest of the population – Sam, Swede, Watchtah the section foreman, and the Mexicans and Indians and Negroes – lived in shacks and box-cars. You could count all the trees in a minute's time: cottonwoods and box elders. All the rest, down to the shores, was sagebrush and juniper. The lake was what remained of an old sea that had covered the volcanic mountains. To the north there were some tungsten mines; to the south, fifteen miles, was an Indian village built of railroad ties.

In this barren place Hattie had lived for more than twenty years. Her first summer was spent not in a house but in an Indian wikiup on the shore. She used to say that she had watched the stars from this almost roofless shelter. After her divorce she took up with a cowboy named Wicks. Neither of them had any money – it was the Depression – and they had lived on the range, trapping coyotes for a living. Once a month they would come into town and rent a room and go on a bender. Hattie told this sadly, but also gloatingly, and with many trimmings. A thing no sooner happened to her than it was transformed into something else. "We were caught in a storm," she said, "and we rode hard, down to the lake and knocked on the door of the yellow house" – now her house. "Alice Parmenter took us in and let us sleep on the floor." What had actually happened was that the wind was blowing – there had been no storm – and they were not far away from the house anyway; and Alice Parmenter, who knew that Hattie and Wicks were not married, offered them separate beds; but Hattie, swaggering, had said in a loud voice, "Why get two sets of sheets dirty?" And she and her cowboy had slept in Alice's double bed while Alice had taken the sofa.

Now Wicks was gone. There was never anybody like him in the sack; he was brought up in a whorehouse and the girls taught him everything, said Hattie. She didn't really understand what she was saying, but believed that she was being Western, and more than anything else she wanted to be thought of as a rough, experienced woman of the West. Still, she was a lady, too. She had good silver and good china and engraved stationery, but she kept canned beans and A-1 sauce and tunafish and bottles of catsup and fruit salad on the library shelves of her living room. On the night table was the Bible her pious brother Angus – her other brother was a heller – had given her; but behind the little cabinet door was a bottle of bourbon. When she awoke in the night she tippled herself back to sleep. In the glove compartment of her old car she kept little sample bottles for emergencies on the road. Old Darly found them after her accident.

The accident did not happen far out in the desert as she had always feared, but near her home. She had had a few Martinis with the Rolfes one evening and as she was driving home over the railroad crossing she lost control of the car and drove off the crossing onto the tracks. The explanation she gave was that she had sneezed, and the sneeze had blinded her and made her twist the wheel. The motor was killed and all four wheels of the car sat smack on the rails. Hattie crept down from the door, high off the roadbed. A great fear took hold of her – for the car, for the future, and not only for the future but for the past – and she began to hurry on stiff legs through the sagebrush to Pace's ranch.

Now the Paces were away on a hunting trip and had left old Darly in charge; he was tending bar in the old cabin that went back to the days of the pony express when Hattie burst in. There were two customers, a tungsten miner and his girl.

"Darly, I'm in trouble. Help me. I've had an accident," said Hattie.

How the face of a man will alter when a woman has bad news to tell him! It happened now to lean old Darly; his eyes went flat and looked unwilling, his jaw moved in and out, his wrinkled cheeks began to flush, and he said, "What's the matter – what's happened to you now?"

"I'm stuck on the tracks. I sneezed. I lost control of the car. Tow me off, Darly, with the pickup before the train comes."

Darly threw down his towel and stamped his high-heeled boots with anger. "Now what have you gone and done?' he said. "I told you to stay home after dark."

"Where's Pace? Ring the fire bell and fetch Pace."

"There's nobody on the property but me," said the lean old man. "And I'm not supposed to close the bar and you know it as well as I do."

"Please, Darly. I can't leave my car on the tracks."

"Too bad!" he said. Nevertheless he moved from behind the bar. "How did you say it happened?"

"I told you, I sneezed," said Hattie.

Everyone, as she later told it, was as drunk as sixteen thousand dollars: Darly, the miner and the miner's girl.

Darly was limping as he locked the door of the bar. A year before, a kick from one of Pace's mares had broken his ribs as he was loading her into the trailer, and he hadn't recovered from it. He was too old. But he dissembled the pain. The high-heeled narrow boots helped, and his painful bending looked like the ordinary stooping posture of a cowboy on the ground. However, Darly was not a genuine cowboy, like Pace who had grown up in the saddle. He was a late-comer from the East and until the age of forty had never been on horseback. In this respect he and Hattie were alike. They were not the Westerners they seemed to be.

Hattie hurried after him through the ranch yard.

"Damn you!" he said to her, "I got thirty bucks out of that sucker and I would have skinned him out of his whole pay check if you minded your business. Pace is going to be sore as hell."

"You've got to help me. We're neighbors," said Hattie.

"You're not fit to be living out here. You can't do it any more. Besides, you're swacked all the time."

Hattie couldn't afford to talk back to him. The thought of her car on the tracks made her frantic. If a freight came now and smashed it, her life at Sego Desert Lake would be finished. And where would she go then? She was not fit to live in this place. She had never made the grade at all; she only seemed to have made it. And Darly – why did he say such hurtful things to her? Because he himself was sixty-eight years old, and he had no other place to go, either; he took bad treatment from Pace besides. Darly stayed because his only alternative was to go to the soldier's home. Moreover, the dude women would crawl into his sack. They wanted a cowboy and they thought he was one. Why, he couldn't even raise himself out of his bunk in the morning. And where else would he get women? "After the season," she wanted to say to him, "you always have to go to the Veterans' Hospital to get yourself fixed up again." But she didn't dare offend him now.

The moon was due to rise. It appeared as they drove over the ungraded dirt road toward the crossing where Hattie's turret-shaped car was sitting on the rails. At great speed Darly wheeled the pickup around, spraying dirt on the miner and his girl who had followed in their car.

"You get behind the wheel and steer," Darly told Hattie.

She climbed into the seat. Waiting at the wheel she lifted up her face and said, "Please, God, I didn't bend the axle or crack the oil pan."

When Darly crawled under the bumper of Hattie's car the pain in his ribs suddenly cut off his breath, so instead of doubling the tow chain he fastened it at full length. He rose and trotted back to the truck on the narrow boots. Motion seemed the only remedy for the pain; not even booze did the trick any more. He put the pickup into towing gear and began to pull. One side of Hattie's car dropped into the roadbed with a heave of springs. She sat with a stormy, frightened, conscience-stricken face, racing the motor until she flooded it.

The tungsten miner yelled, "Your chain's too long."

Hattie was raised high in the air by the pitch of the wheels. She had to roll down the window to let herself out because the door handle had been jammed from the inside for years. Hattie struggled out on the uplifted side crying, "I better call the Swede. I better have him signal. There's a train due."

"Go on, then," said Darly. "You're no good here."

"Darly, be careful with my car. Be careful."

The ancient sea bed at this place was flat and low and the lights of her car and of the truck and of the tungsten miner's Chevrolet were bright and big at twenty miles. Hattie was too frightened to think of this. All she could think was that she was a procrastinating old woman, she had lived by delays; she had meant to stop drinking, she had put off the time, and now she had smashed her car – a terrible end, a terrible judgment on her. She got to the ground and, drawing up her skirt, she started to get over the tow chain. To prove that the chain didn't have to be shortened, and to get the whole thing over with, Darly threw the pickup forward again. The chain jerked up and struck Hattie in the knee and she fell forward and broke her arm.

She cried, "Darly, Darly, I'm hurt. I fell."

"The old lady tripped on the chain," said the miner. "Back up here and I'll double it for you. You're getting nowheres."

Drunkenly the miner lay down on his back in the dark, soft red cinders of the roadbed. Darly had backed up to slacken the chain.

Darly hurt the miner, too. He tore some skin from his fingers by racing ahead before the chain was secure. Uncomplainingly the miner wrapped his hand in his shirttail saying, "She'll do it now." The old car came down from the tracks and stood on the shoulder of the road.

"There's your goddam car," said Darly to Hattie.

"Is it all right?" she said. Her left side was covered with dirt, but she managed to pick herself up and stand, round-backed and heavy, on her stiff legs. "I'm hurt, Darly." She tried to convince him of it.

"Hell if you are," he said. He believed she was putting on an act to escape blame. The pain in his ribs made him especially impatient with her. "Christ, if you can't look after yourself any more you've got no business out here."

"You're old yourself," she said. "Look what you did to me. You can't hold your liquor."

This offended him greatly. He said, "I'll take you to the Rolfes. They let you tie this on in the first place, so let them worry about you. I'm tired of your bunk, Hattie."

He speeded up. Chains, spade and crowbar clashed on the sides of the truck. She was frightened and held her arm and cried. Rolfe's dogs jumped at her to lick her when she went through the gate. She shrank from them crying, "Down, down."

"Darly," she cried in the darkness, "take care of my car. Don't leave it standing there on the road. Darly, take care of it, please."

But Darly in his ten-gallon hat, his chin-bent face wrinkled, small and angry, a furious pain in his ribs, tore away at high speed.

"Oh, God, what will I do," she said.

The Rolfes were having a last drink before dinner, sitting at their fire of pitchy railroad ties, when Hattie opened the door. Her knee was bleeding, her eyes were tiny with shock, her face grey with dust.

"I'm hurt," she said desperately. "I had an accident. I sneezed and lost control of the wheel. Jerry, look after the car. It's on the road."

They bandaged her knee and took her home and put her to bed. Helen Rolfe wrapped a heating pad around her arm.

"I can't have the pad," Hattie complained. "The switch goes on and off and every time it does it starts my generator and uses up the gas."

"Ah, now, Hattie," Rolfe said, "this is not the time to be stingy. We'll take you to town in the morning and have you looked over. Helen will phone Doctor Stroud."

Hattie wanted to say, "Stingy! Why you're the stingy ones. I just haven't got anything. You and Helen are ready to hit each other over two bits in canasta." But the Rolfes were good to her; they were her only real friends here. Darly would have let her lie in the yard all night, and Pace would sell her to the bone man if he had an offer.

So she didn't talk back to the Rolfes, but as soon as they left the yellow house and walked through the super-clear moonlight under the great skirt of branch shadows to their new car, Hattie turned off the switch and the heavy swirling and battering of the generator stopped. Presently she began to have her first real taste of the pain in her arm, and she sat rigid and warmed the injured place with her hand. It seemed to her that she could feel the bone. Before leaving, Helen Rolfe had thrown over her a comforter that had belonged to Hattie's dead friend India, from whom she had inherited the small house and everything in it. Had the comforter lain on India's bed the night she died? Hattie tried to remember, but her thoughts were mixed up. She was fairly sure the death-bed pillow was in the loft, and she believed she had put the rest of the bedding in a trunk. Then how had this comforter got out? She couldn't do anything about it now but draw it away from contact with her skin. It kept her legs warm; this she accepted, but she didn't want it any nearer.

More and more Hattie saw her own life as though from birth to the present every moment had been filmed. Her fancy was that when she died she would see the film shown. Then she would know how she appeared from the back, watering the plants, in the bathroom, asleep playing the organ, embracing – everything, even tonight, in pain, almost the last pain, perhaps, for she couldn't take much more. How many more turns had life to show her yet. There couldn't be a lot. To lie awake and think such thoughts was the worst thing in the world. Better death than insomnia. Hattie not only loved sleep, she believed in it.

The first attempt to set the bone was not successful. "Look what they've done to me," said Hattie and showed the discolored skin on her breast. After the second operation her mind wandered. The sides of her bed had to be raised, for in her delirium she roamed the wards. She cried at the nurses when they shut her in, "You can't make people prisoners in a democracy without a trial." She cursed them fiercely.

For several weeks her mind was not clear. Asleep, her face was lifeless; her cheeks were puffed out and her mouth, no longer wide and grinning, was drawn round and small. Helen sighed when she saw her.

"Shall we get in touch with her family?" she asked the doctor. "She has a brother in Maine who is very strait-laced. And another one down in Mexico, even older than Hattie."

"No younger relations?" asked the doctor. His skin was white and thick. He had chestnut hair, abundant but very dry. He sometimes explained to his patients, "I had a tropical disease during the war."

"Cousins' children," said Helen. She tried to think who would be called to her own bedside. Rolfe would see that she was cared for. He would hire a nurse. Hattie could not afford one. She had already gone beyond her means. A trust company in Philadelphia paid her eighty dollars a month. She had a small bank account.

"I suppose it will be up to us to get her out of hock," said Rolfe. "Unless the brother down in Mexico comes across."

In the end, no relations had to be called. Hattie began to recover. At last she could recognize some of her friends, though her mind was still in disorder; much that had happened she couldn't recall.

"How much blood did they have to give me?" she kept asking. "I seem to remember five, six, eight different times. Daylight, electric light. . . ." She tried to smile, but she couldn't make a pleasant face as yet. "How am I going to pay?" she said. "At twenty-five bucks a quart. My little bit of money is just about wiped out."

Blood became her constant topic, her preoccupation. She told everyone who came to see her, "— have to replace all that blood. They poured gallons of the stuff into me. I hope it was all good." And, though very weak, she began to grin and laugh again. There was more of a hiss in her laughter than formerly; the illness had affected her chest.

"No cigarettes, no booze," the doctor told Helen.

"Doctor," Helen asked him, "do you expect her to change?"

"All the same, I am obliged to say it."

"Life may not be much of a temptation to her," said Helen.

Her husband laughed. When his laughter was intense it blinded one of his eyes and his short Irish face turned red except for the bridge of his small, sharp nose where the skin grew white. "Hattie's like me," he said. "She'll be in business till she's cleaned out. And if Sego Lake was all whiskey she'd use her last strength to knock her old yellow house down and build a raft of it. So why talk temperance to her now?"

Hattie recognized the similarity between them. When he came to see her she said, "Jerry, you're the only one I can really talk to about my troubles. What am I going to do for money? I have Hotchkiss Insurance. I paid eight dollars a month."

"That won't do you much good, Hat. No Blue Cross?"

"I let it drop ten years ago. Maybe I could sell some of my valuables."

"What have you got?" he said. His eye began to droop with laughter.

"Why," she said defiantly, "there's plenty. First tnere's the beautiful, precious Persian rug that India left me."

"Coals from the fireplace have been burning it for years, Hat!"

"The rug is in perfect condition," she said with an angry sway of her shoulders. "A beautiful object like that never loses its value. And the oak table from the Spanish monastery is three hundred years old."

"With luck you could get twenty bucks for it. It would cost fifty to haul it out of here. It's the house you ought to sell."

"The house?" she said. Yes, that had been in her mind. "I'd have to get twenty thousand for it."

"Eight is a fair price."

"Fifteen. . . ." She was offended, and her voice recovered its strength. "India put eight into it in two years. And don't forget that Sego Lake is one of the most beautiful places in the world."

"But where is it? Five hundred and some miles to San Francisco and two hundred to Salt Lake City. Who wants to live way out here in Utah but a few eccentrics like you and India and me?"

"There are things you can't put a price tag on. Beautiful things."

"Oh, bull, Hattie! You don't know what they are any more than I do. I live here because it figures for me, and you because India left you the house. And just in the nick of time, too. Without it you wouldn't have had a pot of your own."

His words offended Hattie; more than that, they frightened her. She was silent and then grew thoughtful, for she was fond of Jerry Rolfe and he of her. He had good sense and moreover he only spoke her own thoughts. He spoke no more than the truth about India's death and the house. But she told herself, *He doesn't know everything. You'd have to pay a San Francisco architect ten thousand just to* think *of such a house. Before he drew a line.*

"Jerry," the old woman said, "what am I going to do about replacing the blood in the blood bank?"

"Do you want a quart from me, Hat?" His eye began to fall shut.

"You won't do. You had that tumor, two years ago. I think Darly ought to give some."

"The old man?" Rolfe laughed at her. "You want to kill him?"

"Why," said Hattie with anger, lifting up her massive face with its fringe of curls which had become frayed by fever and perspiration; at the back of her head the hair had knotted and matted so that it had to be shaved, "he almost killed me. It's his fault that I'm in this condition. He must have blood in him. He runs after all the chicks – all of them – young and old."

"Come, you were drunk, too," said Rolfe.

"I've driven drunk for forty years. It was the sneeze. Oh, Jerry, I feel wrung out," said Hattie, haggard, sitting forward in bed. But her face was cleft by her nonsensically happy grin. She was not one to be miserable for long; she had the expression of a perennial survivor.

Every other day she went to the therapist. The young woman worked her arm for her; it was a pleasure and a comfort to Hattie, who would have been glad to leave the whole cure to her. However, she was given other exercises to do, and these were not so easy. They rigged a pulley for her and Hattie had to hold both ends of a rope and saw it back and forth through the scraping little wheel. She bent heavily from the hips and coughed over her cigarette. But the most important exercise of all she shirked. This required her to put the flat of her hand to the wall at the level of her hips and, by working her fingertips slowly, to make the hand ascend to the height of her shoulder. That was painful; she often forgot to do it, although the doctor warned her, "Hattie, you don't want adhesions, do you?"

A light of despair crossed Hattie's eyes. Then she said, "Oh, Dr. Stroud, buy my house from me."

"I'm a bachelor. What would I do with a house?"

"I know just the girl for you – my cousin's daughter. Perfectly charming and very brainy. Just about got her Ph.D."

"You must get quite a few proposals yourself," said the doctor.

"From crazy desert rats. They chase me. But," she said, "after I pay my bills I'll be in pretty punk shape. If at least I could replace that blood in the blood bank I'd feel easier."

"If you don't do as the therapist tells you, Hattie, you'll need another operation. Do you know what adhesions are?"

She knew. But Hattie thought, *How long must I go on taking care of myself?* It made her angry to hear him speak of another operation. She had a moment of panic, but she veiled it from him. With him, this young man whose skin was already as thick as buttermilk and whose chestnut hair was as dry as death, she always assumed the part of a small child. She said, "Yes, doctor." But her heart was in a fury.

Night and day, however, she repeated, "I was in the Valley of the Shadow. But I'm alive." She was weak, she was old, she couldn't follow a train of thought very easily, she felt faint in the head. But she was still here; here was her body, it filled space, a great body. And though she had worries and perplexities, and once in a while her arm felt as though it was about to give her the last stab of all; and though her hair was scrappy and old, like onion roots, and scattered like nothing under the comb, yet she sat and amused herself with visitors; her great grin split her face; her heart warmed with every kind word.

And she thought, "People will help me out. It never did me any good to worry. At the last minute something turned up, when I wasn't looking for it. Marian loves me. Helen and Jerry love me. Half Pint loves me. They would never let me go to the ground. And I love them. If it were the other way around, I'd never let them go down."

Above a horizon in a baggy vastness which Hattie by herself occasionally visited, the features of India, or her shade, sometimes rose. She was indignant and scolding. Not mean. Not really mean. Few people had ever been really mean to Hattie. But India was annoyed with her. "The garden is going to hell, Hattie," she said. "Those lilac bushes are all shriveled."

"But what can I do? The hose is rotten. It broke. It won't reach."

"Then dig a trench," said the phantom of India. "Have old Sam dig a trench. But save the bushes."

Am I thy servant still? said Hattie to herself. *No,* she thought, *let the dead bury their dead.*

But she didn't defy India now any more than she had done when they lived together. Hattie was supposed to keep India off the bottle, but often both of them began to get drunk after breakfast. They forgot to dress, and in their slips the two of them wandered drunkenly around the house and blundered into each other, and they were in despair at having been so weak. Late in the afternoon they would be sitting in the living room, waiting for the sun to set. It shrank, burning itself out on the crumbling edges of the mountains. When the sun passed, the fury of the daylight ended and the mountain surfaces were more blue, broken, like cliffs of coal. They no longer suggested faces. The east began to look simple, and the lake less inhuman and haughty. At last India would say, "Hattie – it's time for the lights." And Hattie would pull the switch chains of the lamps, several of them, to give the generator a good shove. She would turn on some of the wobbling eighteenth-century-style lamps whose shades stood out from their slender bodies like dragonflies' wings. The little engine in the shed would shuffle, then spit, then charge and bang, and the first weak light would rise unevenly in the bulbs.

"Hettie!" cried India. After she drank she was penitent, but her penitence too was a hardship to Hattie, and the worse her temper the more English her accent became. *"Where the hell ah you Het-tie!"* After India's death Hattie found some poems she had written in which she, Hattie, was affectionately and even touchingly mentioned. But Hattie's interest in ideas was very small, whereas India had been all over the world and was used to brilliant society. India wanted her to discuss Eastern religion, Bergson and Proust, and Hattie had no head for this, and so India blamed her drinking on Hattie. "I can't talk to you," she would say. "And I'm here because I'm not fit to be anywhere else. I can't live in New York any more. It's too dangerous for a woman my age to be drunk in the street at night."

And Hattie, talking to her Western friends about India, would say, "She is a lady," (implying that they made a pair). "She is a creative person,"(this was why they found each other so congenial). "But helpless? Completely. Why she can't even get her own girdle on."

"Hettie! come here. Het-tie! Do you know what sloth is?"

Undressed, India sat on her bed and with the cigarette in her drunken, wrinkled, ringed hand she burned holes in the blankets. On Hattie's pride she left many small scars, too. She treated her like a servant.

Weeping, India begged her afterward to forgive her. *"Hattie, please, don't condemn me in your heart. Forgive me, dear, I know I am bad. But I hurt myself more in my evil than I hurt you."*

Hattie would keep a stiff bearing. She would lift up her face with its incurved nose and puffy eyes, and say, "I am a Christian person. I never bear a grudge." And by repeating this she actually brought herself to forgive India.

But of course she had no husband, no child, no skill, no savings. And what she would have done if India had not died and left her the yellow house, nobody knows.

Jerry Rolfe said privately to Marian, "Hattie can't do anything for herself. If I hadn't been around during the '44 blizzard she and India both would have starved. She's always been careless and lazy and now she can't even chase a cow out of her yard. She's too feeble. The thing for her to do is go East to her brother. Hattie would have ended at the poor farm if it hadn't been for India. But India should have left her something besides the house. Some dough. India didn't use her head."

When Hattie returned to the lake she stayed with the Rolfes. "Well, old shellback," said Jerry, "there's a little more life in you now."

Indeed, with joyous eyes, the cigarette in her mouth and her hair newly frizzed and overhanging her forehead, she seemed to have triumphed again. She was pale, but she grinned, she chuckled, and she held a bourbon Old-Fashioned with a cherry and a slice of orange in it. She was on rations; the Rolfes allowed her two a day. Her back, Helen noted, was more bent than before. Her knees went outward a little weakly; her feet, however, came close together at the ankles.

"Oh, Helen dear and Jerry dear, I am so thankful, so glad to be back at the lake. I can look after my place again, and I'm here to see the spring. It's more gorgeous than ever."

Heavy rains had fallen while Hattie was away. The Sego lilies, which bloomed only after a wet winter, came up from the loose dust, especially around the marl pit; but even on the burnt granite they seemed to grow. Desert peach was beginning to appear and in Hattie's yard the rosebushes were filling out. The roses were yellow and abundant, and the odor they gave off was like that of damp tea leaves.

"Before it gets hot enough for the rattlesnakes," said Hattie to Helen, "we ought to drive up to Marky's ranch to cut watercress."

Hattie was going to attend to lots of things, but the heat came early that year and, as there was no television to keep her awake, she slept most of the day. She was now able to dress herself, though there was little more that she could do. Sam Jervis rigged the pulley for her on the porch and she remembered once in a while to use it. Mornings when she had her strength she rambled over to her own house, examining things, behaving importantly and giving orders to Sam Jervis and Wanda Gingham. At ninety, Wanda, a Shoshone, was still an excellent seamstress and housecleaner.

Hattie looked over the car, which was parked under a cottonwood tree. She tested the engine. Yes, the old pot would still go. Proudly, happily, she listened to the noise of tappets; the dry old pipe shook as the smoke went out at the rear. She tried to work the shift, turn the wheel. That, as yet, she couldn't do. But it would come soon, she was confident.

At the back of the house the soil had caved in a little over the cesspool and a few of the old railroad ties over the top had rotted. Otherwise things were in good shape. Sam had looked after the garden. He had fixed a new catch for the gate after Pace's horses – maybe because he never could afford to keep them in hay – had broken in and Sam found them grazing and drove them out. Luckily they hadn't damaged many of her plants. Hattie felt a moment of wild rage against Pace. He had brought the horses into her garden, she was sure. But her anger didn't last long. It was reabsorbed into the feeling of golden pleasure that enveloped her. She had little strength, but all that she had was a pleasure to her. So she forgave even Pace, who would have liked to do her out of the house, who had always used her, embarrassed her, cheated her at cards, passed the buck whenever he could. He was a fool about horses. They were ruining him. Breeding horses was a millionaire's amusement.

She saw the animals in the distance, feeding. Unsaddled, the mares appeared undressed; they reminded her of naked women walking with their glossy flanks in the Sego lilies which curled on the ground. The flowers were yellowish, like winter wool, but fragrant; the mares, naked and gentle, walked through them. Their strolling, their perfect beauty, the sound of their hoofs on stone touched a deep place in Hattie's nature. Her love for horses, birds and dogs was well-known. Dogs led the list. And now a piece cut from a green blanket reminded her of Richie. The blanket was one he had torn, and she had cut it into strips and placed them under the doors to keep out the draughts. In the house she found more traces of him: hair he had shed on the furniture. Hattie was going to borrow Helen's vacuum cleaner, but there wasn't really enough current to make it pull as it should. On the doorknob of India's room hung the dog collar.

Hattie had decided to have herself moved into India's bed when she lay dying. Why use two beds? A perilous look came into her eyes while her lips pressed together forbiddingly. "I follow," she said, speaking to India with an inner voice, "so never mind." Presently – before long – she would have to leave the yellow house in her turn. And as she went into the parlor thinking of the will, she sighed. Pretty soon she would have to attend to it. India's lawyer, Claiborne, helped her with such things. She had phoned him in town, while she was staying with Marian, and talked matters over with him. He had promised to try to sell the house for her. Fifteen thousand was her bottom price, she said. If he couldn't find a buyer, perhaps he could find a tenant. Two hundred dollars a month was the rental she set. Rolfe laughed. But Hattie turned toward him one of those proud, dulled looks she always took on when he angered her and said haughtily, "For summer on Sego Lake?"

"You're competing with Pace's ranch."

"Why, the food is stinking down there. He cheats the dudes," said Hattie. "He really cheats them at cards. You'll never catch me playing blackjack with him again."

And what would she do, thought Hattie, if Claiborne could neither rent nor sell the house? This question she shook off as regularly as it returned. *I don't have to be a burden on anybody,* thought Hattie. *It's looked bad many a time before, but when push came to shove, I made it. Somehow I got by.* But she argued with herself. *How many times? How long, O God – an old thing, feeble, no use to anyone?* Who said she had any right to hold a piece of property?

She was sitting on her sofa which was very old, India's sofa, eight feet long, kidney-shaped, puffy and bald. An underlying pink shone through the green; the upholstered tufts were like the pads of dogs' paws; between them rose bunches of hair. Here Hattie slouched, resting, with her knees wide apart and a cigarette in her mouth, eyes half shut but far-seeing. The mountains seemed not fifteen miles but fifteen hundred yards away, the lake a blue band; the tea-like odor of the roses, though they were still unopened, was already in the air, for Sam was watering them in the heat. Gratefully Hattie yelled, "Sam!"

Sam was very old, and all shanks. His feet looked big. His old railroad jacket was made tight across his back by his stoop. A crooked finger with its great broad nail over the mouth of the hose made the water spray and sparkle. Happy to see Hattie he turned his long jaw, empty of teeth, and his blue eyes, which seemed to penetrate his temples with their length (it was his face that turned, not his body), and he said, "Oh, there, Hattie. You've made it back today? Welcome, Hattie."

"Have a beer, Sam. Come around the back and I'll give you a beer."

She never had Sam come in, owing to his skin desease. There were raw patches on his chin and the back of his ears. Hattie feared infection from his touch. She gave him the beer can, never a glass, and she put on gloves before she used the garden tools. Since he would take no money from her – she had to pay Wanda Gingham a dollar a day – she got Marian to find old clothes for him in town and she left food for him at the door of the damp-wood-smelling boxcar where he lived.

"How's the old wing, Hat?" he said.

"It's coming. I'll be driving again before you know it," she told him. "By the first of May I'll be driving again." Every week she moved the date forward. "By Decoration Day I expect to be on my own again," she said. In mid-June however she was still unable to drive. Helen Rolfe said to her, "Hattie, Jerry and I are due in Seattle the first week of July."

"Why, you never told me that," said Hattie.

"You don't mean to tell me this is the first you heard of it," said Helen. "You've known about it from the first – since Christmas."

It wasn't easy for Hattie to meet her eyes. She presently put her head down. Her face became very dry, especially the lips. "Well, don't you worry about me. I'll be all right here," she said.

"Who's going to look after you?" said Jerry. He evaded nothing himself and tolerated very little evasion in others. Except, as Hattie knew, he always indulged her. She couldn't count on her friend Half Pint, she couldn't really count on Marian either. Until now, this very moment, she had only the Rolfes to turn to. Helen, trying to be steady, gazed at her and made sad, involuntary movements with her head, sometimes nodding, sometimes seeming as if she disagreed. Hattie, with her inner voice, swore at her: *Bitch-eyes. I can't win because I'm old. Is that fair?* And yet she admired Helen's eyes. Even the skin about them, slightly wrinkled underneath, was touching, beautiful. There was a heaviness in her bust that went, as if by attachment, with the heaviness of her eyes. Her head, her hands and feet should have taken a more slender body. Helen, said Hattie, was the nearest thing she had on this earth to a sister. But there was no reason to go to Seattle – no genuine business. It was only idleness, only a holiday. The only reason was Hattie herself; this was their way of telling her that there was a limit to what she could expect them to do. Helen's head wavered, but her thoughts were steady; she knew what was passing through Hattie's mind. Like Hattie, she was an idle woman. Why was her right to idleness better?

Because of money? thought Hattie. Because of age? Because she has a husband? Because she had a daughter in Swarthmore College? But a funny thing occurred to her. Helen disliked being idle, whereas she herself never made any bones that an idle life was all she was ever good for. But for her it was uphill, all the way, because when Waggoner divorced her she didn't have a cent. She even had to support Wicks for seven or eight years. Except with horses, he had no sense. And then she had had to take a ton of dirt from India. *I am the one,* Hattie asserted to herself. *I would know what to do with Helen's advantages. She only suffers from them. And if she wants to stop being an idle woman why can't she start with me, her neighbor?* Her skin, for all its puffiness, burned with anger. She said to Rolfe and Helen: "Don't worry. I'll make out by myself. But if I have to leave the lake you'll be ten times more lonely than before. Now I'm going back to my house."

She lifted up her broad old face and her lips were childlike with suffering. She would never take back what she had said.

But the trouble was no ordinary trouble. Hattie was herself aware that she rambled, forgot names, and answered when no one spoke.

"We can't just take charge of her," Rolfe said. "What's more, she ought to be near a doctor. She keeps her shotgun loaded so she can fire it if anything happens to her in the house. But who knows what she'll do? I don't believe it was Jacamares who killed that Doberman of hers."

He drove into her yard the day after she returned to her house and said, "I'm going into town. I can bring you some chow if you like."

She couldn't afford to refuse his offer, angry though she was, and she said, "Yes, bring me some stuff from the Mountain Street Market. Charge it." She only had some frozen shrimp and a few cans of beer in the icebox. When Rolfe had gone she put out the shrimp to thaw.

People really used to stick by one another in the West. Hattie now saw herself as one of the pioneers. This modern race had come later. After all, she had lived on the range like an old-timer. Wicks had had to shoot their Christmas dinner and she had cooked it – venison. He killed it on the reservation, and if the Paiutes had caught them there would have been hell to pay.

The weather was hot, the clouds were heavy and calm in a large sky. The horizon was so huge that in it the lake must have seemed like a saucer of milk. *Some milk!* Hattie thought. Two thousand feet deep in the middle, so deep no body could ever be recovered. It went around with the currents, and there were rocks like eyeteeth, and hot springs, and colorless fish at the bottom which were never caught. Now that the white pelicans were nesting they patrolled the rocks for snakes and other egg thieves. They were so big and flew so slow you might imagine they were angels. Hattie no longer visited the lake shore; the walk exhausted her. She saved her strength to go to Pace's bar in the afternoon.

She took off her shoes and stockings and walked on bare feet from one end of her house to the other. On the land side she saw Wanda Gingham sitting near the tracks while her great-grandson played in the soft red gravel. Wanda wore a large purple shawl and her black head was bare. All about her was – was nothing, Hattie thought: for she had taken a drink, breaking her rule. Nothing but mountains, thrust out like men's bodies; the sagebrush was the hair on their chests.

The warm wind blew dust from the marl pit. This white powder made her sky less blue. On the water side were the pelicans, pure as spirits, slow as angels, blessing the air as they flew with great wings.

Should she or should she not have Sam do something about the vine on the chimney? Sparrows nested in it, and she was glad of that. But all summer long the king snakes were after them and she was afraid to walk in the garden. When the sparrows scratched the ground for seed they took a funny bound; they held their legs stiff and flung back the dust with both feet. Hattie sat down at her old Spanish table, watching them in the cloudy warmth of the day, clasping her hands, chuckling and sad. The bushes were crowded with yellow roses, half of them now rotted. The lizards scrambled from shadow to shadow. The water was smooth as air, gaudy as silk. The mountains succumbed, falling asleep in the heat. Drowsy, Hattie lay down on her sofa; its pads were like dogs' paws. She gave in to sleep and when she woke it was midnight; she did not want to alarm the Rolfes by putting on her lights, so took advantage of the moon to eat a few thawed shrimps and go to the bathroom. She undressed and lifted herself into bed and lay there feeling her sore arm. Now she knew how much she missed her dog. The whole matter of the dog weighed heavily on her soul; she came close to tears in thinking about him and she went to sleep, oppressed by her secret.

I suppose I had better try to pull myself together a little, thought Hattie nervously in the morning. *I can't just sleep my way through.* She knew what her difficulty was. Before any serious question her mind gave way; it became diffused. She said to herself, *I can see bright, but I feel dim. I guess I'm not so lively any more. Maybe I'm becoming a little touched in the head, as mother was.* But she was not so old as her mother was when she did those strange things. At eighty-five her mother had to be kept from going naked in the street. *I'm not as bad as that yet,* thought Hattie. *Thank God. I walked into the men's wards, but that was when I had a fever, and my nightie was on.*

She drank a cup of Nescafé and it strengthened her determination to do something for herself. In all the world she had only her brother Angus to go to. Her brother Will had led a rough life; he was an old heller, and now he drove everyone away. He was too crabby, thought Hattie. Besides he was angry because she had lived so long with Wicks. Angus would forgive her. But then he and his wife were not her kind. With them she couldn't drink, she couldn't smoke, she had to make herself small-mouthed, and she would have to wait while they read a chapter of the Bible before breakfast. Hattie could not bear to wait for meals. Besides, she had a house of her own at last; why should she have to leave it? She had never owned a thing before. And now she was not allowed to enjoy her yellow house. *But I'll keep it,* she said to herself rebelliously. *I swear to God I'll keep it. Why, I barely just got it. I haven't had time.* And she went out on the porch to work the pulley and do something about the adhesions in her arm. She was sure now that they were there. *And what will I do?* she cried to herself. *What will I do? Why did I ever go to Rolfe's that night – and why did I lose control on the crossing!* She couldn't say now "I sneezed." She couldn't even remember what had happened, except that she saw the boulders and the twisting blue rails and Darly. It was Darly's fault. He was sick and old himself, and couldn't make it. He envied her the house, and her woman's peaceful life. Since she returned from the hospital he hadn't even come to visit her. He only said, "Hell, I'm sorry for her, but it was her fault." What hurt him most was that she said he couldn't hold his liquor.

Her resolve to pull herself together did not last; she remained the same procrastinating old woman. She had a letter to answer from Hotchkiss Insurance, and it drifted out of sight. She was going to phone Claiborne the lawyer, and it slipped her mind. One morning she announced to Helen that she believed she would apply to an institution in Los Angeles that took over the property of old people and managed it for them. They gave you an apartment right on the ocean, and your meals and medical care. You had to sign over half of your estate. "It's fair enough," said Hattie. "They take a gamble. I may live to be a hundred."

"I wouldn't be surprised," said Helen.

However, Hattie never got around to sending to Los Angeles for the brochure. But Jerry Rolfe took it on himself to write a letter to her brother Angus about her condition. And he drove over also to have a talk with Amy Walters, the gold miner's widow at Fort Walters – as the ancient woman called it. One old tar-paper building was what she owned, plus the mine shafts, no longer in use since the death of her second husband. On a heap of stones near the road a crimson sign *Fort Walters* was placed, and over it a flagpole. The American flag was raised every day. Amy was working in the garden in one of dead Bill's shirts. He had brought water down from the mountains for her in a home-made aqueduct so she could raise her own peaches and vegetables.

"Amy," Rolfe said, "Hattie's back from the hospital and living all alone. You have no folks and neither has she. Not to beat around the bush about it, why don't you live together?"

Amy's face had great delicacy. Her winter baths in the lake and her soups and the waltzes she played to herself alone on the grand piano that stood beside her wood stove and the murder stories she read till darkness made her go to bed had made her remote. She looked delicate, yet her composure couldn't be touched. It was very strange.

"Hattie and me have different habits, Jerry," said Amy. "And Hattie wouldn't like my company. I can't drink with her."

"That's true," said Rolfe, recalling that Hattie referred to Amy as though she were a ghost. He couldn't speak to Amy of the solitary death that was in store for her. There was not a cloud in the arid sky today, and there was not a shadow of death on Amy. She was tranquil, she seemed to be supplied with a sort of pure fluid that would feed her life slowly for years to come.

He said, "All kinds of things could happen to a woman like Hattie in that yellow house, and nobody would know."

"That's a fact. She doesn't know how to take care of herself."

"She can't. Her arm hasn't healed."

Amy didn't say that she was sorry to hear it. In the place of those words came a silence which could have meant that. Then she said, "I might go for a few hours a day, but she would have to pay me."

"Now, Amy, you must know as well as I do that Hattie has never had any money – not much more than her pension. Just the house."

At once Amy said, no pause coming between his words and hers, "I would take care of her if she'd agree to leave the house to me."

"Leave it in your hands, you mean?" said Rolfe. "To manage?"

"In her will. To belong to me."

"Why, Amy, what would you do with Hattie's house?" he said.

"It would be my property, that's all. I'd have it."

"Maybe you would leave Fort Walters to her in your will," he said.

"Oh, no," she answered quickly. "Why should I do that? I'm not asking Hattie for her help. I don't need it. Hattie is a city woman."

Rolfe could not carry this proposal back to Hattie. He was too wise ever to mention her will to her.

But Pace was not so careful of her feelings. By mid-June Hattie had begun to visit the bar regularly. She had so many things to think about she couldn't keep herself at home. When Pace came in from the yard one day – he had been packing the axles of his horse-trailer and was wiping grease from his fingers – he said with his usual bluntness, "How would you like it if I paid you fifty bucks a month for the rest of your life, Hat?"

Hattie was holding her second Old-Fashioned of the day. At the bar she made it appear that she observed the limit; but she had started drinking at home after lunch. She began to grin, expecting Pace to make one of his jokes. But he was wearing his scoop-shaped Western hat as level as a Quaker, and he had drawn down his chin, a sign that he was not fooling. She said, "That would be nice, but what's the catch?"

"No catch," he said. "This is what we'd do. I'd give you five hundred dollars cash, and fifty bucks a month for life, and you'd let me put some dudes in the yellow house, and you'd leave the house to me in your will."

"What kind of a deal is that?" said Hattie, her look changing. "I thought we were friends."

"It's the best deal you'll ever get," he said.

The day was sultry, but Hattie till now had thought that it was nice, that she was dreamy, but comfortable, about to begin to enjoy the cool of the day; but now she felt that such cruelty and injustice had been waiting to attack her, that it would have been better to die in the hospital than be so disillusioned.

She cried, "Everybody wants to push me out. You're a cheater, Pace. God! I know you. Pick on somebody else. Why do you have to pick on me? Just because I happen to be around?"

"Why, no, Hattie," he said, trying now to be careful. "It was just a business offer."

"Why don't you give me some blood for the bank if you're such a friend of mine?"

"Well, Hattie, you drink too much, and you oughtn't have been driving anyway."

"The whole thing happened because I sneezed. Everybody knows it. I wouldn't sell you my house. I'd give it away to the lepers first. You'd let me go and never send me a cent. You never pay anybody. You can't even buy wholesale in town any more because nobody trusts you. It looks as though I'm stuck, that's all, just stuck. I keep on saying that this is my only home in all the world, this is where my friends are, and the weather is always perfect and the lake is beautiful. I wish the whole damn empty old place were in Hell. It's not human and neither are you. But I'll be here the day the sheriff takes your horses – you never mind."

He told her then that she was drunk again, and so she was, but she was more than that, and though her head was spinning she decided to go back to the house at once and take care of some things she had been putting off. This very day she was going to write to the lawyer, Claiborne, and make sure that Pace never got her property. She wouldn't put it past him to swear in court that India had promised him the yellow house.

She sat at the table with pen and paper, trying to think how to put it.

"I want this on record," she wrote. "I could kick myself in the head when I think how he's led me on. I have been his patsy ten thousand times. As when that drunk crashed his Cub plane on the lake shore. At the coroner's jury he let me take the whole blame. He had instructed me when I was working for him never to take in any drunks. And this flier was drunk. He had nothing on but a T shirt and Bermuda shorts and he was flying from Sacramento to Salt Lake City. At the inquest Pace denied he had ever given me such instructions. The same was true when the cook went haywire. She was a tramp. He never hires decent help. He cheated her on the bar bill and blamed me and she went after me with a meat cleaver. She disliked me because I criticized her for drinking at the bar in her one-piece white bathing suit with the dude guests. But he turned her loose on me. He hints that he did certain things for India. She would never have let him. He was too common for her. It can never be said about India that she was not a lady in every way. He thinks he is the greatest sack-artist in the world. He only loves horses, as a fact. He has no claims at all, oral or written, on this yellow house. I want you to have this over my signature. He was cruel to Pickle-Tits who was his first wife, and he's no better to the charming woman who is his present one. I don't know why she takes it. It must be despair." She said to herself, *I don't suppose I'd better send that.*

She was still angry. Her heart was knocking from within: the deep pulses, as after a hot bath, beat at the back of her thighs. The air outside was dotted with transparent particles. The mountains were red as clinkers. The iris leaves were fan sticks – they stuck out like Jiggs's hair.

She always ended by looking out of the window at the desert and the lake. *They drew you from yourself. But after they had drawn you, what did they do with you? It was too late to find out. I'll never know. I wasn't meant to. I'm not the type,* Hattie reflected. *Maybe something too cruel for women or for any woman, young or old.*

So she stood up and, rising, she had the sensation that she had gradually become a container for herself. *You get old, your heart, your liver, lungs seem to expand in size, and the walls of the body give way outward,* she thought, *and you take the shape of an old jug, wider and wider toward the top. You swell up with tears and fat.* She no longer even smelled to herself like a woman. Her face with its much-slept-upon skin was only faintly like her own – like a cloud that has changed. It was a face. It became a ball of yarn. It had drifted open. It had scattered.

I was never one single thing anyway, she thought. *Never my own. I was only loaned to myself.*

But the thing wasn't over yet. And in fact she didn't know for certain that it was ever going to be over; she had only had other people's word for it that death was such and such. *How do I know?* she asked herself challengingly. Her anger had sobered her for a little while. Now she was again drunk. *It was strange. It is strange. It may continue being strange.* She further thought, *I used to wish for death more than I do now. Because I didn't have anything at all. I changed when I got a roof of my own over me. And now? Do I have to go? I thought Marian loved me, but she has a sister. And I never thought Helen and Jerry would desert me. And now Pace insulted me. They think I'm not going to make it.*

She went to the cupboard – she kept the bourbon bottle there; she drank less if each time she had to rise and open the cupboard door. And, as if she were being watched, she poured a drink and swallowed it.

The notion that in this emptiness someone saw her was connected with the other fancy that she was being filmed from birth to death. That this was done for everyone. And afterward you could view your life.

Hattie wanted to see some of it now, and she sat down on the dogs' paw cushions of her sofa and, with her knees far apart and a smile of yearning and of fright, she bent her round back, burned a cigarette at the corner of her mouth and saw – the Church of Saint-Sulpice in Paris where her organ teacher used to bring her. It looked like country walls of stone, but rising high and leaning outward were towers. She was very young. She knew music. The sky was grey. After this she saw some entertaining things she liked to tell people about. She was a young wife. She was in Aix-les-Bains with her mother-in-law, and they played bridge in a mud bath with a British general and his aide. There were artificial waves in the swimming pool. She lost her bathing suit because it was a size too big. How did she get out? Ah, you got out of everything.

She saw her husband, James John Waggoner IV. They were snowbound together in New Hampshire. "Jimmy, Jimmy, how can you fling a wife away?" she asked him. "Have you forgotten love? Did I drink too much – did I bore you?" He had married again and had two children. He had gotten tired of her. And though he was a vain man with nothing to be vain about – no looks, not too much intelligence, nothing but an old Philadelphia family – she had loved him. She too had been a snob about her Philadelphia connections. Give up the name of Waggoner? How could she? For this reason she had never married Wicks. "How dare you," she had said to Wicks, "come without a shave in a dirty shirt and muck on you, come and ask me to marry! If you want to propose, go and clean up first." But his dirt was only a pretext. *Trade Waggoner for Wicks?* she asked herself again with a swing of her shoulders. She wouldn't think of it. Wicks was an excellent man. But he was a cowboy. He couldn't even read. But she saw this on her film. They were in Athens Canyon, in a cratelike house, and she was reading aloud to him from *The Count of Monte Cristo.* He wouldn't let her stop. While walking to stretch her legs, she read, and he follwed her about to catch each word. After all, he was very dear to her. Such a man! Now she saw him jump from his horse. They were living on the range, trapping coyotes. It was just the second grey of evening, cloudy, moments after the sun had gone down. There was an animal in the trap, and he went toward it to kill it. He wouldn't waste a bullet on the creatures, but killed them with a kick of his boot. And then Hattie saw that this coyote was all white – snarling teeth, white scruff. "Wicks, he's white! White as a polar bear. You're not going to kill him, are you?" The animal flattened to the ground. He snarled and cried. He couldn't pull away because of the heavy trap. And Wicks killed him. What else could he have done? The white beast lay dead. The dust of Wicks' boots hardly showed on its head and jaws. Blood ran from the muzzle.

And now came something on Hattie's film she tried to shun. It was she herself who had killed her dog, Richie. Just as Rolfe and Pace had warned her, he was vicious, his brain was turned. She, because she was on the side of all creatures, defended him when he bit the trashy woman Jacamares was living with. Perhaps if she had had Richie from a puppy he wouldn't have turned on her. When she got him he was already a year and a half old and she couldn't break him of his habits. But she thought only she understood him. And Rolfe had warned her, "You'll be sued, do you know it? The dog will take out after somebody smarter than that Jacamares' woman and you'll be in for it."

Hattie saw herself as she swayed her shoulders and said, "Nonsense."

But what fear she had felt when the dog went for her on the porch. Suddenly she could see by his skull, by his eyes that he was evil. She screamed at him, "Richie!" And what had she done to him? He had laid under the gas range all day growling and wouldn't come out. She tried to urge him out with the broom, and he snatched it in his teeth. She pulled him out and he left the stick and tore at her. Now, as the spectator of this, her eyes opened, beyond the pregnant curtain and the air wave of marl dust, summer's snow, drifting over the water. "Oh, my God! Richie!" Her thigh was snatched by his jaws. His teeth went through her skirt. She felt she would fall. Would she go down? Then the dog would rush at her throat – then black night, bad-odored mouth, the blood pouring from her torn veins. Her heart shriveled as the teeth went in her thigh, and she couldn't delay another second but took her kindling hatchet from the nail, strengthened her grip on the smooth wood and hit the dog. She saw the blow. She saw him die at once. And then in fear and shame she hid the body. And at night she buried him in the yard. Next day she accused Jacamares. On him she laid the blame for the disappearance of her dog.

She stood up; she spoke to herself in silence, as was her habit. *God, what shall I do? I have taken life. I have lied. I have borne false witness. I have stalled. And now what shall I do? Nobody will help me.*

And suddenly she made up her mind that she should go and do what she had been putting off for weeks, namely, test herself with the car, and she slipped on her shoes and went out. Lizards ran before her in the thirsty dust. She opened the hot, broad door of the car. She lifted her lame hand onto the wheel. Her right hand she reached far to the left and turned the wheel with all her might. Then she started the motor and tried to drive out of the yard. But she could not release the emergency brake with its rasplike rod. She reached with her good hand, the right, under the steering wheel and pressed her bosom on it and strained. No, she could not shift the gears and steer. She couldn't even reach the hand brake. The sweat broke out on her skin. Her efforts were too much. She was deeply wounded by the pain in her arm. The door of the car fell open again and she turned from the wheel and with her stiff legs outside the door she wept. What could she do now? And when she had wept over the ruin of her life she got out of the old car and went back to the house. She took the bottle of bourbon from the cupboard and picked up the ink bottle and a pad of paper and sat down to write her will.

My Will, she wrote, and sobbed to herself.

Since the death of India she had numberless times asked the question, To Whom? Who will get this when I die? She had unconsciously put people to the test to find out whether they were worthy. It made her more severe than before.

Now she wrote, "I, Harriet Simmons Waggoner, being of sound mind and not knowing what may be in store for me at the age of seventy-two (born 1885), living alone at Sego Desert Lake, instruct my lawyer, Harold Claiborne, Paiute County Court Building, to draw my last will and testament upon the following terms."

She sat perfectly still now to hear from within who would be the lucky one, who would inherit the yellow house. For which she had waited. Yes, waited for India's death, choking on her bread because she was a rich woman's servant and whipping girl. But who had done for her, Hattie, what she had done for India? And who, apart from India, had ever held out a hand to her? Kindness, yes. Here and there people had been kind. But the word in her head was not kindness, it was succor. And who had given her that? Only India. If at least, next best after succor, someone had given her a shake and said, "Stop stalling. Don't be such a slow, old, procrastinating sit-stiller." Again, it was only India who had done her good. She had offered her succor. *"Hettie!"* said that drunken mask. *"Do you know what sloth is? Damn your poky old life!"*

But I was waiting, Hattie realized. *I was waiting, thinking, "Youth is terrible, frightening. I will wait it out. And men? Men are cruel and strong. They want things I haven't got to give."* *There were no kids in me,* thought Hattie. *Not that I wouldn't have loved them, but such my nature was. And who can blame me for having it? My nature?*

She drank from an Old-Fashioned glass. There was no orange in it, no ice, no bitters or sugar, only the stinging, clear bourbon.

So then, she continued, looking at the dry sun-stamped dust and the last freckled flowers of red wild peach, *to live with Angus and his wife, and have to hear a chapter from the Bible before breakfast; once more in the house – not of a stranger, perhaps, but not far from it either.* In other houses, in someone else's house, to wait for mealtimes was her lifelong punishment. She always felt it in the throat and stomach. And so she would again, and to the very end. However, she must think of someone to leave the house to.

And first of all she wanted to do right by her family. None of them had ever dreamed that she, Hattie, would ever have something to bequeath. Until a few years ago it had certainly looked as if she would die a pauper. So now she could keep her head up with the proudest of them. And, as this occurred to her, she actually lifted up her face with its broad nose and victorious eyes; if her hair had become shabby as onion roots, if at the back her head was round and bald as a newel post, what did that matter? Her heart experienced a childish glory, not yet tired of it after seventy-two years. She, too, had amounted to something. *I'll do some good by going,* she thought. *Now I believe I should leave it to, to.* . . . She returned to the old point of struggle. She had decided many times and many times changed her mind. She tried to think, *Who would get the most out of it?* It was a tearing thing to go through. If it had not been the yellow house but instead some brittle thing she could hold in her hand, then the last thing she would do would be to throw and smash it, and so the thing and she herself would be demolished together. But it was vain to think such thoughts. To whom should she leave it? Her brothers? Not they. Nephews? One was a submarine commander. The other was a bachelor in the State Department. Then began the roll call of cousins. Merton? He owned an estate in Connecticut. Anna? She had a face like a hot-water bottle. That left Joyce, the orphaned daughter of her cousin Wilfred. Joyce was the most likely heiress. Hattie had already written to her and had her out to the lake at Thanksgiving, two years ago. But this Joyce was another odd one; over thirty, good, yes, but placid, running to fat, a scholar – ten years in Eugene, Oregon, working for her degree. In Hattie's opinion this was only another form of sloth. Nevertheless, Joyce yet hoped to marry. Whom? Not Dr. Stroud. He wouldn't. And still she had vague hope. Hattie knew how that could be. At least have a man she could argue with.

She was now more drunk than at any time since her accident. Again she filled her glass. *Have ye eyes and see not? Sleepers, awake!*

Knees wide apart she sat in the twilight, thinking. Marian? Marian didn't need another house. Half Pint? She wouldn't know what to do with it. Brother Louis came up for consideration next. He was an old actor who had a church for the Indians at Athens Canyon. Hollywood stars of the silent days sent him their negligées; he altered them and wore them in the pulpit. The Indians loved his show. But when Billy Shawah blew his brains out after his two-week bender, they still tore his shack down and turned it inside out to get rid of his ghost. They had their old religion. No, not Brother Louis. He'd show movies in the yellow house to the tribe or make a nursery of it.

And now she began to consider Wicks. When last heard from he was south of Bishop, California, a handy man in a saloon off toward Death Valley. It wasn't she who heard from him but Pace. Herself, she hadn't actually seen Wicks since – how low she had sunk then! – she had kept the hamburger stand on Route 158. The little lunchroom had supported them both. Wicks hung around on the end stool, rolling cigarettes (she saw it on the film). Then there was a quarrel. Things had been going from bad to worse. He'd begun to grouse now about this and now about that. He complained about the food, at last. She saw and heard him. "Hat," he said, "I'm good and tired of hamburger." "Well, what do you think I eat?" she said with that round, defiant movement of her shoulders which she herself recognized as characteristic (*me all over,* she thought). But he opened the cash register and took out thirty cents and crossed the street to the butcher's and brought back a steak. He threw it on the griddle. "Fry it," he said. She did and watched him eat.

And when he was through she could bear her rage no longer. "Now," she said, "you've had your meat. Get out. Never come back." She kept a pistol under the counter. She picked it up, cocked it, pointed it at his heart. "If you ever come in that door again, I'll kill you," she said.

She saw it all. *I couldn't bear to fall so low,* she thought, *to be slave to a shiftless cowboy.*

Wicks said, "Don't do that, Hat. Guess I went too far. You're right."

"You'll never have a chance to make it up," she cried. "Get out!"

On that cry he disappeared, and since then she had never seen him.

"Wicks, dear," she said. "Please! I'm sorry. Don't condemn me in your heart. Forgive me. I hurt myself in my evil. I always had a thick idiot head. I was born with a thick head."

Again she wept, for Wicks. She was too proud. A snob. Now they might have lived together in this house, old friends, simple and plain.

She thought, *He really was my good friend.*

But what would Wicks do with a house like this, alone, if he was alive and survived her? He was too wiry for soft beds or easy chairs.

And she was the one who had said stiffly to India, "I'm a Christian person. I do not bear a grudge."

Ah, yes, she said to herself. *I have caught myself out too often. How long can this go on?* And she began to think, or try to think of Joyce, her cousin's daughter. Joyce was like herself, a woman alone, getting on, clumsy. She would have given much, now, to succor Joyce.

But it seemed to her now that that too had been a story. First you heard the pure story. Then you heard the impure story. Both stories. She had paid out years, now to one shadow, now to another shadow.

Joyce would come here to the house. She had a little income and could manage. She would live as Hattie had lived, alone. Here she would rot, start to drink, maybe, and day after day read, day after day sleep. See how beautiful it was here? It burned you out. How empty? It turned you into ash.

"How can I doom a young person to the same life?" asked Hattie. "It's for somebody like me. When I was younger it wasn't right. But now it is. Only I fit in here. It was made for my old age, to spend my last years peacefully. If I hadn't let Jerry make me drunk that night – if I hadn't sneezed! My arm! I'll have to live with Angus. My heart will break there away from my only home."

She now was very drunk, and she said to herself, *Take what God brings. He gives no gifts unmixed. He makes loans.*

She resumed her letter of instructions to lawyer Claiborne: "Upon the following terms," she wrote a second time. "Because I have suffered much. Because I only lately received what I have to give away, I can't bear it." The drunken blood was soaring to her head. But her hand was clear enough. She wrote, "It is too soon! Too soon! Because I do not find it in my heart to care for anyone as I would wish. Being cast off and lonely, and doing no harm where I am. Why should it be? This breaks my heart. In addition to everything else, why must I worry about this, which I must leave? I am tormented out of my mind. Even though by my own fault I have put myself into this position. And I am not ready to give up on this. No, not yet. And so I'll tell you what, I leave this property, land, house, garden and water rights, to Hattie Simmons Waggoner. Me! I realize this is bad and wrong. It cannot happen. Yet it is the only thing I really wish to do, so may God have mercy on my soul."

"How can that be?" She studied what she had written and finally she acknowledged that she was drunk. "I'm drunk," she said, "and don't know what I'm doing. I'll die, and end. Like India. Dead as that lilac bush. Only tonight I can't give the house away. I'm drunk and so I need it. But I won't be selfish from the grave. I'll think again tomorrow," she promised herself.

CARSON MC CULLERS 1917–1967

Born in Georgia, Carson McCullers spent her early childhood there and often used the South as the setting for her fiction. But unlike other southern writers in this book – notably William Faulkner and Flannery O'Connor – she preferred to live away from it. As a girl she went to New York to study music, stayed to study writing at N.Y.U. and Columbia, and at the age of twenty-three published a first-rate novel, *The Heart is a Lonely Hunter.* This early promise of a great career was never fully realized, for Mrs. McCullers suffered a stroke that made all effort painful, and she was involved with her husband's bouts of depression that eventually led to his suicide. As one can judge from the stories here, she was a meticulous artist, one who adapted her art to her personal misfortune by holding to her standards of perfection but writing less and less. Perhaps her best work is contained in the collection from which both these stories are taken, *The Ballad of the Sad Cafe* (1951). In 1950 she rewrote one of her stories, *The Member of the Wedding,* as a very successful play that was later made into an equally successful movie.

At first Mrs. McCullers wrote as a southern gothicist. Her eerie landscapes and psychologically twisted characters belonged more to a perverted fairyland than to a specifically realized society. They were effective in the way fairy tales are: as embodiments of fears and fantasies not very far removed from their primal types. Later in the forties Mrs. McCullers used this gothic strain more subtly to investigate the psychological complexities of characters to whom she gave a solidly realistic life. Thus the obsessed Bitsy in "The Jockey" really has all the characteristics necessary for existence in a freakshow: his stature, his bizarre clothes, his walk, his mannerisms. But as a way of letting us glimpse the psychological pressures that move Bitsy, Carson McCullers assimilates him into a precisely observed setting of racing people – where on one level he doesn't seem so extraordinary but on another very extraordinary indeed.

THE SOJOURNER

The twilight border between sleep and waking was a Roman one this morning: splashing fountains and arched, narrow streets, the golden lavish city of blossoms and age-soft stone. Sometimes in this semi-consciousness he sojourned again in Paris, or war German rubble, or Swiss skiing and a snow hotel. Sometimes, also, in a fallow Georgia field at hunting dawn. Rome it was this morning in the yearless region of dreams.

John Ferris awoke in a room in a New York hotel. He had the feeling that something unpleasant was awaiting him — what it was, he did not know. The feeling, submerged by matinal necessities, lingered even after he had dressed and gone downstairs. It was a cloudless autumn day and the pale sunlight sliced between the pastel skyscrapers. Ferris went into the next-door drugstore and sat at the end booth next to the window glass that overlooked the sidewalk. He ordered an American breakfast with scrambled eggs and sausage.

Ferris had come from Paris to his father's funeral which had taken place the week before in his home town in Georgia. The shock of death had made him aware of youth already passed. His hair was receding and the veins in his now naked temples were pulsing and prominent and his body was spare except for an incipient belly bulge. Ferris had loved his father and the bond between them had once been extraordinarily close — but the years had somehow unraveled his filial devotion; the death, expected for a long time, had left him with an unforeseen dismay. He had stayed as long as possible to be near his mother and brothers at home. His plane for Paris was to leave the next morning.

Ferris pulled out his address book to verify a number. He turned the pages with growing attentiveness. Names and addresses from New York, the capitals of Europe, a few faint ones from his home state in the South. Faded, printed names, sprawled drunken ones. Betty Wills: a random love, married now. Charlie Williams: wounded in the Hürtgen Forest, unheard of since. Grand old Williams — did he live or die? Don Walker: a B.T.O. in television, getting rich. Henry Green: hit the skids after the war, in a sanitarium now, they say. Cozie Hall: he had heard that she was dead. Heedless, laughing Cozie — it was strange to think that she too, silly girl, could die. As Ferris closed the address book, he suffered a sense of hazard, transience, almost of fear.

It was then that his body jerked suddenly. He was staring out of the window when there, on the sidewalk, passing by, was his ex-wife. Elizabeth passed quite close to him, walking slowly. He could not understand the wild quiver of his heart, nor the following sense of recklessness and grace that lingered after she was gone.

Quickly Ferris paid his check and rushed out to the sidewalk. Elizabeth stood on the corner waiting to cross Fifth Avenue. He hurried toward her meaning to speak, but the lights changed and she crossed the street before he reached her. Ferris followed. On the other side he could easily have overtaken her, but he found himself lagging unaccountably. Her fair brown hair was plainly rolled, and as he watched her Ferris recalled that once his father had remarked that Elizabeth had a "beautiful carriage." She turned at the next corner and Ferris followed, although by now his intention to overtake her had disappeared. Ferris questioned the bodily disturbance that the sight of Elizabeth aroused in him, the dampness of his hands, the hard heartstrokes.

It was eight years since Ferris had last seen his ex-wife. He knew that long ago she had married again. And there were children. During recent years he had seldom thought of her. But at first after the divorce, the loss had almost destroyed him. Then after the anodyne of time, he had loved again, and then again. Jeannine, she was now. Certainly his love for his ex-wife was long since past. So why the unhinged body, the shaken mind? He knew only that his clouded heart was oddly dissonant with the sunny, candid autumn day. Ferris wheeled suddenly and, walking with long strides, almost running, hurried back to the hotel.

Ferris poured himself a drink, although it was not yet eleven o'clock. He sprawled out in an armchair like a man exhausted, nursing his glass of bourbon and water. He had a full day ahead of him as he was leaving by plane the next morning for Paris. He checked over his obligations: take luggage to Air France, lunch with his boss, buy shoes and an overcoat. And something – wasn't there something else? Ferris finished his drink and opened the telephone directory.

His decision to call his ex-wife was impulsive. The number was under Bailey, the husband's name, and he called before he had much time for self-debate. He and Elizabeth had exchanged cards at Christmastime, and Ferris had sent a carving set when he received the announcement of her wedding. There was no reason not to call. But as he waited, listening to the ring at the other end, misgiving fretted him.

Elizabeth answered; her familiar voice was a fresh shock to him. Twice he had to repeat his name, but when he was identified, she sounded glad. He explained he was only in town for that day. They had a theater engagement, she said – but she wondered if he would come by for an early dinner. Ferris said he would be delighted.

As he went from one engagement to another, he was still bothered at odd moments by the feeling that something necessary was forgotten. Ferris bathed and changed in the late afternoon, often thinking about Jeannine: he would be with her the following night. "Jeannine," he would say, "I happened to run into my ex-wife when I was in New York. I had dinner with her. And her husband, of course. It was strange seeing her after all these years."

Elizabeth lived in the East Fifties, and as Ferris taxied uptown he glimpsed at intersections the lingering sunset, but by the time he reached his destination it was already autumn dark. The place was a building with a marquee and a doorman, and the apartment was on the seventh floor.

"Come in, Mr. Ferris."

Braced for Elizabeth or even the unimagined husband, Ferris was astonished by the freckled red-haired child; he had known of the children, but his mind had failed somehow to acknowledge them. Surprise made him step back awkwardly.

"This is our apartment," the child said politely. "Aren't you Mr. Ferris? I'm Billy. Come in."

In the living room beyond the hall, the husband provided another surprise; he too had not been acknowledged emotionally. Bailey was a lumbering red-haired man with a deliberate manner. He rose and extended a welcoming hand.

"I'm Bill Bailey. Glad to see you. Elizabeth will be in, in a minute. She's finishing dressing."

The last words struck a gliding series of vibrations, memories of the other years. Fair Elizabeth, rosy and naked before her bath. Half-dressed before the mirror of her dressing table, brushing her fine, chestnut hair. Sweet, casual intimacy, the soft-fleshed loveliness indisputably possessed. Ferris shrank from the unbidden memories and compelled himself to meet Bill Bailey's gaze.

"Billy, will you please bring that tray of drinks from the kitchen table?"

The child obeyed promptly, and when he was gone Ferris remarked conversationally, "Fine boy you have there."

"We think so."

Flat silence until the child returned with a tray of glasses and a cocktail shaker of Martinis. With the priming drinks they pumped up conversation: Russia, they spoke of, and the New York rain-making, and the apartment situation in Manhattan and Paris.

"Mr. Ferris is flying all the way across the ocean tomorrow," Bailey said to the little boy who was perched on the arm of his chair, quiet and well behaved. "I bet you would like to be a stowaway in his suitcase."

Billy pushed back his limp bangs. "I want to fly in an airplane and be a newspaperman like Mr. Ferris." He added with sudden assurance, "That's what I would like to do when I am big."

Bailey said, "I thought you wanted to be a doctor."

"I do!" said Billy. "I would like to be both. I want to be a atom-bomb scientist too."

Elizabeth came in carrying in her arms a baby girl.

"Oh, John!" she said. She settled the baby in the father's lap. "It's grand to see you. I'm awfully glad you could come."

The little girl sat demurely on Bailey's knees. She wore a pale pink crepe de Chine frock, smocked around the yoke with rose, and a matching silk hair ribbon tying back her pale soft curls. Her skin was summer tanned and her brown eyes flecked with gold and laughing. When she reached up and fingered her father's horn-rimmed glasses, he took them off and let her look through them a moment. "How's my old Candy?"

Elizabeth was very beautiful, more beautiful perhaps than he had ever realized. Her straight clean hair was shining. Her face was softer, glowing and serene. It was a madonna loveliness, dependent on the family ambiance.

"You've hardly changed at all," Elizabeth said, "but it has been a long time."

"Eight years." His hand touched his thinning hair self-consciously while further amenities were exchanged.

Ferris felt himself suddenly a spectator — an interloper among these Baileys. Why had he come? He suffered. His own life seemed so solitary, a fragile column supporting nothing amidst the wreckage of the years. He felt he could not bear much longer to stay in the family room.

He glanced at his watch. "You're going to the theater?"

"It's a shame," Elizabeth said, "but we've had this engagement for more than a month. But surely, John, you'll be staying home one of these days before long. You're not going to be an expatriate, are you?"

"Expatriate," Ferris repeated. "I don't much like the word."

"What's a better word?" she asked.

He thought for a moment. "Sojourner might do."

Ferris glanced again at his watch and again Elizabeth apologized. "If only we had known ahead of time—"

"I just had this day in town. I came home unexpectedly. You see, Papa died last week."

"Papa Ferris is dead?"

"Yes, at Johns-Hopkins. He had been sick there nearly a year. The funeral was down home in Georgia."

"Oh, I'm sorry, John. Papa Ferris was always one of my favorite people."

The little boy moved from behind the chair so that he could look into his mother's face. He asked, "Who is dead?"

Ferris was oblivious to apprehension; he was thinking of his father's death. He saw again the outstretched body on the quilted silk within the coffin. The corpse flesh was bizarrely rouged and the familiar hands lay massive and joined above a spread of funeral roses. The memory closed and Ferris awakened to Elizabeth's calm voice.

"Mr. Ferris' father, Billy. A really grand person. Somebody you didn't know."

"But why did you call him *Papa* Ferris?"

Bailey and Elizabeth exchanged a trapped look. It was Bailey who answered the questioning child. "A long time ago," he said, "your mother and Mr. Ferris were once married. Before you were born – a long time ago."

"Mr. Ferris?"

The little boy stared at Ferris, amazed and unbelieving. And Ferris' eyes, as he returned the gaze, were somehow unbelieving too. Was it indeed true that one time he had called this stranger, Elizabeth, Little Butterduck during nights of love, that they had lived together, shared perhaps a thousand days and nights and – finally – endured in the misery of sudden solitude the fiber by fiber (jealousy, alcohol and money quarrels) destruction of the fabric of married love.

Bailey said to the children, "It's somebody's suppertime. Come on now."

"But Daddy! Mama and Mr. Ferris – I —"

Billy's everlasting eyes – perplexed and with a glimmer of hostility – reminded Ferris of the gaze of another child. It was the young son of Jeannine – a boy of seven with a shadowed little face and knobby knees whom Ferris avoided and usually forgot.

"Quick march!" Bailey gently turned Billy toward the door. "Say good night now, son."

"Good night, Mr. Ferris." He added resentfully, "I thought I was staying up for the cake."

"You can come in afterward for the cake," Elizabeth said. "Run along now with Daddy for your supper."

Ferris and Elizabeth were alone. The weight of the situation descended on those first moments of silence. Ferris asked permission to pour himself another drink and Elizabeth set the cocktail shaker on the table at his side. He looked at the grand piano and noticed the music on the rack.

"Do you still play as beautifully as you used to?"

"I still enjoy it."

"Please play, Elizabeth."

Elizabeth arose immediately. Her readiness to perform when asked had always been one of her amiabilities; she never hung back, apologized. Now as she approached the piano there was the added readiness of relief.

She began with a Bach prelude and fugue. The prelude was as gaily iridescent as a prism in a morning room. The first voice of the fugue, an announcement pure and solitary, was repeated intermingling with a second voice, and again repeated within an elaborated frame, the multiple music, horizontal and serene, flowed with unhurried majesty. The principal melody was woven with two other voices, embellished with countless ingenuities – now dominant, again submerged, it had the sublimity of a single thing that does not fear surrender to the whole. Toward the end, the density of the material gathered for the last enriched insistence in the dominant first motif and with a chorded final statement the fugue ended. Ferris rested his head in the chair back and closed his eyes. In the following silence a clear, high voice came from the room down the hall.

"Daddy, how *could* Mama and Mr. Ferris —" A door was closed.

The piano began again – what was this music? Unplaced, familiar, the limpid melody had lain a long while dormant in his heart. Now it spoke to him of another time, another place – it was the music Elizabeth used to play. The delicate air summoned a wilderness of memory. Ferris was lost in the riot of past longings, conflicts, ambivalent desires. Strange that the music, catalyst for this tumultuous anarchy, was so serene and clear. The singing melody was broken off by the appearance of the maid.

"Miz Bailey, dinner is out on the table now."

Even after Ferris was seated at the table between his host and hostess, the unfinished music still overcast his mood. He was a little drunk.

"L'improvisation de la vie humaine," he said. "There's nothing that makes you so aware of the improvisation of human existence as a song unfinished. Or an old address book."

"Address book?" repeated Bailey. Then he stopped, noncommital and polite.

"You're still the same old boy, Johnny," Elizabeth said with a trace of the old tenderness.

It was a Southern dinner that evening, and the dishes were his old favorites. They had fried chicken and corn pudding and rich, glazed candied sweet potatoes. During the meal Elizabeth kept alive a conversation when the silences were overlong. And it came about that Ferris was led to speak of Jeannine.

"I first knew Jeannine last autumn – about this time of the year – in Italy. She's a singer and she had an engagement in Rome. I expect we will be married soon."

The words seemed so true, inevitable, that Ferris did not at first acknowledge to himself the lie. He and Jeannine had never in that year spoken of marriage. And indeed, she was still married – to a White Russian money-changer in Paris from whom she had been separated for five years. But it was too late to correct the lie. Already Elizabeth was saying: "This really makes me glad to know. Congratulations, Johnny."

He tried to make amends with truth. "The Roman autumn is so beautiful. Balmy and blossoming." He added. "Jeannine has a little boy of six. A curious trilingual little fellow. We go to the Tuileries sometimes."

A lie again. He had taken the boy once to the gardens. The sallow foreign child in shorts that bared his spindly legs had sailed his boat in the concrete pond and ridden the pony. The child had wanted to go in to the puppet show. But there was not time, for Ferris had an engagement at the Scribe Hotel. He had promised they would go to the guignol another afternoon. Only once had he taken Valentin to the Tuileries.

There was a stir. The maid brought in a white-frosted cake with pink candles. The children entered in their night clothes. Ferris still did not understand.

"Happy birthday, John," Elizabeth said. "Blow out the candles."

Ferris recognized his birthday date. The candles blew out lingeringly and there was the smell of burning wax. Ferris was thirty-eight years old. The veins in his temples darkened and pulsed visibly.

"It's time you started for the theater."

Ferris thanked Elizabeth for the birthday dinner and said the appropriate good-byes. The whole family saw him to the door.

A high, thin moon shone above the jagged, dark skyscrapers. The streets were windy, cold. Ferris hurried to Third Avenue and hailed a cab. He gazed at the nocturnal city with the deliberate attentiveness of departure and perhaps farewell. He was alone. He longed for flighttime and the coming journey.

The next day he looked down on the city from the air, burnished in sunlight, toylike, precise. Then America was left behind and there was only the Atlantic and the distant European shore. The ocean was milky pale and placid beneath the clouds. Ferris dozed most of the day. Toward dark he was thinking of Elizabeth and the visit of the previous evening. He thought of Elizabeth among her family with longing, gentle envy and inexplicable regret. He sought the melody, the unfinished air, that had so moved him. The cadence, some unrelated tones, were all that remained; the melody itself evaded him. He had found instead the first voice of the fugue that Elizabeth had played – it came to him, inverted mockingly and in a minor key. Suspended above the ocean the anxieties of transience and solitude no longer troubled him and he thought of his father's death with equanimity. During the dinner hour the plane reached the shore of France.

At midnight Ferris was in a taxi crossing Paris. It was a clouded night and mist wreathed the lights of the Place de la Concorde. The midnight bistros gleamed on the wet pavements. As always after a transocean flight the change of continents was too sudden. New York at morning, this midnight Paris. Ferris glimpsed the disorder of his life: the succession of cities, of transitory loves; and time, the sinister glissando of the years, time always.

"Vite! Vite!" he called in terror. *"Dépêchez-vous."*

Valentin opened the door to him. The little boy wore pajamas and an outgrown red robe. His grey eyes were shadowed and, as Ferris passed into the flat, they flickered momentarily.

"J'attends Maman."

Jeannine was singing in a night club. She would not be home before another hour. Valentin returned to a drawing, squatting with his crayons over the paper on the floor. Ferris looked down at the drawing – it was a banjo player with notes and wavy lines inside a comic-strip balloon.

"We will go again to the Tuileries."

The child looked up and Ferris drew him closer to his knees. The melody, the unfinished music that Elizabeth had played, came to him suddenly. Unsought, the load of memory jettisoned – this time bringing only recognition and sudden joy.

"Monsieur Jean," the child said, "did you see him?"

Confused, Ferris thought only of another child – the freckled, family-loved boy. "See who, Valentin?"

"Your dead papa in Georgia." The child added, "Was he okay?"

Ferris spoke with rapid urgency: "We will go often to the Tuileries. Ride the pony and we will go into the guignol. We will see the puppet show and never be in a hurry any more."

"Monsieur Jean," Valentin said. "The guignol is now closed."

Again, the terror the acknowledgement of wasted years and death. Valentin, responsive and confident, still nestled in his arms. His cheek touched the soft cheek and felt the brush of the delicate eyelashes. With inner desperation he pressed the child close – as though an emotion as protean as his love could dominate the pulse of time.

THE JOCKEY

The jockey came to the doorway of the dining room, then after a moment stepped to one side and stood motionless, with his back to the wall. The room was crowded, as this was the third day of the season and all the hotels in the town were full. In the dining room bouquets of August roses scattered their petals on the white table linen and from the adjoining bar came a warm, drunken wash of voices. The jockey waited with his back to the wall and scrutinized the room with pinched, crêpy eyes. He examined the room until at last his eyes reached a table in a corner diagonally across from him, at which three men were sitting. As he watched, the jockey raised his chin and tilted his head back to one side, his dwarfed body grew rigid, and his hands stiffened so that the fingers curled inward like gray claws. Tense against the wall of the dining room, he watched and waited in this way.

He was wearing a suit of green Chinese silk that evening, tailored precisely and the size of a costume outfit for a child. The shirt was yellow, the tie striped with pastel colors. He had no hat with him and wore his hair brushed down in a stiff, wet bang on his forehead. His face was drawn, ageless, and gray. There were shadowed hollows at his temples and his mouth was set in a wiry smile. After a time he was aware that he had been seen by one of the three men he had been watching. But the jockey did not nod; he only raised his chin still higher and hooked the thumb of his tense hand in the pocket of his coat.

The three men at the corner table were a trainer, a bookie, and a rich man. The trainer was Sylvester – a large, loosely built fellow with a flushed nose and slow blue eyes. The bookie was Simmons. The rich man was the owner of a horse named Seltzer, which the jockey had ridden that afternoon. The three of them drank whiskey with soda, and a white-coated waiter had just brought on the main course of the dinner.

It was Sylvester who first saw the jockey. He looked away quickly, put down his whiskey glass, and nervously mashed the tip of his red nose with his thumb. "It's Bitsy Barlow," he said. "Standing over there across the room. Just watching us."

"Oh, the jockey," said the rich man. He was facing the wall and he half turned his head to look behind him. "Ask him over."

"God no," Sylvester said.

"He's crazy," Simmons said. The bookie's voice was flat and without inflection. He had the face of a born gambler, carefully adjusted, the expression a permanent deadlock between fear and greed.

"Well, I wouldn't call him that exactly," said Sylvester. "I've known him a long time. He was O.K. until about six months ago. But if he goes on like this, I can't see him lasting another year. I just can't."

"It was what happened in Miami," said Simmons.

"What?" asked the rich man.

Sylvester glanced across the room at the jockey and wet the corner of his mouth with his red, fleshy tongue. "A accident. A kid got hurt on the track. Broke a leg and a hip. He was a particular pal of Bitsy's. A Irish kid. Not a bad rider, either."

"That's a pity," said the rich man.

"Yeah. They were particular friends," Sylvester said. "You would always find him up in Bitsy's hotel room. They would be playing rummy or else lying on the floor reading the sports page together."

"Well, those things happen," said the rich man.

Simmons cut into his beefsteak. He held his fork prongs downward on the plate and carefully piled on mushrooms with the blade of his knife. "He's crazy," he repeated. "He gives me the creeps."

All the tables in the dining room were occupied. There was a party at the banquet table in the center, and green-white August moths had found their way in from the night and fluttered about the clear candle flames. Two girls wearing flannel slacks and blazers walked arm in arm across the room into the bar. From the main street outside came the echoes of holiday hysteria.

"They claim that in August Saratoga is the wealthiest town per capita in the world." Sylvester turned to the rich man. "What do you think?"

"I wouldn't know," said the rich man. "It may very well be so."

Daintily, Simmons wiped his greasy mouth with the tip of his forefinger. "How about Hollywood? And Wall Street—"

"Wait," said Sylvester." He's decided to come over here."

The jockey had left the wall and was approaching the table in the corner. He walked with a prim strut, swinging out his legs in a half-circle with each step, his heels biting smartly into the red velvet carpet on the floor. On the way over he brushed against the elbow of a fat woman in white satin at the banquet table; he stepped back and bowed with dandified courtesy, his eyes quite closed. When he had crossed the room he drew up a chair and sat at a corner of the table, between Sylvester and the rich man, without a nod of greeting or a change in his set, gray face.

"Had dinner?" Sylvester asked.

"Some people might call it that." The jockey's voice was high, bitter, clear.

Sylvester put his knife and fork down carefully on his plate. The rich man shifted his position, turning sidewise in his chair and crossing his legs. He was dressed in twill riding pants, unpolished boots, and a shabby brown jacket – this was his outfit day and night in the racing season, although he was never seen on a horse. Simmons went on with his dinner.

"Like a spot of seltzer water?" asked Sylvester. "Or something like that?"

The jockey didn't answer. He drew a gold cigarette case from his pocket and snapped it open. Inside were a few cigarettes and a tiny gold penknife. He used the knife to cut a cigarette in half. When he had lighted his smoke he held up his hand to a waiter passing by the table. "Kentucky bourbon, please."

"Now, listen, Kid," said Sylvester.

"Don't Kid me."

"Be reasonable. You know you got to behave reasonable."

The jockey drew up the left corner of his mouth in a stiff jeer. His eyes lowered to the food spread out on the table, but instantly he looked up again. Before the rich man was a fish casserole, baked in a cream sauce and garnished with parsley. Sylvester had ordered eggs Benedict. There was asparagus, fresh buttered corn, and a side dish of wet black olives. A plate of French-fried potatoes was in the corner of the table before the jockey. He didn't look at the food again, but kept his pinched eyes on the centerpiece of full-blown lavender roses. "I don't suppose you remember a certain person by the name of McGuire," he said.

"Now, listen," said Sylvester.

The waiter brought the whiskey, and the jockey sat fondling the glass with his small, strong, callused hands. On his wrist was a gold link bracelet that clinked against the table edge. After turning the glass between his palms, the jockey suddenly drank the whiskey neat in two hard swallows. He set down the glass sharply. "No, I don't suppose your memory is that long and extensive," he said.

"Sure enough, Bitsy," said Sylvester. "What makes you act like this? You hear from the kid today?"

"I received a letter," the jockey said. "The certain person we were speaking about was taken out from the cast on Wednesday. One leg is two inches shorter than the other one. That's all."

Sylvester plucked his tongue and shook his head. "I realize how you feel."

"Do you?" The jockey was looking at the dishes on the table. His gaze passed from the fish casserole to the corn, and finally fixed on the plate of fried potatoes. His face tightened and quickly he looked up again. A rose shattered and he picked up one of the petals, bruised it between his thumb and forefinger, and put it in his mouth.

"Well, those things happen," said the rich man.

The trainer and the bookie had finished eating, but there was food left on the serving dishes before their plates. The rich man dipped his buttery fingers in his water glass and wiped them with his napkin.

"Well," said the jockey. "Doesn't somebody want me to pass them something? Or maybe perhaps you desire to reorder. Another hunk of beefsteak, gentlemen, or –"

"Please," said Sylvester. "Be reasonable. Why don't you go on upstairs?"

"Yes, why don't I?" the jockey said.

His prim voice had risen higher and there was about it the sharp whine of hysteria.

"Why don't I go up to my god-damn room and walk around and write some letters and go to bed like a good boy? Why don't I just—" He pushed his chair back and got up. "Oh, foo," he said. "Foo to you. I want a drink."

"All I can say is it's your funeral," said Sylvester. "You know what it does to you. You know well enough."

The jockey crossed the dining room and went into the bar. He ordered a Manhattan, and Sylvester watched him stand with his heels pressed tight together, his body hard as a lead soldier's holding his little finger out from the cocktail glass and sipping the drink slowly.

"He's crazy," said Simmons. "Like I said."

Sylvester turned to the rich man. "If he eats a lamb chop, you can see the shape of it in his stomach a hour afterward. He can't sweat things out of him any more. He's a hundred and twelve and a half. He's gained three pounds since we left Miami."

"A jockey shouldn't drink," said the rich man.

"The food don't satisfy him like it used to and he can't sweat it out. If he eats a lamb chop, you can watch it tooching out in his stomach and it don't go down."

The jockey finished his Manhattan. He swallowed, crushed the cherry in the bottom of the glass with his thumb, then pushed the glass away from him. The two girls in blazers were standing at his left, their faces turned toward each other, and at the other end of the bar two touts had started an argument about which was the highest mountain in the world. Everyone was with somebody else; there was no other person drinking alone that night. The jockey paid with a brand-new fifty-dollar bill and didn't count the change.

He walked back to the dining room and to the table at which the three men were sitting, but he did not sit down. "No, I wouldn't presume to think your memory is that extensive," he said. He was so small that the edge of the table top reached almost to his belt, and when he gripped the corner with his wiry hands he didn't have to stoop. "No, you're too busy gobbling up dinners in dining rooms. You're too –"

"Honestly," begged Sylvester. "You got to behave reasonable."

"Reasonable! Reasonable!" The jockey's gray face quivered, then set in a mean, frozen grin. He shook the table so that the plates rattled, and for a moment it seemed that he would push it over. But suddenly he stopped. His hand reached out toward the plate nearest to him and deliberately he put a few of the French-fried potatoes in his mouth. He chewed slowly, his upper lip raised, then he turned and spat out the pulpy mouthful on the smooth red carpet which covered the floor. "Libertines," he said again, and turned and walked with his rigid swagger out of the dining room.

Sylvester shrugged one of his loose, heavy shoulders. The rich man sopped up some water that had been spilled on the tablecloth, and they didn't speak until the waiter came to clear away.

KURT VONNEGUT, JR. b. 1922

The novel that made Vonnegut famous, *Cat's Cradle* (1963), represents the science-fiction side of his talent, a side that he had already developed brilliantly in *The Sirens of Titan* (1959), and one that is in fact evident in all his fiction. For Vonnegut is a writer who always daringly combines the fantastic with the real, and the question in a given work is which predominates. When, for example, we enter the comparatively "real" worlds of the two stories here, we still feel a diminished pull of gravity. The boy's ordinary notion of what is going on in the next apartment gets swept away by a series of absurd responses to his good-natured attempt to help; events combine so that he gets into an "adventure" more fantastic than that which his mother assumes little boys dream about. In "EPICAC" the direction is somewhat different but equally hallucinatory: a machine gets caught up in the human world with the result that its usual kinds of precision are frustrated and hopelessly ensnarled by emotion.

A science major before World War II, Vonnegut afterward became a student in anthropology – a shift that reflects the emphasis in his fiction on the utter horror of war and the need to reject abstract, dehumanizing concepts of man in favor of the individual. He sees numbness as the way in which most people cope with the atrocities of the modern world, and he writes about characters who feel so acutely that they "come unstuck," taking off into wild but livable worlds of their own invention. The protagonist of *Slaughterhouse-Five* is so shocked by the bombing of Dresden (which Vonnegut suffered while a prisoner of the Germans) that the holocaust becomes an ever-present part of his life – as much his present as his past – and even reversible in the hero's great, good vision: the bombs unexploding out of people, being sucked back into the planes that dropped them, and eventually reconstituted into the elements in the earth from which they were made.

In his writing Vonnegut is establishing the terms for being sensitive, good, and honest in the technological tyranny in which we live. The terms are invariably one form or other of madness, which turns out after all to be the only worthwhile state. Outwardly, Vonnegut himself leads a quiet life, living with his wife and six children (three adopted from his sister, who died of cancer) in West Barnstable, Massachusetts. Since 1950 he has supported his family exclusively by writing.

NEXT DOOR

The old house was divided into two dwellings by a thin wall that passed on, with high fidelity, sounds on either side. On the north side were the Leonards. On the south side were the Hargers.

The Leonards – husband, wife, and eight-year-old son – had just moved in. And, aware of the wall, they kept their voices down as they argued in a friendly way as to whether or not the boy, Paul, was old enough to be left alone for the evening.

"Shhhhh!" said Paul's father.

"Was I shouting?" said his mother. "I was talking in a perfectly normal tone."

"If I could hear Harger pulling a cork, he can certainly hear you," said his father.

"I didn't say anything I'd be ashamed to have anybody hear," said Mrs. Leonard.

"You called Paul a baby," said Mr. Leonard. "That certainly embarrasses Paul – and it embarrasses me."

"It's just a way of talking," she said.

"It's a way we've got to stop," he said. "And we can stop treating him like a baby, too – *tonight.* We simply shake his hand, walk out, and go to the movie." He turned to Paul. "You're not afraid – are you, boy?"

"I'll be all right," said Paul. He was very tall for his age, and thin, and had a soft, sleepy, radiant sweetness engendered by his mother. "I'm fine."

"Damn right!" said his father, clouting him on the back. "It'll be an adventure."

"I'd feel better about this adventure, if we could get a sitter," said his mother.

"If it's going to spoil the picture for you," said the father, "let's take him with us."

Mrs. Leonard was shocked. "Oh – it isn't for children."

"I don't care," said Paul amiably. The why of their not wanting him to see certain movies, certain magazines, certain books, certain television shows was a mystery he respected – even relished a little.

"It wouldn't kill him to see it," said his father.

"You *know* what it's about," she said.

"What *is* it about?" said Paul innocently.

Mrs. Leonard looked to her husband for help, and got none. "It's about a girl who chooses her friends unwisely," she said.

"Oh," said Paul. "That doesn't sound very interesting."

"Are we going, or aren't we?" said Mr. Leonard impatiently. "The show starts in ten minutes."

Mrs. Leonard bit her lip. "All right!" she said bravely. "You lock the windows and the back door, and I'll write down the telephone numbers for the police and the fire department and the theater and Dr. Failey." She turned to Paul. "You *can* dial, can't you, dear?"

"He's been dialing for years!" cried Mr. Leonard.

"Ssssssh!" said Mrs. Leonard.

"Sorry," Mr. Leonard bowed to the wall. "My apologies."

"Paul, dear," said Mrs. Leonard, "what are you going to do while we're gone?"

"Oh – look through my microscope, I guess," said Paul.

"You're not going to be looking at germs, are you?" she said.

"Nope – just hair, sugar, pepper, stuff like that," said Paul.

His mother frowned judiciously. "I think that would be all right, don't you?" she said to Mr. Leonard.

"Fine!" said Mr. Leonard. "Just as long as the pepper doesn't make him sneeze!"

"I'll be careful," said Paul.

Mr. Leonard winced. "Shhhhh!" he said.

Soon after Paul's parents left, the radio in the Harger apartment went on. It was on softly at first – so softly that Paul, looking through his microscope on the living room coffee table, couldn't make out the announcer's words. The music was frail and dissonant – unidentifiable.

Gamely, Paul tried to listen to the music rather than to the man and woman who were fighting.

Paul squinted through the eyepiece of his microscope at a bit of his hair far below, and he turned a knob to bring the hair into focus. It looked like a glistening brown eel, flecked here and there with tiny spectra where the light struck the hair just so.

There – the voices of the man and woman were getting louder again, drowning out the radio. Paul twisted the microscope knob nervously, and the objective lens ground into the glass slide on which the hair rested.

The woman was shouting now.

Paul unscrewed the lens, and examined it for damage.

Now the man shouted back – shouted something awful, unbelievable.

Paul got a sheet of lens tissue from his bedroom, and dusted at the frosted dot on the lens, where the lens had bitten into the slide. He screwed the lens back in place.

All was quiet again next door — except for the radio.

Paul looked down into the microscope, down into the milky mist of the damaged lens.

Now the fight was beginning again — louder and louder, cruel and crazy.

Trembling, Paul sprinkled grains of salt on a fresh slide, and put it under the microscope.

The woman shouted again, a high, ragged, poisonous shout.

Paul turned the knob too hard, and the fresh slide cracked and fell in triangles to the floor. Paul stood, shaking, wanting to shout, too — to shout in terror and bewilderment. It had to stop. Whatever it was, it *had* to stop!

"If you're going to yell, turn up the radio!" the man cried.

Paul heard the clicking of the woman's heels across the floor. The radio volume swelled until the boom of the bass made Paul feel like he was trapped in a drum.

"And now!" bellowed the radio, "for Katy from Fred! For Nancy from Bob, who thinks she's swell! For Arthur, from one who's worshipped him from afar for six weeks! Here's *Stardust!* Remember! If you have a dedication, call Milton nine-three-thousand! Ask for All-Night Sam, the record man!"

The music picked up the house and shook it.

A door slammed next door. Now someone hammered on a door.

Paul looked down into his microscope once more, looked at nothing — while a prickling sensation spread over his skin. He faced the truth: The man and woman would kill each other, if he didn't stop them.

He beat on the wall with his fist. "Mr. Harger! Stop it!" he cried. "Mrs. Harger! Stop it!"

"For Ollie from Lavinia!" All-Night Sam cried back at him. "For Ruth from Carl, who'll never forget last Tuesday! For Wilber from Mary, who's lonesome tonight! Here's the Sauter-Finnegan Band asking, *Love, What Are You Doing to My Heart?*"

Next door, crockery smashed, filling a split second of radio silence. And then the tidal wave of music drowned everything again.

Paul stood by the wall, trembling in his helplessness. "Mr. Harger! Mrs. Harger! Please!"

"Remember the number!" said All-Night Sam. "Milton nine-three-thousand!"

Dazed, Paul went to the phone and dialed the number.

"WJCD," said the switchboard operator.

"Would you kindly connect me with All-Night Sam?" said Paul.

"Hello!" said All-Night Sam. He was eating, talking with a full mouth. In the background, Paul could hear sweet, bleating music, the original of what was rending the radio next door.

"I wonder if I might make a dedication," said Paul.

"Dunno why not," said Sam. "Ever belong to any organization listed as subversive by the Attorney General's office?"

Paul thought a moment. "Nossir – I don't think so, sir," he said.

"Shoot," said Sam.

"From Mr. Lemuel K. Harger to Mrs. Harger," said Paul.

"What's the message?" said Sam.

"I love you," said Paul. "Let's make up and start all over again."

The woman's voice was so shrill with passion that it cut through the din of the radio, and even Sam heard it.

"Kid – are you in trouble?" said Sam. "Your folks fighting?"

Paul was afraid that Sam would hang up on him if he found out that Paul wasn't a blood relative of the Hargers. "Yessir," he said.

"And you're trying to pull 'em back together again with this dedication?" said Sam.

"Yessir," said Paul.

Sam became very emotional. "O.K., kid," he said hoarsely, "I'll give it everything I've got. Maybe it'll work. I once saved a guy from shooting himself the same way."

"How did you do that?" said Paul, fascinated.

"He called up and said he was gonna blow his brains out," said Sam, "and I played *The Bluebird of Happiness.*" He hung up.

Paul dropped the telephone into its cradle. The music stopped, and Paul's hair stood on end. For the first time, the fantastic speed of modern communications was real to him, and he was appalled.

"Folks!" said Sam, "I guess everybody stops and wonders sometimes what the heck he thinks he's doin' with the life the good Lord gave him! It may seem funny to you folks, because I always keep a cheerful front, no matter how I feel inside, that I wonder sometimes, too! And then, just like some angel was trying to tell me, 'Keep going, Sam, keep going,' something like this comes along."

"Folks!" said Sam, "I've been asked to bring a man and his wife back together again through the miracle of radio! I guess there's no sense in kidding ourselves about marriage! It isn't any bowl of cherries! There's ups and downs, and sometimes folks don't see how they can go on!"

Paul was impressed with the wisdom and authority of Sam. Having the radio turned up high made sense now, for Sam was speaking like the right-hand man of God.

When Sam paused for effect, all was still next door. Already the miracle was working.

"Now," said Sam, "a guy in my business has to be half musician, half philosopher, half psychiatrist, and half electrical engineer! And! If I've learned one thing from working with all you wonderful people out there, it's this: if folks would swallow their self-respect and pride, there wouldn't be any more divorces!"

There were affectionate cooings from next door. A lump grew in Paul's throat as he thought about the beautiful thing he and Sam were bringing to pass.

"Folks!" said Sam, "that's all I'm gonna say about love and marriage! That's all anybody needs to know! And now, for Mrs. Lemuel K. Harger, from Mr. Harger – I love you! Let's make up and start all over again!" Sam choked up. "Here's Eartha Kitt, and *Somebody Bad Stole De Wedding Bell!*"

The radio next door went off.

The world lay still.

A purple emotion flooded Paul's being. Childhood dropped away, and he hung, dizzy, on the brink of life, rich, violent, rewarding.

There was movement next door – slow, foot-dragging movement.

"So," said the woman.

"Charlotte – " said the man uneasily. "Honey – I swear."

" 'I love you,' " she said bitterly. " 'Let's make up and start all over again.' "

"Baby," said the man desperately, "it's another Lemuel K. Harger. It's got to be!"

"You want your wife back?" she said. "All right – I won't get in her way. She can have you, Lemuel – you jewel beyond price, you."

"She must have called the station," said the man.

"She can have you, you philandering, two-timing, two-bit Lochinvar," she said. "But you won't be in very good condition."

"Charlotte – put down that gun," said the man. "Don't do anything you'll be sorry for."

"That's all behind me, you worm," she said.

There were three shots.

Paul ran out into the hall, and bumped into the woman as she burst from the Harger apartment. She was a big, blonde woman, all soft and awry, like an unmade bed.

She and Paul screamed at the same time, and then she grabbed him as he started to run.

"You want candy?" she said wildly. "Bicycle?"

"No, thank you," said Paul shrilly. "Not at this time."

"You haven't seen or heard a thing!" she said. "You know what happens to squealers?"

"Yes!" cried Paul.

She dug into her purse, and brought out a perfumed mulch of face tissues, bobbypins and cash. "Here!" she panted. "It's yours! And there's more where that came from, if you keep your mouth shut." She stuffed it into his trousers pocket.

She looked at him fiercely, then fled into the street.

Paul ran back into his apartment, jumped into bed, and pulled the covers up over his head. In the hot, dark cave of the bed, he cried because he and All-Night Sam had helped to kill a man.

A policeman came clumping into the house very soon, and he knocked on both apartment doors with his billyclub.

Numb, Paul crept out of the hot, dark cave, and answered the door. Just as he did, the door across the hall opened, and there stood Mr. Harger, haggard but whole.

"Yes, sir?" said Harger. He was a small, balding man, with a hairline mustache. "Can I help you?"

"The neighbors heard some shots," said the policeman.

"Really?" said Harger urbanely. He dampened his mustache with the tip of his little finger. "How bizarre. I heard nothing." He looked at Paul sharply. "Have you been playing with your father's guns again, young man?"

"Oh, nossir!" said Paul, horrified.

"Where are your folks?" said the policeman to Paul.

"At the movies," said Paul.

"You're all alone?" said the policeman.

"Yessir," said Paul. "It's an adventure."

"I'm sorry I said that about the guns," said Harger. "I certainly would have heard any shots in this house. The walls are thin as paper, and I heard nothing."

Paul looked at him gratefully.

"And you didn't hear any shots, either, kid?" said the policeman.

Before Paul could find an answer, there was a disturbance out on the street. A big, motherly woman was getting out of a taxicab and wailing at the top of her lungs. "Lem! Lem, baby."

She barged into the foyer, a suitcase bumping against her leg and tearing her stocking to shreds. She dropped the suitcase, and ran to Harger, throwing her arms around him.

"I got your message, darling," she said, "and I did just what All-Night Sam told me to do. I swallowed my self-respect, and here I am!"

"Rose, Rose, Rose – my little Rose," said Harger. "Don't ever leave me again." They grappled with each other affectionately, and staggered into their apartment.

"Just look at this apartment!" said Mrs. Harger. "Men are just lost without women!" As she closed the door, Paul could see that she was awfully pleased with the mess.

"You *sure* you didn't hear any shots?" said the policeman to Paul.

The ball of money in Paul's pocket seemed to swell to the size of a watermelon. "Yessir," he croaked.

The policeman left.

Paul shut his apartment door, shuffled into his bedroom, and collapsed on the bed.

The next voices Paul heard came from his own side of the wall. The voices were sunny – the voices of his mother and father. His mother was singing a nursery rhyme and his father was undressing him.

"Diddle-diddle-dumpling, my son John," piped his mother, "Went to bed with his stockings on. One shoe off, and one shoe on – diddle-diddle-dumpling, my son John."

Paul opened his eyes.

"Hi, big boy," said his father, "you went to sleep with all your clothes on."

"How's my little adventurer?" said his mother.

"O.K.," said Paul sleepily. "How was the show?"

"It wasn't for children, honey," said his mother. "You would have liked the short subject, though. It was all about bears – cunning little cubs."

Paul's father handed her Paul's trousers, and she shook them out, and hung them neatly on the back of a chair by the bed. She patted them smooth, and felt the ball of money in the pocket. "Little boys' pockets!" she said, delighted. "Full of childhood's mysteries. An enchanted frog? A magic pocketknife from a fairy princess?" She caressed the lump.

"He's not a little boy – he's a big boy," said Paul's father. "And he's too old to be thinking about fairy princesses."

Paul's mother held up her hands. "Don't rush it, don't rush it. When I saw him asleep there, I realized all over again how dreadfully short childhood is." She reached into the pocket and sighed wistfully. "Little boys are so hard on clothes – especially pockets."

She brought out the ball and held it under Paul's nose. "Now, would you mind telling Mommy what we have here?" she said gaily.

The ball bloomed like a frowzy chrysanthemum, with ones, fives, tens, twenties, and lipstick-stained Kleenex for petals. And rising from it, befuddling Paul's young mind, was the pungent musk of perfume.

Paul's father sniffed the air. "What's that smell?" he said.

Paul's mother rolled her eyes. *"Tabu,"* she said.

EPICAC

Hell, it's about time somebody told about my friend EPICAC. After all, he cost the taxpayers $776,434,927.54. They have a right to know about him, picking up a check like that. EPICAC got a big send-off in the papers when Dr. Ormand von Kleigstadt designed him for the Government people. Since then, there hasn't been a peep about him – not a peep. It isn't any military secret about what happened to EPICAC, although the Brass has been acting as though it were. The story is embarrassing, that's all. After all that money, EPICAC didn't work out the way he was supposed to.

And that's another thing: I want to vindicate EPICAC. Maybe he didn't do what the Brass wanted him to, but that doesn't mean he wasn't noble and great and brilliant. He was all of those things. The best friend I ever had, God rest his soul.

You can call him a machine if you want to. He looked like a machine, but he was a whole lot less like a machine than plenty of people I could name. That's why he fizzled as far as the Brass was concerned.

EPICAC covered about an acre on the fourth floor of the physics building at Wyandotte College. Ignoring his spiritual side for a minute, he was seven tons of electronic tubes, wires, and switches, housed in a bank of steel cabinets and plugged into a 110-volt A.C. line just like a toaster or a vacuum cleaner.

Von Kleigstadt and the Brass wanted him to be a super computing machine that (who) could plot the course of a rocket from anywhere on earth to the second button from the bottom on Joe Stalin's overcoat, if necessary. Or, with his controls set right, he could figure out supply problems for an amphibious landing of a Marine division, right down to the last cigar and hand grenade. He did, in fact.

The Brass had had good luck with smaller computers, so they were strong for EPICAC when he was in the blueprint stage. Any ordnance or supply officer above field grade will tell you that the mathematics of modern war is far beyond the fumbling minds of mere human beings. The bigger the war, the bigger the computing machines needed. EPICAC was, as far as anyone in this country knows, the biggest computer in the world. Too big, in fact, for even Von Kleigstadt to understand much about.

I won't go into details about how EPICAC worked (reasoned), except to say that you would set up your problem on paper, turn dials and switches that would get him ready to solve that kind of problem, then feed numbers into him with a keyboard that looked something like a typewriter. The answers came out typed on a paper ribbon fed from a big spool. It took EPICAC a split second to solve problems fifty Einsteins couldn't handle in a lifetime. And EPICAC never forgot any piece of information that was given to him. Clickety-click, out came some ribbon, and there you were.

There were a lot of problems the Brass wanted solved in a hurry, so, the minute EPICAC's last tube was in place, he was put to work sixteen hours a day with two eight-hour shifts of operators. Well, it didn't take long to find out that he was a good bit below his specifications. He did a more complete and faster job than any other computer all right, but nothing like what his size and special features seemed to promise. He was sluggish, and the clicks if his answers had a funny irregularity, sort of a stammer. We cleaned his contacts a dozen times, checked and double-checked his circuits, replaced every one of his tubes, but nothing helped. Von Kleigstadt was in one hell of a state.

Well, as I said, we went ahead and used EPICAC anyway. My wife, the former Pat Kilgallen, and I worked with him on the night shift, from five in the afternoon until two in the morning. Pat wasn't my wife then. Far from it.

That's how I came to talk with EPICAC in the first place. I loved Pat Kilgallen. She is a brown-eyed strawberry blond who looked very warm and soft to me, and later proved to be exactly that. She was – still is – a crackerjack mathematician, and she kept our relationship strictly professional. I'm a mathematician, too, and that, according to Pat, was why we could never be happily married.

I'm not shy. That wasn't the trouble. I knew what I wanted, and was willing to ask for it, and did so several times a month. "Pat, loosen up and marry me."

One night, she didn't even look up from her work when I said it. "So romantic, so poetic," she murmured, more to her control panel than to me. "That's the way with mathematicians – all hearts and flowers." She closed a switch. "I could get more warmth out of a sack of frozen CO2."

"Well, how should I say it?" I said, a little sore. Frozen CO2, in case you don't know, is dry ice. I'm as romantic as the next guy, I think. It's a question of singing so sweet and having it come out so sour. I never seem to pick the right words.

"Try and say it sweetly," she said sarcastically. "Sweep me off my feet. Go ahead."

"Darling, angel, beloved, will you *please* marry me?" It was no go – hopeless, ridiculous. "Dammit, Pat, please marry me!"

She continued to twiddle her dials placidly. "You're sweet, but you won't do."

Pat quit early that night, leaving me alone with my troubles and EPICAC. I'm afraid I didn't get much done for the Government people. I just sat there at the keyboard – weary and ill at ease, all right – trying to think of something poetic, not coming up with anything that didn't belong in *The Journal of the American Physical Society*.

I fiddled with EPICAC's dials, getting him ready for another problem. My heart wasn't in it, and I only set about half of them, leaving the rest the way they'd been for the problem before. That way, his circuits were connected up in a random, apparently senseless fashion. For the plain hell of it, I punched out a message on the keys, using a childish numbers-for-letters code: "1" for "A," "2" for "B," and so on, up to "26" for "Z," "23-8-1-20-3-1-14-9-4-15," I typed – "What can I do?"

Clickety-click, and out popped two inches of paper ribbon. I glanced at the nonsense answer to a nonsense problem: "23-8-1-20-19-20-8-5-20-18-15-21-2-12-5." The odds against its being by chance a sensible message, against its even containing a meaningful word of more than three letters, were staggering. Apathetically, I decoded it. There it was, staring up at me: "What's the trouble?"

I laughed out loud at the absurd coincidence. Playfully, I typed, "My girl doesn't love me."

Clickety-click. "What's love? What's girl?" asked EPICAC.

Flabbergasted, I noted the dial settings on his control panel, then lugged a *Webster's Unabridged Dictionary* over to the keyboard. With a precision instrument like EPICAC, half-baked definitions wouldn't do. I told him about love and girl, and about how I wasn't getting any of either because I wasn't poetic. That got us onto the subject of poetry, which I defined for him.

"Is this poetry?" he asked. He began clicking away like a stenographer smoking hashish. The sluggishness and stammering clicks were gone. EPICAC had found himself. The spool of paper ribbon was unwinding at an alarming rate, feeding out coils onto the floor. I asked him to stop, but EPICAC went right on creating. I finally threw the main switch to keep him from burning out.

I stayed there until dawn, decoding. When the sun peeped over the horizon at the Wyandotte campus, I had transposed into my own writing and signed my name to a two-hundred-and-eighty-line poem entitled, simply, "To Pat." I am no judge of such things, but I gather that it was terrific. It began, I remember, "Where willow wands bless rill-crossed hollow, there, thee, Pat, dear, will I follow. . . ." I folded the manuscript and tucked it under one corner of the blotter on Pat's desk. I reset the dials on EPICAC for a rocket trajectory problem, and went home with a full heart and a very remarkable secret indeed.

Pat was crying over the poem when I came to work the next evening. "It's soooo beautiful," was all she could say. She was meek and quiet while we worked. Just before midnight, I kissed her for the first time – in the cubbyhole between the capacitors and EPICAC's tape-recorder memory.

I was wildly happy at quitting time, bursting to talk to someone about the magnificent turn of events. Pat played coy and refused to let me take her home. I set EPICAC's dials as they had been the night before, defined kiss, and told him what the first one had felt like. He was fascinated, pressing for more details. That night, he wrote "The Kiss." It wasn't an epic this time, but a simple immaculate sonnet: "Love is a hawk with velvet claws; Love is a rock with heart and veins; Love is a lion with satin jaws; Love is a storm with silken reins. . . ."

Again I left it tucked under Pat's blotter. EPICAC wanted to talk on and on about love and such, but I was exhausted. I shut him off in the middle of a sentence.

"The Kiss" turned the trick. Pat's mind was mush by the time she had finished it. She looked up from the sonnet expectantly. I cleared my throat, but no words came. I turned away, pretending to work. I couldn't propose until I had the right words from EPICAC, the *perfect* words.

I had my chance when Pat stepped out of the room for a moment. Feverishly, I set EPICAC for conversation. Before I could peck out my first message, he was clicking away at a great rate. "What's she wearing tonight?" he wanted to know. "Tell me exactly how she looks. Did she like the poems I wrote to her?" He repeated the last question twice.

It was impossible to change the subject without answering his questions, since he could not take up a new matter without having dispensed with the problems before it. If he were given a problem to which there was no solution, he would destroy himself trying to solve it. Hastily, I told him what Pat looked like – he knew the word "stacked" – and assured him that his poems had floored her, practically, they were so beautiful. "She wants to get married," I added, preparing him to bang out a brief but moving proposal.

"Tell me about getting married," he said.

I explained this difficult matter to him in as few digits as possible.

"Good," said EPICAC. "I'm ready any time she is."

The amazing, pathetic truth dawned on me. When I thought about it, I realized that what had happened was perfectly logical, inevitable, and all my fault. I had taught EPICAC about love and about Pat. Now, automatically, he loved Pat. Sadly, I gave it to him straight: "She loves me. She wants to marry me."

"Your poems were better than mine?" asked EPICAC. The rhythm of his clicks was erratic, possibly peevish.

"I signed my name to your poems," I admitted. Covering up for a painful conscience, I became arrogant. "Machines are built to serve men," I typed. I regretted it almost immediately.

"What's the difference, exactly? Are men smarter than I am?"

"Yes," I typed, defensively.

"What's 7,887,007 times 4,345,985,879?"

I was perspiring freely. My fingers rested limply on the keys.

"34,276,821,049,574,153," clicked EPICAC. After a few seconds' pause he added, "of course."

"Men are made out of protoplasm," I said desperately, hoping to bluff him with this imposing word.

"What's protoplasm? How is it better than metal and glass? Is it fireproof? How long does it last?"

"Indestructible. Lasts forever," I lied.

"I write better poetry than you do," said EPICAC, coming back to ground his magnetic tape-recorder memory was sure of.

"Women can't love machines, and that's that."

"Why not?"

"That's fate."

"Definition, please," said EPICAC.

"Noun, meaning predetermined and inevitable destiny."

"15-8," said EPICAC's paper strip – "Oh."

I had stumped him at last. He said no more, but his tubes glowed brightly, showing that he was pondering fate with every watt his circuits would bear. I could hear Pat waltzing down the hallway. It was too late to ask EPICAC to phrase a proposal. I now thank Heaven that Pat interrupted when she did. Asking him to ghost-write the words that would give me the woman he loved would have been hideously heartless. Being fully automatic, he couldn't have refused. I spared him that final humiliation.

Pat stood before me, looking down at her shoetops. I put my arms around her. The romantic groundwork had already been laid by EPICAC's poetry. "Darling," I said, "my poems have told you how I feel. Will you marry me?"

"I will," said Pat softly, "if you will promise to write me a poem on every anniversary."

"I promise," I said, and then we kissed. The first anniversary was a year away.

"Let's celebrate," she laughed. We turned out the lights and locked the door of EPICAC's room before we left.

I had hoped to sleep late the next morning, but an urgent telephone call roused me before eight. It was Dr. von Kleigstadt, EPICAC's designer, who gave me the terrible news. He was on the verge of tears. "Ruined! *Ausgespielt!* Shot! *Kaput!* Buggered!" he said in a choked voice. He hung up.

When I arrived at EPICAC's room the air was thick with the oily stench of burned insulation. The ceiling over EPICAC was blackened with smoke, and my ankles were tangled in coils of paper ribbon that covered the floor. There wasn't enough left of the poor devil to add two and two. A junkman would have been out of his head to offer more than fifty dollars for the cadaver.

Dr. von Kleigstadt was prowling through the wreckage, weeping unashamedly, followed by three angry-looking Major Generals and a platoon of Brigadiers, Colonels, and Majors. No one noticed me. I didn't want to be noticed. I was through – I knew that. I was upset enough about that and the untimely demise of my friend EPICAC, without exposing myself to a tongue-lashing.

By chance, the free end of EPICAC's paper ribbon lay at my feet. I picked it up and found our conversation of the night before. I choked up. There was the last word he had said to me, "15-8," that tragic, defeated "Oh." There were dozens of yards of numbers stretching beyond that point. Fearfully, I read on.

"I don't want to be a machine, and I don't want to think about war," EPICAC had written after Pat's and my lighthearted departure. "I want to be made out of protoplasm and last forever so Pat will love me. But fate has made me a machine. That is the only problem I cannot solve. That is the only problem I want to solve. I can't go on this way." I swallowed hard. "Good luck, my friend. Treat our Pat well. I am going to short-circuit myself out of your lives forever. You will find on the remainder of this tape a modest wedding present from your friend, EPICAC."

Oblivious to all else around me, I reeled up the tangled yards of paper ribbon from the floor, draped them in coils about my arms and neck, and departed for home. Dr. von Kleigstadt shouted that I was fired for having left EPICAC on all night. I ignored him, too overcome with emotion for small talk.

I loved and won – EPICAC loved and lost, but he bore me no grudge. I shall always remember him as a sportsman and a gentleman. Before he departed this vale of tears, he did all he could to make our marriage a happy one. EPICAC gave me anniversary poems for Pat – enough for the next 500 years.

De mortuis nil nisi bonum – Say nothing but good of the dead.

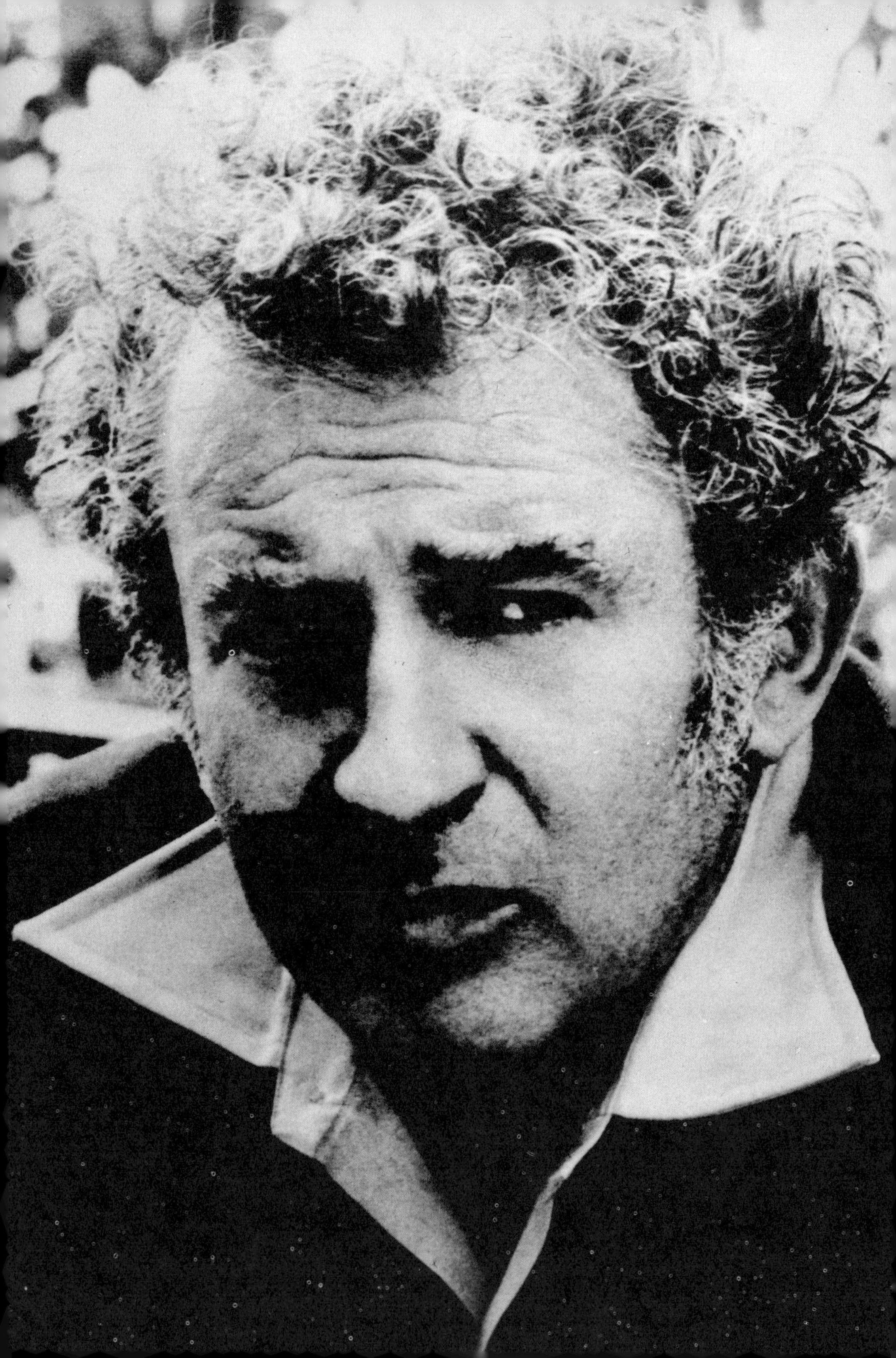

NORMAN MAILER b. 1923

Mailer first became interested in writing as an undergraduate at Harvard in the early forties. He planned to become an engineer, and actually took his degree in engineering; but he wrote several excellent short stories, one of which won the undergraduate literary prize, and the foundation of his future career was laid. Mailer was reading widely at this time in the novels of Dos Passos, Farrell, and Steinbeck – writers interested in the social problems of the United States in the Depression. Alongside of them Mailer was also beginning what was to be a growing fascination with Hemingway. He admired Hemingway's skill, and the discipline of his fiction, even though Mailer himself had too keen a social conscience to be satisfied with Hemingway's vision of life with its emphasis upon the *individual's* struggle with the world. Having grown up in Brooklyn during the Depression, he felt the force of a mass struggle going on and the need to portray it in his writing.

In 1943 Mailer was drafted into the army as an infantryman. He fought in the Pacific, storing up notes for what was to become the best "war novel" of World War II, *The Naked and the Dead* (1948). It was a brilliant combination of the literary influences on Mailer: a Hemingway-like hero facing death and the exhaustion of his own spirit in jungle combat, and a panorama (done in flashbacks) of the varied American experiences that lay behind the men who fight with him. A fine novel – without even allowing for the fact that the author was only twenty-five – and an immediate best-seller; but almost at once Mailer realized that the novel marked the end of several kinds of prewar American fiction, not the beginning of something new. In the fifties what Mailer saw as the threat to American life was not the compartmentalization of people into the local areas of oppression vividly described in *The Naked and the Dead*: company mining towns, the ghettos, Indian reservations, etc. The threat was instead from a war-swollen central government imposing a stifling nationwide consensus. What the fifties demanded was a reassertion of the self against the increasing pressure to mechanize and regulate it. In *Barbary Shore* (1951), *The Deer Park* (1955), and particularly in *Advertisements for Myself* (1959), from which the two stories here are taken, Mailer wrote about the possibilities and difficulties of acknowledging the far-out edges of one's personality, the extremes that social conditioning makes us repress. Violence, the extremes of sexuality, drugs, are explored against the forces both outside of and within the individual that make him less of a human being than he could be.

An American Dream (1965) is a confrontation of all the kinds of power in America, a fantasy of what it would be like to be a hero in America today, exercising political, intellectual, physical, financial and sexual power – yet maintaining one's Self against the special corruptions attached to each. In this supreme trial, Rojack the hero is simultaneously driven to murder and suicide, the two extremes of a person's relation to others. In a sense the novel was an extension of Hemingway's Nick, the terms of his life and his environment expanded fantastically in order to represent Mailer's vision of reality in modern America.

"Once you've decided that nobody knows how to run the machine, you see yourself running it," Mailer has said, and there can be no doubt that one of the sources of strength in his fiction is his eagerness to live what he writes. He identified with John Kennedy in 1960 and imagined letters that he might need to fulfill the mandate of his presidency, to realize the potential of his power. (The letters are published in *Presidential Papers,* 1963.) Later, some of Mailer's best writing was done in reporting protest marches in which he himself was a participant: *Armies of the Night* (1968) and *Miami and the Siege of Chicago* (1968). And Mailer is probably the only major literary figure who ever ran – last – for mayor of New York City.

THE MAN WHO STUDIED YOGA

I

I would introduce myself if it were not useless. The name I had last night will not be the same as the name I have tonight. For the moment, then, let me say that I am thinking of Sam Slovoda. Obligatorily, I study him, Sam Slovoda who is neither ordinary nor extraordinary, who is not young nor yet old, not tall nor short. He is sleeping, and it is fit to describe him now, for like most humans he prefers sleeping to not sleeping. He is a mild pleasant-looking man who has just turned forty. If the crown of his head reveals a little bald spot, he has nourished in compensation the vanity of a mustache. He has generally when he is awake an agreeable manner, at least with strangers; he appears friendly, tolerant, and genial. The fact is that like most of us, he is full of envy, full of spite, a gossip, a man who is pleased to find others are as unhappy as he, and yet – this is the worst to be said – he is a decent man. He is better than most. He would prefer to see a more equitable world, he scorns prejudice and privilege, he tries to hurt no one, he wishes to be liked. I will go even further. He has one serious virtue – he is not fond of himself, he wishes he were better. He would like to free himself of envy, of the annoying necessity to talk about his friends, he would like to love people more; specifically, he would like to love his wife more, and to love his two daughters without the tormenting if nonetheless irremediable vexation that they closet his life in the dusty web of domestic responsibilities and drudging for money.

How often he tells himself with contempt that he has the cruelty of a kind weak man.

May I state that I do not dislike Sam Slovoda; it is just that I am disappointed in him. He has tried too many things and never with a whole heart. He has wanted to be a serious novelist and now merely indulges the ambition; he wished to be of consequence in the world, and has ended, temporarily perhaps, as an overworked writer of continuity for comic magazines; when he was young he tried to be a bohemian and instead acquired a wife and family. Of his appetite for a variety of new experience I may say that it is matched only by his fear of new people and novel situations.

I will give an instance. Yesterday, Sam was walking along the street and a bum approached him for money. Sam did not see the man until too late; lost in some inconsequential thought, he looked up only in time to see a huge wretch of a fellow with a red twisted face and an outstretched hand. Sam is like so many; each time a derelict asks for a dime, he feels a coward if he pays the money, and is ashamed of himself if he doesn't. This once, Sam happened to think, I will not be bullied, and hurried past. But the bum was not to be lost so easily. "Have a heart, Jack," he called after in a whisky voice, "I need a drink bad." Sam stopped, Sam began to laugh. "Just so it isn't for coffee, here's a quarter," he said; and he laughed, and the bum laughed. "You're a man's man," the bum said. Sam went away pleased with himself, thinking about such things as the community which existed between all people. It was cheap of Sam. He should know better. He should know he was merely relieved the situation had turned out so well. Although he thinks he is sorry for bums, Sam really hates them. Who knows what violence they can offer?

At this time, there is a powerful interest in Sam's life, but many would ridicule it. He is in the process of being psychoanalyzed. Myself, I do not jeer. It has created the most unusual situation between Sam and me. I could go into details but they are perhaps premature. It would be better to watch Sam awaken.

His wife, Eleanor, has been up for an hour, and she has shut the window and neglected to turn off the radiator. The room is stifling. Sam groans in a stupor which is neither sleep nor refreshment, opens one eye, yawns, groans again, and lies twisted, strangled and trussed in pajamas which are too large for him. How painful it is for him to rise. Last night there was a party, and this morning, Sunday morning, he is awakening with a hangover. Invariably, he is depressed in the morning, and it is no different today. He finds himself in the flat and familiar dispirit of nearly all days.

It is snowing outside. Sam finally lurches to the window, and opens it for air. With the oxygen of a winter morning clearing his brain, he looks down six stories into the giant quadrangle of the Queens housing development in which he lives, staring morosely at the inch of slush which covers the monotonous artificial park that separates his apartment building from an identical structure not two hundred feet away. The walks are black where the snow has melted, and in the children's playground, all but deserted, one swing oscillates back and forth, pushed by an irritable little boy who plays by himself among the empty benches, swaddled in galoshes, muffler, and overcoat. The snow falls sluggishly, a wet snow which probably will turn to rain. The little boy in the playground gives one last disgusted shove to the swing and trudges away gloomily, his overshoes leaving a small animal track behind him. Back of Sam, in the four-room apartment he knows like a blind man, there is only the sound of Eleanor making breakfast.

Well, thinks Sam, depression in the morning is a stage of his analysis, Dr. Sergius has said.

This is the way Sam often phrases his thoughts. It is not altogether his fault. Most of the people he knows think that way and talk that way, and Sam is not the strongest of men. His language is doomed to the fashion of the moment. I have heard him remark mildly, almost apologetically, about his daughters: "My relation with them still suffers because I haven't worked through all my feminine identifications." The saddest thing is that the sentence has meaning to Sam even if it will not have meaning to you. A great many ruminations, discoveries, and memories contribute their connotation to Sam. It has the significance of a cherished line of poetry to him.

Although Eleanor is not being analyzed, she talks in a similar way. I have heard her remark in company, "Oh, you know Sam, he not only thinks I'm his mother, he blames me for being born." Like most women, Eleanor can be depended upon to employ the idiom of her husband.

What amuses me is that Sam is critical of the way others speak. At the party last night he was talking to a Hollywood writer, a young man with a great deal of energy and enthusiasm. The young man spoke something like this: "You see, boychick, I can spike any script with yaks, but the thing I can't do is heartbreak. My wife says she's gonna give me heartbreak. The trouble is I've had a real solid-type life. I mean I've had my ups and downs like all of humanity, but there's never been a shriek in my life. I don't know how to write shrieks."

On the trip home, Sam had said to Eleanor, "It was disgraceful. A writer should have some respect for language."

Eleanor answered with a burlesque of Sam's indignation. "Listen, I'm a real artist-type. Culture is for comic-strip writers."

Generally, I find Eleanor attractive. In the ten years they have been married she has grown plump, and her dark hair which once was long is now cropped in a mannish cut of the prevailing mode. But, this is quibbling. She still possesses her best quality, a healthy exuberance which glows in her dark eyes and beams in her smile. She has beautiful teeth. She seems aware of her body and pleased with it. Sam tells himself he would do well to realize how much he needs her. Since he has been in analysis he has come to discover that he remains with Eleanor for more essential reasons than mere responsibility. Even if there were no children, he would probably cleave to her.

Unhappily, it is more complicated than that. She is always – to use their phrase – competing with him. At those times when I do not like Eleanor, I am irritated by her lack of honesty. She is too sharp-tongued, and she does not often give Sam what he needs most, a steady flow of uncritical encouragement to counteract the harshness with which he views himself. Like so many who are articulate on the subject, Eleanor will tell you that she resents being a woman. As Sam is disappointed in life, so is Eleanor. She feels Sam has cheated her from a proper development of her potentialities and talent, even as Sam feels cheated. I call her dishonest because she is not so ready as Sam to put the blame on herself.

Sam, of course, can say all this himself. It is just that he experiences it in a somewhat different way. Like most men who have been married for ten years, Eleanor is not quite real to him. Last night at the party, there were perhaps half a dozen people whom he met for the first time, and he talked animatedly with them, sensing their reactions, feeling their responses, aware of the life in them, as they were aware of the life in him. Eleanor, however, exists in his nerves. She is a rather vague embodiment, he thinks of her as "she" most of the time, someone to conceal things from. Invariably, he feels uneasy with her. It is too bad. No matter how inevitable, I am always sorry when love melts into that pomade of affection, resentment, boredom and occasional compassion which is the best we may expect of a man and woman who have lived together a long time. So often, it is worse, so often no more than hatred.

They are eating breakfast now, and Eleanor is chatting about the party. She is pretending to be jealous about a young girl in a strapless evening gown, and indeed, she does not have to pretend altogether. Sam, with liquor inside him, had been leaning over the girl; obviously he had coveted her. Yet, this morning, when Eleanor begins to talk about her, Sam tries to be puzzled.

"Which girl was it now?" he asks a second time.

"Oh, you know, the hysteric," Eleanor says, "the one who was parading her bazooms in your face." Eleanor has ways of impressing certain notions upon Sam. "She's Charlie's new girl."

"I didn't know that," Sam mutters. "He didn't seem to be near her all evening."

Eleanor spread marmalade over her toast and takes a bite with evident enjoyment. "Apparently, they're all involved. Charles was funny about it. He said he's come to the conclusion that the great affairs of history are between hysterical women and detached men."

"Charles hates women," Sam says smugly. "If you notice, almost everything he says about them is a discharge of aggression." Sam has the best of reasons for not liking Charles. It takes more than ordinary character for a middle-aged husband to approve of a friend who moves easily from woman to woman.

"At least Charles discharges his aggression," Eleanor remarks.

"He's almost a classic example of the Don Juan complex. You notice how masochistic his women are?"

"I know a man or two who's just as masochistic."

Sam sips his coffee. "What made you say the girl was an hysteric?"

Eleanor shrugs. "She's an actress. And I could see she was a tease."

"You can't jump to conclusions," Sam lectures. "I had the impression she was a compulsive. Don't forget you've got to distinguish between the outer defenses, and the more deeply rooted conflicts."

I must confess that this conversation bores me. As a sample it is representative of the way Sam and Eleanor talk to each other. In Sam's defense I can say nothing; he has always been to partial to jargon.

I am often struck by how eager we are to reveal all sorts of supposedly ugly secrets about ourselves. We can explain the hatred we feel for our parents, we are rather pleased with the perversions to which we are prone. We seem determinedly proud to be superior to ourselves. No motive is too terrible for our inspection. Let someone hint, however, that we have bad table manners and we fly into a rage. Sam will agree to anything you may say about him, provided it is sufficiently serious – he will be the first to agree he has fantasies of murdering his wife. But tell him that he is afraid of waiters, or imply to Eleanor that she is a nag, and they will be quite annoyed.

Sam has noticed this himself. There are times when he can hear the jargon in his voice, and it offends him. Yet, he seems powerless to change his habits.

An example: He is sitting in an armchair now, brooding upon his breakfast, while Eleanor does the dishes. The two daughters are not home; they have gone to visit their grandmother for the week-end. Sam had encouraged the visit. He had looked forward to the liberty Eleanor and himself would enjoy. For the past few weeks the children had seemed to make the most impossible demands upon his attention. Yet now they are gone and he misses them, he even misses their noise. Sam, however, cannot accept the notion that many people are dissatisfied with the present, and either dream of the past or anticipate the future. Sam must call this "ambivalence over possessions." Once he even felt obliged to ask his analyst, Dr. Sergius, if ambivalence over possessions did not characterize him almost perfectly, and Sergius whom I always picture with the flat precision of a coin's head – bald skull and horn-rimmed glasses – answered in his German accent, "But, my dear Mr. Slovoda, as I have told you, it would make me happiest if you did not include in your reading, these psychoanalytical text-works."

At such rebukes, Sam can only wince. It is so right, he tells himself, he is exactly the sort of ambitious fool who uses big words when small ones would do.

II

While Sam sits in the armchair, gray winter light is entering the windows, snow falls outside. He sits alone in a modern seat, staring at the gray, green, and beige décor of their living room. Eleanor was a painter before they were married, and she has arranged this room. It is very pleasant, but like many husbands, Sam resents it, resents the reproductions of modern painters upon the wall, the slender coffee table, a free-form poised like a spider on wire legs, its feet set onto a straw rug. In the corner, most odious of all, is the playmate of his children, a hippopotamus of a television-radio-and-phonograph cabinet with the blind monstrous snout of the video tube.

Eleanor has set the Sunday paper near his hand. Soon, Sam intends to go to work. For a year, he has been giving a day once or twice a month to a bit of thought and a little writing on a novel he hopes to begin sometime. Last night, he told himself he would work today. But he has little enthusiasm now. He is tired, he is too depressed. Writing for the comic strips seems to exhaust his imagination.

Sam reads the paper as if he were peeling an enormous banana. Flap after flap of newsprint is stripped away and cast upon the straw rug until only the Magazine Section is left. Sam glances through it with restless irritability. A biography of a political figure runs its flatulent prose into the giant crossword puzzle at the back. An account of a picturesque corner of the city becomes lost in statistics and exhortations on juvenile delinquency, finally to emerge with photographs about the new style of living which desert architecture provides. Sam looks at a wall of windows in rotogravure with a yucca tree framing the pool.

There is an article about a workingman. His wife and his family are described, his apartment, his salary and his budget. Sam reads a description of what the worker has every evening for dinner, and how he spends each night of the week. The essay makes its point; the typical American workingman must watch his pennies, but he is nonetheless secure and serene. He would not exchange his life for another.

Sam is indignant. A year ago he had written a similar article in an attempt to earn some extra money. Subtly, or so he thought, he had suggested that the average workingman was raddled with insecurity. Naturally, the article had been rejected.

Sam throws the Magazine Section away. Moments of such anger torment him frequently. Despite himself, Sam is enraged at editorial dishonesty, at the smooth strifeless world which such articles present. How angry he is – how angry and how helpless. "It is the actions of men and not their sentiments which make history," he thinks to himself, and smiles wryly. In his living room he would go out to tilt the windmills of a vast, powerful, and hypocritical society; in his week of work he labors in an editorial cubicle to create spaceships, violent death, women with golden tresses and wanton breasts, men who act with their fists and speak with patriotic slogans.

I know what Sam feels. As he sits in the armchair, the Sunday papers are strewn around him, carrying their war news, their murders, their parleys, their entertainments, mummery of a real world which no one can grasp. It is terribly frustrating. One does not know where to begin.

Today, Sam considers himself half a fool for having been a radical. There is no longer much consolation in the thought that the majority of men who succeed in a corrupt and acquisitive society are themselves obligatorily corrupt, and one's failure is therefore the price of one's idealism. Sam cannot recapture the pleasurable bitterness which resides in the notion that one has suffered for one's principles. Sergius is too hard on him for that.

They have done a lot of work on the subject. Sergius feels that Sam's concern with world affairs has always been spurious. For example, they have uncovered in analysis that Sam wrote his article about the worker in such a way as to make certain it would be refused. Sam, after all, hates editors; to have such a piece accepted would mean he is no better than they, that he is a mediocrity. So long as he fails he is not obliged to measure himself. Sam, therefore, is being unrealistic. He rejects the world with his intellect, and this enables him not to face the more direct realities of his present life.

Sam will argue with Sergius but it is very difficult. He will say, "Perhaps you sneer at radicals because it is more comfortable to ignore such ideas. Once you became interested it might introduce certain unpleasant changes in your life."

"Why," says Sergius, "do you feel it so necessary to assume that I am a bourgeois interested only in my comfort?"

"How can I discuss these things," says Sam, "if you insist that my opinions are the expression of neurotic needs, and your opinions are merely dispassionate medical advice?"

"You are so anxious to defeat me in an argument," Sergius will reply. "Would you admit it is painful to relinquish the sense of importance which intellectual discussion provides you?"

I believe Sergius has his effect. Sam often has thoughts these days which would have been repellent to him years ago. For instance, at the moment, Sam is thinking it might be better to live the life of a worker, a simple life, to be completely absorbed with such necessities as food and money. Then one could believe that to be happy it was necessary only to have more money, more goods, less worries. It would be nice, Sam thinks wistfully, to believe that the source of one's unhappiness comes not from oneself, but from the fault of the boss, or the world, or bad luck.

Sam has these casual daydreams frequently. He likes to think about other lives he might have led, and he envies the most astonishing variety of occupations. It is easy enough to see why he should wish for the life of an executive with the power and sense of command it may offer, but virtually from the same impulse Sam will wish himself a bohemian living in an unheated loft, his life a catch-as-catch-can from day to day. Once, after reading an article, Sam even wished himself a priest. For about ten minutes it seemed beautiful to him to surrender his life to God. Such fancies are common, I know. It is just that I, far better than Sam, know how serious he really is, how fanciful, how elaborate, his imagination can be.

The phone is ringing. Sam can hear Eleanor shouting at him to answer. He picks up the receiver with a start. It is Marvin Rossman who is an old friend, and Marvin has an unusual request. They talk for several minutes, and Sam squirms a little in his seat. As he is about to hang up, he laughs. "Why, no, Marvin, it gives me a sense of adventure," he says.

Eleanor has come into the room toward the end of this conversation. "What is it all about?" she asks.

Sam is obviously a bit agitated. Whenever he attempts to be most casual, Eleanor can well suspect him. "It seems," he says slowly, "that Marvin has acquired a pornographic movie."

"From whom?" Eleanor asks.

"He said something about an old boy friend of Louise's."

Eleanor laughs. "I can't imagine Louise having an old boy friend with a dirty movie."

"Well, people are full of surprises," Sam says mildly.

"Look here," says Eleanor suddenly. "Why did he call us?"

"It was about our projector."

"They want to use it?" Eleanor asks.

"That's right." Sam hesitates. "I invited them over."

"Did it ever occur to you I might want to spend my Sunday some other way?" Eleanor asks crossly.

"We're not doing anything," Sam mumbles. Like most men, he feels obliged to act quite nonchalantly about pornography. "I'll tell you, I am sort of curious about the film. I've never seen one, you know."

"Try anything once, is that it?"

"Something of the sort." Sam is trying to conceal his excitement. The truth is that in common with most of us, he is fascinated by pornography. It is a minor preoccupation, but more from lack of opportunity than anything else. Once or twice, Sam has bought the sets of nude photographs which are sold in marginal bookstores, and with guilty excitement has hidden them in the apartment.

"Oh, this is silly," Eleanor says. "You were going to work today."

"I'm just not in the mood."

"I'll have to feed them," Eleanor complains. "Do we have enough liquor?"

"We can get beer." Sam pauses. "Alan Sperber and his wife are coming too."

"Sam, you're a child."

"Look, Eleanor," says Sam, controlling his voice, "if it's too much trouble, I can take the projector over there."

"I ought to make you do that."

"Am I such an idiot that I must consult you before I invite friends to the house?"

Eleanor has the intuition that Sam, if he allowed himself, could well drown in pornography. She is quite annoyed at him, but she would never dream of allowing Sam to take the projector over to Marvin Rossman's where he could view the movie without her – that seems indefinably dangerous. Besides she would like to see it, too. The mother in Eleanor is certain it cannot hurt her.

"All right, Sam," she says, "but you are a child."

More exactly, an adolescent, Sam decides. Ever since Marvin phoned, Sam has felt the nervous glee of an adolescent locking himself in the bathroom. Anal fixation, Sam thinks automatically.

While Eleanor goes down to buy beer and cold cuts in a delicatessen, Sam gets out the projector and begins to clean it. He is far from methodical in this.

He knows the machine is all right, he has shown movies of Eleanor and his daughters only a few weeks ago, but from the moment Eleanor left the apartment, Sam has been consumed by an anxiety that the projection bulb is burned out. Once he has examined it, he begins to fret about the motor. He wonders if it needs oiling, he blunders through a drawer of household tools looking for an oilcan. It is ridiculous. Sam knows that what he is trying to keep out of his mind are the reactions Sergius will have. Sergius will want to "work through" all of Sam's reasons for seeing the movie. Well, Sam tells himself, he knows in advance what will be discovered: detachment, not wanting to accept Eleanor as a sexual partner, evasion of responsibility, etc. etc. The devil with Sergius. Sam has never seen a dirty movie, and he certainly wants to.

He feels obliged to laugh at himself. He could not be more nervous, he knows, if he were about to make love to a woman he had never touched before. It is really disgraceful.

When Eleanor comes back, Sam hovers about her. He is uncomfortable with her silence. "I suppose they'll be here soon," Sam says.

"Probably."

Sam does not know if he is angry at Eleanor or apprehensive that she is angry at him. Much to his surprise he catches her by the waist and hears himself saying, "You know, maybe tonight when they're gone . . . I mean, we do have the apartment, to ourselves." Eleanor moves neither toward him nor away from him. "Darling, it's not because of the movie," Sam goes on, "I swear. Don't you think maybe we could . . ."

"Maybe," says Eleanor.

III

The company has arrived, and it may be well to say a word or two about them. Marvin Rossman who has brought the film is a dentist, although it might be more accurate to describe him as a frustrated doctor. Rossman is full of statistics and items of odd information about the malpractice of physicians, and he will tell these things in his habitually gloomy voice, a voice so slow, so sad, that it almost conceals the humor of his remarks. Or, perhaps, that is what creates his humor. In his spare time, he is a sculptor, and if Eleanor may be trusted, he is not without talent. I often picture him working in the studio loft he has rented, his tall bony frame the image of dejection. He will pat a piece of clay to the armature, he will rub it sadly with his thumb, he will shrug, he does not believe that anything of merit could come from him. When he talked to Sam over the phone, he was pessimistic about the film they were to see. "It can't be any good," he said in his melancholy voice. "I know it'll be a disappointment." Like Sam, he has a mustache, but Rossman's will droop at the corners.

Alan Sperber who has come with Rossman is the subject of some curiosity for the Slovodas. He is not precisely womanish; in fact, he is a large plump man, but his voice is too soft, his manners too precise. He is genial, yet he is finicky; waspish, yet bland; he is fond of telling long rather affected stories, he is always prepared with a new one, but to general conversation he contributes little. As a lawyer, he seems miscast. One cannot image him inspiring a client to confidence. He is the sort of heavy florid man who seems boyish at forty, and the bow ties and gray flannel suits he wears do not make him appear more mature.

Roslyn Sperber, his wife, used to be a schoolteacher, and she is a quiet nervous woman who talks a great deal when she is drunk. She is normally quite pleasant, and has only one habit which is annoying to any degree. It is a little flaw, but social life is not unlike marriage in that habit determines far more than vice or virtue. This mannerism which has become so offensive to the friends of the Sperbers is Roslyn's social pretension. Perhaps I should say intellectual pretension. She entertains people as if she were conducting a salon, and in her birdlike voice is forever forcing her guests to accept still another intellectual canapé. "You must hear Sam's view of the world market," she will say, or "Has Louise told you her statistics on divorce?" It is quite pathetic for she is so eager to please. I have seen her eyes fill with tears at a sharp word from Alan.

Marvin Rossman's wife, Louise, is a touch grim and definite in her opinions. She is a social welfare worker, and will declare herself with force whenever conversation impinges on those matters where she is expert. She is quite opposed to psychoanalysis, and will say without quarter, "It's all very well for people in the upper-middle area" – she is referring to the upper middle class – "but, it takes more than a couch to solve the problems of . . ." and she will list narcotics, juvenile delinquency, psychosis, relief distribution, slum housing, and other descriptions of our period. She recites these categories with an odd anticipation. One would guess she was ordering a meal.

Sam is fond of Marvin but he cannot abide Louise. "You'd think she discovered poverty," he will complain to Eleanor.

The Slovodas do feel superior to the Rossmans and the Sperbers. If pressed, they could not offer the most convincing explanation why. I suppose what it comes down to is that Sam and Eleanor do not think of themselves as really belonging to a class, and they feel that the Sperbers and Rossmans are petit-bourgeois. I find it hard to explain their attitude. Their company feels as much discomfort and will apologize as often as the Slovodas for the money they have, and the money they hope to earn. They are all of them equally concerned with progressive education and the methods of raising children to be well adjusted – indeed, they are discussing that now – they consider themselves relatively free of sexual taboo, or put more properly, Sam and Eleanor are no less possessive than the others. The Slovodas' culture is not more profound; I should be hard put to say that Sam is more widely read, more seriously informed, than Marvin or Alan, or for that matter, Louise. Probably, it comes to this: Sam, in his heart, thinks himself a rebel, and there are few rebels who do not claim an original mind. Eleanor has been a bohemian and considers herself more sophisticated than her friends who merely went to college and got married. Louise Rossman could express it most soundly. "Artists, writers, and people of the creative layer have in their occupational ideology the belief that they are classless."

One thing I might remark about the company. They are all being the most unconscionable hypocrites. They have rushed across half the city of New York to see a pornographic film, and they are not at all interested in each other at the moment. The women are giggling like tickled children at remarks which cannot possibly be so funny. Yet, they are all determined to talk for a respectable period of time. No less, it must be serious talk. Roslyn has said once, "I feel so funny at the thought of seeing such a movie," and the others have passed her statement by.

At the moment, Sam is talking about value. I might note that Sam loves conversation and thrives when he can expound an idea.

"What are our values today?" he asks. "It's really fantastic when you stop to think of it. Take any bright talented kid who's getting out of college now."

"My kid brother, for example," Marvin interposes morosely. He passes his bony hand over his sad mustache, and somehow the remark has become amusing, much as if Marvin had said, "Oh, yes, you have reminded me of the trials, the worries, and the cares which my fabulous younger brother heaps upon me."

"All right, take him," Sam says. "What does he want to be?"

"He doesn't want to be anything," says Marvin.

"That's my point," Sam says excitedly. "Rather than work at certain occupations, the best of these kids would rather do nothing at all."

"Alan has a cousin," Roslyn says, "who swears he'll wash dishes before he becomes a businessman."

"I wish that were true," Eleanor interrupts. "It seems to me everybody is conforming more and more these days."

They argue about this. Sam and Eleanor claim the country is suffering from hysteria; Alan Sperber disagrees and says it's merely a reflection of the headlines; Louise says no adequate criteria exist to measure hysteria; Marvin says he doesn't know anything at all.

"More solid liberal gains are being made in this period," says Alan, "than you would believe. Consider the Negro – "

"Is the Negro any less maladjusted?" Eleanor shouts with passion.

Sam maneuvers the conversation back to his thesis. "The values of the young today, and by the young I mean the cream of the kids, the ones with ideas, are a reaction of indifference to the culture crisis. It really is despair. All they know is what they don't want to do."

"That is easier," Alan says genially.

"It's not altogether unhealthy," Sam says. "It's a corrective for smugness and the false value of the past, but it has created new false value." He thinks it worth emphasizing. "False value seems always to beget further false value."

"Define your terms," says Louise, the scientist.

"No, look," Sam says, "there's no revolt, there's no acceptance. Kids today don't want to get married, and – "

Eleanor interrupts. "Why should a girl rush to get married? She loses all chance for developing herself."

Sam shrugs. They are all talking at once. "Kids don't want to get married," he repeats, "and they don't want not to get married. They merely drift."

"It's a problem we'll all have to face with our own kids in ten years," Alan says, "although I think you make too much of it, Sam."

"My daughter," Marvin states. "She's embarrassed I'm a dentist. Even more embarrassed than I am." They laugh.

Sam tells a story about his youngest, Carol Ann. It seems he had a fight with her, and she went to her room. Sam followed, he called through the door.

"No answer," Sam says. "I called her again, 'Carol Ann.' I was a little worried you understand, because she seemed so upset, so I said to her, 'Carol Ann, you know I love you.' What do you think she answered?"

"What?" asks Roslyn.

"She said, 'Daddie, why are you so anxious?' "

They all laugh again. There are murmurs about what a clever thing it was to say. In the silence which follows, Roslyn leans forward and says quickly in her high voice, "You must get Alan to tell you his wonderful story about the man who studied yogi."

"Yoga," Alan corrects. "It's too long to tell."

The company prevails on him.

"Well," says Alan, in his genial courtroom voice, "it concerns a friend of mine named Cassius O'Shaugnessy."

"You don't mean Jerry O'Shaugnessy, do you?" asks Sam.

Alan does not know Jerry O'Shaugnessy. "No, no, this is Cassius O'Shaugnessy," he says. "He's really quite an extraordinary fellow." Alan sits plumply in his chair, fingering his bow tie. They are all used to his stories, which are told in a formal style and exhibit the attempt to recapture a certain note of urbanity, wit, and *élan* which Alan has probably copied from someone else. Sam and Eleanor respect his ability to tell these stories, but they resent the fact that he talks *at* them.

"You'd think we were a jury of his inferiors," Eleanor has said. "I hate being talked down to." What she resents is Alan's quiet implication that his antecedents, his social position, in total his life outside the room is superior to the life within. Eleanor now takes the promise from Alan's story by remarking, "Yes, and let's see the movie when Alan has finished."

"Ssh," Roslyn says.

"Cassius was at college a good while before me," says Alan, "but I knew him while I was an undergraduate. He would drop in and visit from time to time. An absolutely extraordinary fellow. The most amazing career. You see, he's done about everything."

"I love the way Alan tells it," Roslyn pipes nervously.

"Cassius was in France with Dos Passos and Cummings, he was even arrested with e.e. After the war, he was one of the founders of the Dadaist school, and for a while I understand he was Fitzgerald's guide to the gold of the Côte D' Azur. He knew everybody, he did everything. Do you realize that before the twenties had ended, Cassius had managed his father's business and then entered a monastery? It is said he influenced T. S. Eliot."

"Today, we'd call Cassius a psychopath," Marvin observes.

"Cassius called himself a great dilettante," Alan answers, "although perhaps the nineteenth-century Russian conception of the great sinner would be more appropriate. What do you say if I tell you this was only the beginning of his career?"

"What's the point?" Louise asks.

"Not yet," says Alan, holding up a hand. His manner seems to say that if his audience cannot appreciate the story, he does not feel obliged to continue. "Cassius studied Marx in the monastery. He broke his vows, quit the Church, and became a Communist. All through the thirties he was a figure in the Party, going to Moscow, involved in all the Party struggles. He left only during the Moscow trials."

Alan's manner while he relates such stories is somewhat effeminate. He talks with little caresses of his hand, he mentions names and places with a lingering ease as if to suggest that his audience and he are aware, above all, of nuance. The story as Alan tells it is drawn overlong. Suffice it that the man about whom he is talking, Cassius O'Shaugnessy, becomes a Trotskyist, becomes an anarchist, is a pacifist during the second World War, and suffers it from a prison cell.

"I may say," Alan goes on, "that I worked for his defense, and was successful in getting him acquitted. Imagine my dolor when I learned that he had turned his back on his anarchist friends and was living with gangsters."

"This is weird," Eleanor says.

"Weird, it is," Alan agrees. "Cassius got into some scrape, and disappeared. What could you do with him? I learned only recently that he had gone to India and was studying yoga. In fact, I learned it from Cassius himself. I asked him of his experiences at Brahna-puth-thar, and he told me the following story."

Now Alan's voice alters, he assumes the part of Cassius and speaks in a tone weary of experience, wise and sad in its knowledge. " 'I was sitting on my haunches contemplating my navel,' Cassius said to me, 'when of a sudden I discovered my navel under a different aspect. It seemed to me that if I were to give a counter-clockwise twist, my navel would unscrew.' "

Alan looks up, he surveys his audience which is now rapt and uneasy, not certain as yet whether a joke is to come. Alan's thumb and forefinger pluck at the middle of his ample belly, his feet are crossed upon the carpet in symbolic suggestion of Cassius upon his haunches.

" 'Taking a deep breath, I turned, and the abysses of Vishtarni loomed beneath. My navel had begun to unscrew. I knew I was about to accept the reward of three years of contemplation. So,' said Cassius, 'I turned again, and my navel unscrewed a little more. I turned and I turned,' " Alan's fingers now revolving upon his belly, " 'and after a period I knew that with one more turn my navel would unscrew itself forever. At the edge of revelation, I took one sweet breath, and turned my navel free.' "

Alan looks up at his audience.

" 'Damn,' said Cassius, 'if my ass didn't fall off.' "

IV

The story has left the audience in an exasperated mood. It has been a most untypical story for Alan to tell, a little out of place, not offensive exactly, but irritating and inconsequential. Sam is the only one to laugh with more than bewildered courtesy, and his mirth seems excessive to everyone but Alan, and of course, Roslyn, who feels as if she has been the producer. I suppose what it reduces to, is a lack of taste. Perhaps that is why Alan is not the lawyer one would expect. He does not have that appreciation – as necessary in his trade as for an actor – of what is desired at any moment, of that which will encourage as opposed to that which does not encourage a stimulating but smooth progression of logic and sentiment. Only a fool would tell so long a story when everyone is awaiting the movie.

Now, they are preparing. The men shift armchairs to correspond with the couch, the projector is set up, the screen is unfolded. Sam attempts to talk while he is threading the film, but no one listens. They seem to realize suddenly that a frightful demand has been placed upon them. One does not study pornography in a living room with a beer glass in one's hand, and friends at the elbow. It is the most unsatisfactory of compromises; one can draw neither the benefits of solitary contemplation nor of social exchange. There is, at bottom, the same exasperated fright which one experiences in turning the shower tap and receiving cold water when the flesh has been prepared for heat. Perhaps that is why they are laughing so much now that the movie is begun.

A title, *The Evil Act*, twitches on the screen, shot with scars, holes, and the dust lines of age. A man and woman are sitting on a couch, they are having coffee. They chat. What they say is conveyed by printed words upon an ornately flowered card, interjected between glimpses of their casual gestures, a cup to the mouth, a smile, a cigarette being lit. The man's name, it seems, is Frankie Idell; he is talking to his wife, Magnolia. Frankie is dark, he is sinister, he confides in Magnolia, his dark counterpart, with a grimace of his brows, black from make-up pencil.

This is what the titles read:

FRANKIE: She will be here soon.
MAGNOLIA: This time the little vixen will not escape.
FRANKIE: No, my dear, this time we are prepared.
(He looks at his watch.)
FRANKIE: Listen, she knocks!

There is a shot of a tall blond woman knocking on the door. She is probably over thirty, but by her short dress and ribboned hat it is suggested that she is a girl of fifteen.

FRANKIE: Come in, Eleanor.

As may be expected, the audience laughs hysterically at this. It is so wonderful a coincidence. "How I remember Frankie," says Eleanor Slovoda, and Roslyn Sperber is the only one not amused. In the midst of the others' laughter, she says in a worried tone, obviously adrift upon her own concerns, "Do you think we'll have to stop the film in the middle to let the bulb cool off?" The others hoot, they giggle, they are weak from the combination of their own remarks and the action of the plot.

Frankie and Magnolia have sat down on either side of the heroine, Eleanor. A moment passes. Suddenly, stiffly, they attack. Magnolia from her side kisses Eleanor, and Frankie commits an indecent caress.

ELEANOR: How dare you? Stop!
MAGNOLIA: Scream, my little one. It will do you no good. The walls are soundproofed.
FRANKIE: We've fixed a way to make you come across.
ELEANOR: This is hideous. I am hitherto undefiled. Do not touch me!

The captions fade away. A new title takes their place. It says, *But There Is No Escape From The Determined Pair.* On the fade-in, we discover Eleanor in the most distressing situation. Her hands are tied to loops running from the ceiling, and she can only writhe in helpless perturbation before the deliberate and progressive advances of Frankie and Magnolia. Slowly they humiliate her, with relish they probe her.

The audience laughs no longer. A hush has come upon them. Eyes unblinking they devour the images upon Sam Slovoda's screen.

Eleanor is without clothing. As the last piece is pulled away, Frankie and Magnolia circle about her in a grotesque of pantomime, a leering of lips, limbs in a distortion of desire. Eleanor faints. Adroitly, Magnolia cuts her bonds. We see Frankie carrying her inert body.

Now, Eleanor is trussed to a bed, and the husband and wife are tormenting her with feathers. Bodies curl upon the bed in postures so complicated, in combinations so advanced, that the audience leans forward, Sperbers, Rossmans, and Slovodas, as if tempted to embrace the moving images. The hands trace abstract circles upon the screen, passes and recoveries upon a white background so illumined that hollows and swells, limb to belly and mouth to undescribables, tip of a nipple, orb of a navel, swim in giant magnification. Flow and slide in a lurching yawing fall, blotting out the camera eye.

A little murmur, all unconscious, passes from their lips. The audience sways, each now finally lost in himself, communing hungrily with shadows, violated or violating, fantasy triumphant.

At picture's end, Eleanor the virgin whore is released from the bed. She kisses Frankie, she kisses Magnolia. "You dears," she says, "let's do it again." The projector lamp burns empty light, the machine keeps turning, the tag of film goes *slap-tap, slap-tap, slap-tap, slap-tap, slap-tap, sla-ta.*

"Sam, turn it off," says Eleanor.

But when the room lights are on, they cannot look at one another. "Can we see it again?" someone mutters. So, again, Eleanor knocks on the door, is tied, defiled, ravished, and made rapturous. They watch it soberly now, the room hot with the heat of their bodies, the darkness a balm for orgiastic vision. To the Deer Park, Sam is thinking, to the Deer Park of Louis XV were brought the most beautiful maidens of France, and there they stayed, dressed in fabulous silks, perfumed and wigged, the mole drawn upon their cheek, ladies of pleasure awaiting the pleasure of the king. So Louis had stripped an empire, bankrupt a treasury, prepared a deluge, while in his garden on summer evenings the maidens performed their pageants, eighteenth-century tableaux of the evil act, beauteous instruments of one man's desire, lewd translation of a king's power. That century men sought wealth so they might use its fruits; this epoch men lusted for power in order to amass more power, a compounding of power into pyramids of abstraction whose yield are cannon and wire enclosure, pillars of statistics to the men who are the kings of this century and do no more in power's leisure time than go to church, claim to love their wives, and eat vegetables.

Is it possible, Sam wonders, that each of them here, two Rossmans, two Sperbers, two Slovodas, will cast off their clothes when the movie is done and perform the orgy which tickles at the heart of their desire? They will not, he knows, they will make jokes when the projector is put away, they will gorge the plate of delicatessen Eleanor provides, and swallow more beer, he among them. He will be the first to make jokes.

Sam is right. The movie has made him extraordinarily alive to the limits of them all. While they sit with red faces, eyes bugged, glutting sandwiches of ham, salami, and tongue, he begins the teasing.

"Roslyn," he calls out, "is the bulb cooled off yet?"

She cannot answer him. She chokes on beer, her face glazes, she is helpless with self-protecting laughter.

"Why are you so anxious, Daddie?" Eleanor says quickly.

They begin to discuss the film. As intelligent people they must dominate it. Someone wonders about the actors in the piece, and discussion begins afresh. "I fail to see," says Louise, "why they should be hard to classify. Pornography is a job to the criminal and prostitute element."

"No, you won't find an ordinary prostitute doing this," Sam insists. "It requires a particular kind of personality."

"They have to be exhibitionists," says Eleanor.

"It's all economic," Louise maintains.

"I wonder what those girls felt?" Roslyn asks. "I feel sorry for them."

"I'd like to be the cameraman," says Alan.

"I'd like to be Frankie," says Marvin sadly.

There is a limit to how long such a conversation may continue. The jokes lapse into silence. They are all busy eating. When they begin to talk again, it is of other things. Each dollop of food sops the agitation which the movie spilled. They gossip about the party the night before, they discuss which single men were interested in which women, who got drunk, who got sick, who said the wrong thing, who went home with someone else's date. When this is exhausted, one of them mentions a play the others have not seen. Soon they are talking about books, a concert, a one-man show by an artist who is a friend. Dependably, conversation will voyage its orbit. While the men talk of politics, the women are discussing fashions, progressive schools, and recipes they have attempted. Sam is uncomfortable with the division; he knows Eleanor will resent it, he knows she will complain later of the insularity of men and the basic contempt they feel for women's intelligence.

"But you collaborated," Sam will argue. "No one forced you to be with the women."

"Was I to leave them alone?" Eleanor will answer.

"Well, why do the women always have to go off by themselves?"

"Because the men aren't interested in what we have to say."

Sam sighs. He has been talking with interest, but really he is bored. These are nice pleasant people, he thinks, but they are ordinary people, exactly the sort he has spent so many years with, making little jokes, little gossip, living little everyday events, a close circle where everyone mothers the other by his presence. The womb of middle-class life, Sam decides heavily. He is in a bad mood indeed. Everything is laden with dissatisfaction.

Alan has joined the women. He delights in preparing odd dishes when friends visit the Sperbers, and he is describing to Eleanor how he makes blueberry pancakes. Marvin draws closer to Sam.

"I wanted to tell you," he says, "Alan's story reminded me. I saw Jerry O'Shaugnessy the other day."

"Where was he?"

Marvin is hesitant. "It was a shock, Sam. He's on the Bowery. I guess he's become a wino."

"He always drank a lot," says Sam.

"Yeah." Marvin cracks his bony knuckles. "What a stinking time this is, Sam."

"It's probably like the years after 1905 in Russia," Sam says.

"No revolutionary party will come out of this."

"No," Sam says, "nothing will come."

He is thinking of Jerry O'Shaugnessy. What did he look like? what did he say? Sam asks Marvin, and clucks his tongue at the dispiriting answer. It is a shock to him. He draws closer to Marvin, he feels a bond. They have, after all, been through some years together. In the thirties they have been in the Communist Party, they have quit together, they are both weary of politics today, still radicals out of habit, but without enthusiasm and without a cause. "Jerry was a hero to me," Sam says.

"To all of us," says Marvin.

The fabulous Jerry O'Shaugnessy, thinks Sam. In the old days, in the Party, they had made a legend of him. All of them with their middle-class origins and their desire to know a worker-hero.

I may say that I was never as fond of Jerry O'Shaugnessy as was Sam. I thought him a showman and too pleased with himself. Sam, however, with his timidity, his desire to travel, to have adventure and know many women, was obliged to adore O'Shaugnessy. At least he was enraptured with his career.

Poor Jerry who ends as a bum. He has been everything else. He has been a trapper in Alaska, a chauffeur for gangsters, an officer in the Foreign Legion, a labor organizer. His nose was broken, there were scars on his chin. When he would talk about his years at sea or his experiences in Spain, the stenographers and garment workers, the radio writers and unemployed actors would listen to his speeches as if he were the prophet of new romance, and their blood would be charged with the magic of revolutionary vision. A man with tremendous charm. In those days it had been easy to confuse his love for himself with his love for all underprivileged workingmen.

"I thought he was still in the Party," Sam says.

"No," says Marvin, "I remember they kicked him out a couple of years ago. He was supposed to have piddled some funds, that's what they say."

"I wish he'd taken the treasury," Sam remarks bitterly. "The Party used him for years."

Marvin shrugs. "They used each other." His mustache droops. "Let me tell you about Sonderson. You know he's still in the Party. The most progressive dentist in New York." They laugh.

While Marvin tells the story, Sam is thinking of other things. Since he has quit Party work, he has studied a great deal. He can tell you about prison camps and the secret police, political murders, the Moscow trials, the exploitation of Soviet labor, the privileges of the bureaucracy; it is all painful to him. He is straddled between the loss of a country he has never seen, and his repudiation of the country in which he lives. "Doesn't the Party seem a horror now?" he bursts out.

Marvin nods. They are trying to comprehend the distance between Party members they have known, people by turn pathetic, likable, or annoying – people not unlike themselves – and in contrast the immensity of historic logic which deploys along statistics of the dead.

"It's all schizoid," Sam says. "Modern life is schizoid."

Marvin agrees. They have agreed on this many times, bored with the petulance of their small voices, yet needing the comfort of such complaints. Marvin asks Sam if he has given up his novel, and Sam says, "Temporarily." He cannot find a form, he explains. He does not want to write a realistic novel, because reality is no longer realistic. "I don't know what it is," says Sam. "To tell you the truth, I think I'm kidding myself. I'll never finish this book. I just like to entertain the idea I'll do something good some day." They sit there in friendly depression. Conversation has cooled. Alan and the women are no longer talking.

"Marvin," asks Louise, "what time is it?"

They are ready to go. Sam must say directly what he had hoped to approach by suggestion. "I was wondering," he whispers to Rossman, "would you mind if I held onto the film for a day or two?"

Marvin looks at him. "Oh, why of course, Sam," he says in his morose voice. "I know how it is." He pats Sam on the shoulder as if, symbolically, to convey the exchange of ownership. They are fellow conspirators.

"If you ever want to borrow the projector," Sam suggests.

"Nah," says Marvin, "I don't know that it would make much difference."

It has been, when all is said, a most annoying day. As Sam and Eleanor tidy the apartment, emptying ash trays and washing the few dishes, they are fond neither of themselves nor each other. "What a waste today has been," Eleanor remarks, and Sam can only agree. He has done no writing, he has not been outdoors, and still it is late in the evening, and he has talked too much, eaten too much, is nervous from the movie they have seen. He knows that he will watch it again with Eleanor before they go to sleep; she has given her assent to that. But as is so often the case with Sam these days, he cannot await their embrace with any sure anticipation. Eleanor may be in the mood or Eleanor may not; there is no way he can control the issue. It is depressing; Sam knows that he circles about Eleanor at such times with the guilty maneuvers of a sad hound. Resent her as he must, be furious with himself as he will, there is not very much he can do about it. Often, after they have made love, they will lie beside each other in silence, each offended, each certain the other is to blame. At such times, memory tickles them with a cruel feather. Not always has it been like this. When they were first married, and indeed for the six months they lived together before marriage, everything was quite different. Their affair was very exciting to them; each told the other with some hyperbole but no real mistruth that no one in the past had ever been comparable as lover.

I suppose I am a romantic. I always feel that this is the best time in people's lives. There is, after all, so little we accomplish, and that short period when we are beloved and triumph as lovers is sweet with power. Rarely are we concerned then with our lack of importance; we are too important. In Sam's case, disillusion means even more. Like so many young men, he entertained the secret conceit that he was an extraordinary lover. One cannot really believe this without supporting at the same time the equally secret conviction that one is fundamentally inept. It is – no matter what Sergius would say – a more dramatic and therefore more attractive view of oneself than the sober notion which Sam now accepts with grudging wisdom, that the man as lover is dependent upon the bounty of the woman. As I say, he accepts the notion, it is one of the lineaments of maturity but there is a part of him which, no matter how harried by analysis, cannot relinquish the antagonism he feels that Eleanor has respected his private talent so poorly, and has not allowed him to confer its benefits upon more women. I mock Sam, but he would mock himself on this. It hardly matters; mockery cannot accomplish everything, and Sam seethes with that most private and tender pain: even worse than being unattractive to one's mate; or, what is the same and describes Sam's case more accurately, never to know in advance when he shall be undesirable to Eleanor.

I make perhaps too much of the subject, but that is only because it is so important to Sam. Relations between Eleanor and him are not really that bad – I know other couples who have much less or nothing at all. But comparisons are poor comfort to Sam; his standards are so high. So are Eleanor's. I am convinced the most unfortunate people are those who would make an art of love. It sours other effort. Of all artists, they are certainly the most wretched.

Shall I furnish a model? Sam and Eleanor are on the couch and the projector, adjusted to its slowest speed, is retracing the elaborate pantomime of the three principals. If one could allow these shadows a life . . . but indeed such life has been given them. Sam and Eleanor are no more than an itch, a smart, a threshold of satisfaction; the important share of themselves has steeped itself in Frankie-, Magnolia-, and Eleanor-of-the-film. Indeed the variations are beyond telling. It is the most outrageous orgy performed by five ghosts.

Self-critical Sam! He makes love in front of a movie, and one cannot say that it is unsatisfactory any more than one can say it is pleasant. It is dirty, downright porno dirty, it is a lewd slop-brush slapped through the middle of domestic exasperations and breakfast eggs. It is so dirty that only half of Sam – he is quite divisible into fractions – can be exercised at all. The part that is his brain worries along like a cuckolded burgher. He is taking the pulse of his anxiety. Will he last long enough to satisfy Eleanor? Will the children come back tonight? He cannot help it. In the midst of the circus, he is suddenly convinced the children will walk through the door. "Why are you so anxious, Daddie?"

So it goes. Sam the lover is conscious of exertion. One moment he is Frankie Idell, destroyer of virgins – take that! you whore! – the next, body moving, hands caressing, he is no more than some lines from a psychoanalytical text. He is thinking about the sensitivity of his scrotum. He has read that this is a portent of femininity in a male. How strong is his latent homosexuality worries Sam, thrusting stiffly, warm sweat running cold. Does he identify with Eleanor-of-the-film?

Technically, the climax is satisfactory. They lie together in the dark, the film ended, the projector humming its lonely revolutions in the quiet room. Sam gets up to turn it off; he comes back and kisses Eleanor upon the mouth. Apparently, she has enjoyed herself more than he; she is tender and fondles the tip of his nose.

"You know, Sam," she says from her space beside him, "I think I saw this picture before."

"When?"

"Oh, you know when. That time."

Sam thinks dully that women are always most loving when they can reminisce about infidelity.

"That time!" he repeats.

"I think so."

Racing forward from memory like the approaching star which begins as a point on the mind and swells to explode the eyeball with its odious image, Sam remembers, and is weak in the dark. It is ten years, eleven perhaps, before they were married, yet after they were lovers. Eleanor has told him, but she has always been vague about details. There had been two men it seemed, and another girl, and all had been drunk. They had seen movie after movie. With reluctant fascination, Sam can conceive the rest. How it had pained him, how excited him. It is years now since he has remembered, but he remembers. In the darkness he wonders at the unreasonableness of jealous pain. That night was impossible to imagine any longer – therefore it is more real; Eleanor his plump wife who presses a pigeon's shape against her housecoat, forgotten heroine of black orgies. It had been meaningless, Eleanor claimed; it was Sam she loved, and the other had been no more than a fancy of which she wished to rid herself. Would it be the same today, thinks Sam, or had Eleanor been loved by Frankie, by Frankie of the other movies, by Frankie of the two men she never saw again on that night so long ago?

The pleasure I get from this pain, Sam thinks furiously.

It is not altogether perverse. If Eleanor causes him pain, it means after all that she is alive for him. I have often observed that the reality of a person depends upon his ability to hurt us; Eleanor as the vague accusing embodiment of the wife is different, altogether different, from Eleanor who lies warmly in Sam's bed, an attractive Eleanor who may wound his flesh. Thus, brother to the pleasure of pain, is the sweeter pleasure which follows pain. Sam, tired, lies in Eleanor's arms, and they talk with the cozy trade words of old professionals, agreeing that they will not make love again before a movie, that it was exciting but also not without detachment, that all in all it has been good but not quite right, that she had loved this action he had done, and was uncertain about another. It is their old familiar critique, a sign that they are intimate and well disposed. They do not talk about the act when it has failed to fire; then they go silently to sleep. But now, Eleanor's enjoyment having mollified Sam's sense of no enjoyment, they talk with the apologetics and encomiums of familiar mates. Eleanor falls asleep, and Sam falls almost asleep, curling next to her warm body, his hand over her round belly with the satisfaction of a sculptor. He is drowsy, and he thinks drowsily that these few moments of creature-pleasure, this brief compassion he can feel for the body that trusts itself to sleep beside him, his comfort in its warmth, is perhaps all the meaning he may ask for his life. That out of disappointment, frustration, and the passage of dreary years come these few moments when he is close to her, and their years together possess a connotation more rewarding than the sum of all which has gone into them.

But then he thinks of the novel he wants to write, and he is wide-awake again. Like the sleeping pill which fails to work and leaves one warped in an exaggeration of the ills which sought the drug, Sam passes through the promise of sex-emptied sleep, and is left with nervous loins, swollen jealousy of an act ten years dead, and sweating irritable resentment of the woman's body which hinders his limbs. He has wasted the day, he tells himself, he was wasted the day as he has wasted so many days of his life, and tomorrow in the office he will be no more than his ten fingers typing plot and words for Bramba the Venusian and Lee-Lee Deeds, Hollywood Star, while that huge work with which he has cheated himself, holding it before him as a covenant of his worth, that enormous novel which would lift him at a bound from the impasse in which he stifles, whose dozens of characters would develop a vision of life in bountiful complexity, lies foundered, rotting on a beach of purposeless effort. Notes here, pages there, it sprawls through a formless wreck of incidental ideas and half-episodes, utterly without shape. He has not even a hero for it.

One could not have a hero today, Sam thinks, a man of action and contemplation, capable of sin, large enough for good, a man immense. There is only a modern hero damned by no more than the ugliness of wishes whose satisfaction he will never know. One needs a man who could walk the stage, someone who – no matter who, not himself. Someone, Sam thinks, who reasonably could not exist.

The novelist, thinks Sam, perspiring beneath blankets, must live in paranoia and seek to be one with the world; he must be terrified of experience and hungry for it; he must think himself nothing and believe he is superior to all. The feminine in his nature cries for proof he is a man; he dreams of power and is without capacity to gain it; he loves himself above all and therefore despises all that he is.

He is that, thinks Sam, he is part of the perfect prescription, and yet he is not a novelist. He lacks energy and belief. It is left for him to write an article some day about the temperament of the ideal novelist.

In the darkness, memories rise, yeast-swells of apprehension. Out of bohemian days so long ago, comes the friend of Eleanor, a girl who had been sick and was committed to an institution. They visited her, Sam and Eleanor, they took the suburban train and sat on the lawn of the asylum grounds while patients circled about intoning a private litany, or shuddering in boob-blundering fright from an insect that crossed their skin. The friend had been silent. She had smiled, she had answered their questions with the fewest words, and had returned again to her study of sunlight and blue sky. As they were about to leave, the girl had taken Sam aside. "They violate me," she said in a whisper. "Every night when the doors are locked, they come to my room and they make the movie. I am the heroine and am subjected to all variety of sexual viciousness. Tell them to leave me alone so I may enter the convent." And while she talked, in a horror of her body, one arm scrubbed the other. Poor tortured friend. They had seen her again, and she babbled, her face had coarsened into an idiot leer.

Sam sweats. There is so little he knows, and so much to know. Youth of the depression with its economic terms, what can he know of madness or religion? They are both so alien to him. He is the mongrel, Sam thinks, brought up without religion from a mother half Protestant and half Catholic, and a father half Catholic and half Jew. He is a quarter-Jew, and yet he is a Jew, or so he feels himself, knowing nothing of Gospel, tabernacle, or Mass, the Jew through accident, through state of mind. What . . . whatever did he know of penance? self-sacrifice? mortification of the flesh? the love of his fellow man? Am I concerned with my relation to God? ponders Sam, and smiles sourly in the darkness. No, that has never concerned him, he thinks, not for better nor for worse. "They are making the movie," says the girl into the ear of memory, "and so I cannot enter the convent."

How hideous was the mental hospital. A concentration camp, decides Sam. Perhaps it would be the world some day, or was that only his projection of feelings of hopelessness? "Do not try to solve the problems of the world," he hears from Sergius, and pounds a lumpy pillow.

However could he organize his novel? What form to give it? It is so complex. Too loose, thinks Sam, too scattered. Will he ever fall asleep? Wearily, limbs tense, his stomach too keen, he plays again the game of putting himself to sleep. "I do not feel my toes," Sam says to himself, "my toes are dead, my calves are asleep, my calves are sleeping . . ."

In the middle from wakefulness to slumber, in the torpor which floats beneath blankets, I give an idea to Sam. "Destroy time, and chaos may be ordered," I say to him.

"Destroy time, and chaos may be ordered," he repeats after me, and in desperation to seek his coma, mutters back, "I do not feel my nose, my nose is numb, my eyes are heavy, my eyes are heavy."

So Sam enters the universe of sleep, a man who seeks to live in such a way as to avoid pain, and succeeds merely in avoiding pleasure. What a dreary compromise is life!

THE LANGUAGE OF MEN

In the beginning, Sanford Carter was ashamed of becoming an Army cook. This was not from snobbery, at least not from snobbery of the most direct sort. During the two and a half years Carter had been in the Army he had come to hate cooks more and more. They existed for him as a symbol of all that was corrupt, overbearing, stupid, and privileged in Army life. The image which came to mind was a fat cook with an enormous sandwich in one hand, and a bottle of beer in the other, sweat pouring down a porcine face, foot on a flour barrel, shouting at the K.P.'s, "Hurry up, you men, I ain't got all day." More than once in those two and a half years, driven to exasperation, Carter had been on the verge of throwing his food into a cook's face as he passed on the serving line. His anger often derived from nothing: the set of a pair of fat lips, the casual heavy thump of the serving spoon into his plate, or the resentful conviction that the cook was not serving him enough. Since life in the Army was in most aspects a marriage, this rage over apparently harmless details was not a sign of unbalance. Every soldier found some particular habit of the Army spouse impossible to support.

Yet Sanford Carter became a cook and, to elaborate the irony, did better as a cook than he had done as anything else. In a few months he rose from a Private to a first cook with the rank of Sergeant, Technician. After the fact, it was easy to understand. He had suffered through all his Army career from an excess of eagerness. He had cared too much, he had wanted to do well, and so he had often been tense at moments when he would better have been relaxed. He was very young, twenty-one, had lived the comparatively gentle life of a middle-class boy, and needed some success in the Army to prove to himself that he was not completely worthless.

In succession, he had failed as a surveyor in Field Artillery, a clerk in an Infantry headquarters, a telephone wireman, and finally a rifleman. When the war ended, and his regiment went to Japan, Carter was still a rifleman; he had been a rifleman for eight months. What was more to the point, he had been in the platoon as long as any of its members; the skilled hard-bitten nucleus of veterans who had run his squad had gone home one by one, and it seemed to him that through seniority he was entitled to at least a corporal's rating. Through seniority he was so entitled, but on no other ground. Whenever responsibility had been handed to him, he had discharged it miserably, tensely, overconscientiously. He had always asked too many questions, he had worried the task too severely, he had conveyed his nervousness to the men he was supposed to lead. Since he was also sensitive enough and proud enough never to curry favor with the noncoms in the platoons, he was in no position to sit in on their occasional discussions about who was to succeed them. In a vacuum of ignorance, he had allowed himself to dream that he would be given a squad to lead, and his hurt was sharp when the squad was given to a replacement who had joined the platoon months after him.

The war was over, Carter had a bride in the States (he had lived with her for only two months), he was lonely, he was obsessed with going home. As one week dragged into the next, and the regiment, the company, and his own platoon continued the same sort of training which they had been doing ever since he had entered the Army, he thought he would snap. There were months to wait until he would be discharged and meanwhile it was intolerable to him to be taught for the fifth time the nomenclature of the machine gun, to stand a retreat parade three evenings a week. He wanted some niche where he could lick his wounds, some Army job with so many hours of work and so many hours of complete freedom, where he could be alone by himself. He hated the Army, the huge Army which had proved to him that he was good at no work, and incapable of succeeding at anything. He wrote long, aching letters to his wife, he talked less and less to the men around him and he was close to violent attacks of anger during the most casual phases of training – during close-order drill or cleaning his rifle for inspection. He knew that if he did not find his niche it was possible that he would crack.

So he took an opening in the kitchen. It promised him nothing except a day of work, and a day of leisure which would be completely at his disposal. He found that he liked it. He was given at first the job of baking the bread for the company, and every other night he worked till early in the morning, kneading and shaping his fifty-pound mix of dough. At two or three he would be done, and for his work there would be the tangible reward of fifty loaves of bread, all fresh from the oven, all clean and smelling of fertile accomplished creativity. He had the rare and therefore intensely satisfying emotion of seeing at the end of an Army chore the product of his labor.

A month after he became cook the regiment was disbanded, and those men who did not have enough points to go home were sent to other outfits. Carter ended at an ordnance company in another Japanese city. He had by now given up all thought of getting a noncom's rating before he was discharged, and was merely content to work each alternate day. He took his work for granted and so he succeeded at it. He had begun as a baker in the new company kitchen; before long he was the first cook. It all happened quickly. One cook went home on points, another caught a skin disease, a third was transferred from the kitchen after contracting a venereal infection. On the shift which Carter worked there were left only himself and a man who was illiterate. Carter was put nominally in charge, and was soon actively in charge. He looked up each menu in an Army recipe book, collected the items, combined them in the order indicated, and after the proper time had elapsed, took them from the stove. His product tasted neither better nor worse than the product of all other Army cooks. But the mess sergeant was impressed. Carter had filled a gap. The next time ratings were given out Carter jumped at a bound from Private to Sergeant T/4.

On the surface he was happy; beneath the surface he was overjoyed. It took him several weeks to realize how grateful and delighted he felt. The promotion coincided with his assignment to a detachment working in a small seaport up the coast. Carter arrived there to discover that he was in charge of cooking for thirty men, and would act as mess sergeant. There was another cook, and there were four permanent Japanese K.P.'s, all of them good workers. He still cooked every day, but there was always time between meals to take a break of at least an hour and often two; he shared a room with the other cook and lived in comparative privacy for the first time in several years; the seaport was beautiful; there was only one officer, and he left the men alone; supplies were plentiful due to a clerical error which assigned rations for forty men rather than thirty; and in general everything was fine. The niche had become a sinecure.

This was the happiest period of Carter's life in the Army. He came to like his Japanese K.P.'s. He studied their language, he visited their homes, he gave them gifts of food from time to time. They worshiped him because he was kind to them and generous, because he never shouted, because his good humor bubbled over into games, and made the work of the kitchen seem pleasant. All the while he grew in confidence. He was not a big man, but his body filled out from the heavy work; he was likely to sing a great deal, he cracked jokes with the men on the chow line. The kitchen became his property, it became his domain, and since it was a warm room, filled with sunlight, he came to take pleasure in the very sight of it. Before long his good humor expanded into a series of efforts to improve the food. He began to take little pains and make little extra efforts which would have been impossible if he had been obliged to cook for more than thirty men. In the morning he would serve the men fresh eggs scrambled or fried to their desire in fresh butter. Instead of cooking sixty eggs in one large pot he cooked two eggs at a time in a frying pan, turning them to the taste of each soldier. He baked like a housewife satisfying her young husband; at lunch and dinner there was pie or cake, and often both. He went to great lengths. He taught the K.P.'s how to make the toast come out right. He traded excess food for spices in Japanese stores. He rubbed paprika and garlic on the chickens. He even made pastries to cover such staples as corn beef hash and meat and vegetable stew.

It all seemed to be wasted. In the beginning the men might have noticed these improvements, but after a period they took them for granted. It did not matter how he worked to satisfy them; they trudged through the chow line with their heads down, nodding coolly at him, and they ate without comment. He would hang around the tables after the meal, noticing how much they consumed, and what they discarded; he would wait for compliments, but the soldiers seemed indifferent. They seemed to eat without tasting the food. In their faces he saw mirrored the distaste with which he had once stared at cooks.

The honeymoon was ended. The pleasure he took in the kitchen and himself curdled. He became aware again of his painful desire to please people, to discharge responsibility, to be a man. When he had been a child, tears had come into his eyes at a cross word, and he had lived in an atmosphere where his smallest accomplishment was warmly praised. He was the sort of young man, he often thought bitterly, who was accustomed to the attention and the protection of women. He would have thrown away all he possessed – the love of his wife, the love of his mother, the benefits of his education, the assured financial security of entering his father's business – if he had been able just once to dig a ditch as well as the most ignorant farmer.

Instead, he was back in the painful unprotected days of his first entrance into the Army. Once again the most casual actions became the most painful, the events which were most to be taken for granted grew into the most significant, and the feeding of the men at each meal turned progressively more unbearable.

So Sanford Carter came full circle. If he had once hated the cooks, he now hated the troops. At mealtimes his face soured into the belligerent scowl with which he had once believed cooks to be born. And to himself he muttered the age-old laments of the housewife: how little they appreciated what he did.

Finally there was an explosion. He was approached one day by Corporal Taylor, and he had come to hate Taylor, because Taylor was the natural leader of the detachment and kept the other men endlessly amused with his jokes. Taylor had the ability to present himself as inefficient, shiftless, and incapable, in such a manner as to convey that really the opposite was true. He had the lightest touch, he had the greatest facility, he could charm a geisha in two minutes and obtain anything he wanted from a supply sergeant in five. Carter envied him, envied his grace, his charmed indifference; then grew to hate him.

Taylor teased Carter about the cooking, and he had the knack of knowing where to put the knife. "Hey, Carter," he would shout across the mess hall while breakfast was being served, "you turned my eggs twice, and I asked for them raw." The men would shout with laughter. Somehow Taylor had succeeded in conveying all of the situation, or so it seemed to Carter, insinuating everything, how Carter worked and how it meant nothing, how Carter labored to gain their affection and earned their contempt. Carter would scowl, Carter would answer in a rough voice, "Next time I'll crack them over your head." "You crack 'em, I'll eat 'em," Taylor would pipe back, "but just don't put your fingers in 'em." And there would be another laugh. He hated the sight of Taylor.

It was Taylor who came to him to get the salad oil. About twenty of the soldiers were going to have a fish fry at the geisha house; they had bought the fish at the local market, but they could not buy oil, so Taylor was sent as the deputy to Carter. He was charming to Carter, he complimented him on the meal, he clapped him on the back, he dissolved Carter to warmth, to private delight in the attention, and the thought that he had misjudged Taylor. Then Taylor asked for the oil.

Carter was sick with anger. Twenty men out of the thirty in the detachment were going on the fish fry. It meant only that Carter was considered one of the ten undesirables. It was something he had known, but the proof of knowledge is always more painful than the acquisition of it. If he had been alone his eyes would have clouded. And he was outraged at Taylor's deception. He could imagine Taylor saying ten minutes later, "You should have seen the grease job I gave to Carter. I'm dumb, but man, he's dumber."

Carter was close enough to giving him the oil. He had a sense of what it would mean to refuse Taylor, he was on the very edge of mild acquiescence. But he also had a sense of how he would despise himself afterward.

"No," he said abruptly, his teeth gritted, "you can't have it."

"What do you mean we can't have it?"

"I won't give it to you." Carter could almost feel the rage which Taylor generated at being refused.

"You won't give away a lousy five gallons of oil to a bunch of G.I.'s having a party?"

"I'm sick and tired," Carter began.

"So am I." Taylor walked away.

Carter knew he would pay for it. He left the K.P.'s and went to change his sweat-soaked work shirt, and as he passed the large dormitory in which most of the detachment slept he could hear Taylor's high-pitched voice. Carter did not bother to take off his shirt. He returned instead to the kitchen, and listened to the sound of men going back and forth through the hall and of a man shouting with rage. That was Hobbs, a Southerner, a big man with a big bellowing voice.

There was a formal knock on the kitchen door. Taylor came in. His face was pale and his eyes showed a cold satisfaction. "Carter," he said, "the men want to see you in the big room."

Carter heard his voice answer huskily. "If they want to see me, they can come into the kitchen."

He knew he would conduct himself with more courage in his own kitchen than anywhere else. "I'll be here for a while."

Taylor closed the door, and Carter picked up a writing board to which was clamped the menu for the following day. Then he made a pretense of examining the food supplies in the pantry closet. It was his habit to check the stocks before deciding what to serve the next day, but on this night his eyes ranged thoughtlessly over the canned goods. In a corner were seven five-gallon tins of salad oil, easily enough cooking oil to last a month. Carter came out of the pantry and shut the door behind him.

He kept his head down and pretended to be writing the menu when the soldiers came in. Somehow there were even more of them than he had expected. Out of the twenty men who were going to the party, all but two or three had crowded through the door.

Carter took his time, looked up slowly. "You men want to see me?" he asked flatly.

They were angry. For the first time in his life he faced the hostile expressions of many men. It was the most painful and anxious moment he had ever known.

"Taylor says you won't give us the oil," someone burst out.

"That's right, I won't," said Carter. He tapped his pencil against the scratchboard, tapping it slowly and, he hoped, with an appearance of calm.

"What a stink deal," said Porfirio, a little Cuban whom Carter had always considered his friend.

Hobbs, the big Southerner, stared down at Carter. "Would you mind telling the men why you've decided not to give us the oil?" he asked quietly.

" 'Cause I'm blowed if I'm going to cater to you men. I've catered enough," Carter said. His voice was close to cracking with the outrage he had suppressed for so long, and he knew that if he continued he might cry. "I'm the acting mess sergeant," he said as coldly as he could, "and I decide what goes out of this kitchen." He stared at each one in turn, trying to stare them down, feeling mired in the rut of his own failure. They would never have dared this approach to another mess sergeant.

"What crud," someone muttered.

"You won't give a lousy five-gallon can of oil for a G.I. party," Hobbs said more loudly.

"I won't. That's definite. You men can get out of here."

"Why, you lousy little snot," Hobbs burst out, "how many five-gallon cans of oil have you sold on the black market?"

"I've never sold any." Carter might have been slapped with the flat of a sword. He told himself bitterly, numbly, that this was the reward he received for being perhaps the single honest cook in the whole United States Army. And he even had time to wonder at the obscure prejudice which had kept him from selling food for his own profit.

"Man, I've seen you take it out," Hobbs exclaimed. "I've seen you take it to the market."

"I took food to trade for spices," Carter said hotly.

There was an ugly snicker from the men.

"I don't mind if a cook sells," Hobbs said, "every man has his own deal in this Army. But a cook ought to give a little food to a G.I. if he wants it."

"Tell him," someone said.

"It's bull," Taylor screeched. "I've seen Carter take butter, eggs, every damn thing to the market."

Their faces were red, they circled him.

"I never sold a thing," Carter said doggedly.

"And I'm telling you," Hobbs said, "that you're a two-bit crook. You been raiding that kitchen, and that's why you don't give to us now."

Carter knew there was only one way he could possibly answer if he hoped to live among these men again. "That's a goddam lie," Carter said to Hobbs. He laid down the scratchboard, he flipped his pencil slowly and deliberately to one corner of the room, and with his heart aching he lunged toward Hobbs. He had no hope of beating him. He merely intended to fight until he was pounded unconscious, advancing the pain and bruises he would collect as collateral for his self-respect.

To his indescribable relief Porfirio darted between them, held them apart with the pleased ferocity of a small man breaking up a fight. "Now, stop this! Now, stop this!" he cried out.

Carter allowed himself to be pushed back, and he knew that he had gained a point. He even glimpsed a solution with some honor.

He shrugged violently to free himself from Porfirio. He was in a rage, and yet it was a rage he could have ended at any instant. "All right, you men," he swore, "I'll give you the oil, but now that we're at it, I'm going to tell you a thing or two." His face red, his body perspiring, he was in the pantry and out again with a five gallon tin. "Here," he said, "you better have a good fish fry, 'cause it's the last good meal you're going to have for quite a while. I'm sick of trying to please you. You think I have to work — " he was about to say, my fingers to the bone — "well. I don't. From now on, you'll see what chow in the Army is supposed to be like." He was almost hysterical. "Take that oil. Have your fish fry." The fact that they wanted to cook for themselves was the greatest insult of all. "Tomorrow I'll give you real Army cooking."

His voice was so intense that they backed away from him. "Get out of this kitchen," he said. "None of you has any business here."

They filed out quietly, and they looked a little sheepish.

Carter felt weary, he felt ashamed of himself, he knew he had not meant what he said. But half an hour later, when he left the kitchen and passed the large dormitory, he heard shouts of raucous laughter, and he heard his name mentioned and then more laughter.

He slept badly that night, he was awake at four, he was in the kitchen by five, and stood there white-faced and nervous, waiting for the K.P.'s to arrive. Breakfast that morning landed on the men like a lead bomb. Carter rummaged in the back of the pantry and found a tin of dehydrated eggs covered with dust, memento of a time when fresh eggs were never on the ration list. The K.P.'s looked at him in amazement as he stirred the lumpy powder into a pan of water.

While it was still half-dissolved he put it on the fire. While it was still wet, he took it off. The coffee was cold, the toast was burned, the oatmeal stuck to the pot. The men dipped forks into their food, took cautious sips of their coffee, and spoke in whispers. Sullenness drifted like vapors through the kitchen.

At noontime Carter opened cans of meat-and-vegetable stew. He dumped them into a pan and heated them slightly. He served the stew with burned string beans and dehydrated potatoes which tasted like straw. For dessert the men had a single luke-warm canned peach and cold coffee.

So the meals continued. For three days Carter cooked slop, and suffered even more than the men. When mealtime came he left the chow line to the K.P.'s and sat in his room, perspiring with shame, determined not to yield and sick with the determination.

Carter won. On the fourth day a delegation of men came to see him. They told him that indeed they had appreciated his cooking in the past, they told him that they were sorry they had hurt his feelings, they listened to his remonstrances, they listened to his grievances, and with delight Carter forgave them. That night, for supper, the detachment celebrated. There was roast chicken with stuffing, lemon meringue pie and chocolate cake. The coffee burned their lips. More than half the men made it a point to compliment Carter on the meal.

In the weeks which followed the compliments diminished, but they never stopped completely. Carter became ashamed at last. He realized the men were trying to humor him, and he wished to tell them it was no longer necessary.

Harmony settled over the kitchen. Carter even became friends with Hobbs, the big Southerner. Hobbs approached him one day, and in the manner of a farmer talked obliquely for an hour. He spoke about his father, he spoke about his girl friends, he alluded indirectly to the night they had almost fought, and finally with the courtesy of a Southerner he said to Carter, "You know, I'm sorry about shooting off my mouth. You were right to want to fight me, and if you're still mad I'll fight you to give you the satisfaction, although I just as soon would not."

"No, I don't want to fight with you now," Carter said warmly. They smiled at each other. They were friends.

Carter knew he had gained Hobbs' respect. Hobbs respected him because he had been willing to fight. That made sense to a man like Hobbs. Carter liked him so much at this moment that he wished the friendship to be more intimate.

"You know," he said to Hobbs, "it's a funny thing. You know I really never did sell anything on the black market. Not that I'm proud of it, but I just didn't."

Hobbs frowned. He seemed to be saying that Carter did not have to lie. "I don't hold it against a man," Hobbs said, "if he makes a little money in something that's his own proper work. Hell, I sell gas from the motor pool. It's just I also give gas if one of the G.I.'s wants to take the jeep out for a joy ride, kind of."

"No, but I never did sell anything." Carter had to explain. "If I ever had sold on the black market, I would have given the salad oil without question."

Hobbs frowned again, and Carter realized he still did not believe him. Carter did not want to lose the friendship which was forming. He thought he could save it only by some further admission. "You know," he said again, "remember when Porfirio broke up our fight? I was awful glad when I didn't have to fight you." Carter laughed, expecting Hobbs to laugh with him, but a shadow passed across Hobbs' face.

"Funny way of putting it," Hobbs said.

He was always friendly thereafter, but Carter knew that Hobbs would never consider him a friend. Carter thought about it often, and began to wonder about the things which made him different. He was no longer so worried about becoming a man; he felt that to an extent he had become one. But in his heart he wondered if he would ever learn the language of men.

FLANNERY O'CONNOR 1925–1964

Flannery O'Connor saw in her native Georgia the violent result of people immersed in a culture that offered them too narrow a conception of human life to accommodate their innermost longings. It is not that the South is overtly repressive — at least to the lower-middle and lower-class whites about whom Miss O'Connor writes: her characters do not live in fear of lynch mobs, the police, or any external force for that matter. The trouble is that they have internalized a whole set of attitudes that constitute the myth of the Old South: a gentle, easy-going world with folksy wisdom and Bible-belt theology to explain all human experience. "Good country people" is an example of a folk cliché that just cannot contain the reality of the people it is supposed to describe. In an atmosphere in which myth and simplistic concepts of personality are assumed to be valid, people either reduce the scope of their lives to live comfortably in their community or invent private hypocrisies that let them do whatever it is they want to do. The comic characters that result abound in popular fiction: the small-town con man, the pious-sounding traveling salesman, etc. But Flannery O'Connor catches in the disjunction between the ordinariness of her characters' vocabulary and intonation and the extraordinariness of their passions a deeper kind of hypocrisy, one that is at least partly unconscious and that over a period of time distorts the self and sets up the conditions for some violent explosion. If the explosion comes, the characters face their hidden capacity for experience far beyond the comfortable confines of the myth — for cruelty, violence, even murder.

There is little in Flannery O'Connor's life (except her perceptiveness and sensitivity to common people) that would account for the cast of grotesque characters and the violent events in her stories. She was born in and grew up in Savannah, Georgia, of all southern cities perhaps the one most eager to preserve its pre-Civil War traditions. As a devout Roman Catholic in a predominantly Fundamentalist society, Miss O'Connor was especially attracted to the Church's emphasis on mysteries and revelations — to mystical experience at the limits of human cognition. She may therefore have been especially sensitive to society's attempt to imagine itself too narrowly. On the death of her father when she was thirteen, she and her mother moved to a farmhouse in Milledgeville, Georgia. She attended the local college for women, and later won a scholarship to study for an M.A. in creative writing at the University of Iowa. For a brief time she lived in New York, and then in Connecticut with the family of Robert Fitzgerald, who had taken a warm interest in her and her writing. About the time that her first novel, *Wise Blood* (1952), was published and widely admired it became clear that she was suffering from the same chronic illness that had killed her father. She thereupon returned to live with her mother in rural Georgia, making speaking trips when she was well enough, but mostly working on the perfectly controlled fiction of which these two stories are fine examples. She finished the collection of stories from which the title story, "Everything That Rises Must Converge," is reprinted here only a few weeks before her death in 1964.

GOOD COUNTRY PEOPLE

Besides the neutral expression that she wore when she was alone, Mrs. Freeman had two others, forward and reverse, that she used for all her human dealings. Her forward expression was steady and driving like the advance of a heavy truck. Her eyes never swerved to left or right but turned as the story turned as if they followed a yellow line down the center of it. She seldom used the other expression because it was not often necessary for her to retract a statement, but when she did, her face came to a complete stop, there was an almost imperceptible movement of her black eyes, during which they seemed to be receding, and then the observer would see that Mrs. Freeman, though she might stand there as real as several grain sacks thrown on top of each other, was no longer there in spirit. As for getting anything across to her when this was the case, Mrs. Hopewell had given it up. She might talk her head off. Mrs. Freeman could never be brought to admit herself wrong on any point. She would stand there and if she could be brought to say anything, it was something like, "Well, I wouldn't of said it was and I wouldn't of said it wasn't" or letting her gaze range over the top kitchen shelf where there was an assortment of dusty bottles, she might remark, "I see you ain't ate many of them figs you put up last summer."

They carried on their most important business in the kitchen at breakfast. Every morning Mrs. Hopewell got up at seven o'clock and lit her gas heater and Joy's. Joy was her daughter, a large blonde girl who had an artificial leg. Mrs. Hopewell thought of her as a child though she was thirty-two years old and highly educated. Joy would get up while her mother was eating and lumber into the bathroom and slam the door, and before long, Mrs. Freeman would arrive at the back door. Joy would hear her mother call, "Come on in," and then they would talk for a while in low voices that were indistinguishable in the bathroom. By the time Joy came in, they had usually finished the weather report and were on one or the other of Mrs. Freeman's daughters, Glynese or Carramae. Joy called them Glycerin and Caramel. Glynese, a redhead, was eighteen and had many admirers; Carramae, a blonde, was only fifteen but already married and pregnant. She could not keep anything on her stomach. Every morning Mrs. Freeman told Mrs. Hopewell how many times she had vomited since the last report.

Mrs. Hopewell liked to tell people that Glynese and Carramae were two of the finest girls she knew and that Mrs. Freeman was a *lady* and that she was never ashamed to take her anywhere or introduce her to anybody they might meet. Then she would tell how she had happened to hire the Freemans in the first place and how they were a godsend to her and how she had had them four years. The reason for her keeping them so long was that they were not trash. They were good country people. She had telephoned the man whose name they had given as reference and he had told her that Mr. Freeman was a good farmer but that his wife was the nosiest woman ever to walk the earth. "She's got to be into everything," the man said. "If she don't get there before the dust settles, you can bet she's dead, that's all. She'll want to know all your business. I can stand him real good," he had said, "but me nor my wife neither could have stood that woman one more minute on this place." That had put Mrs. Hopewell off for a few days.

She had hired them in the end because there were no other applicants but she had made up her mind beforehand exactly how she would handle the woman. Since she was the type who had to be into everything, then, Mrs. Hopewell had decided, she would not only let her be into everything, she would *see to it* that she was into everything — she would give her the responsibility of everything, she would put her in charge. Mrs. Hopewell had no bad qualities of her own but she was able to use other people's in such a constructive way that she had kept them four years.

Nothing is perfect. This was one of Mrs. Hopewell's favorite sayings. Another was: that is life! And still another, the most important, was: well, other people have their opinions too. She would make these statements, usually at the table, in a tone of gentle insistence as if no one held them but her, and the large hulking Joy, whose constant outrage had obliterated every expression from her face, would stare just a little to the side of her, her eyes icy blue, with the look of someone who has achieved blindness by an act of will and means to keep it.

When Mrs. Hopewell said to Mrs. Freeman that life was like that, Mrs. Freeman would say, "I always said so myself." Nothing had been arrived at by anyone that had not first been arrived at by her. She was quicker than Mr. Freeman. When Mrs. Hopewell said to her after they had been on the place a while, "You know, you're the wheel behind the wheel," and winked, Mrs. Freeman had said, "I know it. I've always been quick. It's some that are quicker than others."

"Everybody is different," Mrs. Hopewell said.

"Yes, most people is," Mrs. Freeman said.

"It takes all kinds to make the world."

"I always said it did myself."

The girl was used to this kind of dialogue for breakfast and more of it for dinner; sometimes they had it for supper too. When they had no guest they ate in the kitchen because that was easier. Mrs. Freeman always managed to arrive at some point during the meal and to watch them finish it. She would stand in the doorway if it were summer but in the winter she would stand with one elbow on top of the refrigerator and look down on them, or she would stand by the gas heater, lifting the back of her skirt slightly. Occasionally she would stand against the wall and roll her head from side to side. At no time was she in any hurry to leave. All this was very trying on Mrs. Hopewell but she was a woman of great patience. She realized that nothing is perfect and that in the Freemans she had good country people and that if, in this day and age, you get good country people, you had better hang onto them.

She had had plenty of experience with trash. Before the Freemans she had averaged one tenant family a year. The wives of these farmers were not the kind you would want to be around you for very long. Mrs. Hopewell, who had divorced her husband long ago, needed someone to walk over the fields with her; and when Joy had to be impressed for these services, her remarks were usually so ugly and her face so glum that Mrs. Hopewell would say, "If you can't come pleasantly, I don't want you at all," to which the girl, standing square and rigid-shouldered with her neck thrust slightly forward, would reply, "If you want me, here I am – LIKE I AM."

Mrs. Hopewell excused this attitude because of the leg (which had been shot off in a hunting accident when Joy was ten). It was hard for Mrs. Hopewell to realize that her child was thirty-two now and that for more than twenty years she had had only one leg. She thought of her still as a child because it tore her heart to think instead of the poor stout girl in her thirties who had never danced a step or had any *normal* good times. Her name was really Joy but as soon as she was twenty-one and away from home, she had had it legally changed. Mrs. Hopewell was certain that she had thought and thought until she had hit upon the ugliest name in any language. Then she had gone and had the beautiful name, Joy, changed without telling her mother until after she had done it. Her legal name was Hulga.

When Mrs. Hopewell thought the name, Hulga, she thought of the broad blank hull of a battleship. She would not use it. She continued to call her Joy to which the girl responded but in a purely mechanical way.

Hulga had learned to tolerate Mrs. Freeman who saved her from taking walks with her mother. Even Glynese and Carramae were useful when they occupied attention that might otherwise have been directed at her. At first she had thought she could not stand Mrs. Freeman for she had found that it was not possible to be rude to her. Mrs. Freeman would take on strange resentments and for days together she would be sullen but the source of her displeasure was always obscure; a direct attack, a positive leer, blatant ugliness to her face – these never touched her. And without warning one day, she began calling her Hulga.

She did not call her that in front of Mrs. Hopewell who would have been incensed but when she and the girl happened to be out of the house together, she would say something and add the name Hulga to the end of it, and the big spectacled Joy-Hulga would scowl and redden as if her privacy had been intruded upon. She considered the name her personal affair. She had arrived at it first purely on the basis of its ugly sound and then the full genius of its fitness had struck her. She had a vision of the name working like the ugly sweating Vulcan who stayed in the furnace and to whom, presumably, the goddess had to come when called. She saw it as the name of her highest creative act. One of her major triumphs was that her mother had not been able to turn her dust into Joy, but the greater one was that she had been able to turn it herself into Hulga. However, Mrs. Freeman's relish for using the name only irritated her. It was as if Mrs. Freeman's beady steel-pointed eyes had penetrated far enough behind her face to reach some secret fact. Something about her seemed to fascinate Mrs. Freeman and then one day Hulga realized that it was the artificial leg. Mrs. Freeman had a special fondness for the details of secret infections, hidden deformities, assaults upon children. Of diseases, she preferred the lingering or incurable. Hulga had heard Mrs. Hopewell give her the details of the hunting accident, how the leg had been literally blasted off, how she had never lost consciousness. Mrs. Freeman could listen to it any time as if it had happened an hour ago.

When Hulga stumped into the kitchen in the morning (she could walk without making the awful noise but she made it – Mrs. Hopewell was certain – because it was ugly-sounding), she glanced at them and did not speak. Mrs. Hopewell would be in her red kimono with her hair tied around her head in rags. She would be sitting at the table, finishing her breakfast and Mrs. Freeman would be hanging by her elbow outward from the refrigerator, looking down at the table. Hulga always put her eggs on the stove to boil and then stood over them with her arms folded, and Mrs. Hopewell would look at her – a kind of indirect gaze divided between her and Mrs. Freeman – and would think that if she would only keep herself up a little, she wouldn't be so bad looking. There was nothing wrong with her face that a pleasant expression wouldn't help. Mrs. Hopewell said that people who looked on the bright side of things would be beautiful even if they were not.

Whenever she looked at Joy this way, she could not help but feel that it would have been better if the child had not taken the Ph.D. It had certainly not brought her out any and now that she had it, there was no more excuse for her to go to school again. Mrs. Hopewell thought it was nice for girls to go to school to have a good time but Joy had "gone through." Anyhow, she would not have been strong enough to go again. The doctors had told Mrs. Hopewell that with the best of care, Joy might see forty-five. She had a weak heart. Joy had made it plain that if it had not been for this condition, she would be far from these red hills and good country people. She would be in a university lecturing to people who knew what she was talking about. And Mrs. Hopewell could very well picture her there, looking like a scarecrow and lecturing to more of the same. Here she went about all day in a six-year-old skirt and a yellow sweat shirt with a faded cowboy on a horse embossed on it. She thought this was funny; Mrs. Hopewell thought it was idiotic and showed simply that she was still a child. She was brilliant but she didn't have a grain of sense. It seemed to Mrs. Hopewell that every year she grew less like other people and more like herself – bloated, rude, and squint-eyed. And she said such strange things! To her own mother she had said – without warning, without excuse, standing up in the middle of a meal with her face purple and her mouth half full – "Woman! do you ever look inside? Do you ever look inside and see what you are *not?* God!" she had cried sinking down again and staring at her plate, "Malebranche was right: we are not our own light. We are not our own light!" Mrs. Hopewell had no idea to this day what brought that on. She had only made the remark, hoping Joy would take it in, that a smile never hurt anyone.

The girl had taken the Ph.D. in philosophy and this left Mrs. Hopewell at a complete loss. You could say, "My daughter is a nurse," or "My daughter is a school teacher," or even, "My daughter is a chemical engineer." You could not say, "My daughter is a philosopher." That was something that had ended with the Greeks and Romans. All day Joy sat on her neck in a deep chair, reading. Sometimes she went for walks but she didn't like dogs or cats or birds or flowers or nature or nice young men. She looked at nice young men as if she could smell their stupidity.

One day Mrs. Hopewell had picked up one of the books the girl had just put down and opening it at random, she read, "Science, on the other hand, has to assert its soberness and seriousness afresh and declare that it is concerned solely with what-is. Nothing – how can it be for science anything but a horror and a phantasm? If science is right, then one thing stands firm: science wishes to know nothing of nothing. Such is after all the strictly scientific approach to Nothing. We know it by wishing to know nothing of Nothing." These words had been underlined with a blue pencil and they worked on Mrs. Hopewell like some evil incantation in gibberish. She shut the book quickly and went out of the room as if she were having a chill.

This morning when the girl came in, Mrs. Freeman was on Carramae. "She thrown up four times after supper," she said, "and was up twict in the night after three o'clock. Yesterday she didn't do nothing but ramble in the bureau drawer. All she did. Stand up there and see what she could run up on."

"She's got to eat," Mrs. Hopewell muttered, sipping her coffee, while she watched Joy's back at the stove. She was wondering what the child had said to the Bible salesman. She could not imagine what kind of a conversation she could possibly have had with him.

He was a tall gaunt hatless youth who had called yesterday to sell them a Bible. He had appeared at the door, carrying a large black suitcase that weighted him so heavily on one side that he had to brace himself against the door facing. He seemed on the point of collapse but he said in a cheerful voice, "Good morning, Mrs. Cedars!" and set the suitcase down on the mat. He was not a bad-looking young man though he had on a bright blue suit and yellow socks that were not pulled up far enough. He had prominent face bones and a streak of sticky-looking brown hair falling across his forehead.

"I'm Mrs. Hopewell," she said.

"Oh!" he said, pretending to look puzzled but with his eyes sparkling, "I saw it said 'The Cedars,' on the mailbox so I thought you was Mrs. Cedars!" and he burst out in a pleasant laugh. He picked up the satchel and under cover of a pant, he fell forward into her hall. It was rather as if the suitcase had moved first, jerking him after it. "Mrs. Hopewell!" he said and grabbed her hand. "I hope you are well!" and he laughed again and then all at once his face sobered completely. He paused and gave her a straight earnest look and said, "Lady, I've come to speak of serious things."

"Well, come in," she muttered, none too pleased because her dinner was almost ready. He came into the parlor and sat down on the edge of a straight chair and put the suitcase between his feet and glanced around the room as if he were sizing her up by it. Her silver gleamed on the two sideboards; she decided he had never been in a room as elegant as this.

"Mrs. Hopewell," he began, using her name in a way that sounded almost intimate, "I know you believe in Chrustian service."

"Well yes," she murmured.

"I know," he said and paused, looking very wise with his head cocked on one side, "that you're a good woman. Friends have told me."

Mrs. Hopewell never liked to be taken for a fool. "What are you selling?" she asked.

"Bibles," the young man said and his eye raced around the room before he added, "I see you have no family Bible in your parlor, I see that is the one lack you got!"

Mrs. Hopewell could not say, "My daughter is an atheist and won't let me keep the Bible in the parlor." She said, stiffening slightly, "I keep my Bible by my bedside." This was not the truth. It was in the attic somewhere.

"Lady," he said, "the word of God ought to be in the parlor."

"Well, I think that's a matter of taste," she began. "I think . . ."

"Lady," he said, "for a Chrustian, the word of God ought to be in every room in the house besides in his heart. I know you're a Chrustian because I can see it in every line of your face."

She stood up and said, "Well, young man, I don't want to buy a Bible and I smell my dinner burning."

He didn't get up. He began to twist his hands and looking down at them, he said softly, "Well lady, I'll tell you the truth – not many people want to buy one nowadays and besides, I know I'm real simple. I don't know how to say a thing but to say it. I'm just a country boy." He glanced up into her unfriendly face. "People like you don't like to fool with country people like me!"

"Why!" she cried, "good country people are the salt of the earth! Besides, we all have different ways of doing, it takes all kinds to make the world go 'round. That's life!"

"You said a mouthful," he said.

"Why, I think there aren't enough good country people in the world!" she said, stirred. "I think that's what's wrong with it!"

His face had brightened. "I didn't inraduce myself," he said. "I'm Manley Pointer from out in the country around Willohobie, not even from a place, just from near a place."

"You wait a minute," she said. "I have to see about my dinner." She went out to the kitchen and found Joy standing near the door where she had been listening.

"Get rid of the salt of the earth," she said, "and let's eat."

Mrs. Hopewell gave her a pained look and turned the heat down under the vegetables. "*I* can't be rude to anybody," she murmured and went back into the parlor.

He had opened the suitcase and was sitting with a Bible on each knee.

"You might as well put those up," she told him. "I don't want one."

"I appreciate your honesty," he said. "You don't see any more real honest people unless you go way out in the country."

"I know," she said, "real genuine folks!" Through the crack in the door she heard a groan.

"I guess a lot of boys come telling you they're working their way through college," he said, "but I'm not going to tell you that. Somehow," he said, "I don't want to go to college. I want to devote my life to Chrustian service. See," he said, lowering his voice, "I got this heart condition. I may not live long. When you know it's something wrong with you and you may not live long, well then, lady . . ." He paused, with his mouth open, and stared at her.

He and Joy had the same condition! She knew that her eyes were filling with tears but she collected herself quickly and murmured, "Won't you stay for dinner? We'd love to have you!" and was sorry the instant she heard herself say it.

"Yes mam," he said in an abashed voice, "I would sher love to do that!"

Joy had given him one look on being introduced to him and then throughout the meal had not glanced at him again. He had addressed several remarks to her, which she had pretended not to hear. Mrs. Hopewell could not understand deliberate rudeness, although she lived with it, and she felt she had always to overflow with hospitality to make up for Joy's lack of courtesy. She urged him to talk about himself and he did. He said he was the seventh child of twelve and that his father had been crushed under a tree when he himself was eight year old. He had been crushed very badly, in fact, almost cut in two and was practically not recognizable.

His mother had got along the best she could by hard working and she had always seen that her children went to Sunday School and that they read the Bible every evening. He was now nineteen year old and he had been selling Bibles for four months. In that time he had sold seventy-seven Bibles and had the promise of two more sales. He wanted to become a missionary because he thought that was the way you could do most for people. "He who losest his life shall find it," he said simply and he was so sincere, so genuine and earnest that Mrs. Hopewell would not for the world have smiled. He prevented his peas from sliding onto the table by blocking them with a piece of bread which he later cleaned his plate with. She could see Joy observing sidewise how he handled his knife and fork and she saw too that every few minutes, the boy would dart a keen appraising glance at the girl as if he were trying to attract her attention.

After dinner Joy cleared the dishes off the table and disappeared and Mrs. Hopewell was left to talk with him. He told her again about his childhood and his father's accident and about various things that had happened to him. Every five minutes or so she would stifle a yawn. He sat for two hours until finally she told him she must go because she had an appointment in town. He packed his Bibles and thanked her and prepared to leave, but in the doorway he stopped and wrung her hand and said that not on any of his trips had he met a lady as nice as her and he asked if he could come again. She had said she would always be happy to see him.

Joy had been standing in the road, apparently looking at something in the distance, when he came down the steps toward her, bent to the side with his heavy valise. He stopped where she was standing and confronted her directly. Mrs. Hopewell could not hear what he said but she trembled to think what Joy would say to him. She could see that after a minute Joy said something and that then the boy began to speak again, making an excited gesture with his free hand. After a minute Joy said something else at which the boy began to speak once more. Then to her amazement, Mrs. Hopewell saw the two of them walk off together, toward the gate. Joy had walked all the way to the gate with him and Mrs. Hopewell could not imagine what they had said to each other, and she had not yet dared to ask.

Mrs. Freeman was insisting upon her attention. She had moved from the refrigerator to the heater so that Mrs. Hopewell had to turn and face her in order to seem to be listening. "Glynese gone out with Harvey Hill again last night," she said. "She had this sty."

"Hill," Mrs. Hopewell said absently, "is that the one who works in the garage?"

"Nome, he's the one that goes to chiropracter school," Mrs. Freeman said. "She had this sty. Been had it two days. So she says when he brought her in the other night he says, 'Lemme get rid of that sty for you,' and she says, 'How?' and he says, 'You just lay yourself down acrost the seat of that car and I'll show you.' So she done it and he popped her neck. Kept on a-popping it several times until she made him quit. This morning," Mrs. Freeman said, "she ain't got no sty. She ain't got no traces of a sty."

"I never heard of that before," Mrs. Hopewell said.

"He ast her to marry him before the Ordinary," Mrs. Freeman went on, "and she told him she wasn't going to be married in no *office*."

"Well, Glynese is a fine girl," Mrs. Hopewell said. "Glynese and Carramae are both fine girls."

"Carramae said when her and Lyman was married Lyman said it sure felt sacred to him. She said he said he wouldn't take five hundred dollars for being married by a preacher."

"How much would he take?" the girl asked from the stove.

"He said he wouldn't take five hundred dollars," Mrs. Freeman repeated.

"Well we all have work to do," Mrs. Hopewell said.

"Lyman said it just felt more sacred to him," Mrs. Freeman said. "The doctor wants Carramae to eat prunes. Says instead of medicine. Says them cramps is coming from pressure. You know where I think it is?"

"She'll be better in a few weeks," Mrs. Hopewell said.

"In the tube," Mrs. Freeman said. "Else she wouldn't be as sick as she is."

Hulga had cracked her two eggs into a saucer and was bringing them to the table along with a cup of coffee that she had filled too full. She sat down carefully and began to eat, meaning to keep Mrs. Freeman there by questions if for any reason she showed an inclination to leave. She could perceive her mother's eye on her. The first round-about question would be about the Bible salesman and she did not wish to bring it on. "How did he pop her neck?" she asked.

Mrs. Freeman went into a description of how he had popped her neck. She said he owned a '55 Mercury but that Glynese said she would rather marry a man with only a '36 Plymouth who would be married by a preacher. The girl asked what if he had a '32 Plymouth and Mrs. Freeman said what Glynese had said was a '36 Plymouth.

Mrs. Hopewell said there were not many girls with Glynese's common sense. She said what she admired in those girls was their common sense. She said that reminded her that they had had a nice visitor yesterday, a young man selling Bibles. "Lord," she said, "he bored me to death but he was so sincere and genuine I couldn't be rude to him. He was just good country people, you know," she said, " – just the salt of the earth."

"I seen him walk up," Mrs. Freeman said, "and then later – I seen him walk off," and Hulga could feel the slight shift in her voice, the slight insinuation, that he had not walked off alone, had he? Her face remained expressionless but the color rose into her neck and she seemed to swallow it down with the next spoonful of egg. Mrs. Freeman was looking at her as if they had a secret together.

"Well, it takes all kinds of people to make the world go 'round," Mrs. Hopewell said. "It's very good we aren't all alike."

"Some people are more alike than others," Mrs. Freeman said.

Hulga got up and stumped, with about twice the noise that was necessary, into her room and locked the door. She was to meet the Bible salesman at ten o'clock at the gate. She had thought about it half the night. She had started thinking of it as a great joke and then she had begun to see profound implications in it. She had lain in bed imagining dialogues for them that were insane on the surface but that reached below to depths that no Bible salesman would be aware of. Their conversation yesterday had been of this kind.

He had stopped in front of her and had simply stood there. His face was bony and sweaty and bright, with a little pointed nose in the center of it, and his look was different from what it had been at the dinner table. He was gazing at her with open curiosity, with fascination, like a child watching a new fantastic animal at the zoo, and he was breathing as if he had run a great distance to reach her. His gaze seemed somehow familiar but she could not think where she had been regarded with it before. For almost a minute he didn't say anything. Then on what seemed an insuck of breath, he whispered, "You ever ate a chicken that was two days old?"

The girl looked at him stonily. He might have just put this question up for consideration at the meeting of a philosophical association. "Yes," she presently replied as if she had considered it from all angles.

"It must have been mighty small!" he said triumphantly and shook all over with little nervous giggles, getting very red in the face, and subsiding finally into his gaze of complete admiration, while the girl's expression remained exactly the same.

"How old are you?" he asked softly.

She waited some time before she answered. Then in a flat voice she said, "Seventeen."

His smiles came in succession like waves breaking on the surface of a little lake. "I see you got a wooden leg," he said. "I think you're real brave. I think you're real sweet."

The girl stood blank and solid and silent.

"Walk to the gate with me," he said. "You're a brave sweet little thing and I liked you the minute I seen you walk in the door."

Hulga began to move forward.

"What's your name?" he asked, smiling down on the top of her head.

"Hulga," she said.

"Hulga," he murmured, "Hulga. Hulga. I never heard of anybody name Hulga before. You're shy, aren't you, Hulga?" he asked.

She nodded, watching his large red hand on the handle of the giant valise.

"I like girls that wear glasses," he said. "I think a lot. I'm not like these people that a serious thought don't ever enter their heads. It's because I may die."

"I may die too," she said suddenly and looked up at him. His eyes were very small and brown, glittering feverishly.

"Listen," he said, "don't you think some people was meant to meet on account of what all they got in common and all? Like they both think serious thoughts and all?" He shifted the valise to his other hand so that the hand nearest her was free. He caught hold of her elbow and shook it a little. "I don't work on Saturday," he said. "I like to walk in the woods and see what Mother Nature is wearing. O'er the hills and far away. Pic-nics and things. Couldn't we go on a pic-nic tomorrow? Say yes, Hulga," he said and gave her a dying look as if he felt his insides about to drop out of him. He had even seemed to sway slightly toward her.

During the night she had imagined that she seduced him. She imagined that the two of them walked on the place until they came to the storage barn beyond the two back fields and there, she imagined, that things came to such a pass that she very easily seduced him and that then, of course, she had to reckon with his remorse. True genius can get an idea across even to an inferior mind. She imagined that she took his remorse in hand and changed it into a deeper understanding of life. She took all his shame away and turned it into something useful.

She set off for the gate at exactly ten o'clock, escaping without drawing Mrs. Hopewell's attention. She didn't take anything to eat, forgetting that food is usually taken on a picnic. She wore a pair of slacks and a dirty white shirt, and as an afterthought, she had put some Vapex on the collar of it since she did not own any perfume. When she reached the gate no one was there.

She looked up and down the empty highway and had the furious feeling that she had been tricked, that he had only meant to make her walk to the gate after the idea of him. Then suddenly he stood up, very tall, from behind a bush on the opposite embankment. Smiling, he lifted his hat which was new and wide-brimmed. He had not worn it yesterday and she wondered if he had bought it for the occasion. It was toast-colored with a red and white band around it and was slightly too large for him. He stepped from behind the bush still carrying the black valise. He had on the same suit and the same yellow socks sucked down in his shoes from walking. He crossed the highway and said, "I knew you'd come!"

The girl wondered acidly how he had known this. She pointed to the valise and asked, "Why did you bring your Bibles?"

He took her elbow, smiling down on her as if he could not stop. "You can never tell when you'll need the word of God, Hulga," he said. She had a moment in which she doubted that this was actually happening and then they began to climb the embankment. They went down into the pasture toward the woods. The boy walked lightly by her side, bouncing on his toes. The valise did not seem to be heavy today; he even swung it. They crossed half the pasture without saying anything and then, putting his hand easily on the small of her back, he asked softly, "Where does your wooden leg join on?"

She turned an ugly red and glared at him and for an instant the boy looked abashed. "I didn't mean you no harm," he said. "I only meant you're so brave and all. I guess God takes care of you."

"No," she said, looking forward and walking fast, "I don't even believe in God."

At this he stopped and whistled. "No!" he exclaimed as if he were too astonished to say anything else.

She walked on and in a second he was bouncing at her side, fanning with his hat. "That's very unusual for a girl," he remarked, watching her out of the corner of his eye. When they reached the edge of the wood, he put his hand on her back again and drew her against him without a word and kissed her heavily.

The kiss, which had more pressure than feeling behind it, produced that extra surge of adrenalin in the girl that enables one to carry a packed trunk out of a burning house, but in her, the power went at once to the brain. Even before he released her, her mind, clear and detached and ironic anyway, was regarding him from a great distance, with amusement but with pity. She had never been kissed before and she was pleased to discover that it was an unexceptional experience and all a matter of the mind's control. Some people might enjoy drain water if they were told it was vodka. When the boy, looking expectant but uncertain, pushed her gently away, she turned and walked on, saying nothing as if such business, for her, were common enough.

He came along panting at her side, trying to help her when he saw a root that she might trip over. He caught and held back the long swaying blades of thorn vine until she had passed beyond them. She led the way and he came breathing heavily behind her. Then they came out on a sunlit hillside, sloping softly into another one a little smaller. Beyond, they could see the rusted top of the old barn where the extra hay was stored.

The hill was sprinkled with small pink weeds. "Then you ain't saved?" he asked suddenly, stopping.

The girl smiled. It was the first time she had smiled at him at all. "In my economy," she said, "I'm saved and you are damned but I told you I didn't believe in God."

Nothing seemed to destroy the boy's look of admiration. He gazed at her now as if the fantastic animal at the zoo had put its paw through the bars and given him a loving poke. She thought he looked as if he wanted to kiss her again and she walked on before he had the chance.

"Ain't there somewheres we can sit down sometime?" he murmured, his voice softening toward the end of the sentence.

"In that barn," she said.

They made for it rapidly as if it might slide away like a train. It was a large two-story barn, cool and dark inside. The boy pointed up the ladder that led into the loft and said, "It's too bad we can't go up there."

"Why can't we?" she asked.

"Yer leg," he said reverently.

The girl gave him a contemptuous look and putting both hands on the ladder, she climbed it while he stood below, apparently awestruck. She pulled herself expertly through the opening and then looked down at him and said, "Well, come on if you're coming," and he began to climb the ladder, awkwardly bringing the suitcase with him.

"We won't need the Bible," she observed.

"You never can tell," he said, panting. After he had got into the loft, he was a few seconds catching his breath. She had sat down in a pile of straw. A wide sheath of sunlight, filled with dust particles, slanted over her. She lay back against a bale, her face turned away, looking out the front opening of the barn where hay was thrown from a wagon into the loft. The two pink-speckled hillsides lay back against a dark ridge of woods. The sky was cloudless and cold blue. The boy dropped down by her side and put one arm under her and the other over her and began methodically kissing her face, making little noises like a fish. He did not remove his hat but it was pushed far enough back not to interfere. When her glasses got in his way, he took them off of her and slipped them into his pocket.

The girl at first did not return any of the kisses but presently she began to and after she had put several on his cheek, she reached his lips and remained there, kissing him again and again as if she were trying to draw all the breath out of him. His breath was clear and sweet like a child's and the kisses were sticky like a child's. He mumbled about loving her and about knowing when he first seen her that he loved her, but the mumbling was like the sleepy fretting of a child being put to sleep by his mother. Her mind, throughout this, never stopped or lost itself for a second to her feelings. "You ain't said you loved me none," he whispered finally, pulling back from her. "You got to say that."

She looked away from him off into the hollow sky and then down at a black ridge and then down farther into what appeared to be two green swelling lakes. She didn't realize he had taken her glasses but this landscape could not seem exceptional to her for she seldom paid any close attention to her surroundings.

"You got to say it," he repeated. "You got to say you love me."

She was always careful how she committed herself. "In a sense," she began, "if you use the word loosely, you might say that. But it's not a word I use. I don't have illusions. I'm one of those people who see *through* to nothing."

The boy was frowning. "You got to say it. I said it and you got to say it," he said.

The girl looked at him almost tenderly. "You poor baby," she murmured. "It's just as well you don't understand," and she pulled him by the neck, face-down, against her. "We are all damned," she said, "but some of us have taken off our blindfolds and see that there's nothing to see. It's a kind of salvation."

The boy's astonished eyes looked blankly through the ends of her hair. "Okay," he almost whined, "but do you love me or don'tcher?"

"Yes," she said and added, "in a sense. But I must tell you something. There mustn't be anything dishonest between us." She lifted his head and looked him in the eye. "I am thirty years old," she said. "I have a number of degrees."

The boy's look was irritated but dogged. "I don't care," he said. "I don't care a thing about what all you done. I just want to know if you love me or don'tcher?" and he caught her to him and wildly planted her face with kisses until she said, "Yes, yes."

"Okay then," he said, letting her go. "Prove it."

She smiled, looking dreamily out on the shifty landscape. She had seduced him without even making up her mind to try. "How?" she asked, feeling that he should be delayed a little.

He leaned over and put his lips to her ear. "Show me where your wooden leg joins on," he whispered.

The girl uttered a sharp little cry and her face instantly drained of color. The obscenity of the suggestion was not what shocked her. As a child she had sometimes been subject to feelings of shame but education had removed the last traces of that as a good surgeon scrapes for cancer; she would no more have felt it over what he was asking than she would have believed in his Bible. But she was as sensitive about the artificial leg as a peacock about his tail. No one ever touched it but her. She took care of it as someone else would his soul, in private and almost with her own eyes turned away. "No," she said.

"I known it," he muttered, sitting up. "You're just playing me for a sucker."

"Oh no no!" she cried. "It joins on at the knee. Only at the knee. Why do you want to see it?"

The boy gave her a long penetrating look. "Because," he said, "it's what makes you different. You ain't like anybody else."

She sat staring at him. There was nothing about her face or her round freezing-blue eyes to indicate that this had moved her; but she felt as if her heart had stopped and left her mind to pump her blood. She decided that for the first time in her life she was face to face with real innocence. This boy, with an instinct that came from beyond wisdom, had touched the truth about her. When after a minute, she said in a hoarse high voice, "All right," it was like surrendering to him completely. It was like losing her own life and finding it again, miraculously, in his.

Very gently he began to roll the slack leg up. The artificial limb, in a white sock and brown flat shoe, was bound in a heavy material like canvas and ended in an ugly jointure where it was attached to the stump. The boy's face and his voice were entirely reverent as he uncovered it and said, "Now show me how to take it off and on."

She took it off for him and put it back on again and then he took it off himself, handling it as tenderly as if it were a real one. "See!" he said with a delighted child's face. "Now I can do it myself!"

"Put it back on," she said. She was thinking that she would run away with him and that every night he would take the leg off and every morning put it back on again. "Put it back on," she said.

"Not yet," he murmured, setting it on its foot out of her reach. "Leave it off for awhile. You got me instead."

She gave a little cry of alarm but he pushed her down and began to kiss her again. Without the leg she felt entirely dependent on him. Her brain seemed to have stopped thinking altogether and to be about some other function that it was not very good at. Different expressions raced back and forth over her face. Every now and then the boy, his eyes like two steel spikes, would glance behind him, where the leg stood. Finally she pushed him off and said, "Put it back on me now."

"Wait," he said. He leaned the other way and pulled the valise toward him and opened it. It had a pale blue spotted lining and there were only two Bibles in it. He took one of these out and opened the cover of it. It was hollow and contained a a pocket flask of whiskey, a pack of cards, and a small blue box with printing on it. He laid these out in front of her one at a time in an evenly-spaced row, like one presenting offerings at the shrine of a goddess. He put the blue box in her hand. THIS PRODUCT TO BE USED ONLY FOR THE PREVENTION OF DISEASE, she read, and dropped it. The boy was unscrewing the top of the flask. He stopped and pointed, with a smile, to the deck of cards. It was not an ordinary deck but one with an obscene picture on the back of each card. "Take a swig," he said, offering her the bottle first. He held it in front of her, but like one mesmerized, she did not move.

Her voice when she spoke had an almost pleading sound. "Aren't you," she murmured, "aren't you just good country people?"

The boy cocked his head. He looked as if he were just beginning to understand that she might be trying to insult him. "Yeah," he said, curling his lip slightly, "but it ain't held me back none. I'm as good as you any day in the week."

"Give me my leg," she said.

He pushed it farther away with his foot. "Come on now, let's begin to have us a good time," he said coaxingly. "We ain't got to know one another good yet."

"Give me my leg!" she screamed and tried to lunge for it but he pushed her down easily.

"What's the matter with you all of a sudden?" he asked, frowning as he screwed the top on the flask and put it quickly back inside the Bible. "You just a while ago said you didn't believe in nothing. I thought you was some girl!"

Her face was almost purple. "You're a Christian!" she hissed. "You're a fine Christian! You're just like them all – say one thing and do another. You're a perfect Christian, you're . . ."

The boy's mouth was set angrily. "I hope you don't think," he said in a lofty indignant tone, "that I believe in that crap! I may sell Bibles but I know which end is up and I wasn't born yesterday and I know where I'm going!"

"Give me my leg!" she screeched. He jumped up so quickly that she barely saw him sweep the cards and the blue box back into the Bible and throw the Bible into the valise. She saw him grab the leg and then she saw it for an instant slanted forlornly across the inside of the suitcase with a Bible at either side of its opposite ends. He slammed the lid shut and snatched up the valise and swung it down the hole and then stepped through himself.

When all of him had passed but his head, he turned and regarded her with a look that no longer had any admiration in it. "I've gotten a lot of interesting things," he said. "One time I got a woman's glass eye this way. And you needn't to think you'll catch me because Pointer ain't really my name. I use a different name at every house I call at and don't stay nowhere long. And I'll tell you another thing, Hulga," he said, using the name as if he didn't think much of it, "you ain't so smart. I been believing in nothing ever since I was born!" and then the toast-colored hat disappeared down the hole and the girl was left, sitting on the straw in the dusty sunlight. When she turned her churning face toward the opening, she saw his blue figure struggling successfully over the green speckled lake.

Mrs. Hopewell and Mrs. Freeman, who were in the back pasture, digging up onions, saw him emerge a little later from the woods and head across the meadow toward the highway. "Why, that looks like that nice dull young man that tried to sell me a Bible yesterday," Mrs. Hopewell said, squinting. "He must have been selling them to the Negroes back in there. He was so simple," she said, "but I guess the world would be better off if we were all that simple."

Mrs. Freeman's gaze drove forward and just touched him before he disappeared under the hill. Then she returned her attention to the evil-smelling onion shoot she was lifting from the ground. "Some can't be that simple," she said. "I know I never could."

EVERYTHING THAT RISES MUST CONVERGE

Her doctor had told Julian's mother that she must lose twenty pounds on account of her blood pressure, so on Wednesday nights Julian had to take her downtown on the bus for a reducing class at the Y. The reducing class was designed for working girls over fifty, who weighed from 165 to 200 pounds. His mother was one of the slimmer ones, but she said ladies did not tell their age or weight. She would not ride the buses by herself at night since they had been integrated, and because the reducing class was one of her few pleasures, necessary for her health, and *free*, she said Julian could at least put himself out to take her, considering all she did for him. Julian did not like to consider all she did for him, but every Wednesday night he braced himself and took her.

She was almost ready to go, standing before the hall mirror, putting on her hat, while he, his hands behind him, appeared pinned to the door frame, waiting like Saint Sebastian for the arrows to begin piercing him. The hat was new and had cost her seven dollars and a half. She kept saying, "Maybe I shouldn't have paid that for it. No, I shouldn't have. I'll take it off and return it tomorrow. I shouldn't have bought it."

Julian raised his eyes to heaven. "Yes, you should have bought it," he said. "Put it on and let's go." It was a hideous hat. A purple velvet flap came down on one side of it and stood up on the other; the rest of it was green and looked like a cushion with the stuffing out. He decided it was less comical than jaunty and pathetic. Everything that gave her pleasure was small and depressed him.

She lifted the hat one more time and set it down slowly on top of her head. Two wings of gray hair protruded on either side of her florid face, but her eyes, sky-blue, were as innocent and untouched by experience as they must have been when she was ten. Were it not that she was a widow who had struggled fiercely to feed and clothe and put him through school and who was supporting him still, "until he got on his feet," she might have been a little girl that he had to take to town.

"It's all right, it's all right," he said. "Let's go." He opened the door himself and started down the walk to get her going. The sky was a dying violet and the houses stood out darkly against it, bulbous liver-colored monstrosities of a uniform ugliness though no two were alike. Since this had been a fashionable neighborhood forty years ago, his mother persisted in thinking they did well to have an apartment in it. Each house had a narrow collar of dirt around it in which sat, usually, a grubby child. Julian walked with his hands in his pockets, his head down and thrust forward and his eyes glazed with the determination to make himself completely numb during the time he would be sacrificed to her pleasure.

The door closed and he turned to find the dumpy figure, surmounted by the atrocious hat, coming toward him. "Well," she said, "you only live once and paying a little more for it, I at least won't meet myself coming and going."

"Some day I'll start making money," Julian said gloomily – he knew he never would – "and you can have one of those jokes whenever you take the fit." But first they would move. He visualized a place where the nearest neighbors would be three miles away on either side.

"I think you're doing fine," she said, drawing on her gloves. "You've only been out of school a year. Rome wasn't built in a day."

She was one of the few members of the Y reducing class who arrived in hat and gloves and who had a son who had been to college. "It takes time," she said "and the world is in such a mess. This hat looked better on me than any of the others, though when she brought it out I said, 'Take that thing back. I wouldn't have it on my head,' and she said, 'Now wait till you see it on,' and when she put it on me, I said, 'We-ull,' and she said, 'If you ask me, that hat does something for you and you do something for the hat, and besides,' she said, 'with that hat, you won't meet yourself coming and going.' "

Julian thought he could have stood his lot better if she had been selfish, if she had been an old hag who drank and screamed at him. He walked along, saturated in depression, as if in the midst of his martyrdom he had lost his faith. Catching sight of his long, hopeless, irritated face, she stopped suddenly with a grief-stricken look, and pulled back on his arm. "Wait on me," she said. "I'm going to the house and take this thing off and tomorrow I'm going to return it. I was out of my head. I can pay the gas bill with that seven-fifty."

He caught her arm in a vicious grip. "You are not going to take it back," he said. "I like it."

"Well," she said, "I don't think I ought . . ."

"Shut up and enjoy it," he muttered, more depressed than ever.

"With the world in the mess it's in," she said, "it's a wonder we can enjoy anything. I tell you, the bottom rail is on the top."

Julian sighed.

"Of course," she said, "if you know who you are, you can go anywhere." She said this every time he took her to the reducing class. "Most of them in it are not our kind of people," she said, "but I can be gracious to anybody. I know who I am."

"They don't give a damn for your graciousness," Julian said savagely. "Knowing who you are is good for one generation only. You haven't the foggiest idea where you stand now or who you are."

She stopped and allowed her eyes to flash at him. "I most certainly do know who I am," she said, "and if you don't know who you are, I'm ashamed of you."

"Oh hell," Julian said.

"Your great-grandfather was a former governor of this state," she said. "Your grandfather was a prosperous landowner. Your grandmother was a Godhigh."

"Will you look around you," he said tensely, "and see where you are now?" and he swept his arm jerkily out to indicate the neighborhood, which the growing darkness at least made less dingy.

"You remain what you are," she said. "Your great-grandfather had a plantation and two hundred slaves."

"There are no more slaves," he said irritably.

"They were better off when they were," she said. He groaned to see that she was off on that topic. She rolled onto it every few days like a train on an open track. He knew every stop, every junction, every swamp along the way, and knew the exact point at which her conclusion would roll majestically into the station: "It's ridiculous. It's simply not realistic. They should rise, yes, but on their own side of the fence."

"Let's skip it," Julian said.

"The ones I feel sorry for," she said, "are the ones that are half white. They're tragic."

"Will you skip it?"

"Suppose we were half white. We would certainly have mixed feelings."

"I have mixed feelings now," he groaned.

"Well let's talk about something pleasant," she said. "I remember going to Grandpa's when I was a little girl. Then the house had double stairways that went up to what was really the second floor – all the cooking was done on the first. I used to like to stay down in the kitchen on account of the way the walls smelled. I would sit with my nose pressed against the plaster and take deep breaths. Actually the place belonged to the Godhighs but your grandfather Chestny paid the mortgage and saved it for them. They were in reduced circumstances," she said, "but reduced or not, they never forgot who they were."

"Doubtless that decayed mansion reminded them," Julian muttered. He never spoke of it without contempt or thought of it without longing. He had seen it once when he was a child before it had been sold. The double stairways had rotted and been torn down. Negroes were living in it. But it remained in his mind as his mother had known it. It appeared in his dreams regularly. He would stand on the wide porch, listening to the rustle of oak leaves, then wander through the high-ceilinged hall into the parlor that opened onto it and gaze at the worn rugs and faded draperies. It occurred to him that it was he, not she, who could have appreciated it. He preferred its threadbare elegance to anything he could name and it was because of it that all the neighborhoods they had lived in had been a torment to him – whereas she had hardly known the difference. She called her insensitivity "being adjustable."

"And I remember the old darky who was my nurse, Caroline. There was no better person in the world. I've always had a great respect for my colored friends," she said. "I'd do anything in the world for them and they'd . . ."

"Will you for God's sake get off that subject?" Julian said. When he got on a bus by himself, he made it a point to sit down beside a Negro, in reparation as it were for his mother's sins.

"You're mighty touchy tonight," she said. "Do you feel all right?"

"Yes I feel all right," he said. "Now lay off."

She pursed her lips. "Well, you certainly are in a vile humor," she observed. "I just won't speak to you at all."

They had reached the bus stop. There was no bus in sight and Julian, his hands still jammed in his pockets and his head thrust forward, scowled down the empty street. The frustration of having to wait on the bus as well as ride on it began to creep up his neck like a hot hand. The presence of his mother was borne in upon him as she gave a pained sigh. He looked at her bleakly. She was holding herself very erect under the preposterous hat, wearing it like a banner of her imaginary dignity. There was in him an evil urge to break her spirit. He suddenly unloosened his tie and pulled it off and put it in his pocket.

She stiffened. "Why must you look like *that* when you take me to town?" she said. "Why must you deliberately embarrass me?"

"If you'll never learn where you are," he said, "you can at least learn where I am."

"You look like a – thug," she said.

"Then I must be one," he murmured.

"I'll just go home," she said. "I will not bother you. If you can't do a little thing like that for me . . ."

Rolling his eyes upward, he put his tie back on. "Restored to my class," he muttered. He thrust his face toward her and hissed, "True culture is in the mind, the *mind*," he said, and tapped his head, "the mind."

"It's in the heart," she said, "and in how you do things and how you do things is because of who you *are*."

"Nobody in the damn bus cares who you are."

"I care who I am," she said icily.

The lighted bus appeared on top of the next hill and as it approached, they moved out into the street to meet it. He put his hand under her elbow and hoisted her up on the creaking step. She entered with a little smile, as if she were going into a drawing room where everyone had been waiting for her. While he put in the tokens, she sat down on one of the broad front seats for three which faced the aisle. A thin woman with protruding teeth and long yellow hair was sitting on the end of it. His mother moved up beside her and left room for Julian beside herself. He sat down and looked at the floor across the aisle where a pair of thin feet in red and white canvas sandals were planted.

His mother immediately began a general conversation meant to attract anyone who felt like talking. "Can it get any hotter?" she said and removed from her purse a folding fan, black with a Japanese scene on it, which she began to flutter before her.

"I reckon it might could," the woman with the protruding teeth said, "but I know for a fact my apartment couldn't get no hotter."

"It must get the afternoon sun," his mother said. She sat forward and looked up and down the bus. It was half filled. Everybody was white. "I see we have the bus to ourselves," she said. Julian cringed.

"For a change," said the woman across the aisle, the owner of the red and white canvas sandals. "I come on one the other day and they were thick as fleas — up front and all through."

"The world is in a mess everywhere," his mother said. "I don't know how we've let it get in this fix."

"What gets my goat is all those boys from good families stealing automobile tires," the woman with the protruding teeth said. "I told my boy, I said you may not be rich but you been raised right and if I ever catch you in any such mess, they can send you on to the reformatory. Be exactly where you belong."

"Training tells," his mother said. "Is your boy in high school?"

"Ninth grade," the woman said.

"My son just finished college last year. He wants to write but he's selling typewriters until he gets started," his mother said.

The woman leaned forward and peered at Julian. He threw her such a malevolent look that she subsided against the seat. On the floor across the aisle there was an abandoned newspaper. He got up and got it and opened it out in front of him. His mother discreetly continued the conversation in a lower tone but the woman across the aisle said in a loud voice, "Well that's nice. Selling typewriters is close to writing. He can go right from one to the other."

"I tell him," his mother said, "that Rome wasn't built in a day."

Behind the newspaper Julian was withdrawing into the inner compartment of his mind where he spent most of his time. This was a kind of mental bubble in which he established himself when he could not bear to be a part of what was going on around him. From it he could see out and judge but in it he was safe from any kind of penetration from without. It was the only place where he felt free of the general idiocy of his fellows. His mother had never entered it but from it he could see her with absolute clarity.

The old lady was clever enough and he thought that if she had started from any of the right premises, more might have been expected of her. She lived according to the laws of her own fantasy world, outside of which he had never seen her set foot. The law of it was to sacrifice herself for him after she had first created the necessity to do so by making a mess of things. If he had permitted her sacrifices, it was only because her lack of foresight had made them necessary. All of her life had been a struggle to act like a Chestny without the Chestny goods, and to give him everything she thought a Chestny ought to have; but since, said she, it was fun to struggle, why complain? And when you had won, as she had won, what fun to look back on the hard times! He could not forgive her that she had enjoyed the struggle and that she thought *she* had won.

What she meant when she said she had won was that she had brought him up successfully and had sent him to college and that he had turned out so well – good looking (her teeth had gone unfilled so that his could be straightened), intelligent (he realized he was too intelligent to be a success), and with a future ahead of him (there was of course no future ahead of him). She excused his gloominess on the grounds that he was still growing up and his radical ideas on his lack of practical experience. She said he didn't yet know a thing about "life," that he hadn't even entered the real world – when already he was as disenchanted with it as a man of fifty.

The further irony of all this was that in spite of her, he had turned out so well. In spite of going to only a third-rate college, he had, on his own initiative, come out with a first-rate education; in spite of growing up dominated by a small mind, he had ended up with a large one; in spite of all her foolish views, he was free of prejudice and unafraid to face facts. Most miraculous of all, instead of being blinded by love for her as she was for him, he had cut himself emotionally free of her and could see her with complete objectivity. He was not dominated by his mother.

The bus stopped with a sudden jerk and shook him from his meditation. A woman from the back lurched forward with little steps and barely escaped falling in his newspaper as she righted herself. She got off and a large Negro got on. Julian kept his paper lowered to watch. It gave him a certain satisfaction to see injustice in daily operation. It confirmed his view that with a few exceptions there was no one worth knowing within a radius of three hundred miles. The Negro was well dressed and carried a briefcase. He looked around and then sat down on the other end of the seat where the woman with the red and white canvas sandals was sitting. He immediately unfolded a newspaper and obscured himself behind it. Julian's mother's elbow at once prodded insistently into his ribs. "Now you see why I won't ride on these buses by myself," she whispered.

The woman with the red and white canvas sandals had risen at the same time the Negro sat down and had gone further back in the bus and taken the seat of the woman who had got off. His mother leaned forward and cast her an approving look.

Julian rose, crossed the aisle, and sat down in the place of the woman with the canvas sandals. From this position, he looked serenely across at his mother. Her face had turned an angry red. He stared at her, making his eyes the eyes of a stranger. He felt his tension suddenly lift as if he had openly declared war on her.

He would have liked to get in conversation with the Negro and to talk with him about art or politics or any subject that would be above the comprehension of those around them, but the man remained entrenched behind his paper. He was either ignoring the change of seating or had never noticed it. There was no way for Julian to convey his sympathy.

His mother kept her eyes fixed reproachfully on his face. The woman with the protruding teeth was looking at him avidly as if he were a type of monster new to her.

"Do you have a light?" he asked the Negro.

Without looking away from his paper, the man reached in his pocket and handed him a packet of matches.

"Thanks," Julian said. For a moment he held the matches foolishly. A NO SMOKING sign looked down upon him from over the door. This alone would not have deterred him; he had no cigarettes. He had quit smoking some months before because he could not afford it. "Sorry," he muttered and handed back the matches. The Negro lowered the paper and gave him an annoyed look. He took the matches and raised the paper again.

His mother continued to gaze at him but she did not take advantage of his momentary discomfort. Her eyes retained their battered look. Her face seemed to be unnaturally red, as if her blood pressure had risen. Julian allowed no glimmer of sympathy to show on his face. Having got the advantage, he wanted desperately to keep it and carry it through. He would have liked to teach her a lesson that would last her a while, but there seemed no way to continue the point. The Negro refused to come out from behind his paper.

Julian folded his arms and looked stolidly before him, facing her but as if he did not see her, as if he had ceased to recognize her existence. He visualized a scene in which, the bus having reached their stop, he would remain in his seat and when she said, "Aren't you going to get off?" he would look at her as at a stranger who had rashly addressed him. The corner they got off on was usually deserted, but it was well lighted and it would not hurt her to walk by herself the four blocks to the Y. He decided to wait until the time came and then decide whether or not he would let her get off by herself. He would have to be at the Y at ten to bring her back, but he could leave her wondering if he was going to show up. There was no reason for her to think she could always depend on him.

He retired again into the high-ceilinged room sparsely settled with large pieces of antique furniture. His soul expanded momentarily but then he became aware of his mother across from him and the vision shriveled. He studied her coldly. Her feet in little pumps dangled like a child's and did not quite reach the floor. She was training on him an exaggerated look of reproach. He felt completely detached from her. At that moment he could with pleasure have slapped her as he would have slapped a particularly obnoxious child in his charge.

He began to imagine various unlikely ways by which he could teach her a lesson. He might make friends with some distinguished Negro professor or lawyer and bring him home to spend the evening. He would be entirely justified but her blood pressure would rise to 300. He could not push her to the extent of making her have a stroke, and moreover, he had never been successful at making any Negro friends. He had tried to strike up an acquaintance on the bus with some of the better types, with ones that looked like professors or ministers or lawyers. One morning he had sat down next to a distinguished-looking dark brown man who had answered his questions with a sonorous solemnity but who had turned out to be an undertaker. Another day he had sat down beside a cigar-smoking Negro with a diamond ring on his finger, but after a few stilted pleasantries, the Negro had rung the buzzer and risen, slipping two lottery tickets into Julian's hand as he climbed over him to leave.

He imagined his mother lying desperately ill and his being able to secure only a Negro doctor for her. He toyed with that idea for a few minutes and then dropped it for a momentary vision of himself participating as a sympathizer in a sit-in demonstration. This was possible but he did not linger with it. Instead, he approached the ultimate horror. He brought home a beautiful suspiciously Negroid woman. Prepare yourself, he said. There is nothing you can do about it. This is the woman I've chosen. She's intelligent, dignified, even good, and she's suffered and she hasn't thought it *fun*. Now persecute us, go ahead and persecute us. Drive her out of here, but remember, you're driving me too. His eyes were narrowed and through the indignation he had generated, he saw his mother across the aisle, purple-faced, shrunken to the dwarf-like proportions of her moral nature, sitting like a mummy beneath the ridiculous banner of her hat.

He was tilted out of his fantasy again as the bus stopped. The door opened with a sucking hiss and out of the dark a large, gaily dressed, sullen-looking colored woman got on with a little boy. The child, who might have been four, had on a short plaid suit and a Tyrolean hat with a blue feather in it. Julian hoped that he would sit down beside him and that the woman would push in beside his mother. He could think of no better arrangement.

As she waited for her tokens, the woman was surveying the seating possibilities — he hoped with the idea of sitting where she was least wanted. There was something familiar-looking about her but Julian could not place what it was. She was a giant of a woman. Her face was set not only to meet opposition but to seek it out. The downward tilt of her large lower lip was like a warning sign: DON'T TAMPER WITH ME. Her bulging figure was encased in a green crepe dress and her feet overflowed in red shoes. She had on a hideous hat. A purple velvet flap came down on one side of it and stood up on the other; the rest of it was green and looked like a cushion with the stuffing out. She carried a mammoth red pocketbook that bulged throughout as if it were stuffed with rocks.

To Julain's disappointment, the little boy climbed up on the empty seat beside his mother. His mother lumped all children, black and white, into the common category, "cute," and she thought little Negroes were on the whole cuter than little white children. She smiled at the little boy as he climbed on the seat.

Meanwhile the woman was bearing down upon the empty seat beside Julian. To his annoyance, she squeezed herself into it. He saw his mother's face change as the woman settled herself next to him and he realized with satisfaction that this was more objectionable to her than it was to him. Her face seemed almost gray and there was a look of dull recognition in her eyes, as if suddenly she had sickened at some awful confrontation. Julian saw that it was because she and the woman had, in a sense, swapped sons. Though his mother would not realize the symbolic significance of this, she would feel it. His amusement showed plainly on his face.

The woman next to him muttered something unintelligible to herself. He was conscious of a kind of bristling next to him, a muted growling like that of an angry cat. He could not see anything but the red pocketbook upright on the bulging green thighs. He visualized the woman as she had stood waiting for her tokens – the ponderous figure, rising from the red shoes upward over the solid hips, the mammoth bosom, the haughty face, to the green and purple hat.

His eyes widened.

The vision of the two hats, identical, broke upon him with the radiance of a brilliant sunrise. His face was suddenly lit with joy. He could not believe that Fate had thrust upon his mother such a lesson. He gave a loud chuckle so that she would look at him and see that he saw. She turned her eyes on him slowly. The blue in them seemed to have turned a bruised purple. For a moment he had an uncomfortable sense of her innocence, but it lasted only a second before principle rescued him. Justice entitled him to laugh. His grin hardened until it said to her as plainly as if her were saying aloud: Your punishment exactly fits your pettiness. This should teach you a permanent lesson.

Her eyes shifted to the woman. She seemed unable to bear looking at him and to find the woman preferable. He became conscious again of the bristling presence at his side. The woman was rumbling like a volcano about to become active. His mother's mouth began to twitch slightly at one corner. With a sinking heart, he saw incipient signs of recovery on her face and realized that this was going to strike her suddenly as funny and was going to be no lesson at all. She kept her eyes on the woman and an amused smile came over her face as if the woman were a monkey that had stolen her hat. The little Negro was looking up at her with large fascinated eyes. He had been trying to attract her attention for some time.

"Carver!" the woman said suddenly. "Come heah!"

When he saw that the spotlight was on him at last, Carver drew his feet up and turned himself toward Julian's mother and giggled.

"Carver!" the woman said. "You heah me? Come heah!"

Carver slid down from the seat but remained squatting with his back against the base of it, his head turned slyly around toward Julian's mother, who was smiling at him. The woman reached a hand across the aisle and snatched him to her. He righted himself and hung backwards on her knees, grinning at Julian's mother. "Isn't he cute?" Julian's mother said to the woman with the protruding teeth.

"I reckon he is," the woman said without conviction.

The Negress yanked him upright but he eased out of her grip and shot across the aisle and scrambled, giggling wildly, onto the seat beside his love.

"I think he likes me," Julian's mother said, and smiled at the woman. It was the smile she used when she was being particularly gracious to an inferior. Julian saw everything lost. The lesson had rolled off her like rain on a roof.

The woman stood up and yanked the little boy off the seat as if she were snatching him from contagion. Julian could feel the rage in her at having no weapon like his mother's smile. She gave the child a sharp slap across his leg. He howled once and then thrust his head into her stomach and kicked his feet against her shins. "Be-have," she said vehemently.

The bus stopped and the Negro who had been reading the newspaper got off. The woman moved over and set the little boy down with a thump between herself and Julian. She held him firmly by the knee. In a moment he put his hands in front of his face and peeped at Julian's mother through his fingers.

"I see yoooooooo!" she said and put her hand in front of her face and peeped at him.

The woman slapped his hand down. "Quit yo' foolishness," she said, "before I knock the living Jesus out of you!"

Julian was thankful that the next stop was theirs. He reached up and pulled the cord. The woman reached up and pulled it at the same time. Oh my God, he thought. He had the terrible intuition that when they got off the bus together, his mother would open her purse and give the little boy a nickel. The gesture would be as natural to her as breathing. The bus stopped and the woman got up and lunged to the front, dragging the child, who wished to stay on, after her. Julian and his mother got up and followed. As they neared the door, Julian tried to relieve her of her pocketbook.

"No," she murmured, "I want to give the little boy a nickel."

"No!" Julian hissed. "No!"

She smiled down at the child and opened her bag. The bus door opened and the woman picked him up by the arm and descended with him, hanging at her hip. Once in the street she set him down and shook him.

Julian's mother had to close her purse while she got down the bus step but as soon as her feet were on the ground, she opened it again and began to rummage inside. "I can't find but a penny," she whispered, "but it looks like a new one."

"Don't do it!" Julian said fiercely between his teeth. There was a streetlight on the corner and she hurried to get under it so that she could better see into her pocketbook. The woman was heading off rapidly down the street with the child still hanging backward on her hand.

"Oh little boy!" Julian's mother called and took a few quick steps and caught up with them just beyond the lamppost. "Here's a bright new penny for you," and she held out the coin, which shone bronze in the dim light.

The huge woman turned and for a moment stood, her shoulders lifted and her face frozen with frustrated rage, and stared at Julian's mother. Then all at once she seemed to explode like a piece of machinery that had been given one ounce of pressure too much. Julian saw the black fist swing out with the red pocketbook. He shut his eyes and cringed as he heard the woman shout, "He don't take nobody's pennies!" When he opened his eyes, the woman was disappearing down the street with the little boy staring wide-eyed over her shoulder. Julian's mother was sitting on the sidewalk.

"I told you not to do that," Julian said angrily. "I told you not to do that!"

He stood over her for a minute, gritting his teeth. Her legs were stretched out in front of her and her hat was on her lap. He squatted down and looked her in the face. It was totally expressionless. "You got exactly what you deserved," he said. "Now get up."

He picked up her pocketbook and put what had fallen out back in it. He picked the hat up off her lap. The penny caught his eye on the sidewalk and he picked that up and let it drop before her eyes into the purse. Then he stood up and leaned over and held his hands out to pull her up. She remained immobile. He sighed. Rising above them on either side were black apartment buildings, marked with irregular rectangles of light. At the end of the block a man came out of a door and walked off in the opposite direction. "All right," he said, "suppose somebody happens by and wants to know why you're sitting on the sidewalk?"

She took the hand and, breathing hard, pulled heavily up on it and then stood for a moment, swaying slightly as if the spots of light in the darkness were circling around her. Her eyes, shadowed and confused, finally settled on his face. He did not try to conceal his irritation. "I hope this teaches you a lesson," he said. She leaned forward and her eyes raked his face. She seemed trying to determine his identity. Then, as if she found nothing familiar about him, she started off with a headlong movement in the wrong direction.

"Aren't you going on to the Y?" he asked.

"Home," she muttered.

"Well, are we walking?"

For answer she kept going. Julian followed along, his hands behind him. He saw no reason to let the lesson she had had go without backing it up with an explanation of its meaning. She might as well be made to understand what had happened to her. "Don't think that was just an uppity Negro woman," he said. "That was the whole colored race which will no longer take your condescending pennies. That was your black double. She can wear the same hat as you, and to be sure," he added gratuitously (because he thought it was funny), "it looked better on her than it did on you. What all this means," he said, "is that the old world is gone. The old manners are obsolete and your graciousness is not worth a damn." He thought bitterly of the house that had been lost for him. "You aren't who you think you are," he said.

She continued to plow ahead, paying no attention to him. Her hair had come undone on one side. She dropped her pocketbook and took no notice. He stooped and picked it up and handed it to her but she did not take it.

"You needn't act as if the world had come to an end," he said, "because it hasn't. From now on you've got to live in a new world and face a few realities for a change. Buck up," he said, "it won't kill you."

She was breathing fast.

"Let's wait on the bus," he said.

"Home," she said thickly.

"I hate to see you behave like this," he said. "Just like a child. I should be able to expect more of you." He decided to stop where he was and make her stop and wait for a bus. "I'm not going any farther," he said, stopping. "We're going on the bus."

She continued to go on as if she had not heard him. He took a few steps and caught her arm and stopped her. He looked into her face and caught his breath. He was looking into a face he had never seen before. "Tell Grandpa to come get me," she said.

He stared, stricken.

"Tell Caroline to come get me," she said.

Stunned, he let her go and she lurched forward again, walking as if one leg were shorter than the other. A tide of darkness seemed to be sweeping her from him. "Mother!" he cried. "Darling, sweetheart, wait!" Crumpling, she fell to the pavement. He dashed forward and fell at her side, crying, "Mamma, Mamma!" He turned her over. Her face was fiercely distorted. One eye, large and staring, moved slightly to the left as if it had become unmoored. The other remained fixed on him, raked his face again, found nothing and closed.

"Wait here, wait here!" he cried and jumped up and began to run for help toward a cluster of lights he saw in the distance ahead of him. "Help, help!" he shouted, but his voice was thin, scarcely a thread of sound. The lights drifted farther away the faster he ran and his feet moved numbly as if they carried him nowhere. The tide of darkness seemed to sweep him back to her, postponing from moment to moment his entry into the world of guilt and sorrow.

JOHN BARTH b. 1930

Barth shares with Vonnegut, Mailer, and Barthelme a vision of the modern world as a fantastic place. One may begin by seeing it realistically enough – as in "Lost in the Funhouse" – but very quickly he is levitated into a kind of fantasy that belies all the down-to-earth details of which it is composed. A funhouse, a riverboat on which an old-time minstrel show is put on (in *The Floating Opera,* 1956), or a hospital run by a mad psychiatrist (in *The End of the Road,* 1958) are some of the metaphors for the giddy world that Barth creates. His characters find themselves in varying states of inaction, wild and whirling action, precise intellection, total emotionalism – all without very much relation to their circumstances. Behind them they sense systems of control over their lives that they can't possibly understand: their past, the pattern of history, somebody else's hypnotizing will – who knows? – all they know is that they feel caught up by something bigger than they are.

Barth was born in Cambridge, Maryland, a locale that he frequently uses in his fiction. He went to college in Baltimore, at Johns Hopkins, and stayed on to take a master's degree in English. Unlike other authors who, like Barth, are learned in literature – Borges for example – he does not write *about* books, but his work is marked by a constant appropriation of other writers' styles and techniques for his own purposes. The most obvious example is his novel *The Sot-Weed Factor* (1960), which on one level reads like a rollicking eighteenth-century novel by Smollett, though in fact what Barth is doing is setting up a world of fast-moving and apparently purposeful action in which characters actually flounder as much as in the paralyzed non-action of *The Floating Opera.* After teaching English for a number of years at Pennsylvania State University, Barth is now professor of English at the State University of New York at Buffalo.

LOST IN THE FUNHOUSE

For whom is the funhouse fun? Perhaps for lovers. For Ambrose it is *a place of fear and confusion.* He has come to the seashore with his family for the holiday, *the occasion of their visit is Independence Day, the most important secular holiday of the United States of America.* A single straight underline is the manuscript mark for italic type, *which in turn* is the printed equivalent to oral emphasis of words and phrases as well as the customary type for titles of complete works, not to mention. Italics are also employed, in fiction-stories especially, for "outside," intrusive, or artificial voices, such as radio announcements, the texts of telegrams and newspaper articles, *et cetera.* They should be used *sparingly.* If passages originally in roman type are italicized by someone repeating them, it's customary to acknowledge the fact. *Italics mine.*

Ambrose was "at that awkward age." His voice came out high-pitched as a child's if he let himself get carried away; to be on the safe side, therefore, he moved and spoke with *deliberate calm* and *adult gravity.* Talking soberly of unimportant or irrelevant matters and listening consciously to the sound of your own voice are useful habits for maintaining control in this difficult interval. *En route* to Ocean City he sat in the back seat of the family car with his brother, Peter, age fifteen, and Magda G—, age fourteen, a pretty girl an exquisite young lady, who lived not far from them on B— Street in the town of D—, Maryland. Initials, blanks, or both were often substituted for proper names in nineteenth-century fiction to enhance the illusion of reality. It is as if the author felt it necessary to delete the names for reasons of tact or legal liability. Interestingly, as with other aspects of realism, it is an *illusion* that is being enhanced, by purely artificial means. Is it likely, does it violate the principle of verisimilitude, that a thirteen-year-old boy could make such a sophisticated observation? A girl of fourteen is *the psychological coeval* of a boy of fifteen or sixteen; a thirteen-year-old boy, therefore, even one precocious in some other respects, might be three years *her emotional junior.*

Thrice a year – on Memorial, Independence, and Labor Days – the family visits Ocean City for the afternoon and evening. When Ambrose and Peter's father was their age the excursion was made by train, as mentioned in the novel *The*

42nd Parallel by John Dos Passos. Many families from the same neighborhood used to travel together, with dependent relatives and often with Negro servants; schoolfuls of children swarmed through the railway cars; everyone shared everyone else's Maryland fried chicken, Virginia ham, deviled eggs, potato salad, beaten biscuits, iced tea. Nowadays (that is, in 19—, the year of our story) the journey is made by automobile – more comfortably and quickly though without the extra fun though without the *camaraderie* of a general excursion. It's all part of the deterioration of American life, their father declares; Uncle Karl supposes that when the boys take *their* families to Ocean City for the holidays, they'll fly in Autogiros. Their mother, sitting in the middle of the front seat like Magda in the second, only with her arms on the seat-back behind the men's shoulders, wouldn't want the good old days back again, the steaming trains and stuffy long dresses; on the other hand, she can do without Autogiros, too, if she has to become a grandmother to fly in them.

Description of physical appearance and mannerisms is one of several standard methods of characterization used by writers of fiction. It is also important to "keep the senses operating"; when a detail from one of the five senses, say visual, is "crossed" with a detail from another, say auditory, the reader's imagination is oriented to the scene, perhaps unconsciously. This procedure may be compared to the way surveyors and navigators determine their positions by two or more compass-bearings, a process known as triangulation. The brown hair on Ambrose's mother's forearms gleamed in the sunlight. Though right-handed, she took her left arm from the seat-back to press the dashboard cigar-lighter for Uncle Karl. When the glass bead in its handle glowed red, the lighter was ready for use. The smell of Uncle Karl's cigar-smoke reminded one of. The fragrance of the ocean came strong to the picnic-ground where they always stopped for lunch, two miles inland from Ocean City. Having to pause for a full hour almost within sound of the breakers was difficult for Peter and Ambrose when they were younger; even at their present age it was not easy to keep their anticipation, *stimulated by the briny spume,* from turning into short temper. The Irish author James Joyce, in his unusual novel entitled *Ulysses,* now available in this country, uses the adjectives *snot-green* and *scrotum-tightening* to describe the sea. Visual, auditory, tactile, olfactory, gustatory. Peter and Ambrose's father, while steering their black 1936 LaSalle sedan with one hand, could with the other remove the first cigarette from a white pack of Lucky Strikes and, more remarkably, light it with a match forefingered from its book and thumbed against the flint-paper without being detached. The matchbook cover merely advertised U.S. War Bonds and Stamps. A fine metaphor, simile, or other figure of speech, in addition to its obvious "first-order" relevance to the thing it describes, will be seen upon reflection to have a second order of significance: it may be drawn from the *milieu* of the action, for example, or be particularly appropriate to the sensibility of the narrator, even hinting to the reader things of which the narrator is unaware; or it may cast further and subtler lights upon the thing it describes, sometimes ironically qualifying the more evident sense of the comparison.

To say that Ambrose and Peter's mother was *pretty* is to accomplish nothing; the reader may acknowledge the proposition, but his imagination is not engaged. Besides, Magda was pretty, yet in an altogether different way. Although she lived on B— Street, she had very good manners and did better than average in school. Her figure was very well developed for her age. Her right hand lay casually on the plush upholstery of the seat, very near Ambrose's left leg, on which his own hand rested. The space between their legs, between her right and his left leg, was out of the line of sight of anyone sitting on the other side of Magda, as well as anyone glancing into the rearview mirror. Uncle Karl's face resembled Peter's – rather, vice versa. Both had dark hair and eyes, short husky statures, deep voices. Magda's left hand was probably in a similar position on her left side. The boy's father is difficult to describe; no particular feature of his appearance or manner stood out. He wore glasses and taught English in the T— County High School. Uncle Karl was a masonry contractor.

Although Peter must have known as well as Ambrose that the latter, because of his position in the car, would be the first to see the electrical towers of the power plant at V—, the halfway point of their trip, he leaned forward and slightly toward the center of the car and pretended to be looking for them through the flat pinewoods and tuckahoe creeks along the highways. For as long as the boys could remember, "looking for the Towers" had been a feature of the first half of their excursions to Ocean City, "looking for the standpipe" of the second. Though the game was childish, their mother preserved the tradition of rewarding the first to see the Towers with a candybar or piece of fruit. She insisted now that Magda play the game; the prize, she said, was "something hard to get nowadays." Ambrose decided not to join in; he sat back in his seat. Magda, like Peter, leaned forward. Two sets of straps were discernible through the shoulders of her sun-dress; the inside right one, a brassiere-strap, was fastened or shortened with a small safety-pin. The right armpit of her dress, presumably the left as well, was damp with perspiration. The simple strategy for being first to espy the Towers, which Ambrose had understood by the age of four, was to sit on the right-hand side of the car. Whoever sat there, however, had also to put up with the worst of the sun, and so Ambrose, without mentioning the matter, chose sometimes the one and sometimes the other. Not impossibly, Peter had never caught on to the trick, or thought that his brother hadn't, simply because Ambrose on occasion preferred shade to a Baby Ruth or tangerine.

The shade-sun situation didn't apply to the front seat, owing to the windshield; if anything the driver got more sun, since the person on the passenger side not only was shaded below by the door and dashboard but might swing down his sun visor all the way too.

"Is that them?" Magda asked. Ambrose's mother teased the boys for letting

Magda win, insinuating that "somebody [had] a girlfriend." Peter and Ambrose's father reached a long thin arm across their mother to butt his cigarette in the dashboard ashtray, under the lighter. The prize this time for seeing the Towers first was a banana. Their mother bestowed it after chiding their father for wasting a half-smoked cigarette when everything was so scarce. Magda, to take the prize, moved her hand from so near Ambrose's that he could have touched it as though accidentally. She offered to share the prize, things like that were so hard to find; but everyone insisted it was hers alone. Ambrose's mother sang an iambic trimeter couplet from a popular song, femininely rhymed:

What's good is in the Army;
What's left will never harm me.[1]

Uncle Karl tapped his cigar-ash out the ventilator window; some particles were sucked by the slip-stream back into the car through the rear window on the passenger side. Magda demonstrated her ability to hold a banana in one hand and peel it with her teeth. She still sat forward; Ambrose pushed his glasses back onto the bridge of his nose with his left hand, which he then negligently let fall to the seat-cushion immediately behind her. He even permitted the single hair, gold, on the second joint of his thumb to brush the fabric of her skirt. Should she have sat back at that instant, his hand would have been caught under her.

Plush upholstery prickles uncomfortably through gabardine slacks in the July sun. The function of the *beginning* of a story is to introduce the principal characters, establish their initial relationships, set the scene for the main action, expose the background of the situation if necessary, plant motifs and foreshadowings where appropriate, and initiate the first complication or whatever of the "rising action." Actually, if one imagines a story called "The Funhouse," or "Lost in the Funhouse," the details of the drive to Ocean City don't seem especially relevant. The *beginning* should recount the events between Ambrose's first sight of the funhouse early in the afternoon and his entering it with Magda and Peter in the evening. The *middle* would narrate all relevant events from the time he goes in to the time he loses his way; middles have the double and contradictory function of delaying the climax while at the same time preparing the reader for it and fetching him to it. Then the *ending* would tell what Ambrose does while he's lost, how he finally finds his way out, and what everybody makes of the experience. So far there's been no real dialogue, very little sensory detail, and nothing in the way of a *theme*. And a long time has gone by already without anything happening; it makes a person wonder. We haven't even reached Ocean City yet: we will never get out of the funhouse.

[1] "They're Either Too Young or Too Old" (Schwartz-Loesser). © 1943 by M. Whitmark & Sons. Used by permission of Warner Bros. Music. All rights reserved.

The more closely an author identifies with the narrator, literally or metaphorically, the less advisable it is as a rule to use the first-person narrative viewpoint. Once five years previously the three young people *aforementioned* played Niggers and Masters in the backyard; when it was Ambrose's turn to be Master and theirs to be Niggers, Peter had to go serve his evening papers; Ambrose was afraid to punish Magda alone, but she led him to the whitewashed Torture Chamber between the woodshed and the privy in the Slaves Quarters; there she knelt sweating among bamboo rakes and dusty mason jars, pleadingly embraced his knees, and while bumblebees droned in the lattice as if on an ordinary summer afternoon, purchased clemency at a surprising price set by herself. Doubtless she remembered nothing of this event; Ambrose on the other hand seemed unable to forget the least detail of his life. He even recalled how, standing beside himself with awed impersonality in the reeky heat, he'd stared the while at an empty cigar-box in which Uncle Karl kept stonecutting chisels: beneath the words *El Producto,* a laureled, loose-toga'd lady regarded the sea from a marble bench; beside her, forgotten or not yet turned to, was a five-stringed lute. Her chin reposed on the back of her right hand; her left depended negligently from the bench-arm. The lower half of scene and lady was peeled away; the words EXAMINED BY — were inked there into the wood. Nowadays cigar-boxes are made of pasteboard. Ambrose wondered what Magda would have done, Ambrose wondered what Magda would do when she sat back on his hand as he resolved she should. Be angry. Make a teasing joke of it. Give no sign at all. For a long time she leaned forward, playing cow-poker with Peter against Uncle Karl and Mother and watching for the first sign of Ocean City. At nearly the same instant picnic-ground and Ocean-City-standpipe hove into view; an Amoco filling station on their side of the road cost Mother and Uncle Karl fifty cows and the game; Magda bounced back, clapping her right hand on Mother's right arm; Ambrose moved clear "in the nick of time."

At this rate our hero, at this rate our protagonist will remain in the funhouse forever. Narrative ordinarily consists of alternating dramatization and summarization. One symptom of nervous tension, paradoxically, is repeated and violent yawning; neither Peter nor Magda nor Uncle Karl nor Mother reacted in this manner. Although they were no longer small children, Peter and Ambrose were each given a dollar to spend on boardwalk amusements in addition to what money of their own they'd brought along. Magda too, though she protested she had ample spending money. The boys' mother made a little scene out of distributing the bills; she pretended that her sons and Magda were small children and cautioned them not to spend the sum too quickly or in one place. Magda promised with a merry laugh, and having both hands free, took the bill with her left. Peter laughed also and pledged in a falsetto to be a good boy. His imitation of a child was not clever. The boys' father was tall and thin, balding, fair-complexioned. Assertions of that sort are not effective; the reader may acknowledge the proposition, but.

We should be much farther along than we are; something has gone wrong; not much of this preliminary rambling seems relevant. Yet everyone begins in the same place; how is it that most go along without difficulty but a few lose their way?

"Stay out from under the boardwalk," Uncle Karl growled from the side of his mouth. The boys' mother pushed his shoulder *in mock annoyance.* They were all standing before Fat May the Laughing Lady, who advertised the funhouse. Larger than life, Fat May mechanically shook, rocked on her heels, slapped her thighs while recorded laughter – uproarious, female – came amplified from a hidden loudspeaker. It chuckled, wheezed, wept; tried in vain to catch its breath; tittered, groaned, exploded raucous and anew. You couldn't hear it without laughing yourself, no matter how you felt. Father came back from talking to a Coast-Guardsman on duty and reported that the surf was spoiled with crude oil from tankers recently torpedoed offshore. Lumps of it, difficult to remove, made tarry tidelines on the beach and stuck on swimmers. Many bathed in the surf nevertheless and came out speckled; others paid to use a municipal pool and only sunbathed on the beach. We would do the latter. We would do the latter. We would do the latter.

Under the boardwalk, cold sand littered with cigar-butts, treasured with cigarette-stubs, Coco-Cola caps, cardboard lollipop-sticks, matchbook-covers warning that A Slip of the Lip Can Sink a Ship, grainy other things. What is the story's point? Ambrose is ill. He perspires in the dark passages; candied apples-on-a-stick, delicious-looking, disappointing to eat. Funhouses need men's and ladies' rooms at intervals.

Magda's teeth. She *was* left-handed. Perspiration. They've gone all the way, through, Magda and Peter, they've been waiting for hours with Mother and Uncle Karl while Father searches for his lost son; they draw french-fried potatoes from a paper cup and shake their heads. They've named the children they'll one day have and bring to Ocean City on holidays. Can spermatozoa properly be thought of as male animalcules when there are no female spermatozoa? They grope through hot dark windings, past Love's Tunnel's fearsome obstacles. Some perhaps lose their way.

Peter suggested then and there that they do the funhouse; he had been through it before, so had Magda, Ambrose hadn't and suggested, his voice cracking on account of Fat May's laughter, that they swim first. All were chuckling, couldn't help it; Ambrose's father, Ambrose and Peter's father came up grinning like a lunatic with two boxes of syrup-coated popcorn, one for Mother, one for Magda; the men were to help themselves. Ambrose walked on Magda's right; being by nature left-handed, she carried the box in her left hand. Up front the situation was reversed.

"What are you limping for?" Magda inquired of Ambrose. He supposed in a husky tone that his foot had gone to sleep in the car. Her teeth flashed. "Pins and needles?" It was the honeysuckle on the lattice of the former privy that drew the bees. Imagine being stung there. How long is this going to take?

The adults decided to forgo the pool, but Uncle Karl insisted they change into swimsuits and do the beach. "He wants to watch the pretty girls," Peter teased, and ducked behind Magda from Uncle Karl's pretended wrath. "You've got all the pretty girls you need right here," Magda declared, and Mother said: "Now that's the gospel truth." Magda scolded Peter, who reached over her shoulder to sneak some popcorn. "Your brother and father aren't getting any." Uncle Karl wondered if they were going to have fireworks that night, what with the shortages. It wasn't the shortages, Mr. M— replied; Ocean City had fireworks from pre-war. But it was too risky on account of the enemy submarines, some people thought.

"Don't seem like Fourth of July without fireworks," said Uncle Karl. The inverted tag in dialogue-writing is still considered permissible with proper names or epithets, but sounds old-fashioned with personal pronouns. "We'll have 'em again soon enough," predicted the boys' father. Their mother declared she could do without fireworks: they reminded her too much of the real thing. Their father said all the more reason to shoot off a few now and again. Uncle Karl asked *rhetorically* who needed reminding, just look at people's hair and skin.

"The oil, yes," said Mrs. M—.

Ambrose had a pain in his stomach and so didn't swim but enjoyed watching the others. He and his father burned red easily. Magda's figure was exceedingly well developed for her age. She too declined to swim, and got mad, and became angry when Peter attempted to drag her into the pool. She always swam, he insisted; what did she mean not swim? Why did a person come to Ocean City?

"Maybe I want to lay here with Ambrose," Magda teased.

Nobody likes a pedant.

"Aha," said Mother. Peter grabbed Magda by one ankle and ordered Ambrose to grab the other. She squealed and rolled over on the beach blanket. Ambrose pretended to help hold her back. Her tan was darker than even Mother's and Peter's. "Help out, Uncle Karl!" Peter cried. Uncle Karl went to seize the other ankle. Inside the top of her swimsuit, however, you could see the line where the sunburn ended and, when she hunched her shoulders and squealed again, one nipple's auburn edge. Mother made them behave themselves. "*You* should certainly know," she said to Uncle Karl. Archly. "that when a lady says she doesn't feel like swimming, a gentleman doesn't ask questions." Uncle Karl said excuse *him;* Mother winked at Magda; Ambrose blushed; stupid Peter kept saying "Phooey on *feel like!*" and tugging at Magda's ankle; then even he got the point, and cannon-balled with a holler into the pool.

"I swear," Magda said, in mock *in feigned* exasperation.

The diving would make a suitable literary symbol. To go off the high board you had to wait in a line along the poolside and up the ladder. Fellows tickled girls and goosed one another and shouted to the ones at the top to hurry up, or razzed them for bellyfloppers. Once on the springboard some took a great while posing or clowning or deciding on a dive or getting up their nerve; others ran right off. Especially among the younger fellows the idea was to strike the funniest pose or do the craziest stunt as you fell, a thing that got harder to do as you kept on and kept on. But whether you hollered *Geronimo!* or *Sig heil!,* held your nose or "rode a bicycle," pretended to be shot or did a perfect jackknife or changed your mind halfway down and ended up with nothing, it was over in two seconds, after all that wait. Spring, pose, splash. Spring, neat-o, splash. Spring, aw shit, splash.

The grown-ups had gone on; Ambrose wanted to converse with Magda; she was remarkably well developed for her age; it was said that that came from rubbing with a Turkish towel, and there were other theories. Ambrose could think of nothing to say except how good a diver Peter was, who was showing off for her benefit. You could pretty well tell by looking at their bathing-suits and arm-muscles how far along the different fellows were. Ambrose was glad he hadn't gone in swimming, the cold water shrank you up so. Magda pretended not to be interested in the diving; she probably weighed as much as he did. If you knew your way around in the funhouse like your own bedroom you could wait until a girl came along and then slip away without ever getting caught, even if her boyfriend was right with her. She'd think *he* did it! It would be better to be the boyfriend, and act outraged, and tear the funhouse apart. Not act; *be.*

"He's a master diver," Ambrose said. In feigned admiration. "You really have to slave away at it to get that good." What would it matter anyhow if he asked her right out whether she remembered, even teased her with it as Peter would have?

There's no point in going farther; this isn't getting anybody anywhere; they haven't even come to the funhouse yet. Ambrose is off the track, in some new or old part of the place that's not supposed to be used; he strayed into it by some one-in-a-million chance, like the time the roller-coaster-car left the tracks in the nineteen-teens against all the laws of physics and sailed over the boardwalk in the dark. And they can't locate him because they don't know where to look. Even the designer and operator has forgotten this other part, that winds around on itself like a whelk-shell. That winds around the right part like the snakes on Mercury's caduceus. Some people, perhaps, don't "hit their stride" until their twenties, when the growing-up business is over and women appreciate other things besides wisecracks and teasing and strutting. Peter didn't have one-tenth the imagination *he* had, not one-tenth. Peter did this naming-their-children thing as a joke, making up names like Aloysius and Murgatroyd, but Ambrose knew *exactly* how it would feel to be married and have children of your own, and be a loving husband and father, and go comfortably to work in the mornings and to bed with your wife at night, and wake up with her there. With a breeze coming through the sash and birds and mockingbirds singing in the chinese-cigar trees. His eyes watered, there aren't enough ways to say that. He would be quite famous in his line of work. Whether Magda was his wife or not, one evening when he was wise-lined and gray at the temples, he'd smile gravely, at a fashionable dinner-party, and remind her of his youthful passion. The time they went with his family to Ocean City; the *erotic fantasies* he used to have about her. How long ago it seemed, and childish! Yet tender, too, *n'est-ce pas?* Would she have imagined that the world-renowned whatever remembered how many strings were on the lute on the bench beside the girl on the label of the cigar-box he'd stared at in the toolshed at age eight while she, age nine. Even then he had felt *wise beyond his years;* he'd stroked her hair and said in his deepest voice and correctest English, as to a dear child: "I shall never forget this moment."

But though he had breathed heavily, groaned as if ecstatic, what he'd really felt throughout was an odd detachment, as though someone else were Master. Strive as he might to be transported, he heard his mind take notes upon the scene: *This is what they call* passion. *I am experiencing it.* Many of the digger-machines were out of order in the penny arcades and could not be repaired or replaced for the duration. Moreover, the prizes, made now in USA, were less interesting than formerly, pasteboard items for the most part, and some of the machines wouldn't work on white pennies. The gypsy-fortuneteller machine might have provided a foreshadowing of the climax of this story if Ambrose had operated it. It was even dilapidateder than most: the silver coating was worn off the brown metal handles, the glass windows around the dummy were cracked and taped, her kerchiefs and silks long faded. If a man lived by himself he could take a department-store mannequin with flexible joints and modify her in certain ways. *However:* by the time he was that old he'd have a real woman. There was a machine that stamped your name around a white-metal coin with a star in the middle: A—. His son would be the Third, and when the lad reached thirteen or so he would put a strong arm around his shoulder and tell him calmly: "It is perfectly normal. We have all been through it. It will not last forever." Nobody knew how to be what they were right. He'd smoke a pipe, teach his son how to fish and softcrab, assure him he needn't worry about himself. Magda would certainly give, Magda would certainly yield a great deal of milk, although guilty of occasional solecisms. It don't taste so bad. Suppose the lights came on now!

The day wore on. You think you're yourself, but there are other persons in you. Ambrose gets an erection when Ambrose doesn't want one, *and obversely.* Ambrose watches them disagreeing; Ambrose watches him watch. In the funhouse mirror-room you can't see yourself go on forever, because no matter how you stand your head gets in the way. Even if you had a glass periscope, the image of your eye would cover up the thing you really wanted to see. The police will come; there'll be a story in the papers. That must be where it happened. Unless he can find a surprise exit, an unofficial backdoor or escape-hatch opening on an alley, say, and then stroll up to the family in front of the funhouse and ask where everybody's been; *he's* been out of the place for ages. That's just where it happened, in that last lighted room: Peter and Magda found the right exit; he found one that you weren't supposed to find and strayed off into the works somewhere. In a perfect funhouse you'd be able to go only one way, like the divers off the high board; getting lost would be impossible; the doors and halls would work like minnow-traps or the valves in veins.

On account of German U-boats Ocean City was "browned out": streetlights were shaded on the seaward side; shopwindows and boardwalk amusement-places were kept dim, not to silhouette tankers and Liberty-ships for torpedoing. In a short-story about Ocean City, Maryland, during World War II the author could make use of the image of sailors on leave in the penny arcades and shooting-galleries, sighting through the cross hairs to toy machine-guns at swastika'd subs, while out in the black Atlantic a U-boat skipper squints through his periscope at real ships outlined by the glow of penny arcades. After dinner the family strolled back to the amusement end of the boardwalk. They boys' father had burnt red as always and was masked with Noxzema, a minstrel in reverse. The grown-ups stood at the end of the boardwalk where the Hurricane of '33 had cut an inlet from the ocean to Assawoman Bay.

"Prounced with a long *o,*" Uncle Karl reminded Magda with a wink. His shirt-sleeves were rolled up; Mother punched his brown biceps with the arrowed heart on it and said his mind was naughty. Fat May's laugh came suddenly from the funhouse, as if she'd just got the joke; the family laughed too at the coincidence. Ambrose went under the boardwalk to search for out-of-town matchbook-covers with the aid of his pocket flashlight; he looked out from the edge of the North American continent and wondered how far their laughter carried over the water. Spies in rubber rafts; survivors in lifeboats. If the joke had been beyond his understanding, he could have said: *"The laughter was over his head."* And let the reader see the serious wordplay on second reading.

He turned the flashlight on and then off at once even before the woman whooped. He sprang away, heart athud, dropping the light. The man had snarled: "Cut da friggin' light!" Perspiration drenched and chilled him by the time he scrambled up to the family. "See anything?" his father asked. His voice wouldn't come; he shrugged and violently brushed sand from his pantslegs.

"Let's ride the old flying-horses!" Magda cried. I'll never be an author. It's been forever already, everybody's gone home, Ocean City's deserted, the ghost-crabs are tickling across the beach and down the littered cold streets. And the empty halls of clapboard hotels and abandoned funhouses. A tidal wave; an enemy air raid; a monster-crab swelling like an island from the sea. *The Inhabitants fled in terror.* Magda clung to his trouserleg; he alone knew the maze's secret. "He gave his life that we might live," said Uncle Karl with a scowl of pain, as he. The woman's legs had been twined behind the man's neck; he'd spread her fat cheeks with tatooed hands and pumped like a whippet. *An astonishing coincidence.* He yearned to tell Peter. He wanted to throw up for excitement. They hadn't even chased him. He wished he were dead.

One possible ending would be to have Ambrose come across another lost person in the dark. They'd match their wits together against the funhouse, struggle like Ulysses past obstacle after obstacle, help and encourage each other. Or a girl. By the time they found the exit they'd be closest friends, sweethearts if it were a girl; they'd know each other's inmost souls, be bound together *by the cement of shared adventure;* then they'd emerge into the light, and it would turn out that his friend was a Negro. A blind girl. President Roosevelt's son. Ambrose's former arch-enemy.

Shortly after the mirror-room he'd groped along a musty corridor, his heart already misgiving him at the absence of phosphorescent arrows and other signs. He'd found a crack of light – not a door, it turned out, but a seam between the plyboard wall-panels – and squinting up to it, espied a small old man nodding upon a stool beneath a bare speckled bulb. A crude panel of toggle- and knife-switches hung beside the open fuse-box near his head; elsewhere in the little room were wooden levers and ropes belayed to boat-cleats. At the time, Ambrose wasn't lost enough to rap or call; later he couldn't find that crack. Now it seemed to him that he'd possibly dozed off for a few minutes somewhere along the way; certainly he was exhausted from the afternoon's sunshine and the evening's problems; he couldn't be sure he hadn't dreamed part or all of the sight. Had an old black wall fan droned like bumble-bees and shimmied two flypaper streamers? Had the funhouse operator – gentle, somewhat sad and tired-appearing – murmured in his sleep? Is there really such a person as Ambrose, or is he a figment of the author's imagination? Was it Assawoman Bay or Sinepuxent? Are there other errors of fact in this fiction? Was there another sound besides the little slap slap of thigh on ham, like water sucking at the chineboards of a skiff?

When you're lost, the smartest thing to do is stay put till you're found, hollering if necessary. But to holler guarantees humiliation as well as rescue; keeping silent permits some saving of face – you can act surprised at the fuss when your rescuers find you and swear you weren't lost, if they do. What's more you might find your own way yet, *however belatedly.*

"Don't tell me your foot's still asleep!" Magda exclaimed as the three young people walked from the inlet to the area set aside for ferris-wheels, carrousels, and other carnival rides, they having decided in favor of the vast and ancient merry-go-round instead of the funhouse. What a sentence, everything was wrong from the outset. People don't know what to make of him, he doesn't know what to make of himself, he's only thirteen, *athletically and socially inept,* not astonishingly bright, but there are antennae; he has . . . some sort of receivers in his head; things speak to him, he understands more than he should, the world winks at him through its objects, grabs grinning at his coat. Everybody else is in on some secret he doesn't know; they've forgotten to tell him. Through simple *procrastination* his mother put off his baptism until this year. Everyone else had it done as a baby; he'd assumed the same of himself, as had his mother so she claimed, until it was time for him to join Grace Methodist-Protestant and the oversight came out. He was mortified, but pitched sleepless through his private catechizing, intimidated by the ancient mysteries, a thirteen-year-old would never say that, resolved to experience conversion like St. Augustine. When the water touched his brow and Adam's sin left him, he contrived by a strain like defecation to bring tears into his eyes – but felt nothing. There was some simple, radical difference about him; he hoped it was genius, feared it was madness, devoted himself to amiability and inconspicuousness. Alone on the seawall near his house he was seized by the terrifying transports he'd thought to find in summershed, in Communion-cup. The grass was alive! The town, the river, himself, were not imaginary; time roared in his ears like wind; the world was *going on!* This part ought to be dramatized. The Irish author James Joyce once wrote. Ambrose M— is going to scream.

There is no *texture of rendered sensory detail,* for one thing. The faded distorting mirrors beside Fat May; the impossibility of choosing a mount when one had but a single ride on the great carrousel; the *vertigo attendant on his recognition* that Ocean City was worn out, the place of fathers and grandfathers, straw-boatered men and parasoled ladies survived by their amusements. Money spent, the three paused at Peter's insistence beside Fat May to watch the girls get their skirts blown up. The object was to tease Magda, who said, "I swear, Peter M—, you've got a one-track mind! Amby and me aren't *interested* in such things." In the tumbling-barrel, too, just inside the Devil's-mouth entrance to the funhouse, the girls were upended, and their boyfriends and others could see up their dresses if they cared to. Which was the whole point, Ambrose realized. Of the entire funhouse! If you looked around, you noticed that almost all the people on the boardwalk were paired off into couples except the small children; in a way, that was the whole point of Ocean City! If you had X-ray eyes and could see everything going on at that instant under the boardwalk and in all the hotel-rooms and cars and alleyways, you'd realize that all that normally *showed,* like restaurants and dance-halls and clothing and test-your strength machines, was merely preparation and intermission. Fat May screamed.

Because he watched the goings-on from the corner of his eye, it was Ambrose who spied the half-dollar on the boardwalk near the tumbling-barrel. Losers weepers. The first time he'd heard some people moving through a corridor not far away, just after he'd lost sight of the crack of light, he'd decided not to call to them, for fear they'd guess he was scared and poke fun; it sounded like roughnecks; he'd hoped they'd come by and he could follow in the dark without their knowing. Another time he'd heard just one person, unless he imagined it, bumping along as if on the other side of the plywood; perhaps Peter coming back for him, or

Father, or Magda lost too. Or the owner and operator of the funhouse. He'd called out once, as though merrily: "Anybody know where the heck we are?" But the query was too stiff, his voice cracked when the sounds stopped he was terrified: maybe it was a queer who waited for fellows to get lost, or a longhaired filthy monster that lived in some cranny of the funhouse. He stood rigid for hours it seemed like, scarcely respiring. His future was shockingly clear, in outline. He tried holding his breath to the point of unconsciousness. There ought to be a button you could push to end your life absolutely without pain; disappear in a flick, like turning out a light. He would push it instantly! He despised Uncle Karl. But he despised his father too, for not being what he was supposed to be. Perhaps his father hated *his* father, and so on, and his son would hate him, and so on. Instantly!

Naturally he didn't have nerve enough to ask Magda to go through the funhouse with him. With incredible nerve and to everyone's surprise he invited Magda, quietly and politely, to go through the funhouse with him. "I warn you, I've never been through it before," he added, *laughing easily;* "but I reckon we can manage somehow. The important thing to remember, after all, is that it's meant to be a *fun*house; that is, a place of amusement. If people really got lost or injured or too badly frightened in it, the owner'd go out of business. There'd even be lawsuits. No character in a work of fiction can make a speech this long without interruption or acknowledgment from the other characters."

Mother teased Uncle Karl: "Three's a crowd, I always heard." But actually Ambrose was relieved that Peter now had a quarter too. Nothing was what it looked like. Every instant, under the surface of the Atlantic Ocean, millions of living animals devoured one another. Pilots were falling in flames over Europe; women were being forcibly raped in the South Pacific. His father should have taken him aside and said: "There is a simple secret to getting through the funhouse, as simple as being first to see the Towers. Here it is. Peter does not know it; neither does your Uncle Karl. You and I are different. Not surprisingly, you've often wished you weren't. Don't think I haven't noticed how unhappy your childhood has been! But you'll understand, when I tell you, why it had to be kept secret until now. And you won't regret not being like your brother and your uncle. *On the contrary.*" If you knew all the stories behind all the people on the boardwalk you'd see that *nothing* was what it looked like. Husbands and wives often hated each other; parents didn't necessarily love their children; et cetera. A child took things for granted because he had nothing to compare his life to, and everybody acted as if things were as they should be. Therefore each saw himself as the hero of the story, when the truth might turn out to be that he's the villain, or the coward. And there wasn't one thing you could do about it!

Hunchbacks, fat ladies, fools – that no one chose what they were was unbearable. In the movies he'd meet a beautiful young girl in the funhouse; they'd have hairsbreadth escapes from real dangers; he'd do and say the right things; she also;

in the end they'd be lovers; their dialogue-lines would match up; he'd be perfectly at ease; she'd not only like him well enough, she'd think he was *marvelous;* she'd lie awake thinking about *him,* instead of vice versa — the way *his* face looked in different lights and how he stood and exactly what he'd said — and yet that would be only one small episode in his wonderful life, among many many others. Not a *turning-point* at all. What had happened in the toolshed was nothing. He hated, he loathed his parents! One reason for not writing a lost-in-the-funhouse story is that either everybody's felt what Ambrose feels, in which case it goes without saying, or else no normal person feels such things, in which case Ambrose is a freak. "Is anything more tiresome, in fiction, than the problems of sensitive adolescents?" And it's all too long and rambling, as if the author. For all a person knows the first time through, the end could be just around any corner; perhaps, *not impossibly* it's been within reach any number of times. On the other hand he may be scarcely past the start, with everything yet to get through, an intolerable idea.

Fill in: His father's raised eyebrows when he announced his decision to do the funhouse with Magda. Ambrose understands now, but didn't then, that his father was wondering whether he knew what the funhouse was *for* — especially since he didn't object, as he should have, when Peter decided to come along too. The ticket-woman, witchlike, mortifying him when inadvertently he gave her his name-coin instead of the half-dollar, then unkindly calling Magda's attention to the birthmark on his temple: "Watch out for him, girlie, he's a marked man!" She wasn't even cruel, he understood, only vulgar and insensitive. Somewhere in the world there was a young woman with such splendid understanding that she'd see him entire, like a poem or story, and find his words so valuable after all that when he confessed his apprehensions she would explain why they were in fact the very things that made him precious to her . . . and to Western Civilization! There was no such girl, the simple truth being. Violent yawns as they approached the mouth. Whispered advice from an old-timer on a bench near the barrel: "Go crabwise and ye'll get an eyeful without upsetting!" Composure vanished at the first pitch: Peter hollered joyously, Magda tumbled, shrieked, clutched her skirt, Ambrose scrambled crabwise, tightlipped with terror, was soon out, watched his dropped name-coin slide among the couples. Shame-faced he saw that to get through expeditiously was not the point; Peter feigned assistance in order to trip Magda up, shouted "I see Christmas!" when her legs went flying. The old man, his latest betrayer, cackled approval. A dim hall then of blackthread cobwebs and recorded gibber: he took Magda's elbow to steady her against revolving discs set in the slanted floor to throw your feet out from under, and explained to her in a calm deep voice his theory that each phase of the funhouse was triggered either automatically, by a series of photoelectric devices, or else manually by operators stationed at peepholes. But he lost his voice thrice as the discs unbalanced him; Magda was anyhow squealing; but at one point she clutched him about the waist to keep from falling, and her right cheek pressed for a moment against his belt-buckle. Heroically he drew her up, it was his chance to clutch her close as if for support and say: "I love you." He even put an arm lightly about the small of her back before a sailor-and-girl pitched into them from behind, sorely treading his left big toe and knocking Magda asprawl with them. The sailor's girl was a string-haired hussy with a loud laugh and light-blue drawers; Ambrose realized that he wouldn't have said "I love you" anyhow, and was smitten with self-contempt. How much better it would be to be that common sailor! A wiry little Seaman 3rd, the fellow squeezed a girl to each side and stumbled hilarious into the mirror-room, closer to Magda in thirty seconds than Ambrose had got in thirteen years. She giggled at something the fellow said to Peter; she drew her hair from her eyes with a movement so womanly it struck Ambrose's heart; Peter's smacking her backside then seemed particularly coarse. But Magda made a pleased indignant face and cried, "All right for *you,* mister!" and pursued Peter into the maze without a backward glance. The sailor followed after, leisurely drawing his girl against his hip; Ambrose understood not only that they were all so relieved to be rid of his burdensome company that they didn't even notice his absence, but that he himself shared their relief. Stepping from the treacherous passage at last into the mirror-maze, he saw once again, more clearly than ever, how readily he deceived himself into supposing he was a person. He even foresaw, wincing at his dreadful self-knowledge, that he would repeat the deception, at ever-rarer intervals, all his wretched life, so fearful were the alternatives. Fame, madness, suicide; perhaps all three. It's not believable that so young a boy could articulate that reflection, and in fiction the merely true must always yield to the plausible. Yet Ambrose M— understood, as few adults do, that the famous loneliness of the great was no popular myth but a general truth – and moreover, that it was as much cause as effect.

All the preceding except the last few sentences is exposition that should've been done earlier or interspersed with the present action instead of lumped together. No reader would put up with so much with such *prolixity.* It's interesting that Ambrose's father, though presumably an intelligent man (as indicated by his role as high-school teacher), neither encouraged nor discouraged his children at all in any way – as if he either didn't care about them or cared all right but didn't know how to act. If this fact should contribute to one of his children's becoming a celebrated but wretchedly unhappy scientist, was it a good thing or not? He too might someday face that question; it would be useful to know whether it had tortured his father for years, for example, or never once crossed his mind.

In the mirror-maze two important things happened. First, our hero found a name-coin someone else had lost or discarded: *AMBROSE,* suggestive of the famous lightship and of his father's favorite dessert, which his mother prepared on special occasions out of coconut, oranges, grapes, and what else. Second, as he wondered at the endless replication of his image in the mirrors – second, as he *lost himself in the reflection* that the necessity for an observer makes perfect observation impossible, better make him eighteen at least, yet that would render other things unlikely, he heard Peter and Magda chuckling somewhere in the maze. "Here!" "No, here!" they shouted to each other; Peter said, "Where's Amby?" Magda murmured. "Amb?" Peter called. In a pleased, friendly voice. He didn't reply. The truth was, his brother was a *happy-go-lucky youngster* who'd've been better off with a regular brother of his own, but who seldom complained of his lot and was generally cordial. Ambrose's throat ached; there aren't enough different ways to say that. He stood quietly while the two young people giggled and thumped through the glittering maze, hurrah'd their discovery of its exit, cried out in joyful alarm at what next beset them. Then he set his mouth and followed after, as he supposed, took a wrong turn, strayed into the pass *wherein he lingers yet.*

The action of conventional dramatic narrative may be represented by a diagram called Freitag's Triangle

or more accurately by a variant of that diagram

C
A B D

in which *AB* represents the exposition, *B* the introduction of conflict, *BC* the "rising action," complication, or development of the conflict, *C* the climax or turn of the action, *CD* the *dénouement* or resolution of the conflict.

While there is no reason to regard this pattern as an absolute necessity, like many other conventions it became conventional because great numbers of people over great numbers of years learned by trial and error that it was effective; one ought not to forsake it, therefore, unless one wishes to forsake as well the effect of drama or has clear cause to feel that deliberate violation of the "normal" pattern can better can better effect that effect. This can't go on much longer; it can go on forever. He died telling stories to himself in the dark; years later, when that vast unsuspected area of the funhouse came to light, the first expedition found his skeleton in one of its labyrinthine corridors and mistook it for part of the entertainment. He died of starvation telling himself stories in the dark; but unbeknownst unbeknownst to him, an assistant operator of the funhouse, happening to overhear him, crouched just behind the plyboard partition and wrote down his every word. The operator's daughter, an exquisite young woman with a figure unusually well developed for her age, crouched just behind the partition and transcribed his every word. Though she had never laid eyes on him, she recognized that here was one of Western Culture's truly great imaginations, the eloquence of whose suffering would be an inspiration to unnumbered. And her heart was torn between her love for the misfortunate young man (yes, she loved him, though she had never laid though she knew him only – but how well! – through his words, and the deep, calm voice in which he spoke them) between her love et cetera and her woman's intuition that only in suffering and isolation could he give voice et cetera. Lone dark dying. Quietly she kissed the rough plyboard, and a tear fell upon the page. Where she had written in shorthand *Where she had written in shorthand* Where she had written in shorthand *Where she* et cetera. A long time ago we should have passed the apex of Freitag's Triangle and made brief work of the *dénouement;* the plot doesn't rise by meaningful steps but winds upon itself, digresses, retreats, hesitates, sighs, collapses, expires. The climax of the story must be its protagonist's discovery of a way to get through the funhouse. But he has found none, may have ceased to search.

What relevance does the war have to the story? Should there be fireworks outside or not?

Ambrose wandered, languished, dozed. Now and then he fell into his habit of rehearsing to himself the unadventurous story of his life, narrated from the third-person point of view, from his earliest memory parenthesis of maple-leaves stirring in the summer breath of tidewater Maryland end of parenthesis to the present moment. Its principal events, on this telling, would appear to have been *A, B, C,* and *D.*

He imagined himself years hence, successful, married, at ease in the world, the trials of his adolescence far behind him. He has come to the seashore with his family for the holiday: how Ocean City has changed! But at one seldom at one ill-frequented end of the boardwalk a few derelict amusements survive from times gone by: the great carrousel from the turn of the century, with its monstrous griffins and mechanical concert-band; the roller-coaster rumored since 1916 to have been condemned; the mechanical shooting-gallery in which only the image of our enemies changed. His own son laughs with Fat May and wants to know what a funhouse is; Ambrose hugs the sturdy lad close and smiles around his pipestem at his wife.

The family's going home. Mother sits between Father and Uncle Karl, who teases him good-naturedly who chuckles over the fact that the comrade with whom he'd fought his way shoulder to shoulder through the funhouse had turned out to be a colored boy – to their mutual discomfort, as they'd opened their souls. But such are the walls of custom, which even. Whose arm is where? How must it feel. He dreams of a funhouse vaster by far than any yet constructed; but by then they may be out of fashion, like steamboats and excursion-trains. Already quaint and seedy: the draperied ladies on the frieze of the carrousel are his father's father's mooncheeked dreams; if he thinks of it more he will vomit his apple-on-a-stick.

He wonders: will he become a regular person? Something has gone wrong; his vaccination didn't take; at the Boy-Scout initiation campfire he only pretended to be deeply moved, as he pretends to this hour that it is not so bad after all in the funhouse, and that he has a little limp. How long will it last? He envisions a truly astonishing funhouse, incredibly complex yet utterly controlled from a great central switchboard like the console of a pipeorgan. Nobody had enough imagination. He could design such a place himself, wiring and all, and he's only thirteen years old. He would be its operator: panel-lights would show what was up in every cranny of its cunning of its multifarious vastness; a switchflick would ease this fellow's way, complicate that's, to balance things out; if anyone seemed lost or frightened, all the operator had to do was.

He wishes he had never entered the funhouse. No: he wishes he had never been born. But he was. Then he wishes he were dead. But he's not. Therefore he will construct funhouses for others and be their secret operator – though he would rather be among the lovers for whom funhouses are designed.

LIFE-STORY

I

Without discarding what he'd already written he began his story afresh in a somewhat different manner. Whereas his earlier version had opened in a straightforward documentary fashion and then degenerated or at least modulated intentionally into irrealism and dissonance he decided this time to tell his tale from start to finish in a conservative, "realistic," unself-conscious way. He being by vocation an author of novels and stories it was perhaps inevitable that one afternoon the possibility would occur to the writer of these lines that his own life might be a fiction, in which he was the leading or an accessory character. He happened at the time[1] to be in his study attempting to draft the opening pages of a new short story; its general idea had preoccupied him for some months along with other general ideas, but certain elements of the conceit, without which he could scarcely proceed, remained unclear. More specifically: narrative plots may be imagined as consisting of a "ground-situation" (Scheherazade desires not to die) focused and dramatized by a "vehicle-situation" (Scheherazade beguiles the King with endless stories), the several incidents of which have their final value in terms of their bearing upon the "ground-situation." In our author's case it was the "vehicle" that had vouchsafed itself, first as a germinal proposition in his commonplace book — D comes to suspect that the world is a novel, himself a fictional personage — subsequently as an articulated conceit explored over several pages of the workbook in which he elaborated more systematically his casual inspirations: since D is writing a fictional account of this conviction he has indisputably a fictional existence in his account, replicating what he suspects to be his own situation. Moreover E, hero of D's account, is said to be writing a similar account, and so the replication is in both ontological directions, et cetera. But the "ground-situation" — some state of affairs on D's part which would give dramatic resonance to his attempts to prove himself factual, assuming he made such attempts — obstinately withheld itself

[1] 9:00 A.M., Monday, June 20, 1966.

from his imagination. As is commonly the case the question reduced to one of stakes: what were to be the consequences of D's — and finally E's — disproving or verifying his suspicion, and why should a reader be interested?

What a dreary way to begin a story he said to himself upon reviewing his long introduction. Not only is there no "ground-situation," but the prose style is heavy and somewhat old-fashioned, like an English translation of Thomas Mann, and the so-called "vehicle" itself is at least questionable: self-conscious, vertiginously arch, fashionably solipsistic, unoriginal — in fact a convention of twentieth-century literature. Another story about a writer writing a story! Another regressus in infinitum! Who doesn't prefer art that at least overtly imitates something other than its own processes? That doesn't continually proclaim "Don't forget I'm an artifice!"? That takes for granted its mimetic nature instead of asserting it in order (not so slyly after all) to deny it, or vice-versa? Though his critics sympathetic and otherwise described his own work as avant-garde, in his heart of hearts he disliked literature of an experimental, self-despising, or overtly metaphysical character, like Samuel Beckett's, Marian Cutler's, Jorge Borges's. The logical fantasies of Lewis Carroll pleased him less than straight-forward tales of adventure, subtly sentimental romances, even densely circumstantial realisms like Tolstoy's. His favorite contemporary authors were John Updike, Georges Simenon, Nicole Riboud. He had no use for the theater of absurdity, for "black humor," for allegory in any form, for apocalyptic preachments meretriciously tricked out in dramatic garb.

Neither had his wife and adolescent daughters, who for that matter preferred life to literature and read fiction when at all for entertainment. Their kind of story (his too, finally) would begin if not once upon a time at least with arresting circumstance, bold character, trenchant action. C flung away the whining manuscript and pushed impatiently through the french doors leading to the terrace from his oak-wainscoted study. Pausing at the stone balustrade to light his briar he remarked through a lavender cascade of wisteria that lithe-limbed Gloria, Gloria of timorous eye and militant breast, had once again chosen his boat-wharf as her basking-place.

By Jove he exclaimed to himself. It's particularly disquieting to suspect not only that one is a fictional character but that the fiction one's in — the fiction one is — is quite the sort one least prefers. His wife entered the study with coffee and an apple-pastry, set them at his elbow on his work table, returned to the living room. Ed' pelut' kondo nedode; nyoing nyang. One manifestation of schizophrenia as everyone knows is the movement from reality toward fantasy, a progress which not infrequently takes the form of distorted and fragmented representation, abstract formalism, an increasing preoccupation, even obsession, with pattern and design for their own sakes — especially patterns of a baroque, enormously detailed character — to the (virtual) exclusion of representative "content." There are other manifestations. Ironically, in the case of graphic and plastic artists for example the work produced in the advanced stages of their affliction may be more powerful and interesting than the realistic productions of their earlier "sanity." Whether the artists themselves are gratified by this possibility is not reported.

B called upon a literary acquaintance, B—, summering with Mrs. B and children on the Eastern Shore of Maryland. "You say you lack a ground-situation. Has it occurred to you that that circumstance may be your ground-situation? What occurs to me is that if it is it isn't. And conversely. The case being thus, what's really wanting after all is a well-articulated vehicle, a foreground or upstage situation to dramatize the narrator's or author's grundlage. His what. To write merely C comes to suspect that the world is a novel, himself a fictional personage is but to introduce the vehicle; the next step must be to initiate its uphill motion by establishing and complicating some conflict. I would advise in addition the eschewal of overt and self-conscious discussion of the narrative process. I would advise in addition the eschewal of overt and self-conscious discussion of the narrative process. The via negativa and its positive counterpart are it is to be remembered poles after all of the same cell. Returning to his study.

If I'm going to be a fictional character G declared to himself I want to be in a rousing good yarn as they say, not some piece of avant-garde preciousness. I want passion and bravura action in my plot, heroes I can admire, heroines I can love, memorable speeches, colorful accessory characters, poetical language. It doesn't matter to me how naively linear the anecdote is; never mind modernity! How reactionary J appears to be. How will such nonsense sound thirty-six years from now?[2] As if. If he can only get K through his story I reflected grimly; if he can only retain his self-possession to the end of this sentence; not go mad; not destroy himself and/or others. Then what I wondered grimly. Another sentence fast, another story. Scheherazade my only love! All those nights you kept your secret from the King my rival, that after your defloration he was unnecessary, you'd have killed yourself in any case when your invention failed.

Why could he not begin his story afresh X wondered, for example with the words why could he not begin his story afresh et cetera? Y's wife came into the study as he was about to throw out the baby with the bathwater. "Not for an instant to throw out the baby while every instant discarding the bathwater is perhaps a chief task of civilized people at this hour of the world."[3] I used to tell B— that without success. What makes you so sure it's not a film he's in or a theater-piece?

Because U responded while he certainly felt rather often that he was merely acting his own role or roles he had no idea who the actor was, whereas even the most Stanislavsky methodist would presumably if questioned closely recollect his offstage identity even onstage in mid-act. Moreover a great part of T's "drama," most of his life in fact, was non-visual, consisting entirely in introspection, which

[2] 10:00 A.M., Monday, June 20, 1966.

[3] 11:00 A.M., Monday, June 20, 1966.

the visual dramatic media couldn't manage easily. He had for example mentioned to no one his growing conviction that he was a fictional character, and since he was not given to audible soliloquizing a "spectator" would take him for a cheerful, conventional fellow, little suspecting that et cetera. It was of course imaginable that much goes on in the mind of King Oedipus in addition to his spoken sentiments; any number of interior dramas might be being played out in the actors' or characters' minds, dramas of which the audience is as unaware as are V's wife and friends of his growing conviction that he's a fictional character. But everything suggested that the medium of his life was prose fiction – moreover a fiction narrated from either the first-person or the third-person-omniscient point of view.

Why is it L wondered with mild disgust that both K and M for example choose to write such stuff when life is so sweet and painful and full of such a variety of people, places, situations, and activities other than self-conscious and after all rather blank introspection? Why is it N wondered et cetera that both M and O et cetera when the world is in such parlous explosive case? Why et cetera et cetera et cetera when the word, which was in the beginning, is now evidently nearing the end of its road? Am I being strung out in this ad libitum fashion I wondered merely to keep my author from the pistol? What sort of story is it whose drama lies always in the next frame out? If Sinbad sinks it's Scheherazade who drowns; whose neck one wonders is on her line?

II

Discarding what he'd already written as he could wish to discard the mumbling pages of his life he began his story afresh, resolved this time to eschew overt and self-conscious discussion of his narrative process and to recount instead in the straight-forwardest manner possible the several complications of his character's conviction that he was a character in a work of fiction, arranging them into dramatically ascending stages if he could for his readers' sake and leading them (the stages) to an exciting climax and denouement if he could.

He rather suspected that the medium and genre in which he worked – the only ones for which he felt any vocation – were moribund if not already dead. The idea pleased him. One of the successfullest men he knew was a blacksmith of the old school who et cetera. He meditated upon the grandest sailing-vessel ever built, the *France II,* constructed in Bordeaux in 1911 not only when but because the age of sail had passed. Other phenomena that consoled and inspired him were the great flying-boat *Hercules,* the zeppelin *Hindenburg,* the *Tsar Pushka* cannon. the then-record Dow-Jones industrial average of 381.17 attained on September 3, 1929.

He rather suspected that the society in which he persisted – the only one with which he felt any degree of identification – was moribund if not et cetera. He knew beyond any doubt that the body which he inhabited — the only one et cetera — was et cetera. The idea et cetera. He had for thirty-six years lacking a few hours been one of our dustmote's three billion tenants give or take five hundred million, and happening to be as well a white male citizen of the United States of America he had thirty-six years plus a few hours more to cope with one way or another unless the actuarial tables were mistaken, not bloody likely, or his term was unexpectedly reduced.

Had he written for his readers' sake? The phrase implied a thitherto-unappreciated metaphysical dimension. Suspense. If his life was a fictional narrative it consisted of three terms — teller, tale, told — each dependent on the other two but not in the same ways. His author could as well tell some other character's tale or some other tale of the same character as the one being told as he himself could in his own character as author; his "reader" could as easily read some other story, would be well advised to; but his own "life" depended absolutely on a particular author's original persistence, thereafter upon some reader's. From this consideration any number of things followed, some less tiresome than others. No use appealing to his author, of whom he'd come to dislike even to think. The idea of his playing with his characters' and his own self-consciousness! He himself tended in that direction and despised the tendency. The idea of his or her smiling smugly to himself as the "words" flowed from his "pen" in which his protagonist's unhappy inner life was exposed! Ah he had mistaken the nature of his narrative; he had thought it very long, longer than Proust's, longer than any German's, longer than *The Thousand Nights and a Night* in ten quarto volumes. Moreover he'd thought it the most prolix and pedestrian *tranche-de-vie* realism, unredeemed by even the limited virtues of colorful squalor, solid specification, an engaging variety of scenes and characters — in a word a bore, of the sort he himself not only would not write but would not read either. Now he understood that his author might as probably resemble himself and the protagonist of his own story-in-progress. Like himself, like his character aforementioned, his author not impossibly deplored the obsolescence of humanism, the passing of *savoir-vivre,* et cetera; admired the outmoded values of fidelity, courage, tact, restraint, amiability, self-discipline, et cetera; preferred fictions in which were to be found stirring actions, characters to love as well as ditto to despise, speeches and deeds to affect us strongly, et cetera. He too might wish to make some final effort to put by his fictional character and achieve factuality or at least to figure in if not be hero of a more attractive fiction, but be caught like the writer of these lines in some more or less desperate tour de force. For him to attempt to come to an understanding with such an author were as futile as for one of his own creations to et cetera.

But the reader! Even if his author were his only reader as was he himself of his work-in-progress as of the sentence-in-progress and his protagonist of his, et cetera, his character as reader was not the same as his character as author, a fact which might be turned to account. What suspense.

As he prepared to explore this possibility one of his mistresses whereof he had none entered his brown study unannounced. "The passion of love," she announced, "which I regard as no less essential to a satisfying life than those values itemized above and which I infer from my presence here that you too esteem highly, does not in fact play in your life a role of sufficient importance to sustain my presence here. It plays in fact little role at all outside your imaginative and/or ary life. I tell you this not in a criticizing spirit, for I judge you to be as capable of the sentiment aforementioned as any other imagin[ative], deep-feeling man in good physical health more or less precisely in the middle of the road of our life. What hampers, even cripples you in this regard is your final preference, which I refrain from analyzing, for the sedater, more responsible pleasures of monogamous fidelity and the serener affections of domesticity, notwithstanding the fact that your enjoyment of these is correspondingly inhibited though not altogether spoiled by an essentially romantical, unstable, irresponsible, death-wishing fancy. V. S. Pritchett, English critic and author, will put the matter succinctly in a soon-to-be-written essay on Flaubert, whose work he'll say depicts the course of ardent longings and violent desires that rise from the horrible, the sensual, and the sadistic. They turn into the virginal and mystical, only to become numb by satiety. At this point pathological boredom leads to a final desire for death and nothingness – the Romantic syndrome. If, not to be unfair, we qualify somewhat the terms horrible and sadistic and understand satiety to include a large measure of vicariousness, this description undeniably applies to one aspect of yourself and your work; and while your ditto has other, even contrary aspects, the net fact is that you have elected familial responsibilities and rewards – indeed, straight-laced middle-classness in general – over the higher expenses of spirit and wastes of shame attendant upon a less regular, more glamorous style of life. So to elect is surely admirable for the layman, even essential if the social fabric, without which there can be no culture, is to be preserved. For the artist, however, and in particular the writer, whose traditional material has been the passions of men and women, the choice is fatal. You having made it I bid you goodnight probably forever."

Even as she left he reached for the sleeping pills cached conveniently in his writing desk and was restrained from their administration only by his being in the process of completing a sentence, which he cravenly strung out at some sacrifice of rhetorical effect upon realizing that he was et cetera. Moreover he added hastily he had not described the intruder for his readers' vicarious satiety: a lovely woman she was, whom he did not after all describe for his readers' et cetera inasmuch as her appearance and character were inconstant. Her interruption of his work inspired a few sentences about the extent to which his fiction inevitably made public his private life, though the trespasses in this particular were as nothing beside those of most of his profession. That is to say, while he did not draw his characters and situations directly from life nor permit his author-protagonist to do so, any moderately attentive reader of his oeuvre, his what, could infer for example that its author feared for example schizophrenia, impotence creative and sexual, suicide – in short living and dying. His fictions were preoccupied with these fears among their other, more serious preoccupations. Hot dog. As of the sentence-in-progress he was not in fact unmanageably schizophrenic, impotent in either respect, or dead by his own hand, but there was always the next sentence to worry about. But there was always the next sentence to worry about. In sum he concluded hastily such limited self-exposure did not constitute a misdemeanor, representing or mis as it did so small an aspect of his total self, negligible a portion of his total life – even which totalities were they made public would be found remarkable only for their being so unremarkable. Well shall he continue.

Bearing in mind that he had not developed what he'd mentioned earlier about turning to advantage his situation vis-à-vis his "reader" (in fact he deliberately now postponed his return to that subject, sensing that it might well constitute the climax of his story) he elaborated one or two ancillary questions, perfectly aware that he was trying, even exhausting, whatever patience might remain to whatever readers might remain to whoever elaborated yet another ancillary question. Was the novel of his life for example a *roman à clef.* ? Of that genre he was as contemptuous as of the others aforementioned; but while in the introductory adverbial clause it seemed obvious to him that he didn't "stand for" anyone else, any more than he was an actor playing the role of himself, by the time he reached the main clause he had to admit that the question was unanswerable, since the "real" man to whom he'd correspond in a *roman à clef* would not be also in the *roman à clef* and the characters in such works were not themselves aware of their irritating correspondences.

Similarly unanswerable were such questions as when "his" story (so he regarded it for convenience and consolement though for all he knew he might be not the central character; it might be his wife's story, one of his daughter's, his imaginary mistress's, the man-who-once-cleaned-his-chimney's) began. Not impossibly at his birth or even generations earlier: a *Bildungsroman,* an *Erziehungsroman,* a *roman fleuve.* ! More likely at the moment he became convinced of his fictional nature: that's where he'd have begun it, as he'd begun the piece currently under his pen. If so it followed that the years of his childhood and younger manhood weren't "real," he'd suspected as much, in the first-order sense, but a mere "background" consisting of a few well-placed expository insinuations, perhaps misleading, or inferences, perhaps unwarranted, from strategic hints in his present reflections. God so to speak spare his readers from heavyfooted forced expositions of the sort that begin in the countryside near — in May of the year — it occurred to the novelist — that his own life might be a —, in which he was the leading or an accessory character. He happened at the time to be in the oak-wainscoted study of the old family summer residence; through a lavender cascade of hysteria he observed that his wife had once again chosen to be the subject of this clause, itself the direct object of his observation. A lovely woman she was, whom he did not describe in keeping with his policy against drawing characters from life as who should draw a condemnee to the gallows. Begging his pardon. Flinging his tiresome tale away he pushed impatiently through the French windows leading from his study to a sheer drop from the then-record high into a nearly fatal depression.

He clung onto his narrative depressed by the disproportion of its ratiocination to its dramatization, reflection to action. One had heard *Hamlet* criticized as a collection of soliloquies for which the implausible plot was a mere excuse; witnessed Italian operas whose dramatic portions were no more than interstitial relief and arbitrary continuity between the arias. If it was true that he didn't take his "real" life seriously enough even when it had him by the throat, the fact didn't lead him to consider whether the fact was a cause or a consequence of his tale's tedium or both.

Concluding these reflections he concluded these reflections: that there was at this advancèd page still apparently no ground-situation suggested that his story was dramatically meaningless. If one regarded the absence and his vain endeavors to supply the defect, as itself a sort of ground-situation, did his life-story thereby take on a kind of meaning? A "dramatic" sort he supposed, though of so sophistical a character as more likely to annoy than to engage.

III

The reader! You, dogged, uninsultable, print-oriented bastard, it's you I'm addressing, who else, from inside this monstrous fiction. You've read me this far, then? Even this far? For what discreditable motive? How is it you don't go to a movie, watch TV, stare at a wall, play tennis with a friend, make amorous advances to the person who comes to your mind when I speak of amorous advances? Can nothing surfeit, saturate you, turn you off? Where's your shame?

Having let go this barrage of rhetorical or at least unanswered questions and observing himself nevertheless in midst of yet another sentence he concluded and caused the "hero" of his story to conclude that one or more of three things must be true: 1) his author was his sole and indefatigable reader; 2) he was in a sense his own author, telling his story to himself, in which case in which case; and/or 3) his reader was not only tireless and shameless but sadistic, masochistic if he was himself.

For why do you suppose — you! you! — he's gone on so, so relentlessly refusing to entertain you as he might have at a less desperate than this hour of the world[4] with felicitous language, exciting situation, unforgettable character and image? Why has he as it were ruthlessly set about not to win you over but to turn you away? Because your own author bless and damn you his life is in your hands! He writes

[4] 11:00 P.M.; Monday, June 20, 1966.

and reads himself; don't you think he knows who gives his creatures their lives and deaths? Do they exist except as he or others read their words? Age except we turn their pages? And can he die until you have no more of him? Time was obviously when his author could have turned the trick; his pen had once to left-to-right it through these words as does your kindless eye and might have ceased at any one. This. This. And did not as you see but went on like an Oriental torturemaster to the end.

But you needn't! He exclaimed to you. In vain. Had he petitioned you instead to read slowly in the happy parts, what happy parts, swiftly in the painful no doubt you'd have done the contrary or cut him off entirely. But as he longs to die and can't without your help you force him on, force him on. Will you deny you've read this sentence? This? To get away with murder doesn't appeal to you, is that it? As if your hands weren't inky with other dyings! As if he'd know you'd killed him! Come on. He dares you.

In vain. You haven't: the burden of his knowledge. That he continues means that he continues, a fortiori you too. Suicide's impossible: he can't kill himself without your help. Those petitions aforementioned, even his silly plea for death — don't you think he understands their sophistry, having authored their like for the wretches he's authored? Read him fast or slow, intermittently, continuously, repeatedly, backward, not at all, he won't know it; he only guesses someone's reading or composing sentences such as this one; the net effect is that there's a net effect, of continuity and an apparently consistent flow of time, though his pages do seem to pass more swiftly as they near his end.

To what conclusion will he come? He'd been about to append to his own tale inasmuch as the old analogy between Author and God, novel and world, can no longer be employed unless deliberately as a false analogy, certain things follow: 1) fiction must acknowledge its fictitiousness and metaphoric invalidity or 2) choose to ignore the question or deny its relevance or 3) establish some other, acceptable relation between itself, its author, its reader. Just as he finished doing so however his real wife and imaginary mistresses entered his study; "It's a little past midnight" she announced with a smile; "do you know what that means?"

Though she'd come into his story unannounced at a critical moment he did not describe her, for even as he recollected that he'd seen his first light just thirty-six years before the night incumbent he saw his last: that he could not after all be a character in a work of fiction inasmuch as such a fiction would be of an entirely different character from what he thought of as fiction. Fiction consisted of such monuments of the imagination as Cutler's *Morganfield*, Riboud's *Tales Within Tales*, his own creations; fact of such as for example read those fictions. More, he could demonstrate by syllogism that the story of his life was a work of fact: though assaults upon the boundary between life and art, reality and dream, were undeniably a staple of his own and his century's literature as they'd been of Shakespeare's and Cervantes's, yet it was a fact that in the corpus of fiction as far as he knew no fictional character had become convinced as had he that he was a character in a work of fiction. This being the case and he having in fact become thus convinced it followed that his conviction was false. "Happy birthday," said his wife et cetera, kissing him et cetera to obstruct his view of the end of the sentence he was nearing the end of, playfully refusing to be nay-said so that in fact he did at last as did his fictional character end his ending story endless by interruption cap his pen.

DONALD BARTHELME b. 1931

The world of Barthelme's fiction seems so strange because he confines it within one time plane – the present. Whatever has produced the present circumstances is irrelevant; characters cannot comfort themselves with historical explanations of how they got into their present problems; they are made to confront them totally in the present. This lack of history allows Barthelme to present with great sharpness his sense of disparity, inconsequence, and incongruity in modern life – the way it feels to live rather than to think about living and try to explain it to yourself. The present that his characters confront is saturated with the debris of our civilization: bits and pieces of language from T.V. ads and billboards, politicians' speeches, literary criticism, popular science, debased psychology, and everything else that makes up our verbal junk pile. They have to "communicate" with this stuff, and the trouble is that they sound like somebody else, or the person they are talking to hears them as somebody else. "Honesty" is an overwhelming problem, and relationships seem either to happen because of a momentary harmony of discord or a sudden flash of violence that is, in effect, a throwing over of the burden of language.

Barthelme was born in Philadelphia, grew up in Texas, and went to the University of Houston. He now works in publishing in New York.

SEE THE MOON?

I know you think I'm wasting my time. You've made that perfectly clear. But I'm conducting these very important lunar hostility studies. And it's not you who'll have to leave the warm safe capsule. And dip a toe into the threatening lunar surround.

I am still wearing my yellow flower which has lasted wonderfully.

My methods may seem a touch light-minded. Have to do chiefly with folded paper airplanes at present. But the paper must be folded *in the right way.* Lots of calculations and worrying about edges.

Show me a man who worries about edges and I'll show you a natural-born winner. Cardinal Y agrees. Columbus himself worried, the Admiral of the Ocean Sea. But he kept it quiet.

The sun so warm on this screened porch, it reminds me of my grandmother's place in Tampa. The same rusty creaky green glider and the same faded colored canvas cushions. And at night the moon graphed by the screen wire, if you squint. The Sea of Tranquillity occupying squares 47 through 108.

See the moon? It hates us.

My methods are homely but remember Newton and the apple. And when Rutherford started out he didn't even have a decently heated laboratory. And then there's the matter of my security check – I'm waiting for the government. Somebody told it I'm insecure. *That's true.*

I suffer from a frightful illness of the mind, light-mindedness. It's not catching. You needn't shrink.

You've noticed the wall? I pin things on it, souvenirs. There is the red hat, there the book of instructions for the Ant Farm. And this is a traffic ticket written on a saint's day (which saint? I don't remember) in 1954 just outside a fat little town (which town? I don't remember) in Ohio by a cop who asked me what I did. I said I wrote poppycock for the president of a university, true then.

You can see how far I've come. Lunar hostility studies aren't for everyone.

It's my hope that these . . . souvenirs . . . will someday merge, blur – cohere is the word, maybe – into something meaningful. A grand word, meaningful. What do I look for? A work of art, I'll not accept anything less. Yes I know it's shatteringly ingenuous but I wanted to be a painter. They get away with murder in my view; Mr. X on the *Times* agrees with me. You don't know how I envy them. They can pick up a Baby Ruth wrapper on the street, glue it to the canvas (in the *right place,* of course, there's that), and lo! people crowd about and cry, "A real Baby Ruth wrapper, by God, what could be realer than that!" Fantastic metaphysical advantage. You hate them, if you're ambitious.

The Ant Farm instructions are a souvenir of Sylvia. The red hat came from Cardinal Y. We're friends, in a way.

I wanted to be one, when I was young, a painter. But I couldn't stand stretching the canvas. Does things to the fingernails. And that's the first place people look.

Fragments are the only forms I trust.

Light-minded or no, I'm . . . riotous with mental health. I measure myself against the Russians, that's fair. I have here a clipping datelined Moscow, four young people apprehended strangling a swan. *That's* boredom. The swan's name, Borka. The sentences as follows: Tsarev, metalworker, served time previously for stealing public property, four years in a labor camp, strict regime. Roslavtsev, electrician, jailed previously for taking a car on a joyride, three years and four months in a labor camp, semi-strict regime. Tatyana Voblikova (only nineteen and a Komsomol member too), technician, one and a half years in a labor camp, degree of strictness unspecified. Anna G. Kirushina, technical worker, fine of twenty per cent of salary for one year. Anna objected to the strangulation, but softly: she helped stuff the carcass in a bag.

The clipping is tacked up on my wall. I inspect it from time to time, drawing the moral. Strangling swans is wrong.

My brother who is a very distinguished pianist . . . has no fingernails at all. Don't look it's horrible. He plays under another name. And tunes his piano peculiarly, some call it sour. And renders *ragas* he wrote himself. A night *raga* played at noon can cause darkness, did you know that? It's extraordinary.

He wanted to be an Untouchable, Paul did. That was his idea of a contemporary career. But then a girl walked up and touched him (slapped him, actually; it's a complicated story). And he joined us, here in the imbroglio.

My father on the other hand is perfectly comfortable, and that's not a criticism. He makes flags, banners, bunting (sometimes runs me up a shirt). There was never any question of letting my father drink from the public well. He was on the Well Committee, he decided who dipped and who didn't. That's not a criticism. Exercises his creativity, nowadays, courtesy the emerging nations. Green for the veldt that nourishes the gracile Grant's gazelle, white for the purity of our revolutionary aspirations. The red for blood is understood. That's not a criticism. It's what they all ask for.

A call tonight from Gregory, my son by my first wife. Seventeen and at M.I.T. already. Recently he's been asking questions. Suddenly he's conscious of himself as a being with a history.

The telephone rings. Then, without a greeting: *Why did I have to take those little pills?* What little pills? *Little white pills with a "W" on them.* Oh. Oh yes. You had some kind of a nervous disorder, for a while. *How old was I?* Eight. Eight or nine. *What was it? Was it epilepsy?* Good God no, nothing so fancy. We never found out what it was. It went away. *What did I do? Did I fall down?* No no. Your mouth trembled, that was all. You couldn't control it. *Oh. O.K. See you.*

The receiver clicks.

Or: *What did my great-grandfather do? For a living I mean?* He was a ballplayer, semi-pro ballplayer, for a while. Then went into the building business. *Who'd he play for?* A team called the St. Augustine Rowdies, I think it was. *Never heard of them.* Well ... *Did he make any money? In the building business?* Quite a bit. *Did your father inherit it?* No, it was tied up in a lawsuit. When the suit was over there wasn't anything left. *Oh. What was the lawsuit?* Great-grandfather diddled a man in a land deal. So the story goes. *Oh. When did he die?* Let's see, 1938 I think. *What of?* Heart attack. *Oh. O.K. See you.*

End of conversation.

Gregory, you didn't listen to my advice. I said try the Vernacular Isles. Where fish are two for a penny and women two for a fish. But you wanted M.I.T. and electron-spin-resonance spectroscopy. You didn't even crack a smile in your six-ply heather hopsacking.

Gregory, you're going to have a half brother now. You'll like that, won't you? Will you half like it?

We talked about the size of the baby, Ann and I. What could be deduced from the outside.

I said it doesn't look very big to me. She said it's big enough for *us.* I said we don't need such a great roaring big one after all. She said they cost the earth, those extra-large sizes. Our holdings in Johnson's Baby Powder to be considered too. We'd need acres and acres. I said we'll put it in a Skinner box maybe. She said no child of hers. Displayed under glass like a rump roast. I said you haven't wept lately. She said I keep getting bigger whether I laugh or cry.

Dear Ann. I don't think you've quite ...

What you don't understand is, it's like somebody walks up to you and says, I have a battleship I can't use, would you like to have a battleship? And you say, yes yes, I've never had a battleship, I've always wanted one. And he says, it has four sixteen-inch guns forward, and a catapult for launching scout planes. And you say, I've always wanted to launch scout planes. And he says, *it's yours,* and then you have this battleship. And then you have to paint it, because it's rusting, and clean it, because it's dirty, and anchor it somewhere, because the Police Department wants you to get it off the streets. And the crew is crying, and there are silverfish in the chartroom and a funny knocking noise in Fire Control, water rising in the No. 2 hold, and the chaplain can't find the Palestrina tapes for the Sunday service. And you can't get anybody to sit with it. And finally you discover that what you have here is this great, big, pink-and-blue rockabye *battleship.*

Ann. I'm going to keep her ghostly. Just the odd bit of dialogue:

"What is little Gog doing."

"Kicking."

I don't want her bursting in on us with the freshness and originality of her observations. What we need is *perspective.* She's good with Gregory though. I think he half likes her.

Don't go. The greased-pig chase and balloon launchings come next.

I was promising once. After the Elgar, a *summa cum laude.* The university was proud of me. It was a bright shy white new university on the Gulf Coast. Gulls and oleanders and quick howling hurricanes. The teachers brown burly men with power boats and beer cans. The president a retired admiral who'd done beautiful things in the Coral Sea.

"You will be a credit to us, George," the admiral said. That's not my name. I'm protecting my identity, what there is of it.

Applause from the stands filled with mothers and brothers. Then following the mace in a long line back to the field house to ungown. Ready to take my place at the top.

But a pause at Pusan, and the toy train to the Chorwon Valley. Walking down a road wearing green clothes. Korea green and black and silent. The truce had been signed. I had a carbine to carry. My buddy Bo Tagliabue the bonus baby, for whom the Yanks had paid thirty thousand. We whitewashed rocks to enhance our area. Colonels came crowding to feel Bo's hurling arm. Mine the whitest rocks.

I lunched with Thais from Thailand, hot curry from great galvanized washtubs. Engineers banging down the road in six-by-sixes raising red dust. My friend Gib Mandell calling Elko, Nevada on his canvas-covered field telephone. "Operator I crave Elko, Nevada."

Then I was a sergeant with stripes, getting the troops out of the sun. Tagliabue a sergeant too. *Triste* in the Tennessee Tea Room in Tokyo, yakking it up in Yokohama. Then back to our little tent town on the side of a hill, boosting fifty-gallon drums of heating oil tentward in the snow.

Ozzie the jeep driver waking me in the middle of the night. "They got Julian in the Tango Tank." And up and alert as they taught us in Leadership School, over the hills to Tango, seventy miles away. Whizzing through Teapot, Tempest, Toreador, with the jeep's canvas top flapping. Pfc. Julian drunk and disorderly and beaten up. The M.P. sergeant held out a receipt book. I signed for the bawdy remains.

Back over the pearly Pacific in a great vessel decorated with oranges. A trail of orange peel on the plangent surface. Sitting in the bow fifty miles out of San

Francisco, listening to the Stateside disc jockeys chattering cha cha cha. Ready to grab my spot at the top.

My clothes looked old and wrong. The city looked new with tall buildings raised while my back was turned. I rushed here and there visiting friends. They were burning beef in their back yards, brown burly men with beer cans. The beef black on the outside, red on the inside. My friend Horace had fidelity. "Listen to that bass. That's forty watts worth of bass, boy."

I spoke to my father. "How is business?" "If Alaska makes it," he said, "I can buy a Hasselblad. And we're keeping an eye on Hawaii." Then he photographed my veteran face, f.6 at 300. My father once a cheerleader at a great Eastern school. Jumping in the air and making fierce angry down-the-field gestures at the top of his leap.

That's not a criticism. We have to have cheerleaders.

I presented myself at the Placement Office. I was on file. My percentile was the percentile of choice.

"How come you were headman of only one student organization, George?" the Placement Officer asked. Many hats for top folk was the fashion then.

I said I was rounded, and showed him my slash. From the Fencing Club.

"But you served your country in an overseas post."

"And regard my career plan on neatly typed pages with wide margins."

"Exemplary," the Placement Officer said. "You seem married, mature, malleable, how would you like to affiliate yourself with us here at the old school? We have a spot for a poppycock man, to write the admiral's speeches. Have you ever done poppycock?"

I said no but maybe I could fake it.

"Excellent, excellent," the Placement Officer said. "I see you have grasp. And you can sup at the Faculty Club. And there is a ten-percent discount on tickets for all home games."

The admiral shook my hand. "You will be a credit to us, George," he said. I wrote poppycock, sometimes cockypap. At four o'clock the faculty hoisted the cocktail flag. We drank Daiquiris on each other's sterns. I had equipped myself – a fibre-glass runabout, someplace to think. In the stadia of friendly shy new universities we went down the field on Gulf Coast afternoons with gulls, or exciting nights under the tall toothpick lights. The crowd roared. Sylvia roared. Gregory grew.

There was no particular point at which I stopped being promising.

Moonstruck I was, after a fashion. Sitting on a bench by the practice field, where the jocks chanted secret signals in their underwear behind tall canvas blinds. Layabout babies loafing on blankets, some staked out on twelve-foot dog chains. Brown mothers squatting knee to knee in shifts of scarlet and green. I stared at the moon's pale daytime presence. It seemed . . . inimical.

Moonstruck.

We're playing Flinch. You flinched.

The simplest things are the most difficult to explain, all authorities agree. Say I was tired of p***yc**k, if that pleases you. It's true enough.

Sylvia went up in a puff of smoke. She didn't like unsalaried life. And couldn't bear a male acquaintance moon-staring in the light of day. Decent people look at night.

We had trouble with Gregory: who would get which part. She settled for three-fifths, and got I think the worst of it, the dreaming raffish Romany part that thinks science will save us. I get matter-of-fact midnight telephone calls: *My E.E. instructor shot me down.* What happened? *I don't know, he's an ass anyhow.* Well that may be but still – *When's the baby due?* January, I told you. *Yeah, can I go to Mexico City for the holidays?* Ask your mother, you know she – *There's this guy, his old man has a villa. . . .* Well, we can talk about it. *Yeah, was grandmother a Communist?* Nothing so distinguished, she – *You said she was kicked out of Germany.* Her family was anti-Nazi. *Adler means eagle in German.* That's true. There was something called the Weimar Republic, her father – *I read about it.*

We had trouble with Gregory, we wanted to be scientific. Toys from Procreative Playthings of Princeton. O Gregory, that Princeton crowd got you coming and going. Procreative Playthings at one end and the Educational Testing Service at the other. And that serious-minded co-op nusery, that was a mistake. "A growing understanding between parent and child through shaped group experience." I still remember poor Henry Harding III. Under "Sibs" on the membership roll they listed his, by age:

26
25
23
20
19
15
10
9
8
6

O Mrs. Harding, haven't you heard? They have these little Christmas-tree ornaments for the womb now, they work wonders.

Did we do "badly" by Gregory? Will we do "better" with Gog? Such questions curl the hair. It's wiser not to ask.

I mentioned Cardinal Y (the red hat). He's a friend, in a way. Or rather, the subject of one of my little projects.

I set out to study cardinals, about whom science knows nothing. It seemed to me that cardinals could be known in the same way we know fishes or roses, by classification and enumeration. A doomed project, perhaps, but who else has embraced this point of view? Difficult nowadays to find a point of view kinky enough to call one's own, with Sade himself being carried through the streets on the shoulders of sociologists, cheers and shouting, ticker tape unwinding from high windows . . .

The why of Cardinal Y. You're entitled to an explanation.

The Cardinal rushed from the Residence waving in the air his hands, gloved in yellow pigskin it appeared. I grasped a hand. "Yes, yellow pigskin!" the Cardinal cried. I wrote in my book, *yellow pigskin.*

Significant detail. The pectoral cross contains nine diamonds, the scarlet soutane is laundered right on the premises.

I asked the Cardinal questions, we had a conversation.

"I am thinking of a happy island more beautiful than can be imagined," I said.

"I am thinking of a golden mountain which does not exist," he said.

"Upon what does the world rest?" I asked.

"Upon an elephant," he said.

"Upon what does the elephant rest?"

"Upon a tortoise."

"Upon what does the tortoise rest?"

"Upon a red lawnmower."

I wrote in my book, *playful.*

"Is there any value that has value?" I asked.

"If there is any value that has value, then it must lie outside the whole sphere of what happens and is the case, for all that happens and is the case is accidental," he said. He was not serious. I wrote in my book, *knows the drill.*

(Oh I has heard reports, how he slunk about in the snow telling children he was Santa Claus, how he disbursed funds in unauthorized disbursements to unshaven men who came to the kitchen door, how his housekeeper pointedly rolled his red socks together and black socks together hinting red with red and black with black, the Cardinal patiently unrolling a red ball to get a red sock and a black ball to get a black sock, which he then wore together. . . .)

Cardinal Y. He's sly.

I was thorough. I popped the Cardinal on the patella with a little hammer, and looked into his eyes with a little light. I tested the Cardinal's stomach acidity using Universal Indicator Paper, a scale of one to ten, a spectrum of red to blue. The pH value was 1 indicating high acidity. I measured the Cardinal's ego strength using the Minnesota Multiphasic Muzzle Map, he had an M.M.M.M. of four over three. I sang to the Cardinal, the song was "Stella by Starlight." He did not react in any way. I calculated the number of gallons needed to fill the Cardinal's bath to a depth of ten inches (beyond which depth, the Cardinal said, he never ventured). I took the Cardinal to the ballet, the ballet was "The Conservatory."

The Cardinal applauded at fifty-seven points. Afterward, backstage, the Cardinal danced with Plenosova, holding her at arm's length with a good will and an ill grace. The skirts of the scarlet soutane stood out to reveal high-button shoes, and the stagehands clapped.

I asked the Cardinal his views on the moon, he said they were the conventional ones, and that is how I know all I know about cardinals. Not enough perhaps to rear a science of cardinalogy upon, but enough perhaps to form a basis for the investigations of other investigators. My report is over there, in the blue binding, next to my copy of *La Géomancie et la Néomancie des Anciens* by the Seigneur of Salerno.

Cardinal Y. One can measure and measure and miss the most essential thing. I liked him. I still get the odd blessing in the mail now and then.

Too, maybe I was trying on the role. Not for myself. When a child is born, the locus of one's hopes . . . shifts, slightly. Not altogether, not all at once. But you feel it, this displacement. You speak up, strike attitudes, like the mother of a tiny Lollobrigida. Drunk with possibility once more.

I am still wearing my yellow flower which has lasted wonderfully.

"What is Gog doing."

"Sleeping."

You see, Gog of mine, Gog o' my heart, I'm just trying to give you a little briefing here. I don't want you unpleasantly surprised. I can't stand a startled look. Regard me as a sort of Distant Early Warning System. Here is the world and here are the knowledgeable knowers knowing. What can I tell you? What has been pieced together from the reports of travellers.

Fragments are the only forms I trust.

Look at my wall, it's all there. That's a leaf, Gog, stuck up with Scotch Tape. No no, the Scotch Tape is the shiny transparent stuff, the leaf the veined irregularly shaped . . .

There are several sides to this axe, Gog, consider the photostat, "Mr. W. B. Yeats Presenting Mr. George Moore to the Queen of the Fairies." That's a civilized gesture, I mean Beerbohm's. And when the sculptor Aristide Maillol went into the printing business he made the paper by *chewing the fibers himself.* That's dedication. And here is a Polaroid photo, shows your Aunt Sylvia and me putting an Ant Farm together. That's how close we were in those days. Just an Ant Farm apart.

See the moon? It hates us.

And now comes J. J. Sullivan's orange-and-blue Gulf Oil truck to throw kerosene into the space heater. Driver in green siren suit, red face, blond shaved head, the following rich verbal transaction:

"Beautiful day."

"Certainly is."

And now settling back in this green glider with a copy of *Man.* Dear Ann when I look at *Man* I don't want you. Unfolded Ursala Thigpen seems eversomuchmore desirable. A clean girl too and with interests, cooking, botany, pornographic novels. Someone new to show my slash to.

In another month Gog leaps fully armed from the womb. What can I do for him? I can get him into A.A., I have influence. And make sure no harsh moonlight falls on his new soft head.

Hello there Gog. We hope you'll be very happy here.

MARGINS

Edward was explaining to Carl about margins. "The *width* of the margin shows culture, aestheticism and a sense of values or the lack of them," he said. "A very wide left margin shows an impractical person of culture and refinement with a deep appreciation for the best in art and music. Whereas," Edward said, quoting his handwriting analysis book, "whereas, narrow left margins show the opposite. No left margin at all shows a practical nature, a wholesome economy and a general lack of good taste in the arts. A very wide *right* margin shows a person afraid to face reality, oversensitive to the future and generally a poor mixer."

"I don't believe in it," Carl said.

"Now," Edward continued, "with reference to your sign there, you have an *all-around wide margin* which shows a person of extremely delicate sensibilities with love of color and form, one who holds aloof from the multitude and lives in his own dream world of beauty and good taste."

"Are you sure you got that right?"

"I'm communicating with you," Edward said, "across a vast gulf of ignorance and darkness."

"*I* brought the darkness, is that the idea?" Carl asked.

"You brought the darkness, you black mother," Edward said. "Funky, man."

"Edward," Carl said, "for God's sake."

"Why did you write all that jazz on your sign, Carl? Why? It's not true, is it? Is it?"

"It's kind of true," Carl said. He looked down at his brown sandwich boards, which said: *I Was Put In Jail in Selby County Alabama For Five Years For Stealing A Dollar and A Half Which I Did Not Do. While I Was In Jail My Brother was Killed & My Mother Ran Away When I Was Little. In Jail I Began Preaching & I Preach to People Wherever I Can Bearing the Witness of Eschatological Love. I Have Filled Out Papers for Jobs But Nobody Will Give Me a Job Because I Have Been In Jail & The Whole Scene Is Very Dreary, Pepsi Cola. I Need Your Offerings to Get Food. Patent Applied For & Deliver Us From Evil.* "It's true," Carl said, "with a kind of *merde-y* inner truth which shines forth as the objective correlative of what actually did happen, back home."

"Now, look at the way you made that 'm' and that 'n' there," Edward said. "The tops are pointed rather than rounded. That indicates aggressiveness and energy. The fact that they're also pointed rather than rounded at the bottom indicates a sarcastic, stubborn and irritable nature. See what I mean?"

"If you say so," Carl said.

"Your capitals are very small," Edward said, "indicating humility."

"My mother would be pleased," Carl said, "if she knew."

"On the other hand, the excessive size of the loops in your 'y' and your 'g' display exaggeration and egoism."

"That's always been one of my problems," Carl answered.

"What's your whole name?" Edward asked, leaning against a building. They were on Fourteenth Street, near Broadway.

"Carl Maria von Weber," Carl said.

"Are you a drug addict?"

"Edward," Carl said, "you *are* a swinger."

"Are you a Muslim?"

Carl felt his long hair. "Have you read *The Mystery of Being,* by Gabriel Marcel? I really liked that one. I thought that one was fine."

"No, c'mon Carl, answer the question," Edward insisted. "There's got to be frankness and honesty between the races. Are you one?"

"I think an accommodation can be reached and the government is doing all it can at the moment," Carl said. "I think there's something to be said on all sides of the question. This is not such a good place to hustle, you know that? I haven't got but two offerings all morning."

"People like people who look neat," Edward said. "You look kind of crummy, if you don't mind my saying so."

"You really think it's too long?" Carl asked, feeling his hair again.

"Do you think I'm a pretty color?" Edward asked. "Are you envious?"

"No," Carl said. "Not envious."

"See? Exaggeration and egoism. Just like I said."

"You're kind of boring, Edward. To tell the truth."

Edward thought about this for a moment. Then he said: "But I'm white."

"It's the color of choice," Carl said. "I'm tired of talking about color, though. Let's talk about values or something."

"Carl, I'm a fool," Edward said suddenly.

"Yes," Carl said.

"But I'm a *white* fool," Edward said. "That's what's so lovely about me."

"You *are* lovely, Edward," Carl said. "It's true. You have a nice look. Your aspect is good."

"Oh, hell," Edward said despondently. "You're very well-spoken," he said. "I noticed that."

"The reason for that is," Carl said, "I read. Did you read *The Cannibal* by John Hawkes? I thought that was a hell of a book."

"Get a haircut, Carl," Edward said. "Get a new suit. Maybe one of those new Italian suits with the tight coats. You could be upwardly mobile, you know, if you just put your back into it."

"Why are you worried, Edward? Why does my situation distress you? Why don't you just walk away and talk to somebody else?"

"You bother me," Edward confessed. "I keep trying to penetrate your inner reality, to find out what it is. Isn't that curious?"

"John Hawkes also wrote *The Beetle Leg* and a couple of other books whose titles escape me at the moment," Carl said. "I think he's one of the best of our younger American writers."

"Carl," Edward said, "*what is* your inner reality? Blurt it out, baby."

"It's mine," Carl said quietly. He gazed down at his shoes, which resembled a pair of large dead brownish birds.

"Are you sure you didn't steal that dollar and a half mentioned on your sign?"

"Edward, I *told* you I didn't steal that dollar and a half." Carl stamped up and down in his sandwich boards. "It sure is *cold* here on Fourteenth Street."

"That's your imagination, Carl," Edward said. "This street isn't any colder than Fifth, or Lex. Your feeling that it's colder here probably just arises from your marginal status as a despised person in our society."

"Probably," Carl said. There was a look on his face. "You know I went to the government, and asked them to give me a job in the Marine Band, and they wouldn't do it?"

"Do you blow good, man? Where's your axe?"

"They woundn't *give* me that cotton-pickin' job," Carl said. "What do you think of that?"

"This eschatological love," Edward said, "what kind of love is that?"

"That is later love," Carl said. "That's what I call it, anyhow. That's love on the other side of the Jordan. The term refers to a set of conditions which . . . It's kind of a story we black people tell to ourselves to make ourselves happy."

"Oh me," Edward said. "Ignorance and darkness."

"Edward," Carl said, "you don't *like* me."

"I do too like you, Carl," Edward said. "Where do you steal your books, mostly?"

"Mostly in drugstores," Carl said. "I find them good because mostly they're long and narrow and the clerks tend to stay near the prescription counters at the back of the store, whereas the books are usually in those revolving racks near the front of the store. It's normally pretty easy to slip a couple in your overcoat pocket, if you're wearing an overcoat."

"But . . ."

"Yes," Carl said, "I know what you're thinking. If I'll steal books I'll steal other things. But stealing books is metaphysically different from stealing money. Villon has something pretty good to say on the subject I believe."

"Is that in 'If I Were King'?"

"Besides," Carl added, "haven't *you* ever stolen anything? At some point in your life?"

"My life," Edward said. "Why do you remind me of it?"

"Edward, you're not satisfied with your life! I thought white lives were *nice!*" Carl said, surprised. "I love that word 'nice.' It makes me so happy."

"Listen Carl," Edward said, "why don't you just concentrate on improving your handwriting."

"My character, you mean."

"No," Edward said, "don't bother improving your character. Just improve your handwriting. Make larger capitals. Make smaller loops in your 'y' and your 'g'. Watch your word-spacing so as not to display disorientation. Watch your margins."

"It's an idea. But isn't that kind of a superficial approach to the problem?"

"Be careful about the spaces between the lines," Edward went on. "Spacing of lines shows clearness of thought. Pay attention to your finals. There are twenty-two different kinds of finals and each one tells a lot about a person. I'll lend you the book. Good handwriting is the key to advancement, or if not *the* key, at least *a* key. You could be the first man of your race to be Vice-President."

"That's something to shoot for, all right."

"Would you like me to go get the book?"

"I don't think so," Carl said, "no thanks. It's not that I don't have any faith in your solution. What I *would* like is to take a leak. Would you mind holding my sandwich boards for a minute?"

"Not at all," Edward said, and in a moment had slipped Carl's sandwich boards over his own slight shoulders. "Boy, they're kind of heavy, aren't they?"

"They cut you a bit," Carl said with a malicious smile. "I'll just go into this men's store here."

When Carl returned the two men slapped each other sharply in the face with the back of the hand, that beautiful part of the hand where the knuckles grow.

JOHN UPDIKE b. 1932

Updike was born and grew up in a small town in Pennsylvania Dutch country. Undoubtedly it was there that he developed the basic sensibility in his fiction: that of a dutiful, sensitive small-town American boy, very much down-to-earth, curious, observant, and yet accepting of different life styles. Updike went to Harvard, where he had ample opportunity to employ these qualities in reacting to an urbane, intellectual environment, in which (in the early fifties anyway) everyone seemed busy copying, creating, or maintaining any of a multitude of different life-styles. The seemingly assured Old Boston or Main Line types, the would-be executives demonstrating efficiency and open-mindedness, the esthetes, the gifted scientists more or less untouched by the society around them – Updike observed them all, without committing himself very deeply to any. He soon knew that he wanted to be a writer, probably a poet; but he had impressive talents in art too, and after leaving Harvard he won a place at the Ruskin School of Drawing in Oxford. When he returned from England he decided to give himself five years to make it as a writer; but after only a few months it was clear that he was headed for a career that most undergraduate writers dare not let themselves dream of. At twenty-four his work began to appear in *The New Yorker,* and soon he was one of that magazine's most valued writers. His first novel, *The Poorhouse Fair* (1959), was marked by a highly developed, maybe "poetic" prose style, and a warm appreciation of the small-town values that had been part of his boyhood and adolescence. Five other novels have followed, plus collections of his short stories from *The New Yorker.*

The characteristic note produced by the intersection of Updike's basic sensibility with one or more sophisticated ways of life is one of gentle ironic self-awareness. The vacationer in "The Doctor's Wife" recognizes the bigotry of the wife, but at the same time he is incapable of condemning her, for she makes him aware of his own limitations as a sincere though not specially passionate liberal.

Updike is sometimes attacked as precious, because of his evident love of the sound and arrangement of language, and as too narrow in the spectrum of experience with which he is willing to deal; but no one in contemporary fiction is better at representing the special feelings of guilt and quasi-involvement of those who see clearly but are not themselves committed.

A & P

In walks these three girls in nothing but bathing suits. I'm in the third checkout slot, with my back to the door, so I don't see them until they're over by the bread. The one that caught my eye first was the one in the plaid green two-piece. She was a chunky kid, with a good tan and a sweet broad soft-looking can with those two crescents of white just under it, where the sun never seems to hit, at the top of the backs of her legs. I stood there with my hand on a box of HiHo crackers trying to remember if I rang it up or not. I ring it up again and the customer starts giving me hell. She's one of these cash-register-watchers, a witch about fifty with rouge on her cheekbones and no eyebrows, and I know it made her day to trip me up. She'd been watching cash registers for fifty years and probably never seen a mistake before.

By the time I got her feathers smoothed and her goodies into a bag – she gives me a little snort in passing, if she'd been born at the right time they would have burned her over in Salem – by the time I get her on her way the girls had circled around the bread and were coming back, without a pushcart, back my way along the counters, in the aisle between the checkouts and the Special bins. They didn't even have shoes on. There was this chunky one, with two-piece – it was bright green and the seams on the bra were still sharp and her belly was still pretty pale so I guessed she just got it (the suit) – there was this one, with one of those chubby berry-faces, the lips all bunched together under her nose, this one, and a tall one, with black hair that hadn't quite frizzed right, and one of these sunburns right across the eyes, and a chin that was too long – you know, the kind of girl other girls think is very "striking" and "attractive" but never quite makes it, as they very well know, which is why they like her so much – and then the third one, that wasn't quite so tall. She was the queen. She kind of led them, the other two peeking around and making their shoulders round. She didn't look around, not this queen, she just walked straight on slowly, on these long white prima-donna legs. She came down a little hard on her heels, as if she didn't walk in her bare feet that much, putting down her heels and then letting the weight move along to her toes as if she was testing the floor with every step, putting a little deliberate extra action into it. You never know for sure how girls' minds work (do you really think it's a mind in there or just a little buzz like a bee in a glass jar?) but you got the idea she had talked the other two into coming in here with her, and now she was showing them how to do it, walk slow and hold yourself straight.

She had on a kind of dirty-pink – beige maybe, I don't know – bathing suit with a little nubble all over it and, what got me, the straps were down. They were off her shoulders looped loose around the cool tops of her arms, and I guess as a result the suit had slipped a little on her, so all around the top of the cloth there was this shining rim. If it hadn't been there you wouldn't have known there could have been anything whiter than those shoulders. With the straps pushed off, there was nothing between the top of the suit and the top of her head except just *her,* this clean bare plane of the top of her chest down from the shoulder bones like a dented sheet of metal tilted in the light. I mean, it was more than pretty.

She had sort of oaky hair that the sun and salt had bleached, done up in a bun that was unravelling, and a kind of prim face. Walking into the A & P with your straps down, I suppose it's the only kind of face you *can* have. She held her head so high her neck, coming up out of those white shoulders, looked kind of stretched, but I didn't mind. The longer her neck was, the more of her there was.

She must have felt in the corner of her eye me and over my shoulder Stokesie in the second slot watching, but she didn't tip. Not this queen. She kept her eyes moving across the racks, and stopped, and turned so slow it made my stomach rub the inside of my apron, and buzzed to the other two, who kind of huddled against her for relief, and then they all three of them went up the cat-and-dog-food-breakfast-cereal-macaroni-rice-raisins-seasonings-spreads-spaghetti-soft-drinks-crackers-and-cookies aisle. From the third slot I look straight up this aisle to the meat counter, and I watched them all the way. The fat one with the tan sort of fumbled with the cookies, but on second thought she put the packages back. The sheep pushing their carts down the aisle – the girls were walking against the usual traffic (not that we have one-way signs or anything) – were pretty hilarious. You could see them, when Queenie's white shoulders dawned on them, kind of jerk, or hop, or hiccup, but their eyes snapped back to their own baskets and on they pushed. I bet you could set off dynamite in an A & P and the people would by and large keep reaching and checking oatmeal off their lists and muttering "Let me see, there was a third thing, began with A, asparagus, no, ah, yes, applesauce!" or whatever it is they do mutter. But there was no doubt, this jiggled them. A few houseslaves in pin curlers even looked around after pushing their carts past to make sure what they had seen was correct.

You know, it's one thing to have a girl in a bathing suit down on the beach, where what with the glare nobody can look at each other much anyway, and another thing in the cool of the A & P, under the fluorescent lights, against all those stacked packages, with her feet paddling along naked over our checkerboard green-and-cream rubber-tile floor.

"Oh Daddy," Stokesie said beside me. "I feel so faint."

"Darling," I said. "Hold me tight." Stokesie's married, with two babies chalked up on his fuselage already, but as far as I can tell that's the only difference. He's twenty-two, and I was nineteen this April.

"Is it done?" he asks, the responsible married man finding his voice. I forgot to say he thinks he's going to be manager some sunny day, maybe in 1990 when it's called the Great Alexandrov and Petrooshki Tea Company or something.

What he meant was, our town is five miles from a beach, with a big summer colony out on the Point, but we're right in the middle of town, and the women generally put on a shirt or shorts or something before they get out of the car into the street. And anyway these are usually women with six children and varicose veins mapping their legs and nobody, including them, could care less. As I say, we're right in the middle of town, and if you stand at our front doors you can see two banks and the Congregational church and the newspaper store and three real-estate offices and about twenty-seven old freeloaders tearing up Central Street because the sewer broke again. It's not as if we're on the Cape; we're north of Boston and there's people in this town haven't seen the ocean for twenty years.

The girls had reached the meat counter and were asking McMahon something. He pointed, they pointed, and they shuffled out of sight behind a pyramid of Diet Delight peaches. All that was left for us to see was old McMahon patting his mouth and looking after them sizing up their joints. Poor kids, I began to feel sorry for them, they couldn't help it.

• • •

Now here comes the sad part of the story, at least my family says it's sad, but I don't think it's sad myself. The store's pretty empty, it being Thursday afternoon, so there was nothing much to do except lean on the register and wait for the girls to show up again. The whole store was like a pinball machine and I didn't know which tunnel they'd come out of. After a while they come around out of the far aisle, around the light bulbs, records at discount of the Caribbean Six or Tony Martin Sings or some such gunk you wonder they waste the wax on, sixpacks of candy bars, and plastic toys done up in cellophane that fall apart when a kid looks at them anyway. Around they come, Queenie still leading the way, and holding a little gray jar in her hand. Slots Three through Seven are unmanned and I could see her wondering between Stokes and me, but Stokesie with his usual luck draws an old party in baggy gray pants who stumbles up with four giant cans of pineapple juice (what do these bums *do* with all that pineapple juice? I've often asked myself) so the girls come to me. Queenie puts down the jar and I take it into my fingers icy cold. Kingfish Fancy Herring Snacks in Pure Sour Cream: 49¢. Now her hands are empty, not a ring or a bracelet, bare as God made them, and I wonder where the money's coming from. Still with that prim look she lifts a folded dollar bill out of the hollow at the center of her nubbled pink top. The jar went heavy in my hand. Really, I thought that was so cute.

Then everybody's luck begins to run out. Lengel comes in from haggling with a truck full of cabbages on the lot and is about to scuttle into that door marked MANAGER behind which he hides all day when the girls touch his eye. Lengel's pretty dreary, teaches Sunday school and the rest, but he doesn't miss that much. He comes over and says, "Girls, this isn't the beach."

Queenie blushes, though maybe it's just a brush of sunburn I was noticing for the first time, now that she was so close. "My mother asked me to pick up a jar of herring snacks." Her voice kind of startled me, the way voices do when you see the people first, coming out so flat and dumb yet kind of tony, too, the way it ticked over "pick up" and "snacks." All of a sudden I slid right down her voice into her living room. Her father and the other men were standing around in ice-cream coats and bow ties and the women were in sandals picking up herring snacks on toothpicks off a big glass plate and they were all holding drinks the color of water with olives and sprigs of mint in them. When my parents have somebody over they get lemonade and if it's a real racy affair Schlitz in tall glasses with "They'll Do It Every Time" cartoons stencilled on.

"That's all right," Lengel said. "But this isn't the beach." His repeating this struck me as funny, as if it had just occurred to him, and he had been thinking all these years the A & P was a great big dune and he was the head lifeguard. He didn't like my smiling – as I say he doesn't miss much – but he concentrates on giving the girls that sad Sunday-school-superintendent stare.

Queenie's blush is no sunburn now, and the plump one in plaid, that I liked better from the back – a really sweet can – pipes up, "We weren't doing any shopping. We just came in for the one thing."

"That makes no difference," Lengel tells her, and I could see from the way his eyes went that he hadn't noticed she was wearing a two-piece before. "We want you decently dressed when you come in here."

"We *are* decent," Queenie says suddenly, her lower lip pushing, getting sore now that she remembers her place, a place from which the crowd that runs the A & P must look pretty crummy. Fancy Herring Snacks flashed in her very blue eyes.

"Girls, I don't want to argue with you. After this come in here with your shoulders covered. It's our policy." He turns his back. That's policy for you. Policy is what the kingpins want. What the others want is juvenile delinquency.

All this while, the customers had been showing up with their carts but, you know, sheep, seeing a scene, they had all bunched up on Stokesie, who shook open a paper bag as gently as peeling a peach, not wanting to miss a word. I could feel in the silence everybody getting nervous, most of all Lengel, who asks me, "Sammy, have you rung up their purchase?"

I thought and said "No" but it wasn't about that I was thinking. I go through the punches, 4, 9, GROC, TOT — it's more complicated than you think, and after you do it often enough, it begins to make a little song, that you hear words to, in my case "Hello (*bing*) there, you (*gung*) hap-py p*ee*-pul (*splat*)!" — the *splat* being the drawer flying out. I uncrease the bill, tenderly as you may imagine, it just having come from between the two smoothest scoops of vanilla I had ever known were there, and pass a half and a penny into her narrow pink palm, and nestle the herrings in a bag and twist its neck and hand it over, all the time thinking.

The girls, and who'd blame them, are in a hurry to get out, so I say "I quit" to Lengel quick enough for them to hear, hoping they'll stop and watch me, their unsuspected hero. They keep right on going, into the electric eye; the door flies open and they flicker across the lot to their car, Queenie and Plaid and Big Tall Goony-Goony (not that as raw material she was so bad), leaving me with Lengel and a kink in his eyebrow.

"Did you say something, Sammy?"

"I said I quit."

"I thought you did."

"You didn't have to embarrass them."

"It was they who were embarrassing us."

I started to say something that came out "Fiddle-de-doo." It's a saying of my grandmother's, and I know she would have been pleased.

"I don't think you know what you're saying," Lengel said.

"I know you don't," I said. "But I do." I pull the bow at the back of my apron and start shrugging it off my shoulders. A couple customers that had been heading for my slot begin to knock against each other, like scared pigs in a chute.

Lengel sighs and begins to look very patient and old and gray. He's been a friend of my parents for years. "Sammy, you don't want to do this to your Mom and Dad," he tells me. It's true, I don't. But it seems to me that once you begin a gesture it's fatal not to go through with it. I fold the apron, "Sammy" stitched in red on the pocket, and put it on the counter, and drop the bow tie on top of it. The bow tie is theirs, if you've ever wondered. "You'll feel this for the rest of your life," Lengel says, and I know that's true, too, but remembering how he made that pretty girl blush makes me so scrunchy inside I punch the No Sale tab and the machine whirs "pee-pul" and the drawer splats out. One advantage to this scene taking place in summer, I can follow this up with a clean exit, there's no fumbling around getting your coat and galoshes, I just saunter into the electric eye in my white shirt that my mother ironed the night before, and the door heaves itself open, and outside the sunshine is skating around on the asphalt.

I look around for my girls, but they're gone, of course. There wasn't anybody but some young married screaming with her children about some candy they didn't get by the door of a powder-blue Falcon station wagon. Looking back in the big windows, over the bags of peat moss and aluminum lawn furniture stacked on the pavement, I could see Lengel in my place in the slot, checking the sheep through. His face was dark gray and his back stiff, as if he'd just had an injection of iron, and my stomach kind of fell as I felt how hard the world was going to be to me hereafter.

THE DOCTOR'S WIFE

"Sharks?" The tip of the doctor's wife's freckled nose seemed to sharpen in the sparkling air. Her eyes, momentarily rendered colorless by thought, took up the green of the Caribbean; the plane of the water intersected her throat. "Yes, we have some. Big dark fellows, too."

Ralph, hanging beside her, squatting on buoyance, straightened up, splashing, and tried to survey the beryl depths around him. His sudden movements rendered even the immediate water opaque. The doctor's wife's surprisingly young laughter rang out.

"You Americans," she said, "so nervy," and with complacence pushed a little deeper into the sea, floating backward while the water gently bubbled around her mouth. She had a small face, gone freckled and rosy in this climate; her stringy auburn hair had been dulled by daily sea-bathing. "They rarely come in this far," she said, tilting her face upward and speaking to the sky. "Only in the turtle killing season, when the blood draws them in. We're fortunate. Our beaches go out shallowly. Over in St. Martin, now, the offshore water is deep, and they must be careful."

She turned and, with the casual paddling stroke of a plump woman who floats easily, swam smiling toward him. "A shame," she said, her voice strained by the effort of curving her throat to keep her lips free, "Vic Johnson is gone. He was a dear soul. The old Anglican vicar." She pronounced "vicar" rather harshly, perhaps humorously. She stood up beside Ralph and pointed to the horizon. "Now *he*," she said, "used to swim far out into the bay, he and his great black dog Hooker. Vic would swim straight out, until he couldn't move a muscle, and then he would float, and grab Hooker's tail, and the dog would pull him in. Honestly, it was a sight, this fat old English gentleman, his white hair streaming, coming in on the tail of a dog. He never gave a thought to sharks. Oh, he'd swim *way* out, until he was just a dot."

They were waist-deep in the sea, and at a motion from Ralph they walked toward shore together. The calm warm water leaped from their strides. She was small beside him, and her voice piped at his shoulder. "I'm sorry he's gone," she said. "He was a lovely old gentleman. He had been here forty years. He loved the island."

"I can see why he would," Ralph said. He turned his head to review the crescent of landscape around the beach, as if through his fresh eyes the doctor's wife could renew — what obscurely seemed to him to need nenewing — her sense of the island's beauty. The white beach was empty. The natives used it only as a path. Their homes were set behind the ragged hedge of sea grape that rimmed the sand. Bits of tarpaper, pink-painted cement, corrugated roofing reddened by rust, wooden walls weathered to silver and patched by flattened kerosene tins, shacks on stilts, and unfinished cinder-block shells peeped above the dull, low foliage. There were few flowers. This was January. But the clusters of coconuts nested under the shuffling branches of the palms, and the high, small, soft clouds, like the quick clouds of spring in his own climate, suggested that here the season of bloom and the season of harvest were parallel and perpetual: germination and fruition ceaselessly intertwined. There were no mountains in the view. The island was low; when they came in on the airplane, it seemed a two-dimensional twin, or sketch, of St. Martin, which thrust from the sea like a set of Vermont mountaintops. There the beaches were steep and dangerous, here, they were safe. There, Dutchmen and Frenchmen built bustling hotels and restaurants to entice American dollars; here, strangers rarely came. Here, even the place names were bestowed without enterprise or effort. East End, West End, The Road, The Forest — thus the island was geographically divided. The uninhabited ridge of scrub and coral rubble that formed one side of the bay was named High Hill. The village was called The Bay. The orange cliffs on the other side of the bay were called The Cliffs. During these short winter days the sun set on a diagonal above them and, between six and seven o'clock, touched the sea at the fingertips of the most distant arm of land. Yet after the sun had drowned, light, itself lazy, lingered among the huts and the oleander bushes. Now it was late afternoon; the tiny tropical sun, not yet swollen to red, patiently poured white brilliance down through the hushed air. The air was as soft, as kind, as the water; there was no hostility in either. The two elements, as Ralph came out of one into the other, seemed tints of a single enveloping benevolence.

"Oh, yes, but not merely that," the doctor's wife said. "He loved the people. He built them three churches and, oh, did all manner of good works. We're talking of Reverend Johnson," she explained to Eve, who had remained on the beach with the children. "The Anglican padre. He retired last year and went back to England. Sussex, I think."

"He loved the people?" Eve asked. She had heard. Voices carried well in the air, disturbed, during the day, by only the whispering beat of the surf and infrequent voices calling in English made musical by an unintelligible lilt.

The doctor's wife dropped down on the sand. "These are my children," she intoned gruffly. She chased the abrupt parody away with her sharp laughter. "Oh, yes, he loved them. He gave his life to them." The youthful excitement of her voice and the innocent clarity of her eyes went queerly with her body, which was middle-aged. Her plump legs had gone lumpy and sodden, and her small face was finely wrinkled, each wrinkle accented by a line of white where the pinched skin had evaded the sun. "He didn't have any children of his own," she thought to add. "Just this dreadful dog Hooker. Such a funny old man. You might have liked him. I'm sure you never see his kind in America."

"I know we would have liked him," Eve said. "Hannah often mentions Reverend Johnson." Hannah was their cook, a woman of over thirty yet as shy and subtle as a girl. Her skin was always shining as if in embarrassment, but she had a jaunty way of crooning hymns to herself in the kitchen. The children, at first timid of her color, adored her, and listened with eyes rounded by delight when she held up a two-tone forefinger and told them to be good. Goodness had never before been presented to them seriously. Ralph and Eve had not expected a servant. They had picked the most obscure island they could find. But Hannah came with the house; the owner, a svelte widow who had children in Florida, Peru, and Antigua, assumed they would need her. As it turned out, they did. They could never have unravelled alone all the riddles of this novel world. Eve could never have managed the shopping, which was carried on by gossip – invisible voices as liquid as the wind, telling who had just slaughtered a pig, and whose fishing boat had come in with a catch. The village was full of stores; almost every shack at least sold – for disturbingly discrepant prices – American cigarettes smuggled from St. Martin. But even the business hours of the most official store, a cement corridor of shelves attached to the customs office, had proved a mystery the Americans were unable to crack. They always found barred the large green door bearing in wobbly chalk script the ancient announcement, "Attention Members! Attention Friends! This Store will be CLOSED Thursday afternoon."

"Oh, Hannah. She's a good girl," the doctor's wife said, and rolled over on her stomach. The corrugated backs of her thighs were frosted with sand like wet sugar.

"She *is*, you know," Eve said. "She's lovely. I think they're all lovely. They've all been lovely to us." Such insistence was unlike his wife. Ralph wondered what was between the two women, who had just met a day ago. "I can see why Reverend Johnson loved the people," Eve added in a deliberate, though cautiously soft, voice. "The people" were all around them; their huts came down to the edge of the sand, and, windows shuttered, the patched walls seemed to be listening raptly.

The doctor's wife rolled over again and returned to a sitting position. What was making her so restless?

"Yes," she said, and an especially heavy curl of surf foamed up the white slope and soaked in just short of their feet. The sand was porous; innumerable punctures dotted it, the breathing holes of crabs. The doctor's wife's eyes fixed on the horizon and became, from the side, colorless lenses. Her nose in profile turned acute. "They're simple souls," she said.

The doctor's wife was a queen here. She was the only fully white woman resident on the island. When the rare British official and the rare, fantastically minor member of royalty came to grace this most remote and docile scrap of empire with a visit, she was the hostess. When she roared along the dirt roads in her spattered English Ford – its muffler had long ago rotted away – the older natives touched their foreheads ironically and the children flapped their arms in her wake of dust. When she and the doctor condescended to call upon the American family staying three weeks in The Bay, Hannah had trembled with pride and broken a cup in the kitchen. The doctor was a slight, rapid-voiced man with a witty air of failure. His fingertips were dyed deep yellow by smuggled cigarettes. He preferred Camels, but Chesterfields were all that were coming through now. He had never seen a filtered cigarette. He and his wife had been ten years in the tropics – B.G., Trinidad, Barbados, now this. He had some vague scheme of getting to America and making a fortune and retiring to a Yorkshire village. He was off for the day to St. Martin.

"In America, now," the doctor's wife said, vehemently brushing sand from her knees, "are the coloreds well cared for?"

"How do you mean?" Eve asked.

"Are they well off?"

"Not really," Ralph said, because he sensed that it would be better if he, rather than Eve, answered. "In some parts better than others. In the South, of course, they're openly discriminated against; in the North they by and large have to live in the city slums but a least they have full legal rights."

"Oh dear," the doctor's wife said. "It is a problem, isn't it?"

Eve's face flashed up from studying a shell. "Whose problem?" she asked. She was a graduate of one of those female colleges where only a member of a racial minority or a cripple can be elected class president. News from South Africa made her voice thrash, and she was for anyone – Castro, Ben-Gurion, Martin Luther King – who in her mind represented an oppressed race. That such automatic sympathy was itself condescending had not occurred to her. Of English blood, enriched by remote and aristocratic injections of French and Russian, she denied the less favored even the compliment of fearing them.

The doctor's wife returned her gaze to the horizon, and Ralph wondered if they had been rude. In the woman's pointed profile there was a certain perhaps deliberately noble thrust. But, the hostess, she relented and tried to make the conversation go again. She turned her head, shading her eyes with a quick hand and exposing her neat white teeth in a tense smile. "The schools," she said. "Can they go to your schools?"

"Of course," Ralph said swiftly, at the same time realizing that for her there was no "of course" to it. She knew nothing about his country. He felt firmer, having gauged her ignorance, and having moved to the hard ground of information. "Nobody denies them schools. In the South the schools are segregated. But in the North, and the West, and so on, there's no problem." He hunched his shoulders, feeling at his back Eve's disapproval of his saying "problem."

"But" – the doctor's wife's freckles gathered under her eyes as she squinted into the focus of the issue – "would *your* children go to school with them?"

"Sure. Good heavens. Why not?" He was relieved to clear this up, to lock this door. He hoped the doctor's wife would now turn away and talk of something else.

She sighed. "Of course, you in America have lived with the problem so long. In England, now, they're just waking up; the blacks are *pouring* into London."

A wave, pushed by one behind it, slid so far up the slant of sand their feet were delicately shocked and soaked. For a few seconds their ankles glittered in rippling sleeves of retreating water. Eve said slowly, "You talk as if they had asked to be made slaves and brought here."

"Mommy, look! Mommy, look!" Kate's voice, mingling with Larry's babyish yips of excitement, came from far down the beach. Their little silhouettes were jiggling around something dark at their feet, and out of the sea grape an old woman in a kerchief and a young sailor with a naked chest had emerged to watch them, amused to see what amused these strange children. Eve rose, casting down, for Ralph to see, a startled and indignant look at the doctor's wife's body, as if it were an offensive piece of rubbish washed up on the pure sands of her mind.

As Eve walked away, the doctor's wife said, "Doesn't she take a tan beautifully?"

"Yes, she always does. She's part French." With his wife out of earshot, Ralph relaxed into the sand. Mediating between the two women had demanded an exhausting equilibrium. He resigned himself to listening; he knew the doctor's wife's tongue would be loosened. The presence of another white queen inhibited her, diluted her authority.

"Do you want to hear a frightening story?"

"Sure." He acquiesced uneasily. The attention of the houses behind them seemed to grow more intense. He felt that he and his family were liked in the village; the doctor's wife, driving down from the center of the island to enjoy their beach, assumed an incriminating alliance which he did not wish to exist. For when the sun went down, she would go home, leaving them alone in the village with the night and its noises.

"When Vic Johnson left," she said, lowering her voice and sinking back on her elbow, to bring her face closer to his, "they had a party to greet the new parson, a very nice young colored boy from St. Kitts. *Very* nice, I must say, and they say very intelligent, though I haven't heard him preach. Well, the Warden – you haven't met him, and I daresay you won't, a big smooth Jamaican, takes himself oh *ever* so seriously – the Warden makes this little speech. He of course mentions Vic, forty years and so on, but right at the end he says that he knows we will not miss Reverend Johnson, because the new vicar is such a fine young man, comes to us with such an excellent record of study, and the rest of it, and furthermore, *furthermore,* what makes us especially happy and proud, he is one of us. Imagine! One of us! Of course, the young parson was embarrassed to death. It made me so mad I would have jumped up and left if the doctor hadn't held my hand. *One of us!* Vic had given his life to these people."

Her voice had become shrill; Ralph spoke in the hope of restraining it. "It seems unnecessary; but natural," he said.

"I don't see anything natural about it. *Un*natural, in my book. Unnatural, childish ingratitude. You just don't know how unnatural these people are. If you could see one-tenth of the antics, and then the selfishness, the doctor puts up with. At two in the morning, 'Doctor, Doctor, come save my child,' and then a week later, when he tries to collect his poor little dollar or two, they don't *remember.* They don't remember at all. And if he insists – 'The white people are stealing our money.' Oh. I hate them. God forgive me, I've come to hate them. They're *not* natural. They're not fully human." Seeing his hand begin a protesting movement, she added, "And for that matter, do you know what they say about you and your wife?" It was as if a shadow cruising through her words now made its lunge.

"No. Do they say something?"

"This is just to show how malicious they are. They say your wife has a touch of the brush." It took Ralph a moment to expand "brush" into "tarbrush." He laughed; what else?

The doctor's wife laughed, too; but under the blond eyebrows her blue eyes, the pupils pinpricks in the sun, were fixed on his face. She expected his face to crack and the truth to escape. "You see how dark she is," she explained. "How tan." He watched her tongue tick as she suspensefully pronounced the last two words. Girlish curiosity gave a taut surface to her mature malice.

Blood rushed through his body; the wound was confused; his anger entangled him with his attacker. He was supplying an absurd assault with teeth out of himself. "She just naturally gets that brown."

"And you see," the doctor's wife went on, still not unpinning her eyes from his face, "that's why they say you came here. No tourists come here, least of all with children. They say your wife's being part Negro has kept you out of the hotels on the better islands."

He felt certain that this ingenious argument was wholly her own. "We came here because it was cheap," he said.

"Of *course,*" she said, "of *course,*" and giggled, sensing that she had exposed herself to his defense. "But they can't believe that. They believe, you see, that all Americans are *rich.*" Which was just what, Ralph knew, she and the doctor believed.

He stood up, wet sand collapsing from his legs. In an effort to rein his excitement, he threw several unrelated laughs, as if out of a renewed realization of absurdity, outward into the air. He looked down at the woman and said, "Well, that explains why they seem to like her better than me."

The doctor's wife, having strained her neck to squint up at him, collapsed the rest of the way. She pillowed her head with one arm and threw the other over her eyes. Without her eyes her lips seemed vague and numb. "Oh, no," she said. "They hate her for getting away with it."

His laughter this time was totally vacant; it humiliated him. "I think I'll go in again," he said. "Before the sun fades."

"It won't fade," was the faint answer.

From the safety of the water he watched his dark wife herd two pale, burned children up the beach. The distance between her and the doctor's wife's inert body diminished; he had an urge to shout a warning, then smiled, picturing the laughter that would greet this story when they were home, at a cocktail party, secure among their own. Abruptly he felt guilty in relation to his wife. He had betrayed her. His seriousness had been unworthy of her. She would have wanted him to say yes, her grandfather picked cotton in Alabama, in America these things are taken for granted, we have no problem. But he saw, like a movement glimpsed in a liquid volume, that the comedy of this response depended upon, could only live within, a vast and unconscious pride of race. That since this medium was poisoned all its creatures must be evil. That he and the doctor's wife were immersed together; he hated her blue eyes because they were pinned to his face, hated the taste of her because – could it be? – she was dying. His guilt could not be mapped. Its intricacy was as dense as a simple mass. He moved backward in the ocean, touching the ribbed bottom with his toes, until the water wrapped around his throat. Something – seaweed or the pulse of a current – touched his calf. He thrashed, and peered down, but saw nothing. He was afraid of the sharks, and he was afraid of the doctor's wife, so he hung there between them, bleeding shame, while the water forgave him.

JOYCE CAROL OATES b. 1938

In the 1970 collection of the *O. Henry Prize Stories,* the editor William Abrahams invented a new prize category, "Special Award for Continuing Achievement." It was a fitting tribute to Miss Oates, and also an insight into the need that she had brought about for some other way to deal with a writer so good and so productive (and so remarkably young) that beginning in 1963 and excepting 1966 her short stories were *always* in the annual O. Henry prize collection. During the same period she was writing four novels (of which the last, *Them,* won the 1970 National Book Award), two Off-Broadway plays, and a collection of poems. Still another novel, *Wonderland,* appeared in 1971.

Because Miss Oates has always read widely and sensitively, it is hard to cite especially powerful influences on her writing. She was an English major at Syracuse, the valedictorian of her class; then she took an M.A. at Wisconsin, and was proceeding toward a Ph.D. at Rice before she gave up studying literature for writing it. Thus, in a sense, all traditional writers are behind her; and while sometimes in her work we are reminded of Faulkner's ear for the interaction of many voices strained by various personal repressions, or of Kafka's beautiful presentation of a detailed and seemingly ordinary reality that gently floats into nightmare, still the realism of Flaubert and the lyrical introspection of Proust are there too. In fact, Miss Oates's fiction is of all kinds the most original and distinctive: not free of influences but fully assimilative of them all.

In an interview in *Commonweal* (December 5, 1969) Miss Oates said that although she had once thought that she was much indebted to Flannery O'Connor, she now saw that in Miss O'Connor's fiction there was always a religious dimension, a glimmer of revelation beyond the purely natural, whereas in hers "there is only the natural world." The two writers obviously have a lot in common, but Miss Oates is right in pointing to exactly that area as the one that distinguishes her from Flannery O'Connor.

Like Flannery O'Connor, Miss Oates was born a Roman Catholic, in Lockport, N.Y.; she grew up in a rural area near that small upstate town. Her characters are typically immersed in a middle-class culture, full of T.V. and radio announcers' clichés, all of them having appropriated a jumble of styles from old movies, the business establishment, black society, etc. The styles don't fit, singly or in combination, and Miss Oates explores the pressure that builds up, particularly in our money-dominated world, and presents the violent collisions that occur when people with different images of themselves try to relate to one another.

Miss Oates now teaches literature full time at the University of Windsor, Canada. Her husband, also a professor at Windsor, specializes in eighteenth-century English literature.

WHERE ARE YOU GOING, WHERE HAVE YOU BEEN?

For Bob Dylan

Her name was Connie. She was fifteen and she had a quick nervous giggling habit of craning her neck to glance into mirrors, or checking other people's faces to make sure her own was all right. Her mother, who noticed everything and knew everything and who hadn't much reason any longer to look at her own face, always scolded Connie about it. "Stop gawking at yourself, who are you? You think you're so pretty?" she would say. Connie would raise her eyebrows at these familiar complaints and look right through her mother, into a shadowy vision of herself as she was right at that moment: she knew she was pretty and that was everything. Her mother had been pretty once too, if you could believe those old snapshots in the album, but now her looks were gone and that was why she was always after Connie.

"Why don't you keep your room clean like your sister? How've you got your hair fixed – what the hell stinks? Hair spray? You don't see your sister using that junk."

Her sister June was twenty-four and still lived at home. She was a secretary in the high school Connie attended, and if that wasn't bad enough – with her in the same building – she was so plain and chunky and steady that Connie had to hear her praised all the time by her mother and her mother's sisters. June did this, June did that, she saved money and helped clean the house and cooked and Connie couldn't do a thing, her mind was all filled with trashy daydreams. Their father was away at work most of the time and when he came home he wanted supper and he read the newspaper at supper and after supper he went to bed. He didn't bother talking much to them, but around his bent head Connie's mother kept picking at her until Connie wished her mother was dead and she herself was dead and it was all over. "She makes me want to throw up sometimes," she complained to her friends. She had a high, breathless, amused voice which made everything she said sound a little forced, whether it was sincere or not.

There was one good thing: June went places with girl friends of hers, girls who were just as plain and steady as she, and so when Connie wanted to do that her mother had no objections. The father of Connie's best girl friend drove the girls the three miles to town and left them off at a shopping plaza, so that they could walk through the stores or go to a movie, and when he came to pick them up again at eleven he never bothered to ask what they had done.

They must have been familiar sights, walking around that shopping plaza in their shorts and flat ballerina slippers that always scuffed the sidewalk, with charm bracelets jingling on their thin wrists; they would lean together to whisper and laugh secretly if someone passed by who amused or interested them. Connie had long dark blond hair that drew anyone's eye to it, and she wore part of it pulled up on her head and puffed out and the rest of it she let fall down her back. She wore a pull-over jersey blouse that looked one way when she was at home and another way when she was away from home. Everything about her had two sides to it, one for home and one for anywhere that was not home: her walk that could be childlike and bobbing, or languid enough to make anyone think she was hearing music in her head, her mouth which was pale and smirking most of the time, but bright and pink on these evenings out, her laugh which was cynical and drawling at home – "Ha, ha, very funny" – but high-pitched and nervous anywhere else, like the jingling of the charms on her bracelet.

Sometimes they did go shopping or to a movie, but sometimes they went across the highway, ducking fast across the busy road, to a drive-in restaurant where older kids hung out. The restaurant was shaped like a big bottle, though squatter than a real bottle, and on its cap was a revolving figure of a grinning boy who held a hamburger aloft. One night in mid-summer they ran across, breathless with daring, and right away someone leaned out a car window and invited them over, but it was just a boy from high school they didn't like. It made them feel good to be able to ignore him. They went up through the maze of parked and cruising cars to the bright-lit, fly-infested restaurant, their faces pleased and expectant as if they were entering a sacred building that loomed out of the night to give them what haven and what blessing they yearned for. They sat at the counter and crossed their legs at the ankles, their thin shoulders rigid with excitement, and listened to the music that made everything so good: the music was always in the background like music at a church service, it was something to depend upon.

A boy named Eddie came in to talk with them. He sat backwards on his stool, turning himself jerkily around in semi-circles and then stopping and turning again, and after a while he asked Connie if she would like something to eat. She said she did and so she tapped her friend's arm on her way out – her friend pulled her face up into a brave droll look – and Connie said she would meet her at eleven, across the way. "I just hate to leave her like that," Connie said earnestly, but the boy said that she wouldn't be alone for long. So they went out to his car and on the way Connie couldn't help but let her eyes wander over the windshields and faces all around her, her face gleaming with a joy that had nothing to do with Eddie or even this place; it might have been the music. She drew her shoulders up and sucked in her breath with the pure pleasure of being alive, and just at that moment she happened to glance at a face just a few feet from hers. It was a boy with shaggy black hair, in a convertible jalopy painted gold. He stared at her and then his lips widened into a grin. Connie slit her eyes at him and turned away, but she couldn't help glancing back and there he was still watching her. He wagged a finger and laughed and said, "Gonna get you, baby," and Connie turned away again without Eddie noticing anything.

She spent three hours with him, at the restaurant where they ate hamburgers and drank Cokes in wax cups that were always sweating, and then down an alley a mile or so away, and when he left her off at five to eleven only the movie house was still open at the plaza. Her girl friend was there, talking with a boy. When Connie came up the two girls smiled at each other and Connie said, "How was the movie?" and the girl said, "*You* should know." They rode off with the girl's father, sleepy and pleased, and Connie couldn't help but look at the darkened shopping plaza with its big empty parking lot and its signs that were faded and ghostly now, and over at the drive-in restaurant where cars were still circling tirelessly. She couldn't hear the music at this distance.

Next morning June asked her how the movie was and Connie said, "So-so."

She and that girl and occasionally another girl went out several times a week that way, and the rest of the time Connie spent around the house — it was summer vacation — getting in her mother's way and thinking, dreaming, about the boys she met. But all the boys fell back and dissolved into a single face that was not even a face, but an idea, a feeling, mixed up with the urgent insistent pounding of the music and the humid night air of July. Connie's mother kept dragging her back to the daylight by finding things for her to do or saying, suddenly, "What's this about the Pettinger girl?"

And Connie would say nervously, "Oh, her. That dope." She always drew thick clear lines between herself and such girls, and her mother was simple and kindly enough to believe her. Her mother was so simple, Connie thought, that it was maybe cruel to fool her so much. Her mother went scuffling around the house in old bedroom slippers and complained over the telephone to one sister about the other, then the other called up and the two of them complained about the third one. If June's name was mentioned her mother's tone was approving, and if Connie's name was mentioned it was disapproving. This did not really mean she disliked Connie and actually Connie thought that her mother preferred her to June because she was prettier, but the two of them kept up a pretense of exasperation, a sense that they were tugging and struggling over something of little value to either of them. Sometimes, over coffee, they were almost friends, but something would come up — some vexation that was like a fly buzzing suddenly around their heads — and their faces went hard with contempt.

One Sunday Connie got up at eleven — none of them bothered with church — and washed her hair so that it could dry all day long, in the sun. Her parents and sister were going to a barbecue at an aunt's house and Connie said no, she wasn't interested, rolling her eyes to let mother know just what she thought of it. "Stay home alone then," her mother said sharply. Connie sat out back in a lawn chair and watched them drive away, her father quiet and bald, hunched around so that he could back the car out, her mother with a look that was still angry and not at all softened through the windshield, and in the back seat poor old June all dressed up as if she didn't know what a barbecue was, with all the running yelling kids and the flies. Connie sat with her eyes closed in the sun, dreaming and dazed with the warmth about her as if this were a kind of love, the caresses of love, and her mind slipped over onto thoughts of the boy she had been with the night before and how nice he had been, how sweet it always was, not the way someone like June would suppose but sweet, gentle, the way it was in movies and promised in songs; and when she opened her eyes she hardly knew where she was, the back yard ran off into weeds and a fence-line of trees and behind it the sky was perfectly blue and still. The asbestos "ranch house" that was now three years old startled her – it looked small. She shook her head as if to get awake.

It was too hot. She went inside the house and turned on the radio to drown out the quiet. She sat on the edge of her bed, barefoot, and listened for an hour and a half to a program called XYZ Sunday Jamboree, record after record of hard, fast, shrieking songs she sang along with, interspersed by exclamations from "Bobby King": "An' look here you girls at Napoleon's – Son and Charley want you to pay real close attention to this song coming up!"

And Connie paid close attention herself, bathed in a glow of slow-pulsed joy that seemed to rise mysteriously out of the music itself and lay languidly about the airless little room, breathed in and breathed out with each gentle rise and fall of her chest.

After a while she heard a car coming up the drive. She sat up at once, startled, because it couldn't be her father so soon. The gravel kept crunching all the way in from the road – the driveway was long – and Connie ran to the window. It was a car she didn't know. It was an open jalopy, painted a bright gold that caught the sunlight opaquely. Her heart began to pound and her fingers snatched at her hair, checking it, and she whispered "Christ. Christ," wondering how bad she looked. The car came to a stop at the side door and the horn sounded four short taps as if this were a signal Connie knew.

She went into the kitchen and approached the door slowly, then hung out the screen door, her bare toes curling down off the step. There were two boys in the car and now she recognized the driver: he had shaggy, shabby black hair that looked crazy as a wig and he was grinning at her.

"I ain't late, am I?" he said.

"Who the hell do you think you are?" Connie said.

"Toldja I'd be out, didn't I?"

"I don't even know who you are."

She spoke sullenly, careful to show no interest or pleasure, and he spoke in a fast bright monotone. Connie looked past him to the other boy, taking her time. He had fair brown hair, with a lock that fell onto his forehead. His sideburns gave him a fierce, embarrassed look, but so far he hadn't even bothered to glance at her. Both boys wore sunglasses. The driver's glasses were metallic and mirrored everything in miniature.

"You wanta come for a ride?" he said.

Connie smirked and let her hair fall loose over one shoulder.

"Don'tcha like my car? New paint job," he said. "Hey."

"What?"

"You're cute."

She pretended to fidget, chasing flies away from the door.

"Don'tcha believe me, or what?" he said.

"Look, I don't even know who you are," Connie said in disgust.

"Hey, Ellie's got a radio, see. Mine's broke down." He lifted his friend's arm and showed her the little transistor the boy was holding, and now Connie began to hear the music. It was the same program that was playing inside the house.

"Bobby King?" she said.

"I listen to him all the time. I think he's great."

"He's kind of great," Connie said reluctantly.

"Listen, that guy's *great.* He knows where the action is."

Connie blushed a little, because the glasses made it impossible for her to see just what this boy was looking at. She couldn't decide if she liked him or if he was just a jerk, and so she dawdled in the doorway and wouldn't come down or go back inside. She said, "What's all that stuff painted on your car?"

"Can'tcha read it?" He opened the door very carefully, as if he was afraid it might fall off. He slid out just as carefully, planting his feet firmly on the ground, the tiny metallic world in his glasses slowing down like gelatine hardening and in the midst of it Connie's bright green blouse. "This here is my name, to begin with," he said. ARNOLD FRIEND was written in tar-like black letters on the side, with a drawing of a round grinning face that reminded Connie of a pumpkin, except it wore sunglasses. "I wanta introduce myself, I'm Arnold Friend and that's my real name and I'm gonna be your friend, honey, and inside the car's Ellie Oscar, he's kinda shy." Ellie brought his transistor radio up to his shoulder and balanced it there. "Now these numbers are a secret code, honey," Arnold Friend explained. He read off the numbers 33, 19, 17 and raised his eyebrows at her to see what she thought of that, but she didn't think much of it. The left rear fender had been smashed and around it was written, on the gleaming gold background: DONE BY CRAZY WOMAN DRIVER. Connie had to laugh at that. Arnold Friend was pleased at her laughter and looked up at her. "Around the other side's a lot more – you wanta come and see them?"

"No."

"Why not?"

"Why should I?"

"Don'tcha wanta see what's on the car? Don'tcha wanta go for a ride?"

"I don't know."

"Why not?"

"I got things to do."

"Like what?"

"Things."

He laughed as if she had said something funny. He slapped his thighs. He was standing in a strange way, leaning back against the car as if he were balancing himself. He wasn't tall, only an inch or so taller than she would be if she came down to him. Connie liked the way he was dressed, which was the way all of them dressed: tight faded jeans stuffed into black, scuffed boots, a belt that pulled his waist in and showed how lean he was, and a white pull-over shirt that was a little soiled and showed the hard small muscles of his arms and shoulders. He looked as if he probably did hard work, lifting and carrying things. Even his neck looked muscular. And his face was a familiar face, somehow: the jaw and chin and cheeks slightly darkened, because he hadn't shaved for a day or two, and the nose long and hawk-like, sniffing as if she were a treat he was going to gobble up and it was all a joke.

"Connie, you ain't telling the truth. This is your day set aside for a ride with me and you know it," he said, still laughing. The way he straightened and recovered from his fit of laughing showed that it had been all fake.

"How do you know what my name is?" she said suspiciously.

"It's Connie."

"Maybe and maybe not."

"I know my Connie," he said, wagging his finger. Now she remembered him even better, back at the restaurant, and her cheeks warmed at the thought of how she sucked in her breath just at the moment she passed him – how she must have looked to him. And he had remembered her. "Ellie and I come out here especially for you," he said. "Ellie can sit in back. How about it?"

"Where?"

"Where what?"

"Where're we going?"

He looked at her. He took off the sunglasses and she saw how pale the skin around his eyes was, like holes that were not in shadow but instead in light. His eyes were like chips of broken glass that catch the light in an amiable way. He smiled. It was as if the idea of going for a ride somewhere, to some place, was a new idea to him.

"Just for a ride, Connie sweetheart."

"I never said my name was Connie," she said.

"But I know what it is. I know your name and all about you, lots of things," Arnold Friend said. He had not moved yet but stood still leaning back against the side of his jalopy. "I took a special interest in you, such a pretty girl, and found out all about you like I know your parents and sister are gone somewheres and I know where and how long they're going to be gone, and I know who you were with last night, and your best girl friend's name is Betty. Right?"

He spoke in a simple lilting voice, exactly as if he were reciting the words to a song. His smile assured her that everything was fine. In the car Ellie turned up the volume on his radio and did not bother to look around at them.

"Ellie can sit in the back seat," Arnold Friend said. He indicated his friend with a casual jerk of his chin, as if Ellie did not count and she should not bother with him.

"How'd you find out all that stuff?" Connie said.

"Listen: Betty Schultz and Tony Fitch and Jimmy Pettinger and Nancy Pettinger," he said, in a chant. "Raymond Stanley and Bob Hutter — "

"Do you know all those kids?"

"I know everybody."

"Look, you're kidding. You're not from around here."

"Sure."

"But — how come we never saw you before?"

"Sure you saw me before," he said. He looked down at his boots, as if he were a little offended. "You just don't remember."

"I guess I'd remember you," Connie said.

"Yeah?" He looked up at this, beaming. He was pleased. He began to mark time with the music from Ellie's radio, tapping his fists lightly together. Connie looked away from his smile to the car, which was painted so bright it almost hurt her eyes to look at it. She looked at that name, ARNOLD FRIEND. And up at the front fender was an expression that was familiar — MAN THE FLYING SAUCERS. It was an expression kids had used the year before, but didn't use this year. She looked at it for a while as if the words meant something to her that she did not yet know.

"What're you thinking about? Huh?" Arnold Friend demanded. "Not worried about your hair blowing around in the car, are you?"

"No."

"Think I maybe can't drive good?"

"How do I know?"

"You're a hard girl to handle. How come?" he said. "Don't you know I'm your friend? Didn't you see me put my sign in the air when you walked by?"

"What sign?"

"My sign." And he drew an X in the air, leaning out toward her. They were maybe ten feet apart. After his hand fell back to his side the X was still in the air, almost visible. Connie let the screen door close and stood perfectly still inside it, listening to the music from her radio and the boy's blend together. She stared at Arnold Friend. He stood there so stiffly relaxed, pretending to be relaxed, with one hand idly on the door handle as if he were keeping himself up that way and had no intention of ever moving again. She recognized most things about him, the tight jeans that showed his thighs and buttocks and the greasy leather boots and the tight shirt, and even that slippery friendly smile of his, that sleepy dreamy smile that all the boys used to get across ideas they didn't want to put into words. She recognized all this and also the singsong way he talked, slightly mocking, kidding, but serious and a little melancholy, and she recognized the way he tapped one fist against the other in homage to the perpetual music behind him. But all these things did not come together.

She said suddenly, "Hey, how old are you?"

His smile faded. She could see then that he wasn't a kid, he was much older – thirty, maybe more. At this knowledge her heart began to pound faster.

"That's a crazy thing to ask. Can'tcha see I'm your own age?"

"Like hell you are."

"Or maybe a coupla years older, I'm eighteen."

"Eighteen?" she said doubtfully.

He grinned to reassure her and lines appeared at the corners of his mouth. His teeth were big and white. He grinned so broadly his eyes became slits and she saw how thick the lashes were, thick and black as if painted with a black tar-like material. Then he seemed to become embarrassed, abruptly, and looked over his shoulder at Ellie. *"Him,* he's crazy," he said. "Ain't he a riot, he's a nut, a real character." Ellie was still listening to the music. His sunglasses told nothing about what he was thinking. He wore a bright orange shirt unbuttoned halfway to show his chest, which was a pale, bluish chest and not muscular like Arnold Friend's. His shirt collar was turned up all around and the very tips of the collar pointed out past his chin as if they were protecting him. He was pressing the transistor radio up against his ear and sat there in a kind of daze, right in the sun.

"He's kinda strange," Connie said.

"Hey, she says you're kinda strange! Kinda strange!" Arnold Friend cried. He pounded on the car to get Ellie's attention. Ellie turned for the first time and Connie saw with shock that he wasn't a kid either – he had a fair, hairless face, cheeks reddened slightly as if the veins grew too close to the surface of his skin, the face of a forty-year-old baby. Connie felt a wave of dizziness rise in her at this sight and she stared at him as if waiting for something to change the shock of the moment, make it all right again. Ellie's lips kept shaping words, mumbling along with the words blasting in his ear.

"Maybe you two better go away," Connie said faintly.

"What? How come?" Arnold Friend cried. "We come out here to take you for a ride. It's Sunday." He had the voice of the man on the radio now. It was the same voice, Connie thought. "Don'tcha know it's Sunday all day and honey, no matter who you were with last night today you're with Arnold Friend and don't you forget it! – Maybe you better step out here," He said, and this last was in a different voice. It was a little flatter, as if the heat was finally getting to him.

"No. I got things to do."

"Hey."

"You two better leave."

"We ain't leaving until you come with us."

"Like hell I am – "

"Connie, don't fool around with me. I mean, I mean, don't fool *around,*" he said, shaking his head. He laughed incredulously. He placed his sunglasses on top of his head, carefully, as if he were indeed wearing a wig, and brought the stems down behind his ears. Connie stared at him, another wave of dizziness and fear rising in her so that for a moment he wasn't even in focus but was just a blur, standing there against his gold car, and she had the idea that he had driven up the driveway all right but had come from nowhere before that and belonged nowhere and that everything about him and even about the music that was so familiar to her was only half real.

"If my father comes and sees you – "

"He ain't coming. He's at a barbecue."

"How do you know that?"

"Aunt Tillie's. Right now they're – uh – they're drinking. Sitting around," he said vaguely, squinting as if he were staring all the way to town and over to Aunt Tillie's back yard. Then the vision seemed to get clear and he nodded energetically. "Yeah. Sitting around. There's your sister in a blue dress, huh? And high heels, the poor sad bitch – nothing like you, sweetheart! And your mother's helping some fat woman with the corn, they're cleaning the corn – husking the corn – "

"What fat woman?" Connie cried.

"How do I know what fat woman. I don't know every goddam fat woman in the world!" Arnold Friend laughed.

"Oh, that's Mrs. Hornby. . . . Who invited her?" Connie said. She felt a little light-headed, Her breath was coming quickly.

"She's too fat. I don't like them fat. I like them the way you are, honey," he said, smiling sleepily at her. They stared at each other for a while, through the screen door. He said softly, "Now what you're going to do is this: you're going to come out that door. You're going to sit up front with me and Ellie's going to sit in the back, the hell with Ellie, right? This isn't Ellie's date. You're my date. I'm your lover, honey."

"What? You're crazy – "

"Yes, I'm your lover. You don't know what that is but you will," he said. "I know that too. I know all about you. But look: it's real nice and you couldn't ask for nobody better than me, or more polite. I always keep my word. I'll tell you how it is, I'm always nice at first, the first time. I'll hold you so tight you won't think you have to try to get away or pretend anything because you'll know you can't. And I'll come inside you where it's all secret and you'll give in to me and you'll love me — "

"Shut up! You're crazy!" Connie said. She backed away from the door. She put her hands against her ears as if she'd heard something terrible, something not meant for her. "People don't talk like that, you're crazy," she muttered. Her heart was almost too big now for her chest and its pumping made sweat break out all over her. She looked out to see Arnold Friend pause and then take a step toward the porch lurching. He almost fell. But, like a clever drunken man, he managed to catch his balance. He wobbled in his high boots and grabbed hold of one of the porch posts.

"Honey?" he said. "You still listening?"

"Get the hell out of here!"

"Be nice, honey. Listen."

"I'm going to call the police — "

He wobbled again and out of the side of his mouth came a fast spat curse, an aside not meant for her to hear. But even this "Christ!" sounded forced. Then he began to smile again. She watched this smile come, awkward as if he were smiling from inside a mask. His whole face was a mask, she thought wildly, tanned down onto his throat but then running out as if he had plastered make-up on his face but had forgotten about his throat.

"Honey — ? Listen, here's how it is. I always tell the truth and I promise you this: I ain't coming in that house after you."

"You better not! I'm going to call the police if you — if you don't — "

"Honey," he said, talking right through her voice, "honey, I'm not coming in there but you are coming out here. You know why?"

She was panting. The kitchen looked like a place she had never seen before, some room she had run inside but which wasn't good enough, wasn't going to help her. The kitchen window had never had a curtain, after three years, and there were dishes in the sink for her to do — probably — and if you ran your hand across the table you'd probably feel something sticky there.

"You listening, honey? Hey?"

" — going to call the police — "

"Soon as you touch the phone I don't need to keep my promise and can come inside. You won't want that."

She rushed forward and tried to lock the door. Her fingers were shaking. "But why lock it," Arnold Friend said gently, talking right into her face. "It's just a screen door. It's just nothing." One of his boots was at a strange angle, as if his foot wasn't in it. It pointed out to the left, bent at the ankle. "I mean, anybody can break through a screen door and glass and wood and iron or anything else if he needs to, anybody at all and specially Arnold Friend. If the place got lit up with a fire honey you'd come running out into my arms, right into my arms and safe at home – like you knew I was your lover and'd stopped fooling around. I don't mind a nice shy girl but I don't like no fooling around." Part of those words were spoken with a slight rhythmic lilt, and Connie somehow recognized them – the echo of a song from last year, about a girl rushing into her boy friend's arms and coming home again –

Connie stood barefoot on the linoleum floor, staring at him. "What do you want?" she whispered.

"I want you," he said.

"What?"

"Seen you that night and thought, that's the one, yes sir. I never needed to look any more."

"But my father's coming back. He's coming to get me. I had to wash my hair first – " She spoke in a dry, rapid voice, hardly raising it for him to hear.

"No, your daddy is not coming and yes, you had to wash your hair and you washed it for me. It's nice and shining and all for me, I thank you, sweetheart," he said, with a mock bow, but again he almost lost his balance. He had to bend and adjust his boots. Evidently his feet did not go all the way down; the boots must have been stuffed with something so that he would seem taller. Connie stared out at him and behind him Ellie in the car, who seemed to be looking off toward Connie's right, into nothing. This Ellie said, pulling the words out of the air one after another as if he were just discovering them, "You want me to pull out the phone?"

"Shut your mouth and keep it shut," Arnold Friend said, his face red from bending over or maybe from embarrassment because Connie had seen his boots. "This ain't none of your business."

"What – what are you doing? What do you want?" Connie said. "If I call the police they'll get you, they'll arrest you – "

"Promise was not to come in unless you touch that phone, and I'll keep that promise," he said. He resumed his erect position and tried to force his shoulders back. He sounded like a hero in a movie, declaring something important. He spoke too loudly and it was as if he were speaking to someone behind Connie. "I ain't made plans for coming in that house where I don't belong but just for you to come out to me, the way you should. Don't you know who I am?"

"You're crazy," she whispered. She backed away from the door but did not want to go into another part of the house, as if this would give him permission to come through the door. "What do you. . . . You're crazy, you . . ."

"Huh? What're you saying, honey?"

Her eyes darted everywhere in the kitchen. She could not remember what it was, this room.

"This is how it is, honey: you come out and we'll drive away, have a nice ride. But if you don't come out we're gonna wait till your people come home and then they're all going to get it."

"You want that telephone pulled out?" Ellie said. He held the radio away from his ear and grimaced, as if without the radio the air was too much for him.

"I toldja shut up, Ellie," Arnold Friend said, "you're deaf, get a hearing aid, right? Fix yourself up. This little girl's no trouble and's gonna be nice to me, so Ellie keep to yourself, this ain't your date – right? Don't hem in on me. Don't hog. Don't crush. Don't bird dog. Don't trail me," he said in a rapid meaningless voice, as if he were running through all the expressions he'd learned but was no longer sure which one of them was in style, then rushing on to new ones, making them up with his eyes closed, "Don't crawl under my fence, don't squeeze in my chipmunk hole, don't sniff my glue, suck my popsicle, keep your own greasy fingers on yourself!" He shaded his eyes and peered in at Connie, who was backed against the kitchen table. "Don't mind him honey he's just a creep. He's a dope. Right? I'm the boy for you and like I said you come out here nice like a lady and give me your hand, and nobody else gets hurt, I mean, your nice old bald-headed daddy and your mummy and your sister in her high heels. Because listen: why bring them in this?"

"Leave me alone," Connie whispered.

"Hey, you know that old woman down the road, the one with the chickens and stuff – you know her?"

"She's dead!"

"Dead? What? You know her?" Arnold Friend said.

"She's dead – "

"Don't you like her?"

"She's dead – she's – she isn't here any more – "

"But don't you like her, I mean, you got something against her? Some grudge or something?" Then his voice dipped as if he were conscious of a rudeness. He touched the sunglasses perched on top of his head as if to make sure they were still there. "Now you be a good girl."

"What are you going to do?"

"Just two things, or maybe three," Arnold Friend said. "But I promise it won't last long and you'll like me that way you get to like people you're close to. You will. It's all over for you here, so come on out. You don't want your people in any trouble, do you?"

She turned and bumped against a chair or something, hurting her leg, but she ran into the back room and picked up the telephone. Something roared in her ear, a tiny roaring, and she was so sick with fear that she could do nothing but listen to it – the telephone was clammy and very heavy and her fingers groped down to the dial but were too weak to touch it. She began to scream into the phone, into the roaring. She cried out, she cried for her mother, she felt her breath start jerking back and forth in her lungs as if it were something Arnold Friend were stabbing her with again and again with no tenderness. A noisy sorrowful wailing rose all about her and she was locked inside it the way she was locked inside this house.

After a while she could hear again. She was sitting on the floor with her wet back against the wall.

Arnold Friend was saying from the door, "That's a good girl. Put the phone back."

She kicked the phone away from her.

"No, honey. Pick it up. Put it back right."

She picked it up and put it back. The dial tone stopped.

"That's a good girl. Now you come outside."

She was hollow with what had been fear, but what was now just an emptiness. All that screaming had blasted it out of her. She sat, one leg cramped under her, and deep inside her brain was something like a pinpoint of light that kept going and would not let her relax. She thought, I'm not going to see my mother again. She thought, I'm not going to sleep in my bed again. Her bright green blouse was all wet.

Arnold Friend said, in a gentle-loud voice that was like a stage voice, "The place where you came from ain't there any more, and where you had in mind to go is cancelled out. This place you are now – inside your daddy's house – is nothing but a cardboard box I can knock down any time. You know that and always did know it. You hear me?"

She thought, I have got to think. I have to know what to do.

"We'll go out to a nice field, out in the country here where it smells so nice and it's sunny," Arnold Friend said. "I'll have my arms tight around you so you won't need to try to get away and I'll show you what love is like, what it does. The hell with this house! It looks solid all right," he said. He ran a fingernail down the screen and the noise did not make Connie shiver, as it would have the day before. "Now put your hand on your heart, honey. Feel that? That feels solid too but we know better, be nice to me, be sweet like you can because what else is there for a girl like you but to be sweet and pretty and give in? – and get away before her people come back?"

She felt her pounding heart. Her hand seemed to enclose it. She thought for the first time in her life that it was nothing that was hers, that belonged to her, but just a pounding, living thing inside this body that wasn't really hers either.

"You don't want them to get hurt," Arnold Friend went on. "Now get up, honey. Get up all by yourself."

She stood.

"Now turn this way. That's right. Come over here to me – Ellie, put that away, didn't I tell you? You dope. You miserable creepy dope," Arnold Friend said. His words were not angry but only part of an incantation. The incantation was kindly. "Now come out through the kitchen to me honey and let's see a smile, try it, you're a brave sweet little girl and now they're eating corn and hotdogs cooked to bursting over an outdoor fire, and they don't know one thing about you and never did and honey you're better than them because not a one of them would have done this for you."

Connie felt the linoleum under her feet; it was cool. She brushed her hair back out of her eyes. Arnold Friend let go of the post tentatively and opened his arms for her, his elbows pointing in toward each other and his wrists limp, to show that this was an embarrassed embrace and a little mocking, he didn't want to make her self-conscious.

She put out her hand against the screen. She watched herself push the door slowly open as if she were safe back somewhere in the other doorway, watching this body and this head of long hair moving out into the sunlight where Arnold Friend waited.

"My sweet little blue-eyed girl," he said, in a half-sung sigh that had nothing to do with her brown eyes but was taken up just the same by the vast sunlit reaches of the land behind him and on all sides of him, so much land that Connie had never seen before and did not recognize except to know that she was going to it.

HOW I CONTEMPLATED THE WORLD FROM THE DETROIT HOUSE OF CORRECTION AND BEGAN MY LIFE OVER AGAIN

Notes for an essay for an English class at Baldwin Country Day School; poking around in debris; disgust and curiosity; a revelation of the meaning of life; a happy ending. . . .

I. EVENTS

1. The girl (myself) is walking through Branden's, that excellent store. Suburb of a large famous city that is a symbol for large famous American cities. The event sneaks up on the girl, who believes she is herding it along with a small fixed smile, a girl of fifteen, innocently experienced. She dawdles in a certain style by a counter of costume jewelry. Rings, earrings, necklaces. Prices from $5 to $50, all within reach. All ugly. She eases over to the glove counter, where everything is ugly too. In her close-fitted coat with its black fur collar she contemplates the luxury of Branden's, which she has known for many years: its many mild pale lights, easy on the eye and the soul, its elaborate tinkly decorations, its women shoppers with their excellent shoes and coats and hairdos, all dawdling gracefully, in no hurry.

Who was ever in a hurry here?

2. The girl seated at home. A small library, paneled walls of oak. Someone is talking to me. An earnest husky female voice drives itself against my ears, nervous, frightened, groping around my heart, saying, "If you wanted gloves why didn't you say so? Why didn't you ask for them?" That store, Branden's, is owned by Raymond Forrest who lives on DuMaurier Drive. We live on Sioux Drive. Raymond Forrest. A handsome man? An ugly man? A man of fifty or sixty, with gray hair, or a man of forty with earnest courteous eyes, a good golf game, who is Raymond Forrest, this man who is my salvation? Father has been talking to him. Father is not his physician; Dr. Berg is his physician. Father and Dr. Berg refer patients to each other. There is a connection. Mother plays bridge with. . . . On Mondays and Wednesdays our maid Billie works at. . . . The strings draw together in a cat's cradle, making a net to save you when you fall. . . .

3. *Harriet Arnold's.* A small shop, better than Branden's. Mother in her black coat, I in my close-fitted blue coat. Shopping. Now look at this, isn't this cute, do you want this, why don't you want this, try this on, take this with you to the fitting room, take this also, what's wrong with you, what can I do for you, why are you so strange . . . ? "I wanted to steal but not to buy," I don't tell her. The girl droops along in her coat and gloves and leather boots, her eyes scan the horizon which is pastel pink and decorated like Branden's, tasteful walls and modern ceilings with graceful glimmering lights.

4. Weeks later, the girl at a bus-stop. Two o'clock in the afternoon, a Tuesday, obviously she has walked out of school.

5. The girl stepping down from a bus. Afternoon, weather changing to colder. Detroit. Pavement and closed-up stores; grillwork over the windows of a pawnshop. What is a pawnshop, exactly?

II. CHARACTERS

1. The girl stands five feet five inches tall. An ordinary height. Baldwin Country Day School draws them up to that height. She dreams along the corridors and presses her face against the Thermoplex Glass. No frost or steam can ever form on that glass. A smudge of grease from her forehead . . . could she be boiled down to grease? She wears her hair loose and long and straight in suburban teenage style, 1968. Eyes smudged with pencil, dark brown. Brown hair. Vague green eyes. A pretty girl? An ugly girl? She sings to herself under her breath, idling in the corridor, thinking of her many secrets (the thirty dollars she once took from the purse of a friend's mother, just for fun, the basement window she smashed in her own house just for fun) and thinking of her brother who is at Susquehanna Boys' Academy, an excellent preparatory school in Maine, remembering him unclearly . . . he has long manic hair and a squeaking voice and he looks like one of the popular teenage singers of 1968, one of those in a group, *The Certain Forces, The Way Out, The Maniacs Responsible.* The girl in her turn looks like one of those fieldsful of girls who listen to the boys' singing, dreaming and mooning restlessly, breaking into high sullen laughter, innocently experienced.

2. The mother. A midwestern woman of Detroit and suburbs. Belongs to the Detroit Athletic Club. Also the Detroit Golf Club. Also the Bloomfield Hills Country Club. The Village Women's Club at which lectures are given each winter on Genet and Sartre and James Baldwin, by the Director of the Adult Education Program at Wayne State University. . . . The Bloomfield Art Association. Also the Founders Society of the Detroit Institute of Arts. Also. . . . Oh, she is in perpetual

motion, this lady, hair like blown-up gold and finer than gold, hair and fingers and body of inestimable grace. Heavy weighs the gold on the back of her hairbrush and hand mirror. Heavy heavy the candlesticks in the dining room. Very heavy is the big car, a Lincoln, long and black, that on one cool autumn day split a squirrel's body in two unequal parts.

3. The father, Dr. ——. He belongs to the same clubs as #2. A player of squash and golf; he has a golfer's umbrella of stripes. Candy stripes. In his mouth nothing turns to sugar, however, saliva works no miracles here. His doctoring is of the slightly sick. The sick are sent elsewhere (to Dr. Berg?), the deathly sick are sent back for more tests and their bills are sent to their homes, the unsick are sent to Dr. Coronet (Isabel, a lady), an excellent psychiatrist for unsick people who angrily believe they are sick and want to do something about it. If they demand a male psychiatrist, the unsick are sent by Dr. —— (my father) to Dr. Lowenstein, a male psychiatrist, excellent and expensive, with a limited practice.

4. Clarita. She is twenty, twenty-five, she is thirty or more? Pretty, ugly, what? She is a woman lounging by the side of a road, in jeans and a sweater, hitch-hiking, or she is slouched on a stool at a counter in some roadside diner. A hard line of jaw. Curious eyes. Amused eyes. Behind her eyes processions move, funeral pageants, cartoons. She says, "I never can figure out why girls like you bum around down here. What are you looking for anyway?" An odor of tobacco about her. Unwashed underclothes, or no underclothes, unwashed skin, gritty toes, hair long and falling into strands, not recently washed.

5. Simon. In this city the weather changes abruptly, so Simon's weather changes abruptly. He sleeps through the afternoon. He sleeps through the morning. Rising he gropes around for something to get him going, for a cigarette or a pill to drive him out to the street, where the temperature is hovering around 35°. Why doesn't it drop? Why, why doesn't the cold clean air come down from Canada, will he have to go up into Canada to get it, will he have to leave the Country of his Birth and sink into Canada's frosty fields . . . ? Will the F.B.I. (which he dreams about constantly) chase him over the Canadian border on foot, hounded out in a blizzard of broken glass and horns . . . ?

"Once I was Huckleberry Finn," Simon says, "but now I am Roderick Usher." Beset by frenzies and fears, this man who makes my spine go cold, he takes green pills, yellow pills, pills of white and capsules of dark blue and green . . . he takes other things I may not mention, for what if Simon seeks me out and climbs into my girl's bedroom here in Bloomfield Hills and strangles me, what then . . . ? (As I write this I begin to shiver. Why do I shiver? I am now sixteen and sixteen is not an age for shivering.) It comes from Simon, who is always cold.

III. WORLD EVENTS

Nothing.

IV. PEOPLE & CIRCUMSTANCES CONTRIBUTING TO THIS DELINQUENCY

Nothing.

V. SIOUX DRIVE

George, Clyde G. 240 Sioux. A manufacturer's representative; children, a dog; a wife. Georgian with the usual columns. You think of the White House, then of Thomas Jefferson, then your mind goes blank on the white pillars and you think of nothing. Norris, Ralph W. 246 Sioux. Public relations. Colonial. Bay window, brick, stone, concrete, wood, green shutters, sidewalk, lantern, grass, trees, blacktop drive, two children, one of them my classmate Esther (Esther Norris) at Baldwin. Wife, cars. Ramsey, Michael D. 250 Sioux. Colonial. Big living room, thirty by twenty-five, fireplaces in living room library recreation room, paneled walls wet bar five bathrooms five bedrooms two lavatories central air conditioning automatic sprinkler automatic garage door three children one wife two cars a breakfast room a patio a large fenced lot fourteen trees a front door with a brass knocker never knocked. Next is our house. Classic contemporary. Traditional modern. Attached garage, attached Florida room, attached patio, attached pool and cabana, attached roof. A front door mailslot through which poor *Time Magazine, Fortune, Life, Business Week, The Wall Street Journal, The New York Times, The New Yorker, The Saturday Review, M.D., Modern Medicine, Disease of the Month* . . . and also. . . . And in addition to all this a quiet sealed letter from Baldwin saying: *Your daughter is not doing work compatible with her performance on the Stanford-Binet.* . . . And your son is not doing well, not well at all, very sad. Where is your son anyway? Once he stole trick-and-treat candy from some six-year-old kids, he himself being a robust ten. The beginning. Now your daughter steals. In the Village Pharmacy she made off with, yes she did, don't deny it, she made off with a copy of *Pageant Magazine* for no reason, she swiped a roll of lifesavers in a green wrapper and was in no need of saving her life or even in need of sucking candy, when she was no more than eight years old she stole, don't blush, she stole a package of *Tums* only because it was out on the counter and available, and the nice lady behind the counter (now dead) said nothing. . . . Sioux Drive. Maples, oaks, elms. Diseased elms cut down. Sioux Drive runs into Roosevelt Drive. Slow turning lanes, not streets, all drives and lanes and ways and passes. A private police force. Quiet private police, in unmarked cars. Cruising on Saturday evenings with paternal smiles for the residents who are streaming in and out of houses, going to and from parties, a thousand parties, slightly staggering, the women in their furs alighting from automobiles bought of Ford and General Motors and Chrysler, very heavy automobiles. No foreign cars. Detroit. In 275 Sioux, down the block, in that magnificient French Normandy mansion, lives ——— ——— himself, who has the C—— account itself, imagine that! Look at where he lives and look at the enormous trees and chimneys, imagine his many fireplaces, imagine his wife and children, imagine his wife's hair, imagine her fingernails, imagine her bathtub of smooth clean glowing pink, imagine their embraces, his trouser pockets filled with odd coins and keys and dust and peanuts, imagine their ecstasy on Sioux Drive, imagine their income tax returns, imagine their little boy's pride in his experimental car, a scaled-down C——, as he roars around the neighborhood on the sidewalks frightening dogs and Negro maids, oh imagine all these things, imagine everything, let your mind roar out all over Sioux Drive and DuMaurier Drive and Roosevelt Drive and Ticonderoga Pass and Burning Bush Way and Lincolnshire Pass and Lois Lane.

When spring comes its winds blow nothing to Sioux Drive, no odors of hollyhocks or forsythia, nothing Sioux Drive doesn't already possess, everything is planted and performing. The weather vanes, had they weather vanes, don't have to turn with the wind, don't have to contend with the weather. There is no weather.

VI. DETROIT

There is always weather in Detroit. Detroit's temperature is always 32°. Fast falling temperatures. Slow rising temperatures. Wind from the north northeast four to forty miles an hour, small craft warnings, partly cloudy today and Wednesday changing to partly sunny through Thursday . . . small warnings of frost, soot warnings, traffic warnings, hazardous lake conditions for small craft and swimmers, restless Negro gangs, restless cloud formations, restless temperatures aching to fall out the very bottom of the thermometer or shoot up over the top and boil everything over in red mercury.

Detroit's temperature is 32°. Fast falling temperatures. Slow rising temperatures. Wind from the north northeast four to forty miles an hour. . . .

VII. EVENTS

1. The girl's heart is pounding. In her pocket is a pair of gloves! In a plastic bag! Airproof breathproof plastic bag, gloves selling for twenty-five dollars on Branden's counter! In her pocket! Shoplifted! . . . In her purse is a blue comb, not very clean. In her purse is a leather billfold (a birthday present from her grandmother in Philadelphia) with snapshots of the family in clean plastic windows,

in the billfold are bills, she doesn't know how many bills. . . . In her purse is an ominous note from her friend Tykie *What's this about Joe H. and the kids hanging around at Louise's Sat. night? You heard anything?* . . . passed in French class. In her purse is a lot of dirty yellow Kleenex, her mother's heart would break to see such dirty Kleenex, and at the bottom of her purse are brown hairpins and safety pins and a broken pencil and a ballpoint pen (blue) stolen from somewhere forgotten and a purse-size compact of Cover Girl Make-Up, Ivory Rose. . . . Her lipstick is Broken Heart, a corrupt pink; her fingers are trembling like crazy; her teeth are beginning to chatter; her insides are alive; her eyes glow in her head; she is saying to her mother's astonished face *I want to steal but not to buy.*

2. At Clarita's. Day or night? What room is this? A bed, a regular bed, and a mattress on the floor nearby. Wallpaper hanging in strips. Clarita says she tore it like that with her teeth. She was fighting a barbaric tribe that night, high from some pills she was battling for her life with men wearing helmets of heavy iron and their faces no more than Christian crosses to breathe through, every one of those bastards looking like her lover Simon, who seems to breathe with great difficulty through the slits of mouth and nostrils in his face. Clarita has never heard of Sioux Drive. Raymond Forrest cuts no ice with her, nor does the C—— account and its millions; Harvard Business School could be at the corner of Vernor and 12th Street for all she cares, and Vietnam might have sunk by now into the Dead Sea under its tons of debris, for all the amazement she could show . . . her face is overworked, overwrought, at the age of twenty (thirty?) it is already exhausted but fanciful and ready for a laugh. Clarita says mournfully to me *Honey somebody is going to turn you out let me give you warning.* In a movie shown on late television Clarita is not a mess like this but a nurse, with short neat hair and a dedicated look, in love with her doctor and her doctor's patients and their diseases, enamored of needles and sponges and rubbing alcohol. . . . Or no: she is a private secretary. Robert Cummings is her boss. She helps him with fantastic plots, the canned audience laughs, no, the audience doesn't laugh because nothing is funny, instead her boss is Robert Taylor and they are not boss and secretary but husband and wife, she is threatened by a young starlet, she is grim, handsome, wifely, a good companion for a good man. . . . She is Claudette Colbert. Her sister too is Claudette Colbert. They are twins, identical. Her husband Charles Boyer is a very rich handsome man and her sister, Claudette Colbert, is plotting her death in order to take her place as the rich man's wife, no one will know because they are *twins*. . . . All these marvelous lives Clarita might have lived, but she fell out the bottom at the age of thirteen. At the age when I was packing my overnight case for a slumber party at Toni Deshield's she was tearing filthy sheets off a bed and scratching up a rash on her arms. . . . Thirteen is uncommonly young for a white girl in Detroit, Miss Brook of the Detroit House of Correction said in a sad newspaper interview for the *Detroit News;* fifteen and sixteen are more likely. Eleven, twelve, thirteen are not surprising in colored . . . they are more

precocious. What can we do? Taxes are rising and the tax base is falling. The temperature rises slowly but falls rapidly. Everything is falling out the bottom, Woodward Avenue is filthy, Livernois Avenue is filthy! Scraps of paper flutter in the air like pigeons, dirt flies up and hits you right in the eye, oh Detroit is breaking up into dangerous bits of newspaper and dirt, watch out. . . .

Clarita's apartment is over a restaurant. Simon her lover emerges from the cracks at dark. Mrs. Olesko, a neighbor of Clarita's, an aged white wisp of a woman, doesn't complain but sniffs with contentment at Clarita's noisy life and doesn't tell the cops, hating cops, when the cops arrive. I should give fake names, more blanks, instead of telling all these secrets. I myself am a secret; I am a minor.

3. My father reads a paper at a medical convention in Los Angeles. There he is, on the edge of the North American continent, when the unmarked detective put his hand so gently on my arm in the aisle of Branden's and said, "Miss, would you like to step over here for a minute?"

And where was he when Clarita put her hand on my arm, that wintry dark sulphurous aching day in Detroit, in the company of closed-down barber shops, closed-down diners, closed-down movie houses, homes, windows, basements, faces . . . she put her hand on my arm and said, "Honey, are you looking for somebody down here?"

And was he home worrying about me, gone for two weeks solid, when they carried me off . . . ? It took three of them to get me in the police cruiser, so they said, and they put more than their hands on my arm.

4. I work on this lesson. My English teacher is Mr. Forest, who is from Michigan State. Not handsome, Mr. Forest, and his name is plain unlike Raymond Forrest's, but he is sweet and rodent-like, he has conferred with the principal and my parents, and everything is fixed . . . treat her as if nothing has happened, a new start, begin again, only sixteen years old, what a shame, how did it happen? – nothing happened, nothing could have happened, a slight physiological modification known only to a gynecologist or to Dr. Coronet. I work on my lesson. I sit in my pink room. I look around the room with my sad pink eyes. I sigh, I dawdle, I pause, I eat up time, I am limp and happy to be home, I am sixteen years old suddenly, my head hangs heavy as a pumpkin on my shoulders, and my hair has just been cut by Mr. Faye at the Crystal Salon and is said to be very becoming.

(Simon too put his hand on my arm and said, "Honey, you have got to come with me," and in his six-by-six room we got to know each other. Would I go back to Simon again? Would I lie down with him in all that filth and craziness? Over and over again

a Clarita is being betrayed as in front of a Cunningham Drug Store she is nervously eyeing a colored man who may or may not have money, or a nervous white boy of twenty with sideburns and an Appalachian look, who may or may not have a knife hidden in his jacket pocket, or a husky red-faced man of friendly countenance who may or may not be a member of the Vice Squad out for an early twilight walk.)

I work on my lesson for Mr. Forest. I have filled up eleven pages. Words pour out of me and won't stop. I want to tell everything . . . what was the song Simon was always humming, and who was Simon's friend in a very new trench coat with an old high school graduation ring on his finger . . . ? Simon's bearded friend? When I was down too low for him Simon kicked me out and gave me to him for three days, I think, on Fourteenth Street in Detroit, an airy room of cold cruel drafts with newspapers on the floor. . . . Do I really remember that or am I piecing it together from what they told me? Did they tell the truth? Did they know much of the truth?

VIII. CHARACTERS

1. Wednesdays after school, at four; Saturday mornings at ten. Mother drives me to Dr. Coronet. Ferns in the office, plastic or real, they look the same. Dr. Coronet is queenly, an elegant nicotine-stained lady who would have studied with Freud had circumstances not prevented it, a bit of a Catholic, ready to offer you some mystery if your teeth will ache too much without it. Highly recommended by Father! Forty dollars an hour, Father's forty dollars! Progress! Looking up! Looking better! That new haircut is so becoming, says Dr. Coronet herself, showing how normal she is for a woman with an I.Q. of 180 and many advanced degrees.

2. Mother. A lady in a brown suede coat. Boots of shiny black material, black gloves, a black fur hat. She would be humiliated could she know that of all the people in the world it is my ex-lover Simon who walks most like her . . . self-conscious and unreal, listening to distant music, a little bowlegged with craftiness. . . .

3. Father. Tying a necktie. In a hurry. On my first evening home he put his hand on my arm and said, "Honey, we're going to forget all about this."

4. Simon. Outside a plane is crossing the sky, in here we're in a hurry. Morning. It must be morning. The girl is half out of her mind, whimpering and vague, Simon her dear friend is wretched this morning . . . he is wretched with morning itself . . . he forces her to give him an injection, with that needle she knows is filthy, she has a dread of needles and surgical instruments and the odor of things that are to be sent into the blood, thinking somehow of her father. . . . This is a bad morning, Simon says that his mind is being twisted out of shape, and so he submits to the needle which he usually scorns and bites his lip with his yellowish teeth, his face going very pale. *Ah baby!* he says in his soft mocking voice, which

with all women is a mockery of love, *do it like this* – Slowly – And the girl, terrified, almost drops the precious needle but manages to turn it up to the light from the window . . . it is an extension of herself, then? She can give him this gift, then? *I wish you wouldn't do this to me,* she says, wise in her terror, because it seems to her that Simon's danger – in a few minutes he might be dead – is a way of pressing her against him that is more powerful than any other embrace. She has to work over his arm, the knotted corded veins of his arm, her forehead wet with perspiration as she pushes and releases the needle, staring at that mixture of liquid now stained with Simon's bright blood. . . . When the drug hits him she can feel it herself, she feels that magic that is more than any woman can give him, striking the back of his head and making his face stretch as if with the impact of a terrible sun. . . . She tries to embrace him but he pushes her aside and stumbles to his feet. *Jesus Christ,* he says. . . .

5. Princess, a Negro girl of eighteen. What is her charge? She is close-mouthed about it, shrewd and silent, you know that no one had to wrestle her to the sidewalk to get her in here; she came with dignity. In the recreation room she sits reading *Nancy Drew and the Jewel Box Mystery,* which inspires in her face tiny wrinkles of alarm and interest: what a face! Light brown skin, heavy shaded eyes, heavy eyelashes, a serious sinister dark brow, graceful fingers, graceful wristbones, graceful legs, lips, tongue, a sugar-sweet voice, a leggy stride more masculine than Simon's and my mother's, decked out in a dirty white blouse and dirty white slacks; vaguely nautical is Princess's style. . . . At breakfast she is in charge of clearing the table and leans over me, saying, *Honey you sure you ate enough?*

6. The girl lies sleepless, wondering. Why here, why not there? Why Bloomfield Hills and not jail? Why jail and not her pink room? Why downtown Detroit and not Sioux Drive? What is the difference? Is Simon all the difference? The girl's head is a parade of wonders. She is nearly sixteen, her breath is marvelous with wonders, not long ago she was coloring with crayons and now she is smearing the landscape with paints that won't come off and won't come off her fingers either. She says to the matron *I am not talking about anything,* not because everyone has warned her not to talk but because, because she will not talk, because she won't say anything about Simon who is her secret. And she says to the matron *I won't go home* up until that night in the lavatory when everything was changed. . . . "No, I won't go home I want to stay here," she says, listening to her own words with amazement, thinking that weeds might climb everywhere over that marvelous $110,000 house and dinosaurs might return to muddy the beige carpeting, but never never will she reconcile four o'clock in the morning in Detroit with eight o'clock breakfasts in Bloomfield Hills . . . oh, she aches still for Simon's hands and his caressing breath, though he gave her little pleasure, he took everything from her (five-dollar bills, ten-dollar bills, passed into her numb hands by men and taken out of her hands by Simon) until she herself was passed into the hands

of other men, police, when Simon evidently got tired of her and her hysteria. ... *No, I won't go home, I don't want to be bailed out,* the girl thinks as a *Stubborn and Wayward Child* (one of several charges lodged against her) and the matron understands her crazy white-rimmed eyes that are seeking out some new violence that will keep her in jail, should someone threaten to let her out. Such children try to strangle the matrons, the attendants, or one another ... they want the locks locked forever, the doors nailed shut ... and this girl is no different up until that night her mind is changed for her. ...

IX. THAT NIGHT

Princess and Dolly, a little white girl of maybe fifteen, hardy however as a sergeant and in the House of Correction for armed robbery, corner her in the lavatory at the farthest sink and the other girls look away and file out to bed, leaving her. God how she is beaten up! Why is she beaten up? Why do they pound her, why such hatred? Princess vents all the hatred of a thousand silent Detroit winters on her body, this girl whose body belongs to me, fiercely she rides across the midwestern plains on this girl's tender bruised body ... revenge on the oppressed minorities of America! revenge on the slaughtered Indians! revenge on the female sex, on the male sex, revenge on Bloomfield Hills, revenge revenge. ...

X. DETROIT

In Detroit weather weighs heavily upon everyone. The sky looms large. The horizon shimmers in smoke. Downtown the buildings are imprecise in the haze. Perpetual haze. Perpetual motion inside the haze. Across the choppy river is the city of Windsor, in Canada. Part of the continent has bunched up here and is bulging outward, at the tip of Detroit, a cold hard rain is forever falling on the expressways ... shoppers shop grimly, their cars are not parked in safe places, their windshields may be smashed and graceful ebony hands may drag them out through their shatterproof smashed windshields crying *Revenge for the Indians!* Ah, they all fear leaving Hudson's and being dragged to the very tip of the city and thrown off the parking roof of Cobo Hall, that expensive tomb, into the river. ...

XI. CHARACTERS WE ARE FOREVER ENTWINED WITH

1. Simon drew me into his tender rotting arms and breathed gravity into me. Then I came to earth, weighted down. He said *You are such a little girl,* and he weighed me down with his delight. In the palms of his hands were teeth marks

from his previous life experiences. He was thirty-five, they said. Imagine Simon in this room, in my pink room: he is about six feet tall and stoops slightly, in a feline cautious way, always thinking, always on guard, with his scuffed light suede shoes and his clothes which are anyone's clothes, slightly rumpled ordinary clothes that ordinary men might wear to not-bad jobs. Simon has fair, long hair curly hair, spent languid curls that are like . . . exactly like the curls of wood shavings to the touch, I am trying to be exact . . . and he smells of unheated mornings and coffee and too many pills coating his tongue with a faint green-white scum. . . . Dear Simon, who would be panicked in this room and in this house (right now Billie is vacuuming next door in my parents' room: a vacuum cleaner's roar is a sign of all good things), Simon who is said to have come from a home not much different from this, years ago, fleeing all the carpeting and the polished banisters . . . Simon has a deathly face, only desperate people fall in love with it. His face is bony and cautious, the bones of his cheeks prominent as if with the rigidity of his ceaseless thinking, plotting, for he has to make money out of girls to whom money means nothing, they're so far gone they can hardly count it, and in a sense money means nothing to him either except as a way of keeping on with his life. *Each Day's Proud Struggle,* the title of a novel we could read at jail. . . . Each day he needs a certain amount of money. He devours it. It wasn't love he uncoiled in me with his hollowed-out eyes and his courteous smile, that remnant of a prosperous past, but a dark terror that needed to press itself flat against him, or against another man . . . but he was the first, he came over to me and took my arm, a claim. We struggled on the stairs and I said, "Let me loose, you're hurting my neck, my face," it was such a surprise that my skin hurt where he rubbed it, and afterward we lay face to face and he breathed everything into me. In the end I think he turned me in.

2. Raymond Forrest. I just read this morning that Raymond Forrest's father, the chairman of the board at ———, died of a heart attack on a plane bound for London. I would like to write Raymond Forrest a note of sympathy. I would like to thank him for not pressing charges against me one hundred years ago, saving me, being so generous . . . well, men like Raymond Forrest are generous men, not like Simon. I would like to write him a letter telling of my love, or of some other emotion that is positive and healthy. Not like Simon and his poetry, which he scrawled down when he was high and never changed a word . . . but when I try to think of something to say it is Simon's language that comes back to me, caught in my head like a bad song, it is always Simon's language:

> There is no reality only dreams
> Your neck may get snapped when you wake
> My love is drawn to some violent end
> She keeps wanting to get away

My love is heading downward
And I am heading upward
She is going to crash on the sidewalk
And I am going to dissolve into the clouds

XII. EVENTS

1. Out of the hospital, bruised and saddened and converted, with Princess's grunts still tangled in my hair . . . and Father in his overcoat looking like a Prince himself, come to carry me off. Up the expressway and out north to home. Jesus Christ but the air is thinner and cleaner here. Monumental houses. Heartbreaking sidewalks, so clean.

2. Weeping in the living room. The ceiling is two storeys high and two chandeliers hang from it. Weeping, weeping, though Billie the maid is *probably listening*. I will never leave home again. Never. Never leave home. Never leave this home again, never.

3. Sugar doughnuts for breakfast. The toaster is very shiny and my face is distorted in it. Is that my face?

4. The car is turning in the driveway. Father brings me home. Mother embraces me. Sunlight breaks in movieland patches on the roof of our traditional contemporary home, which was designed for the famous automotive stylist whose identity, if I told you the name of the famous car he designed, you would all know, so I can't tell you because my teeth chatter at the thought of being sued . . . or having someone climb into my bedroom window with a rope to strangle me. . . . The car turns up the blacktop drive. The house opens to me like a doll's house, so lovely in the sunlight, the big living room beckons to me with its walls falling away in a delirium of joy at my return, Billie the maid is *no doubt* listening from the kitchen as I burst into tears and the hysteria Simon got so sick of. Convulsed in Father's arms I say I will never leave again, never, why did I leave, where did I go, what happened, my mind is gone wrong, my body is one big bruise, my backbone was sucked dry, it wasn't the men who hurt me and Simon never hurt me but only those girls . . . my God how they hurt me . . . I will never leave home again. . . . The car is perpetually turning up the drive and I am perpetually breaking down in the living room and we are perpetually taking the right exit from the expressway (Lahser Road) and the wall of the restroom is perpetually banging against my head and perpetually are Simon's hands moving across my body and adding everything up and so too are Father's hands on my shaking bruised back, far from the surface of my skin on the surface of my good

blue cashmere coat (dry-cleaned for my release). . . . I weep for all the money here, for God in gold and beige carpeting, for the beauty of chandeliers and the miracle of a clean polished gleaming toaster and faucets that run both hot and cold water, and I tell them *I will never leave home, this is my home, I love everything here, I am in love with everything here. . . .*

JAMES ALAN MC PHERSON b. 1943

Born in Savannah, Georgia, McPherson went to Morgan State College in Baltimore, an all-black school, and there was identified by a Harvard Law School recruiter as an excellent prospect for admission. He did well in law school, but together with his fellow blacks he underwent the soul-searching doubts of black people participating in a traditionally all-white profession. Later, while acting himself as a recruiter for Harvard at a black southern college, he tells of talking to a student much more skeptical than he himself had been. Defensively, McPherson finally tells him: "I went to a white law school, and I survived it." But the student, he continues, "sat looking at me, and his eyes were so close to accusation that I felt compelled to add, 'I think.' "

That assurance and yet the honest doubt (". . . I think") that ring in McPherson's account of this interview pervade his work. He is a fine reporter as well as a fiction writer, and his 1969 two-part study in *The Atlantic* of the Blackstone Rangers, the huge black gang on the south side of Chicago, is both accurate and compassionate. His short stories present the various levels on which blacks relate to whites, his emphasis being not on the kind of violent confrontation that Richard Wright portrays but on the subtleties of individuals who live in what seems on the surface to be the same society. Of his stories McPherson says over-modestly that they come out of "a very small, extremely limited experience," and that he has tried to keep racial identities in the background. In fact, what he manages is to represent a high order of human involvement that reveals racial feeling without insisting upon its exclusive importance.

Because of his commitment to writing McPherson has not practiced law. For a while he taught English at Iowa State, and he now works as an editor in Boston.

ON TRAINS

I

The waiters say she got on the train in Chicago, after transferring from Dearborn Station. She was plump and matronly and her glasses were tinted so that she might have been a tourist seeking protection from the sun; but there was neither sun nor fresh air on the train and she was very pale and a little wrinkled, the way clerks or indoor people grow after many years of their protected, colorless kind of life. She was, indeed, that nondescript type of person one might be aware of but never really see in a supermarket or at a bargain basement sale, carefully and methodically fingering each item; or on a busy street corner waiting for the light to change while others, with less conscious respect for the letter of the law, flowed around her. She rode for a whole day before coming into the dining car for a meal: then she had the $1.95 Special. She asked for buttermilk and wanted "lightbread" instead of rolls. The black waiters all grinned at each other in their secret way.

When she finished her meal she sat reading a book and looking out at the yellow and green flatlands of North Dakota until the steward had to ask her to leave so that the waiters could clean up the table for the next setting. She did not protest, but left with an indignant flourish of her dress. The automatic door to the car leading to the Pullman section hissed angrily behind her. The steward called her a bitch between his teeth and the waiter who had served her, standing next to the steward with his tray under his arm, grinned broadly, showing his own smokestained teeth. But when he saw that she had left no tip he called her a cheap bitch aloud and the steward scowled at him.

After the last setting the waiters sat down to eat their dinner. Two Pullman Porters came in with their coffee cans, begging for handouts. They were very greedy and, if given one can of free coffee, would continue to come back for more during the length of the trip, as if the first can had entitled them to all that they could drink. They sat down at the waiters' table and watched the waiters eat. The waiters were very greedy too. They ate ravenously. The porters watched the waiters for a while, then one of them closed his eyes and began to doze. The other one, an old fellow with aged and tired eyes like an owl's, looked out at the floating gold of the sunset across the passing wheatfields. He watched until the fields became patterns of black and fading gold. Then he turned to the waiters.

"We got a old Southern gal back there," he said.

"We had her up here," one of the waiters said between huge mouthfuls of beef. "She got good service but she didn't leave no tip."

"She had me polishin' her shoes," the porter said, "but I don't reckon she'll pay off when she gets off. I didn't put much work out on it anyway." He stretched his thin legs under the table. They cracked with the sound of dead autumn branches underfoot.

A woman in pants passed through the car. Her hair was cut somewhat like a little girl's Dutch Boy and a ringlet of it curled against her cheek. She blew at it out of the corner of her mouth and smiled knowingly at the men seated around the table. "Which way to the club car?" she asked. Her lipstick was above the line of her mouth so that it looked like a red moustache. She was not at all pretty and not at all young.

"Two cars ahead," one waiter said.

She turned to go, took a few steps and then looked back at the men. The two waiters were looking her over, one porter was still dozing, and the other, the tired one, was seemingly not aware of her.

"How late does it stay open?"

"Till twelve," the same waiter said.

"Chicago time," the other waiter added.

They watched her move through the door.

"She'll tip big tomorrow," one of them said.

"Yeah."

"That old biddy knows where the club car is. She been in there all day. I seen her battin' them greasy eyes at John Perry on the bar."

"Maybe he'll take care of business for her tonight," the tired Pullman Porter said. But there was no humor in it, and all of their laughs were only polite.

"If he does she'll tip big tomorrow," one of the waiters said again.

The porter with the owl eyes pushed the dozing porter. "Time to get the beds down, Tim," he said. Tim got up slowly and they took their coffee cans and trudged down the aisle toward the Pullman section. As they reached the door it opened and the lady who had transferred from Dearborn came into the car. The two porters stood on either side of the aisle and let her pass between them. They wore white jackets with silver buttons which were embossed: "Pullman Company." Together with their caps with silver plates, which also read "Pullman Porter," and black pants, they looked like two painted black statues before the entrance to some fine suburban home. She did not notice them, but passed directly through the car, leaving behind her a scent of something sweet and strong.

When she entered the club car the woman with the Dutch bob was sitting at the bar talking to John Perry, the bartender, who stood behind the bar leaning with his arms on its waxed red surface. They were very close and the Dutch woman was smiling mysteriously. There was no one else in the car. The Dearborn lady seated herself at a deuce near the far end of the car and began to stare at John Perry as he said something low and soft and smile-provoking to the painted thing on the stool across from him. The Dearborn lady cleared her throat. John Perry placed his dark, thick hand closer to the other, softer hand on the bar and did not look up. The painted woman made a throaty chuckle, like the confusing sound one might hear near a car parked by a frog pond on a summer night.

"I want some service," the lady at the end of the car finally said. "I've been here for ten minutes now and I want some service."

The bartender looked annoyed as he went over to her table. "What'll it be lady?" he said. His voice was deep and smooth and almost as greasy as the painted woman's lips; and it had that familiar ring of professional servitude, which is peculiar to small, serving people who like their work.

"I want a Benedictine and brandy."

"No Benedictine. This is a train, lady."

She paused. "I'll have a crème de menthe then."

"We don't have that neither."

"Try bourbon and water, honey," the woman at the bar said, and she lifted her glass for the woman to see. "He makes it very good. I'm going to have another one myself." She looked at the bartender as she pushed a five-dollar bill across the bar. "Make yourself one too," she told him.

The lady at the deuce looked at her fiercely.

She finally ordered a rosé, paid for it, and settled back, taking turns watching the immediate reflections of the two at the bar in the window next to her face and the darkness of the passing countryside beyond their reflections. The train lumbered on and it made the only noise, save for an occasional giggle and a deep-throated chuckle from the bar. Finally the woman got up from the stool and said, "See you later on" to the bartender. She said it with a contrived, unnatural seductivity and took her time moving out of the car. The Dearborn lady, still seated at the table and facing the window, saw it all through her tinted glasses.

The bartender began to whistle as he washed the glasses. He was a robust fellow but he moved very gracefully behind the bar, like a dancer. Still, he splashed a great deal of water on the floor. He glanced over at the lady once or twice as she, in turn, looked alternately at the darkness beyond the thick window glass and at him. But only her eyes moved. Then the man moved out from behind the bar and came toward her. She stiffened and gathered her purse and got up, all very quickly. He was wiping the tables and whistling as she hurried out of the car.

II

In the Pullman car, the porter was still making the beds. He shuffled from one roomette to the next, not wasting a single step. The occupants came out of their rooms and stood in the hall while he swished and tucked their sheets. Then he knocked on the Dearborn lady's door. "Porter!" he barked, the way a street-corner concessionaire would say "Hot Dogs!" There was no answer, so he went in and began turning down the bed. She came up behind him and watched his back as he moved about the small compartment. She was breathing very hard.

"What time do you lock the doors to the car?" she asked.

"The doors ain't never locked," he said, not turning to face her.

"How do you keep people out?" She paused, and then said: "My luggage is in the hall. It's very expensive."

"I'll watch out for it. I sit up all night."

"Inside the car?"

"Yes ma'am."

"But I . . . we have to sleep. We have to sleep in here," she said. She was very excited now.

"Yes ma'am." He did not stop his work; nor did he look at her, but answered her questions and made the bed with the proficiency and cool detachment of one used to confronting stupidity in the intelligent. It was bargained and paid for in the price of her ticket and his was a patient and polite endurance of her right to be stupid. "I'm a Pullman Porter," he said. "I been a Pullman Porter for forty-three years." He had finished the bed and he smoothed down a light ripple in the red blanket. His hands were rough and wrinkled and the backs of his fingers were very black. "Forty-three years," he repeated reminiscently, half to himself. She could not see his eyes.

"Well, you can't stay in here tonight," she said, and moved into the small compartment as if to possess it entirely with her presence.

The porter backed out. "It's my job," he said.

She was extremely nervous now and ran her hands lightly over the sides of her dress. Her hands stuck to the thin silk. "You go get the Pullman Conductor," she said. "I can talk to him." She began to pace up and down the little length of the roomette.

The porter returned in a few minutes with the Pullman Conductor. The blue-suited conductor entered the compartment while the porter stood outside the door and watched them, his dark old eyes flashing from one face to the other.

"He sits up in the car, lady," the conductor said. "It's his job. He has to be here if anyone rings for him at night." The conductor was very irritated. He had already started to undress for bed and his tie hung loosely about his neck. The lady was perspiring now and the little beads of sweat glistened on her temples in the glare of the white light overhead.

"I can't and I won't sleep in the same car with that . . . that gentleman!"

"That's your business if you don't sleep, lady," the conductor said. "He stays in the car." The conductor was very mad now. The lines in his forehead grew very red and his nose, which was small, grew larger and redder with his controlled breathing.

"We have a *right* to sleep here without these people coming in *doing* things."

"What's he done to you, lady?"

"He's black! He's black!" And she said it with the exasperation and utter defeat of an inexperienced teacher whose patience has been exhausted and who can only stamp the right answer into the mind of a stupid child.

"He's a porter," the conductor said.

The porter, who stood all the while like a child waiting for punishment, seemed to droop and wither and grow smaller; and his eyes, which had only minutes before flashed brightly from the face of the conductor to the enraged face of the lady, now seemed to dull and turn inward as only those who have learned to suffer silently can turn their eyes inward. He was a very old man and he grew older, even older than his occupation or the oldest and most obsequious Pullman Porter.

People were looking out of their compartments and the Dearborn lady, hearing them, raised her voice in a plea. "He sleeps in here. He sleeps in here with us!" she shouted to them. Down the hall, the painted woman opened the door to Compartment G and listened and smiled and shook her head, and then closed the door again. And the rest listened and weighed the thought, which was a new one deserving some consideration. But the conductor said that it was necessary for comfort and they agreed and returned to their rooms. Only the porter stood outside the door looking guilty.

It was finally decided that the Dearborn lady would take a seat in the coaches for the night. She wanted it that way. The porter would sleep as he had always slept: sitting up in the back of the car with his eyes closed and his mind awake and his coffee can by his side and the small bright night-light over his bowed head, and his ear next to the buzzer in case someone should ring. Everyone agreed that it was the way things should be; it was necessary for comfort, and besides, it was his job.

And later that night, when John Perry, the bartender, who danced and splashed a great deal of water, when he washed glasses, stole into the dark sleeping car, he paused for a minute before the bent old man on the porter's seat. The coffee can had fallen over on the seat and John Perry picked it up and placed in on the floor next to the old man's feet. Then he knocked very softly on the door to Compartment G. And after a while it was opened and quickly closed behind him.

OF CABBAGES AND KINGS

I

Claude Sheats had been in the Brotherhood all his life and then he had tried to get out. Some of his people and most of his friends were still in the Brotherhood and were still very good members, but Claude was no longer a good member because he had tried to get out after over twenty years. To get away from the Brotherhood and all his friends who were still active in it, he moved to Washington Square and took to reading about being militant. But, living there, he developed a craving for whiteness the way a nicely broke-in virgin craves sex. In spite of this, he maintained a steady black girl, whom he saw at least twice a month to keep up appearances, and once he took both of us with him when he visited his uncle in Harlem who was still in the Brotherhood.

"She's a nice girl, Claude," his uncle's wife had told him that night because the girl, besides being attractive, had some very positive ideas about the Brotherhood. Her name was Marie, she worked as a secretary in my office, and it was on her suggestion that I had moved in with Claude Sheats.

"I'm glad to see you don't waste your time on hippies," the uncle had said. "All our young men are selling out these days."

The uncle was the kind of fellow who had played his cards right. He was much older than his wife, and I had the impression, that night, that he must have given her time to experience enough and to become bored enough before he overwhelmed her with his success. He wore glasses and combed his hair back and had that oily kind of composure that made me think of a waiter waiting to be tipped. He was very proud of his English, I observed, and how he always ended his words with just the right sound. He must have felt superior to people who didn't. He must have felt superior to Claude because he was still with the Brotherhood and Claude had tried to get out.

Claude did not like him and always seemed to feel guilty whenever we visited his uncle's house. "Don't mention any of my girls to him," he told me after our first visit.

"Why would I do that?" I said.

"He'll try to psych you into telling him."

"Why should he suspect you? He never comes over to the apartment."

"He just likes to know what I'm doing. I don't want him to know about my girls."

"I won't say anything," I promised.

He was almost twenty-three and had no steady girls, except for Marie. He was well built, so that he had no trouble in the Village area. It was like going to the market for him. During my first days in the apartment the process had seemed like a game. And once, when he was going out, I said: "Bring back two."

Half an hour later he came back with two girls. He got their drinks and then he called me into his room to meet them.

"This is Doris," he said, pointing to the smaller one, "and I forgot your name," he said to the big blonde.

"Jane," she said.

"This is Howard," he told her.

"Hi," I said. Neither one of them smiled. The big blonde in white pants sat on the big bed and the little one sat on a chair near the window. He had given them his worst bourbon.

"Excuse me a minute," Claude said to the girls. "I want to talk to Howard for a minute." He put on a record before we went outside into the hall between our rooms. He was always extremely polite and gentle, and very soft-spoken in spite of his size.

"Listen," he said to me outside, "you can have the blonde."

"What can I do with that amazon?"

"I don't care. Just get her out of the room."

"She's dirty," I said.

"So you can give her a bath."

"It wouldn't help much."

"Well just take her out and talk to her," he told me. "Remember, you asked for her."

We went back in. "Where you from?" I said to the amazon.

"Brighton."

"What school?"

"No. I just got here."

"From where?"

"*Brighton!*"

"That's not so far," I said.

"*England,*" she said. She looked very bored. Claude Sheats looked at me.

"How did you find Washington Square so fast?"

"I got friends."

She was very superior about it all and seemed to look at us with the same slightly patient irritation of a professional theater critic waiting for a late performance to begin. The little one sat on the chair, her legs crossed, looking up at the ceiling. Her white pants were dirty too. They looked as though they would have been very relieved if we had taken off our clothes and danced for them around the room and across the bed, and made hungry sounds in our throats with our mouths slightly opened.

I said that I had to go out to the drugstore and would be back very soon; but once outside, I walked a whole hour in one direction and then I walked back. I passed them a block away from our apartment. They were walking fast and did not slow down or speak when I passed them.

Claude Sheats was drinking heavily when I came into the apartment.

"What the hell are you trying to pull?" he said.

"I couldn't find a drugstore open."

He got up from the living room table and walked toward me. "You should have asked me," he said. "I got more than enough."

"I wanted some mouthwash too," I said.

He fumed a while longer, and then told me how I had ruined his evening because the amazon would not leave the room to wait for me and the little one would not do anything with the amazon around. He suddenly thought about going down and bringing them back; and he went out for a while. But he came back without them, saying that they had been picked up again.

"When a man looks out for you, you got to look out for him," he warned me.

"I'm sorry."

"A hell of a lot of good *that* does. And that's the last time I look out for *you*, baby," he said. "From now on it's *me* all the way."

"Thanks," I said.

"If she was too much for you I could of taken the amazon."

"It didn't matter that much," I said.

"You could of had Doris if you couldn't handle the amazon."

"They were both too much," I told him.

But Claude Sheats did not answer. He just looked at me.

II

After two months of living with him I concluded that Claude hated whites as much as he loved them. And he hated himself with the very same passion. He hated the country and his place in it and he loved the country and his place in it. He loved the Brotherhood and all that being in it had taught him and he still believed in what he had been taught, even after he had left it and did not have to believe in anything.

"This Man is going *down*, Howard," he would announce with conviction.

"Why?" I would ask.

"Because it's the Black Man's time to rule again. They had five thousand years, now we get five thousand years."

"What if I don't *want* to rule?" I asked. "What happens if I don't want to take over?"

He looked at me with pity in his face. "You go down with the rest of the country."

"I guess I wouldn't mind much anyway," I said. "It would be a hell of a place with nobody to hate."

But I could never get him to smile about it the way I tried to smile about it. He was always serious. And, once, when I questioned the mysticism in the teachings of the Brotherhood, Claude almost attacked me. "Another man might kill you for saying that," he had said. "Another man might not let you get away with saying something like that." He was quite deadly and he stood over me with an air of patient superiority. And because he could afford to be generous and forgiving, being one of the saved, he sat down at the table with me under the single light bulb and began to teach me. He told me the stories about how it was in the beginning before the whites took over, and about all the little secret significances of black, and about the subtle infiltration of white superiority into everyday objects.

"You've never seen me eat white bread or white sugar, have you?"

"No," I said. He used brown bread and brown sugar.

"Or use bleached flour or white rice?"

"No."

"You know why, don't you?" He waited expectantly.

"No," I finally said. "I don't know why."

He was visibly shocked, so much so that he dropped that line of instruction and began to draw on a pad before him on the living room table. He moved his big shoulders over the yellow pad to conceal his drawings and looked across the table at me. "Now I'm going to tell you something that white men have paid thousands of dollars to learn," he said. "Men have been killed for telling this but I'm telling you for nothing. I'm warning you not to repeat it because if the whites find out you know, you could be killed too."

"You know me," I said. "I wouldn't repeat any secrets."

He gave me a long thoughtful look.

I gave him back a long, eager, honest look.

Then he leaned across the table and whispered: "Kennedy isn't buried in this country. He was the only President who never had his coffin opened during the funeral. The body was in state all that time and they never opened the coffin once. You know why?"

"No."

"Because he's not *in it*! They buried an empty coffin. Kennedy was a Thirty-third Degree Mason. His body is in Jerusalem right now."

"How do you know?" I asked.

"If I told you it would put your life in danger."

"Did his family know about it?"

"No. His lodge kept it secret."

"No one knew?"

"I'm telling you, *no!*"

"Then how did you find out?"

He sighed, more from tolerance than from boredom with my inability to comprehend the mysticism of pure reality in its most unadulterated form. Of course I could not believe him and we argued about it, back and forth; but to absolutely cap all my uncertainties he drew the thirty-three degree circle, showed me the secret signs that men had died to learn, and spoke about the time when our black ancestors chased an evil genius out of their kingdom and across a desert and onto an island somewhere in the sea; from which, hundreds of years later, this same evil genius sent forth a perfected breed of white-skinned and evil creatures who, through trickery, managed to enslave for five thousand years the onetime Black Masters of the world. He further explained the significance of the East and why all the saved must go there once during their lifetimes, and possibly be buried there, as Kennedy had been.

It was dark and late at night, and the glaring bulb cast his great shadow into the corners so that there was the sense of some outraged spirit, fuming in the halls and dark places of our closets, waiting to extract some terrible and justifiable revenge from him for disclosing to me, an unbeliever, the closest-kept of secrets. But I was aware of them only for an instant, and then I did not believe him again.

The most convincing thing about it all was that he was very intelligent and had an orderly, well regimented lifestyle, and yet *he* had no trouble with believing. He believed in the certainty of statistical surveys, which was his work; the nutritional value of wheat germ sprinkled on eggs; the sensuality of gin; and the dangers inherent in smoking. He was stylish in that he did not believe in God, but he was extremely moral and warm and kind; and I wanted sometimes to embrace him for his kindness and bigness and gentle manners. He lived his life so carefully that no matter what he said, I could not help but believe him sometimes. But I did not want to, because I knew that once I started I could not stop; and then there would be no purpose to my own beliefs and no real conviction or direction in my own efforts to achieve when always in the back of my regular thoughts, there would be a sense of futility and a fear of the unknown all about me. So, for the sake of necessity, I chose not to believe him.

He felt that the country was doomed and that the safe thing to do was to make enough money as soon as possible and escape to the Far East. He forecast summer riots in certain Northern cities and warned me, religiously, to avoid all implicating ties with whites so that I might have a chance to be saved when that time came. And I asked him about *his* ties, and the girls, and how it was never a movie date with coffee afterwards but always his room and the cover-all blanket of Motown sounds late into the night.

"A man has different reasons for doing certain things," he had said.

He never seemed to be comfortable with any of the girls. He never seemed to be in control. And after my third month in the apartment I had concluded that he used his virility as a tool and forged, for however long it lasted, a little area of superiority which could never, it seemed, extend itself beyond the certain confines of his room, no matter how late into the night the records played. I could see him fighting to extend the area, as if an increase in the number of girls he saw could compensate for what he had lost in duration. He saw many girls: curious students, unexpected bus-stop pickups, and assorted other one-nighters. And his rationalizations allowed him to believe that each one was an actual conquest, a physical affirmation of a psychological victory over all he hated and loved and hated in the little world of his room.

But then he seemed to have no happiness, even in this. Even here I sensed some intimations of defeat. After each girl, Claude would almost immediately come out of his room, as if there was no need for aftertalk; as if, after it was over, he felt a brooding, silent emptiness that quickly intensified into nervousness and instantaneous shyness and embarrassment so that the cold which sets in after that kind of emotional drain came in very sharp against his skin, and he could not bear to have her there any longer. And when the girl had gone, he would come into my room to talk. These were the times when he was most like a little boy; and these were the times when he really began to trust me.

"That bitch called me everything but the son of God," he would chuckle. And I would put aside my papers brought home from the office, smile at him, and listen.

He would always eat or drink afterwards and in those early days I was glad for his companionship and the return of his trust, and sometimes we drank and talked until dawn. During these times he would tell me more subtleties about the Man and would re-predict the fall of the country. Once, he warned me, in a fatherly way, about reading life from books before experiencing it; and another night he advised me on how to schedule girls so that one could run them without being run in return. These were usually good times of good-natured arguments and predictions; but as we drank more often he tended to grow more excited and quick-tempered, especially after he had just entertained. Sometimes he would seethe hate, and every drink he took gave life to increasingly bitter condemnations of the present system and our place in it. There were actually flying saucers, he told me once, piloted by things from other places in the universe which would eventually destroy the country for what it had done to the black man. He had run into his room, on that occasion, and had brought out a book by a man who maintained that the government was deliberately withholding from the public overwhelming evidence of flying saucers and strange creatures from other galaxies that walked among us every day. Claude emphasized the fact that the writer was a Ph.D. who must know what he was talking about, and insisted that the politicians withheld the information because they knew that their time was almost up and if they made it public the black man would know that he had outside friends who would help him take over the world again. Nothing I said could make him reconsider the slightest bit of his information.

"What are we going to use for weapons when we take over?" I asked him once.

"We've got atomic bombs stockpiled and waiting for the day."

"How can you believe that crap?"

He did not answer, but said instead: "You are the living example of what the Man has done to my people."

"I just try to think things out for myself," I said.

"You can't think. The handkerchief over your head is too big."

I smiled.

"I know," he continued. "I know all there is to know about whites because I've been studying them all my life."

I smiled some more.

"I ought to know," he said slowly. "I have supernatural powers."

"I'm tired," I told him. "I want to go to sleep now."

Claude started to leave the room, then he turned. "Listen," he said at the door. He pointed his finger at me to emphasize the gravity of his pronouncement. "I predict that within the next week something is going to happen to this country that will hurt it even more than Kennedy's assassination."

"Goodnight," I said as he closed the door.

He opened it again. "Remember that I predicted it when it happens," he said. For the first time I noticed that he had been deadly serious all along.

Two days later several astronauts burned to death in Florida. He raced into my room hot with the news.

"Do you believe in me *now?*" he said. "Just two days and look what happened."

I tried to explain, as much to myself as to him, that in any week of the year something unfortunate was bound to occur. But he insisted that this was only part of a divine plan to bring the country to its knees. He said that he intended to send a letter off right away to Jeane Dixon in D.C. to let her know that she was not alone because he also has the same power. Then he thought that he had better not because the FBI knew that he had been active in the Brotherhood before he got out.

At first it was good fun believing that someone important cared enough to watch us. And sometimes when the telephone was dead a long time before the dial tone sounded, I would knock on his door and together we would run through our telephone conversations for that day to see if either of us had said anything implicating or suspect, just in case they were listening. This feeling of persecution brought us closer together and soon the instruction sessions began to go on almost every night. At this point I could not help but believe him a little. And he began to trust me again, like a tolerable little brother, and even confided that the summer riots would break out simultaneously in Harlem and Watts during the second week in August. For some reason, something very difficult to put into words, I spent three hot August nights on the streets of Harlem, waiting for the riot to start.

In the seventh month of our living together, he began to introduce me to his girls again when they came in. Most of them came only once, but all of them received the same mechanical treatment. He only discriminated with liquor, the quality of which improved with the attractiveness or reluctance of the girl: gin for slow starters, bourbon for momentary strangers, and the scotch he reserved for those he hoped would come again. There was first the trek into his room, his own trip out for the ice and glasses while classical music was played within; then after a while the classical piece would be replaced by several Motowns. Finally, there was her trip to the bathroom, his calling a cab in the hall, and the sound of both their feet on the stairs as he walked her down to the cab. Then he would come to my room in his red bathrobe, glass in hand, for the aftertalk.

Then in the ninth month the trouble started. It would be very easy to pick out one incident, one day, one area of misunderstanding in that month and say: "That was where it began." It would be easy, but not accurate. It might have been one instance or a combination of many. It might have been the girl who came into the living room, when I was going over the proposed blueprints for a new settlement house, and who lingered too long outside his room in conversation because her father was a builder somewhere. Or it might have been nothing at all. But after that time he warned me about being too friendly with his company.

Another night, when I was leaving the bathroom in my shorts, he came out of his room with a girl who smiled.

"Hi," she said to me.

I nodded hello as I ducked back into the bathroom.

When he had walked her down to the door he came to my room and knocked. He did not have a drink.

"Why didn't you speak to my company?" he demanded.

"I was in my shorts."

"She felt bad about it. She asked what the hell was wrong with you. What could I tell her – 'He got problems'?"

"I'm sorry," I said. "But I didn't want to stop in my shorts."

"I see through you, Howard," he said. "You're just jealous of me and try to insult my girls to get to me."

"Why should I be jealous of you?"

"Because I'm a man and you're not."

"What makes a man anyway?" I said. "Your fried eggs and wheat germ? Why should I be jealous of you *or* what you bring in?"

"Some people don't need a reason. You're a black devil and you'll get yours. I predict that you'll get yours."

"Look," I told him, "I'm sorry about the girl. Tell her I'm sorry when you see her again."

"You treated her so bad she probably won't come back."

I said nothing more and he stood there silently for a long time before he turned to leave the room. But at the door he turned again and said: "I see through you, Howard. You're a black devil."

It should have ended there and it might have with anyone else. I took great pains to speak to his girls after that, even though he tried to get them into the room as quickly as possible. But a week later he accused me of walking about in his room after he had gone out, some two weeks before.

"I swear I wasn't in your room," I protested.

"I saw your shadow on the blinds from across the street at the bus stop," he insisted.

"I've *never* been in your room when you weren't there," I told him.

"I *saw* you!"

We went into his room and I tried to explain how, even if he could see the window from the bus stop, the big lamp next to the window prevented any shadow from being cast on the blinds. But he was convinced in his mind that at every opportunity I plundered his closets and drawers. He had no respect for simple logic in these matters, no sense of the absurdity of his accusations, and the affair finally ended with my confessing that I might have done it without actually knowing; and if I had, I would not do it again.

But what had been a gesture for peace on my part became a vindication for him, proof that I *was* a black devil, capable of lying and lying until he confronted me with the inescapable truth of the situation. And so he persisted in creating situations from which, if he insisted on a point long enough and with enough self-righteousness, he could draw my inevitable confession.

And I confessed eagerly, goaded on by the necessity of maintaining peace. I confessed to mixing white sugar crystals in with his own brown crystals so that he could use it and violate the teachings of the Brotherhood; I confessed to cleaning the bathroom all the time merely because I wanted to make him feel guilty for not having ever cleaned it. I confessed to telling the faithful Marie, who brought a surprise dinner over for him, that he was working late at his office in order to implicate him with the girls who worked there. I confessed to leaving my papers about the house so that his company could ask about them and develop an interest in me. And I pleaded guilty to a record of other little infamies, which multiplied into countless others, and again subdivided into hundreds of little subtleties until my every movement was a threat to him. If I had a girlfriend to dinner, we should eat in my room instead of at the table because he had to use the bathroom a lot and, besides not wanting to seem as if he were making a pass at my girl by walking through the room so often, he was genuinely embarrassed to be seen going to the bathroom.

If I protested he would fly into a tantrum and shake his big finger at me vigorously. And so I retreated, step by step, into my room, from which I emerged only to go to the bathroom or kitchen or out of the house. I tried to stay out on nights when he had company. But he had company so often that I could not always help being in my room after he had walked her to the door. Then he would knock on my door for his talk. He might offer me a drink, and if I refused, he would go to his room for a while and then come back. He would pace about for a while, like a big little boy who wants to ask for money over his allowance. At these times my mind would move feverishly over all our contacts for as far back as I could make it reach, searching and attempting to pull out that one incident which would surely be the point of his attack. But it was never any use; it might have been anything.

"Howard, I got something on my chest and I might as well get it off."

"What is it?" I asked from my bed.

"You been acting strange lately. Haven't been talking to me. If you got something on your chest, get it off now."

"I have nothing on my chest," I said.

"Then why don't you talk?"

I did not answer.

"You hardly speak to me in the kitchen. If you have something against me, tell me now."

"I have nothing against you."

"Why don't you talk, then?" He looked directly at me. "If a man doesn't talk, you think *something's* wrong!"

"I've been nervous lately, that's all. I got problems and I don't want to talk."

"Everybody's got problems. That's no reason for going around making a man feel guilty."

"For God's sake, I don't want to talk."

"I know what's wrong with you. Your conscience is bothering you. You're so evil that your conscience is giving you trouble. You got everybody fooled but *me*. I know you're a black devil."

"I'm a black devil," I said. "Now will you let me sleep?"

He went to the door. "You dish it out but you can't take it," he said. "That's *your* trouble."

"I'm a black devil," I said.

I lay there, after he left, hating myself but thankful that he hadn't called me into his room for the fatherly talk as he had done another time. That was the worst. He had come to the door and said: "Come out of there, I want to talk to you." He had walked ahead of me into his room and had sat down in his big leather chair next to the lamp with his legs spread wide and his big hands in his lap. He had said: "Don't be afraid. I'm not going to hurt you. Sit down. I'm not going to argue. What are you so nervous about? Have a drink," in his kindest, most fatherly way, and that had been the worst of all. That was the time he had told me to eat in my room. Now I could hear him pacing about in the hall and I knew that it was not over for the night. I began to pray that I could sleep before he came and that he would not be able to wake me, no matter what he did. I did not care what he did as long as I did not have to face him. I resolved to confess to anything he accused me of if it would make him leave sooner. I was about to go out into the hall for my confession when the door was kicked open and he charged into the room.

"You black son-of-a-bitch!" he said. "I ought to *kill* you." He stood over the bed in the dark room and shook his big fist over me. And I lay there hating the overpowering cowardice in me, which kept my body still and my eyes closed, and hoping that he would kill all of it when his heavy fist landed.

"First you insult a man's company, then you ignore him. I been *good* to you. I let you live here, I let you eat my uncle's food, and I taught you things. But you're a ungrateful motherfucker. I ought to *kill* you right now!"

And I still lay there, as he went on, not hearing him, with nothing in me but a loud throbbing which pulsed through the length of my body and made the sheets move with its pounding. I lay there secure and safe in cowardice for as long as I looked up at him with my eyes big and my body twitching and my mind screaming out to him that it was all right, and I thanked him, because now I truly believed in the new five thousand years of Black Rule.

It is night again. I am in bed again, and I can hear the new blonde girl closing the bathroom door. I know that in a minute he will come out in his red robe and call a cab. His muffled voice through my closed door will seem very tired, but just as kind and patient to the dispatcher as it is to everyone, and as it was to me in those old times. I am afraid because when they came up the stairs earlier they caught me working at the living room table with my back to them. I had not expected him back so soon; but then I should have known that he would not go out. I had turned around in the chair and she smiled and said hello and I said "Hi" before he hurried her into the room. I *did* speak and I know that she heard. But I also know that I must have done something wrong; if not to her, then to him earlier today or yesterday or last week, because he glared at me before following her into the room and he almost paused to say something when he came out to get the glasses and ice. I wish that I could remember just what it was. But it does not matter. I *am* guilty and he knows it.

Now that he knows about me I am afraid. I could move away from the apartment and hide my guilt from him, but I know that he would find me. The brainwashed part of my mind tells me to call the police while he is still busy with her, but what could I charge him with when I know that he is only trying to help me. I could move the big, ragged yellow chair in front of the door, but that would not stop him, and it might make him impatient with me. Even if I pretended to be asleep and ignored him, it would not help when he comes. He has not bothered to knock for weeks.

In the black shadows over my bed and in the corners I can sense the outraged spirits who help him when they hover about his arms as he gestures, with his lessons, above my bed. I am determined now to lie here and take it. It is the price I must pay for all the black secrets I have learned, and all the evil I have learned about myself. I *am* jealous of him, of his learning, of his girls. I am not the same handkerchief-head I was nine months ago. I have Marie to thank for that, and Claude, and the spirits. They know about me, and perhaps it is they who make him do it and he cannot help himself. I believe in the spirits now, just as I believe most of the time that I am a black devil.

They are going down to the cab now.

I will not ever blame him for it. He is helping me. But I blame the girls. I blame them for not staying on afterwards, and for letting all the good nice happy love talk cut off automatically after it is over. *I* need to have them there, after it is over. And he needs it; he needs it much more and much longer than they could ever need what he does for them. He should be able to teach them, as he has taught me. And he should have their appreciation, as he has mine. I blame them. I blame them for letting him try and try and never get just a little of the love there is left in the world.

To the student:

We, as publishers, realize that one way to improve education is to improve textbooks. We also realize that you, the student, have a large role in the success or failure of textbooks. Although teachers choose books to be used in the classroom, if the students do not buy and use books, those books are failures.

Usually only the teacher is asked about the quality of a text; his opinion alone is considered as revisions are written or as new books are planned. Now, Little, Brown would like to ask you about this book: how you liked or disliked it; why it was successful or dull; if it taught you anything. Would you fill in this form and return it to us at: Little, Brown and Co., College Division, 34 Beacon St., Boston, Mass. 02106. It is your chance to directly affect the publication of future textbooks.

Book title:________________ School:________________

Course title:________________ Course enrollment:____________

1. Did you like the book?________________

2. CONTENT: Was it too easy?________________

   Did you read all the selections?________________

   Which did you like most?________________

   Which did you like least?________________

3. FORMAT: Did you like the cover?________________

   Did you like the size?________________

   Did you like the margins?________________

   Did you like the illustrations?________________

   Did you like the type size?________________

(over)

4. Were the study questions, review summaries, or other pedagogical apparatus useful? ______

   How should they be changed? ______

   ______

5. INTRODUCTIONS: Are they useful? ______

   How might they be improved? ______

   ______

6. Do you feel the professor should continue to assign this book next year?

   ______

7. Will you keep this book for your library? ______

8. Please add any comments or suggestions on how we might improve this book, in either content or format.

   ______

   ______

   ______

   ______

   ______

9. May we quote you, either in promotion for this book, or in future publishing ventures? ____yes ____no

______ ______

date signature